WANDA'S TOWER

ROBERT BEATTY

authorHOUSE®

AuthorHouse™
1663 Liberty Drive
Bloomington, IN 47403
www.authorhouse.com
Phone: 833-262-8899

Published by AuthorHouse 06/11/2021

ISBN: 978-1-6655-2904-4 (sc)
ISBN: 978-1-6655-2902-0 (hc)
ISBN: 978-1-6655-2903-7 (e)

Library of Congress Control Number: 2021911965

Print information available on the last page.

This book is printed on acid-free paper.

1

"You don't need to know my name," the woman said in a voice that was half whisper and half calculated huskiness as she rubbed her body slowly against his.

The press and sway of the woman's body had started out in time with the slow dance the country-and-western band was playing but had become more independently timed to her internal rhythm as they had come to a mutual agreement on their subsequent purpose and course for the rest of the evening.

The tune the local country band was playing was meant to be the obvious belly-rubbing kind. The woman had picked up on the obvious body-rubbing purpose of the slow-dance tune and was running with it—rubbing with it, actually. Whether the woman was discovering how to body-rub for the first time and was working on instinct or whether she knew how to body-rub from long practice, the obvious points of her body that she was pressing up against the man's chest effectively rendered any curiosity he might have otherwise had about her reluctance to state her name a moot point.

There were a lot more immediate and driving points of consideration than first names, and the woman knew how to press home all of her points. By now, the man couldn't particularly remember how he had struck up a conversation with the well-built standout woman standing by the bar without learning her name during the introduction phase. Now that the woman had proven to be a fantasy in reality and not just in his mind and things were approaching the final stage that such barroom conversation between single men and women often was intended to lead to, the man wasn't about to press the point of the woman's name if that might cause her to pull back the full and warm parts of her body pressing against his.

"You aren't here looking for a name. You're here looking for a woman by any name. I'm not here looking to be named. I'm not here looking for promises. I'm not here looking for commitment. I'm not here looking for ever after. I'm here looking for one night of complete and full coming together. But that's where anything between us ends.

"Tomorrow we'll both be gone from this place and off on our separate ways. Neither of us will look back and think longingly of each other. In fact, neither of us will think of each other. You won't see me after tonight. You may not even see me leave in the morning. The two of us are like two winds blowing into town from different directions that come together in an open field and swirl around each other long enough to kick up some dust. I'll be your midnight wind. But I won't be a name in any little black brag book of male conquests. I won't be a name tattooed on your arm.

"If you give me half a chance, I'll burn myself into your memory. I'll be as soft and warm or as hard and sweaty as you want me to be tonight. I'll leave you with any kind of memory you want to conjure up when you need fond remembering. But I will otherwise be leaving you after we make that memory together. There will be no lingering thoughts or longings trailing off after our parting. There will be no stretching out of anything beyond the one night of our coming together. That's the way I have it planned. That's the way you're thinking."

It sort of was the way the man was thinking. It was kind of a fantasy pickup encounter with a drop-dead sensual woman who had seemingly come out of nowhere and was talking about exactly what he had been thinking. Since the first moment he had danced with the woman in his arms and felt the warm press of her full body against his, he had been thinking in terms of fortuitous gratification with the sensual woman. As far as communications went, subliminal or otherwise, they seemed to be on the same wavelength.

"You can savor the memory of me all you want for all your days if you're inclined to carry memories that long. But it will have to be a memory without a name attached to it. That you won't have a name to go with your memory of me won't hurt you one little bit. It will probably make the memory of me all the more memorable and intriguing."

The music continued. The woman's body continued swaying against his. The feel of her body filled the man's senses to near overloading. The smell of her perfume filled his head.

"I'm ready, willing, and able to be all you want in a woman for a night without complications for you or anything further asked of you. All I ask in return is that you don't make any complications for me and that you accept that I'll be gone after our night together is over. After that, you won't be seeing me again. That's the way you want it. That's the way I want it. For us, there will be no morning after or day after. For us, there is only the night together. So fuck me. Fuck me long, hard, and deep. Fuck me all night. Tomorrow I'll be only a memory—a memory whose name you'll never know."

The man was a truck driver making an overnight stop on a cross-country delivery run. In one sense, the woman had it right that he would soon be off and back on the road. He hadn't explained to her that he could linger awhile to enjoy the favors she was generously extending to him. He assumed the woman was a hot-to-trot local woman who was bored with small-town life and cruised the bars for excitement and casual sex. She wore no wedding ring. Maybe she was put off by the men in the town or had worked her way through them all. Maybe that was why she frequented a bar where transients passed through, looking for the spontaneous thrill of being picked up by a new man. If that was the demon that drove her, the man considered himself ready, willing, and able to quench the devil in her.

"I'll be your devil in bed for the night, but I won't be an angel of the morning to you. We'll be gone from each other before the sun dries out the dew on the windows of the cars in the parking lot of the motel where we'll be spending the night with each other. We're going to be nothing more than memories to each other by the time the sun has burned the mist off the grass in the fields we'll pass by outside the town while going in our opposite directions. We both live on the road. Neither of us plans to leave the road. I don't want to leave the road any more than you do. We'll do better by each other by leaving each other with a memory and getting away before the sun gets fully on us. I live on the horizon. I live to move to the next horizon. We both live on and for the next horizon. It'll be a lot better for both of us if I remain a nameless horizon to you tonight, and we'll remain distant horizons to each other after our night is over."

The woman spoke with a country accent and used country analogies. Her accent both amplified the huskiness of her voice and made it sound a bit corny and incongruous at the same time. But as husky female voices went, hers worked all the way down the line. The woman sounded a bit like a country girl who had been instructed in life-lived-on-the-road

3

philosophy by Jack Kerouac and coached in talking huskily by Lauren Bacall, and she was decked out in a cleavage display that rivaled that of Jane Russell.

"It's nothing personal, ma'am," the man said. That was bunk by definition. What the man was planning, which the woman apparently wanted as much as he did, was about as personal as a man and woman could get with each other. "It's just that at the climactic moment, I wanted to be able to shout out something more than 'Oh, woman, woman!' I kind of thought it would be polite and a favor to you if I could call out your name. It seems like a more respectable thing to do with a woman in that moment than to just grunt and call her nothing. I kind of thought you would rather me use your name on you rather than call you Miss Nameless or shout out, 'To whom it may concern!'"

The man looked down at the woman's face. Though he was six foot tall, he didn't have all that far to look. The woman was about five ten or five eleven. The whole of her head was framed by thick, shoulder-length medium to dark blonde hair. The woman's hair color looked natural, not like it had come off the shelf in the beauty-aids section of a drugstore or out of a Miss Clairol bottle. She had wide hazel eyes and full lips. Her face was slightly upturned toward his. She had a gracefully curved neck that was a bit thicker than the necks preferred on rail-thin fashion models, but it provided a proportionate offset for the woman's full face and left one with the impression she had a good head on her shoulders.

From the man's close-in perspective, he couldn't see her neck directly. Past the woman's chin, there was a straight visual drop down to her chest, which revealed an ample amount of cleavage. The woman's breasts pushed together against each other under the constricting wrap of her tight blouse. The restrictions imposed by clothing and nature made it impossible to see the full depth to which the woman's cleavage ran, leaving the man's imagination to run the depths. The woman must have been wearing a sheer bra with no seams. Through his denim shirt, the man could feel the pointed outline of the woman's large nipples pressing into his chest with no fabric creases in tactile evidence.

The woman's tight blouse had started out the night with the two top buttons strategically unbuttoned. As the night had progressed, somewhere along the line, the third button had also come unbuttoned. It could have easily popped open by itself. There was enough weight behind it. Then again, the woman could have unbuttoned it herself when he was looking

4

in another direction. With the third button unbuttoned, the amount of cleavage now on casual display kept the man's attention focused in that particular direction. He was tempted to look away to see if a fourth button came undone by the time he looked back.

"You came in here looking for a woman," the woman said, speaking truth to the man. "You weren't looking for anything more than a woman, and you weren't looking for anything chaste and demure. You aren't looking for a woman with depth of character. You aren't looking for social-register, proper sex. You're looking for willing, hot, hard, and sweaty. A woman is all you want. A woman is all I want to be tonight. You found a woman who's willing to be all woman with you. You don't need to know the name of a woman in order for her to be a woman and make love like a sweet woman. Or make love like a whore. You don't need to know my name for me to be a woman for you. Knowing my name won't make me any more of a woman to you. All you came in here looking to find was a woman who would act like a woman without any questions asked or any return engagements sought. I came in here looking to be a woman without having to answer questions or be plied for promises. You're looking for a woman to make the night full for you. All I came in here looking to find was a man who would make one night on the road a little less empty for me."

The man still figured the woman was probably a local who wanted to keep her name quiet in the face of potential local gossip that could destroy her reputation if her bar-hopping activity and the knowledge that she was picking up men in the bars and was hard romping with them in the local no-tell motel ever got out. There was also the possibility that she was married and cheating on her husband or was cheating on her regular boyfriend. The man had never seen such a good-looking, unattached single woman in a redneck bar before. Women as good looking as she was who weren't married and who bellied up to the bar and did belly-rubbing dances with men in bars were a rarity indeed in country bars or any bar. If they were not married, they usually were escorted by burly redneck types who looked half psycho. Generally, women as sexy as she was did not appear alone in bars. They usually were on the arm of a muscularly built and dangerous-looking man. When women as well built as she was came into a bar alone, they didn't tend to remain alone for long.

When the man had first met her, he had wondered a bit how an attractive woman her age had managed to stay single so long, especially in a country setting, where women, especially ones as stacked as she was, were prone to marrying early. He wondered if she was a married woman who had the habit of taking herself off to the cheatin' side of town. She was country sounding enough to talk in that sort of accent. She was country sounding enough to think in those terms. The man was at first a bit worried about the possibility the woman was a married farm wife with a dull but big farmer husband she had grown discontented with and was out catting around, looking for thrills with passing truckers. He didn't need some big, burly redneck farmer type storming into the bar with a tire iron in his hand, shouting, "You picked a fine time to leave me, Lucille!" One had to watch out for that sort of thing in country-bar pickup situations.

But the woman didn't fit any of the ready stereotypes of women who let themselves get picked up in bars or went to bars with the proactive idea of getting themselves picked up. The woman wasn't a randy teenager on the make, nor did she look like a divorcée on the rebound, a wayward wife on the sly, or a fading honky-tonk queen trying to recapture past glory. The woman didn't sound or act like a newcomer to bars or to the subject she and the man were planning on pursuing after they left the bar. The woman had some mileage on her. There was more than a hint of mileage in the tone of her voice. But she didn't have an air of desperation about her. She looked to be in her late twenties to early thirties. She was about the man's age. It appeared to him that she might even have been a year or two older than he was.

As the woman pressed her chest into the man and her hands brushed his back, the woman's age brushed on the question of her possible marital status. Getting into her thirties was a bit of a long time for a country girl to go without getting married, especially an all-woman country girl who came with the looks and recommendations she came with. If the woman wasn't a divorcée, she could be currently married, he thought. Country girls were big on marriage. Women with her looks and big measurements often had big husbands.

"The road is all that's ever been there for me. The road is the only life I've known or wanted. You're a trucker. You live on the road like I do. You know the story. You're here one day and gone the next. The road is all there is. The road is all there ever has been for either of us."

The woman's statement caught the man by surprise. Unless she was a liar, she wasn't a local after all. He wondered what she did on the road that she said was all there was for her. There almost seemed to be a certain amount of hidden pain in the woman's voice as she said the road was all there was in her life. The man figured maybe she was cruising bars and making herself available to be picked up as a way to fill the emptiness she felt. The man was sure he could do that for her for one night—and maybe for return engagements when he came through town on his usual route.

"That's why there can be nothing further between us after tonight. There's no need for names. What we're going to be sharing goes way beyond names. But there won't be any sharing between us beyond that. The only life I want is the open road. The only thing I share myself with long-term is the open road and the next horizon up ahead. Since there can't be anything between us beyond the rest of the night, there's no reason for names tonight. Let's just leave names out of it. I'll be fully yours for the rest of the night. I'll be fully gone in the morning. When I'm gone, you'll remember that I was yours for one night. You'll have my body tonight. The road and the next horizon already have my soul. When I've left to take myself off to my next horizon, you won't know who I was, but you will know I was all yours, body and soul, for a night. That's all you'll ever know about me. That's all you'll ever need to know."

The woman's hands ran tightly but smoothly over the man's back and down his sides as they danced. The feel of her touch and the press of her body distracted him from asking what she did on the open road she said was all there was for her.

The woman seemed to pull herself tighter against him, though there wasn't a whole lot of empty space between them left to fill. There was a certain amount of controlled anticipatory tension in the woman's touch. While the woman's hands rubbed slowly and semisoftly in an open-palmed manner, they seemed to convey the unspoken need to grip tighter and rub faster and harder. The woman's full thighs bumped and rubbed the man's legs in a rhythm set more and more by her own internal cadence than by the band. In response, the man rubbed his hands in counter-rotating circular patterns across the back of the woman's silky blouse. He more or less—more than less, actually—wanted to reach his hands down and grab hold of the woman's full hips pressing tightly from inside her blue jeans, which looked to be a size too small or possibly two sizes too small.

The woman wore pointed, open-top shoes that were a bright liquid red in color. The shoes were the type and color proverbially worn by all seductresses. The woman's red shoes rounded out the come-on outfit that accentuated her rounded figure. The shoes weren't high heels; they were flats. In that sense, the shoes weren't the typical shoes women wore when they wanted to maximize their wardrobe for a high-sex look, but they were more practical for dancing and walking. In that time-suspended moment in the bar, all the man could think of was the extra volume that would spill out of the woman's tight clothes she had agreed to spill herself out of for him.

The man was reasonably handsome. He had frequented bars before. To date, he had made two one-night-stand pickups in the past. Looking at the woman and feeling the sensual press of her erotically constructed body, the man thought he had made the pickup of his life. He probably had. The other women he had picked up in his few scattered pickups hadn't been insistent that he take prompt leave of them in the morning. They had more or less wanted him to stay. But the other women hadn't been nearly as good looking as the one he was looking at now and was looking to experience more of. His other pickups had been easy to leave the following morning. He felt this woman would not be as easy to leave.

Why the woman had proven receptive to him wasn't fully clear to the man. He was as vain on average as other good-looking men. He figured the woman might be out after a good time and had picked him because she had epicurean tastes when it came to sex. That possibility was flattering to the man's ego. Still, it was a mercenary world, and when he put his ego aside, the man figured there could be a somewhat more mercenary reason for the woman's quick interest in him. Now that they had gotten to talking and it had become clear where the woman was taking things, and where she wanted him to take her, the man wondered if the woman was a hooker working the bar on a commercial basis and was going to charge him the going street price. Having sex with a hooker didn't bother the man. He had patronized prostitutes before. It was the commercial end of the transaction that presented the possible problem. A woman with her looks could command top dollar, he knew, possibly more than he could afford on a trucker's salary. If the woman had been peddling her wares on the streets of Vegas, only high rollers would have been able to afford her rates. If the woman was a hooker, the man hoped that small-town hookers charged more reasonable fees.

But talk of fees hadn't entered their conversation at any stage. Unless she was planning on turning around on him by holding out a mercenary hand and springing a surprise economic demand on him at the door of her motel room, the woman wasn't a hooker. If it proved she was a hooker, they would discuss price, although the man would express his displeasure over her bait-and-switch tactics. If her price was reasonable, the transaction would go through. But even at the final stage of their agreement, the woman still wasn't talking anything about money. She was talking only about some kind of love-on-the-run philosophy.

An alternate possibility was that the woman was picking up men in bars because she was a nymphomaniac who had an insatiable need to have a different man every night. The woman's looks put having a new man every night within a reachable range of possibility for her. If it was the case that the woman was a nympho, it didn't bother the man. He could do nymphos as well as randy wives.

But these country types liked things in overdrive. They liked souped-up cars like the ones raced on country roads and the NASCAR circuit. They liked souped-up trucks with huge mounted tractor wheels and names like Bigfoot. They liked souped-up tractors like the ones in tractor-pull contests. If the woman was a bit souped-up in her personal sexual realm, her appetite for the form of soup she personally liked was her concern. If the woman had an underlying need to be laid over every night, that was her need. He was only too happy to satisfy for one night a need that probably could never be fully satisfied. But he could do a nympho and get what he wanted out of it. They would both get what they needed out of the night. The man just wouldn't have to pay anything for it.

"I'll take you for my lover tonight. I'll let you take me for your lover. But the open road is the only lover I will ever let take me for life. The road is the only lover I want for life. Distant horizons are the beds I sleep in, and I make it a habit to wake up in the bed of a new horizon every new morning. I'll be your horizon for the night. I'll be all you can see before we turn the lights off. I'll be all you can feel with the lights off. I'll wrap myself around you closer than the darkness that surrounds both of us when we're in my room alone. You may see my outline in the faint light of the room as we cross the room to lie down in my bed. You may catch sight of me from close in as we make love together in the dark. But you won't catch sight of me in the light of the rising sun.

"You'll feel good when you have me tonight. I want you tonight. I need you tonight. I'll be yours for one night. But there's no way I'll be yours in any day that follows. But don't feel bad about not having me beyond next morning. Like they say, two out of three ain't bad."

The man had bought the woman only two drinks that night, though he would have plied her with more if he could have. The woman had spaced out her drinking slowly over the course of the evening. The two drinks hadn't washed the woman's lipstick off. Her glossy red lipstick seemed to shine in the low light of the bar as she spoke her less-than-luminescent assessment of the possibility of the two of them being together for any extended number of days. The smooth upper curves of the woman's rounded breasts seem to glow with a semiliquid light in the reduced light of the country bar. The effect created made it look as if the woman had rubbed herself with bath oil. The effect on the man was increasing. As he stood with the woman's chest pressing against his, the man had to fight off an urge to thrust his head down into the cleavage between the swell of the woman's breasts and let his extended tongue wash from side to side as he pushed his face down into the depths of her chest. Given the volume of the woman's breasts, he thought he might be able to push his head down far enough to the point where the woman's breasts covered his ears and shut out the words she was saying.

"You can trust me for a good time tonight, but you can't trust me past tonight. I'm not trustworthy beyond next morning or any morning of my days. I've never been trustworthy beyond sunrise. I can't be faithful to you or any man. I gave myself to be the mistress of the road a long time ago. The road is the only lover I will ever be faithful to."

Faithfulness wasn't an issue for the man. If the woman was at the bar cheating on her husband, faithfulness apparently was even less of an issue for the woman than she claimed it to be. He sort of wished the woman would forget her philosophizing and get on with everything she was talking about before her enraged redneck husband slammed through the front door with a pump shotgun in hand, looking to do in his faithless, philandering wife and the man she was being unfaithful with at the moment.

"I'll give myself to you tonight. I'll be your total woman for you tonight. Tomorrow I'll be totally gone from you."

A tightness was developing in the place where he was pressing deep into the enhanced volume of territory between the woman's full hips. In the worst way, the man wanted to reach down, grab the woman's hips, and pull himself hard in against them right then and there. But even though the woman had agreed in open conversation to said actions to come, the man figured if he acted too crudely, it could cause the woman to change her mind and walk away, leaving him with a overwound main spring and nowhere to empty out his heated anticipation except into his pants.

"But if you want to take me fully for the night, you first have to fully take me as I am and accept what I say. If you want me to accept you for the night, you have to accept me when I say that we cannot be together or have any further contact after this night is over. If you want me to be yours tonight, you have to accept me when I say that I won't be yours after tonight. If you won't accept that we won't have any days together after this night, then we must part ways right here and now and not have a night together."

At that moment, the man could see only the contours of the woman's body and the shape of the evening she was promising him. He would have agreed to most any condition she demanded in order to keep the rest of the evening on track. Whether or not he was as eager to put the distance the woman wanted between them when the morning rolled around was something he might feel differently about in the morning. At present, with the woman pressing her body against him, the man was interested only in getting on with the rest of the night. That immediate consideration was all the man was thinking of and wanted to think of.

"If you accept me the way I am, take me as I am, and take me the way I want to be taken, I will be all yours for the rest of the night. But if anything is to pass between us tonight, you must accept the condition that there won't be anything between us beyond this night. That is the main condition you must agree to if there is to be a night between us at all. That is the condition under which I will be yours tonight. If you meet that condition, I will be yours in the way you want me tonight.

"I'm not trying to manipulate you. I'm not trying to trap you. All I ask is that you don't try to trap me into staying with you. I'm not trying to get anything out of you, except that you fill in one lonely night for me. The only thing I ask is that you treat me gently and hold me for a night. The only other thing I ask is that you don't try to hold me after our night is over. Your agreement that we won't see each other after tomorrow is the only condition I set on my being yours tonight. It's my one condition, but it's a set condition. You must meet that condition the way I want, or I won't meet you the way you want me to meet you tonight."

As far as agreeing to the woman's conditions, the man was in full agreement with any condition she wanted to set as long as she was still agreeable to meeting him fully naked in her motel room. The only thing he wanted to share with the woman was his swelling desire. To that end, he had no desire to disagree with any of the woman's conditions in a way that might cause her to restrict what she would be to him for the rest of the night.

In the light of the morning, which the woman had set as the cutoff time for any further contact, the man knew he might find the conditions the woman had set to be limiting. He might start thinking of ways to extend their time together and exploring ways to keep in contact. He might see her again if the woman was from the area, as the man's truck route often brought him this way.

At the moment, the woman was doing all the talking and all the limit setting. But the man considered himself pretty good at sweet-talking women in bed. In the light of the morning, he might be able to talk himself into an extension of the horizon the woman said she was always looking to. If he could keep the woman agreeable by agreeing to whatever condition she set tonight, he might be able to talk her into a different arrangement in the morning. If he could insert himself into her tonight, he might be able to find a way to insert himself into her life. But first, he had to get himself into her that night.

"The one other condition I ask is that you do not ask me my name. If you do, I'll just lie to you. Whatever you do for me and with me tonight, you'll have to do it without knowing my name. In a way, I don't have a name. I've lived on the road so long I don't really have a name of my own anymore. The name of the road I'm on is the only name I have."

Any list of names the woman may or may not have had was irrelevant compared to the physical immediacy of the body she was pressing against his body and the immediacy of both their needs. What was the exchange of a social superficiality, such as a first name, compared to the substantive body and the primal exchange the woman was prepared to share with him? When it all came to a head, the man hardly cared what the woman did or didn't want to be called. With the woman pressing her body next to his in his arms and with their bodies soon to be pressed even closer together in her motel room bed, the man had achieved the realization of more fantasy than he might achieve again in life. If the woman wanted to fantasize herself as a woman of mystery, he would let her have her way when it came to the subject of personal nomenclature as long as she let him have his way with the personal and personable physical rest of her.

"If you need me to have a name so bad, you give me a name. Call me by any name you want to. Name me after a woman or a girl you once knew. Name me after a teacher you were found of. Name me after your brother's girlfriend you had the hots for or after your cousin's wife you had the hots for. Name me after a woman you fantasized about. Name me after any girl or woman you wanted but couldn't have. Name me after a lost love. Whoever you want me to be, I'll be her for you tonight. You can shout out any name you want. It won't offend me or put me off or cause me to push you off onto the floor. I'll go by any name you want to call me. Just don't try to call me yours."

The woman's offer to play the role of any fantasy woman the man might have in mind was another accommodation on top of the way in which she had already agreed to be accommodating. The woman's reasoning behind her juggling of names was still obscure to the man, but he wasn't about to let obscurities about names stand between him and the woman's body, which was anything but obscure. The man thought for a moment, but he was distracted by thoughts of other things that had more physically direct and less romantic underpinnings than reminiscing back in time and looking for the name of a lost love.

"Well, there was a girl I had a crush on when I was eight years old," the man said. "It's like the way the character Charlie Brown in the *Peanuts* cartoon strip has a crush on the little redheaded girl. I had a crush on my own little redheaded girl."

Actually, the man's little redheaded girl had been a carrottop with curly orange-red hair. As cartoon characters went, she'd looked a bit more like Little Orphan Annie than Chuck Brown's little redheaded girl.

This woman had long, slightly wavy blonde hair that extended down past her shoulders. Whatever she was, whatever generalized needs and desires had brought her to the bar that night, and whatever immediate and pressing needs had sent her to press herself into a man's arms and press her body against his, the woman was anything but a cartoon character. As a woman, she was as real as they got.

"I'm blonde," the woman who wished to remain nameless said. "But it's real. It's not out of a bottle."

"Her name was Ashley." The man went on. "I never got anywhere with her. We were too young anyway. But I never tried very hard. I just kind of worshipped her from a distance. I guess I was too shy back then."

"Then I'll be your Ashley for the night," the blonde woman said.

13

The bit with the name was sort of a strange beginning for a quickie pickup affair. But the man wasn't going to quibble in front of the awesome real-world numbers of the woman's measurements. If the nameless woman of his about-to-be-realized fantasies wanted him to call her Ashley, he would call her Ashley. Besides, this would be an indirect way of finally having Ashley and doing so with a woman whose body was a lot fuller and more maturely sensual than Ashley's preteen body had been.

The woman's particular hang-up over identity still wasn't clear. Maybe it simply had to do with her not wanting to let her name get out as a bar-hopping bed-bouncer. Maybe it had something to do with her wanting to leave the men she encountered with an air of mystery hanging on after she was gone. If it was her personal fantasy to think of herself as a mystery woman and be thought of as a mystery woman, he would call her Mata Hari if that was what she wanted. When it came to names, he would do it any way the woman wanted as long as she let him do her.

The man mumbled something barely audible in assent to naming the nameless woman Ashley. The man pulled the nameless woman who would temporarily bear the name of his childhood sweetheart from afar even closer to him and continued dancing.

The bar was a typical country redneck type of bar: only half lit, with a wood-surfaced bar; wood floors covered with peanut shells; wood tables; wood booths; and wood walls punctuated with neon signs advertising various type of beer, pictures with cowboy themes, and copies of autographed pictures of sports stars. The wood tables were covered in longneck beer bottles, pitchers of beer, thick drinking glasses, and thick glass ashtrays. The tables were also marked by cigarette burns. Apparently, use of the ashtrays was only a sometimes thing. But then again, one of the joys and definitions of being a redneck was to let one's cigarette burn his or her mark into the table instead of using an ashtray. The manager might have deliberately left cigarettes to smolder across the tables in order to give them and the bar a macho look.

The local country band was adequate for the bar and the night, but they would never be found playing backup for Willie Nelson or Johnny Cash. They probably didn't play outside the local area. The middling talent of the band probably set the middling rate the group could charge, which put the group within reach of the kind of bars they played. The wooden dance floor was small, but there weren't many couples dancing, and the man and woman were pulled together in a small knot that occupied minimal space on the dance floor. Soon enough, the couple would yield that small space to the other patrons when they went off to a private dance floor where the woman had agreed to yield herself. The bar was the kind of bar where a wayfaring cross-country trucker who lived on the road could meet an anonymous woman who also lived on the road. Or lived in town and wanted to remain anonymous because she wanted to keep her wayfaring ways a secret.

The man and his nameless female conquest for the night, the woman who had conquered him more than he had conquered her, finished the rest of the dance, pressing in close and tight to each other, rubbing and moving against each other in a rhythm that was by now almost totally theirs. As the music wound down as the end of the dance approached, the woman took one hand off the man's back and brought it up and placed it behind his neck. Gently but firmly, the woman pulled the man's face in to hers. With her eyes still open, the woman kissed him a lingering, twisting kiss, intertwining her full lips with his. As the final bar of the song faded on the floor and the other dancers turned to leave, the woman continued moving her lips on the man's mouth, rotating and undulating her kiss as she worked her lips on the man's.

The man's pulse quickened even more at the feel of the warm wetness of the woman's full mouth and the taste of her lipstick. They were the last of the dancers, as the others had cleared the floor. It now seemed the woman was not a local who was worried that other locals might see her, as she didn't seem to mind the possibility that someone who knew her might see her french-kissing a man on the dance floor in front of all the patrons of the bar. The woman seemed to be signaling that she didn't care who saw her or what she was doing. She also seemed to be signaling that the time for open-road philosophizing and any spoken words was over.

The woman had declared her name to be superfluous. There came a time when specific words were also superfluous. With a slow, lingering parting of lips, the woman pulled back from her kiss. As their lips parted, the man didn't know or particularly care whether the woman's lipstick was smeared on his mouth. As the woman pulled back from the kiss, the man looked into her hazel eyes.

"Let's go, Ashley," the man said just loudly enough for her to hear.

Without saying another superfluous word, the woman relaxed her pressing against the man and pulled away from him. The couple walked off the floor and back to the booth they had been sitting at, but they did not sit down. Sitting back down would have been superfluous. The woman paused at the booth, reached down to the seat, and picked up her leather cowgirl hat. The western-style wrangler hat was in keeping with the woman's country accent and demeanor, but from the look of her, the man had the feeling the only time in her life she ever bulldogged a steer was when she wrestled a frozen steak out of a freezer to defrost it.

The couple walked silently out of the bar and into the warm summer country night. The woman didn't have a car in the bar parking lot. She said she had walked over from her motel room, which was only three blocks away. The man had walked to the bar too. The truck stop he was spending the night at was a farther walk in the other direction. It would have made no sense to walk back to the truck stop, start up his eighteen-wheeler big rig, and drive to the woman's motel. There probably wouldn't have been any place to park something that big in a motel parking lot anyway.

As soon as they were out the door of the bar, the man wrapped his right arm around the woman's waist and pulled her in close to his side. For her part, and for all the parts that came with her that would play a part in what was to come, the woman took the man's hand in her own right hand and intertwined her fingers with his. With her free hand, she put on her cowgirl hat. From that place just outside the barroom door, the couple started walking silently toward the woman's motel room. The woman still didn't tell him her name. The man still didn't mind as long as she was still in agreement with the exchange to come.

The couple walked past the darkened and closed small shops and businesses on the commercial street of the small town. The only conversation that passed between them was the woman's giving directions to the motel where she was staying. But again, the man was distracted by thoughts of what would soon pass between them.

The man still suspected the woman actually lived elsewhere in the town. All the stuff about the road being her lover was poetic, but she could have gotten it out of a Jack Kerouac book, from a hippie guru, or from any second-rate romance novel. The woman seemed to know her way around the town. That was the main thing that made the man suspect she was from the area. But then again, the motel was only three blocks from the bar where they had met. If the woman was actually from out of town, as he was, it would have been an easy distance and route for the woman to memorize in a short time. She might have surveyed the lay of the land earlier that afternoon as she set her plans to get herself laid that night. *She could be from out of town. Then again, she could be on familiar ground*, he thought. The man wondered if, and how many times, the woman had walked the same route before with other men. When it came to sex, the woman gave the impression she knew her way around the subject a lot more than she knew her way around a small town.

The man kept the woman pulled in close to him as they walked. He enjoyed watching the tight, shapely, generous portions and parts of the woman's body work as she walked. The man deliberately moved his right leg over slightly to the side so the woman's leg brushed his when she walked. He enjoyed the feel of the woman's leg in her tight jeans bumping and rubbing against his. The woman's shiny white blouse reflected the lights of the town at night. He could feel the smooth slip of the woman's silky blouse against his side. He could feel the undulating rub of the woman's full left hip as it moved against his right hip. He could feel her side as it moved next to his. He enjoyed the feel of her body as it worked against his.

It all served to remind him that in a short while, all of the woman's body would be working naked against his in a full-frontal mode. The woman's body swayed and undulated. Her thick blonde hair swayed and bounced in the light of the occasional streetlights they passed under. The woman reached her left arm around behind the man and gripped his belt just above his left hip. The rest of the night was in view. Up ahead, the motel came into view.

2

The motel was a bit sleazy looking to the woman's country way of thinking.

"Are you sure you want to stay in this place, Fred?" Wanda's mother asked as her husband slowed down to turn the car into the driveway of the motel. "It looks kind of seedy to me."

"Wanda's old enough that she needs her own room," Wanda's father said as he applied the squeaky brakes on the old car. "We'll be paying double for two rooms. We're not Waldorf Astoria people. If we don't want to go broke on this trip, we're going to have to stay in less expensive accommodations."

"It still looks a bit tacky," Wanda's mother said.

"As long as there aren't cockroaches crawling the walls, piss stains or vomit on the bed, or drunks passed out on the floor, it will do," Wanda's father said.

Wanda's father turned the car into the driveway of the motel. The car bumped over a pothole at the entrance. In the backseat, sixteen-year-old Wanda put her hand on the car door to steady herself as the wheel hit the pothole, but she said nothing.

"Besides," Wanda's father said, "it's getting dark. We need to get dinner. The desk clerk can point us to a local restaurant. I don't want to drive on for half the night on an empty stomach, looking for a Waldorf hotel that's up to your standards. You aren't going to find much better than this around here anyway. Not something we could afford."

The sun was setting. Long orange-tinged shadows crossed the crumbling asphalt of the motel driveway as Wanda's father steered the car in the direction of the motel office. A neon sign lit the minimal marquee next to the road: Vacancy.

The motel was a typical low-rate motel of its time and country locale. There weren't separate cabins. The motel was a single long one-story row

18

of small rooms side by side with a common wall between the individual rooms. The motel office sat alone in a separate building at one end of the driveway and parking lot. Each room had a single window facing the driveway and parking lot. The rooms looked small and a bit cramped, but they would be staying only one night and would be back on the road early the next morning.

Though Wanda's family was poor, Wanda's mother had a country-style streak of fastidiousness about her. The motel looked as if the rooms probably weren't cleaned properly. Just to be on the safe side, Wanda's mother figured she would probably have to wash off the toilet seats before they could use them. A person could pick up all sorts of strange diseases from toilet seats in public places or toilet seats in motel rooms, which had so many customers the washrooms might as well have been public toilets.

Besides, Wanda's mother suspected the motel didn't particularly cater to or attract the highest of clientele. She just hoped it wasn't the kind of place where one's feet stuck to the floor. Wanda's mother reminded herself to remind her daughter to wash off the toilet seat in her own room and wear slippers on the rug, which probably hadn't been shampooed in years.

For her part, the sixteen-year-old, nearly seventeen-year-old, who was developed enough to be taken for twenty-one, hadn't developed the same degree of fastidiousness as her mother. Teenagers were like that. When it came to practical considerations of accommodations for the night, Wanda didn't want to drive on after dark any more than her father did. To the resilient teenage Wanda, the place would do for the night. After all, they weren't going to live there. They would be moving on as soon as the sun was up.

Wanda's full first name was Wanda Jean. Her mother liked full-length two-part country names like that. Wanda rarely used the second part of her first name. Though she never revealed it to her mother, Wanda wished her mother had given her a name a little less country and corny sounding than Wanda. She was a country girl, and she didn't disparage her cultural roots, but to Wanda, the name Wanda sounded a bit too hillbilly for her taste. Wanda wished her mother had given her a name with a bit more of an exotic or romantic ring to it. Dulcenia would have been a nice name. Or Lucinda, Allison, Marissa, Ramona, or anything else romantic sounding. Wanda had never obsessed over her name. With country-girl practicality, she figured, *You can't change what you can't change,* though in the back of her mind, she felt she could do better for herself with her name. But Wanda wasn't thinking of names at all as her father drove toward the motel office.

Wanda's father pulled the car up to the front door of the motel office. He stopped the engine, got out, and went into the office, leaving his wife and daughter in the car. A short time later, he came back out with two keys to adjoining rooms and instructions on how to get to a local diner. Without stopping to drop off luggage or even look at their rooms, Wanda's father drove the family from the motel to dinner at the restaurant the desk clerk had suggested.

After dinner, they came back to their adjoining rooms at the motel.

The motel was an eleven-room affair with rooms numbered from 10 to 20. Wanda's parents had room number 17. Wanda got room number 18. It was dark by the time they returned. The motel rooms didn't even have televisions in them. There was not much else to do but go to bed. Wanda's father gave Wanda the key to her motel room, and Wanda's mother gave her a short lecture reminding her to wash the toilet seat in her bathroom and keep shoes or slippers on her feet, especially when she was in the bathroom. She said there could be all sorts of germs on the surfaces in places like the one they were in. She also told Wanda to keep the drapes on the window closed.

Wanda made agreement noises. After that, she took her suitcase out of the car and went into her room. Wanda's suitcase wasn't actually a suitcase; it was a simple overnight case that contained her nightie, a few basics of clothing, and a few other needed items. Wanda was a practical girl. When she traveled, she traveled light.

The motel room was a small, square room with an attached bathroom separated from the rest of the room by a half wall. The decor of the room was minimalist to go along with the minimalist function of the minimal roadside accommodations. The complement of furniture was limited to a bed, a dresser, a single small end table, two chairs, and two lamps. The wood of the dresser was nicked and gouged. The carpet was worn thin on the parts that had seen the most traffic. There was a stain of lighter color bleached into the carpet next to the end table, where it seemed some kind of liquid caustic enough to bleach the color out of carpet fiber had spilled. To Wanda, it looked as if a bottle of hair dye had been knocked over by a woman trying to make herself blonde and the coloring had bleached a light spot where it had fallen. Or the stain could have been caused by a bottle of whiskey that had spilled when a patron in a drunken stupor tried to set it down on the end table and missed. The alcohol in the whiskey could have faded the carpet. Or the stain could have alternately been caused when a drunken patron of the motel vomited on the floor and was too drunk that night to clean it up. Perhaps the vomit had soaked into the carpet overnight, and the stomach acid in the vomit had faded the carpet even more effectively than alcohol from any bourbon bottle. The carpet was threadbare and pulling up on some of the edges. There was a short tear in one part of the carpet. Strands of carpet string stretched out from the tear. Wanda kept her shoes on, as her mother had directed.

Wanda set the chain on the door, as her mother had told her to do and as she would have done anyway. Then she closed the drapes, as her mother had directed and as she would have done anyway. It was a bit difficult to get the frayed drapes to cling to each other at the center. A vertical line kept falling open between the drapes, through which someone on the outside could have looked in. Wanda didn't have any safety pins to hold the drapes shut. She had to wrap the drapes together to get them to stay shut.

After securing the drapes, Wanda took off her clothes. She didn't put her clothes in the drawers of the dresser. The drawers looked as if they might stick if she tried to use them. Instead of using the drawers, Wanda draped her clothes over the back of a chair, laying them on top of each other in the same order she had taken them off, arranging her clothes for a fast exit the next morning. That way, she could dress quickly in the morning when it was time to go.

For a while, Wanda stood dressed in only her slippers, with her freshness and relative innocence otherwise exposed in the worn, faded, stained, and soiled room that her mother would have considered sleazy. Wanda glanced toward the window to see if the drapes had fallen open again. Satisfied that the drapes were closed, Wanda reached into her night case and took out her toothbrush and hairbrush.

Wearing only her slippers, she walked into the bathroom and brushed her teeth and her hair. Wanda's mother would probably have objected to seeing Wanda "parade herself around unadorned" the way she was, especially in the place she was in. But in truth—a truth Wanda didn't particularly want to be known by her mother—Wanda enjoyed the feeling of being unadorned and naked in the unadorned and bare setting. She left her nightie in the night case instead of putting it on before going into the washroom, as a way of prolonging the feeling of being unadorned.

The sink in the washroom was a simple one-faucet sink that dripped. A rust stain had set in on the porcelain where the water from the faucet dripped on it, perhaps for years. It looked as if the stain was set deep into the porcelain itself and probably couldn't be scrubbed out.

When Wanda finished washing up in the washroom, she walked back into the bedroom. She walked a bit slower than her usual walking pace. It was another way of prolonging the exposed and unadorned feeling.

As Wanda walked back toward her night case, she again checked to see whether the drapes had fallen open to leave a thin strip of opening between them. In the back of Wanda's mind, she was sort of intrigued by the idea that someone passing by in the parking lot might catch a fleeting and narrow glimpse of a youthful, slim, trim, and tight female figure walking past the window and the slit between the drapes—a distant figure briefly seen passing by in an unadorned state, a quick flash of skin shining in the half-light of the room. She just hoped that anyone who caught a fleeting glimpse of her passing by in her unadorned state would not be a Peeping Tom who snuck in for a closer look and pressed his face to the window, moving his head around, trying to get a fuller view.

Her mother probably would have found Wanda's mental flirtation with exhibitionism a bit wicked, but Wanda hadn't done anything that could be considered exhibitionistic. The drapes hadn't come open. Wanda left the thought of widening the gap between the drapes in the back of her mind and left the drapes the way she had arranged them. She figured the unadorned room had seen a lot of unadorned bodies in its years. For this one night only, the room would see her naked.

When Wanda arrived back at the night case sitting on the dresser she wasn't using, she put the brushes back into the case, where they would be ready to go in the morning without her having to gather them.

Wanda took her two-piece nightie out of her night case and put it on. The nightie was made of flimsy material that was designed as much to be seen through as it was to cover up anything. When Wanda had bought the nightie, Wanda's mother had considered it a bit risqué for a girl her age to wear something like that. At the time, Wanda had reminded her mother that she was going to wear it only at home and that it was comfortable.

The top half of the flimsy nightie didn't offer any support for Wanda's developing chest. Wanda was getting big for her age in that regard. At sixteen, she was past the training-bra stage and had developed into full women's bra sizes. Wanda's mother had suggested it would be a good idea if Wanda wore a bra at all times, even at night, in order to keep things trained and prevent sagging. She did so at home. But bras were tight, and she was growing out of the one she had. In the unadorned motel room, Wanda wanted the relief of being out of the constraint of one for the night.

Wanda took a magazine out of her night case to read. Low-end motels of that day did not have televisions in the rooms. Then Wanda walked over to the bed, took off her slippers, pulled back the covers on the bed, and lay down in the bed to read, leaving only the lamp on the end table next to the bed lit in order to ready by. The covering on the bed was going threadbare. The bed frame squeaked when Wanda climbed in. The mattress was thin and lumpy.

For a while, Wanda read the magazine. When she was finished reading, instead of laying the magazine down on the nightstand, she got back out of bed, walked across the room in her bare feet, and put the magazine back in her night case. Then she walked back to bed in her bare feet. She got back in bed and turned out the light. Despite her mother's cautioning admonition about the potentially less-than-sanitary condition of the rug, Wanda had gotten her feet dirty.

Since they had left the house of the uncle they had been visiting, the only activity Wanda had experienced had been sitting in the backseat of the car. She hadn't done much that would tire her out, and she wasn't particularly sleepy. For some time, Wanda lay awake in bed. A square outline of faint light from the residual light of the summer night and the motel sign shone from around the edges of the drawn drapes. Otherwise, the room was dark. From outside, Wanda heard the occasional distant sound of a car or truck passing in the night on the road just beyond the outer edge of the motel. Cars driven by night drivers approached at random from both directions. They passed the motel, traveling on, heading off to whatever horizon they would be in when the sun rose in the morning.

The pattern of bypassing was broken by the sound of a car pulling into the motel parking lot. From the sound of it, the car headed toward the motel office. A few minutes later, the car returned, pulled up, and parked somewhere near the outside of Wanda's room. Wanda heard the sound of a car door open and shut. A moment later, she heard the door in the next room open and shut.

The room Wanda's parents were in was just beyond the wall on the side of the room across from Wanda's bed. The room in which the door had opened and closed was the room on the other side of Wanda's room, where her bed was up next to the wall. Wanda was in room 19. The room next to hers beyond the wall across from her bed, the one her parents were in on the far side, was room 18. Beyond the wall that the head of Wanda's bed was up against was room 20, the last room in the line of connected rooms sharing thin common walls.

Wanda could hear the sounds of two people talking as they walked into the room. One voice was a man's. The other voice was a woman's. The couple weren't talking particularly loudly, but the walls between the rooms of the motel had been built with an eye on the cheapness of the construction cost. They were thin and flimsy enough that the sounds of conversation from the adjoining room came through the walls without significant attenuation. If the couple had been talking in louder voices, Wanda probably would have been able to make out everything they said. As it was, their voices were just below the level of intelligibility.

For a while, the couple spoke in a normal stream of conversation. But as Wanda listened, the pacing of the voices seemed to grow more fragmented and spaced out. Then the voices stopped entirely. There was a period of rustling sounds without anything being said. From the closeness of the sound coming through the wall, the couple seemed to be standing next to the wall on the other side of the room, close to Wanda's bed.

Then even the rustling sounds stopped. After a few seconds of silence, Wanda heard a series of random and sporadic squeaks coming through the wall. The squeaks sounded identical to the squeaks the frame of Wanda's bed had made when she'd climbed into it. Apparently, all the beds in the motel were made of equally shoddy construction, or they had become equally worn and loose over the years. From the angle and closeness of the sound, the bed in the adjoining room was positioned on the other side of the wall from Wanda's bed. The headboards of the two beds were right across from each other, separated by only the thin wall. The squeaking paused momentarily. Then there was a single heavy squeak.

From out of the darkness and the room beyond the wall came a drawn-out, gasping scream. At least it sort of sounded like a scream. It was definitely the cry of a woman. Wanda sort of gasped herself. She froze in place in her bed at the sudden eruption of sound. She lay motionless in her bed, listening to the sounds that started coming in rapid-fire succession and barely diminished volume from the other side of the wall.

The squeaking of the bed, which had initially been disjointed and random, started coming in a fast-paced, regular rhythm. The squeaking of the bed was matched by a stream of equally fast-paced screams and cries from the woman. The cries of the woman increased in speed and pace as the speed of the squeaking of the bed ramped up. From the sound, Wanda could tell that the cries of the woman were neither screams of terror nor cries of pain.

The woman ran the decibel spectrum from low moans to gasping, shuddering yells that seemed near the top of her voice in intensity. She shouted, but her words, if they were an attempt at words, came out unintelligibly. She gasped. She cried. Several times, she seemed to sob. Sometimes she almost seemed to be wailing. The duration of the woman's sounds ran from long, drawn-out moans at the low end of the audio frequency spectrum to rapid-fire bursts of high-pitched, sharp staccato cries. The woman's intensities and sounds constantly shifted in a random pattern. The only constant was that the woman's gasps, moans, cries, yells, shouts, and other sound effects kept pace with the frenzied squeaking of the bed she was surging around in with her partner for the night. The rickety bed squeaked so loudly it seemed it would fly apart at any moment. The headboard of the bed bumped up against the wall. If there had been a picture hanging on the wall over Wanda's bed, it might have been jarred off the wall and fallen onto Wanda's head. The largely unattenuated sounds of unvarnished pleasure filled Wanda's room almost as much as they filled the room next door.

It was not a celebration of innocence going on in the next room, and the sounds coming through the wall were not falling on totally innocent ears that did not know what was happening in the bed in the next room. Wanda wasn't a naive country innocent. Sixteen-year-old Wanda knew what sex was. She didn't know about sex from personal experience, but she knew the basics of sex. Most of what she knew she had picked up on the streets and on the playground of her high school from other children through secondhand schoolyard chatter and girlish gossip. The only visual association Wanda had with sex to date was what she had glanced on the covers of the types of magazines her parents wouldn't let her read. This was Wanda's first audio encounter with real-time, real-life, hard-core sex. It was coming through the wall in full, unvarnished intensity from an act of primal and unsentimental sex.

Wanda knew enough about sex to know that sex could be illicit. She also knew that illicit sex with a low-rent rendezvous often took place in the kind of cheap no-tell motel she was staying in. What was happening in the next room wasn't something blessed by the white-lace and chiffon trimmings of *Modern Bride* magazine. The liaison happening in the room next door probably hadn't been blessed by the benefit of clergy either.

Though she hadn't been around the block where sex was concerned, Wanda was under no illusion that the sex taking place in the next room was a chaste, pure, romantic encounter between Prince Charming and Snow White. Wanda didn't know who the people in the next room were. She didn't know what race they were. She didn't know what age they were. They could have been a married couple like her parents. But given the setting, Wanda doubted their marital status. Married people had their own homes and residences to have sex in. Unmarried couples tended to patronize motels when coming together from two directions not otherwise attached to each other. Motels were the only open ground to meet on without their, probably illicit, liaisons being known. Though the ages of the couple in the next room were indeterminate from the sound, the man and woman sounded a lot younger and more energetic than an old married couple tired out from driving all day while returning from visiting relatives.

Wanda lay in her bed, not moving or making a sound. She didn't call out through the wall to let the couple know the sound of their coming together was carrying beyond the room they were carrying on in. For one, Wanda was afraid the couple might become angry if their passionate wrestle were interrupted by a teenager banging on the wall and telling them to keep the noise down. For another, Wanda didn't want them to stop. And she didn't want them to know they were being overheard. It might have dampened their ardor completely. Wanda wanted to hear it all.

Wanda was transfixed by the sounds coming through the wall from the adjoining room and the advanced plane of sex going on. She knew about sex. She knew that sex was physical, and she had the general idea that sex could at times be energetic. But what she was hearing wasn't the genteel and ladylike sex only hinted at in her mother's copies of *Good Housekeeping* magazine. This wasn't the powdered and perfumed sex that proper young country ladies were supposed to be exposed to in only minute doses at a time and were supposed to think of only in limited powdered and perfumed terms. This was all sex and all-at-once sex. It wasn't detached, theoretical sex. Wanda was hearing real-life sex happening in real time. It was probably also real-world illicit. It was real-life, real-screaming, real-sweat full-tilt sex. What was going on in the next room was shuddering, grinding, thrashing sex. It was the kind of sex during which a woman threw herself onto a man, wrapped her arms and legs around him, yelled her head off, flopped around frantically like a boated marlin, worked her muscles like a sharecropper hoeing a field by hand under a hot summer sun, sweat like a field hand lugging bales of cotton on a hot summer day, got down and crawled under and got greased up and dirty like an auto mechanic working on a car, bent all the rules of ladylike behavior, broke all the rules of decorum, broke the sound barrier, and broke the bed frame.

The impressionable Wanda was hearing sex of a kind that she had only heard about distantly before that night. She had wondered if it existed. Wanda knew that sex was supposed to feel good, but she hadn't thought it could feel that good. To Wanda's ears, it seemed that good and better to the woman in the next room.

The woman in the next room sounded as if she were lost in pleasure. From the sounds the woman was making—and she was doing a lot of vocalization—she sounded totally submerged in passion and pleasure. Wanda hadn't known that a woman could lose herself in pleasure the way the woman in the next room was. She'd had no idea that pleasure could be as pure as what the woman in the next room seemed to be experiencing. She'd had no idea sex could be as raw and unvarnished as the sex going on in the adjoining room. From the intensity, tone, depth, and modulation of her screams and moans, the female member of the unseen couple sounded as if she had eagerly abandoned herself to her pleasure. The unseen woman seemed to be lost in total pleasure.

To Wanda's way of hearing it and imagining it, the narrow confines of the motel room had expanded outward to become the entire universe for the woman. The horizon of the room and the sex she was having in the room had become the only horizon the woman could see. It was the only horizon she wanted to see. The woman had abandoned herself to her horizon. She was presently engaged in running as hard as she could to embrace her horizon as she ran hard with her lover.

However intensely the more sexually advanced couple in the next room were getting it on, for some time, it had otherwise been coming on with Wanda.

Sixteen-year-old Wanda was just past the beginning stages of puberty and picking up steam fast. The hormones of her maturing body were kicking in stronger by the day as Wanda's preteen years gave way to the beginning of her teenage years at sixteen and the beginning of the sexual drive that could make the teen years so giddy, swirling, and confusing. All the hallmarks of developing puberty and the firing up of her sexual drive were there in Wanda. She noticed a heightened feeling of clothing next to her body and the feel of her clothes growing tight as she grew out of them. She liked the feel of tight clothes on her. She liked the way the boys looked at her in her tight jeans and blouses. She noticed exaggerated sensitivity of her nipples to the touch of any kind of bra or clothing, the furtive glances of boys looking at her, her furtive glances at boys, and the longer sidelong looks at certain boys. She felt a sense and awareness that boys were looking at her. A tension came over her body when certain boys looked at her and her body. A faintness came over her when certain thoughts came spontaneously into her mind. She wondered how the lips of certain boys would feel on her lips and how their lips would feel sucking languidly on her nipples, which had grown sensitive of late and became embarrassingly erect often. A tightness came between her legs when she had the sense that boys were looking at her. The tightness came when she thought about boys when there weren't any boys around.

She imagined herself alone with a particular boy in a school washroom, with the boy standing only inches away from her body. A faintness grew within her as she imagined the boy's hand sliding smoothly inside her blouse and under her bra. She felt exaggerated tightness between her legs as she imagined the boy's hand sliding down inside her blue jeans, moving toward her dampening crotch. Subtle shuddering passed through her body as she imagined standing motionless and silent, offering no objections or impediment, and sighing heavily as the boy's hand moved the remaining distances upward and downward. As Wanda's imagination grew, she found herself wondering how wider swaths of the boy's skin would feel pressed against her unadorned skin.

All that was going on in Wanda's growing body and in her mind, which was growing more aware of her body by the day, was further enhanced by other feelings growing more pronounced and frequent: the tightness between the legs, the moisture between the legs, and the beginning of longings, the proverbial stirrings that writers were always writing about to great expenditures of ink but to no particular expenditure of wisdom.

It was part of puberty in the country. It was part of puberty everywhere. It was fast becoming a part of the developing landscape of Wanda's stirring and surging adolescence.

━━━━๑/๑/๑━━━━

For her part and all the developing parts that made her up, sixteen-year-old Wanda was good looking enough that she turned the heads of developing pubescent boys, and she drew her own sideling glances back toward them. Some people might have considered sixteen to be a bit young for boys and girls to be thinking about such things, but it hadn't been that long ago that Jerry Lee Lewis got in trouble for marrying his sixteen-year-old cousin. When it came to sex, country folk sometimes jumped on the bandwagon a bit early.

The Japanese martial art of jujitsu was based on shifting balances, catching opponents off balance, and using leverage to pull them off their feet and throw them down onto the mat. In an unintentional act of sexual jujitsu, the couple in the next room had caught the impressionable Wanda at the precise moment in her developing puberty when she was most off balance and at the peak of her forming sexual impressionability. The couple throwing themselves around and throwing themselves onto each other in the next room were throwing Wanda across the floor of the room of her life. In short order, they would throw Wanda out the door and onto the road with the impression they had left firmly in her mind. The gasping, moaning, shouting, pleasure-racked sounds of the couple in the next room would eventually become Wanda's mantra and her vagabond wanderer's song of the open road.

Though the couple were carrying on as if they were recapitulating the coming of original sin and the fall of mankind in the Garden of Eden, Wanda didn't know the couple from Adam, nor did she know what, if anything, the affair meant to the couple beyond the night they were in it together with each other. For all Wanda knew, the affair could have been a one-night stand.

Wanda was old enough and sexually informed enough to be familiar with the term *quickie*. She was also aware that not every act of sex was an entrée into grand, devoted, enduring passion and love between people and that not every night spent together by a couple was the beginning of a happily ever after between them. Instead of walking off together into the

29

sunset to start a life together, in the light of the morning, the couple could shake hands and walk off in different directions.

Since the couple next door had arrived in one car, the driver of the car would have to drop off his or her partner somewhere down the road, and the noisy affair could be the end of the romantic road for the couple. That the affair was taking place in a sleazy motel with soiled rooms instead of a manicured hotel with a bridal suite next to a wedding chapel boded more for the possibility the couple would be making a quick exit from each other after their long penetration than beginning a lifetime commitment to each other.

However much of a quickie the affair otherwise represented, the physical affair didn't end quickly. For an extended period of time, the man and woman ground away at each other. The man kept up what seemed to Wanda an exhausting pace. Whatever position the woman was keeping her end up in, she kept up her end of the sound effects in pace with the man's bed-rocking regimen.

The woman's cries of pleasure continued to run the gamut of sounds as she ran the gauntlet of the man's pressing sexuality. The woman's voice alternately went from a low-pitched, extended, wavering vibrato to high-pitched squeals and then back down again into heavy and heaving gasps and back up again into guttural shouts. That the couple were able to keep up such a sustained pace indicated they were young and in the peak of physical fitness and endurance. The deeper resonance and range of the woman's voice indicated she was older than a teenager. At no time in the energetic abandonment of her shouting did the woman shout the man's name. The fact that no names were used made Wanda further suspect the couple weren't particularly looking toward each other and a life afterward. The motel they were in, the night they were in, and the affair they were in seemed to consume them both as if there were no world or horizon beyond.

Whatever depth might or might not have been contained in the affair, the sounds coming from the next room were transformative to Wanda. The apparent illicitness of the affair going on in the next room only made it all the more compelling to the impressionable girl. Wanda lay on her bed's lumpy mattress, listening to the sounds from the next room. If this sort of thing went on routinely at the motel, Wanda understood why the mattresses were so worn, thin, and lumpy. And stained.

No one could have accused Wanda of not being an imaginative girl. Up to that night, Wanda's imagination had been divided in several different and largely unconnected directions. That feature of Wanda's imagination would return the next day in a modified form, but for the particular night at hand, Wanda's imagination went into overdrive and was focused in one direction. Her surging imagination envisioned the woman's body surging beneath her lover's body. She imagined the couple in the next room thrashing around on their own equally lumpy mattress with their clothing strewn around the floor and wrinkled sheets sliding off them and onto the floor. The couple now were completely naked, exposed, and abandoned to their passion; their bodies heaved together, struggling and surging against each other. Sweat glistened on their bodies in the faint light of the shade-drawn room; the sweat of their love soaked through the sheets beneath them down into the mattress. The stains of their love added to the stains of an already stained mattress. Wanda's innate imagination, working in tandem with the intensity and single direction the experience was taking her in, set the pattern for a large portion of her life to come.

Wanda had never before been exposed to sex like the kind she was hearing from the next room, and she had never reacted to any sexual stimulus the way she reacted that night while lying in her bed. Wanda lay tense and motionless in her bed, listening to the intense motion taking place in the next room. She didn't say anything out loud to the people in the next room. She didn't even say anything to herself. As the couple slid around in their bed, lubricated by the growing liquid of their passion for each other, for Wanda, the experience more or less slid beyond the bonds and boundaries of words. In short order, it would slide Wanda beyond what her country parents and upbringing considered the bounds of propriety.

The same faintness Wanda had experienced in the presence of certain sexual thoughts was back again, stronger in the presence of the raw sex she hadn't thought existed. A faint moistness was rising on Wanda's chest and upper body. Though Wanda wasn't moving at the pace of the couple, though she wasn't moving at all, she was beginning to sweat herself. The moisture forming on her upper body was nothing compared to the wetness rising between her legs. Her wetness was coming on stronger than she had ever felt before. A tension Wanda had never felt before arose in her lower body and legs.

Lying in her bed, sprawled out, Wanda imagined herself in the place of the woman in the next room. She projected herself into the woman's bed. Wanda projected herself into the "shameless hussy" her mother would probably have called the woman. She imagined herself in the bed the woman had thrown herself in, with her legs thrown apart as wide as she could manage. As a cheerleader on the cheerleading squad of her high school, Wanda was able to do the splits. Now Wanda imagined tossing decorum and ladylike behavior as far away from her as she could and tossing her legs as wide open as she could to her lover for the night.

As she imagined herself as the woman surrendered to and lost in passion in the next room, Wanda wasn't imagining herself locked in the arms of and locked in passion with any of the boys in her high school. As she lay there with her breath coming faster and her skin growing moist with a thin mist of sweat, she wasn't thinking in terms of her peer group. As she lay there under the swelling stimulation of her vicarious joining in the passion taking place in the next room, she imagined herself as a grown woman having all-out thrashing sex with a grown man as her lover. From that moment on, as she imagined sex and passion the way she was hearing it, gum-chewing, leering, bra-strap-snapping, immature teenage boys did not rise up into the picture Wanda had of sex and lovers and herself as a lover. She wanted a mature man as a lover. From that moment forward, the pattern of Wanda's desire was set decidedly. The application of her new formula and pattern would have to wait a few years before she fully implemented it. But her decidedness would endure undiminished and uncompromised. But then, Wanda had always been a set and decided girl.

Wanda's vicarious imagining carried her right into the veritable throbbing, sweating, churning scene going on in the next room. She imagined herself in the place of the woman in the bed. The sheets had been cast off the bed by their grappling. She imagined herself soaked with sweat from the moist and intimate struggle she was engaged in with her lover. She imagined sweat glistening on herself instead of the unknown woman. She imagined her sweaty palms repeatedly gripping the man's thrashing buttocks, with her grip slipping on the man's sweat. Wanda imagined drops of sweat splashing off her body as the man splashed his body against hers. She imagined drops of sweat flying through the gap temporarily left between them as the man pulled back before thrusting again. She imagined the thicker, heavier wetness of the other liquid a woman's body produced during sex covering her crotch and her lover's crotch, glistening a creamier sheen in the faint light of the room, soaking a deeper and more luxuriant stain into the bed below. She imagined her muscles straining and pulling, pulling her lover down into her.

She imagined the man slamming into her repeatedly, showing no sign of slowing his pace or abating the force of his thrusts. Wanda imagined herself keeping time to the man's heaving pushing of himself into her. She imagined herself heaving and raising up, arching her back, pushing herself up against her lover in response and rhythm with his thrusts downward into her, pushing herself up to join with her lover, pushing herself to the limit of her ability, rising to the limit of her sexuality as she approached what she knew would turn into a gripping, shuddering, convulsing orgasm.

Wanda imagined small impact waves spreading out across her abdomen from the slamming of the man's waist into hers. She imagined her nipples erect and tense, almost aching with the pleasure of the moment they were part of, longing to be fondled and kissed in their erectness. Wanda imagined the heavy thickness of her lover's manhood filling her vagina to its total depth. She imagined the feeling of pleasure filling her whole body and the whole of her being. Above all, she imagined herself being swept up, swept away, and lost in a vortex of pleasure so intense that time and space seemed to disappear, so total and engulfing that she lost track of where she was and whom she was with, and so complete and dominating that when she was in the swirling center of it, she even forgot her name.

Wanda imagined yelling her head off. She imagined shouting and screaming out no particular recognizable articulation except to give vent to the total pleasure that was shaking her like a rag in a dog's mouth, shouting out no particular name except the name of the passion that had come to take her totally and possess her in its shuddering fullness. Wanda imagined no demand upon herself at the time except the demand of her needs and the total demand her body was putting on her to fulfill those needs. She imagined herself free, with no claim on her except the internal claim her body and passion were placing on her. She imagined hearing no call other than the call of passion. She imagined herself knowing no name and going by no name other than the name of passion.

The grasping, gasping, bed-shaking embrace of the couple next door was lasting longer than Wanda had imagined sex lasted. In retrospect, she would realize it probably wasn't a world record for a sexual clinch, and it probably didn't last as long as it seemed to, but at that moment, to Wanda, it seemed like a proverbial eternity. The developing pubescent Wanda lay wide awake, swathed in the sweat of her body and the sweat of her imaginings, listening to the sounds of the rhythmic squeaking of the bed and the noise of the couple coming through the wall.

Wanda listened, enraptured, to the undulating cries of the woman. She didn't know who the unseen woman was. She didn't know anything about the woman. In the quantum leap her activated pubescence had taken, she only knew that she envied the woman. Wanda imagined herself in the woman's place. In the sudden exponential surge of her pubescence, the only wish Wanda had in that fantasy moment was to trade places with the woman. For another length of time that probably wasn't as long as it seemed, Wanda lay silently in her bed in her motel room, her body trembling, her mind going faint, wishing she could join the couple in the next room.

Then, suddenly, Wanda realized there was a way she could join with the couple, so to speak.

Another wave of faintness came over Wanda at what she was thinking about doing. For a moment, her thoughts wavered. Then the thin membrane of reticence was broken by the silent and shabby illicitness of the motel room she was in and the screaming illicitness of the lovemaking going on in the adjoining room. She was going to do it. Wanda had heard of other girls who had done it. Girls who did it were the subject of gossip. It was speculated that certain girls had done it without there being any evidence that they had done it. Wanda hadn't done it. But she would tonight.

It was looked upon as something not done by proper and chaste young ladies. But she was going to do it. Her mother might have said it was wicked. But she was going to do it. Most of the other mothers in her hometown would probably had said it was wicked. But she was going to do it. The minister of the local church she attended with her parents in her hometown would probably have said it was wicked. But she was going to do it. The teachers in the grade school she had graduated from might have smacked her hands with a ruler if they had known what she would do with them. But she was going to do it. The guidance counselors at her high school would probably have given her a lecture on how that kind of behavior would probably leave her with a distorted view of sex. The home economics teachers in the high school would probably have said that things like that just weren't done by proper young ladies. But she was going to do it. They would have said that proper young men didn't think highly of girls who did that kind of thing. But she was going to do it. Wanda knew what the other girls would think of her if they found out she had done it.

But she was going to do it. She didn't know what the boys would think
of her if word got out and around that she had done it. She didn't know if
she could ever think of herself in the same way again if she did it. But she
was going to do it.

Sitting partway up in bed, Wanda reached down and pulled the pantie
section of her nightie down over her legs and off. With her feet, she pushed
the nightie bottom off to the side under the covers. The moist tension in
Wanda's crotch and waist increased exponentially as she lay back down on
the bed, planning to do what she was going to do.

After Wanda lay back down, she reached up and slowly and deliberately
opened the buttons on the top section of her nightie. After the last button
had been unbuttoned, in a slow and deliberate motion, Wanda pulled
the top of her nightie down until it came off her shoulders. Wanda then
pulled her arms out of the short sleeves of the nightie top, leaving herself
all the way out of the pulled-down nightie, and left it lying under her back.
Once again, Wanda was unadorned in the unadorned motel room that
had probably seen as much unadorned passion and coupling as was going
on in the next room. The walls were so thin that the straining sounds of
unadorned sex next door came through to her as if the passion-absorbed
and taken couple were in the room with her.

Wanda's thighs and upper legs seemed to ache in anticipation of what
was to come. Her now bare shoulders tingled. Her bare back and buttocks
tingled as she wondered how many affairs and mingled naked bodies the
bed she was in had been the scene of over the years. She wondered how
many affairs had left their reminders soaked into the mattress she lay on.
Wanda could feel the cool of the night air of the room on her exposed
chest and waist. Wanda's nipples grew even more erect at the touch of the
sheet and the thought of how many other affairs the sheets may have been
touched by. The tension in Wanda's body and mind grew as she knew that
in her own way, she was about to merge herself into the illicitness of the
motel and the illicitness of what was going on in the next room.

Wanda cupped her hands over her breasts, separating them from the
touch of the sheets. She ran her fingers back and forth over the rubbery tips
of her erect nipples. Little electric shocks of pleasure ran through Wanda's
chest, upper back, and shoulders. Playing with oneself was not considered
polite behavior for girls in Wanda's circle. She would be talked about in
her circle if it became known what she was doing. But Wanda had left that
circle far away behind her. All she could hear talking to her was noise from

the impolite sex going on one room over. That was all Wanda could hear. It was all she wanted to hear. The sounds surrounded and engulfed her.

For several minutes, Wanda massaged her nipples with the tips of her fingers and the palms of her hands. The feeling of pleasure in her chest started out as a series of almost electric shocks. The jolting series of discrete electric shocks merged into a unified wave of pleasure that slowly soaked its way farther down Wanda's body.

The couple in the next room kept moving on, and Wanda moved on deeper into passion and sensual revelation with them. She took her hands off her breasts and laid them down on her chest just below her breasts. With a slow and exaggerated motion, Wanda slid her hands down along her sides, feeling the touch of her hands on her naked skin. She wished it was the touch of the male hands of the woman's lover in the next room. From the bottom of her ribs, Wanda ran her hands over the concave curve of her trim and tight cheerleader's abdomen. She continued to move her hands on down over the front of her lower stomach to her waist and beyond, following the contours and bends of her lower body and the focus of her own internal contours and bend to the natural focus that both led toward. Wanda's hands pressed down on her body as they covered the final distance. Her crotch grew tight with anticipation as her hands neared.

As Wanda moved her hands, she felt as soiled and shabby as the motel room she was in. She also felt as illicit as the probably illicit couple in the next room. But the feelings of shabbiness and illicitness didn't stay or even slow Wanda's hands. The feelings washing over Wanda were the point of the exercise. The shabbiness of the setting and the feelings of illicitness going on in the next room and in her own bed were the icing on the cake.

As Wanda's heart and desire merged with the sounds of the surrender to passion coming from the next room, Wanda's hands merged with and flowed into the growing moistness that had started to flow since she had first heard the sounds of desire and craving coming from the next room.

From the vantage point of her hands and all the vantage points going on in her mind, Wanda thrust the first three fingers of both hands into the warm wetness of her vagina from both sides as deep as she could. The fit was tight but not that tight.

Sixteen-year-old Wanda was a big girl for her age. She had to sit back up partially and lean forward in order to get leverage and depth. Her hands slipped deeply into the creamy concoction the passion of the lovers in the next room and the fantasies of her own mind had prepared for her.

An intense and grabbing wave of pleasure shot through Wanda's body. She gasped and sat up farther under the effect of the sudden rush of sensual eroticism. She hadn't expected anything as intense as the wave of pleasure that ran outward from the center of her waist through her whole body to her extremities. Wanda knew sex was supposed to feel good, but she hadn't known that even autoerotic sex could feel that good. The woman in the next room was still shouting and crying in the throes of the intensity she was experiencing. In the rush of the unexpected intensity of her own pleasure, it was all Wanda could do to keep from crying out in pleasure herself. She had to bite her lip to keep from shouting out.

For a minute or two, Wanda sat in a forward lean, working her fingers in and out of her vagina with increasing speed. She picked up the pace. Successive waves of pleasure surged through Wanda as she worked her fingers in and out rapidly. The speed of Wanda's hands kept time with the tempo of the couple in the next room. She thrust her hands into herself as fast, as hard, as deep, and in as much total abandon to pleasure as the couple in the next room. The remainder of her adolescent innocence flew off and away from her as had the panties she had cast aside. She kept up the rapid pace of her autoerotic physical self-stimulation, in total abandonment of the remainder of her innocence.

The semisitting position Wanda had pushed herself into caused her to arch her back. It was an uncomfortable position and a hard position to hold. To get into a more comfortable position that could be sustained longer and would allow her to work herself and her pleasure longer, Wanda rolled over onto her left side in the bed and drew herself up into the fetal position. That gave her the reach and angle she needed for sustained movement.

The couple in the next room hadn't slowed their pace. Wanda deliberately matched the pace of their mutual pleasuring of each other with the pace of her own self-pleasuring. She worked her hands in and out and from side to side in her vagina. She randomly varied the direction and approach of her hands into her crotch as the woman in the next room randomly varied the form and intensity of the pleasure sounds she was making. But Wanda maintained the same pace as the couple. Wanda gasped silently to herself, but she didn't let any sound out. She didn't want the couple in the next room to think she was somehow making fun of them, and she didn't want them to stop. But she didn't know how long she could hold her silence.

37

Silently, Wanda thrust her fingers into herself in time with the thrusting of the couple in the next room. She worked her fingers in and out, trying to stretch deeper and deeper into herself. She bent forward more at the waist. She thrust her hips up as if trying to push her hips up and around her hands. She worked her upper arms and shoulders as well as her lower arms and hands. Along with all the other feelings flowing through her and out of her, Wanda could feel the flow of her own natural lubricant. In short order, Wanda's fingers were covered in warm, slippery solution. As time stretched out and Wanda stretched to reach deeper, the fluid moved up higher on Wanda's hands and out across her crotch and down the insides of her thighs. While Wanda had lain silently listening to the couple and fantasizing, she had raised only a faint moisture on her body. Under her fast-paced physical exertion, Wanda started to sweat seriously. The bedsheet immediately under her was becoming as soaked as her hands were. The thin liquid of her sweat would penetrate the sheets and soak down into the mattress, which had probably been soaked on innumerable occasions before. In the end, Wanda would add the soil of her own sweat and body fluid to the mattress of the room.

In the next room, locked in her fast-paced reverie of lust, the woman continued to moan, yell, and cry out in pleasure. In the intensity of her own pleasure, Wanda held her silence while she held her mouth open. The other reason Wanda didn't want to make any sound was because she didn't want to wake up her parents. Despite all Wanda had been hearing, she hadn't heard anything from her parents in the next room on the other side. Apparently, the sounds the woman made as she was being penetrated by her lover weren't penetrating through the second wall enough to wake them up. Also, Wanda didn't want the couple to realize they were being heard. That could cause them to pull in their horns.

Wanda was an active but silent participant in the passion going on in the next room. She gasped her own gasps, moaned her own moans, cried her own cries, and shouted her own shouts silently in the darkness of the motel room in time and variation with the loud cries the woman sent out into the darkness of the room next door and through the wall. Wanda moved in the throes of her own pleasure as fast as the couple moved in theirs. Wanda moved her body in both controlled, sensuous rhythm and shuddering, herky-jerky movements, just as the couple in the next room were moving their bodies. Wanda was growing as wet and sweaty as the couple in the next room. She threw herself into her own pleasure with as much abandon as the couple threw themselves onto each other and the man threw himself into the woman. In her own way, Wanda had joined the couple in the next room.

Listening to the couple in the next room was Wanda's first encounter with actual live sex. To her, hearing live sex was more of a turn-on than seeing it in a skin magazine or a dirty movie. It was not staged. If Wanda had seen a couple doing it in a fifteen-minute one-reel stag film of her day, the effect on her wouldn't have been nearly as profound. The people in those movies were paid actors. The people in the next room were real people—people like her. They weren't acting for the camera. They were being swept along by the passion in them. Wanda's experience was magnified because it was real life. It also was magnified because it happened right at a critical juncture when the crossbow string of her developing sexuality was cocked in adolescent intensity. The sounds of the couple making love in the next room had driven Wanda's swelling adolescent sexuality several quantum jumps up at once to an intensity she hadn't known was in her and hadn't realized could exist.

Wanda didn't know the length of time she spent in her exercise in self-stimulation. For Wanda, time in the motel room stretched out into a borderless landscape where the passage of time compared to the outside world was hard to gauge. Time, exacting and relative, had become a detached unknown to Wanda and as much of a detached irrelevance as the names of the couple in the next room. The only relative chronological milepost of significance for the night was that the time when Wanda inserted her fingers into her vagina and masturbated for the first time in her life divided the night into two irrevocable halves the way the night itself would come to irrevocably divide Wanda's life.

As far as relative measures of time and other things went, the time Wanda spent proactively pursuing her own pleasure with her fingers massaging the inside of her vagina was at least as long as the time she had lain passive and motionless while listening to the couple thrash around and fantasizing about joining them. The time might have been one and a half times as long or up to twice as long. Wanda would never be sure what the actual time ratio of the two stages was. While the night itself would stand out sharply in Wanda's memory for the rest of her life and would come to shape the calculations for a large part of her life, certain relative parts of the night would remain a blur.

Actual levels of physical energy expended on both sides of the wall were also a bit relative to Wanda's perceptions. If a more detached and clinical observer had timed the couple with a stopwatch, they might not have come near to setting an all-time land-speed record for sexual velocity. But from the newly sexually initiated Wanda's perspective, the pace of the couple seemed frenetic.

Frenetic or not, the couple kept up their fast pace in the room next door. In her bed, Wanda kept pace with them. She wasn't about to fall behind and drop away. She was determined to hold in there with them as long as they could. She had the cheerleader stamina to do it.

Wanda continued to push her fingers as far into her vagina as physiology and comfort would allow. She continued to work her fingers from side to side and around in circular movements. She drew her legs up closer to her waist. As much as she could, Wanda crossed her legs and wrapped them around her hands. Periodic pleasure contractions pressed the walls of Wanda's vagina against her fingers. She shuddered just as the woman in the next room seemed to periodically shudder. But Wanda held her tongue in a way that the woman in the next room didn't.

Holding her tongue wasn't that easy of a task for Wanda. The natural proclivity she was discovering in herself was to shout her head off the way the woman in the bed in the next room was doing. A mental trick men were supposed to use when trying to prevent themselves from ejaculating was to think about baseball. To keep herself from verbally ejaculating, Wanda used the mental trick of imagining her mouth being filled with something that prevented her from yelling. To hold her tongue, Wanda imagined the man's mouth pressed against hers, with his lips covering her lips and his tongue filling her mouth. In an alternative scenario, she imagined her lips wrapped around another portion of the man's anatomy, with his generous fullness filling her mouth to the point of rendering her lips silent as deep-throated moans gathered in her throat.

Wanda didn't know how long she had lain in bed as a passive yet active partaker of the passion of the couple in the adjoining room. She didn't know how long it had been since she had made herself into an active, if removed, participant. She didn't know how long the couple could keep it up. She especially wondered how long the man could keep it up. But Wanda was sure she could keep up with the couple, and she intended to do exactly that. For a typical teenage cheerleader country girl, Wanda had an organized and set mind. When she set her mind to do something, she usually accomplished it, and she usually did so in an organized and decided manner. Even balled up in the fetal position, caught up head over heels in a vortex of disorienting pleasure, and lost to the thought of time and names, Wanda was still Wanda. She was determined to see her passion through to the end of the passion in the next room as long as the couple in the next room were determined to pursue their passion. Wanda would set her own course in the world and in the world of passion and the pursuit of pleasure. However, at that moment, in the pursuit of passion at the motel, Wanda would let the couple set the duration and speed of their runaway passion, which she was determined to keep pace with.

Like the creamy solution flowing out over Wanda's fingers, pleasure flowed out from the central focus between Wanda's legs. Pleasure flowed out of her in spasmodic spurts that made Wanda gasp. It flowed in a steady, even background flow. The pleasure spurted and flowed from Wanda's body like a newly erupted stream flowing from a mountain for the first time, cutting its own winding path as it flowed down the slope. For Wanda, falling into the undiscovered territory of pleasure was like falling into a formerly unseen and unknown vortex that whirled her around and drew her down into it until she vanished below the surface. At the same time, Wanda's pleasure carried her outside her body in directions she had never been carried before. Wanda was transported by the experience. For a while, in the flow of her imagination, which was flowing with the fluid motion of her hands and the liquid flow of her first experience in mature passion, Wanda was transported outside the former narrow limitations of herself and beyond the immediate confines of the soiled bed she was busy soiling further.

The unknown woman in the adjoining room went into a series of deeply sensual female gasps. As the nameless woman on the other side of the wall gasped and moaned, in her expanding imagination, Wanda's throbbing body lifted off the bed. From midair in the shabby, earthbound motel room that had become a launching pad for Wanda's mounting imagination, Wanda was transported through the worn curtains covering the window and out into the parking lot immediately adjacent to her room. Just beyond her door, Wanda could see the closed door and drawn curtains of the motel room next door. From the outside in the parking lot, the room was as dark as her room was. Inside, it was alive with activity. The next moment, in her imagination, Wanda found herself ascending into the air. In a few moments, the motel was just a vague linear architectural outline in the darkened landscape below. All around her, laid out in silhouette in semidarkness, the moonlit landscape shimmered in all directions from horizon to horizon. Above her, the edges of the darkened clouds glowed silver in the light of the moon. The clouds themselves glowed in pearlescent light as they passed in front of the moon. It was stock erotic boilerplate language to describe sexual experience in quasimystic terms of rapturous transport, soaring, and floating, but for Wanda, it worked for the particular circumstance. Wanda's body was working for her, and she hadn't known her body could function so richly.

But Wanda didn't stay suspended in the air of detached quasimystic, erotic metaphor for long. After gasping during the short interval of Wanda's extramotel transport into the night sky above, the faceless woman in the next room unleashed another round of guttural moans and screams. In a flash, Wanda was back in her shabby motel room, in her bed, which was becoming more soiled by the minute. In the next moment of Wanda's imagination, she was transported through the wall separating her room from the couple next door. In an even faster flash, she was transported into the body of the screaming, writhing woman. Semimystic analogies of transport were all right, but high in the air wasn't where Wanda wanted to go at the moment. Wanda wanted to go fully deep into the moaning, panting, gasping, shouting woman who was faceless but decidedly not voiceless.

Wanda didn't want to be a disembodied sprite floating above the scene. She didn't want to observe the scene in the next room from a detached, drifting distance; she wanted to be the scene in the next room. Wanda didn't want open air. She wanted the close, closed-in confines of the shabby room next door. Wanda didn't want to be in the high air above the ground, no matter how erotically charged the air above ground might have been. She wanted to be rolling around on the dirt of the ground. The only suspension Wanda wanted was to be suspended no more than two feet above the soiled carpet of the room next door, in the soiled bed the unknown couple were dirtying further with the sweat and other wetness of their passions. Wanda longed to be in the woman's place in the bed in the next room. That was the only longitude and latitude Wanda wanted. The woman's position on the bed was the only elevated altitude Wanda wanted or further imagined that night.

As the nameless woman in the next room held the timbre, pitch, and volume of her vocalizations, Wanda held her focus on what the woman was doing and what was going on in the next room. She also held the pace with which and depth to which her fingers moved inside her vagina. However high the moon might have been that night, Wanda wanted nothing higher than the position of the woman on her soaked and disheveled bed. Wanda's autoeroticism was unexpectedly pleasurable, but it still wasn't the real thing.

At sixteen, Wanda felt she was old enough to want the real thing. Though what she was doing for herself for the first time was fun, for Wanda, it was only the author's dedication and introductory paragraph to the novel that lay unread ahead of her. At that moment, Wanda wanted to be the story. She wanted to be the woman writing her story in the shouts of her passion. Wanda wanted to be at the center of the thrust and grasp of the shabby wrestling match going on in the next room. She wanted to be at the center of the wet smacking-together struggle going on between the unknown man and the unknown but decidedly unquiet woman. Wanda wanted to be as deep inside the woman as the woman's lover was inside her.

In the relative stage of her sexual consciousness, a consciousness that was suddenly being accelerated to warp speed, Wanda wanted to be bound up in the arms of a lover as tightly as if she were being wrapped by a constrictor snake. She wanted to hear her screams of pleasure piercing the dark air of the room, not caring whether the sound carried through the walls and into the shocked ears of more sensitive hearers. She wanted to hear and feel her screams of pleasure cut off by the heavy press of her lover's lips squeezing down on her lips, forcing her cries back down her throat as her lover forced himself as deep into her as he could. Instead of using her hands to perform counterfeit pleasure on herself, Wanda wanted to feel her hands and arms running wildly in random directions over her lover's sweaty back, feeling the energetic, rippling work of his muscles. She wanted to feel her fingers and fingernails dig into her lover's back. She wanted to feel her lover grab her arms at the wrists and throw her arms out to the side as he threw her limbs and body wide into a full spread-eagle position. As far as levitating or elevating herself went, the only elevating Wanda wanted to feel was herself arching up in a pleasure spasm, pushing her back and upper body up against the downward pressure of her lover's thrusting body, raising herself and him above the bed in an arch that she held in a pleasure-filled contraction until the seizure broke and she collapsed back onto the bed with her lover still thrusting into her in an unbroken chain.

The imagination of the young but now not quite as young Wanda imagined another contraction wave sweeping over her body that drove her to rise up again in another back-bending wave of pleasure. As fast as the images came into her mind—while she came in her hands—Wanda embraced them as fast and hard as she would have liked to be embraced by the unknown woman's lover. In the fast turnover in her mind, Wanda imagined herself held down by the unknown man while keeping up the same pace he was.

In Wanda's imagination, the man was still faceless, but in the light that her imagination shed on the room, the woman was no longer faceless. Wanda imagined an older version of her own face on the sweating, heaving body of the woman. Images flew into and through her mind as fast as the frenetic sexual pace the couple were keeping up in the next room— images as varied and intense as the sounds the woman was making. In the throbbing of the immediate moment, Wanda thought of the immediate, intense, throbbing, energetic experience the woman was going through in the next room. She energetically thought of herself in the place of the woman. In the exponential leap of sexual awareness she was experiencing, Wanda wasn't aware that sexual maturity or sexual consciousness could take quantum leaps. She wasn't thinking about the long-term. She wasn't thinking in terms of moments that could transform her life or of transition points that could change the direction of her life and set a whole new mold for her life without her realizing it at the time.

For Wanda, it was an experience that changed her life in a cold instant—or, in Wanda's case, in a hot and sweaty hour—but the realization that her life had changed wouldn't come that night. The realization that her life had been set on a different path would subtly develop over an extended period of time beginning the next morning. At the current moment, Wanda was too preoccupied to realize the definitive experience would change and define her life from that night on. At the throbbing present, subtlety was lost on Wanda, just as it was lost on the couple in the next room. Under the stimulating spell of listening to the woman in the next room go through stimulation, Wanda was thinking only of how much she wanted to be in the place of the moaning, shuddering, heaving, sweating, grasping, screaming, thrashing, surging, panting, twisting, yelling, kissing, clawing, grabbing, surrendering, possessed, and possessing woman in the next room.

After a duration of time that Wanda did not measured in absolute or relative terms, the rhythm of the sounds coming from the next room changed. The speed of the encounter picked up to a furious pace. The individual squeaks of the bed came so fast and close on the heels of each other they seemed to merge into one long, drawn-out squeal. The woman's staccato cries turned into one long, continuous, high-volume "Oh!" that hung drawn out in the night air of both rooms. From Wanda's interpretation of the pattern shift, things seemed to be coming to a head, so to speak.

In response to the change in tempo and volume from the next room and to her determination to match the couple's speed and intensity, Wanda rolled over onto her stomach. The reach was once again longer, and Wanda kept her hands pushing at her crotch and her fingers in her vagina. As the increased speed of the lovemaking in the next room plateaued, Wanda thrashed around on the bed, still pushing her fingers into her vagina, writhing in an up-and-down, back-to-front wavelike motion that looked a bit like an out-of-water seal flopping its way across a beach. Wanda had to slow herself down when her own bed started to squeak. She still didn't want the people in the next room to hear her. She figured she would be talked about forever at her school if anyone saw her acting like that. Though her mother had never whipped her, Wanda wondered if her mother might have taken a switch to her wicked, unadorned, upturned butt waving shamelessly in the air if she'd caught her doing what she was doing.

Wanda got control of her sexual exuberance and the bed frame just in time. The squeaking of the bed in the next room faltered and then ceased entirely. From out of the dark came a deeply resonant groan of male release. It was the only male sound Wanda had heard all night. The man was a man of few words as well as stamina. The woman responded with a series of separate and distinct high-pitched half shouts. Then she too fell silent.

Wanda went as silent and still as the couple in the next room. She withdrew her hands from her crotch and lay still, listening. She heard no snippets of conversation coming through the walls. No further sound of any kind came from the room next door. Her mystery couple had gone completely silent. Wanda figured both of them had probably gone right to sleep after the man climaxed. They knew how to start an affair up without much ado. They also knew how to bring an affair to an end without a lot of trivial wrap-up. But then again, both of them were probably bone-tired.

The silence that followed the couple's climax was as full and engulfing as the noise of the couple's passion play had been. After a few minutes of listening in the now silent room, Wanda turned back onto her side and pulled the pillow up under her head more. She did not bother to put her nightie back on.

Only silence now came from the next room. Young Wanda, now mature beyond her age, figured the couple in the next room had probably fallen into an exhausted sleep. As Wanda looked out into the darkness of her own room, trying to focus her thoughts, she fell into an exhausted sleep of her own. As she drifted off into sleep, her thoughts were unformed and random. The only coherent pattern and theme that wound through her mind was the notion that although that experience had ended for the night for the couple in the next room, it wasn't going to end there for her. She had to go on from there in the new life and on the new path that the vicarious experience had set her irrevocably on. The new direction and new path she set for herself might not crystalize and form up immediately, she knew. But when it did, her new life would not be one lived vicariously from a distance. It would be fully and directly personal. It would involve her, take her, and shake her the full length of her body and her life.

As Wanda lay in sweaty silence, listening to the silence all around, she tried to sort out in her mind what had just happened in the next room and in her room. But the experience didn't fully sort itself out for Wanda beyond her knowing she would never be the same again.

But Wanda didn't particularly want to fully sort it out and analyze in a clean and clinical manner what she had heard and done. *Mystery can be much more fun when it takes you by surprise and takes over you*, she thought. With all the contradictions and new feelings circling around in her mind, without bothering to get up to wash her body and hands off, Wanda fell asleep.

3

A pounding on the door jarred Wanda out of her sleep. She opened her eyes and looked in the direction of the sound. A square outline of bright sunlight was coming from around the drawn drapes over the window. There was enough light coming around and through the drapes to partially illuminate the room. The first thing Wanda remembered was that she was stark naked. The second thing Wanda remembered was the night before. The third thing Wanda remembered was that she wasn't the same Wanda.

The knocking on her door resumed.

"Wanda, get up! We've got to get going."

Wanda recognized her mother's voice. "I'm awake!" she called back.

"Well, get up, and get dressed, girl. Your father wants to get back on the road," Wanda's mother called through the door.

Wanda made a grab for her nightie top, thinking her mother might barge through the door at any moment and catch her in the unadorned state she had slept in. If her mother had come through the door at that second, Wanda would not have gotten the nightie top back on in time. Her mother also would have caught her in a messier and more compromised state than merely being out of her nightie top.

But her mother couldn't have come through the door even if she had been of a mind to. Wanda remembered that the door was still locked, and the chain was in place. Wanda relaxed, knowing she had at least a small amount of time to straighten things out. She sat up in the soiled bed. She quickly scrounged around under the sheet, looking for the discarded pieces of her two-piece nightie.

"We've got a long way to go if we want to get home by tonight!" her mother called out. "Get yourself moving."

"I've got to get dressed!" Wanda called to her mother as she gathered up the nightie top and bottom and gathered herself. By virtue of having been off her body and discarded under the sheets, the two portions of her nightie had been spared the soaking Wanda had given herself by virtue of her lack of virtue. At least there would be no telltale hints for her mother to discover and wonder about when she went to wash her clothes. But Wanda would have to wash herself, or her blue jeans and any piece of clothing she wore below the waist would stick to her legs and crotch as if she had rubbed them with crazy glue.

"Well, be quick about it, girl," her mother said from the outside. "Your father's looking to be leaving in about ten minutes."

"I'm coming, Mom. I'm coming," Wanda said out loud. *Tell me about it*, she thought to herself as she swung her soiled legs out of the bed.

The night's activity had thrown a crimp in Wanda's plan for a quick exit in the morning. There was a lot of cleaning up to be done. Wanda's hands were sticky. Her crotch was sticky. The front of her waist was sticky. The tops of her thighs were sticky. Her left hip was sticky. Wanda pushed the top sheet to the side, fished around, and grabbed the bottom of her nightie. The bottom sheet on the bed was sticky. But Wanda figured that was a problem for the maid who cleaned up the rooms. Wanda also figured the maid potentially would have a much bigger mess to clean up in the next room.

Wanda ran into the bathroom, still in her unadorned state, tossing her nightie and her slippers into her night case as she passed by. She grabbed a washcloth from the towel rack by the sink in the washroom, turned on the water, and quickly washed all of her involved and affected areas. When Wanda was finished, she threw the washcloth into the sink—something else for the maid to attend to. Wanda wasn't sure she had gotten herself completely clean. But she sort of had the feeling she wasn't going to ever be fully clean again. She sort of liked the feeling.

Wanda zipped back into the bedroom still in her unadorned state. She dressed quickly and made sure she had everything she had come in with in her night case before she closed it. Whether she had left something of herself, symbolically speaking, in the room and was leaving with less or more than she had come with was a matter of poetic interpretation. Wanda didn't have time to sort through either detached literary-style allusion or real-world implications of what had happened the night before. Allusions and implications could be sorted out at leisure later, she thought. In that real-world moment, she had to leave. She knew she was leaving changed.

Wanda pulled the top sheet back over the sticky stain she had left on the bed. Her come stain would come as a surprise to the maid who cleaned the room. Then again, given the lower-level clientele the motel catered to, maybe it wouldn't come as a surprise. Wanda didn't know if the maid would know it was a sixteen-year-old girl who had left a stain of that size. The maid would probably think an older "shameless hussy" had left the stain. Wanda didn't particularly care if the maid knew how old she was or thought of her as the shameless hussy she had sort of been the night before. She would be gone before the maid made the discovery of her initiation into the ranks of hussies. As long as the maid didn't know her name, Wanda was willing to leave her speculating and guessing as to who she was and what she was. Of course the, maid likely would run into a lot bigger guessing game and cleaning chore in the next room.

As the last act of leaving the room where she had spent the last night of her girlhood and been ushered into the first night of womanhood, so to speak, Wanda pulled the drapes open. She grabbed her night case and the room key and opened the door. There wasn't time for a reflective look around the room where her life had changed. She would at least have liked to take a picture of the room for a secret scrapbook. She would carry a mental picture of the room with her.

Outside, in the parking lot next to her room, Wanda's parents were loading their luggage into the trunk of the car. As Wanda stepped out of the motel room, she paused to glance at the next-door room, where the passionate struggle she had taken an indirect part in had taken place the night before. Wanda hoped to catch a glimpse of the couple who had kept her up and upped the ante in her life. But there was no motion from the adjoining room. The door was shut, and the drapes were drawn. Wanda couldn't see the couple whose passion had carried through the walls and carried her over the line. They were probably still asleep in their disheveled bed. Wanda could understand that. They had probably worn themselves out. They might not get up till sometime after noon, she thought.

Wanda put her night case into the trunk and got in the backseat.

"We'll drive on for a while, and then we'll stop for breakfast somewhere down the road," Wanda's father said as he closed the trunk. "I want to put some miles behind us before we stop for breakfast."

Wanda thought silently that she had put quite a bit of mileage on herself during the night.

49

Wanda's father drove the car to the motel office to check out. At the office, Wanda got out of the car with her father, saying she had to turn in her room key. She could have given the key to her father, but she wanted an excuse to go into the motel office. Maybe they had postcards with a picture of the motel on them. She could use a postcard as a substitute reminder instead of a picture of the actual room.

Wanda dropped her key off at the front desk. They didn't have postcards at the desk, but they did have a magazine rack in the office. The desk clerk also had a radio turned on to provide background music in the office. The disc jockey of the local station wrapped up a commercial as Wanda handed in her key. Then he announced the next song: "And now here's Dion's famous love-'em-and-leave-'em song 'The Wanderer.'"

"I'm going to get a magazine," Wanda said to her father as he prepared to pay the bill. Her father said nothing. Wanda left the desk and walked over to the magazine rack. A punchy downbeat came over the radio as she approached the magazine rack. As Wanda started looking at the magazines, the song cued in:

Oh, well, I'm the type of guy who will never settle down.
Where all the girls are, yeah, you know that I'm around.
I kiss 'em, and I love 'em, 'cause to me they're all the same.
I hug 'em, and I squeeze 'em. They don't even know my name.
They call me the wanderer. Yeah, the wanderer.
I roam around, around, around, around.

The song was already an oldie by that time. Wanda hadn't paid much attention to the song before. Like most of the songs pitched to teenagers, Dion's signature song had been just teenage background noise to Wanda. In the light of Wanda's new day, the song took on subtle new meanings. The meanings wouldn't fully form up for some time, but proverbial seeds had been planted the night before and in the songs of the day:

Well, it's Flo on my left, and it's Mary on my right,
and Janie is the girl, well, that I'll be with tonight.
And when she asks me which one I love the best,
I tear open my shirt; I got *Rosie* on my chest.

'Cause I'm a wanderer. Yeah, a wanderer.
I roam around, around, around, around.

Wanda looked over the magazines on the rack. Included in the fare were typical magazines found on public magazine racks in grocery stores and motels of the day, such as *True Confessions*, *True Love*, *True Romances*, and *Screen Romances*. Despite the word *true* in the titles, Wanda doubted they contained stories that were particularly true, and she was sure the so-called confessions likely had more to do with the inventions of staff writers than with actual, notarized real-life confessions by real people. Wanda thought she could send in her own freshly minted real-world confession, but she figured the editor would probably reject it as too juvenile. Or too sticky to handle. But Wanda could point them in the general direction of a couple who had a much more rollicking real-life confession to share.

Meanwhile, on the radio, Dion's confessional song—or alter-ego fantasy song, more likely—went into its middle chorus:

Well, I roam from town to town.
I go through life without a care,
And I'm as happy as a clown
With my two fists of iron, but I'm goin' nowhere.

Wanda looked over the rack and finally selected a magazine in keeping with her interests and in keeping with a girl who had undergone the transformation she had: a copy of *Popular Electronics*.

Though Wanda had lost a good portion of her childhood innocence the night prior, the editor of a confessions magazine wouldn't have been interested in her transformation or, for that matter, in another aspect of Wanda: she was interested in radio and electronics. Eschewing romance magazines, she immersed herself in publications and periodicals about electronics and mechanics. By studying technical books on radio and electronic theory, Wanda had taught herself the field. She knew more about electronics than any of the girls in her school—or the boys, for that matter. In school, she had no soul mates to project herself over the electronics horizon with.

Of late, Wanda had been gaining practical as well as theoretical experience in the field. Following diagrams and instructions in electronics magazines, Wanda had built and made work several electronics projects, including small radio receivers. Recently, a friend of the family had given Wanda a malfunctioning Hallicrafters model SX-24 Skyrider Defiant combination shortwave and amateur band communications receiver. The radio had been built in the late 1930s. It had been a top-of-the-line receiver of its day, but it had become inoperable. The owner wasn't an electronics technician. He didn't know how to fix the radio. But he knew Wanda was interested in electronics, so he gave her the radio. Wanda's family was relatively poor. She would not have been able to buy it new on her own.

Following the schematic diagram in the instructions and a textbook on radio repair, Wanda traced down the faults, replaced parts as needed, and restored the radio to original operating capacity. It was the first professional communications receiver Wanda ever had had. She spent hours listening to shortwave broadcasts on the commercial broadcast bands and the chatter of ham radio operators on the amateur bands. A girl with a soldering iron in her hand wasn't exactly the proper picture of ladylike behavior to some people of sixteen-year-old Wanda's day and locale. But Wanda wasn't afraid to get her hands dirty in a field that she was interested in and that moved her.

Wanda took the magazine off the rack and headed back to the main desk to pay for it. As she walked back to the desk, the reprise stanza of Dion's signature song unfolded:

> Well, I'm the kind of guy who likes to roam around.
> I'm never in one place; I roam from town to town.
> And when I find myself falling for some girl,
> I hop right into that car of mine, drive around the world,
> 'Cause I'm a wanderer. Yeah, a wanderer.
> I roam around, around, around, around, around.

The instrumental bars of the song played as Wanda's father finished paying the motel bill. As Wanda paid for her magazine, the final stanzas of Dion's song played on the radio. The final stanzas were just a sum-up reprise of the proceeding stanzas. Wanda thought about the song as the desk clerk handed her the change. Wanda decided she preferred Dion's other well-known song, "Runaround Sue." In that song, it was a girl who was the wanderer who loved boys and then left them behind. As far as traveling and wandering were concerned, some of the lines of the song Wanda remembered said,

She likes to travel around.
She'll love you and put you down.
People, let me set you wise.
Sue goes out with other guys.

Wanda hadn't paid much attention to the song before. Now, in the light of a different day, with a new perspective, she kind of liked the song. It evened things up a bit.

She also thought she would have liked the name Sue better than the name Wanda. The name Susan wasn't quite as romantic as Annabel, Desdemona, or Marguerite, but it had more resonance in the field of romance or wandering than did the name Wanda. As a name and reputation, Runaround Sue worked. Runaround Wanda sounded like a character out of a *Li'l Abner* cartoon strip. People probably would have taken it for a hillbilly joke.

Wanda noticed there was a public restroom in the lobby of the motel office. Before she left, she wanted to make sure she had cleaned herself up completely. At least she wanted to check to see if anything further had leaked out.

"I need to use the washroom," Wanda said to her waiting father.

"You should have thought of that while you were still in the room," her father answered. "OK, but make it snappy. We've got to get ourselves going."

Wanda's father turned to go out to the car. Wanda could have said a thing or two about getting herself going.

As Wanda turned to head for the washroom, the DJ on the radio announced the next song: "OK, we've had Dion's classic love-'em-and-leave-'em song. Turnabout is fair play. For all you feminist-minded girls out there, here's Linda Ronstadt's love-the-boys-and-leave-them song, 'Different Drum.'"

As Wanda headed toward the washroom, the strains of a twangy guitar filled the office. The plaintive voice of Linda Ronstadt followed in time:

You and I travel to the beat of a different drum.
Oh, can't you tell by the way I run
Every time you make eyes at me?

Wanda was familiar with the lyrics, but in that time and place, the lyrics had added meaning and satisfaction to them, especially coming on the tail of the Dion song. Somebody had to tweak the nose of male wanderers in the name of the Flos, Marys, Janies, and Rosies of the world.

The level of the music reduced as Wanda shut the door of the washroom behind her, but it was still audible inside the restroom. She quickly unrolled a handful of toilet paper off the roll and moistened it with water from the sink faucet. Then she unfastened the buckle on her belt and unzipped her blue jeans. She checked under her panties and wiped herself to see if there were any lingering residual traces from the night before that she had missed in her hurried cleanup in the morning. Wanda didn't know if her mother would consider her a dirty and soiled child if she found out what she had done in her room in time with the couple in the next room or if she would simply consider her a spoiled and headstrong child. But Wanda didn't need her mother to know that the daughter she thought to be pure had taken an autoerotic step into womanhood in the manner she had. Her mother wasn't ready for her unspoiled daughter to come out at such a tender and supposedly innocent age.

As Wanda worked quickly to ensure all lingering traces of her self-initiated and self-perfumed passage into womanhood were wiped clean, out in the lobby, the song that in later years' remembrance of the night before would become her signature song continued:

> Don't get me wrong; it's not that I knock it.
> It's just that I am not in the market
> For a boy who wants to love only me.
> And I ain't saying you ain't pretty.
> All I'm saying is I'm not ready
> For any person, place, or thing
> To try and pull the reins in on me.

Wanda didn't know what her mother would have made of what she had done. Wanda didn't yet know what to make of the way she had thrown herself to the wind of passion and, vicariously through the couple in the next room, run with the feelings of her own body and her thoughts, which had run away with everything inside of her and outside of her. Wanda knew only that as far as running in any particular direction went, she couldn't go back to where she had been before last night. Whatever would come of what she had done, whatever she would come to be or make of herself, she had to go on from where she was now.

She also knew she had to get going. Her father was waiting in the car. He would probably start honking the horn if she didn't appear soon. Parents were known to grow impatient with dawdling children.

> So goodbye; I'll be leavin'.
> I see no sense for this cryin' and grievin'.
> We'll both live a lot longer if you live without me.

Wanda quickly flushed the ball of toilet paper, zipped herself back up, fastened her belt buckle, grabbed her magazine, and opened the door. She hadn't been in the restroom long. As she walked into the motel lobby, the Linda Ronstadt song was still playing. The last stanzas starting with "Don't get me wrong" repeated verbatim, winding to a repeat of the final kiss-off lines that the singer and her lover would both have better lives and would live a lot longer if they eschewed the shallow romanticism of "ever after," never saw each other again, and lived lives apart from each other.

Wanda walked quickly through the office toward the door as the final stanzas of the song repeated. By the time she reached the door, the vocal part of the song had ended. A few instrumental bars trailed off.

The last few notes of the song followed Wanda as she reached the door. She had never paid much attention to the last notes of the song, but this time, the notes affected her in a way they never had before. Wanda couldn't describe the way the notes affected her. They were just a few lilting, upbeat notes of music without any particular uniqueness to them. But to Wanda, they somehow seemed to speak of sunshine and an open blue sky, the kind of sunshine and open sky that were in the air that morning.

As Wanda pushed the door open, the notes seemed to head out through the door with her into the open sky and the horizon beyond. The feeling wasn't overpowering. It didn't last long. Wanda couldn't define the feeling, but it was reminiscent of the free and drifting feeling of distance and distant horizons she got when she was tuning the shortwave bands in the communications receiver she had rebuilt. In the back of her mind, she would remember the song and the feeling she felt that day as she stepped out of the office into the new day.

Wanda got into the car. To get to the motel exit driveway, her father had to drive past the rooms they had stayed in. As the car passed their rooms, Wanda looked at the room next to hers, hoping the couple might be up so she could catch a glimpse of them as they opened the door. At least she would get to see the couple who had stimulated her from out of the darkness the night before. The thought of the couple continued to intrigue Wanda in the light of the new morning she was heading out into.

But the door was still shut, and the drapes were still drawn. Wanda would never get a look at the mystery couple in the next room who had given her an indirect initiation into sex and passion. She wouldn't know their names. The couple would remain a faceless, nameless, identity-free road sign without any writing on it that she had encountered at the roadside motel that had become a crossroad of her life. But then again, formal introductions hadn't been the point of the evening. The world of sensuality and passion the couple had inadvertently introduced Wanda to and the emergence of the feelings imparted by both had become the real point of the exercise. Any identity the couple might have had was secondary to the new outlook on life the couple had left Wanda with. One couldn't really put a name, not a fully polite one at least, on the transformation Wanda had gone through.

Wanda didn't need to know the names of the unknown couple who had altered the ground rules and the direction of her life. Names hanging in the air were irrelevant to paths on the ground. Wanda would follow her path without knowing the names of the people who had shown her the path. She didn't need names.

As Wanda watched the door to see if it would open at the last minute, the car, driven by her father, pulled out of the driveway. The car hit the same pothole on the way out that it had hit on the way in.

As the motel disappeared behind them, Wanda turned forward in her seat. With nothing else to do, she started reading her electronics magazine. One of the articles described how to build a reasonably simple code transmitter for the twenty-meter amateur radio operator band. After reading the article, Wanda decided to build the transmitter. It would be the biggest construction project she had attempted so far, but she was sure she could complete it and make it work. She could use it on the ham bands along with the communications receiver she had successfully restored. Other than working a CB from her father's base station, Wanda hadn't gone on the air before.

But this was a new day. Horizons beyond the horizon were calling to Wanda. Far horizons had always fascinated her. That was one of the reasons she was an avid shortwave listener. Wanda had listened to shortwave broadcasts coming in over the horizon from distant countries. She had listened to amateur radio hams talking to each other over the horizon. She had listened to other people's signals long enough. It was time to send a few signals of her own. In the light of the new day and the new horizon the car headed down the road toward, Wanda no longer wanted to sit behind her shortwave radio and passively let the horizon come to her. It was time to project herself out into the horizons she had only imagined from a distance.

Wanda didn't have an amateur radio operator's license, but she could probably get a license easily enough, she thought. Getting an amateur radio operator's license required passing tests in sending and receiving Morse code and in electronic theory. Wanda already knew Morse code. She had built a small code practice oscillator and had taught herself the code. She was sure she could handle the theory part well enough.

Wanda knew she could get the proper license without too much trouble. But after a night of being transformed by the sounds of outlaw, bootlegged sex in the next room, Wanda's mind was filled with all sorts of outlaw-operation thoughts. She felt she could just as easily go on the air without a license. Following proper rules and regulations wasn't on Wanda's mind that morning. In order to operate on the ham bands without a license, she would have to bootleg a call, either by borrowing one out of the *Radio Amateur Call Book* or by making up a call sign that hadn't been issued. If she kept changing around the calls she used, she could make plenty of contacts without being detected and caught by the FCC. The point for her was to make contacts out over the horizon and then be gone without the other station knowing who she was and that they would never hear her on the air again—at least not under the same call.

Wanda's technically skilled and organized mind would complete the project and make it work. Whether she got a license or not was optional in her mind as she sat in her father's car rolling down the country road they were on. In more ways than one, the seeds of an unlicensed, outlaw-thinking life had been planted.

Wanda's father drove down the country road away from the motel. As a general rule of driving, Wanda's father liked to get an early start, and he liked to get part of the trip out of the way before they stopped to eat. They would stop for breakfast somewhere down the line after he had put some miles behind them.

Wanda sat in the backseat, pretending to read the magazine she had bought. She was careful to maintain a casual demeanor, as if nothing unusual had happened, so as not to send any subtle signals to her parents that their formerly relatively innocent daughter had become soiled. Wanda didn't know if her parents had heard the noise coming from the room two doors down from theirs. She figured if they had heard it, she would have heard about it from them. Her mother would probably have had something to say about the way the "brazen" couple had "carried on half the night." If her parents had heard the amorous couple two doors away, they would probably have assumed their daughter in the closer room had heard it. Wanda would have been a little hard-pressed to deny that she had. Both her parents would then probably have lectured their presumed innocent and unaffected daughter about avoiding the kind of shameless behavior that had gone on in the room next to hers.

Wanda certainly wasn't about to tell her parents how she had engaged herself in her own act of parallel shameless behavior. She had hurriedly cleaned up the traces of her self-generated lust the morning after. She had done the cleanup job well in the limited time frame allowed her. She wasn't about to casually come clean and tell her parents how their supposedly pure daughter had made herself into a sweating, gasping, panting, writhing, humping, pumping, heaving, wicked, shameless, autoerotic, self-stimulating, voyeuristic, sticky-crotched little slut who had thrown herself vicariously into the middle of another couple's orgy; matched their unbridled lust with unbridled, self-generated sensuality of her own; and soiled her bed and body with the fluid of her own lust while she lubricated her mind with the flowing fluid of her free-running fantasy.

But neither of her parents said anything about the couple or brought up anything vaguely along those lines. Perhaps they had fallen asleep by the time the festivities started in the room next to Wanda's. Perhaps the sound hadn't carried all the way through two walls. Time and distance had apparently combined to spare Wanda a squirmy situation.

In a way, time and distance were the subjects at hand as the car rolled on down the road. Time in the form of a passage that couldn't be gone back on or taken back. Distance in the form of a distant horizon suddenly arrived at and crossed. Wanda lowered her magazine and looked out at the country scenes passing in the bright morning sun. Every definition had changed for Wanda, including the definitions of sex, childhood, innocence, and, especially, horizons. As Wanda looked at the horizon beyond the fields they passed, she didn't feel soiled or spoiled in a loss-of-innocence sense. She didn't feel cold or empty. She didn't feel as if her childhood had been taken from her. But as she looked at the horizon, a strange kind of longing came over her. It wasn't longing in the sexual sense. Wanda couldn't describe the feeling, not even to herself. She knew that longing in her had a lot to do with sex and illicit sex. But it also had something to do with horizons and moving into horizons.

In the near distance outside the car window, fields, meadows, and woods went by, green and gold in the bright morning sun. Farther out, the horizon seemed to hang suspended, clear, blue, and motionless, over the moving landscape. As Wanda watched the countryside go by underneath the horizon that seemed fixed and unmoving, another new feeling she had never felt before came over her. The feeling was similar to the momentary feeling she had felt when she heard the last musical bars of the Linda Ronstadt song as she left the motel office, but the feeling was a lot more systematic and involved. It was a feeling born of the bright green landscape moving past the car and the bright, open sky above. Unlike the waves of sensual feeling that had focused on her body and focused her down into her body the night before, under the new feeling, Wanda felt as if she were being drawn out of her own body. In the mental images the feeling created in Wanda, she rose out of the body she had initiated into lust the night before. In her imagination, Wanda rose out of her father's car up into the clear, bright sky over the green country landscape. In Wanda's imagination, her speed slowed as she left the car. Now she was floating over the road at higher-than-treetop level. In Wanda's elevated imagination, below her, the car with her parents and the girl she used to be continued on its way down the road.

In the continuation of her imagination, Wanda drifted off the road below and out over the open field next to the road. From there, she drifted off in no particular set direction. She felt as if she were drifting like a small cloud through the bright sky over the open country landscape below. Below her, she saw the passage of the farms, fields, woods, and streams she floated above. She wasn't drifting in any specific compass direction. The course of her drifting wasn't directed by any path or road. Her drifting wasn't constrained or restricted by any fence or property boundary. She wasn't drifting in any given direction that had been given to her by anybody or by herself. All she knew was that she was heading toward the horizon.

In Wanda's drifting imagination, the horizon ahead of her was all there was. The open sky around her was, at the same time, the world spread out for her and the conduit that took her toward the horizon beyond. The horizon was what she was drifting to and the reason she was drifting. The horizon was the means and the end of her drifting.

In that moment, Wanda felt as if she were part of the horizon. She felt that the substance of her body and mind was made out of the same material as the horizon. She felt like a shortwave signal coming out of the ionosphere of one horizon and heading out toward another horizon, something separate from the horizon but, at the same time, part of the horizon and dependent on the horizon for transport. In the unfolding climax of Wanda's imagination, everything she was seemed to expand out as wide as the horizons around her. The substance of her body and soul seemed to merge into the horizon. In the momentary oneness of her imagination, Wanda became one with the horizon. For a short moment, the feeling surged exponentially higher. In the momentary burst of intense feeling, Wanda knew she would always want to be one with the horizon.

Wanda didn't try to fight off the strange new feeling that had come upon her. She kind of enjoyed it. In its own way, the feeling was as sensuous to her as what she had felt in the night while listening to the amorous couple in the next room. Wanda didn't know why the new feeling had come over her, but it seemed a little more than coincidental that the feeling was coming upon her so soon after all the new feelings that had swept through her the night before. There wasn't any one-to-one correlation between the new feelings and sensations of the night before and the new feeling she was experiencing in the moving car. But in Wanda's organized mind, which made the schematic connections in the electronics projects she built, she guessed there was some connection between the new feeling she was having in the car and the new feelings she'd had the night before. In Wanda's estimate, the new feeling seemed somehow to be a derivative of the feelings she had experienced the night before. It was a time for new feelings all around.

Wanda believed the new set of energetically moving and immediately involved sensations she had felt in bed the night before were somehow generating the drifting and detached feeling she felt as she sat in the back of the car and watched the landscape and horizon pass. But Wanda's organized mind didn't quite see the connection between the two different sets of feelings. There was no logical connection. But feelings weren't always logical. That was why they were called feelings.

The no-longer-quite-so-young-and-innocent Wanda was reasonably sure that the feeling she had was somehow an extension of what she had felt during the night and that it had something to do with the couple and the transitional passage they had put her through—and she had taken herself through—the night before. As she faced the horizons passing outside the car window, for Wanda, feeling became associated with horizons. She knew the memory of the couple would always be with her and in her. She knew the horizon the couple had carried her over would become one of the horizons that divided her life and would always be with her. As Wanda looked at the horizon, she knew that horizons would be part of her from then on. She knew that horizons would always be in her.

As the couple had been swept along by their passion in the narrow confines and limited horizon of the motel room they had taken each other over the horizon in, they had swept Wanda along with them over a larger horizon. The old horizons of Wanda's life had been suddenly shunted behind her. The compartments and horizons of her childhood had become small, inaccessible, passing, and irrelevant. She couldn't have gotten back to and squeezed back into them even if she had wanted. Maybe Wanda hadn't become a full-fledged woman, but she had been christened into a new and far more advanced horizon of maturity. Soon she would pass into another stage of maturity when summer break ended and she returned to school in the fall.

The horizons of Wanda's life had suddenly grown beyond the limited horizons of the past. Only wide and distant horizons would do for Wanda now. Sitting in her father's car, watching the horizons beyond the country road, Wanda was suddenly flooded with a longing for distant horizons. The feeling was as powerful as any of the feelings Wanda had experienced the night before. As much as the sound of the amorous coupling of the couple in the next room had transported Wanda the night before, her longing for horizons transported her out toward the horizons beyond her. Though Wanda wouldn't be fully able to put formal words to what she was feeling for many years to come, at that moment, she knew her life would be about horizons and the pursuit of horizons. From that moment, she knew that horizons would be her life, and only distant horizons would do.

For several long minutes, Wanda stared out the car window, locked in her yearning for horizons. She was able to control herself and keep her facial expression casual and relaxed in such a way that if her mother turned around and saw her, it would look as if she were merely surveying the countryside, and her mother wouldn't ask if she had gone into some kind of trance. The landscape of the area stayed pretty much the same as it passed outside. But Wanda knew the landscape of her life had changed. She wasn't yet fully sure how. The changes would take some time to fully set in. But when fully realized, they would set the pattern of her life.

Wanda turned back to her magazine and continued studying how to build the ham band transmitter described. As the car drove on, Wanda studied the article and the circuit diagram and list of parts necessary to build the transmitter she had already determined she would use in an unlicensed, outlaw manner.

The circuit seemed rudimentary and straightforward enough. Wanda knew enough about electronics that she was sure she could duplicate the circuit and build it. She wanted to get going and get on the air right away. Proper procedures of passing tests, getting licenses, and studying proper operation procedures could wait for a later day, if ever.

Wanda paused in her reading every now and then to wonder if the couple in the next room had gotten up yet. In the light of her day, she wondered about the conversation in the room. She also wondered if the couple would go in the same direction or different directions when they stepped out into the light of their morning. The direction they took in the rest of their lives was pure speculation. Wanda knew only that they had changed forever the direction of her life.

4

The direction things were taking inside the motel room was obvious. The undulating cries of the woman coming through the cheaply constructed door of the motel room and through the window with the shades drawn were loud enough at close range to be audible to anyone walking by outside. The cries weren't the cries of pain of a woman pulling unwanted facial hair with tweezers. Some things were obvious and left no doubt as to what was going on. The cries and yells coming from the motel room were obviously the sounds of a female experiencing intense pleasure. The cries of the woman might have had a wavering tone to them, but the woman sounded unwavering in the pursuit of what she and her partner were pursuing behind the closed door.

Inside the room, the woman was throwing herself into her role with all the abandon with which the man was throwing himself into the woman. The woman ran through the whole archive of known sounds produced by a human female approaching and during orgasm. Along the way, she seemed to invent a few new sounds that hadn't been recorded by ethnologists. The sounds produced by the woman covered the entire range of volume and intensity as the man tried to cover all of the woman with himself. At the low end of the scale, the woman produced a throaty sound that came up in a low-pitched rumble from the depths of her chest at a frequency so low it was almost in the subaudible range. The man felt the sound that came from the woman's chest more than he heard it. On the high-intensity, high-pitched end of the scale, the woman produced a sustained operatic yell that made her sound like a diva in a tragic opera hitting the climatic high note as she lamented over the body of her dead lover. If there had been a crystal wineglass sitting on the nightstand next to the bed, it might have shattered. Except in tragic operas, it was usually the woman who died.

In the midrange between the two bipolar vocal extremities produced by the woman as the man pushed himself into her single-point extremity, the woman produced a range of sounds accompanied by an equally wide range of form, structure, and modulations. She alternately yelled, moaned, screamed, groaned, shouted, panted, cried, gasped, sighed, grunted, and then reversed the sequence. Lying flat on her back, the woman mixed her delivery up in a random pattern. Although the particular physical activity they were engaged in was producing the sounds the woman made, physical orientation didn't make a difference in the range and style of the sounds delivered by the woman. She delivered the same range and variation of sounds whether she was lying flat on her back on the bottom or sitting vertically on top. In other definitions of sexual delivery that went beyond sound effects, the woman delivered from the top as well as she did from the bottom.

When the man had met the woman in the bar, he had been a bit puzzled by her reluctance to tell him her name. Even in the intensity and variety of sounds the woman was putting out, she hadn't let her name slip out. The man had figured she didn't want to give her name because she was a local who wanted to keep her identity a secret and wanted to keep what she was doing quiet.

If the woman wanted to keep what she was doing quiet, she was sure going about it in the wrong way. When she was running on the high end of the vocalization scale, she practically shouted her head off. Walls in the kind of cheap motel they were in had a reputation for being thin. The man figured the woman was probably being heard in both rooms on either side and possibly in two rooms down on each side. If the motel had had two floors, the sounds made by the woman would probably have carried up or down at least one story. When the woman hit her verbal high notes and went into one of her spasms of sequential yells, the man half expected to hear someone pound on the walls, yelling for them to hold it down. Or maybe the manager would knock at the door, sent to their room by phone calls from angry guests whose sleep was being disturbed.

If the woman was concerned that someone might see her picking men up in bars, she didn't otherwise seem concerned that someone might hear her making love at the top of her voice. By then, they were probably hot news all over the motel. The man had the feeling that when they left the next morning, more than a few guests at the motel would look out their windows, straining their necks to see the supercharged couple who had kept them up and see who the loudmouthed hussy was. If the woman was a local who didn't want her identity revealed, her high-decibel approach to sex was working against keeping her indiscretion under wraps. The noise the woman was making would only draw attention to her. In a way, it almost seemed as if the woman wanted people to know what she was doing.

The only time the woman went silent was when he leaned down to kiss her. The kissing substituted one kind of involvement of the woman's mouth for another. Instead of using her lips and mouth for audible moaning, groaning, and yelling, when the man kissed her, she responded with total immersion in the kissing. She would wrap her arms around the man's shoulders, pull her upper body tight against his chest, pull her face into his face, and run her large lips back and forth wildly across his mouth from all sides and in all directions in a frenzied, almost frantic manner. The lip gloss that had still been in place when the woman first kissed him on the dance floor was long gone. There was nothing artificial between their lips now. The wet fullness of the woman's sensuously large lips was applied directly and with force to his lips. Even while involved in her full-frontal, full-court-press kissing, the woman still made little moaning and sighing sounds in her throat, though they weren't loud enough to cause the neighbors to pound on the walls and tell them to hold it down.

The other time the woman was relatively silent while engaged in the high-volume, passionate tussle was when the man would stick his tongue into the woman's mouth. When he gave the woman his tongue full length, she would wrap her lips and mouth around his tongue as tightly as a clam and suck away, as happy as a clam. While the woman sucked on his tongue, she would rub her hands on his cheeks and through his hair. The woman was as good with using her own tongue as she was with addressing his tongue. Kissing and tonguing were the only times when the woman's mouth was otherwise preoccupied enough to keep the noise level down.

The woman varied her physical routine as much as she varied her sound effects. She thrashed around. She undulated her body from head to foot. She heaved herself up against the man as he came down on her. She arched her back from her hips to her shoulders and pushed her body up against his in a tighter and harder rubbing dance than the one they had done on the barroom dance floor. She rubbed her chest and her generous breasts against him from side to side. In the throes of passion, she threw her legs so wide apart that they stuck out over the edges of the bed almost horizontally. The position made the woman look like a cheerleader doing the splits. The position looked uncomfortable to the man, but it was the woman's body and the woman's pleasure.

When the woman wasn't spreading herself out for the man as wide as she could, she would pull her legs in and wrap them tightly around the man's legs. That made it a bit hard for the man to get a full range of motion from his legs through his waist. In the grip of pleasure spasms, the woman wrapped her arms around the man's back and pulled him in tightly while she shuddered and gasped. When she tightened up with both her arms and legs at the same time, the man could hardly move. It was a bit like being double-teamed by boa constrictors. When the woman had her arms wrapped around the man and a pleasure spasm came on, she would dig her fingers and long fingernails into his back.

About midway through phase one, the man and woman switched places. The woman was just as energetic and adept on the top as she was on the bottom. Part of the time, she would sit in a vertical position and ride the man furiously up and down as her large breasts, now unbound and unimpeded by the flimsy sheer bra she'd worn, bounced and undulated within licking distance of his mouth. Other times, she would lie flat on the man and rub the full length of her body on his, with her large breasts sliding back and forth, their passage lubricated by the moisture of their mutual sweat.

One thing had been established early on in their night together: the woman was not a virgin. That simplified things all around. For one thing, the woman didn't have a hymen the man would have otherwise been forced to plow through. It also meant he didn't have to deal with the crying, second-guessing, and accusations of using someone that often came from deflowered virgins. Nor did the man have to sit and listen to outpourings of regret from a virgin he had defrocked. The woman seemed well beyond regrets for her sexual behavior.

The woman's postvirginal status was further confirmed by the advanced bedroom skills she displayed. With the kind of body the woman displayed, the man wasn't surprised she wasn't a virgin. From the advanced degree of energy and sexual skill the woman possessed, he guessed she probably hadn't been a virgin for a long time. The way she'd come on to him in the bar should have been enough of a clue that she wasn't a virgin. That didn't answer the question as to the woman's identity, nor did it answer the question as to whether she was a nympho on the make or a bored housewife on the cheat. But the man didn't have to give her any lessons when it came to sex. The woman could have taught a master's degree course on the subject.

Whether or not the woman was a local who knew the way to the motels in the area, she knew her way around in a bedroom. Whether or not she had brought other men to the motel was an open question. As far as sex itself went, the woman had been there before.

After what seemed an extended period of expending the output of high physical and audio energy, the man and his pickup without a name arrived at a period of relative quiescence. Having achieved the pickup of his life in the bar, having gotten the nameless woman into bed, and having kept up with her sexually, the man achieved ejaculation. After arriving at and achieving that seminal male achievement, the couple coasted to a slower pace and finally came to a point of dreamy lassitude. They were both kind of tired. But the night hadn't come to an end. Love's labor hadn't been lost. Nor had it gone limp. The raw sexuality of the woman and the desire for more of the same maintained the man's erection. In order to preserve the status quo ante, during their period of relative inaction and the woman's relative verbal quiet, the man maintained a slow, languid motion that maintained that which he was maintaining inside the woman's maintenance bay.

Not all sexual activity had ceased in the room. In the relative quietude of the motel room, the man kissed the woman's upper chest. After all the energetic work the man and woman had done on each other, they were both sweaty. A little body sweat didn't stop the man from continuing to make facial contact with the woman's appreciable body. He kissed the wide, wet horizontal expanse of the woman's shoulders. He licked the deep, wet channel of the woman's cleavage. The woman breathed heavily and sighed huskily in a relatively hushed tone as the man kissed the flat wetness of her shoulders and licked the rounded wetness of her breasts. The man could taste the smoothness of the woman's skin through the salty wetness of her sweat. The sheet under the woman was wet with her sweat and his. The area of the sheet immediately under the woman's vagina was wet with a combination of thicker and shinier solutions. The upper sheet they had started out under had been kicked off long ago by their mutual thrashing.

Even small pretenses that the affair would be respectable or at least partially modest, such as sleeping together under a sheet, had been quickly abandoned. They were both stark naked on a bed without any sheets or anything to cover their grappling. The woman was sweating like a Vegas whore in a small un-air-conditioned room in the heat of a desert afternoon. The man was licking and sticking her like a passing truck driver who had stopped to patronize the local ladies of the evening—or the afternoon. That the man was a truck driver who had stopped to explore the local fare was right on the money—money he wasn't going to have to pay the woman. Whether the woman was a randy local and whom she might have been cheating on locally were open questions.

Those of a romantic turn of mind might have considered the scene to be a romantic one: an attractive woman lay naked on a bed with her long, disheveled blonde hair spread out over the pillow and with her lover gently kissing her neck and chest. The woman's sensual sighs and gasps were the only sounds in the room. Classical scenes like that looked great on canvas and on classical film. But it would have been a bit difficult for an artist to paint a picture by or a director to direct a film by. For one thing, there wasn't much light in the room to paint or shoot film. The only light in the room came indirectly from the streetlights outside. The light filtered in over the top of and around the edges of the drapes drawn over the window. For another thing, the background setting they were in didn't lend itself well to grand art set in romantic settings. The motel room, with its scarred bed and lumpy mattress, was a rather seedy setting for classical romance compared to a canopy bed in a grand hotel with a balcony overlooking the Riviera. As far as settings and casts of attendant characters went, the motel room was far more the type of place frequented by truck drivers and truck stop women than by Cary Grant and Grace Kelly.

The audio offering was also limited at the moment. Beyond the woman's low-level sighs and moans, there wasn't any sound in the room. Anyone listening in room earlier—or through the walls—would have been treated to a barrage of varied sounds from the woman. But the soundtrack of the affair taking place in the room would have fit in far better on the audio track of a porno movie than it would have worked as grand, romantic dialogue in a grand, romantic movie, such as *Anna Karenina*.

There wasn't any grand, romantic dialogue to be heard in the motel room. There weren't any words spoken in the room. Those of a romantic turn of mind might have said words weren't necessary in such a moment. But then again, the type of romance that required words to express wasn't the kind of romance the couple had come into the room looking for.

The respite had given both of them time to catch their breath. The man shifted his focus somewhat. With his hands, he pushed the woman's breasts together from the sides, causing them to bulge upward toward his face. Then he started kissing and sucking the woman's erect nipples. At the first touch of his mouth, the woman gasped and tensed. As the man went on kissing and sucking her nipples, the woman arched her back at the shoulders and rolled her head back on the pillow. The man went on kissing and sucking the woman's nipples. He played with her nipples with his tongue. The woman's gasps and moans became louder. They turned back into growing cries of pleasure. The woman's voice was ramping back up toward the volume and intensity of sounds she had made during their energetic first phase. The woman started to move her body, slowly at first and then picking up speed. She added direction and different types of body movements as she brought herself back up to cruising speed.

During their reprieve, the man hadn't pulled himself out of the woman or gone limp. He was good to go from the position he was in. In response to the woman's reawakening, the man started pumping his manhood into the center of the woman's physical womanhood. Under the man's renewed thrusts, the woman yelled louder. The positive feedback loop shot up on an exponential curve to saturation level. The woman screamed and yelled as loudly as she had at the outset. She thrashed around as she had during the initial phase of their thrashing encounter. The man pushed himself into the woman as hard, fast, and deep as he had when he first entered her. Once again, he felt the lubricated slip of his manhood against the walls of her vagina. Once again, he felt the woman's contractions trying to close the shaft of her vagina around his erect manhood. The man couldn't get deep enough into the woman, and he couldn't get enough of the soft, warm wetness of the nameless woman's vagina.

Soon they were both back up to speed again. The woman was back up to volume again. She ran back and forth through the library of sounds she had at hand. She reached the same high notes she had before. People in the adjoining rooms were being treated to round two of the grappling and wrestling of the mystery couple in the next room. For all the sounds the woman was capable of treating guests in the next room to and the man to, she still didn't treat him to her name.

The woman made a motion to move her legs apart. She could have been preparing to do the splits with her legs again. That would have given the man the chance to spread his legs farther apart to give himself a wider base of operations. But instead of spacing his own legs wider to compensate, the man pulled his legs closer together. According to a popular saying, the devil was in the details. The devil-in-bed details of the woman's sexual style were becoming familiar to the man. The subtle clues in the way the woman moved her legs were different from the clues just before she did the splits. In the time they had been making love, the man had become familiar with the woman's sexual patterns. He knew from the subtle way the woman moved her legs that it was a prelude to her wrapping her legs around his. He also knew by her demonstrated response sequence that the woman usually wrapped her legs instead of spreading them. True to her instinctive pattern, the woman spread her legs out just wide enough to gain leverage and raise them up. Then she again wrapped her legs tightly around the man's. Since the man had already moved his legs together, he was ready for the wrapping press of his mystery woman's shapely thighs and calves. The man was rapidly getting to know the woman's sexual response curve. He still didn't know her name.

When it came to the question of identity, the woman had been right when she declined to share her name in the bar. The only kind of identifying he had come into the bar looking to find with a woman was physical identifying. The only identity he had been looking for in a woman was physical identity. As far as physical identity and identifying went, he had found a lot more than he had expected. In the man's estimate of identity and identifying, not knowing the woman's name was a small price to pay for the identity of her body and the identifying she was handing him along with her body. He hadn't been looking for anything more in the way of identity from a woman when he had gone into the bar looking for a willing woman. He was getting exactly what he wanted in that regard. He was getting a nameless body. He hadn't expected that the woman would take the nameless part to such a literal degree.

The man loved the way the woman sat on him when she was on the top. Still, it didn't quite sit well with him that she wouldn't tell him her name. It was more of an ego thing than a romantic thing. Somehow, he didn't quite feel in full control of the situation. He also didn't quite feel in full control of the woman. Although she wasn't holding anything back in bed, there was a part of her she was holding back from him.

The woman had basically given herself to him, but in the back of his mind, the man's male ego sort of turned that around. Though the woman had more or less given herself to him, while coming in the woman, he had sort of come to think of himself as having taken possession of the woman. But despite the sexual fullness the woman was letting him take, if she wouldn't tell him her name, he really hadn't taken full possession of her. One couldn't take possession of a piece of land if the title deed didn't say where the land was.

The man was still planning on leaving the next day. He had to get back on the road and make his delivery, or he would get fired. The night with the woman had turned out to be an unexpected bonus and a great diversion. In the man's male way of thinking, he had also made a great conquest. But in one small way, it wasn't a full conquest. In the back of the man's male ego, it would have been a more complete conquest to savor if he left the woman dreamy-eyed at the memory of his masculinity and yearning for his return. That way, she would be even more his than she was in bed at the moment. Even if he didn't return, if he left the woman carrying a torch for him, she would be his beyond the night. Leaving the woman pining for him in her life would be a male ego boost almost as good as having the woman in bed. A woman he managed to lull and love into a dreamy state would tell him her name, even if she was married. If she didn't tell him her name, then he hadn't won her over and hadn't left her dreaming of him. If she didn't fall under his spell and tell him her name, he really hadn't had her. In a way, she would be the one who had him.

How to get the woman to share her name with him as well as her body was a question for which no immediate answer presented itself. In the back of his mind—the back of his ego, actually, though one could have said they were one and the same—the man sort of figured his masculine charm and lovemaking ability might melt the woman and render her more amenable to sharing the only thing about her that she hadn't yet been willing to share with him: her name. If he could get the woman into a dreamy enough state, she might open her soul and identity to him the way she had opened her motel room door and her legs to him. Maybe after the woman had slept with him and slept on what had happened between them, she would be willing to tell him her name in the morning.

In keeping with her natural timing, after a while, the woman unwrapped her legs from around his and spread them out again, though not as wide as if she were a cheerleader doing the splits at a college football game. In a quasiorgasmic outburst, the woman took her arms off his back and threw her arms up over her head and to the sides. The man reached out, grabbed the woman's wrists in his hands, and held her arms out to the sides as far as they would stretch. The woman's arms and legs, extended out at their angles, created an X-shaped figure that was an extension of the woman's X-shaped figure, with her narrow waist and heavy chest and full hips. The man had the woman pinned and spread eagle on the bed. At that moment, in the symbolic sense, he had the woman even more thoroughly than he'd had her at any time in the night up to that point. In the back of his mind, and under the full length of his torso, the man had the woman completely open to him. At least in a symbolic sense.

If the woman saw anything symbolically objectionable to the position, she gave no indication she objected. She didn't try to pull her arms back in next to her body. The man started pushing himself into the woman at the top end of his operating speed. The woman's wailing cries of pleasure increased in tempo with the man's increase. She arched her back again. The woman seemed to like the position he had her in. She seemed to like the way he was making love to her while holding her in the totally open position he had her in. If she liked being opened up the way she was and liked the loving he was delivering while he had her open to him, maybe he could get her to open up to him tomorrow and give him her name and address, he thought. At least he then would know how to contact her the next time he was in the area. Maybe a future rendezvous could be arranged between them in the morning. Beyond the morning and beyond a single repeat engagement, he might be able to set up an ongoing liaison and repeat affair with the woman while he was on the road. If he could leave the woman pining for his loving, he was halfway home to seducing her into the affair, even if he was seducing her out of her home.

As far as homes went, she was probably cheating on someone anyway. She might have been out cruising bars because she had an unhappy home life. Maybe the main man in her life was a jerk. Maybe he wasn't much of a man in her estimate and according to her demanding sexual requirements. Maybe he didn't measure up to her bedroom standards. Maybe all that stuff about how she lived on the open road was just a cover story for a local cheat who could prove willing to cheat again and go on serially cheating with a man who was a real man. Maybe the woman didn't fully know what she wanted. Maybe she didn't know what or whom she was looking for. Maybe all she needed was a real man to keep her satisfied. In the man's estimate of the situation, of the woman, and of himself, if he was man enough with her, he might be able to redirect her away from her man at home and from the bars she was hopping in order to compensate for her less-than-satisfactory life at home. Maybe he could redirect her to him. While he was in town at least.

That didn't necessarily mean she wouldn't still go bar-hopping while he was away on the road. But maybe his manly prowess could entice her to fit him into her schedule and his schedule on the road on a regular basis. If sailors could have a woman in every port, why couldn't truckers have women waiting for them in small towns along their regular routes? Truckers fantasized about such things. Even if they had only one woman waiting for them in some roadside rendezvous, a few over-the-road truckers managed to make the fantasy into reality to one degree or another. A woman waiting in a small town who would give him a little nookie on the side would go a long way to easing the boredom and monotony of a trucker's life on the open road. Especially if it was a woman with the shapely nooks and crannies she had and who knew how to nookie the way she did.

In the symbolically open position, the couple went on thrashing around and throwing themselves against each other. The fact that the man was more or less running on empty kept his manhood up and in the fray. While the man was managing to keep his manhood up, the woman kept up her varied and unique sound effects. She also maintained the seemingly endless variety of ways she had of moving her body next to his. The continuous sounds the woman was making were starting to become a bit wearying on the man, but at least she didn't just lie there and moan, as some women did.

Aside from the woman's sounds, the man was starting to get a bit weary across the board. Whatever the woman called herself, she wasn't ready to call it quits. The man started to have visions of himself collapsing in exhaustion on top of the woman while she was still in frenetic motion. In the back of his mind, the thought that the woman might outlast him was becoming a bit of a threat to his male ego. While the man continued to cast himself on the woman, he started casting around for a face-saving way to bring their orgy to a conclusion.

It wasn't the man's face or mind that finally provided the end sequence. After spending about one and a half times longer in their second phase than they had in the first, the man felt a buildup of tension in the area that had been tapped earlier and that he thought had been tapped out. He felt like he was going to achieve a doubleheader for the evening. But a good woman had been known to bring out the best in a man.

Like water heading for the nozzle of a fire hose, the building tension surged through the man, following the one path of escape and focusing on the one orifice of release. As his sexual mainspring took one last final turn and his sexual wellspring prepared to vent again, in the spasm of the immediate lead-up to the greater spasmodic moment of male orgasm, the man grabbed the woman's shoulders with his hands.

"Oh, Ashley!" he shouted into the darkness a foot above the face of the woman he couldn't fully see and whose name he still didn't know. In lieu of knowing her real name, the man went with the name she had let him give her. Given all the woman had otherwise given him, he more or less felt he had to shout something as a courtesy to her.

The assumed alias he shouted into the night was more or less the only male sound that had been produced in the room during the energetic tryst. At least it was the only sound made by the man loudly enough to match the woman's sounds. It was also the only male sound loud enough to carry through the walls the way the woman's yells and cries had. If there were people listening in the next room, they would think they knew the name of one of the participants in the next-door orgy keeping them awake. But as for the actual identity of the woman involved, they wouldn't know any more than the man did.

Though he thought his tank was empty, the man ejaculated hard for the second time that night. He came like a freight train. At least that was the proverbial male analogy he would have used to describe the experience. He tapped a reservoir he hadn't known was there. But a good woman had been known to bring out more in a man than he thought was there.

For her part, and the part all her parts had played in bringing the man to secondary climax, the woman tensed her body as tightly as the man's. At the rush of secondary male orgasm, she gripped his shoulders with her hands and dug her nails into the skin. If the timing of the event had been split up into individual frames and analyzed, a sexual forensic examiner would have noted that the woman's final contraction didn't commence the moment the man came. The woman's sympathetic contraction started a moment earlier. The woman actually grabbed the man's shoulders at the moment he shouted the alternate name. An examiner who picked up on the subtle detail of the timing of the woman's response might have speculated that the woman found the man's use of the false name to be as much of a point of orgasm as she found his coming inside her to be. But whether there was actually anything to that little bit of Freudian speculation was as unknown as the woman's name.

As the man came inside her for a second time that night, the woman let out a second long, sustained, modulated moan similar to the one she had let out the first time. As their mutual orgasm proceeded forward in immediate time, both the man and the woman fell silent. For several long moments in the darkness of the room, the man and the woman gripped each other in mutual seizure. Then the wave passed.

When it was over, it was over. The man sort of collapsed in place on top of the woman. His head went to the pillow off to the side of the woman's head, with his lips an inch from the side of the woman's face. The woman relaxed her grip on the man's shoulders. She lay on her back, breathing heavily up into the darkened air of the room. The man and woman lay there in the dark of the motel room, in the middle of the soaked bed, in the midst of their mutual satisfaction, with their mutual bodies covered by the wetness of their mutual sweat. The sudden relaxation after the intense concentration of orgasmic energy left both of them with a heightened sense of feeling. In their heightened awareness of feeling, both the man and the woman could feel the subtle tracings of little drops of sweat as they ran down the exposed sides of their bodies.

The man wasn't one given to subtle reflection in general. At the moment, he was too tired to do any kind of reflecting on much of anything. But earlier, he had been contemplating ways to try to learn the woman's name and address. As far as the use of names went, if the man had been able to reflect on the small and hidden things that had passed between him and the woman, he would have realized that in the grip of the orgasm just past, he had shouted out the name the woman had given him to use. Though he had ended the night on top of the woman, as far as knowing and using names went, the woman was one up on him.

For several long minutes, the man and the woman lay there quietly in the dark, not moving. Then the woman touched the man's side with her hand.

"Let me up," the woman said softly but decidedly. "I have to wash up."

The man could understand the feminine desire to clean up after a sweaty encounter like the one they had just completed. Many people preferred to shower after sex. At the moment, the man was tired. For that and other reasons, he wanted to remain in the woman's bed. The sheets off the bed were sweaty. The lower part of the sheet was wet from other body fluids. The man didn't particularly care, though. To his way of thinking, there was something masculine about sleeping in a soiled bed with a soiled woman he had just compromised. Or further compromised, in her case.

Without saying anything, the man rolled over onto his side off the woman, leaving only one of her arms still pinned beneath his body. The woman slowly sat up in the bed. In a signal to the man concerning his positional oversight, she pulled on her arm to let him know he still had her pinned. Still silent, the man rose up enough for the woman to get her arm out from under him. Then she got up out of bed. For a moment, the man wondered if she was planning to leave, as she had kept saying she would do in the bar. Then he remembered they were in the woman's motel room. He didn't think she was going to leave her own room and go sleep in her car in the parking lot. The woman's getting up could be a prelude to her throwing him out, though, he thought. He was convinced he wasn't going to let the woman throw him out. Not after all the work he had put in on her.

The man remained on his side as the woman walked around the bed in the dark room toward the washroom. The light came on in the washroom. For several minutes, he heard the sound of water running in the sink. Then the light went off.

In the darkness, the man heard the woman walk back into the room. She seemed to stop at the foot of the bed. For a few seconds, there was the rustle of cloth. Then he felt the sheet being pulled up around him. The woman was putting the sheet they had earlier knocked off the bed back on. The gesture of covering him up dispelled his idea that she was planning to throw him out. Why cover him up if she was planning to give him his walking papers?

As she replaced the sheet, the woman left the side of the sheet facing him partially pulled back, as if she were planning on crawling back under the sheet next to him. The man figured that apparently, his manliness had won her over. She was going to spend the rest of the night with him. To the man's way of thinking, he was halfway home to finding out what her name was and where she called home. That secondary climax would probably come the next day. At that particular postorgasm moment, the man didn't say anything one way or the other about any subject. In the back of his mind, it was a masculine thing to go right to sleep after sex in the bed he'd just had sex in with the woman he'd just had sex with.

The woman walked around to the same side of the bed she had gotten up on. But instead of climbing into the bed next to him, she seemed to bend down and pick something up off the floor in the same area where they had both discarded their clothes in a scattered heap when they undressed in hurried heat. The woman seemed to be fiddling around with an item of clothing. From the sound and the shadowy outline of the woman's motions, she seemed to be putting her bra back on. If she wasn't planning on leaving, the man wondered why the woman would be putting her clothing back on.

"I hope you don't mind if I put my bra back on," the woman said in the dark, answering a question the man hadn't asked. "Mother always told me to wear a bra even at night in order to keep from getting stretch marks."

Given the size of the woman's breasts, the man could understand how she could develop stretch marks if her breasts weren't corralled. There was a lot there for gravity to work on. The man could understand the feminine desire not to develop stretch marks. He could especially understand why a woman with the kind of knockout body she had would want to keep her figure trim and hold off any signs of aging.

The woman moved around for a while in the darkness. Then she lifted the cover and slipped into bed next to the man. He reached out and brushed the woman's chest. The quick gesture confirmed she had indeed put her sheer bra back on. The flimsy bra didn't seem to offer much support in or out of bed, but if she felt it helped ward off stretch marks, that was her concern. The man didn't reach anywhere else or touch any other part of the woman's body lower than her chest. He wasn't aware the woman had also put her panties back on.

The man was lying on his left side. The woman climbed into bed; lay down on her right side, facing the man; and pulled the sheet the rest of the way up to their shoulders. The man draped his free arm over the woman's side. In response, the woman took the man's hand in both of her hands. Holding his hand, she moved his arm down into the space between them. The man didn't say anything. He hadn't said much to the woman after their sex started. He had hardly said a word after he called out the name he and the woman had agreed would be her name for the night. In his masculine way, the man didn't want to talk. Talking after sex was a chick thing. He preferred the masculine directness of going to sleep with a woman he had just slept with, so to speak. It made no masculine sense to the man to stay awake and chatter with the woman as if they were a pair of magpies. There would be plenty of time to talk in the morning before he had to get back on the road. There might even be time for a morning quickie before he pulled out of town and got back on the road after pulling out of the woman. He would get the woman's name and address in the morning.

With their hands between them, the woman continued to hold the man's hand. The woman whispered something in a dreamy-sounding voice to the effect that he had been a great lover and that he should go to sleep. The man didn't argue with the woman on either point. He was tired after a long, pounding day on the road and a long night of pounding the woman in bed. With the woman's warm and full body next to his and with her hands holding his free hand, the man drifted off toward sleep.

⟞⟝ᴄ/ᴏ/ᴏᴄ⟝⟞

As the man could attest, the woman worked well in the dark, guided by touch and her senses. But her senses were also attuned to first light. After long practice, the woman had calibrated her visual awareness to the point that she would wake up when the first premorning light became visible over the horizon before the sun had even risen. The ability gave the woman the advantage of usually being able to wake up before the man did.

The light of predawn was starting to show in the square outline around the drawn drapes covering the window. The level of light was still faint, but it was enough to wake the woman up. If she had been alone in the room, she would probably have slept longer. But her long practice had also disciplined the automatic responses of the woman's mind to instinctively know when an early rise was called for to facilitate an early departure.

The man was still sleeping on his left side, facing the woman, in the same position he had been in when he fell asleep. The woman was still on her right side, facing the man. Fortunately, neither of them tossed and turned in their sleep. But then again, they had done enough tossing and turning the night before to equal a whole motel full of restless sleepers for a month.

With the woman's hands folded around his hand, the man had gone to sleep confident she would be there in the morning. The woman's hands had already dropped away from the man's hand while she slept. She had known from experience that physiological response would happen. Sleep had mostly detached her hands from the man's hand. It only took a simple sliding move of her hands to fully separate them the rest of the way from the man's hand without the move registering in the sleeping man's subconscious.

The man did not wake up at the move. The woman slowly slid the sheet off of her, taking care to keep the sheet over the man while not moving it against his skin. Skin could have a high sensitivity to touch. The woman rolled over onto her back next to the edge of the bed. Before sitting up, she hung her left leg over the side of the bed and placed her foot on the floor in order to get maximum leverage to get out of the bed with a minimum of jostling of the bed. They had jostled the bed quite a bit the night before. The man had found the practiced movements the woman employed on him to be quite good at the time. The woman's movements that morning were equally as skilled and practiced as the ones she had employed the night before. But it was a different skill set she was employing now, and her movements had a different end in mind.

Steadying herself for the move, the woman swung her body enough to place her other foot on the floor. Using her legs only, without pushing on the bed with her hands, the woman stood up next to the bed. She was still dressed in her bra and panties. Her low-light vision was good. She quickly located the rest of her clothes and her shoes on the floor. Instead of throwing her clothes in with the pile of the man's clothes when they had thrown their clothes off the night before, the woman had systematically dropped her clothes in one specific spot she remembered near the bed, which made her clothes easier to find without her having to rummage around in the semidark and walk around in the room.

Moving surely and silently, the woman put back on the clothes she had shed so readily and eagerly last night. Since she already had her panties and bra on, the number of clothing items she needed to put back on and the possible attention-getting motions necessary to get dressed were reduced. She also had put her bra and panties on before bed by design. She hadn't worn her bra to bed because she was afraid of getting stretch marks; it was just another way of not stretching out her departure.

The woman silently slipped the red shoes she had worn at the bar back onto her feet. Then she glanced around. She had prepositioned everything she needed for a quick exit in one place close to the door, where they could be grabbed together without her having to make several trips across the room to gather everything up. Her keys, including the motel room key, were ready to go in the pocket of the blue jeans she had put back on. She would have to turn the room key back in at the front desk when she checked out. Her suitcase was already packed. Her brush was in her night

79

case, but she could brush out her tangled hair while sitting in her vehicle after she put some distance between herself and the motel.

She gathered up her night case, which contained most everything she had brought with her into the room, including the nightie she hadn't needed to wear. She picked up her purse, which she had strategically left next to the night case when she came back into the room with the man. Then she put the cowgirl hat she had worn at the bar, which she had also strategically left next to her night case, on her head. Without any further ado or any quiet words directed at the man who had been her lover or further thoughts about him, the woman stepped over to the motel room door and carefully opened it, making as little noise as possible.

The woman quickly stepped through the door into the gathering morning. Then she closed the door behind her as silently as she had opened it. As she walked away, the woman did the man the favor of leaving the little plastic Do Not Disturb sign hanging on the doorknob.

Having accomplished her withdrawal the way she wanted, the woman walked quickly down the length of the motel parking lot to her vehicle, which she had strategically parked at the other end of the parking lot, away from her room. She threw the loose items she was carrying into the passenger-side front seat, got into the vehicle, started it up, and drove it the short distance to the motel office, where she strategically parked it in a position that placed the motel office between the vehicle and the room she'd just left. The woman got back out of the vehicle and walked quickly into the motel office to check out.

The man's mind, responding on an instinctive level to the lack of something rather than to noise or movement, woke him up. Still half asleep, the man didn't know why he had woken up. The space next to him was empty. He moved his arm into the darkness next to him. He remembered the woman. He remembered her lying next to him before he'd gone to sleep. Instead of encountering a soft and warm barrier, the man's hand found nothing. At that point, he woke up fully to reality. The woman was gone.

He waved his arm around in a wider arc, thinking maybe the woman had slipped farther down on the bed. When his reaching hand found nothing, he realized she was no longer in the bed. He rolled over onto to his back and opened his eyes fully. He wondered if the woman was in the bathroom, washing up some more. Women liked to wash up a lot. It was dawn outside. Light was coming in around the drapes. But there was no light coming from the washroom. He heard no sound of running water. He wondered if she was using the toilet. He listened for a while, but he heard no sounds that indicated a toilet was being used. Aside from the occasional distant road sound filtering in through the window, there was only silence in the room that the woman had filled with sound last night.

"Ashley?" the man called out into the fading darkness, using the only name he had to go on.

There was no answer.

He called twice more. When he still received no response, the man reached over to the nightstand next to the bed, groping around for the switch on the lamp on the nightstand. He found the switch and turned the light on. When he looked around, he didn't see the woman anywhere in the room. Another call brought no response.

The man looked around the room some more, wondering where the woman could have gone. Then his peripheral vision caught sight of another absence. He remembered seeing a suitcase sitting across the room. He hadn't paid the suitcase much attention when he and the woman came into the room the night before. He had assumed the suitcase was the woman's, but he hadn't given it any thought beyond that. He had been distracted by thoughts of the night of coming to come. Now the suitcase was conspicuously absent. Then he noticed that the woman's western-style hat, which she had casually dropped onto the suitcase when they entered the room, was gone along with the suitcase. Then he noticed that the woman's purse was gone. Women didn't go anywhere outside the house without their purses.

In the light of the new day and the light of the motel lamp, the man glanced down at the floor. His clothes were still there, but the woman's clothes were gone, including the standout shiny candy-apple-red shoes she had been wearing.

The man sat up in bed, trying to calculate what had happened. The first obvious, logical assumption, as presented by the absence of the woman and her possessions, was that she had dressed in the night and left. That wasn't particularly the deduction he wanted to go with. Maybe the woman was an early riser. Maybe she was dressing in the bathroom with the door to the toilet closed and hadn't heard him when he called.

The man threw the single sheet off. Walking buck naked, he went into the washroom. The door to the toilet was open. There was no light on. There was no Ashley. The woman was gone from his bed and gone from the room. She was apparently gone from his life, and it looked as if she had planned it that way as much as she had planned her exit.

The man rushed back into the room and stopped by the foot of the now quiet and empty bed. His first thought was that the woman was some kind of shill who seduced men and then drugged and robbed them while they were unconscious or after they went to sleep. He rushed over to where he had left his wallet laying on the nightstand and opened it. His money was still there in the original amount. So were his credit cards. The woman had left, but she hadn't robbed him of anything. Except her name and the chance to see her again.

The man grabbed his underpants and jeans and quickly pulled them on. He didn't have any idea where the woman had gone. He didn't know how long she had been gone before he woke up. She might have been gone for an hour, or she might have just left a minute earlier. Maybe her leaving had woken him up. If he moved fast, he might spot her walking to her car in the parking lot, he thought.

Wearing only his boxer shorts and blue jeans, the man opened the already unlatched door of the motel room and stepped outside. He had to be careful not to let the door shut behind him. He didn't have the key to the room, so if the door closed and locked, he would be stuck outside wearing only his pants.

It was starting to become light in the world outside the room. The streetlights were still on, but the buildings around the motel were outlined by the light of the sun that would rise in a short time. An occasional early morning car went by on the road that ran past the motel.

The man glanced at the cars parked nearest the motel room door, but he didn't see the woman by any of them. He looked around the parking lot, trying to see if he could spot the wave of the woman's shapely hips as she walked away from him, but he couldn't see anyone or any immediate motion within the parking lot. If the woman had come to the motel by car, it appeared she had driven away before he got up.

The man heard the sound of a motor accelerating. The sound wasn't coming from the street. It was coming from somewhere in the area of the motel. His first thought was that it was the woman revving up her car to leave. He thought he might still be able to catch the woman before she got away. He looked in the direction of the motor sound. As the man looked, a van pulled out of the motel driveway, turned onto the semidark street, and accelerated down the street away from the motel. The van looked like a commercial work van, with a high square back divided into compartments with doors and a carrying rack on the top. The van had official lettering stenciled on it and a pattern painted on it that looked like a logo of a public utility company. He looked at the van for a moment as it pulled away. He doubted a classy lady like her had come in that. He figured it must have been a public utility worker who was staying at the motel while on the job and who had to get to work early. The man figured the classy woman had most likely come in a hot sports car of some make.

The man again scanned the parking lot to see if he could spot the shapely body of the woman sliding into the low-slung body of a sports car. But he didn't see any sports cars in the parking lot or pulling away down the road. What if she was the cheating wife of a local out on the prowl on the cheating side of town? He looked to see if she was pulling away in a pickup truck. But beyond the departure of the van, there was no activity to be seen. The early morning parking lot was motionless and devoid of any activity. It was especially devoid of the woman who earlier had filled the man's night. The woman had made it good for the man in bed during the night. In the light of morning, she had made good her escape.

The man stood there in his partially unadorned maleness, trying to make sense of what had happened. Mostly, that involved trying to make sense of the woman. She had been good in bed. She had also been as good as her word that he would not see her again after the morning. He hadn't known she meant it literally. After allowing him all that she had in bed, the man had hoped she would allow him some time in the morning to set up other nights in the future. He'd enjoyed the way the woman moved in bed. She had allowed him plenty of leeway to work with in the sack. She apparently didn't believe in giving a man much leeway to work with when it came to interpreting her meaning when she said she liked to keep moving. Now, along with not knowing the woman's name, the man would never know what made the woman tick or kept her moving. He would not know if the woman was a small-town tease, a lonely woman looking for love in a fast-turnover setting, a local-area cheat, or the premier nympho of the county. She would forever remain an unresolved figure on the horizon of the man's memory. But that was exactly the way she had said she wanted it.

The man stood in the open doorway, looking around as if he thought the woman might change her mind and suddenly walk back to him the way the woman in the old Roy Orbison song "Pretty Woman" changed her mind and came walking back to the narrator.

But his mystery woman did not emerge from the shadows of the morning. Like the utility worker who had hurried away in his van to get back on the job, the man had to get back to his truck and get back on the road himself. He went back into the motel room and finished getting dressed. He checked his wallet again and counted the money in it to see if the woman had taken part of it. All his money was there. While the woman had taken a certain amount of his masculine pride in the way she had duped him and dumped him by sneaking out while he was asleep, she had left him his money. He wondered if she had left the motel room bill for him to pay.

As it turned out, she hadn't. As it also turned out, she hadn't left her name at the front desk.

5

As the man walked back to where his eighteen-wheeler was parked at the truck stop, the work van he had seen pull out of the parking lot of the motel followed its own path down the two-lane blacktop of the main road leading out of town, long gone and on the move. Ahead of the van, the sun was starting to rise above the horizon. The growing light illuminated the farm fields and woodlands the van passed by.

Several miles outside of the town, the van turned off onto a smaller side road. The terrain rose on a gentle grade up to an area of relatively high elevation. It wasn't the highest point of elevation in the state, but it put the top of the rise in the relative clear.

Where the curve of the land plateaued another two miles down the smaller road, the van turned onto a small single-lane dirt access road. At the far end of the short lane, a single tall, square brown building stood out alone and isolated in the green expanse of farm fields and woods that surrounded the building. The building was eight stories tall, taller than any building in the small town it was located beyond the fringes of and decidedly taller than the two-story farmhouses in the immediate area. It could have been considered a skyscraper relative to the other limited human-built structures in the area. The building was of an unusual construction. For all its height, the building was no more than twenty-five feet wide at the base. From the ground, it rose straight up on all sides. It looked as if some demented architect had enclosed a single elevator shaft or stairwell in walls and called it a building. The only windows in the building were small single-pane windows in the sides of each floor, which lit the inside of the staircase that led to the top floor of the incongruous building. On the roof, several large, square metal horns looked out in different directions.

A chain-link fence surrounded the small footprint of the strangely proportioned structure. The van pulled up to the padlocked gate at the end of the access road to the building. At the gate to the incongruous-looking building was an incongruous sight: a shapely woman wearing blue jeans, a satiny blouse, and bright red shoes got out of the van; walked over to the gate; and opened the padlock with a key. The woman pushed the gate open; got back in the van; drove it onto the limited grounds at the foot of the half-story-wide, eight-story-tall building; and parked.

The woman did not immediately get out of the van once she had stopped it. From inside the van, she glanced around to see if anyone was watching her. Satisfied that no one was in the area, sitting behind the driver's seat, the woman took off the satin blouse she was wearing. For a short while, the woman's ample breasts bobbed freer, constrained only by the sheer bra she was wearing. Then the woman reached over and picked up the other shirt she had left strategically positioned on the passenger seat in the cab of the van. She pulled on the work shirt. The work shirt was made of heavier material than the satiny blouse. The shirt wasn't nearly as form-fitting or complementary to the woman as the satin blouse she had just taken off, but it was a lot more practical for the work it was made to be worn while doing. On one side of the shirt, the name of a regional phone company was embroidered just beneath the right shoulder. On the opposite side, in the same position, just below the shoulder, an oval name tag was sewn onto the shirt. The name Wanda was stitched into the oval.

Wanda could have worn her uniform into the bar the night before. The phone company didn't have a stated policy for its techs not to wear their uniforms in bars for fear of sullying the company name by having it displayed in less-than-respectable places, such as redneck bars. It wasn't a corporate-image problem. However, image was a consideration to Wanda in the places she went into to play.

Wanda didn't like to wear her phone company uniform into bars, because a lot of people didn't like phone companies. Phone companies were monopolies. Phone companies were big. Phone companies were so big and ubiquitous they might as well have been a branch of the government. Phone companies were arrogant. Phone companies were surly operators. Phone companies were definitely profit-oriented institutions. Phone companies indulged in what many people thought was bill padding. Phone companies put surcharges on phone bills that customers couldn't understand and that appeared on their bills even if they hadn't called anyone for a month. Phone companies gave customers the runaround when they tried to contact a higher-up in the company to complain about anything. Phone companies gave people static when they questioned their billing practices. Phone companies gave people static on the line when they tried to place a call, despite the efforts of phone company technicians, such as Wanda, to keep the lines clear and open. Phone companies were often considered by critics to be high-fee, low-service organizations.

Though she worked for the phone company, for the right men, Wanda could be a high-service, low-fee woman. But in terms of phone analogies, Wanda was big on the quick disconnect.

For those reasons, which were not obvious, and to accentuate her chest, which was rather obvious, Wanda did not wear her phone company uniform into bars. Instead, she opted for the standard honky-tonk-queen come-on uniform of tight jeans, a tight satin blouse, red shoes, and red lipstick. The cowgirl hat was optional, but it added a ready-to-ride element to the image Wanda was trying to project, especially in bars that had a mechanical bull to ride. Along with being adept at handling electronic equipment functioning at microwave frequencies, Wanda had become pretty adept at handling mechanical bulls, which oscillated at much lower frequencies. The sight of Wanda on a bucking mechanical bull—holding on to the pommel of the saddle with one hand and waving her cowgirl hat in the air with the other, with her upper body undulating and the bucking movement of the mechanical animal accentuating the already accentuated thrust of her chest to the point that it seemed about to split open the shiny blouse she was wearing—had left more than a few men with the impression that the unknown hard-riding woman they had never seen in the bar before likely could keep herself on top of a bucking man as well as she kept herself on the bucking mechanical bull.

The doctrine Wanda followed of no contact with a man beyond the first night wasn't a phone company directive. It was Wanda's rule. Needs and wants were simple the first night. Things could be kept simple the first night. Wanda was a girl who liked to keep things simple. Needs were easy to accommodate the first night. As many men had learned, Wanda could be an accommodating girl the first night. Things were direct the first night. Beyond the evasions of her name and place of employment, Wanda was otherwise a direct girl.

Wanda didn't like complications. Things generally weren't complicated the first night. To Wanda's way of thinking and relating, or not relating in a prolonged manner, complications in relationships set in when things went beyond the first night. As a result of her particular philosophy, Wanda's life was organized around the proposition that there would be a whole lot of first nights for her. In that regard, Wanda was an up-front girl—with an up-front bodily construction. According to her systematic, organized thinking, there would be no second nights beyond the first.

Still sitting in the driver's seat of the phone company van, Wanda took her hairbrush out of her night case and brushed out the tangles imparted by the night of relating just completed. After that, she took off her red shoes and put on a pair of work shoes she had strategically left in the van. Her red shoes were the work shoes of the first proposition of her life. Her gym-shoe-like work shoes, with their flat rubberized soles, weren't nearly as eye-catching as the shoes she had danced in and been romanced out of, but they were a lot more practical for climbing stairs like the ones in the structure she was about to work in without catching a heel and falling headlong down the stairs. Not catching or being caught by a heel was what the second category of Wanda's life was about.

After changing her clothes and persona, Wanda sat back in the seat, opened the aluminum cover on her official phone company repair technician's metal clipboard, and started reading the work order for the repairs needed on the equipment in the phone company microwave relay tower she was parked in front of. She had read the work order earlier and was familiar with what had to be done. She just wanted to review things to see if she had left anything out. Her organized mind had pretty much already planned out the work that would have to be done and the steps the work would have to be performed in. She had performed repairs like this many times before in the past. The incongruous Wanda had been in many incongruous phone company structures like the one before her. From self-supporting structures like the enclosed tower, which a repair tech could walk up inside, to open metal-grid towers supported by guy wires; towers as tall, narrow, and unstable-looking as television-station transmitting antennae; and towers that had to be climbed from the outside using a climbing harness and safety belt, they were all familiar territory to Wanda. Even at the top of the tallest tower the phone company had, she was on familiar ground. As with the bedroom she had just left, Wanda had been there before and had done the job well.

After reviewing the work order, Wanda got out of the van and walked around to the back of the van. From a compartment in the back, she took out her heavy work belt and strapped it on. In a series of holster pouches arranged around the outside, the belt carried several tools most often used by telephone repair technicians. It also carried the portable telephone handset technicians used to tap into the phone lines. Wanda also took a separate larger toolbox and a replacement module still in its factory container carton out of the back of the van. It was early in the morning, and she was getting an early start on the job. She hadn't had breakfast yet, but she liked to get an early start and get part of the work behind her before she stopped for breakfast. Since she was starting the job early, she could have part of the work done before she broke to have breakfast at the little diner she had passed on the way to the tower. Besides, the diner had been closed when Wanda passed it on her way to the relay tower.

There was a small possibility her lover from the night before might show up at the same diner. But she figured the man would be more likely to eat at the truck stop where his semi was parked instead of looking for a local restaurant outside town. The man had also told Wanda he was going to be taking a main road, not the local road the diner was on. All this fit into Wanda's calculations. She calculated that her trucker lover would probably be far down the road by the time she went to eat, and he would be on a different road. He wouldn't show up at the diner.

Wanda also calculated that she would probably have the work completed and checked out by early afternoon. If she did have the work finished in that time frame, she could get an early start back to the maintenance office she worked out of. That would give her time to travel the back roads back instead of using main roads and superhighways. That way, she could drive through the type of country and country scenes she had grown up in as a country girl. On the small two-lane blacktop roads, she could see the kind of farms and fields under the open sky that she had looked out over as a child. She could see the horizons she had seen and dreamed of as a child. She could see the open sky she had gazed into so much as a child as she listened to shortwave stations coming out from over the horizon.

The hometown Wanda had grown up in wasn't far off the route back to the office she was based out of. She could stop home to visit her parents on her way back, she thought. It would be something of a detour off the direct route, but she had the time. In the way bureaucracies had of padding time, the phone company had allocated her several days to do the repair work in the tower. If she could get the work finished and check out in one day, she could use the extra time to stop back home for a visit. She hadn't been home much in the last few years. Her mother liked seeing her.

The route to her hometown also crossed within a reasonable distance of the route she and her parents had taken back home from visiting her uncle many years earlier. She wanted to see if a certain motel was still there on the side of the road. It would be a detour on a detour, but she wanted to drive the road to see the motel where the direction of her life had changed and been set on a path to the motels of her current nights and where she had looked past the horizons of her past to first glimpse the particular horizon she pursued through her present. It would be a homecoming.

Having gathered everything she needed, Wanda walked over to the single door at the base of the tower. Using the other key that had been given to her at the maintenance and repair division office she was based out of, Wanda opened the locked door and went inside the tower. She had been the man's during the night. The tower would be hers for the day.

6

Wanda liked to get to work right away—with the pursuit of men but especially with the pursuit of distant horizons. Her pursuit of horizons had started as soon as she got home from the road trip with her parents to visit her uncle, when she'd faced the fork in the road that changed her life. True to the words of Yogi Berra, when Wanda came to the fork in the road, she took it.

True to her determination and organized mind, when Wanda got back home, she built the ham radio transmitter described in the article in the electronics magazine she had bought at the motel, and true to the outlaw idea she'd had in the car but not true to FCC licensing requirements, she put the transmitter on the air before procuring herself an amateur radio operator's license. In conjunction with the receiver she had rebuilt earlier, she went on the air as a bootleg station. She borrowed amateur radio call signs, invented call signs, and made contacts. She never used the same call sign twice. She limited the number of contacts she made. When she was in a contact, or QSO, with another station, she never gave her real name, or handle. She never told the other station her true location, or QTH. That was Wanda's way of staying one step ahead of the FCC.

She started out by working stateside stations. As she grew more proficient at working the bands, she started working foreign stations, which hams called DX. The sunspot cycle that controlled the reflectivity of the ionosphere was at a peak. Propagation was good that year. Distant stations were out there for the taking. Distant horizons could be reached. Wanda gradually pushed her electronic horizons out farther and farther. The horizons she pursued and projected herself into grew more distant.

That she did it all under a set of assumed and shifting identities didn't bother Wanda. It was enough for her that she had done it. In those days, radio amateurs were required to keep logbooks recording their contacts.

Wanda didn't keep a logbook of the unlicensed contacts, so as not to incriminate herself if the FCC came around. She didn't appear in anybody's logbook under her own name or call. For Wanda's organized and detailed mind, memory was enough.

Wanda could have easily gotten an amateur radio operator's license. She had the technical knowledge and skill proficiency. But Wanda was in no hurry to get herself a license to operate. She was already out there operating. In truth, Wanda enjoyed her unlicensed mode of operating. When she was on the air operating clandestinely, she often got her old feeling of distant horizons, and she didn't feel a whole lot of internal pressure to have the proper paper to operate with. In its own way, being an outlaw operator was as stimulating to Wanda as being any kind of operator.

In the fall of the year following her vicarious coming-of-age at the motel, Wanda returned to high school, where she was a proficient student who got top grades. She wasn't about to hide her intelligence just because some country boys might get their noses put out of joint by the sight and contemplation of a girl who got better grades than they did, nor was Wanda shy about displaying her technological prowess to the other students in her school. During show-and-tell sessions at her school, she demonstrated the electronics projects she had built. Around that time, the CB craze was starting to take off. For her part, Wanda could repair a malfunctioning CB radio, while the boys in her school only knew how to key up and say, "Ten-four, good buddy," and talk in hillbilly language.

If Wanda's display of technological ability put any of the boys in her high school off, the other aspects she was starting to display countered that aspect of her. Wanda wasn't quite as thin and lithe as an Olympic gymnast on the parallel bars. Given the growth pattern she had followed up to that point, it was apparent her developing developments would leave her with a full-ranged figure as opposed to a full range of athletic motion. But Wanda was reasonably trim and athletic.

Wanda didn't go out for girls' sports in high school, though that was more by default than anything. Beyond standard gym, Wanda's high school didn't offer any girls' sports or teams. Girls' sports were still considered a bit unladylike in that time and locale. Budgets were limited too. But her high school did have boys' football and basketball, and they had a cheerleading squad to complete the picture. Wanda became as proficient at the standard and expected high school girl avocation of cheerleading as she was at the nonstandard and unexpected girl avocation of electronics. The one sort of balanced out the other.

Although Wanda looked a bit unbalanced and top-heavy, her balance on the cheerleading field was pretty good. She soon made herself into a top cheerleader on the high school cheerleading squad. As a high school cheerleader, Wanda polished and refined the skills she had started with in junior high cheerleading. She could do the splits like a polished professional. Doing the splits was no problem for Wanda. The less-than-wasp-thinness of her waist wasn't a hindrance or a problem to her cheerleading ability. If any part of Wanda's anatomy presented a problem, it was not her lower body; it was her upper body. Her developing full figure forced her to wear a tightly confining sports bra when she did her cheerleading. The boys often quipped that if Wanda jumped around without a bra on, she would blacken both her eyes.

High school was filled with proverbial coming-of-age stories. Wanda could have followed a standard coming-of-age track in high school, but she had been set on a track of her own. It was a track she would come to set for herself more thoroughly as the horizon unfolded in her mind.

As far as coming-of-age stories went, Wanda had already had her coming-of-age story, so to speak, in the motel room the night she heard the apparently of age and experienced couple making love in the room next to hers. Wanda's coming-of-age that night preempted any more standard coming-of-age she might have had in high school. It would also prefigure the outline of a significant part of her life to come. As far as horizons went, the night at the motel had set Wanda's eyes on a significantly wider personal horizon than the shortwave bands. It also came to set her mind on a method of outlaw operating that went beyond slipping onto the amateur radio operator bands without a license.

It would have been hard to overstate how compelling the sounds of desire and passion coming from the next room had been to Wanda that night. Even with all the coming she had done that night, Wanda underestimated the long-term effect the night would have on her.

Previously, Wanda hadn't thought a woman could feel as much pleasure as the woman in the next room apparently had been lost in. Starting the morning after she heard the couple, Wanda wanted that kind and level of pleasure for herself. The level of pleasure and desire the woman had apparently experienced in the next room set the standard for the level of desire Wanda desired to feel herself. Wanda's high school didn't have

a high-jump team, boys' or girls', but the soaring pleasure of the couple
in the next room set a high bar for Wanda. Though it took a while for
the thought to fully and formally form up in Wanda's high school mind,
Wanda wasn't going to allow herself to settle for less than she had heard
that night. The level of pleasure the couple seemed to have experienced
became the goal Wanda would strive for. It became the elevated and distant
skyline standard she would pursue. Elevated and distant skylines were also
known as horizons.

Wanda still didn't have any idea who the couple were. Beyond the
obvious, she didn't know what had brought the couple to the motel. She
didn't know what the agreement between the couple had been. She didn't
know what kind of contract they had been operating under. It might have
been a romantic story. The couple might have come to the motel while
operating on deep feelings of love for each other. Deep romantic feelings
on the part of the man for the woman could explain as well as anything
why he had been driving himself so deep into the woman.

But the kind of high-level, fast-running noise the couple had made
was generally associated more with high-level, hot-running lust than
with spiritual love that ran deep into the soul of another person, and the
street-level setting the couple had set their passion blowout in was generally
associated more with street-level illicitness than with grand and elevated
Romeo and Juliet–style love affairs. One or both members of the couple
could have been married to someone else and carrying on an extramarital
sex affair. They could have picked each other up in a nearby bar. For
all Wanda knew, it had been a service-for-fee professional transaction.
Wanda had never been a dyed-in-the-wool romantic, and the night had
left her even less so. As her view of the night evolved in her mind and the
influence it would come to have on her continued to form up during her
high school years, Wanda suspected the couple had been there for more
illicit reasons than out of any grand commitment to love in the abstract or
love for each other.

The element of pleasure and the element of illicitness had been there
together in the room next to Wanda's that night. The couple might not
have continued on together after their night together, but the two elements
continued on together in equal measure in Wanda's memory and mind.
As the memory of the night continued to take shape and take on greater
connotation in Wanda's mind, the element of imagined pleasure and the
element of illicitness grew in proportion alongside each other. The couple

might not have stayed attached, but the passion and seeming illicitness remained attached in Wanda's mind. Detached observers might have called it the downside of Wanda's developing pubescent sexual response curve. The definition fit as well as any. But the twin elements of pleasure and illicitness remained joined together in Wanda's definition of what sex was about. Together they fed into Wanda's definition of what she was about. The thought of the possible illicit nature of the affair in the next room had been as much of a turn-on to Wanda that night as had been the thought of the pleasure the woman was feeling. As much as the sex in the next room had been lively, the illicitness of the sex remained alive in Wanda's mind and imagination.

As Wanda had joined the couple in vicarious pleasure, she had also joined them in her own form and measure of illicitness. As passion and pleasure had flowed in both rooms that night, passion, pleasure, and illicitness flowed together in the way Wanda wanted to go with the flow. As the pleasure taking place in her body and the thought of the pleasure taking place in the room next door had left Wanda panting and faint that night, the thought of the illicitness going on in both rooms had left her alert and tingling. Pleasure and illicitness were the twin horizons the night in the motel had opened up for Wanda. She wanted more of both horizons, and she was both organized and dedicated when it came to the pursuit of horizons.

As her high school years passed, the memory of the illicit feeling the night had left in her remained as much of a turn-on to her as the memory of the woman's cries of pleasure. The illicitness remained the other half of the memory. It remained the other half of the feeling. The element and feel of illicitness shaped Wanda's memory of the night as it set the shape and feel of Wanda's thinking. It remained the other half of the systematic life outline package Wanda would come to organize in her organized mind. The outlaw nature of the sex in the next room had directly aroused Wanda that night. It would continue to arouse her during her high school years, when teenage arousal was often the order of the day—and night. The possibly illicit nature of the affair in the next room had indirectly stimulated Wanda to go out on the horizon of the shortwave ham bands in an unlicensed, outlaw manner. Soon enough, her desire to recapitulate the night and make it her own would set Wanda running out after more than one outlaw horizon.

The night had been a definite and easily marked line of passage and point of transition for Wanda. The later transition the memory of the night would bring to Wanda would take longer to set in, but it would color far more of Wanda's nights to come. The pleasure and stimulation of that night would become not just a standard to be reached for. The memory of the night would come to be a pattern and package for Wanda to fashion her life around.

Wanda had been transformed physically and psychologically by what she experienced indirectly and directly that night at the motel. A whole sexual package had been imprinted on Wanda. It was an outlaw package that would take her far beyond any stay-at-home missionary position. To Wanda, the illicitness of that kind of affair had become as stimulating and attractive as sex itself. In her mind, the two were coequals. She could not separate them. She didn't want to separate them.

If she would compromise herself in pursuit of pleasure and illicitness, so be it. *Bring it on*, she thought. Being a compromised woman was exactly what she wanted to be and intended to make herself. She would be the compromised, wanton woman sweating and thrashing in a dirty bed in a sleazy motel, writhing in shameless surrender to overwhelming sensuality, screaming in pleasure in the arms of a lover she had just met that night and would not see again after that night.

The pursuit of sexual pleasure and the transport it would bring her would become both the ends and the vehicle of Wanda's life intent. She had no plan to do it through the vehicle of marriage, nor did she have any plan to do it through the vehicle of any one single man. Wanda's life plan for sex was to spend the rest of her life having a long series of illicit affairs—one one-night stand after another, preferably carried out in sleazy locations, such as the cheap motel where she'd had her first indirect sexual experience. She would reproduce not only the sexual intensity of her first experience but also the setting and the illicitness of the experience.

For Wanda, the cheap and dirty setting and the illicitness of the sex would add to the stimulation and intensity. After having a man or allowing herself to be had by a man, she would make a quick and clean break and move on to the next man. There would be no strings attached. There would be no complications. There would be no commitment. There would be no ever after. There would be no falling in love. There would be no falling into anything that would restrain her or hold her past the morning. There would be no agreements between her and any man except that they would love each other hard that night and part in the morning. There would be no arrangements beyond the arrangements Wanda made to leave the next day. There would be no return engagements with any one man. There would be just the thrill and stimulation of the sex of the moment. That would be followed by the thrill of the open road and the journey to the next horizon.

Whether one would have classified Wanda's particular sexual outlook as a perversion, an obsession, a compulsion, a fixation, or just personal uniqueness, it was the plan she came to for the direction of her life. What had come about that night at the motel and what it eventually expanded into in Wanda's mind did not birth a nymphomaniac, nor was it the beginning of an obsession or a compulsion. Wanda was too organized in her thinking to be obsessive or compulsive about anything. She was also too much in control of herself and proud of being in control of any situation to let herself become an out-of-control nympho. Rather, it was the beginning of a unique sexual outlook and life plan organized for Wanda by Wanda. She would define the horizons in her mind, she would set the horizons of her life, and she would move out into the horizons of the world.

Wanda's ideas of a life spent on the road and on the sexual run didn't come into her mind all at once, fully formed, and ready to go the day after her experience in the motel. Her ideas of a life on the road and on the make didn't come into her at any one given time. They developed slowly over a period of several years while she was in high school.

Her night in the motel and the memory of the throbbing sounds of passion and pleasure coming from the next room stayed on her mind and deepened in her mind. Instead of fading into the background of standard expectations and conventionality, the memory of the surging, shuddering, thrashing passion Wanda had heard from the next room that night remained as compelling to the growing Wanda as it had been the night she heard the passion of the couple and joined with the couple in vicarious passion of her own.

In Wanda's developing mind, the call of conventionality would surrender to the call of open and shameless passion and a life on the open road. In her organized mind, Wanda was a romantic. But her romanticism was an inverse romanticism. To her, thoughts of conventional romanticism paled and faded into the aching romance of distant horizons, the seductive call of the open road, and the stimulating thought of seduction on the open road. To Wanda, the thought of romance with a beer-drinking, butt-scratching, deer-hunting, gun-cleaning, fish-catching (fish for her to clean), pickup-truck-revving, freewheeling redneck good old boy or tractor-jockey farmer type didn't hold much of a candle to the romance of life on the road and outlaw love on the run. Though it would take time to fully gestate, Wanda pretty much knew from the night of listening to vagabond loving going on in the adjacent motel room that she wanted to spend her life as a vagabond lover.

With all that running around in her teenage mind, one might have thought Wanda would do a lot of running around in high school, at least in her senior year. High school girls with that kind of mindset and with minds set on the kind of behavior Wanda had come to set her mind on often turned into promiscuous girls with reputations for being a prick tease or a community chest. Indeed, as Wanda continued her physical development in high school, she came to have a chest that a lot of boys would have liked to get closer to.

But it didn't work out that way. While in high school, Wanda didn't turn into a promiscuous girl with a reputation for being easy and sleazy. For one thing, Wanda prided herself on being in control—of both herself and her life. Promiscuous girls weren't really in full control of themselves. They were often controlled and taken advantage of by the boys who took them. For another thing, in those days, shameless little hussies caught sleeping around often found themselves expelled from school. Wanda wanted to go on with her education after finishing high school and master the fields she wanted to master, technical and sexual. An expulsion would have ended her career plans then and there. Also, in the countrified setting where Wanda lived, marriages were often conventionally required, if not actively forced, between boys and girls caught playing house without benefit of house, home, or clergy.

In the plan already established in Wanda's organized mind, making out in the middle of the school year was too close in time and her high school was too close in distance to be the place to launch her life as a lover on the run. An already established tenet of Wanda's plan was that she would have sex only in situations in which the back door or front door was always open and she could run if things got sticky, before they had a chance to become really sticky. The turn-and-run option didn't apply while she was still in high school. There wasn't much room to run. There wasn't any functional door for a quick exit in high school. She could have been caught and found herself thrown out a door she wasn't prepared to be thrown out of or thrown in front of an altar when she had no plans to ever stand before a marriage altar. Wanda was looking for a life of energizing sex without complications. But she didn't want any entangling complications with any of the boys or men in her high school.

High school boys could be snotty, grabby, drooling, and dorky. They could also be egotistical, jerky, and clumsy. They could be immature, and they were forever bragging about their conquests, real and made up. The rapidly physically and philosophically maturing Wanda was already thinking ahead and in terms of mature men. The only mature men in her high school were the old principal, with wrinkled skin and hanging jowls, and the teachers, all of whom were middle-aged and older. Physically, they were about as stimulating to Wanda as roadkill possums. As the opening days of her sexual awakening opened further, Wanda resolved early on that she would set her own terms. Those terms did not have anything to do with leering high school boys. Or stentorian high school teachers. Or dried-up, wrinkled, leering old men. Wanda had no intention of doing the Lolita bit.

Wanda also did not repeat her autoerotic self-stimulating act she had indulged in on the night she was vicariously initiated into a higher level of sexual arousal. It had felt good and been arousing at the time, but it wasn't real sex. It was a cheap substitute for real sex. It was closet sex in all senses of the word. After her initiation, Wanda wanted only real sex with real, living, sweating, thrusting, possessing men. Though horniness had been born in the pubescent Wanda in full bloom that night, she wanted fully mature sex when she reached maturity.

Wanda had lost her virginity, so to speak, in the motel room that night. She just hadn't lost it in the way the boys in her high school would have liked to relieve her of the burden. Many boys in Wanda's high school wondered if Wanda was a virgin. It was hard for them to believe a girl with her looks and measurements could remain virginal. They wondered if she was keeping time with and sharing her charms and physical attributes with some other boy or a man outside of school. But none of them could offer any evidence or convincing anecdotal story to back up any of the speculation about Wanda or how accommodating she was off to the side out of sight. The speculation that she was a loose girl remained mostly speculation. Wanda remained aloof.

There was an old song that said, "If this isn't love, it will have to do until the real thing comes along." Wanda knew what she wanted in real sex and was willing to wait for it. She was also moving toward her personal conviction that sex didn't have to come with long, involved involvements that went on and on. Or marriage.

After her initiation into nonvirginal thinking in the motel room, Wanda remained a secondary virgin throughout high school, including her senior year, after the summer when she decided to become an over-the-road courtesan, at least until senior prom night. That was when the doors of high school swung open for the last time for seniors.

Wanda had been dating a football stud. They made the logical proverbial high school pair. He was a fullback. She was a cheerleader. She also was the second runner-up for homecoming queen. The honor of being homecoming queen went to the equally good looking but more conventionally blonde Melinda Snodgrass. Melinda's escort for the prom was the quarterback of the football team, the other football stud. Wanda wasn't crushed by not being elected homecoming queen. She hadn't even campaigned for the position. Nor was she miffed by not being taken to the dance by the quarterback. The quarterback had more status as a date, but Wanda's date was better looking. Wanda willingly accorded Melinda the title of homecoming queen and the hassle of having to parade around the dance while trying to keep a plastic crown in place on her head. Wanda also willingly accorded Melinda the status date with the quarterback. Wanda had the better looking of the two boys.

Wanda and the boy had dated casually a few times during the last half of their senior year together. They otherwise hadn't done anything. It was not that the boy didn't want to, but Wanda had held him off.

But everyone was supposed to get laid on senior prom night. While they were dancing and the boy was looking into Wanda's large hazel eyes—when he wasn't looking down at her cleavage showing above her strapless gown—he asked the question that probably more than 50 percent of girls at senior proms got asked. Wanda pulled the boy in closer. In a husky voice he had never heard her use before, to the boy's gratification and surprise, Wanda consented. The boy didn't mind that he was not dating the homecoming queen. She just insisted that she call the shots regarding how it would be done and after.

After the dance, when the couples were supposed to be at the soda fountain—at least that was where they told their parents they were going— and proper young gentlemen were supposed to bring their proper young lady dates back home to their mothers, Wanda had the boy drive her to a local motel. The motel wasn't a typical motel. Instead of one long, continuous line of rooms, it consisted of a series of separate small cabins called tourist cabins. The motel was on the main road outside town. It had a reputation for being a no-tell motel, but the boy didn't mind. His date didn't seem to mind either. In fact, she had specified the place. Wanda's knowledge of the location of less-than-reputable establishments made the boy wonder if she was a virgin after all or not. At the moment, her virginity status didn't make any difference to the boy. He would let the QB of the team kick around questions of status with his status date, Melinda Snodgrass. Melinda was known to be a bit reluctant when it came to making out. She was the type of girl some boys disparaged as a so-called professional virgin. The boy's date seemed to have no such reservations. He was going to get laid that prom night.

The boy went into the office and paid for the room while Wanda waited in the car. After minimal delay, he came back out and drove the car to the designated cabin. As the boy pulled the convertible sports car up to the cabin door, a glitch in his plans seemed to present itself. Wanda held up her hand and stopped him as he went to get out of the car. She seemed to want to say something. For a moment, he thought she had changed her mind. Virgins were fickle like that. Or maybe she was about to put some kind of condition on her consent for the evening, such as that he would respect her in the morning or agree to marry her if she got pregnant. Girls of that day and locale often put those kinds of prior conditions on sexual activity. The boy also wondered if Wanda was going to ask him if he had brought any protection with him. The boy had a condom strategically positioned in his wallet for just such a contingency. He was surprised when Wanda handed him one. It was just the beginning of the contingency planning Wanda would follow in the life she was planning to set in motion, a life contingent on the exploration of horizons and sex. Just not a life contingent on marriage.

The boy didn't know what condition Wanda was about to put on the evening, but he would have assented to about anything she said. Given the way her chest swelled out her strapless dress and the way her lips shone in the moonlight, he would have agreed to stand naked on his head in a pile of cow flop if that was what it took to get her in bed.

As it turned out, Wanda did put a condition on the boy taking her into the room, but it wasn't any of the standard conditions he had imagined. The boy knew that some girls had a hang-up about being respected. They didn't want to be dumped after consenting to have sex with a boy. The boy didn't know all that much about his classmate. She was a bit of a mystery to the boys in high school. The term *hot* had not yet been coined to describe a sexy-looking girl, but in period high school male thinking, she was considered a hot item. But nobody was really sure what her views on proper romance were and where her romantic hot buttons lay. The boy figured she would ask him to call her again later as a condition of their making love that night.

Instead of asking if he would respect her in the morning and not dump her after one night, Wanda effectively reversed all of the boy's assumptions by asking him to effectively dump her after finishing with her. Instead of asking him to call her again soon, she reversed the boy's expectations by asking him not to call her at all. For the boy, it was a bit of a surprising switch. Her demand that he have nothing further to do with her after their night together might have dented his football-stud male ego, but the boy was distracted by the way her bare shoulders looked in the moonlight. In his condition of advanced horniness, he would have agreed to stand naked on his head in a toilet bowl in order to get a yes and get in bed with her.

Wanda said he could remember her all he wanted, but he was not to act on any of his memories in any way, especially not by attempting to contact her. Wanda's condition was that they would not see each other after that night—not on break from college and not even during the summer before they left for their respective institutions of higher learning. She would only agree to go into the room with him if he agreed not to contact her again after that night. Their interaction would end there that night, or there would not be a night together that night. She told the boy she would be fully his for the night, but after that night, their time would be fully over. Wanda told him not to become romantically involved with her or attached to her in any way. While the boy was working himself up to speed to make out with the hot-to-trot girl that night, Wanda was working up to speed on the routine she would use in the wider fields she would go out to play in.

Wanda further said she was going off to school in the fall. The boy understood that. He would be going to a small state university in the fall himself on a football scholarship. He agreed to all Wanda's conditions about what would follow that night and not follow after that night. He could either agree to her conditions or chew a rock in an attempt to relieve the urgency of his own condition.

Having secured the boy's agreement, Wanda leaned over and gave him the type of long, sensual kiss he had only seen in movies and had not experienced up to that date with any date. Afterward, with the agreement struck, Wanda and the boy got out of the car. He opened the cabin door for her. Wanda walked through the door without looking back.

As soon as they got inside the cabin and the boy closed the door, Wanda and the boy went into a clinch. They didn't even bother to turn on the light. There was enough moonlight coming in the window for the purposes of the moment. One didn't need light for the purpose of heavy kissing or for the purpose of undressing. There was enough moonlight in the room for that.

After their extended kiss, the boy reached over with both hands and slowly pulled Wanda's strapless gown down over her body. The elastic flexed as it passed over her chest. With the size of the hurdles it had to traverse, for a second or two, it seemed the dress would hang up on the expanded obstacles. Having cleared the main obstacles to movement, the dress slid down smoothly the rest of the way. As her dress dropped to the floor, there was enough moonlight in the room to illuminate how full and mature Wanda's body looked. The only items of clothing she had left on were a strapless bra and her panties. The level of illumination was sufficient for the boy to see how beautiful she looked almost naked. What had been a giggling, jiggling teenage cheerleader only a half hour earlier at the dance had become a poised and seductive Hollywood starlet in a publicity still—and she was about to star for him alone.

Boys always seemed to have trouble undoing girls' straps. Wanda reached around behind her back and unsnapped her bra so the boy wouldn't embarrass himself by fumbling with it. As Wanda released the bra and it dropped away, there was enough moonlight in the room for the boy to see the size and deep red of her nipples and their erect condition. Almost as an instinctive reaction, the boy bent down and pressed his face up against Wanda's chest. He started licking, kissing, and sucking on Wanda's nipples. Wanda gasped and grabbed the boy's shoulders. Holding his shoulders for balance, she arched her back, gasping and crying softly into the air above her in the dark room. This continued for several minutes as Wanda's nipples grew wet from the boy's mouth. The wetness of the tips of Wanda's breasts caused them to shimmer faintly in the moonlight in the room.

The boy didn't need the moonlight to see Wanda's panties. While he continued to lick and kiss Wanda's nipples, he reached down and thrust his fingers in between the thin side straps of Wanda's panties and her naked hips. With Wanda's hands helping him, the boy pulled her panties down over the rounded fullness of her hips so they dropped to the floor around her ankles.

Wanda didn't need the moonlight to return the favor and carry the process and intended goal of the night forward by undressing the boy. The boy didn't need the moonlight to help him finish the job by himself, although he did work at it somewhat faster than she did. At the end of the undressing affair and the beginning of the wider affair, the boy's wallet was left in his pants on the floor, with his single condom still in it and out of strategic position.

The moonlight was useful in helping Wanda and the boy find the bed without banging their shins. From there on forward, the moonlight was romantically optional. Everything else proceeded mostly by touch. Wanda lay down on the bed, drawing the boy along almost on top of her as they went down together. As the boy quivered in anticipation, Wanda centered herself on the bed. Then he felt her legs spread. There was a momentary pause. Then a simple tug of her hands on his outstretched arms signaled to the boy that she was ready.

Wanda gasped as the boy pushed his swollen football-stud manhood into her now officially christened womanhood. The boy sort of gasped himself in a male way at the feel of the warm wetness of Wanda's vagina. Before he could make another sound, Wanda arched her back and threw her body upward against his. She wrapped her arms around his shoulders in a tight grip. As Wanda's chest pressed against the boy's, she pressed her mouth against his. Her lips moved all over the boy's lips faster than a school of squirming catfish in a net. In short order, the lipstick Wanda had managed to keep in careful shape during the whole prom was smeared all over her mouth and the boy's. While the boy kissed Wanda back, he ran his hands rapidly over her head and through her hair. In short order, almost as quick as the downfall of Wanda's lipstick, the hairdo Wanda had managed to keep in place during the night's dancing looked as if she had put her hands on a highly charged static electricity generator and the discharge had come out through her hair. But Wanda had specifically chosen an easy-to-manage hairdo that could be brushed back into place in a quick manner.

Possibly because they couldn't stay in the room for the whole night, Wanda kissed the boy as if there were no tomorrow. After a minute or two of holding her back tensed in an arched position, she relaxed her back and pulled the boy down onto the bed, stretched out fully on top of her. As Wanda relaxed her lips, the boy didn't get a second chance to gasp. When Wanda's lips came off the boy's, the only sounds heard in the room were hers.

As the boy discovered, Wanda, whose virginity had been speculated on so widely in school, was a virgin after all. But she didn't cry over losing her virginity that night. She did cry out but in raw pleasure. As the boy went farther in and the night and their romping went further on, he also learned that his cheerleader date could throw herself around even better in bed than she could on the cheerleading field. He also learned she could shout as loudly in bed as she did when leading a cheer on the field. With all the noise she was making, the boy thought to himself that she probably woke up every other guest at the motel and everyone living within five miles. As a cheerleader, Wanda threw herself into the role. As cheerleader and noisemaker for her upcoming life as vagabond lover on the road and lover of the open road, she threw herself doubly into her first performance. From the boy's immediate perspective, for a girl who was throwing herself into bed for the first time, Wanda was certainly throwing herself into her new role as lover.

Wanda had hustled the boy into bed before he was able to ask whether she wanted him to wear his condom. Given that he wasn't wearing any male protection, Wanda was taking a bit of a chance by allowing the boy to go barefoot with her. But Wanda knew enough about female timing to know she was in a safe portion of her cycle. The only love child born out of the amorous liaison that night was Runaround Wanda, with Wanda as the obstetrician who organized the delivery. Wanda still didn't like her name. She would have to work on that later. At the moment, she was busy working on the basics.

It was easy to undress by touch. It was a bit harder to get dressed by moonlight filtering through drawn curtains. The couple needed to turn on the light to clean up and get dressed afterward. They had to do a bit of running around to get themselves straightened up again. Wanda did another exemplary job of cleaning herself up and putting her appearance back in order in a short time. She brushed her hair and reapplied her lipstick like a mature woman, which one could have said Wanda had just become. She knew her parents would grow suspicious that their presumably still pure and chaste daughter was out doing something improper if she came back with her hair strung out in all directions like a rag mop. The boy would have liked to linger awhile, either in bed with her or in getting dressed with her. Wanda would have liked to savor the moment longer herself. But after the moves they had put on each other, they had to get a move on. Wanda knew they had to get back home before too much time elapsed. Her parents might grow suspicious if she came in too late.

Though Wanda and the boy straightened themselves up as if nothing had happened, when they went out through the door of the cabin, they left the bed in a mess. But that was nothing new for Wanda.

The boy dropped Wanda off at home before her parents sent out the deputy sheriff. Wanda kissed the boy good night and thanked him for a wonderful evening. Then she turned around and coyly walked into the house. The boy turned his car around and went on his way. As far as the first step in setting her life plan in motion, Wanda was on her way.

Wanda had handled her proverbial first night well, she thought. She handled coming back into what could have been a house full of questions equally well. Following her first act of direct-participation sex in the motel cabin, Wanda came through the door to her waiting-up parents acting as nonplussed and casual as she had acted when she got into her father's car after her night of indirect-participation sex in the other motel room. Wanda acted so cool and unruffled her parents could detect no outward signs that the feathers of Wanda's maidenhood had been thoroughly ruffled. They didn't know the degree to which their unchanged daughter had been changed by the night in the motel room earlier. They didn't know the daughter they thought was still unchanged and had been sitting up for to determine if there had been any change had passed a second quantum mile marker of change.

There were some questions, of course. Wanda's calm and unruffled demeanor kept the directions of the questions from taking an embarrassing turn. As fathers had been known to do, Wanda's father inquired about the boy's intentions toward his daughter. Then he inquired about Wanda's intentions toward the boy and her degree of interest in the boy. Though Wanda wasn't more than an hour from being flat on her back with the boy, she responded flatly that she had no intention of seeing him again. She wasn't lying about that part. She really didn't have any intention of seeing him again. However, her lie of omission was a whopper.

When her parents inquired if she had any intention of seeing him again, she reminded them she was going away to school in the fall.

"I'm going to be going to Racier Tech in the fall," Wanda said with the country twang that never fully left her even in her later years. "I've got things I want to do with my life. I don't have any intent of moping around here carrying a torch for some football player who's off throwing a pass at every girl who walks his way."

True to his agreement, the boy did not try to contact Wanda after he left her that night. True to her word and life plan, Wanda didn't contact the boy again. She didn't see a whole lot of her high school classmates after that night. When it came to football players who threw passes, her date had been a running back. It was actually the quarterback of the team who threw the passes. As for whether the QB of the team threw any passes of his own that night, Wanda never did find out if Melinda Snodgrass got laid or not.

Wanda's unaffected attitude convinced her parents she had gotten through the evening unaffected in the manner in which many girls were affected after their senior prom night. Wanda's father was reassured by her claim that the boy didn't have any untoward intentions toward her. As far as untoward intentions went, Wanda's father had inquired about the wrong person. It was probably better that he remained misdirected and uninformed. He might have had a series of sequential seizures if he'd known of his daughter's untoward intention to turn herself into a serial mistress. He would have been just as put out to know the sweat of his daughter's first step in that direction was still drying on her body under her dress.

Later that night, Wanda lay in bed, recapitulating the evening. Recapitulation was the name of the game Wanda had launched herself into. She had finally joined the couple in the next motel room. It had taken her a while, but she had finally caught up to where they had been that night in their room next to hers. Everything had been for Wanda as it had been for them. She had gasped, shouted, shuddered, and trembled, lost in her own closed-in tourist cabin of pleasure. She had accomplished what the couple had accomplished, and she had done it by her rules. She would have liked for the experience to last longer, but she had been forced to cut things short in order to get back home before her parents became suspicious. But she had stuck to her game plan and had made a clean and quick break from the boy after she accomplished what she had set out to accomplish. There would be plenty of other nights when she wouldn't be as rushed and could linger over the experience longer. She could still make as quick of an exit and as clean of a break in the mornings after to come. Wanda didn't know the identity of the couple who had set her on her road to the night she had just completed and to other nights to come. She didn't know if the couple had continued on together in the morning after their night together. She didn't know if they had joined themselves together again after the night Wanda vicariously joined them in. Wanda knew only that she would be joining them again in all her joinings to come.

With thoughts of the drifter she would become going through her mind, Wanda drifted off to sleep.

Wanda had been true to her word when she told the boy she was going on to school in the fall, though she hadn't been precisely accurate when she said she was going to college. Actually, Wanda attended a technical institute. She wanted to study electronics, and the trade school was the most practical and most reasonably inexpensive place where she could learn the field. At that time, some of the boys at the school didn't think a girl could learn a technical field, such as electronics, but Wanda usually pulled down better grades than they did. In the last part of her training, Wanda specialized in learning about microwave technology and equipment that functioned at microwave frequencies.

Microwave frequencies were much higher than shortwave radio frequencies or the frequencies used by AM and FM and television broadcasts, police, fire departments, and other public service and public utility companies. Microwave technology was more complicated and involved than lower-frequency radio. The equipment that operated at microwave frequencies was also more complicated and involved. Wanda wanted to master microwave technology because it was a challenge. Fiber optics had only recently been experimented with and was still largely off in the future. Microwave was the way communications technology was going at the time. Being a technician who knew microwave technology could take Wanda to a good-paying job. In the back of her mind, she figured knowing microwave technology could take her somewhere else she wanted to go.

Wanda graduated from the technical institute with high grades and started looking for a job as an electronics technician. She found the job she wanted when she went to work for a large regional telephone company. People still called them telephone companies in those days. The wider term *telecommunications* came into use later and hadn't been developed at the time. The specific job Wanda was looking for and landed opened up more than one opportunity path she had been looking to open up.

Specifically, Wanda became a repair technician who serviced, maintained, repaired, and installed electronic equipment in the microwave relay stations of the telephone company she worked for. She hadn't drifted into her electronics-related job or the repair field or chosen the company she worked for at random. It had all been a calculated strategy of her organized mind. The stations and equipment Wanda worked on were often located in far-flung relay towers across the nation. The equipment and towers were located in many different sites, from the heart of cities to out in the heart of the countryside. In Wanda's organized mind, it was part of her overall strategy that combined the two fields she was most interested in: electronics and casual sex on the run. The job required her to travel and be on the road a lot. A life on the road was the first of the main elements Wanda wanted out of life. Her being single facilitated things in that regard for both Wanda and the phone company. Married technicians did not like being away from their families. Wanda was not married and was willing to travel. She volunteered for the distant jobs. As a result, the phone company sent her out on the road a lot.

Wanda chose her on-the-road job because it allowed her to be like the proverbial traveling salesman who used the occasion of being on the road as a way of getting into mischief with local girls. When Wanda was on the road to do her repair work, she used the opportunity to go to local bars at night, where she would pick up men. For Wanda, picking up men came as easily as shooting fish in a barrel. Everything a man might have wanted was there in one tightly focused and confined package.

Wanda did a lot of wrestling with men in bed, but she didn't need to arm-wrestle men to get their attention, and she didn't particularly have to go after them. When Wanda put on her tight jeans and tight blouse and showed cleavage, men would come to her with their tongues hanging down to their belt buckles. The decidedly non-phone-company outfits she wore, usually one size too tight, sent all the signals she wanted to send. When Wanda dressed up in her night work clothes, she could make herself look like a cowgirl queen out on the prowl and out on the howl, a honky-tonk angel, or a honky-tonk devil. She could come on like a hot-blooded woman hot to trot. When she talked, she could make herself sound like all of the above. She could also look like a lonely woman looking for love. They were all acts to Wanda. She could make herself look like anything or any woman she wanted to. When she got into her tight clothes and went into her act, she could come up with and come across with any image she wanted to project. One thing she didn't come across looking like was a phone company technician.

Whatever image or persona Wanda was operating under on any given night in any given bar, if she found a particular man desirable, one way or another, she would convey the idea that she was willing and ready to give herself to the man she wanted to be picked up by. Wanda's choice of bars facilitated this. The clientele of the bars she chose were usually there looking to do some picking up of their own.

Once Wanda made her selection for the night, she would have the man take her to a nearby convenient, cheap motel for the kind of low-rent rendezvous and illicitness-tinged sex she was looking for. Once the man was finished with Wanda and Wanda was finished with the man, she would slip away, leaving the man wondering where she had gone. Usually, she left the men wondering who she was. Many times, Wanda left them thinking it hadn't been enough and left them wanting more.

When Wanda was not servicing microwave equipment during the day, at night, she was servicing men in the bars of the cities and towns where she was doing her repair work. During her workday, Wanda worked hard at her repair or installation work. One could have said that Wanda threw herself into her technician's work. She took both branches of her work seriously. At night, she took herself to bars. If she found a man she liked, she would throw herself into an act and throw herself in his direction. A short time later, she would throw herself into bed with the man, where she would throw herself into duplicating the kind of sex she'd heard in the next-door motel room the night of her sexual initiation.

Once Wanda's work in the bedroom was finished, she would leave the motel. When her phone company equipment repair work was finished, she would leave the area. She would return to the service branch office she was based out of and wait to be sent out on the road again. Wanda didn't have sex with any of the repairmen or any of the male personnel at the company she worked for. It was not that the men at the phone company were technogeeks who weren't interested in sex. Plenty of men Wanda worked with would have quickly picked up her line if she had dialed theirs. But Wanda had a strict policy of not screwing where she worked. It would have caused too much trouble. She wouldn't have been able to get as cleanly away from a man who worked for the same company she did as from her other swains for the night. Having sex with men she worked with would have created complications. Wanda wanted sex without complications. Her organized mind hadn't gone to all the trouble of organizing her life and her routine to throw it all away by carelessly screwing a man she couldn't casually slip away from.

Wanda hit her stride when she became an on-the-road repair woman. The night Wanda picked up the man under the *nom de amour* of Ashley, she had been on the phone company repair circuit for years. She had been on her personal bedroom circuit for the same length of time. By that time, Wanda had her electronics skills down to working order. She had her seduction routine honed as well. She also had her slip-away routine and methods developed to high technical proficiency. As for the telephone relay equipment repair and servicing she was engaged in that day, the company had allocated her several days to do the job, which she would finish in an hour. What she did in her free time was up to her.

Wanda went about doing her work quickly and proficiently. She disconnected and pulled out the malfunctioning S41/RFH014 signal routing unit and set it on the floor. When she left, she would take the unit with her. It was too expensive to junk like an old CB set. Back at the home office lab, it would be refurbished, made operational again, put on a shelf, and kept in storage in case a backup unit was needed anywhere.

Next, she installed the replacement unit and initialized it. As a final check, she attached the handset she had brought with her using the alligator clips on the ends of the wires. Using the handset, she dialed the phone company lab and had them run the circuit through the final continuity test. The test passed with flying colors. The circuit was open and active again, without other circuits having to carry the load and becoming overloaded and jammed. The guys at the lab congratulated Wanda on her work. In return, she made them promise to reward her by buying her a drink after work sometime. She didn't plan to seduce any of them the way she had the man in the far-flung bar, as she lived by a firm adage not to screw where she worked. Doing so would have been reckless. It could have derailed everything.

After her work was finished, instead of walking back down the stairs and exiting the tower, Wanda climbed up the ladder that led to the trapdoor that opened onto the roof of the tower and the arrangement of microwave dishes and horns that collected incoming microwave signals and directed them down to the equipment to be amplified and retransmitted over different circuits and paths. She opened the trapdoor and climbed out into the sunshine on the roof. From there, she walked over to the railing running around the edges of the tower roof and leaned against the railing, looking out over the landscape spread out in all directions around her.

With her upper body leaning partway over the rail, Wanda stood at the top of the tower, several stories high, looking out over the landscape below and the landscape of her life. It was the kind of day Wanda liked when she was on the road. The early afternoon summer air was warm. A gentle breeze blew past the tower at the top floor. At the altitude of the top floor, the breeze cooled the air, which was starting to become sweltering at ground level. The summer country sky was bright from horizon to horizon, without any clouds in sight. The land was several dappled shades of green interspaced with the rust and gold color of the tops of maturing crops in the farm fields that spread out like patches of different colors woven into a country patchwork quilt. Occasional small patches of ground-level blue from farm retention ponds spotted the land, which had seemingly been reserved for greens and browns. It was as if small splotches of the blue sky had melted in the summer heat and run down like wax to pool on the land below. The bright blue sky joined the bright green land at the horizon, which the height of the tower made seem both more distant and more present than it appeared from the ground.

The tower was a full ten stories tall. It had been built that high in order to mount the antennae at a high enough altitude to keep the signal above the ground-level clutter that would absorb and degrade the signal. The tower wasn't anywhere near the highest structure in the state, but it was the highest view one could get anywhere in the immediate area. Down on the road, trees, houses, and buildings blocked the view of the horizon. From the top of Wanda's tower, the diminished landscape shrank in proportion to the sky above. Homes, farms, and passing cars were reduced to miniatures. From the top of the tower, the horizon dominated the picture. From the tower, the horizon was clear and open to her. From the top of the tower, the horizon of Wanda's life was clear and open to her.

Wanda the wanderer stood looking out from the roof of the relay tower built by the telephone company she worked for. The top floor of the tower was the highest view in the area, and the towers Wanda worked in were the high view of Wanda's life. A long time earlier, Wanda had placed herself in a tower of her own making. But along with the open road, the top of a tower was where she most liked to be. At the top of her tower, she could see the world around her. She could see but not be seen.

It was a contemplative moment for Wanda. She had had many such moments before from the high vantage points of many different towers. Along with her primary routine of bar-hopping and picking up men, sitting or standing in towers and looking out on the world had become a routine for Wanda. The towers gave the contemplative Wanda quiet moments to reflect on her life, the path she had chosen, and the hold her chosen path had on her. Some of the towers were open-air metal-framed towers. Others were enclosed towers like the one Wanda was in now. Wanda's towers were often quite different from each other, but they had one thing in common: they all were where Wanda wanted to be. They all gave her the view she was looking for.

One couldn't have said Wanda wasn't introspective. She did reflect on her life. But her reflections on her life almost always took things in a self-satisfied direction. Wanda's reflections usually came to the conclusion that she would keep her life on the track it was on and would keep herself coming around to bars and coming to the same free-romance and romance-free conclusions she came to in bedrooms after leaving the men she had picked up in the bars the night before.

Wanda leaned against the railing of the relay tower, looking out the window over the world outside herself. At the same time, she touched upon the world inside herself. That day, she touched both the outer world and her inner world once again. Wanda felt as if she were merging with the land and sky she was looking at.

While looking out from the microwave relay tower and the isolation it represented, Wanda felt as if she were drifting over and above the world. What Wanda felt in that moment was not a sense of superiority over everyone else or the superiority of her life over conventional life. It was a sense of detachment, but it wasn't a sense of aloofness from life in general. It was, however, a sense of detachment from any particular type of life or view of life, especially any view of life dictated to her by anyone or any convention. The feeling was similar to the one that had come over her in the car as her father drove away from the motel the night after she heard the sounds of consuming passion from the next room—detached sounds that set the pattern of her life from then on.

Wanda felt that she was in the two places she belonged in and that she was in the two places at the same time: she had her feet on the road below and her face toward the horizon. The road and the new horizon were the places Wanda had wanted to be in life since she launched her particular life. Moving hard and sweating with a man in a sweaty bed, being out moving on the road, and moving toward the next horizon were the three dynamic modes of travel and personal transport Wanda wanted the most and the most out of in life.

Some people observing Wanda from a distance might have considered her to be a tragic figure. Romantically inclined people might have considered Wanda to be a woman doomed by her compulsion to a life of loneliness, a life without love. In their romantic formulation, they would have considered Wanda's bar-cruising and bed-hopping to be a method of compensation, a way of temporarily filling in the emptiness at the heart of her life, the emptiness of the heart of a woman without love. Those who knew the story might have said an air of existential loneliness hung about Wanda.

There wasn't any such air of loneliness visible in Wanda's chosen persona when she went into her cowgirl-on-the-make routine or her hot-and-flashy-honky-tonk-woman-out-for-a-night-of-fun routine. When Wanda was out on the track running with one of those routines, she hardly came across as a lonely and introverted woman withdrawn into herself. The only time Wanda carried the air of a lonely woman without love was when she wanted to look and sound like a lonely woman looking for love. As a come-on, that worked as well as any woman-going-wild routine. It was just one more arrow in her quiver.

One who liked to put intellectual-sounding definitions on things might have labeled Wanda's personal philosophy of life on the road and distant horizons as country philosophy existentialism. One could have defined Wanda as a female redneck Jack Kerouac. Anyone who found those kinds of academic terms phony and contrived and liked less esoteric and earthier terms could have labeled her as a redneck woman on the romp. Wanda had certainly let herself be pinned by enough men to get herself pinned with that label. But she was far more and far more involved than that.

Whatever category one put Wanda's thinking in, her thinking centered on a philosophy of open horizons, open sex, and an open-door policy of bedrooms. The philosophy had begun the night she overheard the couple making love in the room next to hers at the motel. It was the philosophy Wanda had organized in her organized mind before she had full, direct sex. It was the active philosophy of life she had set in motion the night of her high school prom. This was where Wanda's thinking had been since her first night. This was the direction her thinking had taken since her first day on the road. This was where her thinking remained as her life continued to unfold on the roads and as she continued to unfold herself for men on the beds of motels alongside the roads.

As hard as it was to put a finger on Wanda's particular personal brand of existentialism, for Wanda, it was a real commodity. It was the commodity that kept her living on the road and making herself a commodity to men. Wanda's romantic existentialism of love on the run and a life of running toward distant horizons was what any man who wanted a life with Wanda was up against. Wanda's enjoyment of outlaw love on the run was the main stud muffin in her life. Her sense of the horizon was a hard lover for any man to beat.

Whether one classified the force driving Wanda's lifestyle and keeping her locked in her lifestyle as an obsession, a fixation, a compulsion, or just a case of hormones on overload, it was the same strange compulsion that had started the night in the motel when the formative Wanda discovered how compelling sex could be. What had started out for Wanda as a pubescent lust attack had morphed into an underlying personal metaphysics that held Wanda to her chosen path, a path that bound her more thoroughly than many married couples became bound at the altar. It was a path Wanda intended to follow for life. She had no intention of following any path to the altar. Some observers listening to Wanda's gripping performances through the walls in adjoining rooms might have said she had a seemingly endless depth to her sexual desire. Be that as it may, Wanda lived in the grip of her desire for a life of outlaw love and moving toward the next horizon. As far as desire went, Wanda had no real desire to change her chosen lifestyle of love on the run, not even for a chance at what others classified as true love.

Wanda's compulsion had turned into what could have been described as a backhanded form of existentialism. As she looked out from the roof of the tower, she felt a combination of the intense and immediate feelings of all-encompassing desire, the aching longing she had felt while lying in her room and listening to the couple next door lose themselves in passion, and the detached and dreamy feeling of drifting through the sky and over the world she had felt while riding away from the motel in the backseat of her father's car the next day. Wanda felt more than just a strange sort of sexual fixation. For Wanda, it was a strange sort of romance. To her way of thinking and philosophizing, it was the romance of a vagabond life on the open road and outlaw love on the run. It was lust in its immediate and primal desire to get laid, overlaid by wanderlust and the call of the freedom of the open road and the gypsy life. It was the compelling romance of distant horizons. It was Wanda's form of inverted romance, and it presented a severe challenge to any man who imagined his manly charms could woo Wanda away from the life she had systematically chosen and pursued. Many men fantasized that romance would win a woman over every time and that love conquered all.

But Wanda was already in love. Any man who imagined that romance would win over Wanda would find that she was already deep in the center of a romance of her own: the romance of the open road, distant horizons, and love on the run. Any man who wanted Wanda would have to counter her romance with the road and horizons. It was a tough romance for any man to contend with. Wanda's lover in the form of the open road was a tough buck for any man to buck.

Wanda realized others might sense a certain air of existential loneliness hanging about her. She sort of encouraged the impression. It was an unintended by-product and auxiliary of the persona she liked to create for herself. Wanda herself occasionally felt a certain measure of existential loneliness in the life she had chosen. But existential thinkers were supposed to be drawn to that kind of achingly lonely and drawn-out feeling. At least they wrote as if they were. The writings of Camus, for example, were more depressing than an economy-size bottle of Valium.

In Wanda's reverse existentialism, the semitragic aspect of her self-created identity as a lone and rootless drifter was one of the strange existential elements that kept her drawn into her life and on the path of life she had organized and set for herself. She was drawn to and liked the feeling itself as much as any of the sensual aspects and feelings her bedroom activities provided. At her stage of life, when, for many people, the second part of the story began, Wanda still found the combination of making love on the run and living on the road to be both compelling and addictive. She had no regrets that she had chosen to follow the compelling call of the open road and open love on the road. She also no intention of changing her life. Wanda didn't feel crowded by any ticking biological clock or shrinking window of time, nor did she feel any crowding desperation to get married.

The big proverbial fear of ending up alone in old age often drove unmarried women to desperation to end their state of unwedded nonbliss. Wanda had long ago adjusted to the fact that she would end up alone in her old age. She knew the trajectory curve of her life would leave her alone toward the end of her days. But it was a curve she didn't have any desire to alter. In her mind, Wanda had compensated for it a long time ago.

Wanda didn't fear being alone. She basically lived alone by herself and for herself. She was self-reliant, self-sufficient, and self-satisfied to be so and remain so. Old age would just slow down the pace and energy she brought to the times when she temporarily stepped out of her isolation and into the role of a connected lover, but the overall isolation of her life wouldn't be much more pronounced at the end of her life than it was at her present moment. Wanda reasoned in her organized mind that if she died alone at the end of her life, it would simply be the last step on a path she had walked since she left home, a path she had chosen for herself and set herself on. One of the main clubs held over Wanda's head by romanticists, moralists, and any lingering romantic lobe of her brain—the threat of finding herself alone at the end—held no terror for Wanda. It wasn't a threat that could be used on her. The thought of being alone in old age inspired no desperation in Wanda and invoked no internal pressure in her to get off the path she was on and move in any direction other than the one she had set herself on.

As far as both short-term and long-term life plans went in Wanda's organized mind, Wanda intended to keep on with her chosen lifestyle. She would keep up with her vagabond lifestyle and keep running toward the next horizon. To fill the empty hours along the way, she would continue to pick up men as fast as she was, bed them just as fast, and then leave them just as fast the next day. As she grew older, she would pick up young men as long as her looks held out. Wanda preferred young men. Her looks were still preferable enough to attract men her age and younger. Even as Wanda entered her thirties, she was still bedding men in their early and midtwenties as well as men her age. If and when her looks slipped below the point that she could attract young men, she would continue to pick up men her own age. When her looks and health failed her entirely, she would live on her memories.

At times, Wanda did feel a certain twinge that she had not chosen a more conventional lifestyle. But the call of the open road rang a lot louder in Wanda's ears than the call of any altar, whether a religious altar or, especially, a wedding altar. The romance of the next horizon was stronger in Wanda's imagination than the love stories in the romance magazines she had passed up that day in the office of the motel. The strange power of the life Wanda had chosen long ago drew her forward with more strength than the pull of conventional life and love.

Wanda was fixated on the romance of life on the road and her romance with distant horizons as much as other women were fixated on romance itself. Standing in the tower, looking out at the horizon beyond, Wanda was as much fixated on and fixed in her chosen horizons and chosen path in life as she had been after the night she heard the couple in the next room. Wanda had enjoyed the hot, sweaty, down-and-dirty feeling of intensely connected sex she had felt in the darkness of the motel room with the man the night before.

In Wanda's own way, she equally enjoyed the clean, clear, drifting feeling she got when looking out from the tower roof on the bright, sunlit landscape spreading out around her. She enjoyed the feeling of total immersion in a world of desire and pleasure. She enjoyed the feeling of drifting disconnected over the world. She had all the physical lovers she needed in the men she made love to on the run. She had the two most important individual lovers she needed most in the form of the open road and the distant horizon. Wanda didn't need other lovers. She didn't need romance, and she didn't need anybody's conventional definition of romance in her life.

In her relations with men and in standing on the roof of the tower while looking out on the world she drifted through, Wanda had the two worlds she most wanted. She didn't need anybody else's world or definition of a world. She especially didn't need any definition of her life curtailed by the view in front of an altar or from the confined corridor of marriage, nor did she feel constrained or redirected by any compelling inner need for the proverbial love for a lifetime.

Wanda the wanderer, telephone company technician, dirty girl, bar cruiser, female pickup artist, bedroom epicurean, sexual adventuress, and mistress of the movable feast stood looking out over the scene of the pleasant green land spread out before her. She also looked out over the landscape of the pleasant and stimulating life she had chosen, ordered, shaped, and prepared for herself. In all the directions she looked, Wanda liked the view from her tower.

7

Son of a buck, Wanda thought as the motel pulled into view. The place was still there. She remembered everything about the night of her secondhand, next-room-over initiation into the world of sexual passion, including the name of the town and the location of the motel out on the western edge of the town. It had to be the same place.

Time hadn't diminished her memories of the night that had changed her life and been the locus of her sexual formulation. But time hadn't been as kind and preserving to the motel. Given that the place had looked run down and on the downside of the curve to oblivion when she had been there the first time, when she'd had her first time, Wanda had figured the place had probably been torn down by then. But it was still there, looking every bit as shabby as, if not shabbier than, it had looked the night she walked into her shabby room where she lost her virginity psychologically and symbolically.

Someone was still eking out a living off the small motel alongside the two-lane country road off the main highway. It looked as if the motel had changed hands in the years since she had been there and experienced her first vicarious sexual experience. The sign was in the same location it had been in when her father pulled into the driveway all those years ago. The road in front of the place had been repaved in the interim. At least the new owners or the road-building contractor had filled in the pothole. The motel was now called the Rosewood Chalet, though Wanda doubted a single stick of the exotic and expensive hardwood had been used anywhere in the place, and the boxy, linear construction of the motel bore no resemblance to a Swiss chalet. The new owner had probably chosen the name in an attempt to give the joint a bit of class. Wanda couldn't remember what the original name of the motel had been. Names hadn't been prominent in Wanda's mind or important that night.

The word *Vacancy* was lit up in neon on the motel sign. It was late in the afternoon. Wanda had arrived at the motel just about when she had figured she would. The sun wouldn't set for at least two hours. With all the miles she had put behind her since leaving the tower she had finished repairing, Wanda could have put some more miles behind her and stayed on the road and driven until dark. But the chance to spend the night at the motel where she had first been put on the road she had been traveling since that night was too much to pass up. Wanda figured she might even be able to use the occasion of her homecoming at the motel to put some more miles on herself.

Wanda turned the phone company service van into the partially remembered driveway of the motel where her fully remembered night had occurred years earlier. As her father had done those many years earlier, Wanda drove the van up to the motel office and parked. Before she got out, she sat in the van for a moment and looked around. The outside walls of the motel rooms looked as if they had been repainted, but the basic construction of the line of motel rooms was the same. The outside of the office looked a bit newer and cleaner. It had apparently been remodeled in some way, but Wanda couldn't remember much of what it had originally looked like, so she couldn't pick out what, if anything, had been altered. Minor improvements had been made, but a major rebuild hadn't taken place. Wanda's life had been altered and redirected in a comprehensive way by her one night in the motel. The motel had done a major remake on her.

After she turned off the ignition and stopped the engine of the van, Wanda sat there running some numbers around in her mind. Her organized mind calculated fast, just as it had calculated a fast life for her. Wanda was thirty-one. She had been sixteen when she stopped at the motel with her parents and had her life changed by the sounds from the next room. It had been fifteen years since that night. It was a bit sobering to Wanda to realize she had lived almost as many years since leaving the motel as she had lived when she first came to—and came in—the motel. Almost half her life so far had passed since she had been there. The last fifteen years of her life had been divided from the first sixteen years of her life by the one night she had spent at the motel. The direction and form of her life afterward had been set by the one night she had spent at the motel she now returned to.

The relative length of the two time periods emphasized the passage of time for Wanda. The passage of time in her life touched on other things that probably would never touch on Wanda's life. She was in her early thirties. She was drawing close to the end of her childbearing years. Her biological clock was ticking itself out, but she had no particular regrets. Just as she wasn't desperate to get married, Wanda wasn't desperate to have children. However driving the biological imperative to procreate might have been in the human species in general, Wanda felt no particular driving need to reproduce. When she had first started out in pursuit of her horizons, she had accommodated her mind to the fact that she would live the life she had chosen alone without the stumbling blocks and drag anchors of marriage, children, or husbands.

Wanda had launched her particular lifestyle the night of her senior prom. In the years since then, she had taken herself into the pursuit of sexual conquest and gratification. She had taken herself out of conventionality and into the depths of sexual involvement. But she had no desire to send a clone of herself into the world.

Wanda had no plan to get herself pregnant by either intention or accident. The pill had come out just before Wanda started putting herself out on the road and in bed with men on the road. With her focused and organized mind, Wanda used birth control routinely and consistently without any gaps in coverage. There would be no son of a buck conceived by accident in Wanda in any motel.

Wanda wasn't feeling the time crunch of the approach of her fertile years, nor was she alarmed by the ticking of her biological clock. Wanda's mother was vicariously feeling it for her. In her concerned country-mother way, Wanda's mother was forever inquiring of her daughter when she was going to settle down, get married, and have children. It wasn't that Wanda's mother was desperate to have grandchildren. In her country-mother way, she was concerned for her daughter's happiness. Wanda's mother was of the old-fashioned country-mother opinion that a woman couldn't really be happy unless she was married and had a family of her own or at least one deep relationship to shore up, anchor, and give meaning to life. Every time Wanda and her mother talked, either on the phone, the lines of which Wanda helped keep open and humming, or during one of Wanda's infrequent trips home, the conversation usually rolled around to when Wanda was going to find a good man and lose her single status. She always put her mother off by saying she might get married if she found the right man. She didn't tell her mother that in her mind, the concepts of "right man" and "for more than one night" were contradictions in terms for her.

Once Wanda put her mother at ease by making the statement that seemed to hold open the possibility of matrimony for her if the right man came along, she would go on to ask her mother if she wanted her daughter to find the right man or just grab the first male who came along because she was desperate and end up in a bad marriage. What could Wanda's mother say in answer to such a loaded, manipulative question? Of course she didn't want her only daughter and only child to end up in a bad situation or an abusive marriage. She would agree with Wanda that she should be careful to pick the right man, but she would usually amend that by saying she was suspicious that Wanda wasn't looking as hard as she could have been for Mr. Right because she was having too much fun being single.

Wanda hadn't outlined for her parents in philosophical detail her attitude toward life on the road, nor had she told them the full story of how she was having fun in the single life her mother suspected she was having too much fun in to step out of and get married. Wanda knew they wouldn't have approved one bit. As far as questions concerning her love life went, she acted casual, nonplussed, coy, evasive, and denying, just as she had the night she came back from the prom. For all her parents knew, their daughter remained as pure, chaste, and unchanged as they assumed she had been the night she came back from the prom in a state that was far from pure, chaste, and unaltered.

Wanda's lies of omission were piling up, but she figured she would be able to go on convincing her parents she was going on with her search for Mr. Right. When it came their turn to die, they would die convinced their overly selective daughter was still looking for the perfect man.

Wanda got out of the van and went into the motel office. The carpet looked newer than she remembered. The front desk counter appeared to have a new top. The magazine rack was gone.

Wanda told the desk clerk she had stayed at the motel in the past. She didn't specify how long past. She said she wanted to get the same room or the room next to the one she had stayed in. She didn't elaborate on the reason she wanted the same room. She specifically asked for room 18 or room 19—the room where she'd had her sexual initiation or the room the couple had used. It would be a homecoming either way.

It turned out that both rooms were taken. But the desk clerk gave Wanda room number 20. That was the room on the other side of room 19. It was also the last room in the line of rooms at the far end of the building. It was a bit disappointing to Wanda that neither room directly related to her past at the motel was available, but the room was otherwise functional. And it was equidistant from the central room. It was on the opposite side from where her room had been, but the walls were just as thin on either side. If the room was still being used by sexual outlaw couples and if a couple came to the room after a pickup, Wanda would be able to hear them equally well. If Wanda came back to the motel after a pickup of her own, the people in room 19 would be able to hear her equally well. She would attend to making the audio part well known as she attended to the man and attended to keeping herself unknown.

Wanda went to the room, thinking of a replay. The room was basically a replay of what she remembered. The furnishings were as sparse as they had been when she was last there. The tables and dresser looked to be of newer vintage than she remembered, but they looked to be low-end, low-priced factory-production knockoffs. The room had a television this time. The carpet was in a bit better shape. The mattress was just about as lumpy. Wanda left her overnight case in the room and headed out to a local restaurant the desk clerk recommended—or was shilling for.

As she finished eating in the restaurant, Wanda contemplated stopping off in the local bar she had passed on the way to the restaurant to see if she could make a pickup to take back to the motel. Before Wanda had gone to the restaurant, she had cruised around the small town in the van, checking out the local establishments. The bar down the road from the restaurant wasn't particularly big. Wanda had been in far bigger bars. The one she had made her most recent conquest in the night before had been almost twice the area. But it was larger than the other bar in town. Apparently, she was in a ten-cent, two-bar town. It looked marginal as a pickup bar, but it appeared to have been there for a while. It might have been the bar where the pickup she heard the night of her sexual initiation started.

One aspect of trying to make a pickup in the town bothered Wanda. It wasn't the timing, coming as soon as she was off the pickup from the night before—and the man coming inside her twice. Wanda had made back-to-back pickups on successive nights in successive bars before. What bothered her the most was that she would have to use the phone company van to take the man back to her motel room. One of Wanda's safety rules was that she was the one who drove to the hotel or motel she was staying at. That way, she was more or less in control of the situation. Problems could develop if she let the man choose the place and do the driving. If the man turned out to be a psycho or a kink who liked rough sex, she could find herself in potentially severe trouble if the man drove her to some isolated farmhouse or open field far out in the countryside. Women had been known to disappear while being taken on that kind of ride. Isolation was the key element guys like that preferred if they were planning on doing anything beyond straight sex. Being in a facility where there were other people around added a measure of deterrent. Even a nutcase would think twice about trying to kill a woman in a public motel where sound carried and cries for help could be heard, especially through walls as thin as the ones in that motel.

The other problem involved with letting the man drive was that letting him take her to his place separated her from her transportation that would take her away in the morning. It messed up her quick-exit strategy.

But that night, Wanda had the phone company service van. The night before, it had been a short walk back to her motel room with the man. It had been easy to slip out in the morning and slip away in the van. But it was too long of a walk in the dark back to the motel. She would have to drive herself and her swain for the night back to the motel in the van. She could slip away, leaving him there, if she wanted to. It wouldn't be all that far of a walk back into town for the man.

The problem was that the man would know she worked for the phone company. She pretty much had to tell him. He was bound to ask questions when she took him back to her place in a phone company van. If the man wanted to find her again, he would know where to start looking. It was easier to keep her workplace identity secret when she was working on a job that didn't require all the tools and test equipment carried in the van and she could carry the tools she needed in her own car or when she was working with other technicians and one of them brought the van with the tools while she traveled to the job location in her car. That made keeping her identity a secret easier. The night before, she had been able to get away with her most recent pickup without using the van except to get away after the night was over. It wouldn't work that simply here, provided there was a man to be worked.

Wanda went back and forth in her mind, trying to decide how to proceed. Finally, she decided that possibly recapitulating her night at the motel with her as the woman of the couple was worth the possible problem of the man finding out she worked for the phone company. She changed out of her uniform with the name tag and into her pickup work clothes. She still didn't have to give her name or tell him which office she worked out of. If she just drove off and left him, he might be a bit pissed. Perhaps the night would be enough, and he would be amenable to her just dropping him off in town and then disappearing from town and from everything except his memory. She didn't have to be anywhere on schedule the next morning. It was a bit of a violation of Wanda's established procedure, but she was willing to chance it if she was able to more fully christen the motel that had christened her years earlier. In the back of her organized mind, it was something Wanda had always wanted to do. It would be quite a homecoming.

Wanda left the restaurant to check out the lay of the land in the bar—and if she could pick up a stud lay from the local land. But the bar proved to be a disappointment. There were only a few old farmer types and one or two scraggly farmhand-looking types. They were probably regulars at the bar. None of them held any interest for Wanda or created any faintness in her at the thought of being held by them. Wanda wasn't a nymphomaniac. She didn't have to have sex every night with any man she could get a hold on. Wanda had high standards for both looks and personality. She wanted handsome men, and she wanted men around her own age or younger, down into their twenties. She didn't want boors, rednecks who snorted all over her and came on as if they were God's gift to country girls and honky-tonk queens, or conceited jerks. If Wanda's standards weren't met by the local fare, she would leave and spend the night alone. She might go to bed a little frustrated, but going to bed with her standards intact was a lot more satisfying than going to bed with some dried-out old coot or an arrogant jerk. In her career as bar-hopper and bed-bouncer, Wanda had walked away from far more men than she had walked away with.

Wanda drank one bottle of beer without talking to anybody in the bar. Then she left, leaving the patrons there to wonder who the attractive woman they had never seen in the bar before was and why they never saw her again after that short time that night. Even by walking in from out of the night and then walking back into it without saying a word, Wanda had the ability to leave men thinking about her and wondering who she was.

Back in the motel room, as she had done two rooms over and years earlier, Wanda walked around for a while unadorned as she got ready for bed. As she had done earlier, she deliberately stretched out the time she remained unadorned. As she had done earlier, she savored the feeling. Then she put on a nightie that was even more transparent and revealing than the one she had worn the night at the motel fifteen years earlier. She watched television for a while and then turned off the set and the light.

Wanda lay awake in the dark for a while, reliving her first night at the motel in her mind. It was a disappointment to Wanda that she hadn't been able to recapitulate the life-shaping night she had had—and that had had her—when she came to, and at, the motel as a teenage girl. Wanda had hoped she could re-create her first night—in more than one sense—at the motel, but not as a wet-behind-the-ears and soon-to-become-wet-other-places teenage girl but as the mature woman of the couple. Given that she wasn't in room 18 or 19, it wouldn't have been as precise of a replay as she wanted, but from whichever room she recaptured the night when her youth had become tainted, Wanda would have re-created the sounds of that night.

Wanda had spent the whole of her sexually active life to date in other motels and hotels, re-creating what she had heard going on in the room next to hers that night at the motel she had now returned to. But in the organized plan in Wanda's organized mind, she didn't just re-create the passion and the illicit sex she had overheard that night. It was part of Runaround Wanda's intent to re-create the sounds of passion and runaway desire she had heard coming from the woman in the next room. In order to make the replay as real to anyone who happened to be listening as it had been to young Wanda that night, it was the practice of present-day Wanda to yell, shout, cry, and moan as loudly as the woman she had heard in the next room that night. Wanda wanted to re-create the full package of that night with herself as center of the full package and in full voice.

Wanda didn't mind that others might hear her. In truth, a truth she still didn't want her parents to find out about, Wanda wanted people to hear her. It wasn't that she was consciously trying to turn on some other pubescent teen of either sex and turn him or her into the kind of randy wanderer she had made herself into. Just as Wanda had always wondered who the woman in the next room was and what her motivations had been, she wanted to leave people wondering who the passion-swept woman in the room next to theirs was. In that sense, making noise with her lovers was an act of vicarious exhibitionism on Wanda's part. She didn't want people to know who she was, but she did want to leave them remembering her as she touched upon their lives and their imaginations and then passed on without them ever seeing her or knowing the name of the mystery woman in the next room. Wanda would leave them wondering who she was but never knowing, just as Wanda never had seen the woman in the next room or learned her name. That was Wanda's way of completing the picture in her mind of the couple in the next room.

As she was completing the picture in her mind, she would leave others with a picture in their minds. If she played her role well, she would leave them with a mental picture in their imaginations they would never forget. Over the years, the picture might grow and become embellished the way the picture of the couple in the next room had grown and become embellished in Wanda's imagination. As with the men whose arms and beds she temporarily filled for a night before she disappeared over the horizon, Wanda was satisfied to be the woman who swept in out of the darkness of the night, riding a wave of passion and pleasure, and then vanished as fast as she had come back out into the distant horizon. If no one ever knew her name, that was all right in Wanda's inverse romanticism. She didn't want anybody to know who she was, but she did want them to know she had been there.

As far as sounds from the next room went, there seemed to be noise and voices coming from room 19 next to hers, the room where the sounds of passion she had heard fifteen years earlier had set the pattern of her life from that night on. Wanda lay in the darkness of her room with the light off and listened with her ears and memory primed. Maybe a replay of what she had heard happening in the room fifteen years earlier was about to develop. It would at least be a secondary entertainment after her efforts to turn up a replay affair of her own in town had fallen flat. Wanda's sexual initiation had begun in the room next door. What she had overheard had overwhelmed her. It had set the pattern and path of her life. In one sense, the experience in the next room that night, which had been transferred vicariously to her, had been the biggest single part of her life. One could have said it had been a large bit of Americana for Wanda. If the walls of the motel could have talked, their tales of the endless forms of sexual Americana they had witnessed could probably have filled encyclopedias.

But no such vicarious revival developed out of the darkness and through the walls. Wanda listened, straining to make out details of what was going on in the room and who the people in the room might have been. The walls of the motel weren't any thicker or more sound-resistant than they had been fifteen years earlier. Sound carried through with only partial attenuation. As Wanda listened, she could hear both male and female voices coming from the room. That was a bit encouraging. Maybe they were an amorous couple like the pair who had occupied the room on the night of her sexual initiation as a voyeur.

But there seemed to be more than a couple in the room. As Wanda listened, it seemed she could hear four distinct and different voices instead of two. Two of the voices seemed to be male. The other two were female. Unless a group sex orgy was about to break out, a family was occupying the room next door. It had been a cheap motel when Wanda's father took them there fifteen years ago. He had chosen the motel because they were poor, and it was cheap. It was still a cheap motel. The poor family probably had chosen it for the same reason her father had.

None of the voices sounded like those of young children. They all sounded more mature. The male voices sounded rough. Wanda heard one of the male voices growl something about kicking someone's ass. Whether the man behind the voice was addressing one of the others in the room or talking about someone more removed, Wanda couldn't hear. If the group in the next room were a family, they didn't seem to be possessed of a deep sense of family values. And they didn't sound like a particularly sensual group. Unlike with the unknown couple who had stimulated her many years earlier, Wanda didn't particularly want to get to know the people in the room where her sexually alternate life had been launched fifteen years earlier. They didn't sound like people she wanted to share anything with. They didn't sound like the kind of people she wanted to know she was there.

Whatever the identities and dispositions of the people in the next room were, they seemed more disposed to break out into a fight than into passionate lovemaking. Either way, the sounds of enthralled and enthralling sexual romping didn't start up in the room. The people next door finally fell silent. With nothing shaking, especially the bed and the walls, there was nothing more to listen to in the dark. Without the possibility of at least a vicarious auditory replay of her special night in the motel developing for her, after a while, Wanda drifted off to sleep.

Later that night, the sound of banging came from room 19. The sound woke Wanda up. It wasn't the kind of banging sound she had hoped for. Someone was banging forcibly on the door of the next room from the outside. The growling bark of a deeply resonant, commanding male voice demanded they open the door, saying something about having a warrant to take them into custody. The martial voice and the direction of the shouted orders sounded like police making a bust. Apparently, that night, room

19 was indeed being employed by outlaws on the run, just not the sexual outlaws Wanda associated with the room. A bit of Americana was taking place in room 19 that night after all, just a different and less pleasant form of Americana than the kind Wanda had heard as an impressionable pubescent teenager fifteen years earlier. Wanda tensed herself and prepared to dive under the bed if shooting started.

Either someone in the room opened the door, or the cops had obtained a pass key from the night clerk. The door of the room next door slammed open. General commotion erupted inside the room. The female voices screamed. Profanity erupted from the male voices in the room. Resonant police-style voices shouted commands for them to lie down on the floor and assume the position. Then Wanda heard a faint clicking sound that she took to be handcuffs being applied. Following that, the commanding voice ordered them to get on their feet. As Wanda listened, the apprehended felons were hustled out the door, where they were ushered into a waiting vehicle. She heard the sounds of the vehicle doors being closed. Wanda assumed the bust was over, and that was that. She figured the police would drive away, taking the captured felons back to the local station house. But suddenly, the door pounding started up again. This time, the authoritative fist was pounding on her door! A different commanding voice shouted through the door for whoever was inside to open up.

Wanda threw off the bedcover and switched on the lamp on the nightstand next to the bed. Apparently, the local cops thought there were more felons in the adjoining room. She wasn't afraid to open the door for the local police, but she hoped she could clear things up and convince them she wasn't connected with whomever they had just busted in the next room. She had some free time on her schedule, but it was limited. If the local cops took her in as a suspect and she lost several days while she cleared her name, she might lose the free time she was planning on using to visit her parents. But Wanda wasn't afraid to face the police. She had nothing to hide. But then again, there was little on her that was hidden. With the transparent two-piece teddy she was wearing, she was close to being buck naked.

Wanda undid the latch and pulled the door open. She expected to see a square-jawed officer standing outside, dressed in a starched uniform with ironed creases, a fatigue-brown police shirt, and a gleaming badge. Instead, she saw a ruggedly handsome, athletically built man in his late twenties to early thirties in blue jeans and street clothes. The man wore no badge. Wanda stopped in her tracks with the door most of the way open and glanced around quickly. In the dim light of the parking lot, she could see a large minivan-type vehicle parked in front of the motel room next door. Two scowling men and two semihysterical women sat in the back seats. The vehicle didn't have official police-style painting on the side or a flashing light on the roof. Two other men were milling around the vehicle. Another came out of the open door of room 19. None of them were wearing police-style uniforms.

Instead of issuing more command directives, the man outside the door stopped with his mouth open. He had expected to find another street-criminal type. Instead, he found himself facing a voluptuous woman who was, for all practical purposes, naked. Wanda wondered if the man was going to rush in, throw her to the ground, and slap handcuffs on her. Instead, he stood there with his mouth half open. Wanda could see the man had been taken by surprise. By instinct, she could also tell the man was no threat to her. She stood with her hand on the open door and a "What can I do for you, big boy?" look on her face.

"Now, what does the law want with little old me?" Wanda asked. Wanda was a country girl. She assumed the apprehending officers were country cops, so she reverted to her roots and spoke in an exaggerated country accent. "I get a little behind in my rent payments at times, but I'm not a bad girl. Not the dangerous kind, that is. I'm not packing heat, if that's what you're worried about. The only concealed stuff I'm packing is for the next fashion show."

Wanda glanced around at the other men wrapping up the arrest. All of them were dressed in the same street clothes as the man in front of her. "Where are your uniforms?" she asked in her practiced coy voice, which was laced with real curiosity. "Are you plainclothes or undercover cops?"

"Ah, no, ma'am," the man stammered. "We're skip tracers. We're bringing in two guys who jumped bail and took off. We've got them on a legal warrant."

That explained the absence of uniforms and official police-type markings on their vehicle.

"You're bounty hunters?" Wanda asked.

"We prefer to think of ourselves as auxiliary law enforcement officers," the man said.

"Whatever you call yourselves, I've always wanted to meet a bounty hunter," Wanda cooed. "You're so Wild West. You're like real-life Texas Rangers."

The streetwise man knew how to handle himself and anything he encountered on the streets. But at the moment, both his street smarts and his concentration were a bit rattled by the sight of the voluptuous, nearly nude woman standing in front of him. The man sort of smiled at being compared to an all-American icon. He didn't know what to say next. He wasn't sure what question to ask. He couldn't even remember what question he had come to the well-stacked, nearly naked woman's door to ask. Wanda jogged his memory for him.

Wanda leaned against the door she held open. She angled her body in an even more provocative way. "What can I do for you auxiliaries of the law?"

The man caught himself staring. "Ah, yeah," he stammered. "I was looking for any accomplices of the men we're taking into custody."

"Now, do I look like a street thug to you?" she asked in an exaggerated coy country voice. If anything, Wanda looked like a stripper in rehearsal.

"There are just a few things I need to check out," the man said. The main thing he wanted to check out was the voluptuous woman he had unexpectedly discovered. Asking a few official-sounding questions would give him more time to ogle her.

"Such as?" Wanda asked in a leading voice.

"To start with," the man said, "ah, what's your name, ma'am?"

"Well now, you can call me Rhonda," Wanda said, making up the name on the spot. She had given a different fake name at the motel lobby desk. "I just use my first name for most occasions. We models go by a first-name basis most of the time."

"Are you in any way associated with the individuals in the next room?" the man asked, getting his full official voice back.

"Why, heavens no," Wanda said in her best "What? Innocent little ole me?" country-girl voice. "I didn't even know who was in the next room. I'm on the road doing fashion shows for the lingerie company I'm a model for. I got in late and checked in. Then I had dinner in town. After that, I came back here and went right to bed. The door to the next room was closed. I didn't see anybody coming or going. I didn't have any idea there were criminals in the next room. If I had known that, I would have just kept on driving all night. I thought it was safe to stop here. Apparently, it wasn't. I guess I have you to thank for keeping me safe."

"Didn't mean to bother you, ma'am," the bounty hunter said. "I'm just trying to make sure we corralled the whole group. That's why I'm checking adjoining rooms."

"Are you going to have to take me in?" Wanda asked in her innocent-little-me voice. "If you take me in like this, you may end up booking me for indecent exposure. Why, I'm hardly dressed for an interrogation. If you put me under the lights, I may start sweating."

The man would have preferred to perform an interrogation behind the closed doors of the motel room. Between the two of them, he figured they could work up quite a sweat.

"What are you doing, Andy?" a dry but authoritative voice asked from the side. An equally rugged but more dogged-looking older man came up alongside his younger compatriot. Wanda took the older man to be the head skip tracer and the younger man a trainee or a junior partner.

"I was just checking out the next room, Chief," the younger man said.

The older skip tracer looked askance at Wanda's revealing lack of dress. "Were you checking out the room or checking out her?" the head bounty hunter asked in an obvious tone.

"I just wanted to see if they had rented two rooms and one of them was hiding in it," the younger skip tracer said. "I didn't want us to lose any of them."

"There were only four named in the warrant," the older man said. "The two guys and their girlfriends. We got all four of them."

"I thought they may have picked up another accomplice on the way," the younger skip tracer said.

Pickup was the operational word all around that night.

The older man glanced again at Wanda and then looked back at his junior deputy. The precaution of checking adjoining rooms was reasonable. The chief bounty hunter could understand why his younger assistant was standing staring at what he had flushed out. He could also understand why he wanted to interrogate the curvaceous woman.

"The warrant said they were all African American." He pointed at Wanda. "Does she look Afro-American to you?"

"Ah, no," Andy said sheepishly. Even in the dim light, he could see about every inch of Wanda, right down to the subtle skin tone and lack of any hint of African American coloration.

"If she's passing for white, she's doing a damned good job of it," the older man said, looking back at Wanda. "The one thing she isn't passing for is dressed." The chief bounty hunter looked back at his younger protégé. "Let's stop embarrassing the poor woman. We got everyone we came here after. She obviously isn't involved." He turned and started to walk away, motioning for the younger man to follow. "We've got to get these scumballs turned in. You can check out the local talent later after hours."

"I'm not local," Wanda said. "I'm just passing through. I'll only be here the one night."

"Sorry to bother you, ma'am," the younger bounty hunter said as he turned to follow the chief skip tracer.

"When you're done fingerprinting and putting them in cells, or whatever you do with the bad guys you catch, come back and tell me all about who you saved me from," Wanda said in a cloying voice to the younger man as he turned to leave.

"There you go; you got yourself an invite," the head bounty hunter said to his younger partner without looking back as he walked away.

"Ah, OK, ma'am," the younger man stammered at the unexpected invitation. Then he turned and followed his boss back to the van. In the van, there would be congratulations handed to him, not for helping to capture the escaped criminals but for apparently having scored a midnight romp with a buxom lady who looked as if she had stepped out of a *Playboy* magazine centerfold.

Not quite believing his possible good luck was real, as he arrived at the van, the young bounty hunter turned back and looked at Wanda's room. The unexpected woman who had handed him an unexpected invitation was still standing in the doorway in her minimally dressed state. She was leaning languidly on the doorframe with one arm up on the frame. She seemed to smile at him. Then she went back inside the room and closed the door. As the man watched, he noticed she left the light in the room on.

—◦◦◦—

The light was still on when the man returned half an hour later after helping to deliver and book the bail jumpers he and his team had caught and after the head bounty hunter dismissed the team for the night. In the man's imagination, he liked to think the woman was waiting up for him.

But he figured that idea was as much of a figment of his imagination as the come-on she had seemed to give him.

The young skip tracer knocked hesitantly on the door. He figured the woman might have left the light on as a night light. For all he knew, she had gone to sleep and had never intended to wait up for him. The man prepared to walk away if he didn't get a response.

But right after he knocked, he heard the faint sound of stirring coming from inside the room. Then the door opened. Standing in the doorway was the woman who had been standing there before. She was dressed in what she had been wearing—or not wearing—when he last saw her. Her figure hadn't diminished since she first opened the door. The man's imagination hadn't diminished either.

"Well now, there you are," Wanda, a.k.a. Rhonda, said. "I'm glad you came back. Did you get those bad boys in the next room locked up tight?"

"Yes, ma'am," the man said. "They've been turned over to the local police department, where they'll be incarcerated until they can be transferred to the state police."

"The police aren't going to turn right around and let them out again, are they?" Wanda asked with an exaggerated sound of concern. "For all I know, they blame me for turning them in. If they get out, they may come back to get me. I need someone to protect me."

"They won't be released, ma'am," the man said in a reassuring voice. "They've already jumped bail. They're now considered a proven flight risk. They won't be released."

Wanda exhaled an exaggerated sigh of relief. "Well now, that makes me feel so good to hear that," she said in a pleased-sounding tone. "I'm so glad they're in jail instead of so close next door to me. Who knows what might have happened to little me if they had known I was in here all alone? I really owe you one for taking them away and keeping me safe. Right now, I need the company of a big, strong man to make me feel safe. Come in, and spend some time with me to calm me down and tell me everything's all right. While you're at it, you can tell me about the men you may have saved me from. I also want to hear all about the work you do and how you go about doing it."

"I'd be only too happy, ma'am," the man said. Half his concentration was focused on the woman's offer. The other half was focused on the woman's cleavage and on her generous and bulging breasts covered in only the most nominal manner by the bikini top of her teddy, which was about as flimsy as and nearly as transparent as Saran wrap. Every inch of her generously full and rounded breasts and her fully erect nipples were outlined and showing in full detail. The woman didn't seem to be aware of how obviously her body was showing through her flimsy nightie, which was more like a veil than a nightie.

"But you're not dressed for company. You're hardly dressed at all."

Wanda made a gesture of glancing down at her top, which was a top in name only and not in opaqueness. "Oh, I wear this stuff all the time when I'm on the road modeling for the lingerie company I model for. I wear it so much I kind of forget I'm wearing it. I must say, I don't even wear this much back home. Back in my apartment, I sleep buck naked. I would have slept in the nude here too, but Mother always said that modesty dictated that I should wear something when I'm on the road. It's such a warm night that I didn't want to wear anything heavier. I might sweat up the sheets."

Wanda pretended to glance around outside the motel door. "There's nobody around to see me except you. Besides, it's not like men haven't seen me dressed in something flimsy like this. The photographers who do the photo shoots see me dressed this way. Men who see the ads and read the company catalogs see me dressed this way. Directly or indirectly, men see me dressed this way all the time. What's one more man? I'm not embarrassed to be wearing it if you're not embarrassed to see me in it."

"Ah, no, ma'am," the man said. "I'm not embarrassed by what you're wearing. What you wear is up to you. You're a big girl."

"I'm a big girl a long way from the office by myself on the open road," Wanda said. "It can get so dull at times on the road, and sometimes I can't sleep. I must say, I never had this kind of excitement happen so close to me before. Now I'm all wound up. I probably won't be able to get to sleep for hours. Right now, I don't want to sleep. I'm too excited to sleep. I find men who do exciting things like you to be exciting. I've always been fascinated by bounty hunters. It's almost like you're outlaws yourself, existing on the edge of the law but working for the law. To me, you're like John Waynes— bad boys who are good boys. I've always wanted to get to know a bounty hunter and get to know what he's really made of."

She pushed the door open farther. "Don't stand out there in the dark. Come on in, and tell me all about yourself and how you do what you do."

As Wanda stepped aside, the man walked into her motel room.

"I'd offer you a drink, but they don't have one of those minibars in this motel," Wanda said. "All I have to offer is my thanks."

The man turned around and looked at the voluptuous, full-figured, nearly naked woman who had invited him into her motel room. When she had been standing in the doorway, the light had been behind her. Her front had been in the shadows. Now the light from the single desk lamp on the nightstand shone directly on her. He could see her womanly body in full-frontal lighting and full, sensuous color. The deep red of her nipples showing through the almost transparent thinness of her wispy top set off and were set off themselves by the deep red of her hair and the natural redness of her full lips. The red of the woman's nipples merged with and transitioned suddenly into the creamy flesh tones of her heavy, rounded breasts. Despite their generous size, her breasts did not sag. They thrust firmly and defiantly forward, retaining their full, rounded shape against the pull of gravity. Her nipples pointed straight out ahead. The flimsy transparent top she wore was one to two sizes too small. The top was stretched almost skintight over her breasts. It conformed itself to every curve, pushing out where her nipples jutted forward. Her breasts were so large that the top, which had been cut deliberately short to begin with, couldn't cover them fully. The bottom third of the woman's breasts were exposed below the bottom seam of the silky, see-through top, which was thinner and more transparent than a silk handkerchief. Below the top that was hardly a top at all, the woman's full figure curved in and out in an hourglass shape where her torso joined her full hips at the waist. The only other clothing the woman had on was a narrow and tight thong made of equally transparent material. The thong didn't leave much of anything to the imagination any more than her top did.

"Tell me all about how you saved me from whatever those guys might have done to me, and I'll show you just how grateful a girl can be." Wanda closed the door behind them.

For an extended interval that night, the motel was treated to the deep-throated sounds of a woman yelling and screaming in abandonment to what sounded like exquisite pleasure. For anyone who heard, it seemed the woman was putting extra effort into her endeavor. The room next door was empty, as the bounty hunters had taken all of the occupants in. There wasn't anyone in the room to hear. There wasn't an impressionable teenage girl at a juncture of sexual maturity listening to sounds of abandonment to pleasure that would set the pattern of her sexual maturity and life path to come. In that sense, Wanda didn't fully duplicate the night that had changed her and made her the Wanda she was. She didn't duplicate herself in the life of an impressionable young girl the way her life course had been set by the unknown, sensual couple fifteen years earlier. But Wanda the wanderer had otherwise returned to her roots at the beginning of her wandering. She didn't know if anyone in the other rooms could hear her or not, but she vocalized as if she were shouting to the world. In a way, she was shouting her name to the world. She was shouting a name no one would ever know any more than she knew the name of the nameless and faceless woman she had heard shouting in pleasure in the adjoining room so many years earlier. Even the man she was shouting into the ear of would not know her name.

Wanda and the bounty hunter finally collapsed into an exhausted sleep. For Wanda, her seduction routine had gone as usual, but the follow-up that night was a bit different. She had spent so much time otherwise engaged that night that she had lost a lot of sleep. After she and the bounty hunter finally went to sleep, instead of waking up at early dawn and slipping out, to catch up on needed sleep, Wanda slept all the way through with the man till mid-dawn.

Not being able to slip away unseen as she preferred didn't present a problem for Wanda. The skip tracer had to leave relatively early in the morning. They had a backlog of cases to work on, and he had to get back to the office for the next assignment. Before he left, the bounty hunter asked Wanda, whom he knew as Rhonda, where he could find her again. Wanda made up the name of a big lingerie company in New York. The skip-tracing company did work all over the country. The tracer said he might be in the New York area sometime and would look her up.

As he left, Wanda stood partially dressed in the open doorway in the light of the rising sun, dressed in her tight country-style jeans and push-up bra, and waved goodbye to him. Not long after the bounty hunter left, Wanda set out driving the phone company van in a direction different from the one she had told the skip tracer she was going in. He wasn't there to see her leave in the phone company van.

⸺⸺ʊ/ʊ/ʊ⸺⸺

In short order, in the new day, Wanda was on her way to her parents' house—the house she had grown up in and the house her unconventional life had started out in conventionally. Behind her, she left the motel where her life had changed fifteen years earlier and where the direction of the life

138

she had chosen for herself had been set. What she had heard through the walls had changed her life and set it on the course she immersed herself in to that day and intended to go on immersing herself in for all the coming days of her life ahead of her on the open road. The benchmark transitional influence on her life had come as an act of unexpected serendipity. For all the years afterward, Wanda had hoped to be able to go back to the motel where her life had changed and re-create the night that had changed her life, staying in the room, this time with her setting the pace and making loud, womanly noises that kept others up and drove them to masturbatory fantasies while visualizing what was going on in the next room and wondering about the mystery woman who sounded so deeply locked in pure, raw pleasure.

When nothing had turned up for her in the dreary and nearly empty bar of the dreary and nearly empty town, Wanda had figured the chance to re-create the life-altering night of her past had gone by and probably wouldn't come again. However, in a second act of unexpected serendipity, she had been able to re-create that night after all, and she had done it with all the gusto and verbalizing she had planned to do it with. Wanda didn't know how many people had heard her performance. She didn't know if the sound had carried to any other room. But she had otherwise managed to retrace the footsteps of her past with her legs thrashing in the bed.

In her mind, Wanda filed the experience away on an equal basis with all the other experiences she had procured for herself and then slipped out of to disappear down the road. For the skip tracer, the experience lingered in his memory. He couldn't forget the gorgeous woman who had practically yanked him through her door and into her bed. He wanted to find her again to try to start something with her. A few weeks later, he decided to try to find the voluptuous woman who had given herself to him so readily and eagerly. He figured it should be easy. After all, he was a skip tracer. Tracking down people was his job. He figured he could find her again anywhere in the country. Besides, she had given him the name of the lingerie company she worked for.

However, when the skip tracer did try to find Wanda, a.k.a. Rhonda, he discovered the lingerie company she'd claimed to be a model for didn't exist and never had existed. The skip tracer went back to the motel to check the motel records for that night to find her identity. But Wanda had given a false name to the motel clerk and left no address to go with it. She had registered under a different name than Rhonda. Now the skip tracer had two names, both of them probably false. She had paid in cash, so she hadn't left a credit card receipt. The bounty-hunting skip tracer was left with no trace he could trace. At that point, he realized he had been given both the shuffle and the dodge. From the way she had talked, the woman had sounded rather dumb to the man. As he stood in the light of day outside the motel, in the light of everything, he realized the woman had been a lot smarter than he had given her credit for. *You've got to be smart to play being that much of an airhead and do it convincingly,* he thought.

For Wanda, her exit had gone as her exit scripts always went: the way she planned it. Her night at the motel of her beginning had gone the way she had hoped it would after all. As far as visiting the motel of her past and as far as revisiting the motel again, Wanda didn't know if she would ever come that way again. As far as what she had done in the motel, Wanda had come that way before many times. As the horizon of the open road expanded in front of her, she planned to go on coming that way.

8

It wasn't Tara. It wasn't Cannery Row. It wasn't a dirt-poor, depressed Appalachian shanty. It wasn't exactly classic country idyllic. The road that wound through the subdivision of scattered houses was paved, but the asphalt was old and crumbling. The driveways to the garages were dirt. Pickup trucks of various ages sat in the garages or in driveways leading to garages that didn't have enough room for vehicles because they were so filled with discarded stuff the owners didn't use but didn't want to part with. The phone company van parked just off the road stood out from the other vehicles in color, configuration, and size.

The wood-framed house was old and somewhat worn looking, but it was reasonably solid. The paint was faded, but the roof didn't leak. The house used a septic tank for sewage removal, but the indoor plumbing functioned as it should have. There was no central air-conditioning, but the furnace worked. The house was country enough that it had a front porch.

Wanda sat on the front porch in the morning sun with her mother.

"I guess you'll be pulling out and leaving soon," Wanda's mother said. "It's like you. It's always been like you. Even as a toddler, you were always in motion, goin' nowhere in particular but always goin'. The same when you were a teenager. I know you enough that I can tell when you're getting anxious to move on. You've got that faraway look in your eye again."

"I've got that 'I've got to get back to work, or I'm going to get fired' look in my eye," Wanda said. "I only had the time to get back home like I did because I got my work on the last job done quick and had three days left in the time slot allotted. I was close enough to home that I could get here with enough time left over to stay over. But the two free days I had left over are run out, and I've got to get back and on to the next job before the phone company starts docking my pay or fires me for being AWOL on company time."

"Well, if you get fired, you can always move back home here with your father and me," Wanda's mother said. "Your room is still available. We left everything pretty much as you left it. We left your old radio station and the radio set you built the same as it was. You used to roam all over the country on that thing. You could have stayed in your room and roamed all over on the air. But you went out and did it for real on the road."

"I never did get a license for that thing," Wanda said. "With a whole *Radio Amateur Call Book* to bootleg calls from out of, I didn't need to get a license. I was thinking about getting one, but I just never got around to getting a station call of my own. I never got caught at bootlegging calls."

She had been clever enough to use a different call every time she went on the air. To further avoid FCC censure, sometimes she would read between the lines of the call book and make up calls that didn't exist.

"I think the real reason you never got a call or handle of your own was that you enjoyed the thrill of bootlegging calls as much as you did getting on the radio," Wanda's mother said.

Wanda's skill at bootlegging radio call signs had prepared her well for bootlegging names for herself.

"I still remember you beep-beeping away up in your room on your radio," her mother said.

"That wasn't the transmitter you heard beeping," Wanda said. "It was my sidetone oscillator. When used during Morse code transmission, a sidetone oscillator allows you to hear and monitor the quality of your signal so you can tell if it's clean or sloppy. I built the sidetone oscillator along with the transmitter."

"Whatever." Wanda's mother's technological acumen did not go beyond running a vacuum cleaner and dishwasher and turning on their old secondhand television. "Either way, you're more than welcome to come back and start beeping away again from here. I promise not to turn you in to the radio police. So does Father."

"How is Father health-wise?" Wanda asked. She hadn't asked about her parents' health in the two days she had been at home. She had been afraid to bring up the subject, as it might have darkened their time together.

"He's fine," Wanda's mother said. "He's still working. Keeps saying he doesn't want to quit and that he has no intention of retiring. Has even less intention of stopping fishing. When he dies, it will probably be with a bass on the line."

A more concerned tone came into Wanda's voice. "How are you feeling?" she asked. "Is your heart still giving you trouble?"

"It hasn't been causing me any real problems, dear," Wanda's mother answered. "It just goes a little flighty on me from time to time. The doctor calls them episodes. Sometimes I get pains in the chest. The doctor says he can't detect anything obviously wrong, but he acts like he seems to think he hears something or detects something he doesn't like. That's why I want to get what I have to say out here and now. I'm not sure if I'll still be around the next time you come home."

"Oh, Mother, don't talk like that," Wanda said in a peeved voice. "Why are you thinking that way? Is that doctor throwin' a scare into you?"

"No. But he wants me to monitor my condition and report to him if anything changes for the worse."

"You do what he says," Wanda replied in a reverse motherly admonition.

"I will," Wanda's mother said. "But right at this moment, the moment before you leave and get back on the road you're lookin' to get back on again, it's the condition of your heart I'm more worried about."

"My heart's in great shape," Wanda said. "At least that's what the doctor who does examinations for the phone company says. The company requires all its employees to have regular medical checkups. I guess they do that in order to weed out anyone they think might drop dead on the job and drive up their workers' comp rates. If they detect anything medically wrong with you, I don't know if they can arbitrarily fire you or pull your health insurance. So I'm probably safe there."

"That's not the state of your heart I'm referring to," Wanda's mother said.

"If it's not atrial fibrillation you're talking about, what about my heart are you referring to?" a puzzled Wanda asked. Her mother had always been straightforward and plain in the way she expressed herself. She had never spoken cryptically, not to the degree she was now.

Wanda's mother paused. She seemed to be trying to form her words. Or she was bracing herself to say something she felt had to be said but was afraid could turn contentious. "I'm talking about the freewheeling, free-lovin' way your father and I pretty much know you've been living your life apart from us out on the road."

Wanda started to say something, but her mother didn't pause for effect or to gauge the effect her words were having on her daughter.

"Though you've never quite said it out loud in so many words, your father and I have pretty much known all along what you've been doin' with your free time while you're out freewheeling and unattached on the road, what with all your talk about not getting tied down and going out over horizons and not planning to get married anytime at all and how much you enjoy enjoying every spontaneous adventure that comes your way and not being constricted in your enjoying it by anybody's opinion or disapproval or by any what you call 'dried-out and shopworn' old morality that would keep you from enjoyin' the moments that come your way and that afterward would keep you tied down and not movin' on. Though you never said it in so many words, your father and I figured you were talkin' about sexual matters and weren't referring to speeding down the highway while blowing off the speed limit."

Wanda opened her mouth to speak. Before she could, her mother held up her hand to cut her off.

"We never said any of this to anybody outside the house. In talkin' about it among ourselves, your father and I never call you a slut or a Jezebel or any of those hard-edged country terms for women said to be of loose morals. Between ourselves, we've on occasion used the term *Ramblin' Rose* concerning you but nothing more hard and harsh. We've never thought of you as a slut or anything along that line, even when we were thinkin' that you've not been thinkin' very well where it comes to your lovin'. You're our daughter no matter how free and wide you may live your love life when you're away from us out on your own. We aren't going to bad-mouth you to anyone, and we're not going to bad-mouth you among ourselves."

Wanda went to open her mouth again. Again, her mother held up her hand to cut her off.

"Now, don't go denying what I'm saying. Denying anything isn't you either. When you've set your mind to do something', you've never been one to back away from it or apologize for doin' it, no matter whose face you're lookin' in or talkin' at. That ain't you. And you've never been one to lie about it or deny it. Denying is just another form of lying. You're not the lying type. I don't want to hear you start lying about anything, even that. However much I may disapprove of your lifestyle on the road, I like the thought of you lying even less than I like the thought of you bed-hopping. So keep any denials you may have to offer to yourself. I don't want to hear you become a liar. The subject's been on my mind for some time. I didn't want to bring the subject up while you were here. I figured it might poison or sour the time we had together."

"If you weren't going to say it while I was here, why are you bringing it up now that I'm about to leave?" Wanda asked, neither denying nor confirming what her mother had said.

"I'm saying what I have to say now because you're about to leave and go back to the way you've been going on. I have to say it now and not some time later because I don't know when you'll be back again. You get back home so rarely. For that matter, I don't know if I'll be around when you do get back, what with my heart being the way it is."

"Oh, Mother, don't talk that way," Wanda snapped in a half-angry voice. "If you don't want to hear me talk about what I'm doing out on the horizon, I don't want to hear you talk about dying."

Wanda leaned in a bit closer to her mother. Her voice became softer but more focused. "If your heart's causing you problems such that you can't do housework or the things you used to, I could move back home and help Father take care of you. I could get a job in town and live here at home."

"And give up the job you say you love so much?" Wanda's mother cut in. "When I speak of my heart having problems, I'm not trying to manipulate you the way some mothers manipulate their daughters into staying close to them by claiming to be sick. I'm not trying to get you to move back home to care for a relative who says she's at death's door. I'm not even talkin' about myself. And I'm not talkin' about the condition of my heart. Like I said at the outset, it's the condition of your heart and what I fear may become of it that I'm talkin' about. It's about the loving that ain't going on in your heart while the lovin' you've been doin' with your body has been goin' on. It's about the love that's draining out of you while you put yourself out in every bed with every man who catches your fancy. It's what you may be doin' to your own heart and the damage you may be doin' to it with your ramblin' love ways that's got me worried about the state of your heart. As fast on your feet as you think you are where it comes to fast lovin', too much of it can trip you up. You may someday find that you can't handle it or the consequences to your heart."

Wanda was a little surprised at her mother's heart talk. Per the necessity of her life situation, Wanda's mother had always been a practical, down-to-earth woman, but inside, she also was something of a romantic. Her romanticism had come out from time to time throughout Wanda's childhood. Now it was coming out full force. Wanda wondered if her mother's feeling of possible impending mortality caused by her heart condition was causing her to try to convert her to romanticism.

"If I can handle working in a high-tech field and keep my wits about me and keep myself moving in a man's job and handle myself in a man's world, I assure you I can handle my own heart and keep my heart from getting stepped on," Wanda said. "I can just as well keep from tripping over my heart and falling on my face. My heart isn't some kind of fragile spun-glass figurine that's going to break at the slightest jostling. I can handle my heart as well as I can handle my life. I don't have a country girl's achy-breaky heart. I'm not the kind of girl who gets led around by the nose and waltzed around by her own romanticism. Romanticism hasn't tripped me up so far in my life, and it's not going to trip me up and bring me down in the rest of my life. The same that goes for my life goes for my heart. My heart's never felt threatened. My heart's never been afflicted with the pain of longing for a soul mate. What's all this mortal threat you see to my heart?"

"The kind of fast-pace-on-a-dirt-track lovin' you're engaged in can be hard on a woman's heart," Wanda's mother said. "Even if she thinks her heart's made of asbestos and can't get burned. That kind of lovin' that isn't real loving can become like scar tissue over the heart. There are no nerves in scar tissue. That's why scar tissue feels numb. Because she can't feel the damage that's been done on the outside layer, she can't feel the damage being done at a deeper level. It hardens her heart to the point she can't love for real at all. Eventually, she comes to a point that she can't love pure and real. And she can't get back to real love. She's lost the ability to love deep and real. She spends her life in a state where she can't either give love or receive love. She ends up hard and stays that way till the end of her life.

"Eventually, she comes to the end of her days without ever having loved or been loved real-like. She gets to where she don't care what effect it's having on her heart or her life. She comes to the end of her life and realizes she never had a real life at all. At that point, she realizes her life, the life she thought so full, was hollow and empty. But by then, it's too late to turn herself around and set herself back on the right track where love is concerned. She gets cold. She gets empty. She gets bitter. But there's nothing that can turn it around back to more tender feeling. All she can feel is gall, and there's no one she can turn to in order to take the gall away."

"You mean a man?" Wanda asked rhetorically. "You say I need a man in my life?"

"You need one special man. One special man can give your life the meaning that playing the field never can and never will."

"One special man in my life?" Wanda said with calculated irony in her voice, circling around like a snake preparing to strike. "A life in which I circumscribe my life around his? A life that I surrender to him? A life I shape and mold around his? A life in which I surrender to him to set the path of my life for me? A life that fades into his until it effectively disappears? A life that's all of him and little or nothing of me? Is that the kind of life you mean?"

Wanda liked to think of herself as an independent thinker and a pacesetter out ahead of conventional thinking and conventional definitions of relationships. The sentiments she expressed to her mother that day weren't all that different from the neofeminist ideas in ascendance and washing around pop-culture thinking at the time.

"I mean a combined life," Wanda's mother said. "A life the both of you bring something into and make something larger and better out of. A blended life. A connected life that's more than the sum of the parts you bring separately. A life that transcends and triumphs over separateness. A life that holds more meaning for each of you than an isolated life can hold for you alone."

Wanda realized she wasn't going to be able to talk her mother into a corner and gain her blessing on her chosen lifestyle. At that point, she started to get an inclination as to where she had gotten the core of her own personal philosophy of life. Her mother's philosophy ran in a direction diametrically opposite her own, but they ran with equally settled focus and determination.

"A blended life with the right man gives you someone to walk through life with. It gives you someone standing with you as life runs its course. It gives you someone with you at the end of your life. While life is still in you, it keeps you from being alone in life and from ending life alone."

Provided you die first, Wanda thought. "As I've said before," Wanda said, "I'm not afraid of being alone. Nor am I afraid of dying alone. I'm not afraid of leaving this life alone. The main thing I'm afraid of losing in this life is control over my life. I'm afraid of anyone setting the direction of my life, even to a partial degree. That kind of blended life isn't for me."

"It's worked just fine for your father and me," Wanda's mother said.

Wanda's father was the manager of a truck repair company in the local town. He could be a bit gruff and stiff at times, but he was a reasonable father to Wanda and a reasonable husband to his wife. He was not abusive, unfaithful, womanizing, alcoholic, wanderlust-prone, or absent for extended times when he wasn't working, except the scattered times when he was fishing. At night, he didn't spend long hours away from home drinking in bars or carousing either alone or with cronies. Though he had grown up in the country and was countrified, he wasn't the kind of hard-drinking, self-indulgent, half-crazy character sung about and adulated in redneck good-old-boy songs. He had married Wanda's mother because he perceived the same characteristics in her. In their years together as a successful couple, they had had a few arguments but no more than other successful, stable couples. There had been no hidden undercurrents of the kind that led to infidelity or country-gothic-murder stories. They had lived a circumscribed, ordered, restrained life together. Their circumscribed, ordered, restrained union had produced a reckless, free-form child in Wanda.

"It's worked for you," Wanda answered. "And more power to you for it having worked for you. I hope it keeps on working for you. But I know myself, and I know that it could never work for me and would never work for my life."

"A man and a woman together for life is the way the Good Lord planned it from the beginning," Wanda's mother said.

Wanda's parents were religious—not in an intense, holy-rolling way, but they took God and his views of marriage to heart. When she had been a young girl, Wanda's parents had sent her to Sunday school. But like the countrified adage of water rolling off a duck's back, religion had not taken in young Wanda. When she'd become older, especially following the incident in the motel, Wanda had become taken with and taken by her own sexual catechism.

"And you think that only a man will be able to round out my life and make me whole?"

Wanda had always loved her mother, and they had always gotten along reasonably well. Tensions occasionally developed between the traditional and romantic-minded mother and the free-spirited daughter, but their life together hadn't been a formulaic story of a tyrannical and possessive mother trying to suppress and hold down a rebellious daughter who wanted to break free and break away to live her own life.

"Your father and I just want you to be happy," Wanda's mother said. "And we were both kind of hoping you would bring some grandchildren into the family."

"Well, I'm not bringing a man into my life and getting married just to bring grandchildren into the world and into the house here just so you can have some grandchildren to pamper and spoil," Wanda said. "Especially when I'm the one who will have to take them home and go through the work of unspoiling them and straightening them out and sidetrack my life to raise them till they're old enough to go off on their own, by which time my life will be gone, and I'll be old and won't have the strength to get my life back again."

Wanda's mother didn't want to invoke God any further because she didn't want to come across as a Bible-thumper thumping her daughter over the head with scripture. She figured doing so would probably just harden her daughter even more against God and the proper order of life as she saw it. In a short while, her daughter would be leaving. She didn't want them to part in contention to any degree. She would leave it there. Her daughter had come to her philosophy of life on her own in her own way. She would have to come to God in her own way.

"Besides, I'd make a lousy mother. You have the instincts for it. I don't. The only things I have an instinct for are the open road and living my life by my instincts."

Wanda's mother did not comment directly. In a few minutes, her daughter would leave home again. She would have to come back home again in her own way. "Well, even if you don't come back here with a husband and children in tow, you're always welcome back home," her mother said.

Wanda thanked her mother and said she had to be going. She asked her mother to say goodbye for her to her father, who was at work. Wanda hugged her mother one last time and then went to the phone company work van she had come in. In a short while, she was back on the road again, traveling down country roads, heading in the direction of the phone company office she was based out of. She stayed off main highways and stayed on country roads because the traffic was lighter, and she liked the landscape scenery better. Though viewed from the lower level of the cab of a phone company van instead of from the top of a tower, the world still spread out around Wanda. Up ahead, the horizon receded as she moved toward it down the road. The horizon was out ahead of her. She felt no need for a man to be waiting for her in a possessive, holding manner over the horizon. No such man appeared on Wanda's horizon.

9

Chuck was self-effacing. It showed on his face. The unconscious lack of arrogance or swagger on his face, in his voice, and in his expression had inadvertently stood him in well with women. It would come to stand him in well with a woman he would want to do a lot more than stand around with.

He no longer had what he had once called a home. He couldn't really call the Hampton Inn he had been put up in during the upcoming installation job his home away from home, but his section of the phone company had been willing to spring for the expense of something more than a minimal, sleazy lodging facility and reimburse him and the other techs on his team for a decent place to stay while he was on the road to supervise the installation. The inn even had a pool.

Chuck didn't go to bars on a regular basis, so he really couldn't call the bar he had gone into his bar away from the bar. But he liked country-and-western music. The punchy beat of CW music was playing in the background as Chuck went in through the front door. The front door was positioned in the center of the building, immediately between a neon Coors beer sign inside the front window on the left and a neon Miller Time sign to the right. The front door was centered under the word *Montana* on the neon sign above the door. The lit sign proclaimed the name of the establishment to be Jake's Montana Bar. The name was a bit of a strange anomaly, as the bar was several states east of Montana. Chuck figured that Jake, the owner, probably had originally come from Montana or wanted to give patrons the impression he had once been a Montana cowboy. Or Jake could just as easily have lived in the state the bar was in all his life. Jake might have put the name of the famous cowboy state in the title of the bar in order to give it a western image—if the owner's name was even Jake. For all Chuck knew, Jake could have been the name of the chairman of the board or the corporate lawyer of the holding company that owned the bar. If there was an actual owner with the first name of Jake, at least he had included the apostrophe and the *s* at the end of his first name. If he had left them out, the bar would have been called the Jake Montana Bar. That would have given the subtle impression that the owner was somehow related to the famous San Francisco 49'ers quarterback Joe Montana. That would have been quite a pretense. Chuck didn't have a lot of pretensions of his own. Pretension had never profited him much.

Chuck wasn't a philosopher, but he was familiar with serendipity—by theory, if not by word. He knew theoretically that one often went looking for one thing and found another. Chuck wasn't thinking in terms of serendipity when he went to the bar that night. He wasn't thinking of serendipity at all. For serendipity to work, Chuck assumed one had to be looking for something particular in order to find something else in particular. He wasn't looking for serendipity. But that night, serendipity would find him.

That night, he didn't go to the bar looking for what guys often looked to find in bars beyond a bottle of beer. He wasn't looking for anything beyond the kind of beer advertised in the neon signs in the bar windows and the good CW music he heard playing in the background as he stepped into the bar. He hadn't come to the bar with any elevated expectations of finding any particular type of experience one found in a bar, whether the experience was elevated or low. He basically was just looking to soak up a little local atmosphere and some local suds. It was more interesting than sitting in his comfortable and clean but standard hotel room and reading technical manuals. There wasn't anything in the hotel room to hold his interest. Chuck figured he might as well go out to a local bar.

He had come to the bar by default as opposed to sneaking out of his hotel room to seek a philanderer's window of opportunity. There wasn't any reason to stay in the room and wait for a phone call from home or make a call home from the room. He no longer had a home to call home to from any room anywhere in the country. He had no one to call to report in and give spoken confirmation that he had arrived safely.

The time of night when Chuck walked through the door of Jake's bar was the same time when he would have called home from the hotel if he had still been married. If his wife had still been home waiting, Chuck would have timed his calls home so that they came in at an hour that would have been prime time for a philandering two-timer on the road to be out at the bars, trying to pick up women. That had been Chuck's way of reassuring his wife he was staying in his hotel room and wasn't using being away from home on the road as a window of opportunity to cheat. To further reassure his wife that he wasn't out cruising for one-night stands, Chuck would invite his wife to call him at some random later time at his hotel room just to prove he was there and not out cheating. Chuck had taken the fact that his wife never took him up on his offer and never called him on the road as a sign she trusted him. He hadn't taken it as a sign that he couldn't trust her.

That night away on the road in a different town, there was no reason for Chuck to call anyone and no home to call. There wasn't anyone waiting at any home for his call, nor was there anyone for whom to stay in his hotel room and behave himself and wait for a call. When he entered the bar, he had nothing on his mind other than a beer.

That particular night, Chuck wasn't immediately out for what other men went to bars for and were out for in an obvious and heavy-handed manner. That he wasn't out for the obvious would, in an inverse way, serve him well with one particular woman at the bar who was particular in more than one sense of the word. Chuck wasn't possessed of the kind of arrogance that some men had seeping out of every pore of their expression and demeanor like tar oozing from a tar baby. Even when they thought they were successfully hiding their arrogance, their efforts only made their arrogance all the more obvious.

Chuck was handsome. He also had an athletic build. But he wasn't a vain mirror-starer, nor did he consider himself to be God's gift to women. One significant woman had already rubbed the gifts he had given her and the life he had wanted to give her into the mud and walked over them on her way out of his life.

Most of Chuck's pretensions that his looks and manly charm could hold a woman who had wanderlust and functional lust in general had disappeared with the functional concept of faithfulness that his ex-wife never had functionally had. Any pretensions left in Chuck had been drained out to the point they were pretty much below any woman's radar screen. Chuck's reasoned humility of omission would turn out to be an even better wardrobe choice for the night than the country-style jeans and shirt he had worn to the bar instead of his work uniform. Not coming on as if he thought of himself as God's gift to women would draw the attention of a woman who wanted to give herself a gift. In the process, she would give him her own particular gift.

Complementary with the name, the bar had a western saloon motif: rough-sawed wood siding on the walls; wood-enclosed metal pillars holding up the ceiling; heavy Santa Fe Spanish-style terra-cotta tile with rounded edges and deep grooves between tiles on the floor; a bar made of heavy dark wood with long, prominent, heavy-headed tap handles that projected straight upward next to each other in a row like a phalanx of phallic symbols; neon signs on the walls advertising even more kinds of beers than the two in the windows next to the door; antique metal signs advertising different country-type products, from tractor motor oil to chewing tobacco; western-scene paintings and posters of country-and-western singing stars on all the walls; a large map of Montana on one wall; a large pair of longhorn steer horns on another wall; a mounted buffalo head on a third wall; live cacti in flowerpots on the ledge between rows of booths; television sets, tuned to some kind of sports event, suspended from the rafters; and guys in denim shirts and leather jackets. Half the leather jackets seemed to have Confederate flags embroidered on them. There was no dance floor, but country-and-western music played on the sound system. The music was not loud enough to be jarring but had been set at a level calculated to reinforce the motif and set the attitude of the bar.

Chuck hadn't worn his phone company uniform into the bar. He was dressed in new pair of dark blue jeans and a light blue denim shirt. He figured his attire was a lot more appropriate for a country-and-western bar and would allow him to blend in better. Besides, a lot of people didn't like phone companies. Phone companies were like power companies to a lot of people. They were arrogant, they were insular, and they sent collection agents out the next day if someone was a day late in paying a bill, but they took forever to get a serviceman out if someone had a problem on the line. And people didn't necessarily like phone company employees.

Chuck was in a town he had never been in before. He was on the locals' turf. He'd felt he might stand out like a sore bureaucratic techno thumb if he wore his phone company uniform. He was at a working-stiff bar. He wanted the local patrons to think of him as a working stiff. Some people had trouble seeing phone company workers as working stiffs like them, even when the employees were technicians out on the road, working with their hands instead of computer printouts, doing manual installation labor. They thought of phone company employees the way they thought of post office employees: as a collection of pinched-faced bureaucrats and snotty employees who got paid for being snotty. Women often thought of phone company technicians as techno geeks little different from computer nerds. Being from a phone company could be a conversation killer at a bar.

When Chuck entered the bar, he didn't hesitate or stand in the doorway, looking around. That could have gotten him pegged for an outsider or at least a first-timer at the bar. Trying to look like he had been there before, Chuck walked straight to the bar. The bartender was engaged at the moment. While Chuck waited for the bartender to finish waiting on the other customer, he looked around. It was a high-traffic hour of the night. The bar was fairly crowded. There were a number of free seats available, but Chuck didn't mind standing. The mix of patrons was about sixty-forty men to women. There were no children in evidence. The place was not a family-environment establishment.

As Chuck's glance came back to the bar he was standing at the center of, he saw a woman standing at the end of the bar, talking with a knot of four men hovering around her. The woman had a cowgirl hat on her head and large, circular gold hoop earrings in her ears. She was wearing a two-piece outfit made of shiny reddish-brown leather. The top was a tube top fastened with pearly buttons. The strapless top was apparently held up by its tightness and the swelling bulge of the woman's chest. From the measurements of what the top had to deal with, it looked as if all the buttons would pop in rapid-fire sequence if the woman inhaled deeply. From what Chuck could see of what the woman had left to be seen by having left the top buttons of her leather blouse strategically unbuttoned, he could understand why the men had been drawn to her like flies with their antennae up and wagging.

The lower half of the woman's matching two-piece western cowgirl-temptress ensemble was a tight, short skirt made of the same leather-looking material, with the same color and liquid shine, as her leather tube top. The bottom of the leather skirt was positioned several inches above the woman's knees. Where the skirt strained to cover the woman's hips, it spread so tightly and was pulled so smoothly it looked as if it had been painted on. The top portion of the woman's come-hither outfit didn't reach all the way to join with the bottom section. A few inches of bare midriff showed above the woman's waist in the subdued light of the bar.

As Chuck glanced her way, the woman seemed to be looking back at him. The men clustered around the woman went on chattering as if they did not notice the shift in the direction and focus of her attention. The woman's long dark blonde hair hung partially over one eye the way Veronica Lake wore her hair in the movies in which she played a gun-moll temptress. It appeared to Chuck that the woman had dressed not to be comfortable but to make herself attractive. Given the eager press of the men around the woman, her wardrobe choice seemed to be doing the job she intended. The brown leather did enhance things well but only because there was a lot to be enhanced. The woman's clothes were a useful adjunct, but any particular wardrobe selection would have been superfluous. To Chuck's way of thinking and sizing things up, given her shape and the size of the things she had to size up, the woman could have filled out an old feed and grain sack and made it look drop-dead sexy.

From the look of the woman, Chuck assumed she was a local who frequented the bar. He didn't know if the woman was just counting coup by trying to see how many men she could attract to herself or if she intended to make a more serious choice for the night. She might have only been playing that she was a serious player. Then again, she might really have been a serious player looking to do some serious relating. Either way, she was seriously dressed for whatever part she was there trying to play.

However far the woman was or wasn't willing to go in her pursuit of fun, Chuck wasn't about to challenge the locals in their hoped-for fun or their local good-time girl. That could have led to even dicier conversations than those that might result if it were found out he worked for the phone company. Besides, there was a lot of competition he would have to buck if he wanted to make himself into her buck for the night. On a relative scale, Chuck was better looking than the men hovering around the woman. But he suspected if he walked over to the woman, she might just add him to her string of males she already had panting around her red high heels. For all Chuck new, the woman might have gotten an ego boost from having guys swarm around her. However much his sexual needs had been put on hold by his wife's infidelity and his divorce, Chuck felt no need to be one more man in the woman's chain of ego gratification. As it had turned out, he had been just another man in the line of his ex-wife's ego-gratification series. In the back of his mind, Chuck wished the woman a wise choice and a fun night.

Chuck turned his attention back to the bar. The bartender became free and asked him what he wanted to drink. Chuck ordered a beer. He paid for the drink, took the longneck bottle, and walked away from the bar.

If a bar didn't have a dance floor and a man was not there to check out the local good-time girls, there wasn't much to do in a bar except drink, sit, and brood. The mysterious stranger sitting at the bar and brooding was in the most clichéd tradition of western movies.

The trouble with Jake's Montana Bar was that there weren't any seats in front of the bar itself, and there weren't many open seats anywhere in the place that night. Chuck walked around with his beer in hand, trying to look casual. On one of his rounds, a couple got up and left, leaving one of the two-person booths open. Chuck sat down in the booth and proceeded to brood a phone company technician's brood.

The booth had a high back with padded red leather seats. It was a bit small and cramped, but at least he was off the floor. In the relative quiet and isolation of the booth, Chuck sat quietly, thinking about the work that would begin the next day. He had been sent to the town to supervise the installation of equipment in a new microwave relay link the phone company was setting up. Construction on the station tower in the area had already been completed. Two installation teams had been sent from two different service facilities. Chuck and his team were based out of the Memphis office. Tomorrow they were scheduled to meet with a similar team from the Columbia, South Carolina, office. Together they would install the microwave receiving and transmitting equipment in the relay tower and bring the system online. Chuck was the project supervisor who would supervise both installation teams.

When not working at the jobsite, Chuck and his team would stay at the Hampton Inn they had been booked into, with expenses paid for by the phone company. The other team were staying in a different hotel arranged and paid for by their office. They would meet every day at the tower until the installation was complete. Even with the two teams working together, the job would take several days to complete.

There were, of course, a lot of temptations that could be encountered by a man away from home alone on the road. The woman in tight leather was just one small example, though her measurements were not so small. Men away from their wives on road trips had been known to have quickie affairs. That was nothing new. Chuck's ex-wife had reversed the usual formula. It was Chuck's wife who had been having the quickie affairs while he was out on the road keeping his nose to the phone company's grindstone and being faithful. Chuck's wife was not the paranoid, suspicious type. She had not had affairs because of an obsessive paranoia that he was cheating on her while on the road and a desire to get even. Chuck's wife had affairs because she liked having affairs.

It had been two years since the unwayward-on-the-road Chuck had divorced his wayward-at-home wife. Technically, the technically proficient Chuck was back in circulation. But even though he was now free to do the on-the-rebound thing and cruise bars, the lingering memory of the way he had been cuckolded on the road kept him brooding in his booth instead of circulating around and hitting on women in the bar. The same reason kept him from approaching the woman with her gaggle of men standing at the end of the bar. His cuckolding wife had liked men in groups and sequential series. The woman at the end of the bar was out on the cuckold howl as much as his wife had been. For all Chuck knew, she might have been at the bar cuckolding her truck-driving husband who was out on the road.

His wife's infidelity hadn't just been the onetime fall of a woman overtaken by a random burst of temptation and loneliness. His wife's unfaithfulness had been systematic. She even had her affairs scheduled in advance of when he would be on the road. The infidelity of the woman he had believed in and trusted with the blind trust of a puppy had left a bitter taste in Chuck's mouth. That she had been practicing her infidelity on such an organized scale had left him feeling naive. More properly sized up, the size, dimension, and duration of his wife's undiscovered infidelity had left Chuck feeling stupid. It wasn't just that his wife had been taking an inch and screwing around while Chuck was miles away on the road. She had been laughing at him every inch of the way while she was doing it.

If Chuck sought a place to sit and brood over the memory of his wife and drown the memory in forgetfulness, the booth wasn't the best choice for that purpose. The small booth reminded Chuck of the booths along the wall in the gaming arcade in the mall he and his wife used to go to. Chuck was good at arcade games. He was especially good at riding the motorcycle simulator. He was good at all kinds of arcade games, from mechanical-skill and dexterity games, such as pinball, to video games. His wife wasn't as good as he was at arcade games, especially ones with a built-in instant-reacting tilt alarm. Her skill lay in playing proverbial cheating games in which it took longer for the alarm to be raised.

As his beer bottle approached the empty point, Chuck's thoughts drifted away from the installation work and back to his wife. He wasn't mourning the loss of his wife, and he wasn't wishing she would come back to him. The chasm of insult and anger separating him from his ex-wife was too great to be bridged from either side. He wasn't even thinking of his ex-wife directly. He was thinking more of himself. Chuck hadn't come all the way to another town in another state to have himself a pity party. He could have done that as well at home, and he was beyond that point anyway. Being on the road caused him to reflect not so much on what his wife had been doing while he was on the road in the past but on where his wife had left him on the proverbial road of life and where the road was going, or not going, for him in the future.

Chuck was well into his thirtieth year, a transitional year that many aging young men and women considered to be one of the major milestones of life. Chuck had put a lot of miles behind him. His wife's infidelity had put a lot of unexpected miles on him. He had done well in his job as a technician and had risen quickly in the ranks. It was a bit unusual in the phone company for a technician to become a full supervisor at the age of thirty.

Thirty was the year by which one was supposed to have become settled down and settled into home and family life. At thirty, he had no wife. He had no home. He had no family. His wife had always said she wanted to wait a bit until they were older to have children. In retrospect, he could see why she had been putting off having children. She had been too busy working on ways to put him off. Having children would have been another layer of inconvenience for her to contend with while she was out contending in bed with her lovers on the side.

Chuck had believed in home and family. He had believed in ever after. He had believed in the home and family track in life. He'd thought he was on that track with his wife. If he'd had a family, he would eventually have been able to persuade the phone company to take him off cross-country duty and assign him to work in the area. Now, at thirty, when home, family, ever after, and rootedness should have been starting to gel for him, Chuck found himself back on the road again. Given that he was single and had no family to accommodate and no home to accommodate them in, the phone company was not likely to pull him off of transient duty. For the foreseeable road ahead, there was nothing ahead of Chuck but the road.

Chuck looked at his beer bottle. There was about one swallow left. Unless he could flag down a wandering waitress and have her bring him another beer, he would have to get up, leave the booth, and get another drink himself. One or more of the standing patrons would probably pounce on the open booth while he was back at the bar getting his drink.

He would be left back on his feet again, as he had been left back on the road again. Whether he sat in the barroom booth or out on the road, as Chuck stared at the beer bottle, he knew he would be alone.

Suddenly, Chuck found himself not quite so alone. A figure swept in from the aisle between the booths and the tables and sat down in the empty seat on the other side of the booth. Even before Chuck could look up, from the roundedness of the figure that his peripheral vision picked up and the bow-wave smell of perfume that proceeded the figure, Chuck could tell the figure was female.

When Chuck looked up, he saw a slightly nonsvelt but sensuously curvaceous body dressed in a tight leather skirt with a bare midriff and a tightly strained leather top sitting in the booth seat directly across from him. As he looked up higher, he saw a sensually elegant face accented by a streak of glossy red lipstick, framed vertically on either side by long and slowly curving waves of honey-blonde hair. Below her face was the shine of reddish-brown leather over two mounds of milky white skin pressed in against each other. The rounded twin mounds were divided into two separate hemispheres by a deep vertical groove. The top-curved mounds of the woman's breasts and the deep canyon of her cleavage shone a semiglossy, creamy white in the indirect light of the bar. The figure that had appeared so suddenly and unexpectedly out of the half-light of the bar was the attractive woman Chuck had seen standing in the middle of the knot of men at the far end of the bar. By the time Chuck had looked all the way up, the woman had already sat down in the seat across from him. She reached across the length of the table and set a small purse down on the inner end of the table. As she swung her legs in fully under the table, they brushed up against Chuck's legs.

"I hope you don't mind if I sit down," the woman said in an apologetic but husky voice. "But I've been on my feet all day, and there's no other open seat in the place."

Out of the corner of his eye, Chuck could see one or two open seats.

"Besides, I saw you walking by yourself. You looked kind of alone."

If she had followed his movements as he left the bar and sat down, apparently, the woman had been watching him more than the single glance she had given him from the end of the bar. Her statement that she had been watching him made Chuck wonder if she had stumbled upon him at random or had planned to just happen by. The hangers-on who had been clustered around the woman at the bar were nowhere in immediate sight.

Chuck wondered if the woman had broken away from them and what excuse she had given to leave. Had she said she had to go to the bathroom or something like that? If the woman had slipped out on her would-be admirers, she had apparently been willing to dump all of them for him.

But then again, Chuck figured he might just be engaging in a revamped pretension.

"When I saw you up close sitting here, you had kind of a sad look on your face. You looked like you could use some company."

Chuck had been thinking about his unfaithful wife and his divorce when the woman approached. He had also been feeling a bit alone and abandoned in a place he had never been in before. If the woman had read that on his face, she was as perceptive as she was stacked.

As he recovered from his surprise at the sudden materialization of the woman, he figured maybe everything he had been thinking about had left him with some kind of lost-puppy look on his face. It might have been that expression the woman clued in on. The only part he had played was to remember the part his wife had played in draining the meaning and direction out of his life. Had his thoughts been so obvious on his face?

For her part, years of bar-hopping and sexual partner selection had honed Wanda's senses to where she could read, if not the sum total of a man by the look on his face, at least an operational part large enough to take her through the night with the man she had chosen. What most men had written on their faces when they came to Wanda was obvious. She was out after precisely that obviousness, so that kind of display in a man didn't bother her.

But Wanda could pick out other signs that could spell out hidden dangers lurking in a man. She could pick out the subtle signs of the kind of arrogance that made a man think a woman was his plaything or punching bag. That kind of look on a man became more apparent in a bar. She could pick out the subtle clues of concealed neuroses, lurking fetishes, and underlying obsessions. She could pretty much instinctively recognize the kind of man who was potentially dangerous. She had systematically steered away from them.

Though she preferred to be on the bottom during sex, Wanda had managed to stay on top of things as far as avoiding dangerous men. The fact that she was constantly moving around brought her in contact with lots of different men. Her instinctive radar had been able to filter out the men with hidden compulsions and hair-trigger anything in their personalities.

The fact that Wanda did not stay in any one given area too long and, after having given herself to a man, was often out of the picture before the man was out of bed prevented any man from becoming possessive with her or obsessive about her. It also prevented pesky romantic complications from developing in her swains for the night.

Wanda couldn't fully read the look on Chuck's face. It seemed like the look of a man who had been hurt. But it wasn't the look of a man who would beat her up when some hidden need to hurt women exploded out of him. The look on the man's face was turned outward. It wasn't the look of a neurosis or an obsession that was turned inward, feeding on itself and chewing on its own festering sores. Wanda was a quick study. As she sized up the man sitting alone, he had a detached and somewhat sad look on his face. It was a faraway look. Wanda figured they at least had one thing in common. She knew all about looking at faraway horizons. She would be far away enough in the morning anyway.

"Ah, sure. Sit down." Chuck sort of stumbled over his words, trying to think of something suave to say to the gorgeous woman who had appeared so suddenly and had already sat down. "You're welcome to the seat. Far be it from me to keep a tired gal on her sore feet."

As Wanda centered herself in the seat across from Chuck, Chuck's gaze more or less centered on the line of deep cleavage that divided the center of her chest. The centerline of her cleavage waved from side to side a bit as she finished settling into her seat.

"I'm on my feet a lot myself. I know how your feet can start to bother you when you've been on them too much. Sit down, and take a load off." Chuck hoped the woman didn't take the "take a load off" portion of his comment to mean he thought she was fat.

She wasn't fat or even plump. She just wasn't as gauntly thin as the supermodels who were just starting to make their appearance at the time. Her face and body were a little thicker than the willowy figures of the models who strutted the latest absurd big-name designer originals down high-fashion runways in New York and LA or posed on the beach for high-glitz fashion photo shoots in exotic locations while wearing bikinis with less total cloth to them than an emergency bandage. Her body more resembled the women one saw splayed over the big chopper bikes in motorcycle magazines or the big-chested models in beer ads pitched to rednecks. What the woman's body lacked in subtle thinness and fluid grace it more than made up for in willingness to put itself forward. Chuck's face

162

was facing the woman, but his eyes were fixed on the compressed cleavage of her chest.

"If you've been on your feet all day in high heels, that's why your feet are probably hurting," Chuck added. He went on staring at the confined and bulging swell of the woman's breasts as they were pushed together by her tight leather tube top.

"It probably wasn't a good idea to wear my heels in here," Wanda said. "Especially with uneven floors like they have here. It will probably only make my feet hurt all the worse."

Chuck continued to focus the direction of his gaze toward her generous breasts and the deep cleavage between them. He nodded in the general direction of her feet, which were out of sight under the table. It gave him an excuse to look in a more direct line at her chest. "The tile on the floor has a high shine on it."

Chuck commented on the hard southwestern-style tile on the floor as he went on looking at the way her upper breasts and cleavage seemed to shine softly in the subdued light of the bar. "It's pretty slippery, especially where some drunk spilled his beer. Your feet could slip out from under you real easy wearing heels in here. The space between the tiles is pretty deep before you get to the grout. The thin tip of your heel could slip into one of the spaces between the tiles, and you could twist your ankle. The floor in this place is a pretty uneven surface to walk around on in shoes already as unstable as high heels. You should have worn some kind of shoes with a lower back and rubber soles. They may not be as fashionable as the stiletto heels you're wearing, but it's better than slipping on the floor, breaking your nose, and chipping a tooth on a table on the way down."

Chuck couldn't see Wanda's fashionable red high-heel shoes under the table. His gaze was still drawn to the way she displayed her fashionable cleavage.

"I suppose I should have worn my flats," Wanda said. "I usually wear them when I go dancing. It's hard to dance in heels. But they don't have dancing here. I just got lazy and didn't change my shoes before I came here."

Somehow, Chuck doubted she worked in the clothes she was wearing and had come straight to the bar after getting off work. If she was a daytime working girl, she had obviously stopped off where she lived and changed from her street clothes into the outfit she was wearing before coming to the bar. She could have just as easily changed her shoes when she changed out of her work clothes.

Unless she worked at night and was wearing her work clothes.

"My big old clodhopper feet are expendable," Chuck said with self-effacing, or foot-effacing, solicitousness toward her feet. "I stumble over my own feet all the time. But from what I could see of you when you were standing down at the end of the bar, you've got the best-looking pair of ankles in the place. I'd hate to see ankles as nice as yours all black and blue from getting twisted up trying to walk in heels on a floor that was made for cowboy boots."

"You saw me standing there?" she asked.

"That I did," Chuck answered. "I must say, you were a lot more pleasant sight to lay eyes on than the bartender."

There was a lot more of his body that he would have liked to lay on the woman besides just his eyes, but he didn't want to come right out and state that obviousness either.

"You should have come over and introduced yourself," Wanda said.

"You seemed to be with friends," Chuck answered. "I didn't want to interrupt."

"They were a bunch of jerks who latched on to me," she said. "A girl could catch pneumonia the way they were breathing down my back and front. I'll probably have a stiff neck in the morning from exposure to all the moist, beer-scented air they were putting out on me. You would have made the time a lot more pleasant for me by getting me away from them."

She leaned forward and shifted around in her seat, trying to get more comfortable. As she leaned forward in the confined space between the booth seat and the table, the bottom of her chest pressed against the table. The displacement caused the upper surfaces of her breasts to temporarily bulge out even more. The trough of her cleavage became even more pronounced. Chuck's gaze on the better part of the woman's chest became even more focused, taking the better part of his face in the same direction.

Chuck was trying to remain suave, but the swelling, fluid motion of the woman's upper body and all it carried with it carried things beyond the point of suaveness for Chuck.

"I'd hate to see you catch a chest cold or get a sore neck any more than I'd want to see you turn your ankle," Chuck said. At least he hadn't come back with any obvious comment about her having the best-looking chest and neck in the place. Other than that, the swelling obviousness of the woman's body was knocking his suaveness into a cocked hat. The effect was starting to affect his cock too. Wanda continued to lean forward against the table, causing her displaced womanhood to remain bulged up and out at the exaggerated curve it had taken on. All Chuck could do with his slipping suaveness was look at her enhanced womanliness.

"I thank you for your brotherly concern for any part of my anatomy." She stretched her arm across the table. With the two forefingers of her right hand, she touched Chuck's chin and tilted his head up to look at her face.

Chuck looked into large hazel eyes accentuated by a trace of eyeshadow. Her fingernails had bright red nail polish on them, but they weren't the long, tapered, manicured nails that fashion-conscious women usually had.

"But my feet aren't where you're looking, honey," Wanda said in a coy and wry voice. "Neither is my neck, my face, or my hairdo, which I paid enough for. If you want to talk to me, look up here. This is the part of me that does the talking."

Chuck figured a lot of men would probably have thought her body was talking a lot louder than anything else. "Sorry, ma'am," he said in apologetic honesty.

Chuck had been staring at her chest, and she had caught him staring. Chuck had his face toward her. He had been staring with the direction of his eyes. He'd thought he had her fooled in that regard, but she had detected the true direction of his eyes. Apparently, she had the ability to pick up on subtle directions.

But Wanda also obviously had dressed in a provocative manner in order to provoke that kind of obvious response. Chuck didn't want to state the obvious fact to her face, which he was now looking directly at.

"I didn't mean to offend. It's just that sometimes my eyes have a head of their own. They're like my second cousin's rowdy set of twin toddler boys. They're always wandering off on her and getting into some kind of mischief. My eyes often go wandering off on me. I can't always keep them in line, no matter how I try. They've gone charging off on me on more than one occasion. They've gotten me into trouble before, going where they shouldn't and prying into things and places they should stay out of."

Chuck hoped the wry little countrified analogy about his wayward-son eyes would deflect any possible sense of violation she felt at his mentally drooling over her chest. She might have been nothing more than a barroom tease, but at that far-flung moment in a faraway town, Chuck wanted little more than for the woman to tease him more.

165

In response to Chuck's countrified analogy, Wanda laughed. "You're forgiven," she said without any rancor in her voice.

Chuck was glad she hadn't taken offense or taken her leave. Whatever game she was playing, at that stage, he didn't want her storming off in a huff.

"I know what you're talking about when you talk about children you can't control," Wanda said. "My parents never could control me. I was always giving my mother no end of fits, going out with boys she said a proper young lady shouldn't be going around with, going out to the kind of places your mother tells you to stay out of, and staying out past the time she told me to be home. My parents never did get me in line."

As far as getting her wardrobe the way she wanted it and getting her chest in line, Chuck thought she otherwise had her ducks in a row. Two of them at least.

Wanda had never been the problem child to her parents that she let on to Chuck. That was just part of the wild-woman-out-of-control persona she had chosen for herself that night. She'd always had a close relationship with her parents, especially with her mother. In Wanda's teen years under her parents' roof and tutelage, she had never gone out with any boys her parents had disapproved of. She hadn't gone out with a lot of boys in high school at all. Even on prom night, when Wanda's wayward-daughter behavior had officially launched and she had been officially christened into wayward womanhood, Wanda still had gotten back home within her parents' prescribed time frame. After taking her first major step across the limits, Wanda had actually gotten home a little after the time limit her parents had set, but it had been close enough that her parents let the discrepancy with their time limit pass. They weren't aware of the wider discrepancy Wanda had slipped into the time limit when she slipped out of her clothes in the motel cabin. Wanda's full-blown waywardness hadn't started until she was out of the house and living on her own and on the road.

"Was I being that obvious?" Chuck asked.

"About as obvious as any man who's ever looked at me the way you were looking," Wanda said. "Some men can be as obvious as they come."

Chuck wondered if she meant the comment as a sexual pun.

She had obviously dressed in a way that would naturally bring men to her with obvious thoughts coming into their minds and projecting out through their eyes.

"I thought I was doing a pretty good job of hiding the orientation of my eyeballs," Chuck said.

"Honey," Wanda said with a calculated sound of experience in her voice, "men have never been very good when it comes to hiding their obvious selves. The more men try to hide their obviousness, the more it shows through."

She paused for a second and then started out on a related path. "I can't say this is the first time a man's locked his eyeballs in place looking at me. I've gotten used to it by now. Men have been getting down-bend hyperextension cricks in their necks by trying to look down my blouse since I was fourteen. Mama always said that if I developed any more than what I had, I'd turn men's heads so fast and hard they'd wring their own necks like a farmer killing a chicken for frying. When they weren't trying to sneak a peek down my open front, they were burning out their brains trying to worm their imagination inside my sweater."

Chuck laughed along with her little country colloquial witticisms. The bar was located in a small southern city with a population of about eighty-five thousand. It wasn't a small town, but it wasn't a center of eastern sophistication. It was country enough to produce people who spoke in country idioms. Wanda's countrified speech and accent reinforced Chuck's belief that she was a local.

"Well, no offense again, ma'am," Chuck said, "but you're bound to draw more than a few sets of wandering eyes dressed the way you're dressed."

Wanda smiled an undefined, enigmatic Mona Lisa half smile. Her smile didn't change shape or go away. She didn't seem to take any offense to his stating of the obvious. But then again, she had probably dressed with the aforementioned obviousness in mind.

"As my father used to say," Chuck said, cuing in on what Wanda's mother had said, "if you display your wares in a store window and you display them well, don't be surprised if people window-shop."

As far as store-window analogies went, at that moment, Chuck would have liked to play a little boy pressing his face against a department store window, longing for a bike or some other toy just out of reach inside the window, except Chuck wanted to press his face into the gap between Wanda's twin bay windows.

As far as shopping and other commercial analogies went, Chuck wondered if the woman dressed the way she did because it was good for business.

Wanda had role-played the part once and had taken money for her services. If only for one night, she'd wanted to feel what it was like to be an actual hooker. For that one night, she hadn't minded thinking of herself as, parading herself as, and performing as a streetwalker. Wanda had enough looks and know-how that she could have turned her avocation into an actual side career to augment her earnings as a phone company service technician.

But being a hooker attracted the wrong kind of crowd, and it didn't give a girl a whole lot of choice. She had to take on all comers. Wanda liked to do the choosing, and her standards were high.

Her job with the phone company gave her the opportunity to indulge her wandering lifestyles, geographic and sexual. If she lost her job as a traveling service tech, she might have to take to the road in a more restricted fashion. Wanda didn't think she would be able to get the feeling of being a drifter and drifting toward her distant horizons if she behaved like a flat-out whore.

"Well, now that you've got me undressed with your wandering eyes and running around unadorned in your wayward mind, don't you think we should at least exchange names?" Wanda asked.

Chuck caught himself. He had been so distracted by her sudden appearance, the attention she was showing him out of the blue, and her earthy country-and-western sexiness that he had completely forgotten the standard first step in a first-time encounter between a couple at a singles' scene or in a barroom pickup.

"Oh yeah. It just sort of slipped my mind," Chuck said, still wanting to slip his fingers between the woman's cleavage. For a moment, names had been distant and unimportant. To Chuck, their names might as well have been lost out over the horizon somewhere. "My given name is Charles. But that name always seemed so formal to me. It makes me sound like one of those snooty English butlers. I don't like Charlie either. You can call me Chuck."

Wanda reached out and took Chuck's hand in hers. She gave his hand a little welcome-greeting squeeze. "Well now, you can call me Ramona," Wanda said.

The choice of name was an art form to Wanda—an art form she polished as much as she worked on and polished her art of seduction. In running through men on the road, she had made it a goal to run through all the women's first names in the dictionary before she repeated any one given name—all the sexy and exotic-sounding first names, that was. She preferred names with a sensual and romantic ring to them. To date, in her string of one-night dates, Wanda had called herself by the names Angelique, Arlena, Aurora, Belinda, Carla, Carmel, Cecila, Clarissa, Cleo, Corrina, Darleen, Dawn, Desiree (the allusion was obvious), Dulcie (short for Dulcenia), Elaina, Eva, Evangeline, Gillian, Helena, Irene (for the famous song "Goodnight, Irene" by Huddie Ledbetter, the one who said, "Good night and goodbye"), Juliana, Kathleen (a good name for an Irish girl, though Wanda wasn't Irish), Kitty, Kristina, Leslie, Libby (a liberated woman), Linda, Lola, Loretta, Lucinda, Marrietta, Melania, Melinda, Miranda, Misty (a woman who came out of the mist and disappeared back into the mist), Mona (for the moaning she did in bed), Nell, Olivia, Pamela, Patricia, Roxanna, Sandra, Shelia, Theresa, Ursula (an alliteration of the word *urgent*, a subtle way of conveying the state of her need), Veronica, Virginia (used in the state of Virginia in an Ursula state of need), Vivian (the vital, vibrant, and vivacious one), and Yolanda. She hadn't gotten to the *Z*s yet, but there weren't many *Z* names to use, though she had considered using the name Zoe at some point in the future. She also had used the names Florence, Maryanne, Janice, and Rosanna in honor of the Flo, Mary, Janie, and Rosie whom the wanderer of the Dion song had romanced and then dumped. This time, she was the wanderer in charge of the romantic situation, using men, dumping them, and moving on.

The only name she never would go by—and go to bed under—was her own name. The name Wanda was just too flat, corny, and unromantic for Wanda's taste. The closest name to her own she had used was Wendy. The name was kind of corny in its own way, but Wanda had used it in a backhanded allusion to one who wended her way through life.

In a quick computation, Wanda came up with the name Ramona. Ramona, the longer and more romantic variant of Mona, was a name she had always wanted to use. This was the first time she would get a chance to exercise the new name she had chosen for herself while indulging herself in the exercise she had performed dozens of times.

When Wanda was in a distant-horizons mood and wanted to stretch the horizon of her behavior, she would not give a name at all. Having no name and making love as a nameless, unknown woman was the epitome of Wanda's sense of inverse romanticism. Making love without a name, even an alias, made Wanda feel like a woman on the horizon. It was the ultimate sexual and romantic role she wanted to play in life: a woman who came out of the horizon and disappeared back over the horizon without anyone ever knowing who she was.

As Wanda had told the earlier man, the road and the horizon were her principal lovers. When she made love without a name, she was giving herself to her two primary lovers as much as to the man. When Wanda was through making love to any man, she returned to her two main lovers, the road and the horizon, the next day. She would not return to any one man again.

When Wanda made love without a name, she was symbolically already back on the road before she was even out of the man's bed. She was moving off toward the next horizon even before she stopped moving with the man in bed. When she made love with no name, the love of her first lover was deep in her soul while the man was deep in her.

"Well, now that we have relative identities established," Wanda said, "I suppose the next question would be the old fallback second-tier question: 'Do you come here often?' After that, I'd ask if you know where around here a girl can go to find a place where they have dancing."

"I'm afraid I can't help you on either of those, ma'am," Chuck answered. "This is the first time I've ever been in this town or in this bar."

"Then you don't live here?" Wanda asked.

"No, ma'am," Chuck said. "I just got in late this afternoon. I drove around looking for a place to get a drink. I pulled into the first country-looking bar I saw. I don't even know where the other bars in this town are."

"Are you a trucker?" Wanda asked.

Things were proceeding just the way Wanda liked for them to proceed. She had initially presumed the man who had caught her interest was a local, but he had just revealed that he was a transient passing through town. If the man was a trucker, as her last one-night-stand lover had been, he would be gone back on the road the next day.

Wanda was going to be in town for several days working on the installation job. Along with getting the installation job done, her other objective for the trip was to try to get herself installed at as many bars and with as many men as she could during the window of opportunity. To Wanda's way of thinking, a different bar and a different man each night was not an unreasonable objective. Given her looks, it was not an unreachable goal.

But complications could arise if she ran into any of the men she had slept with on a previous night. When Wanda had asked Chuck if there were any other bars in the area, she hadn't been just making light conversation. Her question had had a pragmatic intent to it. She was trying to pin down the locations of other bars where she could pick up men she wanted to be pinned down by. Men were creatures of habit. They usually went to the same bar over and over again. In order to avoid running into any one man more than one time, she would have to go to different bars each night.

The choice of bars was important for Wanda. No high-tone, sophisticated, country-club pickup scenes for her. Wanda wanted sex that was as earthy, raw, and raunchy as the sex she'd heard going on in the next room the night the pattern for her life had been set. No discotheque scenes for Wanda. She preferred redneck bars or working-class bars. The man's social class was inversely important to Wanda. No stockbroker lovers for Wanda. She didn't do the crossover-into-high-society bit. Wanda was blue collar and earthy. She wanted blue-collar men, and she wanted blue-collar—and sweaty-collar—affairs with earthy men. Wanda liked working-class men. She liked truckers. She liked construction workers. She liked country and cowboy types. She preferred reasonably handsome men. She also preferred men who were athletic looking. She wasn't extensively picky, but she wasn't about to settle for anything below her standards. She could walk away if those standards were not met.

Once Wanda arrived at any given bar, she would run a visual survey of the men at the bar to see if there was any man she wanted to give herself to and run with for the night. If an attractive man came up to her in the bar, Wanda would go into whatever act she had chosen for the night. If she spotted an attractive man who was alone but didn't come up to her, she would carry whatever act she had chosen and the whatevers of her body up to the man she had chosen and go into the act she had chosen.

Wanda felt she had hit the double jackpot that night. Chuck was the best-looking man she had seen so far. He had the rugged, chiseled male face Wanda liked and the athletic build she preferred. He would be the most handsome man she had had so far. The visual radar of Wanda's organized mind had spotted the man almost as soon as he walked in. The calculating part of her mind had already halfway selected him as her lover for the night as he stepped up to the bar. She had fully made up her mind when he looked at her from the bar. As he'd stepped away from the bar and walked in a different direction, Wanda had figured she would have to be the one who took the initiative.

While she'd continued to chat with the men who had clustered around her, Wanda had watched Chuck out of the corner of her eye as he walked around. When he'd sat down, she'd marked the spot. In Wanda's organized mind, she'd started setting her strategy as the other men chattered on. When she'd decided the time to make her move had come, Wanda had made up an excuse about having to go to the bathroom and slipped away from the men who had clustered around her. She had headed off in the direction of the bathroom and then detoured wide around the men in the crowd of the bar.

Once Wanda had sat down with Chuck and started talking to him, she'd found he also had the personality traits she was looking for. Wanda wasn't shy about taking the initiative and coming on to a man when the situation required it. Though all of the situations Wanda sought to set up required that a man either come on to her on his own or respond to her come-on, paradoxically, she did not like men who came on like an octopus on steroids. If a man was too grabby from the start, he would find himself not getting to the finish he had hoped for. Wanda's radar was also tuned to any hidden signals of arrogance, hard-edged attitudes of disrespect for women, or surface hints of mental conditions that might spell trouble or potential abuse. Wanda didn't mind being treated like a sex object once her objective of sex for the night was out on the track and rolling. A man just had to treat Wanda with respect in order to get her to the kind of yes she had come to build her life around and had come to the bar to find.

Chuck was respectful, polite, and courteous to her. He wasn't coming on with a leering drool and grabbing hands. But he was otherwise responding like a man. Wanda's radar for the focus of men's attentions could see from the way Chuck had been staring at her signature female parts. She didn't mind that he had been staring. She dressed to elicit exactly that type of stare from a man. From the orientation of Chuck's look and the apparent strength and orientation of his attention to her, she didn't think there was a sexual-orientation problem with him. Wanda couldn't fully read the look on his face or the nature of his demeanor. He could have simply been shy and introverted. On the other hand, he still looked and sounded a bit like he was sad. Wanda could deal with shy and introverted men as easily as she could handle the more aggressive, up-front, ready-to-go type of guys.

From what she could see and sense, Chuck had everything she wanted and needed. It might take a little longer, but she would work him up—in all senses of the word.

"No, I'm not a trucker," Chuck said.

"What kind of work do you do?" Wanda asked.

"Ah, let's just say I'm a traveling mechanic. I work for a company servicing the farm machines they make—harvesters, threshers, combines. The stuff's too big for the user to bring into the shop like a broken lawnmower. The company sends me out to wherever the problem is, and I do the repair work in place."

Chuck still didn't want to tell her he worked for the phone company. Her appearance and interest in him had been an unexpected pleasure and bright spot in what would have otherwise been just another dull and empty night spent draining a beer bottle while watching other people mill around before going back to his standard hotel room with no calls waiting and no one home to call. He didn't know the depth of Wanda's interest in him, and he couldn't see the shape of her intent. But he could see the shape of her body quite well.

Even if she was just a tease out playing at being a bad girl and nothing came of it, Chuck liked the shape of her interest in him better than the empty seat he had been looking at before she materialized out of the half-light of the bar and sat down across from him.

Wanda was turning him on. Chuck doubted anything more would come of it, but he didn't want to take the possible chance of turning the unexpected woman off and driving her away by revealing that he worked for the phone company. She might have her own gripe about poor service and surly operators.

"Well, it looks like we're both in the same boat on the same road," Wanda said. "I've never been in this bar before either. I've never been in this town before today either."

Chuck looked at her face in surprise.

"I have a job that keeps me on the road too. I live on the road just like you do. We're birds of a feather who fly alone. We just crossed paths on our migratory routes."

Her statement that she had a traveling job and had come into town from the outside just as he had caught Chuck by surprise. He had figured she was a local. He had also started to wonder if she was a streetwalker.

173

Unless she walked a much longer street than other ladies of the evening, her statement that she had a traveling career undermined that idea.

"Where do you work?" Chuck asked. "I mean, who do you work for, and what do you do that keeps you on the road so much? I must say, you don't look much like a trucker."

"Let's just say I work in the fashion industry," she answered. Wanda then named a fashion house specializing in intimate apparel for women.

Chuck was familiar with the company and their product line. His wife had received catalogs from the company and had purchased various items from the company for use at night over the phone lines he maintained during the day. In his comparative naivete, he had thought his wife was buying the skimpy items of intimate apparel for his eyes only. He had occasionally thumbed through the catalogs when his wife wasn't around. The photographic layouts of models in the—loosely defined—clothing the company manufactured were as good and almost as revealing as anything one could find in *Playboy* magazine, which he had stopped reading when he married his wife, who had kept up her playgirl attitude.

"I never really thought of fashion as an industry," Chuck said, cuing in on her statement that she worked in the fashion industry. "Heavy industry workers are built like linebackers. Their fingers are too thick to do delicate stitching. I thought the kind of things your company made were stitched together by dreamy-eyed young girls in cottages."

Chuck suspected the things were actually stitched together by underpaid young girls working twelve-hour days in sweatshop conditions in foreign countries or by underpaid undocumented immigrant girls. But he thought he might cause the woman to stomp away in a huff if he voiced his real suspicions about the labor practices of the company she worked for.

He said, "Calling it an industry makes it sound like they stamp these things out on an assembly line like car bodies. Do the women who sew the clothes your company makes at least get to sit down, or do they stand around on an assembly line all day like UAW workers in a Detroit auto plant?"

"The women who work behind the sewing machines are sitting down," she answered. "I'm the one who's on her feet most of the time. I travel around all the time and all over the country, checking on dealers, showing new product lines, setting up shows, and things like that. I work a circuit."

Wanda's tongue-in-cheek comment about working circuits was the closest she had come in her chosen lie that night to the truth about the kind of work she actually did.

She continued. "At the end of a long day, my ankles can be as sore as the feet of any guy who's spent an eight-hour shift standing on an assembly line. My feet can end up even more sore when I've been in heels all day like the ones I'm wearing now. But the company thinks it helps push the product if the saleswomen dress fashionably. The company wants its female reps to look the fashion part."

Chuck was hardly a fashion editor, but he noticed there seemed to be a bit of a disconnect between the style line the company she worked for produced and the clothes she was wearing. The clothes she wore looked more like something that had come from Frederick's of Hollywood instead of from the catalogs his wife had read. Chuck couldn't remember seeing anything leather in the silk-, satin-, lace-, and camisole-oriented catalog from the company. The ultimate end of the disparate modes of dress in the catalogs and in the clothes she was wearing was the same. The message of transport was just a bit different. The intimate apparel in the catalogs Chuck had seen from the company had said, "Sweep me into your arms, and sweep me away with tender, passionate, trembling love." The outfit Wanda was wearing was not so much moonlight and roses. It was a bit more direct in its romantic approach. It was what Chuck would have classified as a "Come fuck me" dress.

The way she was dressed made her look a bit like a hooker, but the fact that she worked for a fashion company explained the way she was dressed as much as his initial suspicion. Women in fashion liked to dress in clothing they considered fashionable. She had probably dressed the way she had in order to appear fashionable, as her company had directed. As she'd said, it was a form of advertising for her company and the fashionably provocative clothing line they manufactured.

"Wearing high heels is part of the whole fashion package I'm trying to present. Gym shoes or flats would be a lot more comfortable for the long hours I often put in on my feet, but they wouldn't complete the high-fashion package." Wanda looked down in the general direction of her feet. "I've been on my feet all day in these heels; then I came to this bar without changing into more comfortable shoes. My ankles are giving me gripes about it right now."

"Like I said," Chuck said, "I hate to think of pretty-looking ankles like yours all sore and swollen."

Wanda leaned forward in the seat again. Her breasts compressed and bulged out against the edge of the table again. She reached down below the table. Chuck heard the sound of a shoe dropping to the floor.

The next thing Chuck felt was the woman's leg being pressing against his. He gave sort of a startled reaction, but he managed to keep it from becoming visibly obvious.

"Here you go," Wanda said. "If you find my ankles to be so pretty and you don't like to think of them hurting me, rub them for me, and make them stop hurting."

"Ah, yeah, sure," Chuck said. For the second time, his suaveness split into pieces and ran away from him like a pack of mice in which a cat had suddenly appeared in the middle of licking its paws. "I hate to see a working girl go around footsore."

Wanda moved her leg from the side of Chuck's leg up to the top of his legs and in between. Chuck reached down with both hands, took her ankle in his hands, and started rubbing. Her ankle wasn't tiny and petite, but it wasn't fat or puffy. It was solid and well formed. From what Chuck had seen when she was standing at the end of the bar and from what he could feel, her well-shaped ankle was attached to the end of a shapely leg. As Chuck rubbed her ankle, she pointed her foot at him, closed her eyes, and leaned back in her seat.

"Mmm, that does feel good," Wanda purred.

The smooth and slippery feel of her tight nylons made Chuck's hands tingle. The feel of her leg in his hands made more than his hands tingle. She wasn't shy. Earlier generations would have considered a woman who introduced herself to a man in such an up-front manner to be forward. Earlier generations would have considered any woman who dressed the way she was dressed to be a brazen hussy. What they would have called a woman who stuck her foot in a man's lap and asked for a rubdown probably couldn't have been repeated in polite society. Be that as it historically might have been, Wanda had more than one forward way of introducing herself and her sore feet to a man.

For several long moments, Chuck massaged her ankle as she leaned back dreamily in her seat with her eyes closed.

"Rub my upper leg too," she said with her eyes still closed. "I've been on my legs today every minute that I've been on my feet. My legs are as tired as my ankles."

There were all sorts of ways a woman could be forward about presenting herself to a man. Chuck didn't know how bad Wanda's feet really hurt. He could only take her word for it. From where he was sitting, she was starting to seem more footloose than footsore.

Chuck moved his hands farther up the scale and started massaging the calf of her lower leg with long, slow strokes. Trying to imitate the moves he imagined a professional masseuse would use, with his hands close together, Chuck rubbed both sides of her leg simultaneously. Then, varying the motion, he stroked the full length of her calf in a sequential hand-over-hand motion, following and feeling the curve of her calf. Given the distance between them and that the table prevented him from leaning forward and reaching farther, her knee marked the limit of Chuck's reach. Some days, Chuck was so busy doing involved service work that he wished he had an extra set of arms and hands. Now he found himself wishing his arms were two feet longer—or three feet longer.

Chuck glanced at the booth across the aisle from the booth he was in. The people in the other booth were otherwise engaged and weren't staring at him and the woman. Chuck didn't hold the glance too long, as he didn't want to attract attention. But he was starting not to care whether anyone saw what he was doing.

Wanda sighed more as Chuck rubbed her leg. The smooth feel of her leg and the tone of her voice were starting to make Chuck feel a bit light-headed.

"It should only take you an hour of that to get that leg back in shape," Wanda said. "Then you can work on the other one."

For several more long moments, Chuck continued to massage her lower leg and ankle. She had indicated that both of her legs hurt. So far, she had extended only one leg to him. Chuck wondered when the other shoe would drop.

Wanda opened her eyes. "Are you going to be in town long?" she asked.

Chuck could have lost his suaveness again at the forward and leading implication of the question. But the time of suaveness had passed. *When suaveness deserts you, try being honest*, he thought. Instead of trying to be suave or witty, Chuck gave a direct answer.

177

"I'll be starting the job I'm here to do tomorrow," he said. He was being only partially honest. The job he would be starting was the installation of the phone company relay equipment he would supervise with the crew from his branch office and the other crew coming in from the Columbia office. From the cover story he had told her, she would think he was talking about some kind of mechanical equipment repair job. "I'll be here for a few days. Then I'll be heading back to the home office."

The fact that he would be in town for a few days put a crimp in Wanda's plan to use the same bar for another pickup on a subsequent night. He might come back to the same bar, looking for her again. Even if he thought she wasn't in town anymore, which was what she was planning to tell him, he might come back to the same bar anyway for another drink or hoping to find another pickup. After all, the bar would prove as rewarding to him as it was going to be for Wanda. He might consider it to be a good-luck joint. She would have to start working other bars on other nights after she worked Chuck tonight.

"I'll be heading out tomorrow," Wanda said. Before Chuck could make a trailing response, she led in with another forward move. "That doesn't give us much time to get to know each other, now, does it?"

There was forward, and there was fast-forward. There were leading implications, and there were implications that grabbed one by the collar and pulled. There was suaveness lost, and there was suaveness grabbed at and regained on the fly because one's instinctive reaction would have made him look like a stammering fool.

Chuck's immediate physical response to her loaded statement was to momentarily tighten his grip on her leg, but he simply pushed a little harder with his hands on the rub stroke he was beginning, as if it were all part of the move. She seemed to be taking the rest of the moves into her own hands.

"Then I guess we'll have to make every moment count," Chuck said. It was a rather formulaic response, but at least he didn't sit there with his mouth working open and shut with no sound coming out like a boated catfish. Chuck couldn't say he had no idea where she was taking things. Some leads and implications were self-evident. He didn't know how far she was thinking of running with the leading implications in what she said, but at that moment, in a bar in a state far away from the home that no longer existed for him, Chuck was ready to run with her, no matter how bad her legs hurt.

Wanda paused for a moment. She cocked her head slightly to one side. Then she came back with another leading question. "Before we go any further, are you here on your own without any prior commitments?" she asked in a leading tone. "Or are you here being a bad boy with a lonely wife waiting at home?"

Wanda hadn't caught sight of a wedding ring on Chuck's finger. She hadn't felt anything metallic on his hands as he rubbed her leg. If he had been wearing a wedding ring, she would have felt it. Nor did Wanda see any telltale indentation on his ring finger, as if he had been wearing a ring and taken it off before he came into the bar. Wanda avoided married men as pickup candidates.

Wanda wasn't into marriage, but she wasn't into breaking up preexisting marriages. She wasn't looking to be the proverbial blushing bride carried over the threshold. The only threshold she wanted to be carried over was the threshold of sexual pleasure. The only other threshold she wanted to cross was the threshold of the next horizon she would carry herself over. She didn't intend to make a home with any man. Her home was on the road.

"Do I look like a bad boy to you?" Chuck asked. He asked the question in an "Aw, shucks" tone of voice, but the question was leading in its own way. He wondered why she wanted to know whether he was a proverbial bad boy. Was she trying to avoid bad boys? Or was she out looking for one? Did she think she had radar for bad boys? He wasn't even sure what her definition of a bad boy was.

"Honey, all boys are bad," Wanda said in an experienced-girl-who's-been-around-the-block voice. "Or I should say all boys are bad during at least one stage in their life. It just comes out at different times. It's the wild teenage boys who grow up to be the respectable doctors and ministers. It's the good boys who get good grades in school and don't get into trouble as teenagers who grow up to be the corporate crooks and shady politicians. It's the good boys who don't run around with bad girls when they're young who grow up and run around with bad women after they get married."

Wanda cocked her head slightly again. "While you're here in the bar talking to me, by any chance, is there someone waiting for you to come back to her?" she asked, taking the conversation in a different leading direction. "Are you here being a bad boy while someone's home waiting for you?"

Wanda rejected the proverbial ideal of hearth, home, and marriage for her personal life, but she didn't want to think of herself as a home-wrecker prying apart someone else's life and marriage. There were plenty of single men out there for her to do and who were panting to do her. There were all sorts of complications involved in being named in a divorce petition, including exposure as a wandering vixen, public embarrassment for her and the phone company, and the loss of the job that gave her the opportunity to wander.

Besides, setting out to be a home-wrecker was a mean thing to do. Wanda had always thought that women who were casual or deliberate home-wreckers were mean and nasty. Dirty girls in soap operas were home-wreckers. Wanda would have felt she was dirtying herself up if she knowingly had affairs with married men and took the chance of potentially breaking up marriages and families. When she prowled the bars, she avoided married men. Some moralists might have considered Wanda to be dirty because of her bar-hopping and bed-bouncing in general; however, in her personal morality, Wanda didn't want to think of herself as dirty. She didn't want to cross the line into territory she considered low-level dirty. She wanted to keep her horizons clean.

Chuck stopped rubbing her leg. He sat there for a moment, holding her leg at midcalf with one hand over the top of her leg and one hand under. He had struck a nerve with Wanda when she first saw him. Now Wanda had the feeling she had struck a nerve in him. She had thought her night was made when he walked into the bar. Now she had the feeling she had walked into something else.

"I had someone waiting home for me once," Chuck said, looking at the table more than at Wanda. "At least I thought she was waiting for me. But she had never really been in waiting for me or in waiting for any man. When I was out on the over-the-road jobs I was sent on, while I thought she was waiting for me, I was being a good boy. I stayed in the motel rooms and watched television. While I was watching television from the front, she was out cruising behind my back. She always wanted to know my schedule, right down to the hour when I would come back. In those days, I was a naive enough twit to assume she wanted to know when I was coming back because she loved me. I even allowed my naive, romantic twit self to slip deep enough into romantic twitdom that I assumed the reason she wanted to know the hour when I would be back was because she was counting the hours until I came back. As it turned out, the reason she wanted to know my schedule down to the hour was so she could juggle the time such that she could give herself a time buffer and get back home from the apartment of the man she was sleeping with or could have him hustled out of our apartment, where she had been sleeping with other men in our bed.

"She worked as a legal assistant. When it came to the managerial skill of time management, she was good at it. I didn't even have to be away for her to play. She got to the point that she could slip away from the law office she worked for, slip out legal briefs with a man during her lunch break, and be back in the office on time with every legal filing in order and every hair back in place by the time her lunch break was over. This wasn't a onetime human failing on her part. This was something she was doing on a routine basis. She had probably been planning on carrying on her side affairs while she was planning her wedding trousseau."

"I take it this is your wife you're talking about," Wanda said.

Chuck was still holding her leg. He was still holding his hands motionless in the position they had been in when he stopped. "Ex-wife," Chuck said. "I married her when I was twenty-three. I divorced her four years later when I was twenty-seven. I was country. She was uptown city. I was blue collar; she was an upwardly mobile white-collar yuppie professional. Some people might have called it a crossover romance and thought it was something special and out of the ordinary for that reason. I suppose that's what I thought about it. Now I suppose I should have paused in my supposing and stopped to think and ask why she would be willing to drop her uptown life and her uptown men for a blue-collar worker like me. I guess I was a romantic enough fool that I thought it was love or something along that line. She must have been slumming when she took up with me. I guess she saw me as a high-visibility stud to round out the picture of her life. It took me four years of having stars in my eyes and simplistic notions of romance clouding my brain before the truth finally blew through the pretenses I had about love and about myself."

"She was sleeping with other men in your apartment, in your bed, while you were out on the road?" Wanda asked in a voice that was a bit incredulous for her.

From what little Wanda knew of his ex-wife, she sounded a lot like her as far as having an organized mind. But Wanda was still starting to think of the woman as a nasty bitch. Chuck seemed like a nice guy. In life, it always seemed to be the nice guys who got shafted by untrustworthy and unscrupulous women. They were also the men who were hurt the most by that kind of woman.

"She had that part of it planned right down to the wire too," Chuck answered. "When she was entertaining men in our apartment, she even arranged in advance the hour when I would call to let her know I was in my room being a good boy. That way, she knew when to slow down and take a break so she wouldn't sound out of breath when she picked up the phone when I called. I don't know how she kept the other man quiet. After I found out what she was doing, I had this vision of her leaning over the man in bed, talking to me on the phone, and holding the phone in one hand and her other hand on the man's mouth to keep him from hiccupping or making some other accidental sound."

Chuck's wife had lied to him. By marrying him and implicitly promising ever after and a life together, she had promised him something she apparently had no intention of delivering from the start. Wanda had no plan for a life together with any man for a lifetime or plan for a lifetime of any other romantic proverbial. But she had made it a central part of her coda that she was always honest with the men she made love to and then left. She might have left men wondering where she had gone, but they always knew where they stood with her before she left them standing alone watching her disappear over the horizon.

"You did seem to have a lost-puppy-in-the-rain look on your face when I sat down," Wanda said. "I guess you were thinking about losing your wife."

"You really can't call me a lost puppy," Chuck responded. "My ears aren't floppy enough. And I can't say I'm lost without her. I just lost the life and the home I thought I had but never really had from the beginning. Even when I was still out on the road, I thought I was off the road because I had a home and a life to come back to. After I found out my wife had been two-timing me from the start, I was back on the road again with no home to come home to. If I looked like I was moping, that was more or less what I was thinking about. But I didn't feel like sitting in a hotel room and remembering it. So I came here."

"So you came to this bar to drown your sorrow?" Wanda said.

Chuck took one hand off Wanda's leg, picked up his nearly empty beer bottle, and waved it above the table. "This is all I've had to drink," he said. "I would hardly call one beer drowning myself. I might have another one or two before I leave, but I wouldn't even call three beers a drowning flood."

As Chuck held up his beer bottle, Wanda noticed there was just about one swallow left. "Looks like you're about dry," she said in a country-accent-tinged country euphemism. "Let me buy us another round. It's the least a woman can do for you to make up for what your wife did to you."

Wanda actually had something more comprehensive in mind that she could do for him to make him feel better. She pulled her leg off Chuck's lap, reached down, and slipped her shoe back on.

"I'll go get the drinks for us," Chuck said, shifting in his seat in preparation to get up. It wasn't that he felt his masculine ego was being usurped or damaged by the woman taking on the usual masculine role of getting the drinks. In his proverbial politeness, he just thought of it as a normal courtesy to a woman.

"You stay here and hold the booth," Wanda said as she swung her legs out into the aisle. "If you get up and walk away, one of the guys hanging on to me earlier might come sit down in your spot and try to get himself back in with me."

Both Wanda and Chuck saw the inadvertent sexual pun in that one.

"They may come up to you when you stand at the bar," Chuck said.

"If I'm on my feet, I can keep moving," Wanda said as she stood up.

Chuck was about to remind her that she had been complaining about having tired feet, but he changed his mind. However sore her feet might have been, they weren't sore enough to keep her from walking to the bar.

Wanda picked up her small purse from the table and turned to head back to the bar. As she turned to leave, Chuck wondered if her role reversal in going for drinks was just an excuse to break away from him. He had gone on about his divorce longer than he had talked to her about anything else. Maybe she thought he was boring or a crybaby. Her offer to buy them drinks might have been just a ruse to get away from him and put herself back into circulation. It wouldn't have been the first time a woman dumped him in place.

As she turned to leave, Wanda stopped and turned back. She took off her cowgirl hat. "I'd better mark my seat," she said. "Some other hot-to-trot woman may come sit down in my place while I'm gone."

As Chuck watched, she dropped her hat onto the seat she had just gotten up out of.

"I'll be back," Wanda said in a husky voice. Then she turned and walked toward the bar. The liquid reddish color of her leather tube top and skirt flashed and shone in the subdued light of the bar. The tightness of her leather skirt gave almost a full outline of each of her full hips. The red high heels that were supposedly hurting her feet clicked on the tile floor as she walked.

Chuck watched the curved shine and wave of her full hips as she walked toward the bar. As he watched her walk away, he wondered what he had dropped into the middle of—or what had dropped in on him. Chuck didn't want to let his male ego go running away on him, but from the signals he was picking up from Wanda, it appeared she was coming on to him. There was an old Roman saying: "Some men are born great. Other men achieve greatness. Still other men have greatness thrust upon them." Chuck knew that some men knocked themselves out in trying to pick women up in bars without getting anywhere. Other men achieved pickups. Chuck wondered if he was about to have an all-time-great pickup thrust upon him when he hadn't even come into the bar thinking in terms of a pickup. He had heard of something like that. As he remembered, it was called serendipity.

Chuck finished off the last drink of beer in his bottle and sat there wondering where to take it next. More precisely, given that Wanda was basically taking all the initiative, the question was where she was going to take it next—provided she came back.

That was the direction of Chuck's thinking when she came back to the table.

She approached the booth with two bottles of the same kind of beer Chuck had been drinking, holding the necks of the longneck bottles. When she walked up to the booth, Chuck expected she would move her hat to the side and sit down where she had been sitting on the other side of the table. Instead, she set her purse back down near the outer end of the table and sat down next to Chuck in the same seat.

"Slide over," Wanda said as she sat down. "I'm tired of sitting on the other side of the room from you. There will be a lot of road mileage and a lot of distance between us by the time tomorrow night rolls around. There's no reason we should have all this distance between us tonight."

Chuck slid over to give her room to sit down. The seat in the booth had basically been built for only one person. It was a bit of a tight fit with both of them in the same seat. Wanda pushed up close to Chuck's side. She didn't leave any daylight between them. He could feel the slippery slide of her leather skirt against his leg as she adjusted her position. From her closer proximity, the scent of her perfume was more prominent. The smell of her perfume wasn't intoxicating to Chuck, but it was more intriguing than the smell of beer in the open bottle she had brought him. When a country boy found the scent of a woman better than the aroma of fresh beer or the smell of bass he'd caught himself cooking in a pan over an open fire, he was hooked deeper than any fish. Some of Wanda's long blonde hair spilled up against Chuck's shoulder. Her face and full lips were now only about a foot away from his.

From the closer-in angle, her lips looked even fuller than they had from across the table, and her glossy lipstick seemed to shine even brighter. She paused to take a drink out of her bottle of beer. Her lips fully covered the top lip of the bottle. The exposed upper sections of her breasts swelled upward rounder, fuller, and more curved than they had seemed from the other side of the table. As Wanda was distracted in taking the drink, Chuck used the opportunity to glance down her front. Her cleavage seemed twice as deep as it had from the other side. Chuck couldn't see bottom. There seemed to be no end to the depths of her.

Wanda put down her beer bottle and shifted to one side in her seat in order to face Chuck more directly. She folded her arms in front of her on the table edge and leaned in a bit. Her arms pushed her breasts up.

"Well now, we've already been introduced, honey," she said. "We're not strangers anymore. Don't make yourself a stranger. I like the strong type, but I don't like the strong, silent type. Tell me something about yourself. I don't know a whole lot about you except that you fall in love with the kind of women who do dirt to nice guys. Then you end up in bars in another state, pouring yourself out to the first forward woman who sits herself down beside you. Tell me something about yourself before you got mixed up with the likes of her. Tell me how you fell in love with a woman like her in the first place. When you found out she was two-timing you, did you go on being the silent type, or did you cry over her?"

"However much I did or didn't cry myself, the story would probably bore you to tears," Chuck answered. "Do you really want to sit here for an hour being bored while listening to me tell you I walked into love with my eyes closed and continued walking with my eyes shut until I fell into a hole so big that even I couldn't miss it? Or should I just sing you a short chorus of 'Why Do Fools Fall in Love?'"

"Forget about her," Wanda said. "Tell me about your life before you met her. Where did you grow up? What kind of childhood did you have? I bet you got into all sorts of mischief as a young boy. I imagine you as the kind of mischievous young boy of the kind Red Skelton used to play—the one who went around saying, 'If I dood it, I get a whippin'. I dood it."

"Even my early life is kind of a boring story," Chuck said.

"I'll be the judge of that," Wanda said. "Tell me about yourself as a child. Tell me about how you came of age. I'll bet that's an interesting story."

If she pressed herself any closer to him, Chuck had a feeling he might come of age again all over her.

Chuck started telling her about his childhood. As he spoke, she listened with her head cocked to the side at him. Her hair hung partially over one eye. The effect made Wanda look a bit like Lauren Bacall listening to Humphrey Bogart in the movie *To Have and Have Not*.

Chuck and Wanda shared background details of their earlier lives and how and where they had grown up—that was, they shared details as far as full disclosure would allow honesty to be extended. Outside the boundaries where truth would have grown problematic, different details were substituted. Chuck and Wanda went back and forth telling each other how they had come to be where they were at that particular moment and at that particular point in their lives.

Regarding the details of how they had come to be on the life paths and career paths they were on, the truth was fudged on both sides. Regarding where they would be the next day, details were also fudged. Chuck fudged partially the technical details of what he would be doing the next day, but he was accurate when he said he would be working in the area. Wanda fudged completely the technical side of what she would be doing. She also fudged geographically by claiming she would be in another state by the end of the next day.

Chuck told Wanda about growing up in a small town in Tennessee, which, in fact, he had. He told her the name of the town. Wanda had never heard of the town, but it was on the map. Chuck told her he had always been fascinated by all things mechanical. He told her about working on hot rods as a teenage boy. He told her about how he grew up to translate his love of mechanics into a job as an on-the-road technician who went from town to town repairing the heavy farm and agricultural equipment his company manufactured. The part about the hometown he had grown up in was accurate. The part about growing up liking cars and mechanics and turning his hobby into a career in repairing mechanical equipment was fudged. He had grown up fascinated by all things electronic, not mechanical. He didn't tell her he had built several electronic projects on his own and made them work. He didn't tell her about having an amateur radio operator's license. He didn't mention anything about being interested in electronics.

He wanted to keep her thinking of him as a mechanic. Chuck was afraid if he mentioned electronics, she might press him for more details. From there, it might come out that he worked for a nationwide phone company instead of the nationwide manufacturer of farm equipment he had claimed. She would know he was a liar. That could turn her off on him and might cause her to turn off any plans she had to go any further with him. Chuck was already deep into a lie. He had to go deeper into the lie to maintain the lie. If she found out he was deep in a lie, it might derail any possibility of his getting deeper into her.

For her part and the part she was playing, Wanda told Chuck that she had grown up in a small town in South Carolina, which she had. That confirmed to Chuck that she was a country girl. Though her face, figure, and dress were like those of a woman who had come off the beaches of Côte d'Azur or from the Carnival district of Rio, her accent was down-home American country. Wanda's statement that she had grown up in a small town in South Carolina was accurate, but she casually neglected to mention the name of the town. She didn't need any man going back to her hometown to try to track her down and filling in her parents on what she was doing on the road.

"I'll bet you were a big football star when you were in high school," Wanda said. Country-boy stud types were usually football players in high school, and Wanda knew football players. After all, she had been taken to her prom and, from there, to her christening at the tourist cabin by a boy on her high school football team. Actually, Wanda had taken herself to the starting gate that night more than the boy had. "You were probably the captain of the team. You probably had all the cheerleaders fighting over you. I was a cheerleader when I was in high school. I would have thrown myself all over the field for you if you were quarterbacking my team."

Wanda was good at little indirect sexual double entendres like that.

"My high school was too small to have a football team," Chuck said. "We had gym. We had a baseball team. I played on that. But I didn't break

187

Ted Williams's batting average, and I wasn't good enough to go on to the major leagues. The baseball team was about the only group-sport activity I was involved in." He didn't tell her he had been the president of the radio club. "We didn't have any cheerleaders. Not even for the 4-H club."

Wanda knew how to play around, and she knew how to play with exposed cleavage. She also calculated that if a girl wanted to get a man to play with her in bed, a useful adjunct to cleavage was to play to a man's sexual ego.

"Even if you didn't play football, I bet you were still the big man on campus in high school," Wanda said in a toying voice. "You probably drove the girls wild or sent them into a fantasy state when you walked by. All the girls probably went faint and sweaty if you as much as looked at them."

Since her first night of indirect exposure to sex in the motel room, Wanda had known about going faint at the thought of sex. She knew about real sex and the sweat of real sex from all the other nights of sex she had put herself through, starting with her first night of live and direct sex after her senior prom.

"With all the girls who were probably chasing after you, I'll bet you had to run your legs off to stay ahead of them—the ones you didn't want to get caught by, that is."

"If there was a whole line of girls fainting and dropping in their tracks behind me as I walked by, I never heard them fall," Chuck answered in a self-effacing manner. "My high school was kind of small. There weren't a lot of girls in the school to begin with, and none of them dropped their books, their guard, or their drawers when they saw me. If I was turning on girls left and right, it wasn't very obvious. If I was driving any of the girls in my high school crazy with desire, they all kept it a well-guarded secret. No girl in my high school ever came up to me and let me know straight out that she was turned on by me. I didn't even get any anonymous unsigned notes from secret female admirers stuck through the vent holes of my locker. Where it came to being pursued by high school girls, I didn't have to run an inch to get away from them."

"I'll tell you right now that you turned me right on the first time I saw you," Wanda said in a continuance of her male ego stroking. "You didn't even have to walk by. I was turned on just by the sight of you sitting there with a beer in your hand. Give me half a chance, and I'll make up for all the failures of those other girls all around, starting with what they didn't tell you. A good-looking guy like you should be told every day by a girl that you turn her on. You deserve to have girls throwing themselves at you left and right, and they should be doing it from up front the way I'm doing and not walking past you and away while thinking it from behind your back. If the girls in your school were too dumb or too snitty to say you turned them on, that was their stupidity and their loss. I'm not so proud that I won't come right out and tell you to your face that you're turning on every inch of me I have to offer."

"If we'd had girls in my high school who looked as good as you, they wouldn't have had to come to me," Chuck said in a continuance of his self-effacing. He was ready to rise to Wanda at a moment's notice. He just didn't rise to her bait at that moment. "They wouldn't have had to say that I was turning them on. I would have been all over them, telling them how much they were turning me on. They wouldn't have been able to get a word in edgewise. We just didn't have a whole lot of girls who looked like you. We didn't have any girls who looked as good as you. Even if I had been a high school pickup artist, which I wasn't, there wasn't a lot for a teenage playboy to pick from at my school."

"I'm still sure you dated all the popular girls," Wanda said. "You probably took the homecoming queen to your senior prom. I'll bet you better than even money that you took the homecoming queen out to a motel after the dance and got laid on your prom night. Everyone is supposed to get laid on their prom night. I did."

Chuck hadn't lying when he indicated his high school years hadn't been a teenage bacchanalian coming-of-age blowout. There hadn't been many girls at Chuck small high school. None of the girls in his high school had been standout attractive. A few of the girls had found Chuck attractive. Some of them would have liked to date him, but no girls in Chuck's high school had had a hopeless crush on him. There had been no girl Chuck had had a hopeless case of infatuation with. None of the girls in Chuck's high school ever had developed a heavy thing for him. There hadn't been any girls within the close horizon of Chuck's high school that he ever had had a thing for.

There had been, however, one particular older woman.

"I'm afraid I didn't get laid on my prom night," Chuck answered. "We didn't have a senior prom for me or anyone to get laid after."

The statement was an honest one. He could have made up a story on the fly about tussling in the backseat of a car with the prom queen or some

189

other local Miss Popularity. He didn't want to spin the true story of tussling in the bed of a country matron old enough to be his mother's aunt.

He feared revelation of the truth could send the woman sliding out the door to get away from him. Chuck thought the best strategy was just to slide out to the side and be honest about what he hadn't done on his graduation night and not try to improvise a reputation-building lie on the spot. As far as lies went, he was already sitting on a whopper of omission. At the moment, he didn't feel like adding to the surplus of lies in the world by spinning a lie of commission.

"The only male thing I did on graduation night was some male bonding. Me and a couple of senior boys I graduated with drove out to the side of the river, got drunk, reminisced, and talked about what we were going to do next. A lot of us still didn't know what we were going to do with our lives. We were kind of like the good old boys in the Don McClean song 'American Pie,' who drove a Chevy down to the levee and drank whiskey and rye. Except we were drinking beer and tequila, and we weren't singing, 'This will be the day that I die.' A few of us got so drunk that night we felt like we were going to die, but nobody did. None of us got laid that night either, unless you count lying out on the grass and puking up what I had drunk."

Wanda laughed.

As for what the boys down by the levee that night had planned to do next in life, Chuck told Wanda he had already been signed up to go to a technical college in the fall to study mechanics. It was more of a low-level lie than a whopper, but it was a fib. During that wet night, he had actually been already signed up to go to technical college to study electronics. But mechanics sounded more macho. Electronics sounded wimpy—the kind of stuff that nerds did for a living.

"Now that I've told you about my boring teenage life, you tell me something about your early life," Chuck said. "I'll bet you drove the boys at your school at lot wilder than I drove girls wild at mine. You probably had the boys walking into walls while looking at you when you walked by in your cheerleading outfit and short skirt. You probably caused a few of the male teachers to snap chalk sticks in two between their fingers when you walked into class in your tight letter sweater."

Chuck figured he should return the compliment in kind. He didn't go as far as to sing the old chorus "You must have been a beautiful baby, 'cause, baby, look at you now." But she did look as if she had been a high school temptress.

"We didn't have cheerleader letter sweaters like the jocks had letter sweaters," Wanda said. "We did have knit tops with the school letters on them and short skirts. But we cheerleaders didn't have full-fledged letters that we earned for our performance the way the boys earned letters."

If Wanda had earned a letter for her prom night performance after the prom, it would have been a big red A.

"I'll bet if you came into class one minute late wearing your short skirt, the principal would use the excuse to put you in detention for an hour, with him watching you every minute," Chuck said.

Chuck caught himself. Attractive high school girls had been known to attract sexual abuse from male teachers and school administrators. She might have been sexually approached and manhandled in her school. Chuck had meant his comment as a joke, but he might have been stepping on a sore memory for her.

Wanda laughed again. "Our principal was too old for anything like that," she said. "I didn't get detention in school. I was pretty much a good girl in class. It was outside of class and by myself on the streets and roads that I had a tendency to turn bad. At least by Mother's way of thinking. She never whooped my ass for doing it, though she probably thought I needed a good whooping."

"I'll bet you were the homecoming queen in your school," Chuck said, sidestepping that bit of kinky bait too.

"I was second runner-up to homecoming queen," Wanda answered. "The student homecoming committee gave the crown to Melinda Snodgrass. She was a blonde like me but a light blonde. I think they had the old cultural stereotype that light blonds were supposed to be pure. They probably were also going on the old stereotype that strawberry blondes like me were more outlaw. They weren't all that far off the money concerning me. I had already started to turn a bit outlaw in my junior year. My hair and my reputation may have cost me the title."

"You were robbed," Chuck said, throwing in another compliment. Especially if the homecoming queen crown had gone to a girl with the last name of Snodgrass. "You would have made a better-looking homecoming queen riding on the homecoming float than any blonde. They didn't know what they were missing when the passed you over."

Whether he liked being over or under, Wanda planned that he wasn't going to miss out on what she had to offer.

Wanda confirmed that her high school graduating class had had a senior prom. She didn't volunteer that she had gotten laid on her prom night, and Chuck was too polite to ask. But she wouldn't have denied it if he had asked. Wanda had her own definition of game playing in mind, but she wasn't looking to play a game of sexual one-upmanship with Chuck. That she had indeed gotten laid on her prom night put Wanda one up on Chuck—or one down, depending on how one looked at it. Wanda didn't tell Chuck about her other first night at the motel or the long string of other nights in motels, hotels, cabins, and cabanas since prom night.

After running through the subject of their high school years—without Wanda telling the story of how the boy had run through her on prom night—the conversation turned to what they had done and where they had gone after high school.

Wanda went on to tell how, as she had grown up, she had come to travel farther afield from her small-town home life. She embellished the story by telling how she had already been in the process of traveling further afield from small-town propriety. She elaborated a bit on what she had said about giving her mother fits. She told how, in the last two years of high school, she had started going out with boys who rode motorcycles and drove hot rods. She said her less-than-country-lady behavior with less-than-country-gentleman boys had continued for a year after she left high school. She told Chuck about long rides on the backseat of motorcycles while wearing a black leather jacket with her arms wrapped around the boy driving the bike or sitting in the front seat of an open-top hot rod or muscle car while wearing a tight sweater with her arm leaning on the door.

In the storytelling process, Wanda casually mentioned that several road trips had taken more than one day, with the unspoken implication being that she and the boy had spent the night somewhere other than home. Wanda didn't make up any explicit details of what she and the boys had done, but the way Wanda spun the story sort of left the impression of a girl who had been motorcycle mistress to Marlon Brando and the Wild Ones.

Chuck listened with interest to what she said. He also paid attention to what she didn't say but implied. It was a proverbial teenage-country-girl-from-small-town-Carolina-flirting-with-the-boys-and-flirting-with-getting-a-reputation-of-being-a-bad-girl life story. He also found it to be a rather sexually stimulating story. As he listened with growing interest to the story of how a country girl from a small town in Carolina had grown up to be an on-the-road temptress working for a national lingerie company, Chuck never paused to consider that the name Ramona wasn't exactly a standard small-town South Carolina country-girl name.

In the process of telling how she had departed from the straight and narrow for the straight open road with local bad boys, Wanda basically departed all the way from the truth. She had never done that as a teenager, to herself or her mother. Wanda hadn't even ridden on a motorcycle until she was twenty-seven and picked up a man who owned a motorcycle. The lie was all part of the suggested persona Wanda was portraying that night of a formerly wild and out-of-control teenage girl turned sensual lingerie consultant by day who could revert to her wild teenage ways at night for the right man.

Wanda added that the road trips on motorcycles and hot rods during her wild-in-the-wildwood years had first imparted her love of the open road to her. Wanda thought that portraying herself as a motorcycle mama riding on the backseat of motorcycles and as a tight-sweater-wearing teenage hussy riding in the front seat of a hot rod would provide a more convincing explanation for how she had come to her love of the open road than the story of how she had ridden away from a motel in the backseat of her father's car while dreaming of open roads and open horizons after a night of female masturbation performed while listening to another couple banging their heads off in the next room.

Wanda didn't claim to have gone to college of any kind, including the technical school she had attended and graduated from with honors. Instead, she described how she had drifted around aimlessly for a year after high school. Then she described how she had drifted into the field of fashion. From there, she told how she had worked her way up to become a traveling sales rep for a fashion company. She told him how, in the years since then, she had come to live on the road.

She told how the road had become so much a part of her that she didn't know any other life outside of life on the road, and she told him she didn't want any life other than a life on the road. In conveying her love for the open road and her desire for a life on the open road, Wanda was effectively telling the truth. She started out in the truth and slid off into a lie. In the end, Wanda circled back to the truth. Her circuitous path back to the truth bypassed the phone company entirely.

The two country people on the road exchanged stories about their country childhoods, with their country accents coming out as the stories and the night went on. Afterward, Wanda and Chuck spent a good amount of time exchanging stories of life on the road. It was a subject both of them were familiar with, Chuck by reason of default and Wanda by way of enthusiastic endorsement of her personal country existentialism of the vagabond life on the road. Chuck had to continue to do a partial fudge job concerning his job. He had to remember to substitute mechanical things for electronics.

For the part she was playing, Wanda had to remember she was claiming to be in a field that was entirely different from, detached from, and unrelated to electronics. There wasn't a lot of direct crossover between the phone company and the fashion trade. To maintain his cover story, Chuck only had to step to one side slightly. When it came to talking about her work as a traveling fashion consultant, Wanda had to wing it entirely. But she had been winging it on her own since she had gone on the road. She had a wider front to maintain and put forth, but she was good at maintaining and presenting her front.

One front that Wanda consciously let slip out more was her country accent. Over her years away from home and out on the wider road in the wider world, she had polished away much of the hard country accent she'd had as a child and teenager. In its place, she had developed an urban voice that masked her country origins. When Wanda was employing her act as a fashion consultant, having a more cosmopolitan-sounding voice made her sound more convincing as a cosmopolitan sophisticate. A self-proclaimed big-city lingerie consultant who supposedly worked the fashion circuits from New York to LA but spoke with a southern-cracker accent wouldn't have been very convincing.

But with the country man she had her country-girl cap set on sleeping with, Wanda let herself and her accent revert back to her country origins. Going back to her country roots put Wanda at ease. It seemed to put the country man she wanted to take her leisure with at ease to. Instead of an unapproachable city woman who might consider him a rube, as his unfaithful wife had, she was coming across as a down-home good old country girl who worked in a big-city-oriented profession but was willing shed her affected city ways and get back down to her country origins. Wanda figured that would help her and the man get down to the country type of original relating she had come into the bar looking for.

Along with her ongoing and growing feelings of lust, Wanda felt comfortable with the man. He was handsome, but he wasn't conceited. He was obviously masculine, but he wasn't obvious about it. He was manly, but he didn't come on like a strutting, slavering caricature of maleness, as did professional wrestlers and professional rednecks. Chuck wasn't trying to paw her with every turn of his hands, and he wasn't throwing leering sexual innuendo and suggestion in her face with every turn of phrase. Wanda was ready to be pawed and fondled by a man, but in the organized irony that was Wanda's mind, the fact that he wasn't trying to paw and fondle her at every turn was a bigger turn-on for her than if he had tried. That he wasn't coming on hard and fast was getting him further and faster with Wanda than he knew.

Chuck was handsome and athletically built. He was also friendly, respectful, reasoned, and restrained. Even though Wanda's perspective didn't extend beyond any given night she was willing to extend herself with a man and give herself to a man, Chuck had all the qualifications she was looking for. He was a stud, and he was a gentleman. He was both quantity and quality.

Chuck also had the quality that he could be hurt by a woman. However he equivocated his reactions to his wife's unfaithfulness, however much of a stiff upper lip he was maintaining, however he denied still loving his ex-wife, and however much his love for her had in fact faded, from the way he spoke about his wife's betrayal, it was obvious he had been hurt deeply and was still hurt.

In the inverse thought process of Wanda's organized mind, the fact that a man could be hurt by a woman made him all the more attractive to her. A man who could be hurt when a woman pulled the ground out from under him and pulled the life he'd thought he had away from him was a man who could love a woman for life. He was a quality lover spiritually as well as physically. He was a quality man. By Wanda's estimate, the man sitting close to her side was a man who could stay by a woman's side and love her for life. It was something of a rare quality in men, especially in men one picked up in bars. Wanda wanted to be associated with that kind of love, if even only for one passing night. She wasn't looking to be loved for a lifetime, but it was something special to Wanda to be able to sleep with a man who could love a woman for a lifetime. In that sense, Wanda was a thief of love. But she figured, *If you're going to be a jewel thief, it's better to steal diamonds than rhinestones, especially if you're planning to sell them on the black market. If you're going to be a thief of love, it's better to steal quality love for one night, even if you're going to let it go the next day and put yourself back out on the open market.*

To Wanda's organized way of thinking, it was time to get the ball rolling—in all senses of balling and all senses of rolling around.

"From the way you talk about your wife, you sound like you're still in love with her," Wanda said. She started to wonder if her hope for a lively night of corporeal and earthy lovemaking with him was going to be derailed by a ghost from his past.

"I loved her when I thought she loved me," Chuck answered. He looked at his beer and then away across the table. "But I can't love her now. What she did went beyond a onetime weakness that she was later sorry for and wanted forgiveness for. She was playing fast and loose from the beginning, and she had probably planned it that way from before the day we got married. She was good at maneuvering around me. Legal secretaries learn how to do legal maundering from the lawyers they work for. It was more than just that my masculine pride ended up damaged because she had sex with another man. Make that other men in a conga line. It wasn't one little corner of my pride that got pinched. It wasn't even a punch in the nose. She sucker punched every inch of self-respect I had. She didn't respect me all the nights she was systematically bedroom-romping with other men. She hadn't respected me from day one. She hadn't spent a minute of our marriage respecting me. She always complimented me on having a handsome face, but all she was looking for was a head she could mount on her wall. She never really looked into my face. She spent most of her free time laughing in my face."

Chuck momentarily fell silent. He continued to look away across the table, not quite knowing where to take it next. Wanda already knew where she wanted to take it and where she wanted to take Chuck. Chuck's closing line was the opening Wanda had been looking for.

Chuck turned his beer bottle in his hand, trying to think of what to say. He felt a sense of movement to his right side. He was about to open his mouth and resume random conversation, when his peripheral vision saw Wanda's hand come across the front of his face, below his chin. Her hand touched his cheek softly on the side of his face away from her. Chuck's head jumped slightly in surprise, but she did not remove her hand. With a soft pull of her hand, she turned his head to face her. When Chuck looked around, he saw that she had moved her head and upper body even closer to him. After Wanda turned Chuck's face her way, she left her hand on his cheek.

"Now, that's an awfully nice face to have someone laugh in it," Wanda said in a voice calculated to be both sad and soothing. "That woman was a fool to have dumped you."

Chuck no longer saw his beer, the booth he was sitting in, or the bar beyond. All he saw was Wanda's face. Her large hazel eyes and full lips were now only a few inches from his face. From her closer position, the shine on her lip gloss seemed brighter than any of the lights on the ceiling or neon signs on the walls.

"You can call her a fool if you want," Chuck said. "But I was the fool for falling in love with her in the first place."

"Love has to begin somewhere," Wanda said, trying to sound philosophical. She kept her hand on his cheek. "Sometimes love comes at you from out of the blue. And love doesn't always come with guarantees. When love does come, you have to believe and take a chance. If you're suspicious all the time, you'll never take any chance. You may avoid bad love, but you'll miss the possibility of good love. Your wife may have betrayed the love you extended to her. That was her folly. If you spend your whole life as a skeptic and cynic, you'll never love at any time. Never loving can be the greatest folly of all."

They hadn't taught philosophy in the trade school Wanda attended, but she instinctively figured that a little romantic philosophy could grease the skids for her.

"Then I was a fool for being blind and believing so long that she loved me, when she hadn't loved me from the start," Chuck said. "Love doesn't mean you have to be a turkey, but I was her prize turkey. Loving someone may be honorable enough in itself, but when you let yourself be blinded by love, then you deserve the dunce cap, and you deserve to be called a fool."

"As a philosopher once said," Wanda said, "a fool who loves is nobler in his heart and is wiser in his own folly than all the cynics who ever have been or ever will be." She didn't know if any philosopher had actually said that. It just sounded like something a philosopher would say. She had made it up on the fly as a way of getting closer to unzipping his fly.

"Well, that's very poetic," Chuck said. At that poetic moment, he wasn't concentrating as much on the philosophical implications of what Wanda had said as on the implications of the way she was rubbing his cheek with her fingers. "But poetic rhymes about the value of love in theory don't mean a whole lot when you're the real-world person who's seen the world you thought you had being dumped out the back door and when you're the one who's been walked on and flushed down the toilet like a turd. There's not a lot of romantic poetry you can recite that will make something like that go away or make you feel like writing sonnets about love like Shakespeare or sing praises to love like you were Lord Byron."

Chuck had studied English literature in high school and had something of a lingering familiarity with classic English literary masters, such as Lord Byron. He especially remembered Byron's famous poem that contained the line "She walks in beauty as the night." He thought, *That kind of elevated, romantic language doesn't mean much to you in specific or leave you thinking very highly about love in general when it's your wife who's walking out the office door at noon and shacking up with men in a hotel room during lunch hour or bringing men in through your door and shacking up with them in your own bed while you're out of town.* That kind of thing could leave the average person thinking the non-Byronesque thought *Love sucks.*

"There's not much you can say about love when the one you love and thought loved you says, 'So long, chump. It was fun playing games with you and tricks on you while it lasted, but you found out, and I'm outa here. But I was never really there with you to begin with.'"

Wanda moved her hand from Chuck's cheek and brushed her fingers over his lips. Chuck stopped talking.

"Is this the mouth you used to say goodbye to your wife with?" Wanda asked rhetorically.

"It's the only one I've got," Chuck answered. "It was the divorce court judge instead of me or a poet who pretty much wrote our goodbyes for us. I didn't have a whole lot to say directly to my wife, romantic, poetic, or otherwise, when I took my final leave of her."

"Your wife left you with a bad taste in your mouth," Wanda said.

Chuck couldn't tell if it was another rhetorical question or a rhetorical statement. "I suppose you could put it that way," he said.

Wanda moved her face in closer to his. She took her hand off his lips and wrapped it around the back of his neck. "Well, maybe I can leave you with a better taste in your mouth," she said with a quiet, sensual purr.

Wanda pivoted around on the booth seat on one hip to bring the full front of her body around to Chuck. She thrust one hand around behind Chuck's upper arm and looped her hand over his shoulder. In a quick move, she pulled her body up close against his. In a surprise instant, her large breasts, accentuated by deep cleavage Chuck had been caught staring at from across the table earlier, were no longer out of reach across the table. Suddenly, her breasts were pressing up against his body from a partial angle. Chuck could feel the press of her chest against the denim of his shirt as the soft fullness of her breasts spread out across his chest. The upper extension of her cleavage bulged upward as her chest compressed against his. The press of her body pinned Chuck's arm against his body. His beer bottle was still in his hand.

With the hand she had placed on the back of his neck, Wanda pulled Chuck's head down to meet her face coming up. The half-light of the bar was obscured as her face came up to Chuck's and cut off his view of anything else. Her full and sexy face was now immediately in his face, with little space left between them. Her large eyes filled most of the field of vision of Chuck's eyes. Her nose touched his and then brushed past. The full, sensual lips that had shone with the reflected light of lip gloss from across the table went out of sight as they surged up against and flowed over his lips.

Wanda pressed her sensual-woman-alone-on-the-road face up to Chuck's lost-puppy-dog face and started kissing him long and hard. She worked her full mouth back and forth over his mouth in a quickstep march that covered the full territory of his mouth and then covered it over again and again. As Wanda adjusted the position of her body against Chuck's, she threw her outer leg over his legs beneath the table. The tightness of her leather skirt somewhat restricted her range of motion and the angle to which she could spread her legs apart, but former cheerleader Wanda was not going to let wardrobe limitations keep her from doing the splits. As she pushed her on-the-road sexual behavior far past the limitations the religious mores of the Bible Belt region she had grown up in would have allowed, she pushed her leg past the limitations imposed by the tightness of her wardrobe. Her leather skirt rode up on her legs toward her hips as she threw her free leg over Chuck's legs.

Chuck's suaveness deserted him completely. He didn't even think to try to reach for and grab his suaveness as it ran away from him in the bar. The only thing he wanted to reach out and grab at that moment was Wanda. Two years of living without love, physical, poetic, or conceptual; two years of staring at the dissolved fragments of the home he once had thought he had but never had had; and two years of staring at the open road with no home at the end and nothing ahead but more open road exploded inside Chuck and exploded outward over Wanda.

Chuck practically dropped his beer bottle out of the hand at the end of the arm Wanda had pinned against his body. The bottle wavered on the table and almost fell over. Under the press of her body against his and the fast-paced rotating press of her lips over his, Chuck turned his body around in the booth seat to where he was fully frontally pressed up against her as her front pressed against his. As he did, she further shifted the position of her body and pressed her lower leg against his lower leg. She arched her upper leg at a higher angle over Chuck's legs. Her leather skirt slid farther up on her thighs.

The face of his ex-wife didn't float before Chuck's eyes. The only things his eyes could see in the reduced light of the bar and the limited perspective of Wanda's close-in position were her closed eyes and the faint color of eyeshadow above then. No ghost of failed marriage past hung in the void between Wanda and Chuck. The void that had been there since Chuck's divorce was now filled to overflowing with the sensual fullness of Wanda's body and the dynamic motion of her fully flowing sensuality.

As she kissed him, Chuck pressed his lips against the fullness of her lips and kissed her back as hard as and nearly as frenetically as she was kissing him. The warm wetness of her mouth filled Chuck's mouth as he tried to push his lips and mouth inside hers. It was one of Wanda's definitive moments when words weren't needed. No words were spoken. Physiologically, no words could be spoken. Wanda and Chuck grabbed breaths of air to the side on the run, as if they were Olympic swimmers rotating their heads to grab a quick breath before submerging their faces back into the water in the driving strain of the maximum effort of their full-length sprint.

Chuck couldn't do much with his arm caught between Wanda and the high back of the bench seat of the booth. He didn't want to break the clinch and move back enough to loop his arm up and over her shoulder. All he could do was slip his hand into the tightly confined space between her leg and his. The touch of the leather warmed by her body was almost as sensual as the press of her warm, wet mouth against his. Chuck moved his hand around, probing for her hip. With his free arm and hand, Chuck started rubbing the now more exposed upper thigh of the leg she had draped over his legs. Chuck could feel the smooth slide of her nylon stocking under his hand. He pushed his hand up farther until the nylon fell away, and he could feel the direct warmth and softness of the flesh of her upper thigh. At about the same elevation as he encountered direct flesh, his hand slipped beneath the tight confines of her leather skirt.

The combined feeling of warm skin beneath his palm and the smooth and slippery feel of leather against the top of his hand was a double-rush buzz to Chuck. At that moment, which was proving as definitive to Chuck as it was to Wanda, Chuck didn't think any bartender could have thrown together a mixed drink as intoxicating as what he was feeling.

Wanda's leather skirt was too tight for Chuck to push his hand up any farther. It would have taken some weird contortions and shifting of body position to get his hand farther up her skirt. Besides, if he got that crude, it could turn her off and make her push him away. That was the last thing Chuck wanted her to do. Instead of pushing his hand farther up under her skirt, Chuck pulled his hand out from under her skirt and placed it on top. From there, he ran his hand up her thigh and over the curve of her hip. The full curve of her hip pressed up beneath the tightness of her leather skirt. For several long moments, Chuck ran his hand back and forth over the curve of her hips as he and Wanda ran their lips and mouths over each other's. After a while, spent from tactilely exploring the hemispherical curve of her hip, Chuck set his hand in upward motion again. Just past the inward curve of her waist, he encountered more warm and yielding flesh when his hand arrived at her bare midriff. For another extended period of time, Chuck rubbed his hand over her side above her waist.

With her full lips pressing on his, Chuck slowly worked his hand higher up her side to where he encountered, in the form of her tight leather top, the same impediment to farther linear progress he had encountered with her leather skirt. Chuck managed to push his hand a little farther up her side under her top, but the tightness of the top and the press of her body against his once again put a limit on farther upward mobility. Tightness in a woman's clothing accentuated every turn and aspect of her figure, but it made it more difficult for a man to lay hands on the aspects of her figure that her tight clothes highlighted and prevented him from making direct contact with her skin. Chuck had to back his hand down and make himself content with rubbing her side and running his hand over her back. Though Chuck's hand was blocked from farther upward movement, he managed to run his hand around laterally to the far side of her waist. With his arm wrapped around her waist, Chuck pulled Wanda in even closer. She did not stop kissing him.

By a stopwatch, the whole clinch lasted only about five and a half minutes. In the stretched-out, relative timeline of the moment, it seemed to Chuck to go on as long as the halftime of one of the sporting events playing on the televisions suspended from the ceiling. In the intermittent lucid moments when he was focused on the world beyond the woman, Chuck found himself wondering if he and the woman were providing the halftime entertainment for the bar. Chuck found himself wondering how many other people were watching them. At the same time, he found he did not particularly care who saw them.

Wanda put her hands on the sides of Chuck's face and continued to kiss with undiminished vigor. Chuck took his free hand off her bare midriff and brought it up to the back of her head. He ran his hand over the back of her neck, running his hand through her thick mane of blonde hair. Blood was racing through Chuck's veins and pumping in his temples. Blood was pumping through his whole body. Blood was pumping through the free arm he was running through her hair and around the side of her neck and face. At the same time, his other arm, which had been pinned and squeezed in place between his body, her body, and the back of the booth seat by the press of their clinch, seemed to be going to sleep due to lack of circulation.

Chuck slid his hand that was still free and capable of mobility out of her hair, placed the palm of his hand on the side of her neck, and started rubbing his hand over her neck the way he had been rubbing it through her hair. Wanda responded by kissing him faster. Maybe time and space didn't cease to exist for Chuck, but certain circles in space and time disappeared from immediate and relevant view. Chuck didn't know what it was leading to or where Wanda was leading him.

What Chuck hoped it was leading up to was as obvious as the words they didn't have to say. Chuck was still doubtful it would end up going as far as his detached imagination, fueled by Wanda's undetached manner of contact, wanted to take it. It all still seemed a bit too good to be true to Chuck. Things like that just didn't happen in life.

But there was nothing standing between Chuck and Wanda.

She stopped her movable feast of kisses. She held one long, sustained kiss for over a half minute, and then she slowly backed away from the kiss. Their lips lingered together for a moment and then slipped apart temporarily, leaving a drawn-out strand of saliva between them. Wanda moved her head only a few inches, leaving her face within an easy extension of Chuck's face. She kept her front pressed up against Chuck's chest. Her hands were still on the sides of Chuck's face. Her leg was still wrapped over Chuck's legs. Chuck's free hand was still on the side of her neck. His other arm was still pinned between them and the back of the seat.

"Well now," Wanda said in a low purr, "did that leave a better taste in your mouth than the one your wife left you with?"

"I must admit," Chuck said, "it sure left a better taste than the one left in my mouth by what the guys and I were drinking on graduation night, the night none of us got laid. It tasted a whole lot better than what came up for a lot of us later that night."

Chuck was gracious enough that he didn't want to get into little vengeful ad hominem comparative attacks on figures from his past, even ones who had hurt him. But as far as relative comparisons and flat-out kissing went, Wanda was better than his wife had been. As far as comparisons of other aspects flat and not so flat went, Wanda was a lot less flat than his wife had been.

Chuck glanced quickly around the bar. He half expected to see a large crowd about to break into applause. But the aisle was empty. The bar seemed to be going about its normal nightly business. The people in the adjoining booths didn't seem to be paying attention to them or were pretending not to have seen them. One could start a fight in a redneck bar by leering at someone else's good-time party. The only attention they seemed to have drawn was that of the roving waitress. Apparently, the waitresses hadn't sold tickets.

"I think we gave the waitresses something to talk about for a week," Chuck said.

"That's old hat for me," Wanda said. For a woman to whom sex was old hat, she liked the latest in expensive designer cowgirl hats.

Wanda's story of how she'd started relating to the male sex was an exaggeration. She hadn't gone on any sexual-exploration road trips before her prom night, and then she had gotten her deflowered self back home shortly after midnight. She hadn't had any overnight affairs while she was living at home. She hadn't started up late-night rambling until the last year of her trade school. She hadn't started her hobby as a roving on-the-road paramour until after she started her job as a roving repair woman for the phone company. Wanda's story of how she had farmed herself out to be a bad girl to the local bad boys of her farming community was just a calculated ploy in building her mature-wild-woman-who-started-out-as-a-local-bad-girl-out-of-control image.

"I drove Mother crazy the way I carried on, the way I let the boys carry on with me, where I let them take me, and how I was letting them take me. When I'd come back in after a stay of one or more nights on the open road, she'd grab me by the arm and march me out to Father's toolshed."

Wanda's father didn't have a toolshed.

She continued. "Once she had me in the toolshed and closed the door, she'd make me drop my drawers, which she knew I had dropped the night or nights before. Then she'd make me bend over and grab my ankles. Then she'd take a strap to my bottom so bad I couldn't sit down for a week. It was a little backwoods vignette all around. I'd be yelling my head off from the pain."

Wanda's mother had never spanked her when she was a child or whipped her with a belt when she was a teenager, nor had her father. Wanda's story was an exaggeration. An exaggeration on steroids. Wanda threw the detail in because she figured a small taste of S&M would spice up the story. It also might make Chuck want to soothe her poor abused bottom by rubbing it with his hands.

"She'd be yelling what a tramp I was. Our house was isolated, but I wouldn't have been surprised if the sound carried to the whole town. I'd walk around holding my aching tail out behind me, waddling like a goose. Sometimes the only thing that kept me from riding off with boys on motorcycles and in cars was that my backside was too sore for me to sit down. When I was able to sit down again, I'd be off with another boy to another motel. When it came to the 'If I dood it, I get a whippin'. I dood it' adage of the Red Skelton character of the mean little kid, I dood it, and I got a whippin' for doing it. Then I went out and dood it again."

Chuck kind of wanted to laugh at the way she described the culture clash of her backwoods-bad-girl-on-the-make attitude with the more fundamentalist, moralist outlook of her mother. But her face was still inches from his, and he didn't want to appear to be laughing in her face.

"I don't think my parents would have whipped me if they knew I was making out," Chuck said. "But if either my mother or our local pastor saw us in the kind of clinch we were just in, they'd probably say we have to get married. They'd both say we compromised ourselves."

Chuck wasn't fully sure why he had said what he had. He didn't think his mother or local pastor would have said that, nor was Chuck immediately marriage-minded at the moment. He had only recently come off a bad experience in marriage. Yet after five and a half minutes in Wanda's arms, the thought of marriage was in the back of his mind again.

"Honey," Wanda said in a wry voice with her lips inches from Chuck's, "if I had gotten married every time I went and got myself compromised, by now, I'd have been married more times than Liz Taylor and Marilyn Monroe combined. But my mother and a whole seminary full of pastors or the College of Cardinals wouldn't have been able to whip me into getting married if I hadn't wanted to back then. They still couldn't do it today. I may have compromised myself all over the road and all over the landscape, but marriage is one compromise you're never going to catch me in."

She went back to rubbing Chuck's cheek with the fingers of one hand. The tempo of her voice slowed down and became more drawn out and measured. "There is one slight problem with a life on the road, though. The road is like one of those rich older men who keep young women as mistresses. They can be a sugar daddy to the girl, but by their age and nature, they can be chilly and aloof. The road gives me most everything material I want out of life, but the road can be a cold and distant lover. A girl can get lonely when she's out on the road by herself. She needs something more immediate and substantial in her arms than a vision of the next horizon over the horizon she's looking at. When the sun sets and I can't see the horizon anymore, I can get as lonely as the next girl. I'll be back on the road tomorrow, but right now, I'm just a lonely girl alone on the road."

Wanda started running the tips of her fingers over Chuck's lips. "Without your wife with you or a home to go back to, I have a feeling you're a lonely boy on the road. I'd be willing to make a country-girl wager that you're every bit as lonely as me."

Chuck made some kind of agreement noise. Wanda paused for a second and then started running her fingers over his lips again. She moved her face in another three inches closer. Her leg was still draped over his legs.

"You know," Wanda said in a knowing tone of voice, "when lonely people meet each other on the road with no home waiting for either of them, they've been known to get together and make their night a little less lonely for both of them." She took both of Chuck's hands and cupped them in hers. "If you're as lonely as I am and you don't want to be lonely any more than I do, I'm quite willing and ready to keep you company for the rest of the night."

Any suaveness Chuck had left disappeared. In an automatic reflex that spoke as much as the suave words he didn't have to say, Chuck's body tightened.

Wanda continued. "Take me somewhere I can be myself and make plain to you the kind of girl I am. I can't make myself any plainer to you."

Chuck straightened up all the way in his seat. Another part of his anatomy straightened up more than it already was.

"Since neither of us has a home to go back to, we could make a home for each other here on the road, in our home away from the home we don't have."

The distance left between them disappeared all the way. Without saying another suave word he didn't have, Chuck buried his head in the nape of her neck and started kissing the curve where her shoulders met her neck. The thought had passed through his mind when he first saw her standing at the bar, but as fast as the thought had come into his head that she was looking to be picked up and that he might score with her, Chuck had discarded the thought as being an unlikely pretense on his part. Things like that happened in overheated male fantasies, but they didn't happen in the real world. Now, out of the blue, it was about to happen. *Maybe things like that do happen in the world*, he thought.

Wanda rolled her head slightly to one side as Chuck kissed her neck. "You seem to share my philosophy of not being lonely on the lonely road," she said. "By your reaction, I take it we have a date for the night."

Chuck brought his head back up straight. It wasn't the only point of his anatomy straightening itself up. "Your place or mine or right here?" Chuck said in a semicontrolled voice. He had meant it to sound suave, but it had come out sounding lame. He had come to the limit of his remaining suaveness.

Wanda laughed at his little attempt at a witticism. "Well, for the sake of a girl's safety, I insist on a semipublic place, like a motel or a hotel. But I usually prefer a place with a little more room and four walls around. This booth is too open, and it's too small. Our legs would stick out and trip people walking by. We'd only be taking up space without buying drinks, and we'd be distracting other paying customers from buying drinks. The manager wouldn't like that. He'd probably throw us out after two minutes. Even if he didn't throw us out right away, he would when closing time came around. We might not be finished by then."

There was, however, one little stumbling block that could possibly finish things right then and there.

"Before we go working ourselves out any further," Chuck said, "there's one thing I need to work out now."

Wanda was a bit puzzled at the unexpected interruption. By this phase of the game, everything was usually off and running. The need for further clarification or further words was usually long past by this time.

"What's that?" Wanda asked.

"You asked me if I was here being a bad boy," Chuck said, alluding to her asking earlier if he had someone waiting at home for him. "By any chance, are you here being a bad girl? Is there someone home waiting for you? More accurately put, speaking of danger, is there someone out driving around in a blind, jealous rage looking around for you on the cheatin' side of town? Are we going to walk out into the parking lot and be confronted by a blow-top redneck with a shotgun in his hand, shouting, 'You picked a fine time to leave me, Ramona'? I'm ready to die in your arms tonight, but I don't want to do it off the end of a twelve-gauge pump."

Chuck made up the part about the jealous husband carrying a shotgun instead of saying flat out that he didn't want to make love to her if she was a two-timing wife who was dumping on her husband the way his wife had dumped on him behind his back. But attempting to ascertain if a woman had a potentially dangerous, jealous cuckolded husband was a good general safety precaution. It was good-looking women like her who usually had psycho boyfriends or boyfriends they had driven psycho by their randy behavior.

Wanda reached down and pulled up Chuck's arm still pinned against the back of the seat. With her hand, she directed his fingers to the base of her ring finger. "Feel my finger."

"Do you fart if I pull your finger?" Chuck asked. As horny as he was at the moment, he couldn't resist the obvious line.

Wanda laughed at Chuck's second attempt at a witticism, which wasn't much better than the first. "I just wanted you to feel for yourself that I'm not wearing a ring, and there's no depression in my finger where I took one off," Wanda said.

Chuck felt her finger. There was no depression groove left by a removed ring. There were a lot more parts on her that he would rather have been feeling than her finger.

"There's no ring there, honey," Wanda said as she rubbed the tips of his fingers over the base of her ring finger. "And there isn't an indentation where a ring used to be that I slipped off."

Chuck hadn't seen any ring on her finger earlier. His fingers were a bit tingly from his arm having gone numb from being pressed against the seat of the booth.

"I'm not married. I've never been married. I never will be married. I like my life as it is. I like life on the open road. You may not have a home to go back to. I don't have a home in the usual sense. My home is the road. The road is the only home I know. It's the only home I want. The road is the home I always come back to. I'm not about to exchange life on the road for any life of in-place domesticity that would keep me glued in one place for the rest of my life. Waking up in the same place every morning would drive me crazy. I like waking up in a different place every morning. It's just that I get tired of sleeping alone the night before I wake up in a different place.

"Our lives crossed on this road. I'll spend the night with you here in this town on the road. Since you don't have a home, I'll make a home for you in my body. We can make a home for each other on the road for tonight. Tomorrow I'll be back on the road. We probably won't run into each other again after tonight. We've got this one chance only. That's why we have to make it count. For this night, I'll be the home and lover you lost. For tonight, you can be the kind of lover to me that the road can't. But tomorrow I'll leave you and go back to my first lover. The difference between me and your wife is that there won't be any lies passed between us. You'll know that I'm gone, and you'll know where I've gone off to. If you can agree to that and if you can handle the fact that I've done this with other men before you and will be doing it with other men after you, there's nothing standing in our way."

Chuck would not have been able to accept it if she was out cheating on her husband, but his male ego could handle the fact that she had had other men before him and that there would be other men after him. He could handle it mainly because he wanted to handle the woman.

Wanda continued. "If you can accept that I'll be gone from you and back on the road tomorrow, I'll be yours for tonight. We can be a home to each other for one night."

Chuck had never read anything by Jack Kerouac, but he knew enough about hobos to know that the lure of the open road had quite a hold on certain people. Wanda was convincing in the way she described her love of life on the open road. She had convinced Chuck she was a free spirit who lived her personal form of hobo life on the open road. She just did it out of the trunk of her car as a lingerie distributor instead of out of an open boxcar.

"Then my place on the road or your place on the road?" Chuck asked. "I don't think you'd want to use my car. It's a compact. We'd both need a chiropractor to straighten us out the next day if we tried making love in the backseat."

It would have been even tougher to use the front seat of a phone company repair van. Fortunately, since Chuck was the supervisor, he was able to drive his own car to the installation site. The other members of his crew and the crew from the Columbia office would be bringing the repair vans.

"Where are you staying?" Wanda asked.

"At the Hampton Inn," Chuck said. "It's at the north end of town, beyond the shopping mall, where the main drag joins up with the east–west road that runs past town."

That worked just fine by Wanda's standards for the way she liked to work things. The motel her supervisors had put her and the rest of the installation crew from the Columbia branch office up in was on the other side of town. The hotel was public enough, with enough people in adjoining rooms, that a man wouldn't be likely to try anything crazy. Wanda figured the presence of people in adjoining rooms would provide a measure of safety. They would also be there to hear her sound effects.

Wanda ran her hand over the side of his face again. "I'll drive myself over to your hotel and come up to your room," she said. "I'll meet you there in half an hour."

Wanda prepared to leave. Once things had been set in motion, she didn't believe in wasting time. She pulled her leg off Chuck's lap. "What room are you in?"

"Room 817," Chuck answered.

"I'll knock on your door," Wanda said. "You can wash up after if you like, but don't be running the water when I get there. You might not hear me knock. I don't want to be left standing in the hall. Anyone who sees me in the hall knocking on a door dressed the way I am may think I'm a call girl." She straightened herself up as if preparing to leave. "I'll leave first. You leave five minutes after I do. That way, the other guys I was talking to won't think we're leaving together. If they get a hint of what we're heading out to do, they might get jealous, follow us out, and start something crazy."

It sounded like a reasonable safety precaution. But Wanda wasn't really afraid that some other man in the bar might start stalking them. She just didn't want Chuck to see her drive away in the phone company van she had come to the bar in.

"You don't have to drive yourself over," Chuck said. "I can drive us there in my car."

Wanda shook her head. "I choose the place, and I provide my own transportation," she said in a quiet but settled voice. "It's my rule. I choose who I go with, and I choose when I leave afterward. I've always left the next morning, and I always will leave in the morning. Don't try to stop me from going in the morning. Don't try to follow me when I go. Don't try to find me after tonight. That's another of my main rules. It's the rule you'll have to accept if you want me to stay with you tonight. If you don't accept that rule, we should just turn around and walk away in opposite directions right here and now."

Like many men before him, Chuck was too preoccupied by thinking about what would be coming up between them to voice any objections to any of her rules.

"You can hold me in your arms for the rest of the night. But you'll find that I'm hard to hold if you try to hold me longer than one night. I make my own way in life. I'll go through the rest of my life setting my own path. I won't go through life harnessed to a convention or to any man. It's nothing personal. I'm not saying you're not attractive. All I'm saying is that I'm not ready for any person, place, thing, morality, or concept to put a collar around my neck, put a leash on me, and pull me to heel or put a bit in my mouth and pull the reins in on me. I'm like a wild horse out on the range who's never known a bridal. I'd go crazy and start bucking if some cowboy tried to put a saddle on me or tried to make me pull in harness. I'd drive any man who tried to domesticate me crazy. I'd drive him as crazy as domesticity would drive me crazy. I may be the best woman you'll ever have tonight, but I wouldn't be good for any man long-term. Beyond one night, I wouldn't be good for any man in any sense of being good. In the long run, we'll both live a lot longer and you'll be a lot happier if you live without me."

Her choice of words sounded like something Chuck vaguely remembered hearing in a Linda Ronstadt song.

As Wanda talked on, outlining her rules and philosophy of life and love on the road, Chuck again glanced down at her exposed cleavage and the outline of her full breasts straining against the confinement of her leather top. Wanda caught the direction of his glance.

"Don't fall in love with me. That's another of my rules. It's the rule I insist a man follow with me the most. That rule is for your own good as well as mine. It's a self-defense rule for you as much as it is for me. I can't be faithful to any man. I've left every lover I've had so far in life. I'll leave every lover I ever will have and go back to my first lover, the open road. I'll betray you like I've betrayed all my other lovers except the road. I can't be trusted. In that sense, I'm no different than your wife was. The difference between me and her is that I'll tell you that honestly, up front, and to your face, provided the eyes in your face aren't so busy being distracted by looking at my front that the ears in your head can't hear what the mouth in my face is saying to your face."

What could he have said? What could any man have said in a similar situation?

"Tonight I'll make love to you like there's no tomorrow. But when tomorrow does actually come, I'll be gone. When it comes time for me to leave, I hope you'll understand that I was born a rambling woman. It's not in me to be anything but a rambling woman."

Now Chuck thought that sounded like something taken from the Allman Brothers song "Ramblin' Man."

Chuck looked up from her chest and straight into her eyes. "We'll do it your way," he said in a definitive voice. There weren't a whole lot of other definitive words he could have used. He was afraid to use any other or additional words. Any other words or any further words could possibly have derailed the moment coming up.

Wanda moved back in close to Chuck. "We can do it both my way and your way," she said in a husky and suggestive voice. "I think you'll like my way as much as your way."

She leaned in and kissed Chuck again. She lingered the kiss for a while but not nearly as long as her first kiss. Foreplay was fun in itself, but when Wanda was ready to roll and raring to go, she felt foreplay could be dispensed with.

"Are you really going to come?" Chuck asked instinctively as she broke her kiss.

Wanda stroked his cheek again. "Honey, you get me in your bed and see how fast and how much I can come on to you and with you."

Chuck still wondered if he would actually see her walk through the door into his room.

With a quick move, Wanda swung around in her seat and stood up. For a moment, she looked at Chuck. "If you doubt I'll show," she said, "along with what I'll be doing for you later, I'll tell you what I'll do for you now." She bent over the table, reached over to the other seat, and picked up her cowgirl hat. But instead of putting her hat on, she dropped it onto the table directly in front of Chuck. "I'll leave my hat with you. That way, you know I'll be coming back for it. It will also go on marking my place. There are probably plenty of other hot-to-trot women in this place who would jump at the chance to jump a good-looking man like you. They may come swarming all over you and try to tackle you when you head for the door. If other women see you with my hat, they'll know I'm yours and you're all mine. For this night. If they want you, they'll have to take a number and wait in line for the next night."

Wanda straightened the rest of the way up and looked at Chuck with a knowing look. "You said room 817, didn't you?"

"Yes," Chuck said.

"Just wanted to check," Wanda said. "I wouldn't want to knock on the wrong door and have some old couple come to the door, look at me dressed like this, and think I'm a call girl out on assignment. They might call the manager about me and have me tossed out of the building. We'd both miss a great night."

"The room's on the top floor," Chuck said. "It's the second room down the hall from the northwest corner. My company actually managed to get me a room on the top floor this time. The room looks out to the north, away from the town. It looks out over the landscape instead of toward the shopping mall down the street. In the daylight, you can see the countryside for miles. It's probably the best view in the whole place."

The room also looked out over the main country road that ran past the town. Chuck figured it was probably the road she would take when she took her leave of him in the morning and returned to her life on the road, as she said she would.

"Given that it's dark and the shades will be drawn, I don't think the view is going to make much difference to us," Wanda said. "Unless you're an exhibitionist who likes to leave the curtains open. Personally, I don't mind being exhibitionistic myself now and then. For those watching from the sidewalk, we could put on quite a show. Until we go horizontal."

Even if Wanda didn't see the view out the window of his room, it would still be a symbolic high view for her. The hotel was eight stories high. That was the same height as the last microwave tower she had worked on and savored the view from after a job well done. She would work on him as long as they both lasted. It would be a good job done for both of them. She would savor her triumph as she worked on the installation of the new microwave system the next day.

Wanda picked up her purse from the table and smiled a coy little smile. "Don't be late," she said. "You wouldn't want to keep a poor love-starved country girl waiting, would you?"

Chuck started to open his mouth to issue an emphatic denial. Before he could say anything, Wanda turned and walked away.

She walked off in the direction Chuck's back was to. He had to turn around and look over the back of the booth seat to watch her walk away. Her hair bounced as she walked. Her full hips alternately pumped beneath the tightness of her leather skirt. Her bare midriff seemed to glow softly in the subdued light of the bar. As Chuck watched, she turned the corner at the end of the aisle and headed in the direction of the front door.

After she disappeared from sight, Chuck turned back in his seat. Her presence had been vibrant and filling. By comparison, the booth he was sitting in now suddenly seemed exponentially emptier and quieter than when he had first sat down in it. Most other men would have been high-fiving themselves at that point. Chuck was self-effacing enough that he sat there in the now quiet and empty booth more or less wondering if it had all been real. Chuck still felt that things like that just didn't happen in the world. Perhaps he had fantasized the whole thing. But her hat was there in the booth. A faint taste of Wanda's lip gloss lingered in his mouth. An even fainter trace of her perfume lingered. Chuck wasn't sure if the hint of her perfume was lingering in the air or in his memory.

Chuck picked up his beer bottle and drank the remaining part of the beer Wanda had bought him. After finishing the bottle, he resolved to keep one of the two bottles she had bought them as a souvenir of the night. Even if she didn't show up at his hotel room, it would still make for a memorable enough remembrance.

After finishing his bottle, Chuck set it aside and turned his attention to the identical bottle Wanda had bought for herself. She hadn't drunk much of the beer in the bottle. He tentatively brought the bottle up to his lips, the lips Wanda had not been tentative about kissing only a short while ago. As he took a drink out of the bottle, he got another faint taste of her lip gloss from the rim of the bottle. He resolved that he would keep the bottle she had drunk out of as the souvenir bottle.

Chuck sat in silence and turned her beer bottle around in his hand. At that point, most men would have been thinking about getting themselves into the woman, but Chuck wondered what kind of woman he had gotten himself involved with, provided there would even be any further involvement to come. All he could surmise was that she was a randy rover, as his wife had been; she was just more honest and up front about it. As far as measurements went, Wanda was more up front in that department than his wife had been too. Wanda was sexier too. She had a unique philosophy of life on the road and love on the run that she lived by. That was something else she had in common with his ex-wife. The difference was that she lived her sexually open life honestly and openly on the open road and on a grander scale than his wife, who had lived her sexually randy life in the shadows, behind his back and off his back.

The fact that she lived a vagabond lifestyle became the trigger point for a series of fantasies Chuck had about her. In his first fantasy, a fantasy of the open road, he was a hobo riding alone in an open boxcar in a past era. She was a female hobo who suddenly jumped into his boxcar the way she had unexpectedly dropped into the seat across from him. In his imagination, her long blonde hair was tangled and stained with the soot of railyards and cinders from the smokestacks of coal-burning steam locomotives. Instead of leather, she wore a soiled denim shirt and torn blue jeans. She instinctively knew the price she needed to pay for riding in his boxcar. Without saying a word, she started to unbutton her stained denim shirt. She wasn't wearing a bra underneath. Hobo women couldn't afford the latest in women's foundations. In his imagination, Chuck the hobo approached the beautiful, dirty hobo woman as she finished unbuttoning her shirt. He pulled the road-stained woman in close to him. As their lips pressed together, he pressed her up against the rough wooden boards of the inside wall of the boxcar. Light and shadows from the world passing by outside swept over them as the train rolled across the open countryside.

She'd told him she worked for a manufacturer and distributor of women's intimate apparel. Chuck imagined himself as a fashion photographer who photographed high-fashion models for a high-fashion magazine. The woman was a top model and was in his studio for a one-on-one photo shoot. She was standing in front of a single-color backdrop screen. Her hair was wild and tangled in the high-fashion style. She had a pouty come-hither look on her face. She was modeling only a minimal and flimsy see-through bra and lace thong. Both items were strained to their flimsy limit by the press of her fullness on both ends. Chuck walked up to the posed woman on the pretext of making minor adjustments to her hair. She turned to him, her face a picture of longing, need, and desire. Chuck pulled the woman in close to him. As their lips pressed hard together, Chuck ran his hands wildly over her almost naked back. He fumbled with the single snap on the flimsy strip of sheer material that was her bra. It unsnapped easily.

Chuck looked at Wanda's cowgirl hat. He didn't know if her fashion consultation employment had ever taken her west of the Pecos River, but he fantasized about her in a western setting. In his imagination, Chuck was an itinerant cowboy who had gone to work for a rich rancher with a beautiful and high-spirited daughter who had a reputation for riding broncos and men. In his imagination, the woman was standing in an empty stall in the barn. Her back was to him as he walked into the stall. She was wearing her cowgirl hat. Instead of a leather top, she was wearing a fancy western-style embroidered satin blouse of the kind Dale Evans or Patsy Cline wore. As Chuck closed the door of the stall behind him, the woman turned around. Her fancy western-style blouse was unbuttoned down past her navel. The handsome cowboy Chuck and the spirited rancher's daughter pulled each other in close to each other. Her cowgirl hat fell off as they dropped down onto the hay on the floor of the stall.

Chuck next imagined her skin being a shade browner in color. He imagined her as a Mexican or South American peasant temptress in an off-the-shoulder peasant dress. In his imagination, he was the son of a powerful landowner or the head of a band of *vacaros*. The woman was standing in front of him with her shoulders and upper chest bare down to the top of her peasant dress. Her arms were held straight down at her sides, angled backward behind her back. She might have been simply holding her arms behind her back. Then again, her hands could have been tied behind her back. The imaginary browner-skinned version of the woman looked up at Chuck, her face a mixture of want and surrender. Chuck grabbed her by her hair and pulled her face up to his.

Chuck caught himself and snapped back to reality. The woman might not show up at his hotel room at all. She might not spend a single further minute running with him anywhere, and already he was running through sexual-fantasy scenarios that could have been main fiction features in *Playboy* or *Hustler* magazine. At that moment, she could have been heading for the hills like a Mexican bandit while, in his mind, he had been ravishing her as if he were Pancho Villa or Zorro. Chuck figured that before he gave free rein to his fantasies, he should consider the real-world possibility that he had seen the last of the woman. Given that he might never get ahold of her again, he figured it would be a good idea to get ahold of his fantasies.

Chuck looked at his watch. It had been four minutes since she left. She had asked him to wait five minutes before he left. He figured four minutes was enough lead time for a woman who moved as quickly and surely as she did.

Chuck picked up the beer bottle she had drunk out of and the hat she had left. He got up out of the booth, walked to the front door, and left the bar. Out in the parking, he stopped by his car and poured the rest of the beer out of the bottle. Then he put the bottle and the hat on the backseat of his car, got in the front seat, and drove away. He did not see any phone company vehicles in the area. But then again, he wasn't looking for evidence of phone company presence. At the moment, the phone company was one of the last things on Chuck's mind.

10

As a vehicle of seduction and desire, the room left much to be desired. The room was clean, but as far as romantic accommodations went, even though it was on the top floor, the size and minimalist setting of the room didn't resemble a penthouse suite in the grand hotel overlooking the Mediterranean from a bluff in Monaco in *To Catch a Thief* as much as it resembled the roadside cafeteria a lovesick cowboy dragged Marilyn Monroe off to in *Bus Stop*. Even Cary Grant would have had trouble scoring in such limited facilities. Grace Kelly would probably have taken one look at the place, turned around, and stormed out.

There wasn't a whole lot that could be done to turn an economy-rate hotel room into a passion pit. With the woman's hat still in his hand, Chuck stood for a moment, looking around his hotel room. The only thing he could think to do to enhance the romantic aura of the place was to open up the minibar in his room so he could offer the woman a drink. If she actually showed up, Chuck figured she wouldn't want to be jumped as soon as she got through the door, as if she had stepped into a wrestling ring. She would probably like some kind of romantic lead-in to the main event she had promised. Despite her country background and her youth as a wild and out-of-control motorcycle-riding, motel-bed-hopping teenager, the woman had morphed into a sophisticated-looking and -sounding lady. She would want some semblance of sophistication out of him before they got down to their final entertainment. Offering the woman a drink poured out of an airline-sized miniature bottle from a minibar was about the limit of sophisticated foreplay that could be achieved in his room at the Hampton Inn.

Chuck dropped the hat onto the counter, where the woman would see it when she came into the room—if she ever actually set foot in the room. He walked over to the minibar and broke the seal on it. Opening the bar would cost him extra. Actually, it would cost the phone company extra. The company was paying for the accommodations. Chuck didn't know how closely the accounting department at the company went over expense sheets. It was possible they might reject the extra expense of using the bar and make him reimburse the company for it.

But Chuck was willing to pay the extra out-of-pocket expense to use the minibar. If the woman actually showed up, offering her a drink was the only embellishment he could think of to make things slightly more sophisticated and sensual for the woman and put her in more of a mood for romance. If she didn't show up, he could use the bar to drink himself a dunce's toast for having been led on and dumped by a woman for a second time.

After Chuck broke the seal on the minibar and opened the door, he found there was a minirefrigerator in the bar. But there was no ice in the refrigerator. If the woman wanted ice in her drink, he would have to walk down to the ice machine at the opposite end of the hall and around the corner and bring back a bucket of ice. Not only would that be a bit awkward, but the time delay spent in getting the ice might be long enough for the woman to cool down. He thought of going for the ice right away, but the woman might show up while he was fighting with the ice machine. If he wasn't there to open the door, she might walk away. The woman didn't look or sound like the kind of woman who would wait around.

Chuck paused. When it came to the possibility of pressing the woman in his room, there was a more pressing concern right in the room than away at the ice machine. After breaking the seal on the minibar and opening it, Chuck decided he had better conceal any indication that he had lied about his employment. He hadn't unpacked his suitcase yet. The suitcase was open, with his phone company uniform showing. If the woman happened to spot the uniform, she would know he worked for the phone company and wasn't an itinerant mechanic, as he had claimed. If she found out he had lied to her, she could take offense and take her leave of him, not because he worked for the phone company but because he was a liar. The woman was honest enough about her views of life, love, and sex. She might not appreciate dishonesty in the men she honestly loved and left. If she discovered his uniform and found out he had lied to her, she might leave in a huff without loving him in a state honesty or in any state in the Union—provided she actually showed up at all.

Chuck took his phone company uniform out of the suitcase and put it in the bottom drawer of the dresser with the phone company insignia and his name patch facing down. He then placed several layers of his regular street clothes on top of the uniform. There were some technical manuals dealing with the upcoming installation job that he had brought in from his car earlier and had planned to review in bed before going to sleep. He hadn't anticipated that his bedtime activity was going to be totally different—if the woman actually showed up at the door of his room.

Chuck grabbed the manuals and stuffed them in the bottom drawer of the dresser, burying them underneath his uniform and other clothes. Then he went over to the closet, where he had tossed his baseball cap with the phone company logo above the brim. He took the hat out of the closet and buried it in a likewise manner in the bottom of the drawer.

Having completed cleaning up the room of any evidence that he worked for the phone company, Chuck figured it might be a good idea to clean himself up a bit. He had spent a long day driving on the road to get to the town the jobsite was located outside of. He had planned to take a shower before going to bed. He had assumed he would be going to bed alone. He hadn't taken a shower before heading out to the bar, as he hadn't planned to bring company back from the bar. Chuck wasn't overtly sweaty, but he didn't feel properly clean to be entertaining a lady in the manner she wanted to be entertained—provided she actually showed up for the entertainment she had set in motion. Chuck figured that just to be sure he didn't gross the woman out by emanating any odors he wasn't aware of, he should wash up a bit before she arrived—if she arrived at all.

The woman had cautioned him not to be running the water when she arrived. In line with what the woman he wanted to get in line with had said, Chuck was afraid if he took a full shower, he might not hear her knock on the door. Instead of preparing for a shower, he took off his shirt, dropped it onto the nearest chair, and went over to the sink in the washroom. There he started to wash his upper body off using a washcloth. He ran the water in only quick spurts in order not to miss the woman knocking on the door—if she ever actually came to his door.

As Chuck washed, he looked at his face in the mirror. It was a fairly good-looking face by the standards of either sex. But Chuck no longer harbored any pretensions about the utility of his face when it came to holding any woman past or pending. His good looks hadn't held his wife. The woman who was coming, or maybe wouldn't come at all, was more drop-dead gorgeous than his wife. Chuck wondered what made him think there was anything about him that could hold the woman, when he hadn't been able to hold his wife. Chuck had never been a vain mirror-starer, but he had once thought his looks gave him a better-than-even chance with women. After the revelation that his wife had been systematically unfaithful from the start even as he had thought his manly charms and good luck were captivating her, he now doubted he could hold any woman, especially an exotic-looking and thinking creature like the woman he had met in the bar. She had made it verbally clear that no man could hold her beyond one night. But what made him think he was even necessarily capable of drawing a woman like her in from the road she operated from or from the distant territory of her mind that she operated out of?

Since his own face was in question, Chuck's thoughts switched to the woman's face. Instead of his own face in the mirror, he saw the face of the woman. Her face triggered another series of minifantasies.

The woman might not have been an executive, but as a fashion consultant, he figured she knew something about the fashion business and the business world in general. He assumed that when she wasn't out on the road, she was probably headquartered in a large city, such as New York or LA. In his fantasy, Chuck was a young business school graduate who had just come to work for a large corporation headquartered in a skyscraper in downtown Manhattan or some other large city. The woman was a top-level executive of the company. She was working him late that night. In his imagination, Chuck was standing in the woman's top-floor office. She was wearing a tight, form-fitting black business suit with a silk blouse unbuttoned at the top. Her hair had been initially set in an upward-sweeping fashion, but she had let it down as their discussion of getting down to business proceeded. Corporate executives had been known to let their hair down where heavy-duty business was concerned.

In his fantasy vision, the woman's thick blonde hair was replaced by a shorter, easy-to-manage brunette pageboy or sugar-bowl-style cut. She was wearing tight black slacks and a strained, tight white blouse that seemed stretched to its limit. Her chest was as impressive as her business credentials.

She was sitting behind an impressively large corporate desk, outlining for him exactly what their working relationship would be. She also outlined for him just how close the relationship would need to be between the two of them if he wanted to get anywhere in the company. Over by the large plate-glass window was a futon-style couch made of red leather.

Up in the top-floor office suite, the woman came out from behind her desk and walked toward him. The understanding of the business relationship was complete. The contract between them had been agreed on. In a short while, it would be finalized on the bottom line by both of them. No further words, legal, corporate, or otherwise, were necessary. Fine print was about to become bold text. Bottom lines were about to be gotten down to.

Instead of coming directly to him, the woman walked past him to the door of the office. For a second, Chuck thought she was going to show him the door and put him out through it. Instead, she threw the bolt and locked the door from the inside. Then she switched off the lights from a wall switch next to the door. The room went dark except for the dim light coming through the tall curtains over the large plate-glass window.

In the semidarkness, the woman walked back to where he was standing in front of her large executive desk. She took Chuck's hand and led him across the expanse of the large office over to a leather couch positioned close to the large picture window. Halfway to the couch, she jettisoned her stylish dress-for-success business suit jacket in the middle of the floor.

The high-powered executive woman in Chuck's fantasy left him by the couch and walked over to the window. At the window, she pulled the tall curtains fully open to the cityscape far below. Thus exposed, they could possibly be seen from outside. But the room was dark, and they were on the top floor of one of the tallest buildings in the city. All anyone on the ground or in another building would see was a faraway darkened window high up. Onlookers would have needed a telescope to see up that high, and they would have seen nothing but a darkened window with no depth of view inside. The woman walked back to where he was standing by the couch.

Alongside the couch, the woman and Chuck initialized the first step of their upcoming business relationship with a long, lingering full-mouthed kiss. As Chuck deftly unbuttoned her blouse, the woman loosened the belt of her business suit slacks and then the belt of his pants. Given the height of the building, they would have been only miniature figures to anyone on the ground or in a neighboring building. A voyeur would have needed a telescope to peep on them. The last items of their clothing and inhibitions fell away, and they prepared to get down to real business and the business of real love and his initiation into becoming the kept man of a rich older woman.

With the glistening lights and the night-sky panorama of the city skyline serving as a backdrop, the woman pulled Chuck down toward the leather couch. Outside the top-story window, the lights of the city spread out below like a shining jeweled field. The headlights of cars on the city streets below moved like a liquid river of light; half the stream was red from the taillights of the cars going away from them, and the other half was white from the headlights of the cars coming toward the building where they were engaged in struggling, surging surrender to passion and each other in secret, spread out and grappling with each other in the darkened office room high above the shining lights of the city.

As high-level visions stretching out to distant horizons went, it was a vision Wanda could have appreciated and resonated with. As a rule, Wanda's horizons were always just out of reach. She sought a horizon that always remained a horizon, something to be pursued always but never fully attained. Her horizons were seen but always just out of reach. She liked horizons that were out ahead of her at a distance she had to keep straining to follow.

Chuck, on the other hand, liked to keep his horizons close to him and at hand. Chuck's vision of making high-power love to a high-powered older female executive wasn't all spontaneous imagination conjured up on the fly on the spot. It was drawn from his memory of the time he lost his virginity and his entry-level innocence, not to a citified older female executive on high but to a far more down-to-earth, earthy, and countrified matron three times his age (3.16 times to be exact). However, their disparate ages were just numbers. In a darkened bedroom with the shades drawn, numbers and years of difference sort of disappeared. Faraway horizons disappeared too. In such situations, the only horizon one could touch was the one in his or her arms.

———•/•/•———

Lucinda McAlister was a divorced woman who lived in the town Chuck had grown up on the outskirts of. She had lived there all her life and had never left the town, not even after her husband deserted her and ran off. Though she was fifty-seven, she did not look a day over forty-four. She was tall, about five foot eleven. While not thick or stout, her body was full and firm. Her hair had not turned white but was streaked with white. Her skin, while not the creamy smoothness of a teenage girl's or young woman's and starting to show faint beginnings of an older woman's skin and complexion, had not gone wrinkled or saggy. She had no age spots. Her breasts, while not as ample as Wanda's and flatter and less projecting than Wanda's, were generous in their own country-matron way. While they would later be exponentially eclipsed in comparison by Wanda's, they were sufficient to catch and hold eighteen-year-old pubescent Chuck's attention—and enough for him to want to hold her to him.

People of the town wondered if Lucinda was lonely. Her face did not have a lonely look to it, nor did it carry a hard or angry look, but it was a set one. Her face had a set expression similar to Wanda's, but it didn't have a look that seemed to be looking out over a far horizon, as Wanda's face had. The only horizon Lucinda seemed to be focused on was the horizon of the town she worked in as a checkout woman in the town grocery store—the town she lived in alone, in the house left to her by her deceased parents. The house was just outside the border of the town. She had no children. With no husband, children, or secret lover to give her heart to, people of the town gossiped about her and wondered if her heart had become closed off by her isolation to the point where her heart had died.

To whatever degree her isolation was affecting her heart on a deeper level, the woman bore up under it and kept on going as if it did not affect her. There was an undercurrent of small-town speculation as to whether she was secretly lonely. But the speculation remained speculation, as she did not seem to be on the prowl for a man. She did not go to bars and was not found soliciting dates on the side from men of the town. Most of them were married anyway. The depth of her despair and loneliness, if any, and what kind of man it would take to break through the shell of her closed-off life and reach her soul remained open questions.

Lucinda lived alone on the edge of the town. Her house did not face inward toward the town. It was oriented on its long axis parallel to the main street of the town, where the business district was located. Several blocks away on either side ran the lesser roads that contained the wood-framed one- and two-story houses that lined the residential district streets. Lucinda's house was just on the other side of the last residential street out from the main street, which was called Main Street, out just beyond the outer town boundary line. With that orientation, her front door faced away from the town on an oblique angle to the town.

Being that it was on the outer boundary of the town, her house could be approached without one having to go through the town to get to it. There was a front door but no back door. There was a side door on the side of the house that faced away from the town and could not be seen from the last street out. A person could approach through the woods without being seen from the nearest street.

While Lucinda's house was not a ramshackle wreck out of a Tobacco Road setting, the house was slipping into disrepair. Neither Lucinda nor her husband, while he was there, was handy in performing the low-level maintenance and touch-up work needed to keep the physical problems of the house from spreading, metastasizing, and joining. Though the house was not falling in on itself in end-stage dissolution and decay, there were several areas that needed attention. If those areas were to grow and merge, they could eventually bring about the crumbling and downfall of the house. As it was, the need for repairs on the house would rebound to the advantage of both Chuck and Lucinda.

In his eighteenth year, after having graduated high school and after having sobered up after his drunken future-wondering celebration with his friends down by the levee that wasn't a levee, Chuck was looking to earn some extra money to go to trade school the coming fall.

Chuck was a skilled general repairman and handyman and did different kinds of pickup repair jobs when he could get them. Lucinda's house needed repairs. Chuck's mother knew her from shopping in the grocery store where Lucinda worked. Chuck's mother and Lucinda got to talking one day when there was no rush behind her in the checkout lane. Lucinda said she needed repair work done on her house. There were other handymen in the town, but they could get expensive. Lucinda did not have a lot of free cash for pricey work. Chuck's mother told Lucinda that her son was looking for work and was willing to work for reduced rates to earn money for school. Lucinda told Chuck's mother to send him around, and she would provide him with work she needed done—work that hadn't been done for her for some time.

The repairs to the house took several sessions to complete. While Chuck was doing the needed work on her house, Lucinda rewarded him with sandwiches she made for him and lemonade and soft drinks. After Chuck completed the work on her house, she brought him back to do needed lawn work; the grass needed to be mowed, and bushes needed to be trimmed. Lucinda would sit outside on a lawn chair, dressed in a short country-style skirt and a country-style blouse with a country-style flower pattern printed on it and two buttons opened at the top for comfort and ventilation. She would watch Chuck as he worked on the lawn and landscaping. She kept a pitcher of something cool for him to drink at her side, ready when he needed refreshing. She kept a second lawn chair next to hers for Chuck to sit in next to her when he was on break. As the work progressed, Lucinda would call him to take a break and come sit with her with increasing frequency.

As the work progressed, Chuck concentrated on his work, trying to do a workman-like job to please Lucinda, who was friendly toward him and did not treat him with barely disguised contempt the way some matrons treated menials. Chuck appreciated that. As the work progressed, it became his set plan to do the best job he could for Lucinda. As it was, she was setting plans of her own.

In the summer of his eighteenth year, Chuck had reached close to his maximum physical-maturity development. He was as tall as he would grow. Later years would see him fill out a bit more around the waist, but in the summer of his eighteenth year, his physical development had tightened up into what could have been called classic male-model proportions.

The last day Chuck was scheduled to work for Lucinda was hot. Chuck was working with his shirt off, trying to stay cool in the summer sun. Taking off his shirt to stay cool didn't work all that well. Even dressed only in his blue jeans with no shirt on, he was becoming soaked in sweat. Lucinda sat in her lawn chair next to the wall of her house, in the shade of the house, watching him work. Maybe she wasn't transfixed by the sight of Chuck bare-chested and sweaty, but she followed his motions closely. Even though she was sitting in the shade of the house and was not moving, she was growing a bit sweaty in her own right. If there was such a thing as sympathetic vibration between people at a distance, was there sympathetic sweat between a man and a woman at a distance?

That particular day, Lucinda wore tight country-style blue jeans and a tight country-style blouse with small flower prints on it. On her head, she wore a large, wide-brimmed matron-style hat. The shade of the house and the hat kept the direct sun off her head and face, but she was growing hot herself. She fluttered the open top of her top-buttons-unbuttoned blouse to cool her chest off. Beside her was a pitcher of lemonade. She had poured two glasses for them to drink to cool themselves off with when the final work was finished. She and Chuck were both on the side of the house facing away from the town. Nobody saw them there.

Chuck walked up to where Lucinda was sitting. As he did, she stood up.

"I'm done," Chuck said. "I'll put the tools back in the garage."

"Oh, you poor boy," Lucinda said in a coy voice. "You're all sweaty. Here. Let me cool you off."

Before Chuck could say anything, Lucinda reached down quickly and picked up the pitcher of lemonade. With an equally fast and delft move, she casually tossed the contents of the liquid in the pitcher onto Chuck's bare chest.

Chuck gasped as the icy liquid splashed against his bare chest and ran down to his stomach.

The dousing she had given him wasn't necessarily an ice-breaking moment—she had never been icy to him, and her action was not a contemptuous one but a teasing gesture among friends, something teenage girls did to teenage boys they really liked—but it set things in fluid motion.

Turnabout was fair play, even when performed on a teasing older country matron—or especially on one. In a move even quicker than Lucinda's, he reached down with one hand and picked up a full glass of lemonade with ice cubes in it. With his other hand, he reached over and pulled her loosened blouse forward. Then he proceeded in kind to dump the glass of lemonade and ice cubes down the front of her blouse. Lucinda gasped as loudly as Chuck had as the icy liquid ran down her front inside her blouse. At the line of the country-style leather belt she wore, the liquid ran farther down over her legs, staining her blue jeans a darker shade of blue. Inside her blouse, the ice cubes got hung up halfway down by the tightness of her blouse.

"Oh, you naughty boy," Lucinda said as she tried to work the ice cubes free. She found it necessary to open all the buttons on her blouse.

Chuck assumed she was going to shake the ice cubes out. Instead, she pulled the blouse all the way off and held it to the side in one hand. She was wearing a semisheer bra that outlined the smooth shapes that lay beneath to be outlined.

"Now we're both wet all over. We'll have to go inside to dry off. It's cooler inside than out here in the sun."

Chuck figured they could both dry off faster outside in the sun. He wasn't sure the house would be any cooler inside. The house didn't have any air-conditioning, not central air or a window unit.

Lucinda took Chuck's hand in hers and squeezed it. There was as much a feeling of need in the way she held his hand as there was a sense of her giving him direction. She turned and headed into the house, using the out-of-sight side door. Chuck said nothing and followed her into her house with her holding his hand all the way.

Chuck had never been in her house. The inside of the house was a bit cooler but only because the windows had thick curtains she kept partially drawn to keep out the full sun. Lucinda led him across what he took to be a central living room, with bare wood floors partially covered by large area rugs. He saw a couch and two stuffed chairs that looked as if they were becoming threadbare. Some of the boards of the floor must have worked partially loose. The boards squeaked as they walked over them at the quick pace Lucinda set.

Off to one side of the room was a flight of stairs going up. The wooden stairs were carpeted, but the carpeting looked thin and worn from long use without replacement. Tugging on his hand, Lucinda led Chuck up the stairs. The wood of the stairs also creaked at their passage. Chuck made a mental note to nail down the loose boards of the house.

At the top of the stairs, Lucinda led Chuck down a similarly carpeted hallway and turned him into what appeared to be an upstairs hall bathroom. On the opposite wall was a sink. Above the sink was a large bathroom mirror. With Chuck standing behind her, Lucinda looked at their reflections in the mirror. Chuck couldn't tell if she was looking at herself, at him, or at both of them.

Lucinda picked up a towel and started to pat her chest dry. "Unsnap my bra," she said. "It's wet too. I need to change it. But that's for later. Right now, I have something else I have to attend to."

Chuck hesitated a moment. Another mark had been reached. Another level had been passed. It was a day of level passing. They were coming at him at fast. Being the gentleman that he was, Chuck could not say no to a woman in need.

Trying to figure out how women's bra straps worked often was frustrating for men. They were often far more complicated than they needed to be. Fumbling with them could make a man seem like a dork. It could be a moment killer, especially if he pinched the woman with her own bra snap.

Fortunately for Chuck, Lucinda's bra was a simple and straightforward single-strap arrangement with a single catch. He figured she was accustomed to snapping and unsnapping it with a simple deft move. It should have been an easy thing for her to manipulate.

Chuck's fingers trembled a bit as he reached to do what she had asked. As he fumbled with the catch, he wasn't sure why she had asked him to do for her what she could have easily done for herself after she had him leave the room. He wondered why she wanted him to stay.

The simple catch came apart as it had been designed to do. The two sides of the bra separated and fell off to the sides. Without unsnapping the shoulder straps, Lucinda pulled the bra all the way off. Her sag-free, wrinkle-free mature breasts came into full view, reflected in the mirror she was standing in front of. With a quick move, she tossed her bra onto the floor to the side. She was now fully naked to the waist.

"Hold me by the waist with both hands," she said. "I'm afraid I might fall if I lean too far forward."

Chuck's mouth kind of moved, but no words came out. Like the helpful, supportive-of-women, newly minted man he was, Chuck placed his hands on the naked skin of her sides, one on each side, and held her softly but firmly. As he touched and held her sides, he felt a kind of tremble go through his hands. He wasn't sure if he had trembled or if she had. Or both.

Lucinda leaned inward over the sink. She reached over the counter and picked up a tube of lipstick. As Chuck held her, she opened the tube and started to apply the lipstick. It was a bright red color. She put it on thickly. Chuck assumed that putting on lipstick while he held her to keep her from falling was the other service she wanted him to perform for her.

When she was done applying the lipstick, she leaned back. For a moment, she said nothing.

"Move closer to me," she said finally.

The surprised, dutiful Chuck did what she wanted. He moved to where his naked chest was pressing against her naked back. At the feel of his full-length, body-pressing touch, she sort of sighed and leaned back against him tighter. Her hair hung down.

"Kiss my neck," she said in a hushed voice. She moved her head to the side, as if to give him room to reach her neck with his lips better.

That day, he had been taken through two doors he had not gone through before. A third door was opening for him. But at that open–door moment, Chuck paused. He didn't know where she was taking him. He didn't particularly care. But he was still a gentleman.

"I've been as busy as I can be in throwing myself at you," Lucinda said in a frustrated-sounding tone. "I'm making myself as obvious as I can without begging. I was trying to be subtle about it, hoping you would get my drift without my having to tell you. Now I'm saying out loud that I'm yours for the taking, and I'm saying it out in the open. But you seem to be missing what I'm saying. Why are you holding back? Don't you want me?"

"Ah, no," Chuck stammered, "it's not that. I just didn't want you to think I was taking liberties with you."

"They're my liberties," she said in a decisive voice rising from the hushed voice she had been using. "They're my liberties to give and take and be taken. No one takes them from me. I give them when I want to who I want. From the first moment I saw you, I wanted to take you to me. When I saw you today out in the yard with your shirt off and sweaty, I wanted you more than I could control or wanted to control. Are you a virgin? Have you made love to any of the girls in your school?"

The girls in his small high school were few and far between. Half of them were hard to approach and off-putting. The other half were annoyingly giggly or prone to chewing bubble gum and popping bubbles, even in class. The teachers would make them swallow their gum.

Gentleman that Chuck was, he respected all girls and women, as his father had taught him to do. He never tried to cop a feel of any of the girls in high school. He never snapped their bra straps—he figured they wouldn't like it but had a feeling they secretly did.

"Ah, no," Chuck said, trying not to stammer. "On both accounts. I'm not much interested in the girls in school. The girls in my school are so immature and giggly."

He wondered if Lucinda was looking for an experienced man to share her liberties with. For all he knew, upon hearing of his inexperience and learner's status, she would send him out her side door.

"Could you take an older woman as a lover?"

"Ah, from knowing the girls in school, I've come to want more maturity in a woman than I've ever found in them. I could take an older woman as a lover."

"Even one as old as I am?" she asked, still facing their combined reflections in the mirror. "A woman thirty-seven years older than you? Or would you feel like you were making love to your mother?"

"My mother is fifteen years younger than you," Chuck said. He was immediately embarrassed by what he'd said. A gentleman never asked a woman her age or compared a woman's age to another woman's age to her face.

"Your mother's older sister then," she said. "Would it revolt you to make love to me? Would you think of me as a dirty old woman who's starved for love? I'm both. I just don't usually advertise it like I'm doing now. Would you go running out the door and leave me alone and never come back to me again?"

Chuck wasn't sure what his feelings toward her were. He knew he would be leaving town soon enough. His feelings about how much he wanted to keep seeing her and whether he would come back to her the next day or in the future were still in flux.

"You will be leaving me soon enough to go off to your technical school. Will I never see a trace of you after that?"

It was all moving rather fast—too fast for his feelings to have gelled. Chuck still wasn't sure what his feelings for her were. He wasn't sure if what he felt for her was love or how deep his love for her really went.

"You said you wanted to make love with me when you saw me in the backyard a short while ago," Chuck said. He wasn't sure whether he was trying to convince her or convince himself. "I knew from the first time I saw you that I wanted to be close to you. I will come to you again before I go off to school. We will be close then. After I get my education, graduate, get a job, and become established, I will come back to you."

He said "to you," but he didn't say "for you."

"By that time, I'll probably be seventy-seven years old," Lucinda said. "If I'm even still alive by then. If you come back to me then to look for me, you'll probably find me in a grave. Even if I am still alive, I have a hard time imagining you coming back for a woman my age. You'll probably just go on from where you're standing and keep on going farther away from me. You'll never come back to me again, unless you come back to leave a flower on my grave."

Chuck wanted to say something reassuring to her but wasn't sure he had the words to speak or could come up with any words that wouldn't sound hollow, empty, and lying. Lucinda saw him in the mirror as he opened his mouth, to say what he knew not. She held up her hand to cut him off.

"No more words," she said. "Words are so hollow. They fade and disappear as soon as they're spoken. The time for words is over. No more empty words. No more words that sound assuring and understanding.

Let's just take ourselves to the understanding we came up here to get ourselves to."

She put her hands on his hands holding her above the waist. She gripped his wrists tightly. "Now kiss me like I want you to," she said. She tipped her head to the side again to expose her neck. "Kiss me like you want nothing better than to kiss me and keep kissing me. Kiss me like a lover. Kiss me like you love me, even if you don't."

Chuck couldn't say no to a sad-faced, lonely-sounding woman in sexual need, even one 3.66 times his age, nor could he say no to the need rising in his hormone-charged pubescent body. He buried his face in Lucinda's neck and started rapidly kissing her neck and shoulder on that side. His kisses became heavier and wetter. At midlevel elevation, his grip on her midriff became tighter. Down at ground level, Lucinda kicked off her shoes, one to either side. Back up at midlevel, she fumbled distractedly with and unbuckled her big country-style belt buckle. The loose ends of the belt fell to the sides, removing one small obstacle to deeper involvement in a situation that was fast becoming a growing loose end.

As Chuck continued his accelerated kissing of her shoulder, neck, and cheek, her sighs rose to small gasps and then to midlevel gasps. She stepped up rubbing her naked back against his naked chest. Through his hands, he could feel the workings of the muscles of her midriff as she moved.

For Chuck, time became sort of a blur. Per Lucinda's instructions, he kept kissing her as if he really wanted to. Which he did. He kept kissing her as if he really meant it. Which he did. For an indeterminate length of time, he stood with his bare front pressed up against her naked back and continued kissing her neck, shoulders, and upper back while holding her at her midriff. Despite her age, he did not find a second of what he was doing to be distasteful.

Then the pattern changed. Lucinda grabbed his hands and pulled them off her body. For a second, Chuck wondered if she was about to tell him to go away and throw him out. But instead, she moved his hands down to where her tight blue jeans began. There she hooked his thumbs inside her pants and panties and started to push his hands and her clothing down, wiggling her hips as her jeans and panties passed over them. That she had unbuckled her belt earlier allowed her to do it without pausing to unbuckle her belt. With Chuck's hands in tow, she pushed her clothes past her knees, where she let them fall the rest of the way to the floor, where she kicked them off to the side, as she had done with her blouse and bra.

Lucinda stood up quickly. Before Chuck could casually examine the full length of her nakedness, she wrapped her arms tightly around him and pulled herself up against him. Her mature, soft, and pointed but not saggy breasts flattened out against his chest. At the feel of her warm body and soft skin against him, Chuck's sensations and feelings went sort of blurry again. He had heard the some women threw themselves at men. If this was what it was like to have her throwing herself at him like a baseball outfielder throwing a long ball to home plate, he would play on her team and in her outfield anytime.

Lucinda kissed him long, hard, and deep. She worked her lips around and back and forth over his. He could taste the lipstick she had put on thickly a few minutes ago. For several long minutes, she held the movable feast of her kiss on his lips.

Just as quickly as she had begun, she broke her kiss and pulled her head back. For a moment, she tipped her head downward. Chuck wondered if she was embarrassed by what she had done. Then she looked decisively back up.

"OK, there you have it," she said in a decisive tone with the pace of her words increasing. "There you have me. I'm a dirty, shameless old slut. I suppose I should be ashamed of myself for what I'm doing with you, but I'm not. I'm too old to be shamefaced about anything. I'm a tired woman. I'm tired of being old. I feel dried up and dried out. I'm tired in knowing that my best days are behind me and that all I have to look forward to is getting older and more tired. I'm tired of wondering what people are thinking and probably saying about me. I'm tired of working the same job, where I'll probably die behind the checkout counter. I'm tired of rattling around in an empty house. I'm tired of hearing the sound of my own footsteps but no one else's. I'm tired of hearing the sound of my own voice and no other voice answering me. I'm tired of being alone. I'm tired of being lonely. I'm tired of hearing my own voice in my head. I'm tired of not seeing much of anything coming my way in the future. I'm tired of not having any love coming my way. If it did come my way, I don't know if I have love to give back."

For a woman who said she didn't want to hear any more words, she was coming up with a lot of words.

"I want my old life back. I want something better than my old life. I want to be young again. At least I want to feel young again, even if I'm not. I just want to feel something worth feeling. I want to feel like I can feel again. I want to love and be loved. I want young love or at least what feels like young love. I want a young lover. You will be gone from me and over the horizon soon enough. You will probably forget me as soon as you are over that horizon. You will be a horizon of my memory that I will probably carry close to me always. Be close to me, if only once before you're gone."

Chuck didn't know if he loved her. He didn't know how many more moments they might have together in the future. All he knew at that passing moment was that he couldn't stand to see her sad.

"After you're gone—"

Chuck put his hand softly over her mouth. "No more words, beautiful naked lady I'm about to give myself to as a lover. Take me, and possess me. Make me yours. You've shown me your body. Now show me your heart and the heart of your love."

Wordlessly, Lucinda took his hand and led him through the side door of the washroom, which led into a bedroom the washroom was joined to. In the middle of the room, with its large headboard up against the wall, was a king-sized bed. The bed was sturdy looking, neither baroque fancy nor a secondhand thrift-store look.

Lucinda tugged on Chuck's hand for him to come with her. She didn't have to tug hard. Since the morning, things had been moving fast. Chuck didn't know where things were moving to, beyond the obvious. But they were in motion.

Alongside the bed, Lucinda let go of Chuck's hand. She reached over and grabbed the blanket on the bed. With a quick flourish, she tossed the blanket and the top sheet under it off onto the floor, leaving a large pillow at the head of the bed. She climbed into the bed and lay down with her head on the pillow. She held her arms outstretched toward him in a beckoning way with her hands open. Chuck's interest in what was about to take place was rising—along with something else.

Chuck came up to the side of the bed. He quickly pulled down his pants and underpants. When he went to pull them the rest of the way off, he realized he couldn't get them past his shoes and would have to take off his shoes so he could pull his pants the rest of the way off. He bent down and hopped around clumsily, taking his shoes and socks off, shifting from one side to the other, standing first on one foot and then the other, trying to stay balanced on one leg at a time and keep from falling over. He figured that to an outside observer, he wouldn't have looked at all like a suave and practiced seducer. But he was new to this and new to undressing in the heat of the moment, trying to catch up with a lover out ahead of him.

Chuck climbed into the bed, kicking off a sock he hadn't gotten all the way off, which was hanging on his toe. Lucinda was in the center of the bed. He had to scramble across several feet of the bed to get to her. As he moved toward her, she spread her legs and held her arms out toward him. She knew what was about to transpire. She had made love before. She had been there before, probably in the same bed.

It was daylight outside, but she had drawn the shades to keep out the hot sun. The un-air-conditioned room wasn't as hot as it could have been, not hot enough to raise an immediate sweat. That would come later with exertion.

Regarding the kind of relating he was about to engage in, Chuck was a neophyte. But he wasn't totally wet behind the ears—except for a lingering trace of lemonade. He had heard talk on the streets. He had talked about it with the other boys in school and during drinking bouts down by the levees. He had seen pictures in dirty magazines of the kind his mother would not allow in the house. He knew the anatomical basics. His positional estimate was just initially a bit off.

Chuck drove his stiffened pubescent manhood downward toward the position where he estimated he would come into position inside her. Instead of plunging into a deep shaft of warm wetness that seemed to go on forever, his pubescent male extension pushed up against soft flesh that yielded a bit but would not open up for him.

"Silly boy," Lucinda said in a coy and almost giggling but mature voice. "You've set your sights too high. Where the key to me and my availability begins starts lower than that."

Chuck lowered his extended position to a lower level and drove himself forward. This time, he felt himself plunge into the deep channel of warm, soft wetness he had expected to encounter. He and Lucinda both gasped at the unexpected surge of pleasure they experienced. He had heard sex was supposed to feel good, especially the first time, but he hadn't known it could feel that good. In a spasm of pleasure, Lucinda arched her back up, rising up under him with enough force to lift him up with her rising. Her arms wrapped tightly around him. Her hands gripped his back. Her fingers dug into his skin.

"Take me!" she cried out. "Take me as a lover. Take me as a slut. Take me as you would take a girl your age that you sat next to in school and longed for. Take me as a lonely woman. Take me as a dirty old woman who needs love. Take me for whatever kind of woman you want to take me for. Take me as I am. Just take me, and keep on taking me!"

Thus, they were off to the races, with Chuck racing to thrust himself deeper into her, Lucinda racing to thrust herself up against him, and both of them racing to fill their bodies, hearts, and souls with each other, racing into each other, where they merged with each other in the gap that wasn't there. Chuck strained. Lucinda gasped, cried out, and made unintelligible pleasure sounds.

"Oh yes!" she gasped, breaking her stream of otherwise unintelligible passion. "Oh yes, I remember this! It's all coming back to me. I haven't gone so dead in my body and mind that I can't remember what it was like when it was real. It's becoming real for me again. Love is real again."

She went back to her undecipherable emoting. Her body shuddered and surged.

"Love me!" she gasped out after a short interval of silence. "Love me, love me, love me, love me. Love me like the lover you've made me again. Love me like a princess. Love me like a slut. I'll be either of them for you. I'll be both of them for you. Love me like the shameless woman I am. I'll be your shameless slut. You can love me like the shameless woman I'll make myself for you. Just keep loving me!"

People often said time stood still at moments like that. Einstein said that time was always in (relative) motion. Chuck couldn't really say that time stood still for him. At that particular moment of time- and dimension-crossing intensity, he wasn't thinking about time or Einstein's time–space continuum. He wasn't thinking of any continuum other than Lucinda in his arms in her bed in her room. He needed no other continuum. To the exclusion of time, the rest of the world, and what his future horizon might hold, Chuck's horizons came down to the room he was in, the bed he was in, and the woman he held in his arms.

As far as time went, in the back of his mind, Chuck knew he could not spend the extended amount of time he wanted to spend with her. His mother knew he had planned to go to Lucinda's house to finish the last of the jobs he was doing for her. If he stayed too long, she might grow suspicious. She might confront Lucinda, asking why and how she had detained her son for so long on what was supposed to be a short workday. Tongues could start to wag. Fingers could be wagged at both him and Lucinda.

"Love me now. Love me like there's no tomorrow, and I'll be yours here and now like our time will never end."

As far as time continuums and continuing beyond the now that enveloped them, in the back of his otherwise engaged mind, a question pushed its way into his mind as to where his suddenly arrived at affair with her would or could go and where taking it any further would leave both of them. Chuck wondered how far he was going to go in continuing to see her. For all he knew, she might fall in love with him. For all he knew, she might already have been in love with him. For all he knew, she might have been thinking of marriage with him. For all he knew, he might fall in love with her.

For all Chuck knew, she might come to think of him in terms of age- and social-convention-bucking marriage material. For all he knew, she might already have been thinking of him in those terms. That she might come to want to do a winter–spring marriage could prove problematic all around but more for him than her.

If they were married, or if a marriage was forced, she might feel she had recaptured what she had lost and thought she would never regain; she would have love with the young lover of her older-woman dreams. Her future would be secure. His planned future would be redirected, disrupted, and derailed. He could end up in a dead-end job in a dead-end life in a dead-end town, the husband or kept man and lover of a woman 3.166 times older than he was. As a future technician who valued accuracy in all things, Chuck would later calculate the number to several decimal places of accuracy—they turned out to be all 6s.

In another back lobe of his mind, Chuck realized that a way out of the possible pending dilemma was already in place, functional, and about to kick in. In a few days, he would be going off to the technical school he was enrolled in. That alone would take him out of the picture, and any picture Lucinda might have of a future with him, for two years at least. By that time, her possible ardor for him might have cooled, leaving him off the hook of her expectations and hopes. After a sufficient interval of time had passed, she would not be as hurt as she would have been if he dumped her tomorrow. What hopes she might have been entertaining or might come to entertain in the future of his coming back to her would slowly fade.

Chuck felt dirty that he was thinking in terms of breaking it off with her and putting distance between himself and a lover he had just started up with that day. But the horizon of his life was calling. It was a horizon far bigger than the confines of the small town that was his home. It was a horizon he did not want to jettison, not even for a woman who might have been in love with him.

His conflicted emotions left him feeling somehow dirty. He wasn't sure what would be dirtier: leaving her with no hope of his ever coming back to her or leaving her with false hope that he would come back, when he knew he probably wouldn't.

"Love me like there's no tomorrow, and I'll love you for all my tomorrows."

As the strain built up in his mind, the strain in his body ramped up exponentially. With an uncontrollable, rushing surge, his love for her, as dubious and equivocal as it was, exploded inside her in a gushing surge of hot liquid passion. Chuck tensed uncontrollably. His hands gripped her tighter. Her hands gripped him tighter. A deep groan of release escaped uncontrollably from his mouth, from deep in his throat.

For almost a minute, he remained tensed in the clinch he was caught in, as if he were paralyzed. Then the wave of contraction passed, and Chuck fell exhausted onto Lucinda. The sweat of their mutual exertion blended together between them.

There followed a long moment of silence broken only by their mutual heavy breathing.

"Now see what you've done, you naughty boy?" Lucinda said, breaking her silence and the silence in the room. In the darkened room, Chuck couldn't see much of anything, let alone the horizon. "You've made me feel alive again. You've made me feel loved again. You've made me feel like a woman again. If you keep this up, I may fall in love with you."

Chuck lay his head down next to her head, with his face toward her upturned face. For a while, he kissed her cheek. She sighed and continued to caress his back.

As Chuck lay there with Lucinda in her bed, his thoughts didn't take flight; they just sort of drifted. His thoughts drifted over no horizon in particular. They drifted back over his graduation, the graduation he hadn't gotten laid after. They drifted back to the time after graduation when he and his friends had sat by the levee, drinking whiskey and beer and wondering what their futures would be. His mind drifted out over the horizon, out toward further horizons dim and uncertain.

The next thing Chuck felt was someone poking him in the ribs.

"Wake up, you naughty boy," Lucinda said. "Don't fall asleep on me. It's all very romantic. I enjoy that you love me enough and think of me enough not to have jumped up out of bed and gone running off as soon as you were finished, but you've got to get up, get dressed, and get yourself back home before your mother comes here kicking down my door with a whipping switch in her hands, looking to use it on both of us, shouting that I'm a dirty old woman robbing the cradle and corrupting her innocent son."

Chuck started to stir and move off her.

"Neither of us needs to get that kind of reputation stuck on us. It will stick with both of us like a tar baby for the rest of our lives."

What happened in a small town stayed in the small town. The trouble was that it often stuck around forever.

"Given that you're going away to school, you'll be out and away from all the nasty rumors that might go flying around and the gossip and bad reputations and pointing fingers that could come about if it's discovered that we're lovers. I'll be stuck in the middle of it like a fly caught on flypaper. You'll be out of here, over the horizon."

Chuck pulled himself out of her and sat up on the bed beside her.

"You'll be beyond the horizon of this town. Back here in this town, the horizon will close in on me."

Chuck thought he should say something. It was only properly romantic to say something to the lover one was about to say goodbye to and leave behind. But the words would not come.

"Don't say anything, you silly boy," Lucinda said as Chuck opened his mouth. They stood together by the open side door to the house, the door that was out of sight from the street, the door he would go out through but probably never come back through. "As I said, the time for words is over. Time to go our separate ways. We were never on one way together. I'll stay here in the town. You just go your own way and keep on going."

As the realization that he probably would never come back to her, at least in the near term, set in on him, Chuck felt he had to say something. "As I said," Chuck said, "after I complete my education, get a job, and get established, I may very well come back to you."

"As I say again," Lucinda said, "the time for words is over, especially for words you don't mean or for words you won't act on when the times comes, even if you think you mean them now. You and I both know you won't be coming back to me. I know you won't be coming back to me. You may come back now and then to visit your parents but not to me as a suitor or as a lover. That's a road too far. There's too much distance between us for that to happen. You just go your way and put more distance between us. While you're at it, put distance between you and me in your mind. I will remember you. In time, you will forget me. You may remember me and think of me from time to scattered time, but from here on out, I will remain a distant and fading horizon to you. That's the way it should be. That's the way it will remain. Now, get going. The rest of your life is out over the horizon, waiting for you. Instead of embracing me any further, go out and embrace your life."

Lucinda kissed Chuck and eased him out through the open door. Chuck said nothing. He went out and away without looking back to see if she was watching him or if she had closed the door.

In the few days remaining before he left for school, Chuck did not visit Lucinda again. He went away to school as planned. He studied straight through, not taking any time off to return home during breaks. He graduated in the top of his class in technical school and was hired immediately by the phone company. After he finished his education, in the short time before he started working for the phone company, he came back to his hometown to visit his parents. While he was there, he did not make any attempt to contact Lucinda or even tell her he was around.

As it turned out, Lucinda died suddenly of a heart attack during Chuck's first year as a roving technician. She was in her early sixties at the time, but her heart had weakened faster than the rest of her body. His mother, who was unaware of the affair he had had with Lucinda, casually mentioned it to him in a phone call he made to home. Chuck made a mental note to put flowers on her grave the next time he was in his hometown, but he was not sure when that would be.

Chuck eventually got married to and later divorced from the unfaithful woman who betrayed him and played him fast and loose with more than one man, playing around in secret, taking her lovers in the shadows and not coming out in the open about it. In light of what he discovered his wife was doing, he eventually gave up on finding any kind of love for a lifetime. Eventually, he came to think the only home he would ever have was the road. He didn't like the thought but came to accept that was the way it would be for him. He accepted it but took no pleasure in the thought of a life on the road. In due time, he would meet a woman who would make him again think of love for a lifetime and a home off the road. But he would pin his hopes for a life off the road on a woman whose life was on the road and who sought no other life.

Chuck's memories of Lucinda faded over time. In time, he met, married, and divorced his unfaithful wife. After that, he more or less lived a vagabond drifter's life, going from one remote installation and maintenance job to another.

In the rebound of his wife's unfaithfulness, Chuck eventually gave up on finding any kind of love for a lifetime and a home to go with it. To replace the home he had lost, Chuck made the road and his unsettled rambling as a repair technician on the road into a replacement home and substitute life.

Chuck didn't hate his vagabond life on the road. He found the road to be a great place to go to forget the past. On the downside, open roads and open horizons reminded him of how open-ended and hollow his life had become. He did not exalt in his days on the road. Eventually, he came to think the only home he would ever have would be the road. He didn't like the thought but came to accept that was the way it would be for him.

He accepted but took no pleasure in the thought of a life on the road. In due time, in a bar far from home on the open road, he would meet a woman who made him again think of love for a lifetime and a home off the road. But he would pin his hope for a life off the road on a woman whose life was on the road and who gloried in her life on the road.

11

After he finished washing, Chuck brushed his teeth quickly. He didn't have any of the minty-fresh toothpaste. Regular toothpaste would have to do. At least it would take the lingering beer breath out of his mouth. He wouldn't taste like a redneck when the woman kissed him—if she actually arrived to kiss him. But then again, the taste of beer hadn't stopped her from kissing him in the bar.

Chuck walked back into the main part of the hotel room and checked his watch. It had been about twenty minutes since he left the bar. He was still under the half-hour time frame in which the woman had said she would meet him in his room. He paused, thinking of which shirt he should put on. He hadn't brought any dress clothes, and he hadn't brought a David Niven smoking jacket and white ascot. He hadn't thought he would be eating at any dining establishment more high tone than Burger King or a Ponderosa Steak House, nor had he anticipated that he would be entertaining ladies in his hotel room. He didn't have anything fancy from a country-and-western fashion-statement standpoint. The woman was a fashionable lady who worked for a fashion company, despite how sparse and limited in material their creations functionally were. Chuck didn't have anything fashionable to wear for the upcoming night's encounter, if the encounter and the woman actually materialized.

Chuck had only the working-class clothes of a working-class man out on the road on assignment. The only fashion statement he could offer the fashionable woman was a clean shirt he hadn't driven all day in. As limited as his street clothes were, they were a lot more fashionable than his phone company uniform.

Chuck hoped the woman wouldn't think that he was somehow devaluing her or treating her in a coarse and casual way or that he thought of her as a cheap barroom pickup because he hadn't changed into clothing with more savoir faire to it. But then again, the end point of the encounter was to get both of them out of their clothes. He was afraid she might get turned off by his street clothes and leave before things got to the removal-of-clothing stage—if she actually showed up to remove anything.

As Chuck considered which shirt to put on, another series of fantasies about the woman in various levels of high and low fashion came into his mind.

The woman had told him that as a teenager, she rode as backseat auxiliary to motorcycle-riding bad boys. Chuck's imagination cued in on and embellished the scene as he added himself to the picture. In his imagination, he was the Marlon Brando wild one in black leather on the driver's seat of a big Harley hog. His backseat—and motel room—traveling companion was a slightly younger version of the woman. It was a hot and sunny day on the open road. Instead of the oxblood-colored leathers she had been dressed in at the bar, the woman was dressed in black leather pants with a black leather bikini top and black high-heeled leather boots. She wobbled in a somewhat unstable manner on her boots when she walked. Up top, she wobbled dangerously close to falling out of her tight leather top.

In Chuck's budding imagination, she climbed onto the backseat and wrapped her arms around him. In the press of her grip, even through his own leather jacket, he could feel the outline of her leather top. He could also feel the outline of everything beneath her leather bikini top. They started off down the road.

A few miles later, on a deserted stretch of road, the woman reached up with one hand and unzipped his leather jacket. She started rubbing his chest with both hands. Distractions like that could cause a guy to dump a bike. Chuck decided that for safety's sake, he should fulfill the woman's building desire before they ran off the road head-on at sixty miles an hour. As they passed an area with high bushes, Chuck turned the bike off the road. Concealed from the road in the bushes, he took the woman's hand and helped her off the bike. It was a familiar routine they had done before. As per the usual routine, the woman led Chuck to a spot she chose.

With leathers, the tighter they were, the harder they were to get off. The woman thrashed around, trying to pull her tight leather pants off. They got hung up on her full hips. Chuck imagined himself sitting on the ground by her feet as he worked to pull her tight leather down over her feet while she sat on the ground across from him, trying to push her pants down.

Also with leathers, Chuck figured the pressure of wearing them put pressure on one's bladder, making him or her have to go frequently. Wherever they were heading on the road, it would take them a long time to get there if they had to make a pit stop every twenty miles, not to go to the bathroom or to service the bike but to service the woman's needs, sexual or bathroom-break-wise. It would be sunset before they even got out of the county.

From sunset on the open road, Chuck's imagination switched to a Sunset Boulevard scene. Instead of being a rodeo queen, the woman was an established and famous blonde actress from the classic era of 1930s through 1950s Hollywood who lived on Rodeo Drive or in Bel Air—a Lauren Bacall, Lana Turner, Marilyn Maxwell, Veronica Lake, Mamie Van Doren, Diana Dors, Jayne Mansfield, Lili Saint Cyr, Kim Novak, Barbara Nichols, Anita Ekberg, Virginia Dale, Marie Wilson, Cleo Moore, Carol Landis, Joan Blondell, or Betty Grable.

In the Tinseltown landscape of Chuck's fantasy, he was an upcoming young actor she had taken to be her lover and kept man. He and the woman were standing on the second-floor balcony of her seafront mansion overlooking the Pacific Ocean at night, looking at the moon on the sea. They had just returned from being seen publicly at the Brown Derby or some other Hollywood spot where they would undoubtedly become an item in tabloids and gossip columns the next day. The woman was dressed in an exquisite evening gown with a dangerously plunging neckline. Around her neck, she wore an exquisite, and exquisitely expensive, diamond collar necklace. Chuck was dressed in a tuxedo. The moonlight danced on the waves. A warm ocean breeze was blowing over them. The curtains next to the door waved in the breeze. They had handed out standard statements to gossip reporters at the restaurant.

No more public or private words had to be said. In the wash of the warm Pacific breeze, the slightly older version of the woman turned to Chuck; wrapped her long, cinematic arms around him; and locked him in an extended, cinematic kiss. The two of them then turned and walked slowly across the marble floor of the bedroom to the woman's large canopy bed, which she would cast him into and from which she would proceed to cast him as her new leading man. With the flip of Chuck's hand on a single snap, her designer evening dress slipped off and collapsed around her ankles. Chuck's tuxedo was a bit more involved for the woman to remove, but she had a practiced hand at such things. The tuxedo slipped off easily enough. As the breeze coming through the open balcony door parted the silky curtains on the canopy bed, the famous blonde-bombshell actress led her upcoming male lead through the veil.

In his imagination, Chuck went back to imagining the woman as half white and half native South American, with a browner cast to her skin but blonde hair. In this incarnation, she was a sultry temptress coming out of the smoke of a riverfront bar far up the backwater of the Amazon River. Chuck imagined her with a Eurasian shape to her face. The brownness of her skin set off the blonde of her hair.

In a Western to Eastern Hemisphere shift, in his imagination, the woman became a half-white and half-Chinese dragon lady out of a 1930s movie, wearing a red silk dress slit up to the top of her thigh. She pushed aside a curtain made of oriental beads, coming to him out of the smoke of a Shanghai opium den. She was a woman he could become addicted to.

In a backshift, Chuck's imagination gave the woman back her white skin and the black leather she had worn as a motorcycle mama. He placed in her hand the riding crop she had been holding in his imagined English-equestrian-woman incarnation. Except she wasn't an upper-class English-landed-gentry mistress coming at him in a horse stall. This time, she was the headmistress of an S&M club, coming at him dressed in a semi-see-through bodysuit with the size and coverage of a woman's one-piece bathing suit, a modern-day Betty Page ready to dominate or be dominated, whichever direction her needs were running that particular night. The high-gloss bodysuit had the color and liquid shine of licorice. The semitransparent material seemed closer to a thin layer of opaque plastic than cloth. The semitransparency of the bodysuit outlined everything underneath in detail and left little to the imagination.

The woman wore shiny, thigh-high black leather boots with high heels with pointed toes. Around her neck, she wore a black leather collar with pointed metallic studs mounted in it. She wore long black leather gloves that also had metal studs mounted on them. In her hand, she carried the symbol of her authority as headmistress at the S&M club. It was also the instrument of her method of persuasion and the means with which she satisfied the special cravings that people attended the club to have satisfied in the half-light of the club, out of the limelight of the world. Chuck originally thought the symbol of authority in her hand was a riding crop.

Upon closer inspection, he could see she was holding a braided leather whip.

Chuck caught himself once again. He was really losing it. As his fantasy vision faded, he grabbed the whip from the hand of his kinky S&M fantasy woman and used it to perform self-flagellation on his pretensions. The woman wasn't going to show up. He should have known that from the moment she separated herself from him and left him in the bar. She had been fooling him all along and stringing him along the way his wife had fooled him and strung him along from day one. He had done the main fool job on himself by thinking she was actually attracted to him.

For the woman, it had probably been only a casual and momentary dalliance. When he had responded seriously, she had started looking for a way to back herself out of something she didn't want to go any deeper into. She did not want to have him go deep in her. Everything she had said about coming up to his room had been a ruse to keep him in place while she got away. His wife had been willing to sacrifice their marriage to be rid of him. The woman had probably been so anxious to get away from him that she had been willing to sacrifice her cowgirl hat as a decoy in order to get away.

Chuck kind of laughed to himself. He stopped thinking about which shirt to put on. The woman wasn't coming. There wouldn't be any coming in the hotel room that night. His pretensions had made him think his male looks would make her come to him and would make something come of the night. His pretension of being a masculine stud who could hold a woman hadn't been born out. Chuck had thought he had banished all pretenses and fanciful thinking from his mind and life. Now his fantasies and pretensions were suddenly sprouting all over the place like mushrooms on a damp lawn. He had let his pretensions slip back in to his life as he allowed himself to believe in the bar that the woman would actually come up to his hotel room to service him. He should have learned from his wife that his pretensions didn't service him well at all.

In his surge of reality thinking, Chuck figured he might as well leave his shirt off, pour himself a drink from the bar he would be sharing with no one, and drown the last of his pretensions. If he couldn't drown them, he would sit there with his drink in hand and play bop the gopher with any pretension or wild imagination that popped up. He might as well start with his vision of the woman as a kinky S&M mistress, he thought. If any of the recently budded crop of fantasies and pretensions needed to be knocked down like a sprouting toadstool, it was that one. He could otherwise make use of the imaginary whip he had grabbed from the hand of his imaginary lady. Why not? An imaginary whip would be in line to beat down his imaginary pretensions.

As Chuck raised the whip to administer the coup de grâce to his pretensions, there was a knock at the door.

For an instant, he froze in place, wondering if things like this really did happen in the world. Then, without regard for the shirt he wasn't wearing, he headed quickly over to the door. As he walked to the door, he figured it was just the maid looking to turn down the bed in his room. She was probably late on her rounds and was doing the top floor last.

At the door, Chuck looked through the peephole. Outside the door, rounded and distorted by the magnifying lens of the peephole, he could see a face with large eyes and full lips framed by a mane of long blonde hair. The rounding effect of the peephole lens made the woman's breasts seem even rounder and fuller. Maybe things like that did happen in the world.

As if the vision would pop like a child's soap bubble or the woman would turn and disappear if she didn't get an immediate response, Chuck yanked the door open. He opened it so fast he ran it into his foot. Fortunately, he was wearing his heavy work boots. The boot absorbed the shock. Otherwise, he would have stubbed his toe hard. It was still a hard enough bump to make Chuck pull his foot back as if he had jammed his toe. He shifted his body back to make room for the door to swing open. When he opened the door, he saw the woman from the bar, sans cowgirl hat. She was wearing flat-soled shoes instead of the red high heels she had been wearing in the bar when Chuck massaged her tired feet. She had also taken her hoop earrings off and put her lipstick back on.

"Ah, hello," Chuck said. His Cary Grant suaveness was a bit rusty. "Come on in."

Chuck stood half concealed behind the door. The woman of his visions, who was now a lot closer than any vision and was a lot closer to becoming his reality, walked into the room.

"Well, I seem to have gotten the right room number," Wanda said as she walked casually over the threshold of vision and into the reality of Chuck's hotel room. "I'm not dyslexic, but sometimes I do transpose numbers. I once took Route 96 instead of Route 69. I was halfway out of the state, heading toward the wrong city, before I realized I was on the wrong road. I wasn't fully sure if you said 817 or 871. I half expected some old biddy to come to the door, think I was soliciting, and shout at me to take my hussy self back to the street corner I usually work off of."

"I don't think there is a room 871," Chuck said in what passed for a suave rejoinder. "The hotel isn't big enough to have seventy rooms on a single floor. From the room-number directions on the wall in the hall, I think 835 is the highest room number they go up to."

He waited until she had moved beyond the range of the swing of the door. He didn't want to turn her off by slamming the door into her ankle the way he had bumped his own foot.

"Did you have any trouble getting past the front desk?" Chuck asked. He didn't know what the hotel policy was concerning guests of the hotel entertaining guests of their own in the rooms, especially when it seemed a guest was getting paid instead of the hotel. The desk clerk might have taken Wanda for a streetwalker. The way she was dressed did make her look a bit like one. Wanting to keep the hotel from getting a reputation as a hookers' haven, the desk clerk might have tried to prevent her from coming up to his room.

"Did anybody at the front desk say anything?"

"I didn't even stop at the front desk," Wanda said, as if the move had been no sweat. "I just walked in as big as life and went right to the elevator. They probably thought I was staying here. That's a little trick I picked up in the business world. If you move like you know what you're doing and you act like you own the place, people get the idea you do own the place." When it came to picking up tricks, she was as bold and as big as life. "If you move like you've got a purpose, people think you belong there. It's one of my main sales approaches and my main approach to life. You'd be surprised how much an air of confidence opens doors for you."

As she walked deeper into the room, Chuck closed the door behind them. "I took good care of your hat," he said, trying to make conversation of any kind. He was a bit beyond suaveness. "It's over there on the dresser." He pointed at the dresser on the near wall.

Wanda didn't turn around to look where he was pointing. "Just as long as you didn't sit on it or use it to catch the drain off when you changed the oil on your truck." She stood with her back to Chuck and looked around the room for a moment. "This is a nice room you've got here," she said, looking around. "As far as hotel rooms go. They must give you a better allowance where you work than I get. The expense account at my company is a bit limited. All I can afford on my company allowance is a dingy motel on the other side of town."

Wanda looked around at the lay of the room. Though it was on an upper floor, she calculated she could get out quickly in the morning. A roving girl's calculations were never done.

"Like I said in the bar," Chuck said, trying to make conversation, "the travel department at my company got me a pretty good room. The room has probably one of the best views in the town. This town isn't exactly skyscraper city. I don't know if there's any building taller than eight stories, even in the downtown business district. Probably the only thing taller around here is a grain elevator." For obvious reasons, he didn't want to add, "Or the newly completed telephone company microwave relay tower." He said, "When it's light out and the curtains are open, the view out that window is probably about the best view you can get around here."

Wanda turned around and looked at Chuck standing in all his male glory without a shirt on. "It's nowhere near as nice a view as the one I'm getting now," she said as she scanned Chuck's athletic, naked upper body and proverbial washboard abs. "About the only amenities they have at the motels I stay at are hot and cold running water. If they had rooms that offered hot men running around half naked like this room has, I'd pay the difference out of my own pocket to stay in that place."

Along with the thoughts of coming that were going through his mind, the thought came to Chuck that his appearing in the door already half naked might seem presumptions to her. She might take it that he thought he had her in the bag, in all senses of the word. Despite all she'd said about the great time she was offering to show him, she might have been put off by that kind of display of naked male chauvinistic presumption. It could turn out to be another inadvertent presumption, he thought, and presumptions had never served him well.

"I apologize for only being half dressed," Chuck said. "When you came to the door, you caught me while I was changing clothes after washing up. I hadn't put a clean shirt back on. Give me a minute, and I'll dig one out of the drawer."

Chuck remembered that his clean shirts were in the pile of clothes his phone company uniform was buried under in the dresser drawer. He would have to be careful in getting one out, or she might catch sight of his uniform and start asking questions.

"Don't bother," Wanda said in a voice both decided and suggestive. "I'll just have to rip it back off of you later. Putting a shirt back on would be a system redundancy in this case. It would be a duplication of effort, and the shirt might get shredded if I lose control and tear it off you."

With all that was going through his mind, Chuck never paused to consider that *system redundancy* wasn't a term one heard used often in the fashion industry. Granted, the guiding design ethos of the fashion industry did often have a lot to do with applying a low volume of material to the limited coverage of strategic areas with a minimal overlap of resources. But *system redundancy* was a term more often found in engineering and technical fields like the one he was in.

"Besides, I'd lose my nice view. From where I'm standing, it's a more stimulating view than the road I'm going to be looking at tomorrow. You just leave your shirt off. Let a poor love-starved country girl dream what she may."

"I didn't want to give you the idea that I was presuming on you or that I was getting ready to jump you the minute you walked in the door," Chuck said, offering apologies even though she had indicated none were needed. "After I washed up, I kind of slowed down in getting dressed. I figured you weren't coming, and there was no reason to rush. You kind of took me by surprise when you showed up when you did."

Wanda looked puzzled. Then she glanced down at her watch. Chuck didn't note that her watch wasn't one of the thin, jeweled high-fashion watches that high-fashion women wore. It was a heavier watch with several associated dials and features. It looked more like the kind of watch a gadget-crazy guy, engineer, or technician would wear.

"Why did you think I wasn't coming?" Wanda asked. "It's not like I'm running way late and behind schedule. If anything, I'm ahead of schedule. According to my watch, I got here in under the time I said it would take me. Why did you give up on me so fast?"

"It's not that I thought you couldn't tell time," Chuck said in a straightforward manner. *When suaveness fails, try honesty.* "Or that I thought you got lost and, like a guy, wouldn't ask for directions. As I was thinking about it, I just kind of started thinking that you wanted to get away from me and that you made up the whole thing about coming up to my room as a way to put me off so you could get out of the bar and get away from me. It's not like the experience is all that new or unexpected for me. I've been there before. You wouldn't be the first woman who said she loved me but was just saying it so she could get me out of the house and go on about her own business. Maybe I'm just paranoid in thinking that every woman is going to put me down. But that's pretty much the way I've been thinking for the last two years."

It seemed to Wanda's organized mind that Chuck's wife had damaged his self-confidence more than she had initially thought. She liked him, both in looks and in personality. He was self-effacing in his masculinity instead of throwing his masculinity in her face. Though she had come to his room looking to get pawed and to do some pawing of her own, the fact that he hadn't started pawing her the minute she walked through the door was actually a bigger turn-on than if he had tried to jump her the minute she walked in. Wanda felt sorry for him for what his wife had done to him. She figured he was in need of a little ego boost, and she was just the girl to give him the boost he needed. They both would get something they needed out of the night. She would just have to make it clear to him that she wasn't the ball cutter his wife had been.

The trick was to make it clear that while she wasn't like his wife, she was actually very much like his wife, and he had better not develop any presumptions that she was going to fall in love with him or become attached to him. She would also have to make it clear that he'd better not get any ideas about attaching himself to her. It was a bit of a contradiction in terms, but Wanda had handled contradictions, and men, before. It was familiar territory for her. It was ground she had walked before. It was ground she enjoyed walking. She enjoyed living her life as a contradiction.

Wanda squared her bare shoulders and looked Chuck straight in the eye. "Hey, like I said, I'm not some kind of prick tease who heats up men like a blacksmith heats up horseshoes and then gets her jollies by dropping them into cold water, where they sizzle as they cool off," she said, using a country analogy they both would be familiar with. "I say what I mean, and I mean what I say. I deliver on the promises I make. I deliver myself when I make myself a part of the promise. I take my life seriously. I take my loving anywhere I can get it, but I take my loving seriously. I don't play children's games. I play it serious, but I play it straight.

"I'm not a two-timer. I'm a one-timer for any man, but I'm an honest one-timer. I'm not the same as your wife. I'm not here cheating on my husband with you. We may both be cheating on some higher biblical morality, but I'm not cheating on you by lying to you and saying that I'm going to love you forever the way your wife promised to but had no intention of doing. The point I'm trying to make is that I am the same as your wife. I'm just a more honest version of her. I can't be faithful any more than she was. It isn't in me to be faithful. But I won't tell you lies, claiming I'll love you faithful forever. I'll tell you where we stand together. I'll tell you up front that we won't be standing together after this night. Tonight I'll make love to you like there's no tomorrow, because for us, there will be no tomorrow. I'll make love to you without reservation, but it will be love without pretense to greater love. I'll make love without pretending I'm capable of love for more than one night. I'll deliver the love I promise for one night, but I won't promise long-term love that I have no intention of delivering on."

Wanda didn't toss her head as she talked. She stood with her head cocked slightly to one side in a gesture she meant as a point of honest emphasis. "Like I already told you, if you want, you can hold me for the rest of the night. But don't try to hold me when I leave tomorrow. I'm a girl who lives by the motto 'No promises, no demands.' I make no promises beyond the promise I make for a night. I put no demands on you beyond the demand that you don't put any demands on me to stay with you beyond our one night together. Don't hand me any promises in the morning. Don't make any demands of me now or in the morning. That's the way I am. That's the way I live. That's the way I relate, in bed and out. That's the real me."

Whether Wanda was playing a game was a matter of interpretation. But at that stage of the game, like many men who had stood and listened to Wanda's lectures before, Chuck was amenable to agreeing to any time limit or proviso she put on the temporary relationship so he could see and get his hands on the woman beneath her skintight leathers.

"That's the real me all the time. The way I am now is the way I'll be in the morning. If you want me tonight, you'll have to accept me as I will be in the morning. That means you'll have to accept that I'll be going my way in the morning. I'll be your deep and long lover tonight. By the end of next morning, I'll be long gone."

"Ah, would you like a drink?" Chuck asked, taking things in the direction he assumed suaveness would take things. His changing of the subject was his way of accepting her terms.

"Yeah, sure," Wanda answered casually, going with the change of subject. She assumed his redirection was his way of saying he accepted her terms. "But just a glass of wine. I've already had a couple of drinks tonight, and I don't like the hard stuff very much."

Wanda hadn't meant it as a sexual pun.

"I'll see what they have," Chuck said, pointing to the minibar against the other wall. "The selection may be a bit limited, though."

Chuck started to walk to the minibar. Wanda stopped him. "Before you do, it might be a good idea to put the Do Not Disturb sign outside and turn the dead bolt on the lock," she said. "We don't need some overeager night maid walking in on us during an overeager moment of our own."

Chuck opened the door, hung the plastic sign on the doorknob, closed the door, and set the latch. As Wanda stepped deeper into the room, Chuck walked over to the minibar he had opened and looked inside. As he had suspected, the selection was limited. There was only one choice of wine in the minibar, and it was closer to something one would pick up in a six-pack off the endcap of an aisle at a liquor store than something brought to one in Maxine's by a wine steward with a white towel over his arm.

"I'm afraid the only thing they have in here in the way of wine is a single wine cooler," Chuck said after surveying the fare for a minute. "It's not going to be very gourmet."

"That's fine by me," Wanda said. "I was never much of a wine connoisseur. You didn't get much Dom Pérignon in my hometown. I grew up drinking the cheap stuff. Some people judge wine by the quality of flavor, aroma, and bouquet. I judge wine by how good of a buzz it gives you."

Chuck picked up the wine cooler. "I'm afraid this wine cooler isn't very cool. If you want it cold, I can get you some ice out of the ice machine down the hall."

Wanda didn't want to interrupt the flow any more than Chuck did. "Just bring me the bottle, honey," she said in her been-around-the-block country-girl voice. "That's all I need. It doesn't make any difference to me if it's room temperature going down. It all goes to body temperature once you swallow it."

Chuck reached for a glass to pour the cooler into.

"Forget the drinking glasses," Wanda said. "We'll just pass the bottle around between ourselves. At sixteen, I cut my teeth in the seats of hot rods, passing a bottle between me and the bad boy who owned the car I was in at the time. Sometimes I had to drive them back home in their own hot rods when they got too ripped to drive. They didn't think I could handle a hot car, but I could. I was always a careful driver. Sometimes they tried to get me drunk so they could have their way with me in the backseat. They didn't think I could handle my liquor any more than they thought a girl could handle a hot rod. But I was always a more careful drinker than they were. I didn't swallow down near as much as I made it look like I was. At the end of the drinking bout, they were under the dashboard. I was left standing with my relative virtue intact. I surrendered my virtue when and where I chose to on my own sober timing. I didn't surrender it for what they poured for me out of a bottle they thought they could pour me into."

Wanda hadn't done that as a teenager either. But the story was a useful adjunct to the image she was trying to portray of a wild country girl who had grown up to be a fashionable woman in the fashion trade but still was a wild country woman under the skin.

Chuck, in all his half-naked male glory, walked over to Wanda. As he advanced, he twisted off the twist-off cap of the bottle, breaking the seal and tearing the paper wrapping that covered the top of the bottle. With a side-hand throw, he pitched the cap toward a nearby wastebasket and missed. As he approached Wanda, she reached over and set her small purse down on the nearby desk.

"I wish it was a bottle of Dom Pérignon on ice in a silver bucket in the fanciest restaurant in New York," Chuck said as he handed the wine cooler to her. In his estimate, the line he used and the names he dropped were the top of the line in suaveness.

"Don't sweat it, honey," Wanda answered as she took the bottle with a coy look on her face. She had another form of sweating on her mind that she was eager to get down to. She hoped he wouldn't drag out his attempt at suave foreplay for too long. "I'll take whatever you can give me and whatever I can get. It may not be champagne on ice, but this isn't Studio 54, and I'm not Gia Carangi." Wanda went on dropping her own set of names.

Wanda only knew from afar and by reputation the names of the famous disco in New York and the famous model, who was one of its most well-known patrons. But she was masquerading as a woman in the fashion industry. From what Wanda had heard, mostly from tabloids, the names she used were top-of-the-line names to drop in the fashion world. But she had no direct familiarity with either of them. Wanda wouldn't have known Studio 54 if she had been called out to install a phone in the joint, and she wouldn't have known Gia Carangi if she had tripped her with a phone line she was dragging across the sidewalk and into the disco. That night, Wanda was dressed as she imagined Gia would dress.

For a few quick and fleeting moments, Wanda considered using the name Gia in her next barroom incarnation. But Gia Carangi was well known enough in general popular culture that people in the circuit Wanda made her rounds in might be familiar with her through the tabloids the way Wanda was. If Wanda used the name, it might be obvious it was an alias. Wanda hadn't hit the G names very hard. There were names there to be used. She figured she could choose a name that had an exotic ring to it or was somehow reminiscent of Gia, such as Gloria (Wanda was in her glory when she was out of her clothes), Gisele (Wanda was as limber and active as a gazelle in bed), Gabriella (it was an exotic, French-sounding foreign name just as Gia was an exotic Italian name), or Gilda (it was the name of an oversexed American character played by Rita Hayworth). Choosing a name for a night was a serious consideration for Wanda. But Gia and the Gs would have to wait. For the moment, Wanda had other considerations on her mind.

Wanda took the wine cooler Chuck handed her. She looked at him right up to the moment she put the bottle to her lips. When Wanda drank out of the bottle, she didn't sip it daintily with only her bottom lip, as if she were a refined courtesan in the court of Louis XV or a sophisticate in Parisian society. She wrapped her full lips fully around the mouth of the bottle, upended it at an angle greater than forty-five degrees, and chucked down several big swallows as if she were still a country bad girl sitting in the front seat, or backseat, of the badass car of a country bad boy, passing a bottle with him. Her lips pumped as she drank. Chuck watched the swallows as they rippled from her upturned jaw muscles down her throat to where the movement disappeared into the swelling volume of her chest.

With a quick, small gasp, Wanda brought her head back down and broke off her drinking round. She handed the bottle back to Chuck. Chuck thought to hold up the bottle as if it were a toast and say, "Here's looking at you, kid," before he drank. For a moment, it seemed like the right suave thing to say. But he decided the line was a bit obvious.

Chuck took the bottle and took a drink out of it without saying anything. He didn't chug it quite as hard as Wanda had. The wine cooler didn't have the taste of a special-year vintage that had been aging in a wine cellar for four decades at a big-name vineyard, waiting to be decanted for the highest of high society. The cooler had the bland taste of a recent production run of a low-end beverage aimed at the beer and brats crowd. It was meant to be drunk over a backyard barbecue grill, not from the table of an outdoor café overlooking the Seine River and the skyline of Paris. For Chuck, the bland taste of the wine cooler was embellished by the taste of Wanda's lip gloss on the glass lip of the bottle and the paper wrapping around the neck.

Chuck handed the bottle back to her. "Don't worry," he said. "I'm not trying to get you drunk like your teenage bad-boy friends did."

"Don't give up so fast," Wanda said in a wry voice as she reached to take the bottle back. She ran her hand over his as she took the bottle. At the smooth stroke of her hand, Chuck came close to losing control of the bottle and dropping it.

Instead of turning her head toward the ceiling, upending the bottle, and chugging it again, Wanda kept her head straight forward and looked at Chuck the whole time. She took only a single ladylike drink that didn't threaten to drain the bottle. It was as if she were trying to conserve her resources and prolong the encounter. Instead of a wild country girl knocking them back with the best of them, she now seemed more like a cultured paramour sipping vintage wine with her lover in a street-side Paris café, an ambience and a wine-drinking market the wine cooler hadn't been designed for.

Even for Chuck, there came a time when words weren't necessary. Wanda and Chuck passed the bottle back and forth several more times between them without saying anything. With Wanda sipping instead of slam-drinking, the volume of liquid in the bottle wasn't being depleted as fast. On each exchange, Wanda stepped closer to Chuck. Finally, the rounded projection of her leather-clad chest was a bare inch from his bare chest. She couldn't press her case any more closely without pressing her chest against his. In the light of the wall lamp next to the bed on the other side of the room, Chuck could see the cherry-red shine of her lipstick and the oxblood shine of her leather top. Her long blonde hair hung down over her shoulders in both front and back. From her close position, Chuck could smell not only the scent of her perfume but also the scent of her skin.

Though Wanda was no longer belting her drinks down, the muscles in her neck still moved with a subtle, fluid motion as she swallowed the fluid going down her throat. Her swallows moved in one direction only: downward toward her chest and the rest of her body beneath. The liveliness of the muscles in her neck seemed to carry a hint and a promise of the liveliness of her full body underneath.

As Chuck stood in front of her with his shirt off, thinking about the rest of their clothes falling away, the rest of the world fell away from Chuck. Standing before her in his half-naked male glory, in the imagination of his mind, Chuck drifted into a world that was all male. The only other world in sight was the world of the beautiful and sensual woman standing in front of him. In his all-male world, he would have exploded in fury on any other male or any other force that threatened violence to the woman. But it was not a male world that would lift a finger to do a single act of violence or force to the woman.

In Chuck's mind, time seemed to stand still in the room as he stood with Wanda. Whatever the degree of relative time dilation in Chuck's mind was, in the outside world of the room, the laws of physics and physical resource depletion continued on in their usual form. After several passes, the bottle had been nearly drained. There was only one swallow left for either of them. Chuck handed the bottle back to Wanda to let her finish it. Again, she stroked his hand as she took the bottle from him.

In an ongoing revival of Chuck's imagination, there was a certain Garden of Eden quality to the scene. He was the naked Adam, and Wanda was the naked Eve. The low-end-beverage-market wine cooler was the forbidden fruit being shared by the couple who were committing original sin and who would go on later in the scene to commit more sin, original or not.

Chuck's vision shifted. Instead of the original human, Adam, with few spoken words to his credit, Chuck was an Elizabethan-era Shakespearean writer with a long string of plays and sonnets of romance to his fame. Wanda was his beautiful courtesan mistress in high powdered wig and ruffled off-the-shoulder Elizabethan-era gown who had inspired many of his sonnets. Instead of a top-floor room of a midrange-priced hotel, they were standing together at the foot of a grand palace staircase, attending a royal ball and performance commanded by the queen sovereign of the realm herself.

But the Elizabethan vision was as proverbial as the Garden of Eden one. In a more homegrown incarnation of his imagination, Chuck reverted to his country roots. In his imagination, he was a young country boy out walking through the open fields with his childhood sweetheart. He wasn't bare-chested, and Wanda wasn't bare-shouldered, but they were both barefoot. Instead of sharing a bottle of inexpensive wine cooler, they were sharing drinks out of a Coke can. Chuck could feel the soft bend of the long grass of the field under his feet. The fields were lush and green. They seemed to stretch on forever around them. The sky above them was a clear bright blue that seemed to stretch on and out to an even greater forever.

Chuck's country vision switched from childhood pastoral to a more adult one. Instead of childhood sweethearts, he and Wanda were a pioneer couple—the first pioneer couple in a new and open territory. Instead of a long-haired fashion consultant dressed in high-fashion leathers, Wanda was his long-haired pioneer wife dressed in buckskin leather. Instead of standing at night in a confined room in a hotel in a developed area, they were standing in the bright sunlight in an open field of what would become their new homestead in the new land. The field and the land they were standing on and the sky above them stretched out in all directions to all the horizons around them. In the new land, they would make a life for themselves, facing the new horizons before them. Chuck had his own sense of horizons.

Wanda had come to Chuck's hotel room for precisely what men took women they picked up in bars back to their hotel rooms for. She had said so on her own. The night had been her initiative more than it had been his. Chuck didn't want to come on to her as being grabby, but the obvious purpose of the evening was to be obvious and come on to each other. Chuck didn't want to come on to her as if he were forcing her, but he wanted to get the obvious things going.

Chuck was a man. Men weren't supposed to faint, and they weren't supposed to go weak at a touch. That was a chick thing. But a tremble of human excitement that was neither particularly male nor female spread rapidly through Chuck from his chest to all extensions of his body as he contemplated the next move he was going to make, whatever conclusion his contemplation arrived at. The swelling feeling that passed from his chest to all his extensions took up residence and had a pronounced effect on one extension in particular.

As Wanda raised the bottle to her full lips to take the final drink, Chuck reached out and brushed her hair off one of her shoulders. Then he laid his hand on her shoulder. He held his hand in position for a moment. Then he started slowly caressing her shoulder from one side to the other and up the side of her neck. Her skin was incredibly soft, smooth, and warm. Though he hadn't drunk enough of the wine cooler to feel the effect of it and mistake the effect of alcohol for the feeling of sensual touch, the feel of her body was intoxicating to him. He didn't go faint, but he did go on stroking her naked shoulder.

At his first touch, Wanda stopped moving her hand and froze in place with the lip of the bottle just outside her lips. As he caressed her shoulder, a low sigh of pleasure came out of the part of her mouth that wasn't blocked by the bottle. A dreamy look came over her face. Her head angled back slightly, and her eyes closed partway. For several long moments, she stood in the same position with the bottle poised just in front of her mouth. The long moments stretched out into a long minute. She lowered the angle of the bottle, but she kept the top of the bottle in the vicinity of her mouth.

"It's been too long of a time." Wanda sighed sensuously at half breath. She spoke at half her normal speaking pace, with her eyes more than half closed. "It's been way too long."

With his other hand, Chuck pushed her hair off her other shoulder. Using both hands, he started caressing and massaging both of her shoulders. From her shoulders, he extended his hands down her arms and back up. He ran his hands back over her shoulders and down her back as far as the edge of her leather top. Wanda's eyes closed the rest of the way. She rolled her head back several degrees. Perhaps the feeling wasn't intoxicating to Wanda, but it was close enough for her present purpose and the hoped-for further purposes she seemed on track for.

Wanda continued to hold the bottle up at her lips, but she wasn't looking for an opening to drink the last small swallow of wine in the bottle. As Chuck ran his hands back and forth across her shoulders and upper back, Wanda ran her lips over the top of the bottle as if she were drinking. There was symbolism in her gesture. Then she altered her symbolic style and ran her tongue around the outside lip of the bottle. Her holding up the bottle was getting in the way of Chuck's arm as he massaged her shoulder on that side, so after a while, Wanda lowered her arm and the bottle to give Chuck more room.

As Chuck caressed her shoulders, Wanda wrapped her arms around his bare chest and started rubbing his back with her hands, including the hand still holding the wine-cooler bottle. The bottle was at room temperature. If it had been chilled, Chuck would have probably jumped at the touch of the cold glass.

Wanda pulled herself closer in to Chuck. The bulging swell of her large breasts compressed against the bareness of Chuck's chest. He could feel the smooth slip of her leather top against his chest and the warmth of the body just one thin layer of shiny leather away. Their closeness and their combined body heat aerated and concentrated the smell of her perfume. Her face seemed lustrous. The thick red of her lip gloss made her lips seem even fuller than they were. Her eyeshadow made her eyes seem larger than they were. The spreading press of her breasts made them feel even larger than they actually were. Wanda was as big as life and full of life. Everything about her seemed larger than life. Either she wasn't wearing a bra, or she was wearing a strapless bra that was so thin it didn't have enough substance of its own to register to the sense of touch. It was as if there wasn't anything lying between him and the substance of her chest except the thin layer of her leather top. Once again, Chuck could feel the details of the points of her substance through the leather of her top. The feeling of her pointed substance was even more pointedly immediate and real to Chuck this time because he didn't have a shirt on. All of the full and swelling warmth and life of her substance was only a thin layer away from him.

Chuck wanted to pull all of her substance and life next to and into his. He wanted to again feel the press of her large lips against his. He wanted to feel the full spread of her breasts against his chest without any layer of anything between his chest and hers. He wanted to feel all the points of her womanly substance pressing against the points of his male substance. He wanted to feel the slow spread of her legs as she welcomed the approach of his love and as she made herself welcome to him. He wanted to watch her large eyes roll back and close. He wanted to hear the gasp of pleasure that came from between her full lips as he penetrated her. He wanted to feel every inch of her pressed against every inch of himself. At that moment, Chuck wanted to possess and feel every last ounce of her substance. He wanted to merge every inch and ounce of himself with every last bit of the fullness of her warmth and substance. He wanted to merge his life with the fullness of the life in her. If she would allow it, he would fill in the center of the life of her womanhood that she was offering to share with him. For one night at least, she would more than fill the gap in his life.

Chuck brought his hands up along Wanda's neck and cupped her face in his hands from both sides. He seemed on the verge of drawing her face in to his. Wanda closed her eyes and parted her full lips in anticipation of the kiss that would initiate everything she had wanted to initiate with him since she first saw him in the bar.

But there was one more fundamental, gentlemanly function that Chuck's quasifundamentalist standards compelled him to perform before they could get down to final fundamentals. Instead of kissing Wanda, Chuck looked her in her closed eyes.

"You don't have to do this if you don't want to," Chuck said with all the gentlemanly magnanimity in him. It wasn't just a public-relations ploy before he twisted her arm behind her back and threw her onto the floor. The famous phrase "No means no" hadn't yet come into widespread usage at that time, but the concept was an integral part of Chuck's country moral fiber. If she didn't want to be compromised any further, he would indeed stop where she wanted him to. One of the oldest and most proverbial country sayings said, "Don't look a gift horse in the mouth." As far as spirited mounts went, Wanda was about the best-looking filly he ever had wanted to ride bareback. But it might be a steeplechase she didn't want to be put through. She would be a hard prize to give up, but if she didn't want to go any further, he would respect her enough to stop. He would just have to console himself afterward by chewing on the leg of the bed and drinking the rest of the minibar dry.

It was a nice gesture to offer any woman at any romantic juncture. However, at that moment, it was a bit of a moment killer for Wanda. It threw off the rhythm just as it was getting started. The semidreamy look on her face dropped away. She opened her eyes and looked at Chuck with sort of a "You picked a fine time to leave me hanging out to dry, just when things were about to get rolling" look in her eyes.

"I just don't want you to think I'm forcing you to do something you don't want to do," he said.

The look on Wanda's face changed to more of a "Where do you go getting off breaking my stride just when I was getting ready to get myself off?" look.

Wanda could have purred something soothingly bland, such as "Of course you're not forcing me," and gone on from there. But that might not have been enough to get both him and her past whatever bad memory from the past or moral inhibition had prompted his hesitancy. Wanda didn't know how much damage Chuck's wife had done to his self-confidence. The lingering damage might have been enough to cause him to falter at the critical moment. There was also the possibility he was about to be tripped up by the sudden rising of some latent Sunday-school morality about gentlemanly behavior, a rising that could prevent the rising of anything else. Either one could throw their plans for a fun evening off track, she thought. Sometimes the best seeming of deals could fall apart at the last moment when one least expected them to, just when one thought he or she had everything worked out and set. In Wanda's estimate, Chuck needed the ego boost, and she needed a good time. She just had to focus his attention and kick any mental roadblocks he might have had out of the way. Some guys with sexy eyes and a sexy face couldn't see the obvious when it was right before their eyes and in their face.

"Hey, if I didn't want to do it and didn't want to be here, do you think I'd be here now?" Wanda said, pointing out what should have been obvious logic. "Did you see me trying to push you away from me? Did you see me go running out the back door of the bar?"

"For a while, it kind of looked like you wanted to get away from me," Chuck said. "Like I said, I wasn't sure you would come."

"Well, do you see me here now?" Wanda pointed out more obviousness. "Do you see me kicking and screaming to get away from you now? Nobody drags me into bed. I came up here panting like a female panther in heat. I came here because I wanted to. You didn't drag me here by my hair. Am I going to have to drag you into bed over and above some Sunday-school morality and idea that says you have to be a gentleman to the nth degree, even if the woman is long past the state where she's looking for a squeaky-clean, righteous gentleman?"

Though one might have interpreted what Wanda was saying as a put-down of the concept of gentlemanliness, she was actually appreciative of his telling her that she didn't have to put out. His willingness to back down at such a late and spring-loaded point in the cycle if she objected was the epitome of gentlemanly behavior. That Chuck was that much of a gentleman was an even bigger turn-on for Wanda. It offered final proof that he wouldn't abuse her. She just needed to verbally disabuse him of any notion that she had any objections.

"Don't get me wrong. Don't think I don't appreciate the fact that you don't want to drag me or force me. I appreciate the hell out of it. A real gentleman is a rare find. But too much gentlemanliness can leave a girl out in the cold when she's running hot. I appreciate you thinking of me as a lady and approaching me like I am a lady, but I don't appreciate the delay it's causing us when there's a lot more I'd appreciate getting from you. As far as ladies go, I'm not here pretending to be a lady. You don't have to be every inch the perfect gentleman. I don't need a gentleman who's a good boy to the last degree. Right now, I need a good, hard lover, and I need a good, hard lovin'."

The speech was vintage Wanda. In the heat of her verbally expressing herself while describing how badly she wanted to physically express herself, Wanda's country accent and contractions started coming out. Aspects of her wild-country-woman attitude started coming out.

"If you want to be a gentleman tonight, you can kiss my hand before you start kissing everything else on me. If you want to be a gentleman in the morning, you can help find and pick up my clothes from the floor and the corners where we're going to be throwin' 'em tonight. Then you can help me get dressed in the morning and open the door for me when I leave. Right now, I don't want no gentleman mincing around me, trying to tell me I'm a lady. I just want to do some less-than-ladylike pumping, bouncing, sweating, and screaming over in that bed. When I'm through and all wore out and too tired to move, if you want to do a gentlemanly favor for me, you can clean me up by licking the sweat off my chest."

Chuck didn't think he'd find that suggestion of recommended gentlemanly comportment or required behavior in the pages of *Gentlemen's Quarterly* magazine or in an advice column by Emily Post.

"If you want to do me a favor so bad, stop trying to do some kind of gentleman bit that would leave me out in the cold and out of your arms. Don't stand off from me like some high-society gentleman talking to some standoffish high-society lady at a library fundraiser. You didn't find my name in the social register. You picked me and my body up in bar. Don't make social niceties with me. Make love to me like a woman you picked up in a bar. Make love to me like I am the biggest tramp you ever picked up anywhere."

"You want me to think of you as a tramp?" Chuck asked.

"You can think of me as a tramp, slut, hussy, or any of the puritan definitions of women like me," Wanda answered. "I don't care if you think of me as a lady or a tramp. It's my body that needs servicing, not my ego. Put a less-than-flattering definition of a woman on me if you like. Just lay me like I'm all the woman you ever wanted. If you need a romantic vision of a woman who was both lady and tramp, think of me as Scarlett O'Hara. Throw me over your shoulder, and carry me off to your bed the way Rhett Butler did with Scarlett in the movie *Gone with the Wind*. You won't see me kicking and fighting the way Scarlett did."

The image was a southern icon and a piece of Americana that was still familiar with most people in the country at the time. Still, in the evolving political correctness of the era, even Clark Gable would have been frowned upon for manhandling a woman like that, even if they were married.

"Clark Gable didn't throw Vivien Leigh over his shoulder," Chuck said. "He carried her in front of him forearm-style, and he carried her a long way up a grand staircase. This hotel room is a lot more cramped than a grand plantation. If I threw you over my shoulder, I couldn't take more than two steps across room before I had to dump you off in the bed. It would hardly be worth the effort to hoist you up."

"Then drag me by my bra strap standing up," Wanda said.

"I might snap it," Chuck said.

"I'd probably snap it myself by running out ahead of you to get to the bed," Wanda said. She nodded toward the hotel room bed. "The point is that in my dirty mind, I'm already over there in that bed, ready to rock and roll. Since I'm already running out ahead of you in my mind, what are we standing here in the middle of the room waiting for? Like I said, you've got me anywhere you want me. What more do you think you have to do for me to get me off my feet and get me going on my back?"

Wanda hadn't had to talk to a man this much before in the past. All the talking was getting in the way of the real form of communication she wanted to get down to.

Still, it was the era when communication between the sexes was becoming a pop-culture thing, and women were coming to value sensitive males. The old caveman male who grabbed a woman by her hair and threw her into bed without uttering a single love word or making any love sounds beyond a few grunts was on the way out. The new pop-culture definition of sensitivity often translated into a man being communicative with a woman at all stages of getting her to yes. Chuck wondered if his verbal performance so far was up to her standards.

"I was afraid that maybe you thought I hadn't talked enough or that I wasn't giving you enough foreplay," Chuck said.

Wanda rolled her open eyes. "Foreplay shmoreplay," she said. "Give me more play. I'm past the fore stage. I just want to play. Where it comes to foreplay, there's verbal foreplay, and there's physical foreplay. Physical foreplay has it all over any kind of verbal foreplay, and physical foreplay is only as good as an overture that takes you into the main body of the play. But too long of an overture can be distracting when you want to get down to the first act."

Wanda moved her arm that held the bottle off Chuck's back and laid it alongside his arm. The wine-cooler bottle in her hand touched the top of his arm where it joined his shoulder.

"I wasn't trying to get you drunk when I offered you a drink," Chuck said. "It just seemed like the gentlemanly thing to do."

More with the gentleman stuff. "Honey, you don't need to tank me up with alcohol like I'm some sort of space rocket to get me to lift off your pad here and touch down in your bed."

Wanda touched the top of her own shoulder with the top of the bottle. "Right now, I don't need any kind of fuel in my veins to make me get up and go. With all the high-octane hormones I've got running around in my blood already and the high-power horny thoughts I've got running around in my dirty little mind, you don't need to go trying to get another drink in me in order to get me in the sack. You don't need to ply me with drinks the way the bad boys I dated used to try to do. You don't need to get any more drinks into me in order to lubricate me. I'm all lubed up now in all senses of the word. I'm so wet I could soak up the whole carpet in this room so bad it would take a week of airing to dry out. It's only because I'm wearing leather that it doesn't soak through my skirt and leave me walking around with a big, wet stain on my drawers, advertising what I want and making me look like I spilled all over myself—which is what I'm about to do from the inside out. I was past the drinking stage when I got here. You don't need to go about trying to ply me with drinks like I'm a Sterno can that needs to be soaked with alcohol in order for me to catch fire. I don't need to have any more alcohol poured into my veins in order to light me up and heat me up."

Chuck hadn't been trying to get her drunk. It was kind of hard to get anyone drunk on a single low-end-market wine cooler. He had just been following what he considered the dictates of suaveness. But the woman he badly wanted to roll in the hay with was on too much of a roll for him to get any further words of denial in.

Wanda pulled back from Chuck a bit and shifted to the side slightly in the direction of the hotel room desk. "And I don't need any more words poured in my ear in order to move me off dead center. Don't ply me with either. Just ply me with what a man usually plies a woman with and in the way he plies her when they get through talking and down to the real plying. I've been past the state of needing words for as long as I've been past the stage of needing drinks. You don't need to get any more clever words out and into me. Just get the usual male thing out and into me."

Wanda reached over and set the almost empty bottle down on the hotel room desk next to her purse with a definitive thump. She straightened back up, talking faster and more emphatically. "Verbal foreplay and other forms of beating around the bush are fine for couples just starting out and for girls who aren't sure what they think and are trying to make up their minds what they want. I'm no beginner, and I know what I want. As far as turn-ons go, I've got you. I don't need your words to turn me on any further. Let the dictionary publishers handle words. You just handle me. Don't put your words in my ear; put my body in your bed, and put yourself into me. Stop cranking out more words that I don't need to hear and you don't need to say. Put that mouth of yours to better use. Swallow any words you have left, and use your mouth to kiss me. Stop jumping around the subject, and jump me."

Some guys who were at a loss for words just had to have it spelled out for them.

"I'm not going to be around very long past the morning. We're both on a limited schedule here. Stop taking up valuable time, and take me!"

A wild country girl didn't have to lecture an old country boy like Chuck more than once. He threw his right arm under her left arm and around her lower back at enough of a downward angle that his right hand ended up on the bare space between her leather top and her leather skirt. The fingers of his right hand wrapped around the side of her bare midriff. He brought his left arm up high on her back. With his left hand, he grabbed the back of her neck. He picked up a full handful of her thick hair in the process. In the back of his mind, Chuck figured he had picked himself up a handful all around.

With a full-court press, using both his arms and hands, Chuck pulled Wanda in tightly to him. The length of his reach and the forward press of his upper body bent her back slightly. If the position was a bit awkward and was hurting her back, Wanda didn't seem to mind. As Chuck wrapped his arms around her, she threw her arms back tightly around his bare back and gripped him the way an inexperienced girl riding bareback for the first time might wrap her arms around the neck of a wild horse she was riding. The difference was that Wanda was an experienced rider, and she was the wildest mare Chuck had ever encountered and proposed to ride.

Chuck and Wanda mutually threw their lips together. As she had done in the bar, she ran her full lips over his lips in a random pattern. But the kiss in the bar had been more languid and lingering. This time, she moved her mouth faster and harder over Chuck's mouth. In short order, she repeatedly covered his mouth from what seemed to Chuck like all conceivable angles and then some. A proverbial-minded writer of sensual fiction would have said Wanda "greedily devoured" Chuck's mouth. There was some truth in that description. But the couple were already moving beyond proverbials.

Once again, Wanda's lips virtually submerged Chuck's lips with their fullness. Once again, the taste of her lip gloss filled his mouth. Once again, the warmth, fullness, and active life of Wanda filled all of Chuck's senses to overflowing. As had happened when she kissed him in the bar, the immediate surroundings and the rest of the world around Chuck disappeared. Wanda's face was the only landscape Chuck could see. She was all the world he could see. She was the only world he wanted. At that moment, she was the total world to Chuck. As totality went, she was total woman.

In an analogy from his youth, holding and kissing her was like swinging out on the rope swing attached to the tree branch that hung over the river at the swimming hole on a hot summer day, letting go at the far apex of the swing, and feeling the exhilaration of the plunge and the cooling surge of the full-body splash into the cool water below. The difference was that this time, the temperature gradients were reversed. Given that the air-conditioning was on in the room, it was the hotel room that was cool. Wanda was a pool of warmth he was merging with. Chuck could only imagine the warmth and exhilaration of the plunge into her deep pool of womanliness and the final merging with the warmth and fullness of her body. She gave out a series of little truncated grunts and sighs of pleasure as she kissed. The sounds she made were muffled and stopped in her throat. Her eyes were wide open.

With his left hand on the back of her neck, Chuck pressed her face in even closer to his. He tried to match the frenetic pace of her kisses with his own but found it hard to keep up with the pace she was setting for both of them. As far as raw velocity of kissing went, Chuck found himself in a race for his money—money he wasn't going to have to pay her for her services. The fingers of Chuck's right hand gripped and opened and gripped again her bare side above her waist. His fingers repeatedly sank into the soft and yielding flesh of her bare midriff. Without releasing his grip on the back of her neck, Chuck's left hand felt the smooth, linear fullness of her thick hair. He had a grip on only one section of the length of her hair. On either end of his hand, her long hair slipped out of his grasp and ran off in both directions.

In response to the press of Chuck's hand on the back of her neck, Wanda brought her right arm up and placed her hand behind the back of his head. She started running her fingers through his hair. Given that Chuck's left arm was below her right arm and didn't block the way, it was an easy reach. Chuck's right arm, which he was using to reach down to her bare waist, was above Wanda's left arm. Wanda wanted to bring both her arms up and hold Chuck's face in to hers with both of her hands. It seemed more feminine and romantic that way. But the press of Chuck's arm held Wanda's upper arm pinned down at her side. She was only able to bring her hand up as far as his shoulder.

For several long minutes, Wanda and Chuck stayed locked in their clinch in that pose. Chuck shifted position. As he did, he moved his chest against Wanda's chest. She must have taken the move as a sexual act. In response to Chuck's movement, as she kissed him in a random pattern, Wanda started rubbing her chest against his, first in a rhythmic, undulating vertical pattern and then from side to side in a horizontal oval. Chuck wasn't sure how she was able to maintain and keep separate her erratic and random kissing pattern and her organized rubbing pattern at the same time. A standard insult of the time was that a person couldn't "walk and chew gum at the same time." Apparently, Wanda had enough of an organized mind that she was sexually able to kiss randomly and rub rhythmically at the same time. Her capacity to handle two disparate motions at the same time worked out for Chuck at the lip level and the chest level.

Once again, Chuck felt the warmth and juicy wetness of her full lips cavorting over his from all sides and angles. Once again, he felt the press of her full breasts against him. Once again, he felt the smooth slip of her leather top against his bare skin. Once again, he felt the points of her womanhood drawing their lines of challenge in the sand of his chest, begging him to step over.

Chuck pulled his right hand off and away from her bare midriff. He took his other hand off the back of her neck and placed his hands on either side of her face, covering the back of her cheeks and ears. The switch in position allowed Wanda to come out of the backward bend he had her in and straighten up. If he had hurt her back with the position, she didn't give any indication. Chuck continued to kiss her as hard as he had been. She continued to kiss Chuck back equally emphatically. If the pressure of his kissing was hurting her lips, she didn't seem to give indication or mind. As Chuck continued to kiss her, he rubbed his hands over the sides of her face and her ears, pushing her hair up and back. As he rubbed the sides of her face and her ears where her earrings had been, he understood why she had removed her earrings. In the thrashing heat and the flailing grasps of passion, large hoop earrings of the kind she had been wearing in the bar could easily become snagged by fingers or a watch and get painfully pulled out of her earlobes. She must have removed her earrings in anticipation of just such an occurrence.

That Chuck had moved his arms and was no longer pinning one of her arms allowed her to bring both her arms up. She placed both her hands behind Chuck's head and continued to kiss him with as much abandon as she had from the start of the clinch.

After massaging her lips for a minute or two in that position, Chuck pulled his face away from hers but only far enough to break the almost suction-cup grip their lips had on each other. Chuck wasn't going anywhere. But then again, he was. As quickly as he had broken their kiss, he reapplied his mouth to her cheek and started kissing her again.

But this time, Chuck didn't stay stuck on a single point of her anatomy, as he had when kissing her lips. From the starting point of her cheek, Chuck kissed his way across her cheek and lower jaw, heading toward where her face joined her neck. When he reached her neck, he started kissing his way down her neck. When he reached the base of her neck, he started kissing his way down the curve where her neck spread out and joined her shoulder. For a while, it seemed he would continue on out across the top of her shoulder, but midway across her shoulder, he reversed directions and started kissing his way back toward her neck at a slight downward angle.

Though the overall theme was about as adult as it came, or was going to come, Chuck's kissing was somewhat reminiscent of a child's game of connect the dots, in which a person drew lines from one numbered point to another. The movement seemed random, but the outline of a picture emerged from the connecting of the random-seeming points. The final figure of the game often was apparent from the pattern of the dots even before the game started. The outline of Wanda's figure had been apparent from the first moment he saw her in the bar. The outline of where the couple were heading would have been apparent to anyone watching them through the keyhole. The outline of where Chuck and Wanda were taking each other was already clear to both of them. The foreplay fun was in connecting the dots as they headed toward the predetermined final picture.

Chuck continued to kiss his way across the base of her neck until he was near the center of the base of her neck. From there, he detoured back up the side of her neck, kissing as he went. He left a kiss for every half inch of feminine territory covered. As he kissed his horizontal path to her neck and the vertical path up her neck, she rubbed the back of his head with both hands. She held her arms almost straight out to the sides. She ran the fingers of both her hands rapidly through his hair.

At the bottom of her jaw, Chuck paused in place for several minutes, kissing and nuzzling the curve and hollow of her neck under her jaw. Country boys were good at kissing in hollows, and they were good at kissing the hollows of a woman's anatomy. Wanda rolled her head back to give him more room and give verbal vent to her enjoyment of the sensation. With her lips now free, Wanda's sounds were no longer trapped in her throat and cut off behind her teeth. At the base of Wanda's head, in the space under her jaw, Chuck kissed her hard and fast and nuzzled her long and slow. He opened his mouth as if he were Dracula about to suck the blood out of his next intended beautiful female victim. But he kept his teeth off her neck. Instead of biting, he closed his mouth, drawing his lips over the forward curve of her neck from both sides in a series of long, slow half licks and half sucks. When his lips closed at the center of her neck in the hollow above her Adam's apple, Chuck opened his mouth and repeated the motion.

In response to everything Chuck was doing, Wanda gave out a series of low moans of enjoyment punctuated by half gasps of pleasure. She was reserving her louder sound effects for their later closure. With her head thrown back, Wanda moaned and gasped softly at the feel of the warm and wet caress of Chuck's kisses, but she didn't otherwise say anything. His kisses were becoming a bit wet and sloppy, but Wanda liked her sex wet and sloppy. She didn't utter any complaints. She didn't say anything or make any sound other than the low-level grunts, gasps, and sighs of pleasure that came from deep in her chest and deep in her soul. The time for words had passed for Wanda. But then again, she had been past the word stage from the moment she walked into his hotel room. Though she was holding her vocal cords at an idling pace, she kept the rest of her body in midrange motion. As he kissed and she sighed, Wanda rubbed her body against Chuck's in the same undulating up-and-down motion and side-to-side rotary motion as she had before. It was a little tricky to coordinate her movements with her head thrown back the way it was, but there was an organized mind inside Wanda's thrown-back head. Though Wanda's organized mind was starting to go dreamy at the relative pleasure of the moment and the thought of the more intense pleasure to come, she was still able to coordinate and maintain the divergent expressions of her enjoyment and give subtle and not-so-subtle physical hints as to where and what stage she wanted to take things to next.

Chuck had his own next-stage destinations in mind. He pulled his lips off her neck and leapfrogged his mouth past her neck down to the middle of her breastbone in her upper chest. From his new vantage point, Chuck started kissing again. He also resumed the general downward track of his kissing, which had been interrupted by his detour up her neck. With more territory to cover, Chuck had to spread out the physical separation of his kisses more. Instead of planting a kiss on every half inch along his track across her skin, Chuck spaced his kisses out to one every inch. The vertical distance of her chest was larger than that of her neck. There was also a lot more horizontal territory to explore. Not the additional territory of her expanded three-dimensional dimensions.

The skin of the top of her upper chest was drawn tight over her breastbone where it joined with her collarbones. Her skin was warm where it stretched over the bones beneath, but there was no vertical give to it. Chuck kissed his way down her chest, following the trace road that led across the flat plain of her upper chest toward the mountain pass opening to the deep valley of her cleavage. Chuck wasn't a western country boy, but kissing his way down her chest was a bit like moving from the hardpan lowlands of eastern Montana into the foothills and high plains of the Rocky Mountains. As he kissed his way across the widening expanse of the wide-open west of her bare chest, in his countrified way of thinking and analogizing, Chuck sort of felt like Lewis and Clark exploring the a new frontier no one from their side of the Mississippi River had set eyes on before. To Lewis and Clark and those who'd sent them, the West had been virgin territory. By her own admission, Wanda was no virgin. However many men had had her before, she was new and virgin territory to Chuck. As Lewis and Clark had started their journey of exploration from the flat ground west of Saint Louis with the mountains of the western horizon before them, Chuck started out on the flat ground of Wanda's upper chest.

To the south of his face, the mountains of her horizon rose up before his face.

As Chuck kissed his way down her chest, the firm and tight skin of her upper chest pulled over the outside of her breastbone started to give way to the softer and deeper flesh swelling up at the base of her breasts. Chuck left a wet spot on her skin everywhere he kissed her, but where her flesh grew deeper as it transitioned into the swelling mounds of her breasts, he pushed his kisses deeper into the warm and yielding flesh of the expanding volume of her chest. To the consternation of historical researchers, Lewis and Clark had left no monuments or mile markers, just their reports they submitted to trace the direction of their journey of exploration and their stops along the way. As he proceeded on his journey of discovery and exploration as he approached the boundary of Wanda's leather top, Chuck thought to pause somewhere along the line to give her a hickey she could take away with her in the morning and remember him by for several days. But he decided that would have been a bit immature for a man his age.

Kissing all the way, Chuck entered the high-plains pass of her cleavage. As he pushed deeper into the narrowing pass, the rising slopes of her breasts pressed in against his cheeks equally from both sides. The soft mounds of her breasts yielded to the push of his cheeks, but they pushed back with their own soft and warm press as he pressed on. With his face buried in her cleavage and his nose pushed to the bottom, Chuck reminded himself of the old hound dog his family had had when he was a young boy. The dog had never caught or even chased a criminal in its life. Barring a career in law enforcement, the dog had had the alternate idea that its function in life was to rid the world of gophers. When the dog ran a gopher to ground in its borough, the dog would stand with his front legs and paws angled out in front of him and his head down with his muzzle pushed into the hole where he had caught the scent of the gopher. With his muzzle pushed into the gopher hole, the dog would bark down into the hole. Then he would back his head out and try to dig the gopher out of its hole. The gopher holes were usually too deep for him to dig his way to the bottom. Having failed to dig the gopher out, the dog would stick his muzzle back in the hole and resume barking. Then he would go back to digging. It had been an amusing sight when it happened out in open country, but it had been embarrassing if the dog was tearing up a neighbor's lawn. Chuck would have to drag the barking dog away from the opening to the den of his intended victim. Chuck didn't bark as he thrust his muzzle into Wanda's cleavage, but if he'd had a tail, he would have wagged it.

Like his old country hound when it had caught the scent, Chuck's nose filled with the scent of Wanda, and it wasn't the musty smell of a gopher. She must have strategically rubbed a dab of perfume between her breasts. The scent of her perfume was stronger between her breasts than it had been anywhere around her. But that could have been a simple effect of concentration and lack of airflow. There usually wasn't a lot of wind in a narrow mountain pass. The atmosphere was a bit stuffier and more concentrated in the tight valley between Wanda's breasts. He was sending his face into a tight confine her perfume hadn't had the chance to evaporate out of. Along with the scent of her perfume, as Chuck kissed the floor and sides of her cleavage, he could taste the smooth taste of her flesh. Along with that, he got a residual taste of something else, something not natural to a woman's body, something that came from the shelf in the beauty aisle in a drugstore instead of being secreted by the glands of female skin. Chuck couldn't identify the taste, but he had tasted something like it on his wife before. He wasn't sure if it was bath oil or body powder. It could have been either. But he didn't have time to stop and do a chemical analysis or a taste test. There was far more of the woman he wanted to get a taste of.

Instead of an airheaded dog with his nose in a gopher hole, with his face deep in Wanda's cleavage, Chuck became like a confused alpinist in the Grand Canyon. There was an embarrassment of riches on all sides—so many paths to walk and so much territory to clamber over but so little time. He didn't know which slope he wanted to climb. He only knew he wanted to climb both.

Chuck jumped rapidly from side to side, kissing both of her breasts. Although Chuck considered the quantity of her breasts to be the same as quality, he decided that quantity and velocity in kissing were not necessarily the same as quality. Though he'd started out fast, as he proceeded, he slowed down the pace. He lingered longer over each kiss. He pushed his lips deeper into the warm and yielding mounds of her breasts. As he dragged out the kisses, he dragged his lips and tongue across the surface of her breasts. By this time, Chuck had brought his hands down from the sides of her head and was holding the middle of her upper back, below the shoulder blades.

For her part, at that point in the evening and the further part she wanted to play in the rest of their night together, Wanda brought her hands down from the back of Chuck's head. She positioned her hands behind his neck. She rubbed her hands harder and in widening arcs around the back of his neck and over his shoulders where they joined with his neck. As Chuck kissed her breasts and kissed deeper, Wanda still wasn't expending words, but her breathing became deeper and more forceful. Occasionally, low-level tremors would force Wanda to break the pattern she was using to stroke Chuck's neck and shoulders. She would grab his shoulders and hold on as her body shuddered slightly.

Chuck continued to both kiss and lick both of her breasts until they were wet and shiny from his saliva in dual arcs extending from where the tops of her breasts joined her chest down to where her leather top began. At that point, Chuck's downward progress stalled as if he had hit a leather wall. He tried kissing farther down on the surface of her top. Wanda gasped a bit louder as he did, but for Chuck, the taste and sensation weren't the same. Oceanographers said that nine-tenths of the mass of any iceberg was below the water. Wanda's breasts were a lot warmer and a lot more pliable than an iceberg calved off a glacier, but only about a third of her breasts was exposed above her leather top. Two-thirds of the volume of her breasts was still concealed and confined below and by the chaperoning grip of her tight leather top. Wanda had gone beyond the chaperone stage the night of her senior prom. Chuck wasn't aware of that particular fact any more than he was aware of her real name. But he figured it was time to get her past the chaperone stage and get himself past her leather top, which wrapped and cut off the full volume of her chest and his full realization of her chest as if the tight top were a chastity belt.

Wanda had plenty to show and tell, and Chuck wanted to get the show on the road. With his hands on her upper back, he was already in position to initiate the next stage.

As he continued to kiss down into her cleavage and out onto the expanding territory beyond, Chuck reached his hands down slightly and started feeling around for the zipper on her top. He followed the ridge of her spine. The zipper should have been in the center of her back, just above her spine. The trouble was that Chuck couldn't find the zipper. He ran his hands in widening circles, but he didn't encounter any zipper track or zipper pull. There was nothing there but smooth leather. Then Chuck remembered that her top buttoned in the front instead of being zipped in the back. From his position with his face buried in her chest, he hadn't seen the buttons just beyond his nose. It was a case of not being able to see the forest for the trees—or the buttons for the boobs.

A little embarrassed at himself, Chuck stood fully upright, ready to approach things from the right direction. Another aspect of his anatomy was fully up and ready to go by that time. Chuck brought his hands around front. With a male version of Mona Lisa's half smile on his face, Chuck started unbuttoning the western-style pearl buttons on Wanda's New-York-fashion-house-leather-trying-to-look-western-style leather top. The buttons were actually snaps. Wanda didn't offer any resistance or say anything as he unbuttoned the snaps. She held her hands on his shoulders, at the base of his neck. With her large eyes, which her eyeshadow made look even larger, she looked him straight in his eyes. Her eyes were fully open, and her lips were parted.

As Chuck unsnapped the snaps in a downward progression, her top opened and started falling away to the sides. The light of the room fell on new territory of her breasts as they became exposed. The depth of her cleavage was still in shadow. As Chuck unsnapped the last snap, her top fell away by itself. As it dropped toward their feet, Chuck grabbed the top and tossed it off to the side so they wouldn't trip on it. As he tossed her top to the side, she shook her head, but it wasn't a gesture of disagreement. She was shaking out her hair. When she looked back at Chuck, a wave of her long hair hung over one eye Lauren Bacall style.

Free of the upward and inward pull of the leather top, her full and rounded breasts settled downward a bit, but they didn't sag. There was more than enough life and youth in her breasts to keep them full and round. Her breasts faced Chuck and the world as alert, straight on, and ready as her eyes did, the difference being that the central focal points of her breasts stood out from their surrounding territory instead of being recessed in sockets like her eyes. And they didn't need eyeshadow to outline them. Their presence was pointedly visible and out there for all to see.

Wanda was wearing a bra, but as Chuck had speculated, it was a strapless sheer bra. The bra was flimsy and lacked the leverage of shoulder straps. By itself, the bra didn't look as if it would have had the physical ability to hold her large breasts up if they'd wanted to sag. Her breasts held their shape and angle. The bra was so thin and sheer Chuck couldn't see the point of wearing it. It didn't seem to serve much of any visible support function. It didn't look as if it would even keep her breasts from moving and bouncing when she walked. Apparently, the tight leather top served that function.

Chuck figured she wore the bra just for minor angular adjustment. She probably wore it for politeness and propriety's sake. Women who openly said they weren't wearing underwear were looked upon with suspicion of being openly dirty girls. She might have worn the thin and transparent creation just to technically say she was wearing a bra. Beyond that, the bra seemed superfluous and overwhelmed.

With his libido already in active position and his hands in the ready position, Chuck started running his hands over the full hemispherical curves of her breasts. He started with the top quarter of her breasts, where he had already been. He ran his hands in a downward direction over her breasts, pressing with his fingers as he did. As he ran his hands down over the smooth curve of her breasts, he could feel the soft give of the deep flesh of her breasts as his fingers sank in. He could also feel the lingering moisture left by his kisses and licks. Wanda's breasts turned dry at the top edge of her sheer bra, where it started an inch or two above the extended points of her nipples. It was the same point where his lips had stopped and her leather top had commenced. At that point, just above her other prominent points, Chuck felt her smooth and silky skin transition to the smooth and silky feel of her sheer bra. Her bra was so thin and smooth it was hard to tell where her skin left off and the bra began. As Chuck pressed on, the heels of his hands rode up and over the supple but extended points of her large erect nipples.

At that point, and those points, Chuck rotated his hands to the side, using her nipples as the fulcrum and pivotal points. As he turned his hands, he felt the wide curve of first the sides and then the lower-half expanse of her breasts. Chuck paused with the palms of his hands over her nipples and his fingers cupped under the wide underside curves of her breasts. He was able to wrap his hands probably less than halfway around the full circumferences of her full breasts. There was an old saying that anything more than a handful was a waste. On the other hand, Chuck went by the old Mae West adage that too much of a good thing was wonderful.

With his hands, Chuck started massaging Wanda's breasts. He could feel the slip of her smooth skin and the silky slide of his hands over her sheer bra. He rubbed and squeezed her breasts gently, but he closed his fingers around her breasts deeply enough to feel the sensation of his fingers as they sank into her soft flesh. Wanda tilted her head back slightly and closed her eyes partway again. She started to breathe a little more heavily and leaned a bit on her arms as she held on to Chuck's shoulders. For a few minutes, Chuck massaged her breasts. He couldn't seem to cover all the territory there was to explore. Wherever he felt, there always seemed to be more mounded flesh beyond his fingers. Her breasts seemed to go on forever. Chuck was starting to wish the night would go on forever. From every angle she would let him stand with her, Chuck was starting to feel that he could stand there with her forever.

The dreamy look on Wanda's face made her look as if she were halfway to heaven. But she was still only partway to the original natural state the Lord of heaven and the nature of Earth had made her in. As she seemed to drift off into her removed state, Chuck checked the front of her bra, looking for a hook or strap in front. He had mistaken the side on which her clothing was fastened before. He didn't want to make the same mistake twice. Not seeing any hook in the center front of the bra, he assumed it fastened from behind. He took his hands off her breasts and reached around behind her back once again. He could feel the snap or whatever kind of fastener was in the middle of the bra strap. It was a single fastener, but it wasn't a simple hook. Chuck fumbled blindly with the snap, trying to figure out how it worked by feel, but he couldn't seem to figure out the mechanism and get it open. Wanda's clothing seemed determined to conspire to make him seem like a bumbling male.

Realizing Chuck's predicament, Wanda nimbly reached around behind her back and took over operations. With one quick move of her hands, she unsnapped the fastener that had defeated Chuck. Women were much better at handling snaps. But then again, she had probably been snapping and unsnapping bras like that for years, he thought, probably since before she became a wild country teenager riding in cars and on motorcycles with boys. A figure like hers had probably started to announce itself when she was eight years old in order to become so pronounced at her present age.

Wanda's flimsy bra came off with a fluttering wave, as if it were a silk scarf. With a quick flip of her hand and arm, she tossed the bra off to the side, where it landed farther away than her top. It looked like her prediction that her clothing would end up tossed to the four corners of the room was coming true, with her as the tosser. Wanda hadn't been in that particular hotel room or with that particular man before that night, but when it came to tossing clothes, she had been there before.

With her arms already up and extended from taking off her bra, Wanda threw her arms back around Chuck and pulled herself in close to him again. Chuck reciprocated by again throwing his arms around her.

Together they brought their faces up to each other and threw their lips back together in another kiss that was more assertive and intense than the first. Wanda's lip gloss had been worn away many miles ago. All Chuck could taste were her lips. Free of the constraints of her clothing, which hadn't been all that constraining to begin with, her large breasts compressed and spread out across Chuck's chest. Free of the constraints of conventional mores or Emily Post dictums about proper, ladylike comportment or the proper outline of womanly shame, Wanda started shamelessly rubbing the outline and the underlying fullness of her chest against Chuck's. As she had before in a more full-dressed state, Wanda rubbed herself against Chuck in both an undulating up-and-down pattern and a side-to-side circular pattern.

Her breasts felt incredibly soft and warm against Chuck's chest. In their compressed fullness, they seemed to spread out to where they encompassed the whole width of his chest. He could feel both the full, dispersed, distributed press of the soft mass of her breasts in general and the single specific points of her nipples. The feel of her breasts in all their unadorned and unconstrained naturalness and full fullness was dizzying to Chuck, almost to the point of being disorienting. Chuck responded by pulling his arms tighter around her and kissing harder. He rubbed his hands rapidly back and forth over the bare skin of her back, which was no longer restricted and segmented into limited patchwork sections by her clothing. The whole of her naked upper body was open to the sweep of his touch without the interruption of clothing.

Chuck tried to cover the whole of her naked back with his moving hands. As he swept his hands over her back, he could feel the muscles of her back work in synchronicity as they moved the front of her chest against his. Chuck was getting his wish to feel every inch of her against every inch of him, at least in the upper extremities. The whole front of her warm and throbbing body was pressed against his to the point where no daylight shone between them. Wanda's face was directly in Chuck's face. His eyes looked straight into her open eyes. She was arousing all of Chuck's senses to a greater degree than any woman had ever aroused them or aroused him before, including his wife. His manly senses were out barking and howling like a pack of country dogs on the scent of a bitch female in heat. Whether the woman in his arms was a bitch in heat was a matter of personal interpretation. All Chuck knew at the moment was that the warmth and fullness of her body and the heat of her passion were driving him crazier than his old hound dog ever had gone at the scent of a gopher. As NASA said, all of Chuck's systems were go. It was obvious to him that Wanda was equally ready to go.

The pace with which she rubbed herself against him increased in tandem with the rising level of Chuck's arousal. The two stood locked in place in their frenetic mutual dance, which covered the spectrum of passion but didn't move from the place where they were standing. It was hard to tell who was leading in the dance and whom was being led. As the couple necked furiously, they seemed to be running neck and neck in the run-up of their passion. It was hard to tell who was leading whom in the race to the passion peak. It was also hard to predict who would be leading whom into the passion pit of the bed no more than two yards away.

For several more long minutes, the couple kissed, pressed, and rubbed against each other. Then Chuck broke off kissing her lips and started kissing her cheek. The move started out similar to the way he had kissed his way sequentially down her chest before he removed her upper clothing—with help from Wanda. For a moment, it looked like he was about to repeat the sequence in whole. But Chuck was ready to leap Wanda. In pursuance of this, Chuck leapfrogged things a bit.

Though Chuck didn't necessarily worship at the shrine of Wanda's body, he went to his knees before her. But the supplicant position he assumed was hardly to deliver an altar boy prayer. It was just to keep himself from getting a cramp in his neck.

Wanda was good looking enough to drive most any man to his knees. She had taken that position several times before in her own version of foreplay performed from a similar relative male-to-female positioning, but she had been the party who sank to her knees. Wanda wondered at bit at Chuck's somewhat unusual reversal of roles, positions, and moves. She let her arms slide loose from his back as he slid to his knees in front of her.

On his knees before her, Chuck wrapped his arms around her now fully exposed midriff above her waist. From there, he pulled her closer to him; set his face straight forward, facing the full, proud, rounded, and unmistakable assertions of the totality of her womanliness; set his lips, which had been momentarily idling, back into motion; and started kissing her breasts. His kisses weren't just discrete little pecks on the sides of her breasts, as if he were giving his cousin a kiss on her cheek. Chuck gave her breasts full-male, full-mouthed kisses. As much as he could without snagging her breasts with his teeth, he pushed his lips deep into the soft and satiny depth and swelling volume of her breasts. Keeping his teeth withdrawn and at bay, Chuck worked his lips back and forth, pushing a deep depression into the individual breast he happened to be concentrating on at the moment. Often, he pushed deep enough that his nose also pressed into her breasts. Then he would draw his lips back tightly over the individual breast he was working on, stretching out the point where his lips finally closed and slipped off her breast. If he inadvertently left a hickey on her breast or breasts, so be it, he thought. On more than one occasion, Chuck left a thin trail of saliva stretching out as he withdrew his lips.

As before, Chuck jumped the attention and favors of his mouth back and forth between her breasts, as if he couldn't make up his mind which one he wanted or preferred. He placed long, languid kisses on one after the other in jumping secession. He jumped back and forth from one breast to the other as if he were his old hound dog running back and forth between two gopher holes. As soon as the dog got to one hole, a gopher would pop up in the other, and the dog would go running back to it. Prairie dog mounds were a better spatial analogy to her breasts than gopher holes.

Wanda now understood why Chuck had dropped to his knees. She'd had men kiss her breasts before, but that had usually happened when she was flat on her back and the man was above her on top. This was the first time a man had gotten down on his knees to pleasure her. Wanda appreciated the gesture, along with appreciating everything else he was doing for her and would do for her. Wanda put her hands on Chuck's shoulders and leaned in as he continued to kiss.

After several more long, extended minutes, Chuck narrowed his focus, slowed his pace, and started to kiss and suck the nipples her breasts had been holding extended and ready for him since the moment he first touched her. Taking one breast at a time, Chuck rolled the nipple around with his tongue. The sensation and feel of the rubbery slip of her erect nipples between his lips and around his tongue sent pulses of excitement through him as if her breasts were charged batteries and the wetness of his mouth was completing the circuit. Electronics techs thought in terms of charges and completing circuits. Wanda was thinking in terms of getting on with and completing her circuit for the night in the bed no more than two yards away.

After toying with a nipple with his tongue for a time, Chuck would then suck on it, covering the whole nipple and beyond with his mouth. He drew out the sucking into a long, lingering linger. The goal was to leave the front peaks of her breasts wet and the rest of her body weak and faint. From Wanda's point of view, he was accomplishing both of his goals. As he sucked, Chuck would gently squeeze her breast with both hands, as if he were a Greek shepherd in the hills drinking out of a full wineskin. Given the volume of her breasts, the spatial analogy wasn't that far off.

Wanda's body trembled. She leaned in more and tightened the grip of her fingers on Chuck's shoulders. She spread her legs more, as if to get herself a better stance. She breathed heavier. Little gasps of pleasure came out of her mouth. As Chuck went on, Wanda's squeaking gasps changed to throatier moans. For the most part, Wanda's eyes were wide open, but occasionally, she would close her eyes, tilt her head back, and sigh or moan more deeply.

Chuck used the occasion of her having her head thrown back to pull his head away from sucking her breasts. Bringing his hands down and around front, Chuck reached for the belt on her leather skirt. The belt was a wide leather belt with a heavy cowboy belt buckle. With a quick move of his hands, Chuck unfastened the belt buckle and loosened her belt. Then he reached for the zipper on her skirt and pulled it down. At least the zipper was easily located and worked without complications.

Wanda's full hips and the tightness of the leather skirt held it from dropping after Chuck had pulled the zipper down all the way. Chuck looked up at her. Her head was still tilted backward. From the angle of her head, he couldn't quite make out the look on her face, but it wasn't a disapproving one.

Chuck focused his attention back on what he was doing. He tugged on the skirt from both sides with both hands. The skirt was as tight as it looked. It took a bit of tugging, but Chuck managed to pull it over and past the outward curves of her full hips. After passing her hips, the skirt came loose and fell down to the point where the spread of her legs stopped further downward progress. Wanda obligingly put her legs together so the skirt could fall the rest of the way. When the skirt hit the floor, she obligingly stepped out of it with one leg and used her other leg to kick it off to the side.

As for her underwear, it didn't cover much of anything. Wanda was wearing a narrow thong composed of a red lace strap that ran horizontally around the waist and a strip of thin red satin mesh that ran perpendicular down from the waist strap and curved around under her crotch. The thong was as sheer and see-through as her bra, especially the mesh portion, but it seemed to be composed of even less total material. It was the kind of thing a high-fashion, highly sensual woman who worked for a high-fashion company that made high-fashion, highly sensual clothing would have had access to and worn. Wanda's unadorned and unrestricted full hips curved to the sides, swelling out and away from the small red T of her lace thong. The equally sensuous, rounded curves of her upper thighs rose upward from her knees, expanding outward to the point where they merged with the inward curve of the lower circumference of her abundant hips. From where he knelt on the floor, Chuck could see the shape of things to come and the road ahead of him.

Tentatively, almost apologetically, Chuck inserted the first three fingers of his left hand between her legs, immediately below where the lace thong was doing its minimal job of covering her crotch. He could feel the satiny texture of her red thong. Immediately above that, he could feel the texture and outline of her portal of womanliness. Through the thin covering of the material of the thong, Chuck's fingers felt the smaller curves of the lips of her vagina. There wasn't much left to the imagination. The lace and thin satin mesh of the thong did little to conceal vision of forbidden territory. It didn't do much in the way of blocking sense of touch either. But then again, it hadn't been designed as a defensive barrier of a woman's modesty. It had been designed to be a teaser. Nor had the red thong been intended as a red-flag warning for a man who was hot to proceed not to proceed any further. The red thong served the same purpose for a woman as a red cape a matador waved in the face of a bull. It wasn't designed to slow things down. It was designed to start the charge.

Wanda hadn't been exaggerating when she had claimed to be wet. The red thong was soaked through in the area beneath her crotch. Like a piece of cloth drawing up water or a candle wick drawing melted wax, the thong seemed to be drawing her wetness up its narrow front strip. The sticky moisture of the immediate area gave testimony to the immediateness of her need.

The thin red thong was the last thin red line between virtue and wanton need. With his exploratory fingers in place, Chuck started massaging the entrance to Wanda's vagina. As per its design and minimal purpose, the thong did almost nothing to block the sense of touch and feel. Chuck could feel the outline of her love portal in full detail as his fingers played over the lips of her vagina and sensed the depth of the central gap between as it dropped away from his fingers. The mesh netting of the thong stopped

Chuck's fingers from penetrating any deeper but did nothing to stop the flow of her anticipatory wetness.

Wanda spread her legs back out to give Chuck more room. She gripped Chuck's shoulders tighter. Instead of throwing her head and shoulders back, she dropped her head forward and leaned in, using her arms as braces. Wanda's long hair fell over and off her shoulders and hung down between them in a wavy blonde cascade. Her big eyes were wide open.

For several moments, Chuck massaged her crotch. In a full-body response to his touch, Wanda shuddered and gasped louder. As he worked his fingers around the opening of her vagina, she rolled her hips around in a circular motion and pushed her pelvis in and out, bringing the promise of pleasure it held for him and the demands of pleasure she wanted for herself from him closer to Chuck. Alternately, she would turn her face down and look toward Chuck and then back up. As Wanda undulated her needs in front of Chuck's face, she inched closer and leaned down toward him more. Her face was just above Chuck's head. Her large breasts hung down close to his face.

As Wanda moved closer to Chuck, she was approaching the instability point where if she moved in any closer, she would lose the leverage provided by her arms on his shoulders and topple forward over his back. She stopped moving closer just short of the point of instability and held her position as she held Chuck's shoulders but didn't hold her tongue. Wanda's sound effects were approaching the instability and breakout point. Her gasps and moans were breaking the surface of audibility. If they got much louder, they might break the sound-blocking barriers of the hotel room walls.

Wanda threw her head back and let out a long, sustained moan. Chuck seized the opportunity to grab Wanda's thong with both hands on both sides and pull it down. With Wanda's legs spread out as far as they were, he wasn't able to pull it far down before the increasing separation of her thighs brought it to the point where it was stretched to the limit and threatened to tear apart. Wanda again obliged him by bringing her legs back together to the point that the thong dropped free to the floor. Again, Wanda used her leg and foot to kick away the interfering piece of clothing, sending it sailing in the direction opposite her skirt.

Wanda spread her legs back out. The invitation was clear. The way was clear. The body part or area to further proceed with was Chuck's option. He slid his fingers back along the same warm road they had traveled moments before, following the creamy path to the source and wellhead of her wetness and the primary physical focal point of her passion. Chuck pushed his fingers upward slightly as he proceeded. Without even minimal interference from the thong to block sensation of touch, Chuck could fully feel the warm flex of the skin of the upper curve of her crotch. The path to the center of her physical womanhood had been lubricated and made even smoother and slipperier by the liquid flow of her need.

As his fingers passed the lips of her labia, Chuck turned the direction of his fingers and pushed them into the creamy walls of her warm and slippery vagina. The interior walls of her vagina flexed inward at the press of his touch. Chuck could feel the give and rebound of the flesh of her vagina. Her natural lubrication kept anything from snagging.

Wanda leaned forward again. Her breasts hung down toward Chuck's face, as they had before. She dug her fingers into his shoulders deeper than before. She opened her eyes as before. She opened her mouth wider than before. She gasped and moaned louder than she had before. She shuddered harder than before and undulated her body more than before. Waves of vibration rippled down her breasts. The quivering of each successive wave stopped where her nipples danced in the air, only to be followed by another wave.

Chuck moved his fingers from side to side and in and out of her vagina for several minutes. Wanda's body, now fully naked except for her shoes, continued to wave and undulate at Chuck's deep touch. She was enjoying herself at the preliminary, preintercourse stage. She definitely seemed to like the particular form of foreplay, but to Chuck, it was starting to seem like child's play. Finger-fucking was something done in the backseat of a car by teenagers who didn't want to go all the way. Chuck was beyond that stage. He hadn't even started out at that stage as a teenager; he had launched right into things in a stall of a horse barn. Besides, his hand was getting sticky.

Chuck stood up, bringing Wanda with him. As his body rose—he had already risen up in the other sense of the word—he grabbed Wanda by her naked hips and pulled her hard up next to him. They were both hard up in all senses of the word. Chuck and Wanda started kissing again, but instead of bringing her arms down lower for a better wrapping grip, Wanda kept her arms high and wrapped them around his neck while she kissed, and Chuck kept his arms angled downward at a steep angle. He gripped and pulled up and in on the swelling curves of her southern-end extremities. At least by grabbing her hips, he was able to wipe some of the stickiness off his fingers.

The feel of his hands grabbing and massaging her hips sent Wanda's pulse to a thumping peak. As the passion surged in her body, she could feel the surge of blood going through the veins in her temples and her neck. She wrapped her upper arms tighter around her neck. Her arms crossed each other at a ninety-degree angle behind his neck and bent at the elbows. Her forearms pointed out and away from each other in opposite directions at a 180-degree angle. As Chuck pulled her in by the hips, Wanda pressed her body in against him, rubbing and surging herself against him. She could feel the coolness of the air-conditioned air in the room at her back and the heat of Chuck's body against the front of her chest. As she rotated and rubbed her lower body, she could feel the hard metal of his belt buckle as it moved against her naked skin between her navel and her crotch.

Once again, Wanda was unadorned and in her element. She felt totally naked. She felt totally compromised. She felt she was giving herself totally to him. She felt totally abandoned to passion and sensuality. She felt like a shameless, unapologetic, panting slut. That was precisely how she wanted to feel and the way she wanted to feel about herself. Wanda loved the throbbing feelings surging through her body. Soon enough, she would feel the surging throb of him inside her. She loved the feeling of being out of her clothes. She loved the feeling of being out of control and running away with herself. She loved the feeling of total surrender to passion and runaway desire. She loved the feeling of being totally surrendered to him. She loved all the feelings individually and in combination. This feeling was what she felt she had been born for and made for. Wanda loved the feeling of sinking herself deep into the center of passion and pleasure. The only feeling remaining to be realized was the feeling of Chuck sinking himself deep into the center of her love and lust. For the rest of the night, she would make love to him as if there were no tomorrow. Tomorrow she would look for another man who would fill her with the same feelings. In Wanda's set mind, there would be no turning back from Chuck tonight. There would be no turning back from the life she had set for herself and the life road she had set herself on.

It was time to get the show on the road. Wanda pulled her arms off Chuck's neck. Keeping her body as close to him as she could while leaving room enough for her arms, she reached down between herself and Chuck. Similar to what he had done for her, Wanda started tugging hard on his belt buckle. She had to work by touch, and the angle was a bit hard to work at, but she soon had his belt unbuckled. Still working by touch, Wanda proceeded to pull down the zipper of his pants. As the two front sides of his pants separated to the sides, Wanda paused to run her hand over what lay beneath. Through his underpants, she could feel the hardened obviousness of his desire and passion toward her.

Wanda brought her hands around to his sides and placed them on either side of his loosened belt and pants. Grabbing the top bands of both his jeans and his underpants, Wanda started pulling both of them down at the same time. Chuck took his hands off his hips, placed them on top of Wanda's hands, and helped her pull his pants down. As Chuck's underpants slid down, they snagged on his upturned manhood. The straight extension of Chuck's erect manhood was pulled down, pivoting at the base like a large industrial lever being thrown. When his underpants passed down far enough that they pulled away from the protrusion they had hung up on, Chuck's manhood snapped back to attention.

Chuck and Wanda bent back away from each other as they crouched down to pull Chuck's pants down to the floor. Words weren't necessary when their hands and Chuck's pants mutually arrived at the floor. Without saying anything, Wanda stood back up. With two quick moves, she kicked off her shoes. Things didn't go quite as smoothly from there for Chuck. He was wearing his heavy-laced work shoes. They couldn't be removed as casually as Wanda had kicked off her flats. They had to be untied by hand. Chuck had to bend down, pull his pants back up enough to get to the laces of his shoes, and untie them in a bent-over position. His butt waved in the air as he untied his shoes. The position was a bit unstable. Chuck almost fell over twice as he hurried to untie his shoes. When he was finished untying his shoes, he had to balance precariously on one foot and then the other as he pulled his shoes, pant legs, and socks off each foot in turn.

Words, of course, weren't needed to direct or outline what was coming next. Even a stone sphinx could have told where the couple were headed. Wanda was an enthusiastic enough partner. Chuck didn't have to take her hand and lead her anywhere. She was running out ahead of him. She knew the drill. She was apparently ready and eager to get drilled.

Wanda already had the blanket and sheet on the bed pulled back while Chuck was still halfway through his pants-removal dance. She positioned herself in the bed as Chuck walked toward the light switch that controlled the lights next to the bed. Wanda lay on the bed with her head turned to toward him. She had a ready, willing, eager, and organized look on her face as Chuck turned the button switch that switched off the wall lights next to the bed.

The only lights left in the room were the faint light from the streetlights on the road outside the hotel coming in around the drawn window curtains and the indirect light of the night-light in the bathroom. Wanda was more or less an outline on the bed. But at that moment, lights were as superfluous as words. What couldn't be seen in full, direct clarity and detail could be handled by touch. In the faint light, Chuck could see her legs spread as he approached.

Without any superfluous words that they both silently agreed weren't needed, Chuck threw himself up onto the bed and straddled Wanda with his legs, but he didn't hold the position for long. He quickly brought his legs back together again in the space created by the spread of her legs. She had already gone into a full spread as he arrived, but she spread her legs even farther. For a moment, Chuck slid his knees around on the sheet, positioning himself over her. He mentally calculated his position relative to her and the distance and angle of the last small open space remaining between them. Wanda reached up and grabbed his shoulders. Snapdragon tension flowed through both of them. Chuck was like a racehorse shifting excitedly in the stall before the start of a race. In a second or two, he would explode out of the gate. The starting lineup for the evening wasn't new to Wanda. It wasn't all that new to Chuck either. After all, Chuck knew a thing or two about starting out explosively with sex from the narrow confines of a horse stall.

Wanda was on the same angle she had been on since she launched her sexual career. Chuck had judged his angle correctly. Like an expert fighter pilot guiding the pitot head in during a midair refueling, Chuck plunged himself down into Wanda without missing a beat or missing the target and piling his manhood into her abdomen or the bed. Wanda gasped and dug her fingernails into Chuck's shoulders. She threw her body up against his body, which was still coming down. The imagination that had started up in Chuck's mind when Wanda first sat down next to him in the bar and had been running in a continuous closed loop since then had been rendered true. She had rendered herself to him fully. The pessimistic side of his imagination, which had believed she wouldn't show up, had been rendered wrong. Things like that did happen in the world.

Pretty much every muscle in Chuck tensed as he sank down into the incredible, warm, enfolding dampness of Wanda. Chuck almost gasped himself at the knowledge of where he was and at the feel of her. Her body was soft and warm. She was soft inside and outside. She was soft all over. Oh God, was she soft. Her body was full and warm. Her vagina was full, soft, slippery, and warm. She was warm all over, inside and outside. Oh God, was she warm. She was as wet as she had said. Chuck's manhood sank down into a veritable well of flowing wetness. Oh God, was she wet—and loud.

As Chuck started pumping with all he had to offer in the characteristic male way, Wanda started screaming with all her lungs had to offer in a high-volume female way. Her screams weren't screams of pain. They weren't demure, ladylike, contained expressions of fulfillment, nor were they made with concern about the sound traveling beyond the walls of the room. Anyone who happened to overhear her orgasmic shouts would recognize them immediately as obvious screams of pleasure, the type of screams that women let out in porno movies. Wanda's rollicking sound effects didn't present a recognition or misidentification problem. Anyone who heard the penetrating screams would know right away the manner in which she was being penetrated and that she liked it. People overhearing her exuberance wouldn't think she was being murdered and call the police. They might, however, possibly call the manager to complain about the noise.

Chuck had initially figured Wanda was an illusion who had disappeared out of his life when she disappeared through the front door of the bar. He'd suspected she was a tease who heated him up as part of a game and then ran away. Until she had actually appeared at his door, Chuck had assumed he would never see her again. Now he was in full male sexual stride, achieving full real-world penetration of the woman he had thought would prove to be an illusion.

The question as to how real Wanda and her intentions were was being answered to the full satisfaction of Chuck and Wanda. The lesser question was how far the sounds of her obvious satisfaction were carrying beyond her immediate circle of pleasure. The hotel was better built, with thicker and more sound-deadening walls, than some of the cheaper motels Chuck had stayed in. But given the full-throated volume of the sound effects she was making, Chuck wondered if the people could hear her yelling in the adjoining rooms. Given the decibel levels involved, there was a possibility her shouts and screams were being heard down at the far end of the hall. Chuck figured he could be the talk of the floor the next day, provided people didn't call the front desk, in which case he'd find himself being talked to by the manager that night.

There were other members of the installation team from his branch office staying at the hotel. All sorts of stories could start floating around the office concerning his male prowess and pickup ability. Those kinds of rumors could be flattering to Chuck's male ego, but they could become embarrassing and get out of hand if they started getting around where he worked. Luckily, Chuck had a certain amount of space where that possible problem was concerned, and it wasn't just the insulation space of one wall. None of his coworkers were staying on the same floor. Perhaps because he was a phone company supervisor and the hotel wanted to stay in good with Ma Bell, Chuck was the only member of his team who had been given a room on the top floor. The other members of the installation team from the Memphis office Chuck worked out of had rooms on lower floors. Unless one of them had the room directly below his, the other members of his group were probably removed enough that they wouldn't be able to hear the woman, determine that the sound was coming from his room, and make the connection as to the kind of connection he had made in the bar earlier that night.

Chuck had casually informed the other members of his crew that he was going out to a bar that night. He had told them where he was going that night, because he hadn't thought anything like what had transpired was going to happen. He'd figured he would come back with no more than one or two beers under his belt, not a wild and oversexed woman looking to rip off his belt and pants. If any of his coworkers did hear the sounds coming from his room and from the woman, Chuck was sure he would hear about it the next day. His coworkers would assume he had gotten lucky in the bar. He would be pressed to explain and describe the woman he had picked up. Even if he did explain what had happened, his fellow techs might find the story of how a gorgeous woman come out of nowhere and threw herself all over him to sound a bit contrived and improbable. They would probably think that things like that didn't happen in life. They might also figure that everyday women didn't make sounds like those while having sex.

Wanda was making some pretty professional-level and professional-sounding sounds. If any members of his team heard her shouting the way she was, they might think he had picked up a prostitute. Ladies of the evening had been known to make all kinds of loud and phony sounds as a way of playing to their clients' egos and maybe earning themselves an extra tip at the end of the trick. The only way Chuck could render Wanda silent was to bend his head and face down and kiss her. Then she would stop yelling and kiss him back hard. That would momentarily stop her sound effects, but it threw off Chuck's rhythm, and with his head down, he couldn't get as much windup for each thrust. As soon as Chuck would take his mouth off hers, she would go back to her moaning and shouting. If any of his coworkers were listening in on the goings-on in his room, Chuck figured he might have a hard time convincing them that the woman had approached him and that she wasn't a hooker. She sounded like a hooker—and spread her legs like one.

Wanda didn't make demure sounds, and she didn't hold her legs close together as if she were a modest and proper young lady trying to preserve some kind of secondary modesty. As Chuck slammed himself into her, she slammed her legs apart to an angle approaching 180 degrees. Her lower legs extended out and over the sides of the bed. Her legs were more or less pinned down and held in place by the sequential thrusts of Chuck's lower body. Her lower legs jutted out into the darkened room. They shook and vibrated as Chuck pumped himself into her, and she threw her upper body against him. Given the way she could do the splits, Chuck wondered if she had been a cheerleader in her self-described wild youth.

However, wherever, whenever, and in whatever capacity she had been serving when she developed the ability to open her legs up as far as she could, she threw her legs open for Chuck and threw herself open, panting at him, as he threw his body on top of hers and threw his manhood into the spread-out opening at the center of Wanda's world. In the world of the room and the immediate world of the bed, Chuck drove his rigid and extended manhood into the portal of the world Wanda had thrown her front door wide open to. The front of Chuck's crotch and pelvis smacked into her crotch. Little waves of compression rippled out unseen across her inner waist. Chuck's heavy thrusts stimulated the release of more wetness in her. At the same time, the squeezing thrusts of Chuck's manhood drove the wetness out of her vagina, and the smacking contact of his upper thighs spread it out across their crotch areas and lower waists like a stamping machine extruding plastic into a thin sheet. As their high-impact lovemaking proceeded at its front-and-center fast pace, the front and center of both Wanda's and Chuck's crotches and waists became soaked in her wetness.

As Wanda shouted, yelled, and moaned, she alternately ran her hands over Chuck's back hard or dug her fingernails into the back of his shoulders. As Chuck threw himself onto and into her, she threw her upper body back at him as fast and hard as he threw himself down on her. From the audio portion of their lovemaking, which was provided by Wanda alone, someone in the next room might have gotten the impression that whoever the man was, he was banging a prostitute. If someone had been looking at video of their fast-paced and raunchy lovemaking through a concealed closed-circuit TV camera—fiber optic hadn't yet come into wide use at the time—that person, seeing the shameless way the woman writhed and thrashed around in pleasure and the brazen way she was throwing herself into and at the man, might have concluded she was a prostitute. Hookers acted like that in bed. It was called giving the man his money's worth. Someone getting both audio and video of their lovemaking could just as easily have concluded that the woman was a whore. If any of his coworkers got either an audio or video sample of the woman, Chuck figured he might have trouble convincing them she wasn't a whore. She fucked like one.

At the moment, Wanda didn't care if anyone was listening. She actually hoped there were people listening. She didn't care if they mistook her for a whore, as long as they weren't connected with the phone company and the story didn't get back to her parents.

Lying flat on her back with Chuck running flat out into her, Wanda was in her element. Along with standing on a far horizon, the place she was occupying at the moment was the principal place in the world where she most wanted to be. If individuals she would never see again passed by and came to think of her as a bad girl, it was a price she was willing to pay. It was a price she enjoyed paying. It was a reputation she was aroused and titillated by the thought of having, as long as she could leave behind the people she had left thinking of her as a dirty girl and even an outright slut and walk beyond them to the next distant horizon. Wanda welcomed getting a dirty-girl reputation with people she walked past and away from. She actively encouraged them to think of her along those lines as long as they couldn't follow the line to where she went. Where she was, what she was doing, what she was feeling, and what she would be doing and feeling with a different man on another night meant the world to Wanda. She didn't care if people who happened to overhear her or see her ended up thinking she was the biggest whore they had ever heard or seen. Wanda actually liked the idea that passing people she would never meet again thought she was a big-assed whore. That impression might not have been technically correct, but it was otherwise close enough to what she was doing. It was also close enough to the way Wanda liked to think of herself and think of her life of free love and the freedom of the open road.

Wanda was throwing herself at Chuck, but it was only the latest in a long line of free throws—some might have said foul pitches—she had started many years earlier. A long time ago, Wanda had thrown herself into her life on the open road as much in full drive as she was throwing herself down for Chuck that night. She threw herself into her life of sex on the open horizon with all the abandon with which he was throwing himself into her. Wanda threw herself at him the way she threw herself at her life on the road. She threw her legs open to him and held the charge with all the energy she had always thrown into her life of the pursuit of pleasure. That night, she gave herself to Chuck without reservations, qualms, or regrets and with the full intent to follow her pleasure as far, hard, deep, and throbbing as it could be reached with the help of Chuck that night and with no intention of following him anywhere in the morning.

Pleasure contractions shuddered through Wanda's vagina. From there, they spread out through her lower body like small jolts of electricity that made her gasp between shouts and dig in with her fingers and nails. As Chuck went on, the pleasure surges grew in intensity and effect in Wanda. When bigger surges hit, they sent spasms through her that made her throw her arms out to the sides with fingers spread. The movement was almost an involuntary reflex that Wanda had no control over. As fast as she would throw her arms out, she would regain control, pull her arms back in, and wrap them around Chuck's back until the next spasm made her arch her back and throw her arms out again. She was sliding so deep into pleasure that she was losing control. She was entering a state of full concentration on what she was doing and full surrender to the pleasure she was feeling.

For Wanda, it was a kind of Zen state wherein the world outside disappeared, and she slid down into a deep blue sea of pure and enveloping pleasure. The sea was both soft and engulfing and contained currents that spun her around and sent her tumbling in overpowering surges as if she were a surfer knocked off her board and thrown tumbling end over end through the breaking crest of a monstrous wave. She would come up gasping only to have another wave break over her and sweep her on in another heaving surge of pleasure. Like a bodysurfer without a board, Wanda rode the crest of every wave of pleasure with her body stretched out and straining. As the crests broke over her, she dove headfirst into the trough below, down into the charging, swirling depth of the tumbling tidal surges of pleasure. Wanda had no intention of going in depth into a relationship with Chuck or with any specific man beyond any one specific time, but for that specific night and all the specific nights that would come, she intended to take herself to the depths of pleasure. Wanda had no desire to rein in the heart of any man, and she had no desire to have any man hold position and hold sway in her heart. All she wanted to do for that night and for her life to come was to immerse herself in the heart of pleasure with one man for one night and then head out the door into the sunlight of morning, heading out for the next horizon.

Chuck was well aware there wasn't any depth or possibility of depth to the relationship. Wanda had told him repeatedly at every step that there wouldn't be any depth or any continuance to the relationship after the night was over. At the moment, the only long-term continuance Chuck was thinking about was how long he could keep his continuance up and going with her. For the moment and for the depth of relationship that would never be, all Chuck wanted to do was get himself as deep as he could into her body and soul.

Her vagina was soft, warm, and enveloping. It surrounded his manhood from all sides. It seemed to have a suction that tried to hold him in place and pulled him back inward toward the center of her as he moved back on each stroke to gain leverage to thrust himself inward again. The enveloping fullness and sensual grasp of her sensual orifice seemed to demand every full inch of him at every instant without surrendering a millimeter of him for a millisecond. Her vagina was like the earth surrounding a tree root. It seemed to want to encircle and enclose Chuck's manhood in the warm wetness of its life-giving soil and fix him in place motionless and rooted in her forever. Her body was full, warm, and accepting. At the same time, it was driving, pitching, thrashing, and sweaty. It surrendered itself to him just as she had surrendered herself to him. Other times, it seemed as out of control as its mistress.

At times, Wanda would cease her frenetic motion and lie still. During those intervals, her body lay soft and motionless beneath his body like a content domestic kitten purring in its owner's lap. When she went into motion, her body surged, heaved, and bucked, wild and free like a wild, untamed stallion on the open plains. Chuck knew something about horses and the way they jumped and bounced their riders around. Wanda's breasts, which had already flattened out from her position on her back, further compressed and spread out as Chuck's chest pressed down on them. They swelled back into their mounded shape as far as gravity and their internal fluid dynamics would allow them to rebound when Chuck raised himself up off her chest. Her nipples were erect and alert. Her body seemed to want to draw Chuck in and absorb him as much as her vagina did. Chuck wanted to merge himself with her body well enough, but in a way, it was sort of an exercise in swimming upstream. For Wanda, having sex was like diving over the crest of a wave and being carried along forward with it. For Chuck, making love to her bouncing body was a bit like trying to swim into oncoming waves and feeling the smack of them against his chest.

From experience and practice he had gained with his wife, Chuck had developed a degree of mental and physical discipline that enabled him to prolong the sexual experience and hold off on coming. He had been able to successfully hold off ejaculation for about half an hour, but the surging, sensual pleasure of making love to Wanda's full and flowing body was expanding beyond the control of his male discipline. For the purpose of both his pleasure and hers, Chuck tried to hold back the dam burst for as long as he could, but his love—proverbially, poetically, and physiologically—could not be denied. Chuck's desire and swelling love for her was coming to the point where it could no longer be contained inside him. At any given moment, Chuck's upcoming not-to-be-denied expression of love he could not hold inside himself would be transferred inside Wanda.

Like a thoroughbred horse going out of control, Chuck's disciplined body bolted and ran away with him, heading for an open corral gate. His body tensed along its full head-to-toe length. His hands wrapped around and grabbed Wanda's shoulders from beneath. His eyes closed, and his jaw clenched. Like a champion steeplechase competition horse breaking into a full gallop as it approached the hurdle and launching itself into a jump over a high fence, Chuck exploded inside Wanda in repeated surges of hot liquid passion. In spite of himself, Chuck let out a deeply satisfied groan of male gratification and release. Outside and inside, Wanda felt what was going on with Chuck and what was coming out.

A sympathetic vibration wave of pleasure peaked and ran through her body. Wanda pulled her arms tightly across Chuck's back and gave out with a sustained, gasping cry of her own. Her body tensed up to the same degree as Chuck's body. Sometimes mutual orgasms did happen in the world. As the couple strained and groaned in their mutual clinch, Chuck's hard and extended expression of love continued to surge and strain for all it was worth, sending its hot wetness deep into the hot, absorbing wetness of Wanda. For a long series of straining contractions, Chuck's manhood continued to send its liquid expression of love out and deep down into her encompassing universe of love. He just couldn't stop coming. His manhood had not drawn out its coming with that duration and intensity before, and it hadn't put itself out to quite the same degree for his wife.

At that juncture, most standard couples would have collapsed into each other's arms in exhaustion. But Chuck was hardly through with Wanda, and Wanda wasn't near what she considered finished with him. They both knew their relationship was a one-shot deal. Neither wanted the night to be a one-shot affair.

From his experience with having sex with his wife, Chuck had learned that the best way to keep sex going after coming was simply to keep on going. As the wave of gripping tension passed, even before his manhood had finished squeezing out its last seeming drop, Chuck started pumping himself hard inside her again. The pleasure factor had been reduced a bit by his having come, but the pleasure factor remaining and the raw sexiness of Wanda kept his interest up and kept his manhood up. Chuck had scored doubleheaders with his wife before. He wasn't sure how much he had left in reserve, but he was sure he could score a doubleheader for Wanda. Either way, he was going to have fun trying.

Wanda just as quickly broke her muscular lockup and went back to her initial pattern. Using the twin fulcrums of her shoulders and hips as anchorage points, she arched her back and pushed up against Chuck, thrusting and rubbing with her body from her abdomen to her chest. She went back to rubbing his back with her hands and digging in with her fingernails, as she had before. She also went back to making the same kind of sound effects she had been making. The volume wasn't quite as loud as earlier. After a half hour straight of high-decibel sound effects, she was getting a little hoarse.

With the raw sensuality of Wanda to sustain his interest and the feel of the warm, wet press of her surrounding womanliness to maintain the full attention of his manhood but with no remaining reservoir of pressing fluid to trigger the issue, Chuck's manhood remained locked in rigid, erect stasis as his body continued to drive its fixed rigidness in and out of her, and the rest of his body remained in fluid motion up and down on her body. Chuck did not fade in the stretch, but relative time did. He didn't have his watch on. He couldn't see it on the desk in the darkness, and as the minutes rolled on, he had no particular interest in clock-watching. He didn't know how long it had been since he had come. He only knew that he was lasting longer on his second wind in the second phase.

As time passed, his motions became relatively more grooved and rhythmic. He continued to push himself as deep into Wanda as was reasonably possible without exceeding the point where his deep thrusts would cause her pain. As time passed in the bedroom, Wanda's response slowed down a bit. Sometimes she would push and pull herself up tightly against him and cling to him to the point where Chuck would find himself throwing the weight of both of them around on the bed. Other times, she would lie detached on the bed and moan softly as Chuck continued to make grooved, rhythmic love to her. In those times of relative quietus, Chuck would lean down and kiss her. Kissing her often triggered another round of grabbing, pulling, and pushing on the part of Wanda, using all of her parts. Her sound effects had died down to a conversational level that only occasionally rose back up to wall-penetrating level. They had been at it seemingly as long as a standard opera lasted. Even a big-name opera star with a big chest would have had trouble sustaining an unbroken aria straight through the whole length of the performance. Wanda had a big chest, but it wasn't that big. An opera wasn't supposed to be over till the fat lady sang. Wanda had been singing all across the musical scale from low base to high alto without an intermission for what seemed like almost the length of time it took to complete a performance at La Scala. Chuck liked her sound effects. He didn't mind if people in the next room heard them, but he figured her vocal cords were starting to give out.

Relative identity faded along with relative time. After he came inside her, Chuck came to care even less who she was. He only wanted to get deeper inside her. As Chuck slipped deeper into her body and soul, even her name became unimportant to him. Her obvious identity as a full and obvious woman was all Chuck could see and feel. During the extended duration of their extended lovemaking, Wanda as the full and definitive woman was all the relative identity he wanted or needed from her. She was raw, raunchy, in-your-face sensuality. She was soft and surrendering. She was hot, charging, and aggressive sexuality. She was demure and retiring femininity. One minute, she would be heaving and yelling like a flat-out whore with sweat pouring off her body. The next moment, she would lie quietly sighing like a proper lady. One minute, she would be rubbing the sweat of every pore of her body all over his body. The next minute, she would lie quietly and let him kiss the sweat off her neck and chest. In the suspension of relative time and relative identity of their lovemaking, Wanda was the only world Chuck could see. She was the only world he wanted. She had fully and totally given herself to him. She was a full and total woman. In the relative identity of the world existing between them in the room, she was the full and total world to Chuck. In the morning, she would be fully and totally gone. She had said so enough herself.

As time, real and relative, passed in the room and as love, real and relative, passed between himself and the passing woman, thoughts less centered on passing started to take root in the corners of Chuck's mind. Chuck had his own form of horizon thinking. The first horizon in Chuck's mind was Wanda. She was the immediate and relative horizon he was concentrating on. In that, he was following her instructions and admonitions. She had told him she was a passing horizon who would soon leave him and go off to a horizon of her own.

But Chuck was capable of his own form of far-horizon thinking. His far-horizon thinking occasionally grew quite bold, even in the face of unfavorable mitigating reality—reality past and statements made in the immediate, cautionary present. In the back of his mind, Chuck's over-the-horizon thinking had once grown bold enough to marry a woman he realized in retrospect of time and experience he shouldn't have. Along with the other thing that had risen on him in response to Wanda, his far-horizon thinking was starting to rise again. Though she had openly declared herself to be a passing horizon, in the back of Chuck's mind, thoughts of a horizon a bit more permanent with her were starting to take shape on the margins. The shape and margins of her body had something to do with the shape of Chuck's thoughts on the margin. But as the night progressed, the intensity of their lovemaking remained ratcheted up, and the fullness of her toyed with Chuck's body and soul, thoughts of a more lasting form of love started to toy with Chuck's over-the-horizon-thinking mind.

Chuck had closed the immediate gap with Wanda. But the gap between the more permanent horizon he might wish for with her and real-world horizons was effectively as large as their different lives. She had been specific that there would be no horizon for them together beyond the morning. Before and after she had seduced him, she'd had her exit already planned and set. Tomorrow she would be gone, off to her own horizon, and he would find himself standing alone on his horizon.

Chuck had the physical part under control. He continued to make love to her luscious body at an equilibrium pace that maintained his pleasure and hers, but because he had shot his main wad, the level of feeling in his manhood hovered just below the level of intensity that would have overridden his empty state and triggered a second climax. It was the emotional part that forced the second issue and the second issuing.

As the evening stretched out, Chuck continued to make love to the woman stretched out beneath him. As he continued to make physically balanced love to the unbalanced, top-heavy woman, even though he wasn't fully aware of what was transpiring on the margins of their perspiring, in a deep but rising part of his mind, Chuck started to think in terms of a deeper love for her. Those feelings of love tipped the balance. Gradually, the thoughts of deeper love rose and added themselves into the mix of thoughts and feelings going through Chuck's mind.

Chuck's new rising thoughts of love for Wanda added to the intensity of the feeling of physical pleasure going through his body. Along with his rising thoughts of love for her came a parallel thought of love for a lifetime with her. It was a love that dared not speak its name, but it was a love that added throw weight to the love that Chuck was throwing to and into her.

By the relative measure of time that Chuck wasn't keeping, the time elapsed since his first climax had been more than twice as long as the time interval between when he had penetrated her and when he had come inside her the first time. Chuck's lust for her he was holding at a constant level. His growing feeling of love for her was adding fuel to the fire, even though there might not have been much in the way of reserve fluid left in the tank that fed the fire hose. Familiar sensations were slowly building up below Chuck's waist. Male preorgasmic tension was rising again in him. He could feel the threshold approaching again. It looked like he was going to be able to deliver on his doubleheader after all.

The second installment of Chuck's love for Wanda was on its way. That he would reach a second climax was inevitable. Since it was going to happen, Chuck decided that instead of swimming against the current, he could intensify the coming moment by switching directions and going with the flow. Instead of slowing down as a control tactic to try to reduce the building feelings, like a ski jumper pushing himself off the starting platform of a ski jump and pushing with his ski poles—a single pole in Chuck's case—as he accelerated down the slope, Chuck released his control fully and accelerated the rate of his pumping into her.

The driving feel of pleasure in his driving organ soared up at an exponential rate. His pleasure in everything about his love act with Wanda soared up in tandem with his other more specific feelings. The preorgasmic tension in his body reached a peak. Once again, Chuck gripped her shoulders tightly. Once again, for the swelling moment, she was all the world Chuck could see and the only world he wanted. Once again, the outside world disappeared, and time froze in place as the physical manifestation of Chuck's love for her froze hard in position inside the center of her physical world of love.

The peaking tide of Chuck's physical love for her, reinforced by the growing tide of his emotional love for her, surged out of his body and into her in a second succession of straining waves. Once again, Chuck's muscles and jaw clenched. Once again, his body locked in place in his grip on her and above her. Once again, his mouth groaned out his pleasure in her face. To Chuck's surprise, an amount of liquid expression of his love issued forth, driven by his contraction waves of pleasure.

Once again, Wanda responded with shuddering contractions of her own. Her individual contractions then froze into one long contraction continuous over a short spurt of time and the whole length of her body. Once again, she dug her fingers into Chuck's shoulders. Once again, she angled her head back at the top of her neck. Once again, she gasped out a long gasp.

For several long moments, the couple stayed locked frozen, grasping and motionless, in the gripping throes of the clench of their passion for each other. With their fingernails digging into each other's back, they held their grip. Their muscles started to tremble from the overload. Then the wave passed. First, Chuck's fingers released their grip, and then Wanda's did. Chuck slumped onto her, panting. Chuck's chest, which he had held in sweaty motion above her upper body, merged with the sweat of her chest. His chest settled down upon and covered her full chest. He lowered his head down alongside her head. Their cheeks touched. For several minutes, Chuck lay with his head alongside her head, his open eyes looking down at the sheet immediately under his nose, his body fully on Wanda, and his manhood fully extended inside her and breathed heavily. Wanda lay with her eyes closed and her face toward the ceiling. Verbal sound effects ceased. The only sound in the room was their mutual satisfied panting.

For most couples, that would have been the proverbial end of the affair for the night. Maybe because Chuck knew the morning would bring about the designated end of the affair, as she had declared it would, Chuck wasn't about to let the affair or Wanda go without getting the most out of both. Chuck's manhood was still intact and erect inside her.

With his manhood still in raised condition, Chuck raised his head and looked into her face. "I hope you don't think I'm through with you," he said smoothly to her.

"Oh, I hope you're not," Wanda answered with her eyes closed. She rolled herself onto her side, turning her body toward him. As she rolled herself over, Chuck slipped off her to the side. "You've been doing all the work so far." She repositioned herself and Chuck. "You must be getting tired by now. I can't leave you to wear out your back while I lie here with a big smile on my face and get all the goodies while you do all the cranking. It's my turn to do some of the heavy lifting."

Heavy squat thrusts would have been a better description of what she proposed. Chuck followed the direction her hands were pushing him in. He slipped out of her as he rolled off her and over onto his back on the bed. Wanda splayed herself and her spread legs over Chuck. Since her rollover had moved him toward the edge of the bed, she directed him to slide himself back to the center. After Chuck was through positioning himself on the bed, Wanda grabbed Chuck's still extended and firm manhood in her hand. With the future direction of the affair that night in her hand, she repositioned her body. At the same time, she did a little repositioning of the operational angle of Chuck's manhood. Having completed that, she slid herself down over the still vertical extension of Chuck's manhood.

After positioning herself, Wanda wasted no time in starting to ride him. As she sat with legs off to either side of Chuck's waist, drawn back at the knees; with her wet crotch spread across his crotch; and with her hands on Chuck's sides at the base of his ribs and her warm and wet womanliness enwrapping his masculinity, she started pumping up and down. Once again, the piston of Chuck's desire and love for her was in action, but this time, instead of the piston moving up and down within the cylinder wall, in the reverse mechanical application of their new position, it was the cylinder wall that moved up and down over the fixed-position piston.

Wanda worked her body up and down in a vertical range that extended from raising herself up to a position just short of where Chuck's extended manhood would have popped out of her lubricated guide sheath and then pushing herself all the way back down to where her crotch and the inside surface of her thighs smacked against Chuck's lower waist. Chuck's eyes had grown long accustomed to the dark by that time. In the nearly full darkness of the room, Chuck could see Wanda's body surging up and down on him. Her hair bounced on her shoulders and back. Her big breasts bounced and undulated with all the fleshy and fluid fullness in them. She alternately held her head down, looking down at Chuck along the axial lines of her arms, or threw her head back as spasms of pleasure gripped her. She continued her sound effects, as if being on top and doing all the work hadn't diminished her ardor for the act and the pleasure she was feeling in it. The only thing that limited the sounds she was making was the fact that her vocal cords were getting tired. Chuck thought to suggest that she save something for the next time they made love, frenetic or otherwise. But based on her earlier statements in the bar where he had met her, there wouldn't be a next time.

By Wanda's riding arrangements and by the sustaining drive of his own passion for her, the third phase of their time together stretched out into a time period that came to approach the time interval of the second phase of their lovemaking between Chuck's first and second coming. For an extended length of time, Wanda bounced and tossed herself vertically on Chuck's extended manhood. Then she varied her fare and varied her orientation and thrust vector. While holding her pace constant, she shifted her knees back, shifted her arms forward, took a new grip on Chuck's shoulders, and leaned forward. For a while, she held herself in partial suspension above Chuck while her sexual throttle held her at cruising speed. Her large breasts were now close enough to make contact. They bounced and rubbed on Chuck's chest. Her large nipples touched and dragged across Chuck's less large and nonfunctional male counterparts.

For a while, Wanda held her intermediate position above Chuck, as if she were playing an angel on the wing suspended halfway between heaven and Earth. Though Chuck fit into her spread legs well enough, the analogy of Wanda as an angel suspended between Earth and heaven didn't quite fit. Though she was mounted above him in the air, the hotel room was hardly a sacred temple mount where one drew closer to the divine. Chuck felt earthy enough in her presence. What she was doing felt divine and heavenly enough, but the Bible would probably have classified what they were doing as profane. As far as Wanda's being an angel of love on the wing, in the morning, she would take her love away and take wing. Some might have argued that of all the profane things taking place between them, making love on the run and then running away was the most profane act.

Profane or not, after holding her partially suspended position, Wanda laid herself all the way down and splayed herself out full length on Chuck. Her large breasts compressed and spread out across his chest. Her hair fell around his neck and over his shoulders. For a moment, Chuck thought she was collapsing in exhaustion. Her subsequent moves quickly disproved that idea. Now horizontally oriented, Wanda continued to pump at the speed she had sustained from the start. She surged and heaved herself horizontally across the full length of Chuck's body. Her breasts bulged out under compression. With their front ends stuck in place on Chuck's chest by friction and sweat, the main bodies of her breasts rolled with the surging of her body.

In her new orientation, Wanda's face was now directly above Chuck's face. Whatever she was bringing home to Chuck, whatever she wouldn't be bringing home tomorrow, and whatever she would be taking away in the morning, the position of her face brought home the possibility of kissing. Whatever different lines they traveled off on in the morning, at the moment, Wanda and Chuck were thinking along the same lines. They paused to kiss. It was another long, lips-entwining kiss. Wanda kept her hands gripping the ends of Chuck's shoulders. Chuck put his hands on the sides of her head. He ran his hands through her hair hanging down past the sides of his face.

Wanda sat back fully upright. Instead of resuming her original position with her arms braced on Chuck's sides, she placed her hands on the sides of her hips. Like a hotdogging bronco buster in a rodeo showing off for the audience by riding a bucking bronc without holding on to the reins, Wanda started pumping again, thrusting herself up and down, using her leg and thigh muscles alone. Chuck felt she should have put her cowgirl hat on for that part of the performance.

For some time, Wanda balanced and bucked on Chuck like a circuit rider in a rodeo riding a bronc or a bull. She apparently tired of the position or found it to be unstable. She spread her arms out to the sides, held them straight out, and bumped up and down on Chuck. Instead of a rodeo rider, now she looked like a surfer balancing on a surfboard, sliding down a bumpy wave. Then she brought her arms around parallel to each other and held them out straight in front of her. Now she looked like a skier who'd lost her ski poles, bouncing her way down a rock-strewn slope without any snow on it. The combination of arm moves made her look like a yoga master trying to do a graceful routine on top of the cab of a pickup truck driving over a pothole-filled country road. Finally, she gave up her free-form moves and went back to leaning on her arms with her hands held on Chuck's sides.

The full length of her body seemed to merge with the full length of his body. In their close clinches, her passion flowed over him. Her life flowed over his. The net result of their extensive and extended full-length physical merging was that in Chuck's extended-horizon thinking, Wanda was coming to merge full length with the fuller extension of Chuck's soul.

Time wore on, but neither Chuck nor Wanda had worn out yet. Their surging continued. Wanda showed no sign of growing tired or wanting to quit. She seemed to be reaching for a distant horizon to cross. She had told Chuck she was a horizon that couldn't be achieved. She had basically declared herself to be beyond reach, at least for more than one night. She had put herself existentially beyond reach beyond any long-term horizon.

But Chuck's horizon thinking had a way of running out ahead of itself where women were concerned, especially this woman who had come running after him and whom he had entered. It also had a way of ignoring and mentally jumping barriers that seemed beyond all reach.

Wanda had declared herself beyond reach. But Chuck's horizon thinking was running out ahead of her. Her soft-edged and hard-edged sensuality had been filling his mind and fantasies since he met her in the bar. Her warm and voluptuous body had been filling his arms since she arrived in his hotel room. Her hot, sweaty, free-running passion had been filling his senses to overflowing since they started making love. Her wetness poured out of her to soak his lower body as her desire poured out over the rest of him. Her vagina engulfed and covered the full length of his manhood extension. Her vagina seemed to be absorb and merge with his manhood. In the times when their bodies were pressed together, Wanda rubbed her abandonment to passion all over him. In her coming, she pressed herself along the full length of Chuck's body. She was warmth, life, and energy wherever he touched her and whenever and wherever she pressed her body next to his. Her warmth, life, and energy were saturating his soul down to the deepest level, the level where deeper love, ever after, and for a lifetime lay. Despite her statements that he should not even think about falling in love with her, as their lovemaking drew out into hours, Chuck was falling in love with her.

Wanda had been on top for more than an hour. Except for the interval when she had stretched herself out and down on him, she had been perched vertically above him for most of the time. Once again, the physical pleasure of the encounter was holding constant. That, in turn, held Chuck's manhood in a consistent erect state, but due to exhaustion of limited resources, nothing further had been forthcoming—it was actually a third coming Chuck was looking for. The ongoing physical stimulation held things constant. Everything they were doing, which Wanda was primarily doing in that particular position, still felt good. But the physical stimulation held constant at a level below the threshold that could have overcome the inertia and driven things to a level that would have allowed Chuck to reach the breakthrough point where he achieved the triple-header he had set as his goal.

As Chuck's manhood held its orientation inside Wanda, in his mind, a new orientation to her rose. As his love for her and his over-the-horizon thoughts of a life with her increased, the feeling of pleasure in the act of love he was performing with her increased. The feeling of pleasure in his manhood slowly climbed over and above the neutral level it had been holding at. Once again, love was rising to tip the balance and trip the trigger. Preorgasmic tension rose in Chuck again. He gripped Wanda tighter and kissed her faster.

As the new orientation peaked, Chuck sought out a new physical orientation with her. With Wanda sitting and bouncing on his waist, Chuck pushed himself up into a sitting position facing her, with his legs still pointing straight out behind her hips. As he came fully upright in front of her, while remaining fully upright inside her, Chuck wrapped his arms around her, pulled her in close again, and started kissing her hard once more. The sudden upturn in his ardor coming as it did—and would again soon enough—so late in the game caught Wanda off guard. The thrust of his new love and the sudden change in position it inspired took her by surprise enough that it broke her stride. She stopped pumping. For a minute, she sat there on Chuck's lap as the clinch of his kiss froze her in position. She held her arms out to the sides and down at an angle as Chuck kissed her. Then she recovered and wrapped her arms around Chuck and joined in the active dynamics of kissing.

For several more minutes, the couple kissed. But sitting upright with his legs straight out and the weight of Wanda pressing him backward was an awkward position for Chuck to maintain. He leaned back and dropped down onto the bed, pulling her along with him. As he pulled her down on top of him, he kept his arms wrapped around her and continued kissing her as they went down. He continued his kiss as they arrived flat out on the bed. Once they were back down on the bed, Wanda repositioned her legs behind her and out to the sides the way she had before when she had lain down on Chuck. Instead of pulling her arms out from under Chuck and gripping his shoulders with her hands, as she had done before, she left her arms wrapped around under him.

For a while, the couple just kissed. Then Wanda started up pumping again at the same oblique she had used earlier. She went back to making sound effects, but they were a bit cut off and muffled at her mouth by the press of Chuck's kiss. She rubbed her body over his body as far as the tightness of his embrace and the anchoring of his kiss would permit.

Chuck and Wanda surged against each other and into each other, locked together in their moist and intimate struggle on the wet sheet of the hotel room bed. The fullness of Wanda was merging with the fullness of Chuck's being. In the face of her free-ranging sexuality and free-running passion, in the free run of his desire for her, Chuck's free-running horizon thinking jumped the fence of her words that he had no future horizon with her. His horizon thinking further jumped over her cautions for him not to fall in love with her.

Given the expanded horizons that Chuck's horizon thinking dared to reach for, it was somewhat inevitable that he was starting to think beyond the horizon Wanda had declared off-limits. As he lay wrapped in her arms, wrapped in their hot, wet passion for each other, she was the only world Chuck could see. Despite Wanda's dictum that he shouldn't think about a life with her or look for her on the horizon in the morning, Chuck was starting to think in terms of a wider horizon and a more extended life with her. In an earlier version of horizon thinking, a younger Chuck had once dared to visualize himself as a Lady Chatterley's lover, living as the kept man of the older country matron he had lost his virginity to. Now, in Chuck's more mature horizon thinking, he dared to think of himself and Wanda as life partners keeping company and keeping each other. Given that she liked life on the road so much, Chuck figured she wouldn't want to stay sitting around an apartment, waiting for his return. He would probably have to take her on the road with him when he went out on service calls. They could combine careers. While he did his repair and installation work, she could do her lingerie shows in the cities and towns he was sent to.

Chuck liked the idea of a vagabond life shared with her. At some point, he would have to confess that he worked for the phone company, but he didn't think the truth would present any kind of real problem. One possible problem could be transport. Wanda was a classy lady. She probably drove a classy sports car, he thought. Chuck didn't know how well she would take to riding in a phone company truck.

Chuck's vision of home and a life with a woman had disappeared with the revelation of his wife's infidelity. Since then, his horizons had been empty. Wanda was the most intense vision of warmth, closeness, fullness, life, love, giving, desire, and passion he had experienced since his wife's betrayal left him standing in the void. In the one night Chuck had known her, Wanda had more than filled in the visions he had lost in his wife's betrayal. The sex was even better than it had been with his wife. Wanda had reactivated Chuck's horizon thinking, which had hung suspended in limbo in a dead valley between dead and cold horizons on all sides. Since he had gone into energetic motion with her, his horizon thinking had gone back into motion. As his body had gone into fast-flowing, free-form motion with her, his horizon thinking had gone into its own free-running flow. She had declared herself to be an unattainable horizon. But Chuck's horizon thinking had a mind of its own.

Her full lips felt good pressed on his. Her warm and full body felt incredibly good stretched out on him. Her passion and desire felt good as she poured the intensity of her love over the outside of his body. All the feelings of sensuality that her full body and full sexual appetite delivered had energized Chuck's body. It felt sensual at all levels of his body to be in motion with her. In Chuck's mind, it felt just as sensuous to have a horizon to be moving toward again.

Wanda had awakened and aroused Chuck's horizon thinking and had driven it off the dead neutral it had been stuck in. The rising level of his horizon thinking was slowly charging up his manhood over and above the dead neutral state it had hung suspended in since he came inside her the second time. The stimulation of his rising horizon thinking and the rising level of his horizon feelings for her was generating a rising-level-possibility feeling in his manhood. Despite the drained status and seeming exhaustion of the system, things seemed to be improbably building toward another climax.

The possibility was rising—it had actually been risen for some time—that he might be able to achieve the goal he had never been able to achieve with his wife. The level of possibility thinking in Chuck's mind reached the kickoff point. He came to think it could actually be done. The level of possibility feeling in him had risen, but it remained just below critical mass. It would take a little help from Wanda to get to the tipping point. Given their relative positions, she held the possibility keys all around.

Chuck whispered in her ear that if she sped things up a bit, he might be able to reach a personal best that he hadn't reached before with any woman. Wanda was game for the personal best a man could give her. Getting the personal best out of any man was what her game was all about. As long as the man was up, Wanda was up to trying.

Wanda raised herself partway up in order to gain maneuvering room and a better operational and leverage angle. She accelerated her pumping to a frenetic pace. Her hair bounced and flew. Her body thrashed. Her breasts trembled and undulated. The bed shook and squeaked. Wanda's punctuated cries blended together into a long, sustained wail of pleasure. Wanda reproduced the drawn-out cry she had heard at the climactic moment from the unknown woman in the next room of the motel on the night that had set the pattern she had played out since then and was playing out that night in the hotel room with Chuck. Wanda hit her sprint speed and held her stride for the critical minutes it took to make the critical difference.

Chuck held on to her as best as he could, but there was no stable platform to hold. Every inch of her body was in high-energy motion. He was getting an appreciation for what it was like to be an aquatic acrobat in a show at Sea World, trying to hold on to and stay with a leaping dolphin.

Chuck didn't know how many physicians ever prescribed sex as physical therapy, but the stimulation of Wanda's accelerated humping was just what the doctor ordered. The pleasure and tension in his manhood rose slowly but inexorably above the idling level it had been stuck on and surged into the overload zone. Chuck's entire manhood system went into deep contractions, straining and pushing against the soft, wet walls of Wanda's vagina, struggling to squeeze out the last few drops that weren't there to be expelled. Chuck let out a deep moan of male satiation and release.

At the feeling of Chuck's contractions and the sound of his groan, Wanda stopped moving. She tensed her body and gripped with her hands. The muscles in her butt tensed harder than the rest of her body. She squeezed her thighs together. As his lower body contracted, trying to expel what wasn't there to be expelled, Chuck raised himself up off his shoulders. His neck and head bent forward toward her face frozen in the grip of pleasure just above him. Chuck's forehead touched her forehead. Their noses touched. Her hair hung down in blonde cascades along the sides of her face and his.

As far as reaching sexual far horizons, it was Chuck's first triple-header. Though she didn't keep a logbook of comparative statistical records, it was an endurance record for Wanda too. In high school, Chuck had run track, but he and Wanda were too tired to take a victory lap. Chuck laid his head back down on the bed. Wanda laid her hands on the sides of Chuck's chest and laid her head down on his chest with her cheek resting on his skin just below the base of his neck. Her hair spread out to the sides. For several long moments, there was silence in the room.

"I think we kept the whole wing of the hotel awake the whole time," Chuck said by way of making proverbial postcoital conversation. Wanda's head was turned off to the side. He couldn't see her face in the darkened room, only a disheveled tangle of blonde hair. "If the manager doesn't evict me in the morning, he'll probably go to a local courthouse and have a judge slap a gag order on us. At least he'll probably charge me double for wear and tear on the furniture."

"I was the one making most of the noise, honey," Wanda said. "The night manager may still be on duty when I leave. If he wants to shut me up, he'll have to grab me and tape my mouth shut as I walk by."

As far as taping went, Chuck liked the thought of Wanda in bed with her hands taped behind her back, unable to go anywhere. He liked the vision of being taped into bed by her every bit as much.

"But I'll be on my way out anyway. It will be a bit like closing the barn door behind the horse as it leaves. If I kept anybody up, it won't do any good for me to go around knocking on doors and apologizing after the fact. I don't care who hears me. I like getting as deep into sex as much as men like getting into me. I don't ask them to hold back their energy from me. They can let it all out inside me. By the same token, I don't hold anything back either. I let it all out as much as they do and in any way that moves me. If I make sounds at the top of my lungs and that forces people to put a pillow over their head to keep the noise out, that's their problem. I like my loving too much to hold back on any part of it or curtail any expression of it."

In the darkened room, Chuck could feel the side of her mouth move against the skin of his chest as she spoke.

"I'm not going to be with any one given man for more than one given night. I figure I've got to make the best of any given opportunity that comes my way. When I get going, I want to enjoy myself all the way. I want the man to enjoy me just as much. I appreciate a man loving me. In return, I like to let him know how much I appreciate it and enjoy what he's doing for me. To do that, I let out with what I'm really feeling, even if that means letting out a yell at the top of my lungs. I want to remember the night. I want the man to remember the night. If I end up keeping someone up in the next room all night, well, that'll give them something to remember."

Spoken like a true wild country girl turned wild, urban, sophisticated big-city-woman lingerie consultant, Chuck thought. "You are one hell of a woman when it comes to everything that goes with loving," he said, in complimentary mode and in an obvious pun. "You're quite a little wildcat all around. As far as wildcats go, you're like one of those oil-drilling wildcatters. When it comes to resource extraction, you're a one-woman oil-drilling company. I think you pumped the well dry. I'm going to have to apply for one of those oil-depletion allowances they give oil companies when their wells start running out. I think you drained every last drop out of me."

"Doesn't make a whole lot of sense to keep it to yourself," Wanda said. "Nature made that part of a man's life to be shared with a woman."

Chuck wondered to what degree she ever considered the possibility that men and women were made to share whole lives together as well as passing sexual aspects of their lives.

"I might have had an overflow situation," Chuck said. "My tank hasn't been drained out since my wife left me. For what it's worth, though, I never had a triple-header with her in the time we were together. I guess that puts you one up on my ex-wife."

Wanda shifted her head around a little more toward Chuck's face. "Honey, you're a great guy in bed and all around. If your wife dumped you, she's a snotty bitch or a stupid bimbo to drop a man like you. Tonight her loss is my gain, for the night at least. When I leave here in the morning, it'll be a point of pride on my part to say that I gave you something your wife never did."

The question of leaving touched on the new-horizon thinking that had been going on in Chuck's mind. While they were still undressed, he decided to address the question in one small way.

"We may have worn ourselves out, but we didn't kill the whole night," Chuck said, trying to sound witty and country romantic at the same time. "It's still a long time till morning. You don't have to leave right away. I sure don't want to kick you out of bed. The morning will get here soon enough on its own. You don't have to go sprinting away out ahead of it. You can stay here until the morning."

Wanda turned her head all the way around to face Chuck. She set her chin down on his chest. "I usually make it a habit to keep moving," she said. "But right at the moment, I'm too tired to move another muscle. While I'm down here on the bed with you, I think I'll just take you up on your offer."

Chuck felt almost as gratified by her agreement to stay with him as he had felt when she showed up at his door.

"I will be gone in the morning, like I said," she added. "But like you said, the morning isn't here to see what I do with the rest of my night."

She pushed herself up and off to the side but not to slip away from him. Chuck's manhood disengaged from her and slipped out as her lower body rose up and angled to the side. It was starting to lose erectile tensile cohesion anyway.

"What the morning doesn't know tonight won't bother it when it gets here."

Wanda reached over and grabbed the top sheet and blanket, which had been relegated to the side at the start of their lovemaking and pushed farther away by their thrashings. She wrapped the sheet around her shoulders and laid back down on Chuck, pulling the sheet and blanket over him as well. Her large breasts spread out across his chest, as they had before. She lay flat on top of him, not off to the side, as she had done with her trucker lover earlier. She didn't partially dress herself.

"Like I said, if you don't try to hold me in the morning, you can hold me for the rest of the night." She laid her hand on Chuck's chest, as she had before. She kissed his chest once and then turned her face to the side and laid it down on his chest, as before. Her hair spilled across his chest, as it had before.

She fell silent. Chuck didn't disrupt the moment by interjecting any further question. It was another juncture wherein words weren't necessary.

He feared any more words might derail the status quo. The morning was uncertain, but Chuck didn't want to lose the moment. He brought his arms up and softly wrapped them back around Wanda. Whether he could hold her in the morning in any manner was the universal question over the horizon. But the morning and the question of whether he could hold her or convince her to stay might as well have been out on the other side of the universe. Thus, Chuck held his questions about her plans for leaving for her next horizon and held his tongue. The only thing he wanted to do at the immediate moment was hold her.

Wanda's fingertips moved slightly on the corner of Chuck's shoulder. He felt the warm press of her body laid out full length on top of him. Her thighs laid on top of his. Her legs and feet were on top of his. The warmth of her body filled the bed against the cool of the air conditioner running beneath the blinds drawn over the window. Chuck lay there in the dark, thinking about what had happened.

The home he once had thought was his had become a hollow and empty space since his wife's infidelity. The jobsites he had been sent to since then had been equally hollow and empty, more so because the sites were away from the familiar ground he had once called home. His life had been meaningless movement between a series of hollow and empty spaces. He had come to this town expecting to find another empty place farther away from the empty place of his home city and another series of vacant nights spent sitting in his hotel room or looking out the window of a local bar. He had expected a satellite empty shell in a distant and removed orbit from the primary empty shell of the home he no longer had.

Instead, he had found a woman who filled up the three-way empty space in his bed, his heart, and his mind. She had come out of the horizon and filled the empty and drifting horizon that his life had been. Tomorrow she would disappear over another horizon of her choosing. She was as emphatic that she was going to leave in the morning as she had been about making love to him. Chuck's horizon thinking toyed with ways of trying to get her to stay or at least to tell him where he could find her again, but he didn't think that was going to happen. The way she had come to him out of the blue had been a miracle in itself. Double back-to-back miracles like that just didn't happen in the world.

As Chuck's mind drifted over the improbable future horizons he probably didn't have with her, Chuck and Wanda drifted off to sleep.

During their night of sweaty and intense lovemaking and the quiet aftermath when she had lain peacefully on top of him, Chuck had developed a sensitivity to the horizon idea of staying with the exotic and provocative woman who had come to him out of the half-light of a small-town country bar. In more ways than one, she had become a horizon he could relate to and wanted to keep on relating to.

———

Years of practice had calibrated Wanda's sense of morning and morning light to the point that she would wake up at the first sign of an increase in the rising curve of dawn light. When she woke up the next morning after her night of abandoning herself to passion with the man she had picked up in the bar, Wanda knew instinctively by the level of light filtering into the room through and around the drawn drapes just how much time she had to make her exit, get back to the motel in which she was staying before her coworkers were awake, get herself cleaned up, get to the jobsite, and make it look as if she had spent an uneventful night in her motel room.

Wanda was doing two nonstandard things this time. First, she was trying to work her off-hours game around a full installation crew and keep them from finding out she was cruising bars and cruising men. Usually, she worked alone when on the road or with one other tech. It was a lot easier to indulge her private side career as a roving one-night courtesan if she was working alone. Trying to juggle a whole work crew and keep them from learning about her extracurricular activities presented a lot more problems.

Wanda's second departure from her usual protocol was that she wasn't planning on departing as fast as she usually did. She hadn't partially redressed herself for a quicker getaway in the morning. She had slept on top of Chuck for the night instead of sleeping off to the side so she could slip away from him without waking him up. He would probably feel it and wake up when she crawled off him.

The reason for Wanda's second departure from her usual departure procedure was that she liked Chuck more than any man she had known in the past. He was the best lover she had ever had and the nicest guy she had run into in her life on the run. There wouldn't be any contact between them in the morning. She would be gone when he woke up.

Chuck looked sexy lying there sleeping, the proverbial combination of little boy and grown man. Wanda thought to kiss him as he lay sleeping, but she thought that might wake him up. After all the work he had done for her the night before, he probably needed his sleep.

Instead of kissing him, Wanda eased herself off him. He did not wake up. Then she eased herself off the bed. He did not wake up. She stood up next to the bed and laid the covers back down over him. Then she walked over to the bathroom, turned on the light, and closed the door behind her. Inside the bathroom, she turned on the water, grabbed a washcloth, and started taking a shower.

Chuck wasn't sure whether it was Wanda's movement in getting off him and out of bed or the sound of running water that woke him. All he knew when he came fully awake was that she was gone from the top of him and gone from his bed. At the end of the room, he could see light coming from under the bathroom door, and he could hear water running. She was still there, but apparently, she believed in washing after sex, at least the next morning. Chuck looked over and checked the lit numbers of the standard hotel clock radio on the end table next to the bed. He had about two hours before he was scheduled to meet with his installation crew down in the hotel restaurant for breakfast. From there, they would head out to the jobsite, where they would meet the crew from the Columbia office and start the job.

Chuck turned and sat up on the edge of the bed. He wasn't sure how to proceed next. He could wait for Wanda to emerge from the shower, but knowing the length of time women spent in bathrooms, he figured he might have a long time to wait for her to come out. Sitting up naked in bed with the lights off and waiting for her to come out didn't make much sense. He reached over and turned on the wall light. In the increased light of the room, he looked around for his pants. He spotted his underpants and jeans lying in a heap on the floor where he had been standing when Wanda pulled them down. On either side of his pants were the work shoes he had danced around while unlacing to take his pants off the rest of the way.

Chuck got up out of the soiled bed he and the soiled woman had spent their thrashing night of passion dirtying each other up in, walked unadorned across the room, and stood by the pile, preparing to get dressed. Given the extended length of time they had been naked together during the night and the amount of energy they had expended together in their naked condition, Chuck thought about walking over to the bathroom door and standing there naked while waiting until Wanda walked out of the shower naked herself. Some people might have called it a romantic gesture, but to Chuck, it seemed kind of presumptuous. Greeting her naked might make it appear he wanted sex again immediately, he thought. She might not be in the mood for more sex. She might get the idea he thought of her as a receptacle instead of a woman. It could blow any chance of his talking her into staying longer.

Chuck bent down and untangled his underpants from the pile. There was dried sweat on the upper part of his body, and Wanda's wetness still clung to the lower part of his body. His manhood and crotch were still sticky from the semidried liquid expression of her passion. Chuck figured his underpants would probably stick to him when he tried to take them off. He needed a shower as much as she did. He considered joining her in the shower. Since they had been lovers the night before, he probably had earned the right to barge right in and join her in her shower. Some people might have considered it a romantic thing to do, but Chuck felt it would be a presumptuous thing to do. Besides, the tub and shower were kind of narrow and not all that big. It would be a bit crowded for two. He could wash up after she showered. Given the amount of time women spent in bathrooms, Chuck quipped to himself that he might have enough time to call room service and have breakfast sent up.

Though Wanda hadn't charged him anything for her services, Chuck's mental quip that she would be in the bathroom all morning wasn't the first time he had sold her short. Wanda knew mornings, and she was a practiced hand at moving quickly in the morning. As Chuck bent over to put on his underpants, the water stopped running in the bathroom. She had finished her shower much more quickly than his stereotypical estimate of women spending hours in the bathroom. He pulled on his underpants slowly, listening to the sounds of movement coming from behind the closed bathroom door. Then he picked up his jeans and started putting them on. As he was finishing buckling his belt buckle, the bathroom door opened, and Wanda walked out into the room, drying herself with a towel. She was as quick at drying herself as she was at washing. But her hair wasn't wet. Apparently, she hadn't washed it. That saved washing and drying time.

She walked toward Chuck in the middle of the room. She had already dried her shoulders and chest. As she walked, she dried her midsection. Her large breasts swayed and jostled against each other as she dried herself vigorously.

"Well, look what's up," she said in a wry voice as she walked toward Chuck. "No sexual pun intended." Her quip was sort of a reverse double entendre. His manhood was still asleep after its long workout the night before. "Though we probably both looked a bit bedraggled when we got up. We probably both got out of bed looking like something the cat dragged in. I sure did. I thank you for letting me use your shower. At least I got the sweat off myself."

She ran the fingers of one of her hands through her tangled hair. "My hair's a mess, and I don't have any way of straightening it out here. I didn't think to bring my hairbrush with me. It's back at the motel room I didn't stay in last night. The room was kind of a waste of money, but I'm putting it on the company credit card. I don't plan to fill in the accounting department on the way I was really filling in the night and how I was getting filled in last night."

She stopped in the middle of the floor, just short of the red lace thong she had kicked to the side the night before. "When I get back to my motel room and get my hair brushed, I'll look human again. My legs may be a little sore when I go to reach for the gas pedal, but at least I won't go back on the road looking like I had a bad-hair week. As far as my week goes, I'll probably be walking bowlegged for the rest of the week."

She finished drying her waist. She paused for a moment with the towel positioned in front of the entrance to the restricted landscape Chuck had explored thoroughly the night before. She went back to her complimenting-a-man's-sexual-ego voice. "I must say, that was quite a night all around. I've never had it quite so good before from any man. When I got up this morning, like the country saying goes, I felt like I had been rode hard and put away wet. Or is that rode wet and put away hard? I don't always remember how all these country sayings go, but I guess that one works the same from both ends. Just like you worked well for me from both positions, top and bottom."

Chuck smiled at her calculated compliment.

Wanda started drying her legs. "You were still asleep when I got up. From the workout we gave each other and the way we both fell asleep so fast, I thought you'd probably sleep till noon. Believe me, I'd have liked to stay right there with you, but I don't have time to waste. I've got to get myself up and get going and get back on the road."

She looked up at Chuck. Other than his hair being mussed a bit, he looked as athletic and energetic as he had when she walked in the door. "I must say, you're looking none the worse for wear after last night. You look pretty hale and hearty this morning. I may have drained you out in one way, but you look like I didn't drain the life out of you. At least I won't be leaving you in a crumpled heap when I leave."

Wanda focused in on the fact that Chuck was dressed in his jeans but was bare-chested. "I'll also be leaving you dressed the same way I found you when I walked through the door. It looks like I'll be leaving you just the way I found you all around."

Chuck focused in on her nakedness, which wasn't being concealed to any substantial degree by the towel she was drying her leg with. "Believe me," he said in his own sexually wry voice, "I'd like to leave you here in the state of dress you're in right now. It would make my work a lot more pleasant and make my day go faster to think of you waiting here for me in the condition you're in now." Chuck had been trying to think of a way to broach the subject of getting her to stay for as long as he could persuade her to extend her stay with him. The only thing he could think of at the moment was to use the suggestive humor he had. It was the only opening Chuck could see to test whether she might give him another opening.

"Honey, the word *waiting* doesn't appear anywhere in my dictionary," Wanda said with her head down as she dried her foot with the towel. "I don't sit around waiting for anyone. I don't sit around waiting for any man. I'm not about to spend my life sitting around in an apartment, waiting for a man, even if he's a rich man who's got me stashed in a luxury penthouse overlooking Times Square in New York or in a playboy villa on the Riviera, overlooking the Mediterranean. I'm not a cheap mistress. I'm not even an expensive mistress. I don't intend to live as any man's kept woman. I keep myself."

Since the beginning of the night before, Chuck had been warming to the thought of being her keeper. How he would be able to keep her in a flat in Memphis in the face of her statement that a condo on the Gold Coast wouldn't hold her was a problem.

She continued. "I keep myself, and I keep myself moving. I'd rather be poor and moving on the open road than walking in circles in one place, even in a rich man's digs. I gave myself to be kept by the road a long time ago. The road is the only keeper I have and the only keeper I know. The road is the only thing I want to be kept by. It's the only life I know or want. A man can keep me for the night. He can wave himself around inside me all night the way you did. But in the morning, I'll be leaving for the open road, no matter what kind of inducement any man waves at me to keep me from leaving."

Chuck's method of using his suggestive joke about leaving her naked in his room to test the water to see if he could get her to stay had backfired. He figured that using the words *wait* and *waiting* hadn't been the right approach with her, as half her vocabulary was centered on leaving.

"You don't have to leave so fast out of here right now," Chuck said. "I'm not running you off. I'll toss you onto your back anytime you want me to, but I'm not tossing you out now."

Wanda had her head down, drying her other leg. She spoke without looking up. "It's like I told you last night. I'm on a tight schedule. I've got to get to my next showing." She just wasn't honest about the kind of showing she had in mind. "I've got to get moving and back on the road."

She stood up. With a quick move, she tossed the towel onto the back of a nearby chair. She was as fully naked as she had been the night before. Her body was as full as it had been the night before. In the coming light of the morning, she looked as gorgeous to Chuck as she had looked before their night of coming had begun.

"I'm not in the business of selling big farm combines or the kind of pieces of large farm equipment you repair, which are so expensive you can sell one unit and earn your commission for six months. I sell lingerie." She bent back down and picked up the red lace thong. She stood back up and held the thong out at arm's length, dangling it on the tip of one finger. "I sell this kind of stuff. Things like this are low-priced, low-profit-margin items. You've got to sell a lot of them to make a mark on the balance sheet. I'm not on commission, but I've got to make a lot of sales to earn my keep so the company will think fondly of me and keep me employed."

Chuck figured she could have stayed employed even more easily by modeling the stuff.

"You wouldn't want to get a poor country working girl fired because you kept her from making her rounds, now, would you?" Wanda had a different kind of rounds in mind to keep making, and wedlock and domesticity would have kept her from making them.

"Actually, I wouldn't mind getting you fired if it meant that you would have to stay with me and that I could take you on the road with me," Chuck said.

"Honey, I'd go crazy after five minutes spent sitting in the backseat of someone else's car," Wanda said. "Even if it was the stretch limo of a rich tycoon."

Actually, if she went on the road with him, she would be sitting in the front seat of a phone company van. If she didn't like riding in the backseat of a stretch Mercedes-Benz with a built-in bar, Chuck figured she would be even less thrilled about riding shotgun in the cab of a phone company service truck.

"If it was a chauffeured limo with a good-looking chauffeur, I'd probably be hitting on the driver after the first three miles." Wanda stepped into her thong quickly and pulled it up into place. "I don't ride in anyone's glove compartment. I ride my own road and head out for my own horizons."

She paused and looked around the room as if she were scanning the horizon. "Do you see where my bra landed? I don't remember where it got tossed when we were distracted by stripping each other during the run-up to our night of bed-bouncing. I don't even remember which one of us tossed it."

"It's over here," Chuck said as he spotted the thin, sheer bra lying on the floor in front of the air conditioner at the end of the room. He couldn't remember who had tossed it there either.

Chuck stepped over and picked up the bra. He walked back to her and handed it to her. Wanda bent forward. Her large breasts waved in the air beneath her. She scooped her breasts up into the bra. Given the weight-to-containment ratio of her breasts to the flimsy bra, the scene reminded Chuck of a fisherman trying to net a trophy bass in a pet-store net made to catch goldfish. With a quick movement that bespoke long practice, Wanda reached around behind her back and snapped the single fastener. After a night of rest, the bra once again seemed strained to just short of its operational limit.

"You'll have to eat something before you get back on the road," Chuck said as she straightened up. "You can't be on such a tight schedule that you can't stop to eat. I'd hate to think of you getting faint from hunger behind the wheel while going seventy-five miles an hour on that open road of yours. Why don't you let me take you out to breakfast somewhere?"

Asking her out to breakfast wasn't part of his plan to keep her around. Chuck didn't have any organized strategy at the moment. He was just trying to think up a way to get her to stay a little longer.

"I thank you for the offer," Wanda said as she bent back down and picked up her leather skirt off the floor. "But I want to get some miles behind me before I stop to eat." She quickly stepped into her leather skirt

317

as she spoke. "When I've got someplace I've got to be heading out to, I don't like to dawdle around and delay leaving." She pulled up her skirt, fastened it, and buckled her belt. "That can put me behind schedule. If I have to stop, I like to stop on the way to where I'm going. It makes me feel like I'm on the way to going somewhere. I don't like hanging around where I've been. That gives me a feeling like I'm stuck and going nowhere. It also makes me feel like I'm falling behind the curve."

To Chuck's way of thinking, she had a lot of curves to fall back on.

She was proving to be a much quicker dresser than his wife had been. Chuck had often sat around grumbling, waiting to go somewhere, while his wife spent an interminable amount of time in the bedroom, getting dressed. Maybe she had been a slow dresser only where he was concerned. She might have been a fast dresser in the times when she wasn't concerned with him. Chuck wondered if his wife had dressed as quickly as Wanda at the completion of her lunch-hour trysts.

"Don't worry about the state of my stomach and how it affects the alertness of my driving. I won't pass out from hunger pangs before I stop," Wanda said.

Chuck had struck out with his plan of delaying her leaving by taking her to breakfast. But there had been a problem connected with that idea anyway. He could have taken her to the restaurant in the hotel, but he was scheduled to meet the rest of his installation team in the restaurant for breakfast before they left for the jobsite. He might have had to face some suspicious looks and embarrassing questions from his coworkers if he'd showed up with a woman on his arm who dressed as if she worked in an embarrassing profession. To keep from being seen, he would have had to take her to some local restaurant away from the hotel. He didn't know where the local restaurants were located. After breakfast, he would have brought her back and dropped her off at her car.

If the situation had been different, Wanda might have taken Chuck up on his offer. But there was a problem connected with that. If he took her to breakfast, instead of bringing her back to the hotel afterward, he would want to drop her off at her car. Except Wanda hadn't come to the town in her car. She had driven one of the phone company vans she and the team from her home office would be using to do the installation work. She had driven the van to the hotel and parked it out of sight. If she had Chuck drop her off by the van, he would know she had lied to him about working for a lingerie distributor. He would also know the company she really worked for and where to find her.

In order to be helpful, Chuck picked up her leather top and handed it to her. As she put on her top, Chuck walked over, picked up her shoes where she had kicked them off by the bed, and brought them to her. When he came back with her shoes, she was already snapping the last of the snaps on her top. She was even quicker at getting back into her clothes than getting out of them. The ease with which she had picked him up in the bar bespoke a polished and efficient skill at seducing men for the night. The quickness and dexterity she displayed at getting dressed bespoke long practice at slipping away the morning after. She was as proficient at the art of withdrawal as she was at her approach.

She slipped her shoes on even quicker than she had gotten back into her other items of limited clothing. Chuck's opportunity to get her to stay longer was slipping away fast. He needed to come up with something fast that would get her to stay. The exercise felt like trying to nail down the wind or catch and hold a flashing sparkle of light reflecting off the surface of rippling water.

"We just spent what was probably the greatest night of my life together," Chuck said spontaneously. Plan A hadn't worked. The only plan B he could think of at the waning moment was to follow the old adage: *When you're at a loss for suave words to use on a woman you like, try the last-ditch fallback strategy of saying what you honestly feel.* "Now you're about to walk out the door as casually as if you were leaving a shoe sale."

"I told you I'd be leaving at first light," Wanda said, running her fingers through her tangled hair in lieu of a comb. "You knew I'd be leaving in the morning before we left the bar. You got back here ahead of me, even though I left first. You probably headed out of that bar on winged feet. The knowledge that I was planning on leaving in the morning didn't slow you down or put any drag irons on your ankles then. The deal was that you weren't going to slap any ball and chains on me when I was ready to leave."

"Isn't there anything I can do to get you to stay a little longer?" Chuck asked.

Wanda stepped over and stood in front of him. She placed her hands on his shoulders. She smiled a friendly but set smile. "Honey, going along with me last night is like going out for football," she said in a friendly but decided voice, using a country high school analogy she thought was sure to resonate with him. "You already knew the rules when we went into our first huddle. I laid down the rules before I laid myself down for you. You agreed to those rules without any hesitation. This scrimmage has only one period. You can't change the rules in the middle of the game or run out the clock further, especially after you've scored the touchdown."

Then Wanda remembered Chuck had said he had played baseball, not football, in high school. "You can't add extra innings after you've scored the home run. I'm not pulling any kind of surprise on you like your ex-wife did. I didn't hold back from you last night in bed, and I didn't hold any truth back before we left for bed. I told you I'd be leaving. I told you exactly when I would be leaving. That time has come. I let you know honestly who and what I am. I told you what I'm about. I'm about leaving, and I'm about to leave. But you've known from near to the moment we met that I would be leaving."

"I still don't know your last name, but I'm starting to think that Leaving is your middle name," Chuck said.

"Close enough, honey," Wanda said in an unoffended but decided-sounding voice. "My parents should have given it to me as a first name. That's why I told you not to get attached to me. I told you not to attach yourself to me. We had as great a time together last night as you said. I enjoyed it as much as you did. I wouldn't trade last night for any of the nights I've had. I loved being held by you all last night. I was your angel when you held me last night. I'm an angel when I can see the door in the morning. But I turn antsy and bitchy when any man tries to hold me for more than one night. I wouldn't be the same woman you knew last night if you tried to hold on to me. It would only mess up what we had together. I wouldn't take well to being held. I would only slip out the back door when you weren't looking. You had enough of that from your wife. You would only get more of the same if you tried to hold me. The difference being that when I slipped out and away, I wouldn't be coming back."

She stepped closer to Chuck and laid one hand on his shoulder in a confidential gesture. "I wasn't lying when I said that I enjoyed last night," she said in a confidential voice. "You're the best I've ever had in bed, and you're the nicest guy I've known, all rolled up into one. And I'm not playing to your masculine ego as a way to put you off guard so I can slip out the door. I meant what I said on all parts."

"Somehow, I have the feeling that all of that and all of my charm isn't going to buy me any more time with you," Chuck said.

"I'm being honest about what I said," Wanda said. "I'm going to remember you. I probably will remember you more than any other man I've had or will have. But I was just as honest about leaving, and I was being up-front honest about leaving the whole time you were distracted by looking at my front. We made some great memories last night. But a memory is all any man can ever be to me. A memory is all I can ever be to you or to any man. Let's not ruin the memory we made for each other by you trying to hold me in place and make more memories that can't be. I wouldn't like being held, and you wouldn't like me if you tried to hold me. To me, it would be another form of bondage."

Chuck still kind of liked the vision of her in bondage. He liked the idea of being in bondage to her just as much.

"You'll have a lot more pleasant remembrance of me in the days to come if you let me go this morning. I live for the next horizon. But I can't live in any horizon any man tries to pull in over me."

"Can't you at least give me your address and phone number so I can find you again?" Chuck asked. The question hung in the air as the last question he could ask.

"If you want to find me again, you'll have to look on the open road," Wanda said in a cryptic, poetic tone. "That's where you can find me. That's where I live. The road is my home. It's the only home I want. It's the only life I want. I'll live my life on the road as long as I'm able. So there's no real reason for me to give you an address. Just look down any stretch of open pavement anywhere. You'll have an equal random chance of spotting me in the distance."

"I thought maybe we could arrange to meet from time to time when we're both on the road," Chuck said. He thought maybe she'd be amenable to some kind of serial meeting arrangement. It had worked in the movie *Same Time, Next Year.* If he could persuade her to stay in at least partial contact with him, eventually, he might be able to persuade her to stay all the way close with him. "At least that way, we could keep in touch."

Wanda shook her head. "That's just another way of keeping me on a leash. Maybe it's a long leash, but it's still a leash. If you tried to hold me from a distance, I'd feel just as held, and I'd feel just as much like I had to get away. I live for the next horizon. I couldn't enjoy moving to any horizon if I felt I had a rope on me that trailed out behind and tied me to a horizon I had already left behind. In one way or another, I've been on the road since my days as a teenage bad girl riding on the back of motorcycles and in the front seats of cars with boys. I drive myself on the road now, but I still take my loving on the road, and I take it at my pace when and where I choose. I've had a whole lot of lovers on the road since I started, but the road is the lover I always come back to and stay with. When it comes to length, duration, and staying power, for me, roads go on longer than any man."

Her voice softened a bit. "But of all the lovers I've had so far, I'll probably remember you the most. When I grow older and reach a stage where I start looking back and start regretting leaving anyone behind, it will probably be you I'll regret leaving the most. If I come to miss anyone, it will probably be you I come to miss. There've been a lot of men ahead of you in my life, but in that sense, you're ahead of all the rest of them. That puts you one up on all of them."

Chuck didn't think that little bit of male one-upmanship was going to mean a lot to him when he heard the door shut behind her. "It looks like all my male charms aren't going to get you to stay with me any longer," he said.

"All I can say about my leaving is what I told you at the start and have been telling you all along," Wanda said. "All I can say about you now that I've come to know you better is that I like you, and I like you better than any man I've known so far. I don't know if that means anything to you. I don't know if that gives you any comfort. But it does stand for something. But that something is all that can exist between us."

"All you're going to leave me with is a casual goodbye?" Chuck asked rhetorically.

She looked a bit bemused at his choice of rhetorical words. "Honey, where casual goes, what I gave you last night went far beyond casual," she said in an obvious tone. "So don't give me *casual* like I held you like a dandelion seed in my hand and blew you away with a slight puff. You got a lot more than casual out of me last night. We've both got the sore muscles to prove it. I didn't shortchange you. You got exactly what you wanted and all that you wanted out of me. We wrote a whole book on less-than-casual relating last night. Don't say the whole chapter was casual just because the last paragraph is a bit brief."

Now she seemingly was a literary editor as well as a lingerie consultant, Chuck thought.

She continued. "As far as goodbyes go, a casual goodbye is better than a lot of drawn-out scraping and clawing with you trying to hold me and me trying to get away. Like I said, we made some really great memories last night. Keeping me around a little longer this morning isn't going to add anything of consequence to those memories. Trying to hold me is only going to trip up what we shared and send it all sprawling on its face. Don't dirty up what we shared by trying to turn me into something you can't make me into and that I can't be."

It was familiar territory to Chuck. He felt he was on home ground in more than one sense. "That's the story of my life," he said in a wronged-male tone. "I always seem to get hooked up with women who are bent on leaving. Like my ex-wife."

"Your wife casually lied to you, along with the other ways she treated you casually," Wanda said. "I've been honest with you from the word *go*. You've known from the start where you stand with me."

"All your honesty isn't doing much of anything more for me than my wife's dishonesty," Chuck said. "When you close the door behind you, your much-vaunted honesty is going to leave me standing just as alone."

"Honesty can be a bit rough up front sometimes," Wanda said. "But it's not as hard as a false hope that falls through. A lie that forms the basis of a great hope can hurt twice as bad when it's revealed to be a lie. Don't build me into a hope that cannot be. As you say, I may be leaving you standing alone at the moment, but standing alone isn't all that bad. I do it all the time. I've done it most of my life. I will stand alone for the rest of my life. I decided that a long time ago. My horizon hasn't changed."

Chuck knew he was beaten. He couldn't match her rhetoric of the open road. He knew his love for her couldn't match in kind or degree her love for the road and far horizons. He didn't want to sound like a whining, complaining, spoiled, and manipulative male any more than he wanted to come across like an obsessive and possessive male. Other than the obvious other thing he had left with her, the last impression he created would be the only thing of his that she carried away with her as she left. If that was the only thing of substance, other than the obvious, she took with her, Chuck didn't want to mess up that last and lasting impression. At least he would leave her with a quality memory.

"I can't stop you from leaving," Chuck said in his wounded-and-resigned-but-mature-about-it male voice. "I won't make a scene. I won't try to stop you. As far as passing shadows go, I just want you to know that last night was far more than something passing and casual for me."

Wanda paused for a moment. But only for a moment. "Well now, it wasn't casual for me either. But I'm thinking I've been remiss, and I should leave you with something a little less casual than a few casual words."

She put her hand under Chuck's chin, brought her face up to his, and kissed him on the lips. It was a soft kiss, not as hard and pressing as their other kisses. Chuck didn't fight the kiss, but he didn't press back hard, as he had done earlier. It was more than a friendly peck on the cheek, but it wasn't as extended as their other kisses, and it didn't carry the promise of more to come. Wanda held the kiss for several moments and then released.

"That should prove that I think of you as something more than just a casual pickup," she said. It also proved to be the trigger move for a quick exit. After she kissed him, she turned around and picked up her small, easily portable purse from the table where she had also set the wine-cooler bottle they had shared the night before. Then she turned and walked toward the door.

Chuck stood in place and watched her walk toward the door. Close to the door, Wanda picked up her cowgirl hat from the counter. Without turning back, she walked toward the door. Having spoken what she considered to be a reasonably honest and straightforward goodbye, Wanda turned the dead bolt on the hotel room door, opened the door, stepped quickly through, and closed the door behind her.

Though it was a quick goodbye by Chuck's time frame, for Wanda, it had been a comparatively drawn-out goodbye. Along with everything else Chuck had gotten from Wanda, by comparison, he had gotten exponentially more words of goodbye from her than her trucker lover and many of her other lovers had received. But after leaving the room, she picked up the pace and headed quickly down the hall. Though Chuck had let her go without a fuss at the end, he had tried to hold on to her more than she had expected. Wanda wanted to clear the hall quickly in case he had a sudden change of heart.

The elevators were around the corner, on the other side of the floor. As she reached the end of the hall, Wanda paused and looked back at the door to Chuck's room at the end of the hall. The door remained closed. He didn't suddenly come running out into the hall, chasing after her. But Wanda hadn't looked back to see if she was being pursued. Looking back at the door of her lover's room, Wanda felt a twinge of regret. She hadn't been BSing when she told Chuck that she felt different about him than she did about any other man and that she liked him and would miss him.

There was truth in what she had said. In the future, if she ever missed a man when she looked back on her life, it would probably be him, just as she had said. She probably would miss him more than any other lover. But the call of the road and horizons was in her.

Wanda held the look for about the same length of time she had held her last kiss with him. Then she pulled herself back together and pulled her thinking back in line with her standard operating procedure. She quickly walked to the elevator and rang it up.

To keep from being seen by Chuck from his window as she left, Wanda had parked the phone company van on the south side of the building. She hadn't even parked in the parking lot of the hotel; she had parked in the parking lot of the shopping center across the street from the hotel. To add an extra measure of disconnect, Wanda had parked the van near the center of the shopping mall, in front of a Radio Shack, the kind of place a phone company van would seem in place in front of.

In the gathering light of morning, Wanda crossed the largely empty parking lot of the shopping mall, got in the van, and drove away. She still had enough time to get back to her motel without being seen. From there, she had enough time to change into her phone company work clothes, comb her hair, get breakfast, and get out to the jobsite as if nothing had happened. Though Wanda had tarried and had felt a twinge of sadness at leaving Chuck, it was over. It was time to get something to eat and time to move on. Chuck would soon fade into a pleasant memory. From Wanda's perspective, that was all she could reasonably expect to happen.

For a while, Chuck stood still in place in the middle of his hotel room, where he had been standing when the woman left. In the end, when it came to leaving, the woman had it her way. But then again, as she herself had pointed out, Chuck had had her his way. He had gotten a lot more out of the night than he had bargained for or imagined when he went to the bar. He had gotten a lot more out of her, and had put a lot more in her, than he had expected to come about. He had reached a personal best with her he never had achieved with his wife. But in spite of all that, or possibly because of all that, when the woman left, it felt to Chuck as if she had taken away a bigger part of him than she had left behind in what other men would have considered a well-satiated and satisfied male ego. In the balance of Chuck's heart, the balance sheet of the time they had spent in the sheets was out of balance in favor of the woman.

Chuck stood in place, contemplating what he'd had with the woman and what he had lost when she left. He also contemplated the woman he had never really had and couldn't really call lost. She had come to him out of nowhere in the bar. She had come to him out of the hall of the hotel and into his room when he hadn't expected her to come. They had both come together and had come more than once together in bed. Then she had disappeared back into nowhere. She had filled Chuck's senses. She had filled his arms. She had filled the night for Chuck. She had filled an empty hole in his life that seemed all the larger and emptier now that she had revealed to him how large the hole was and then had filled that hole. Now she was gone from him as quickly as she had come to him. In the emptiness of the room and his life, it almost felt as if the woman had never been there.

Chuck looked at the almost empty bottle of wine cooler for a minute and then drank the swallow remaining in the bottle. He wasn't sure whether he drank the last draft as a way of toasting the fact that he had scored, toasting the woman, drowning his sorrow, or just trying to look suave and sophisticated to himself. Either way, the wine in the bottle had gone warm to room temperature. Chuck figured the warm wine was all the warmth he was going to encounter on the rest of trip.

After drinking the last drink of wine from the bottle, Chuck stood looking at the bottle. He wondered if he should keep the bottle as a souvenir of the woman. The thought was a bit corny, but Chuck had already saved the beer bottle the woman had drunk out of in the bar as a souvenir. It was on the floor in the back of his car. Chuck wondered if he should throw away the beer bottle and keep the wine-cooler bottle. Given that they both had drunk out of the wine-cooler bottle, it seemed to be a more intimate souvenir. But there was more of the woman's lip gloss on the beer bottle. Chuck didn't come to any definitive conclusion as to which bottle to keep. As he stood looking at the bottle, he decided he would keep both bottles as souvenir remembrances of the woman.

There was another souvenir she had left him. Her wetness still covered his manhood, his crotch, and the front of his lower waist. It had already gone semidry by the time they woke up and he put his underpants back on. Now Chuck's underpants were sticking to his body. For a while, he contemplated not washing and leaving the wetness on him for the rest of the day as a remembrance of his night with the now vanished woman. But after a day of drying, it might be a bit of a painful process to pull off his stuck underwear, he thought. Chuck went into the bathroom and took his own shower. He had a little more than an hour until he was scheduled to meet the rest of his work crew in the hotel restaurant for breakfast. Life had to go on. The work schedule had to be met. Phone company customers had to be served. He would have time later to think about the woman, though he would probably have the rest of his life to remember the woman he would never see again.

———◦/◦/◦———

"Some babe was really getting the blocks put to her last night," Paul Anders said. "I could hear her yelling through the ceiling half the night. It sounded better than the movie I was watching on the porno channel."

Paul Anders was known by the nickname of Porno Paul because he was an outspoken fan of porno flicks. Chuck wasn't surprised he had dialed up the adult channel on the hotel's cable network. If the phone company auditor went over the expenses line by line and found the charge for the adult-entertainment channel, the company would probably make Paul reimburse the cost. The phone company didn't block phone-sex lines as long as the subscribers paid, but Chuck didn't think the company would like paying for their technician's personal peccadillos.

"She sure sounded like she was enjoying herself. At least somebody in this two-bit burg was having fun last night."

Chuck and his installation crew sat around the long table the waitress had made by pulling two shorter tables together end to end. They were all dressed in their phone company uniforms. Chuck had on his own phone company uniform and a fresh pair of underpants. Most of the crew were having the buffet breakfast. The breakfast at the local Hampton Inn they were staying at wasn't exactly Waldorf Astoria gourmet fare. The scrambled eggs were a bit dry. The sliced cantaloupe was a bit old. The bacon was a bit tough. The waitress was a bit old, dry, and tough looking herself. But the coffee was good.

"You're up on the floor above me, aren't you?" Paul asked Chuck.

"Yeah," Chuck answered nonchalantly.

"Then you're on the same floor where Little Miss Screaming Bimbo was getting herself fucked cross-eyed. If I could hear her through the ceiling, she could probably be heard in half the rooms down both sides of the hall on your floor. Did she keep you up half the night?"

A lot of men would have used the opportunity to indulge in male one-upmanship and spin a triumphant male tall tale about his conquest, especially if the story was true. The woman had instructed Chuck to keep quiet about what they had done, but she had also left him the rest of his life to spin and embellish the tale. But Chuck wasn't in much of a triumphant mood. As he had lied defensively to the woman, Chuck lied defensively to the rest of the work crew.

"I went out to a local bar last night and had a few brews," Chuck said casually. "When I got back, I was tired from all the driving I did to get here, and the drinks were making me sleepy. I fell asleep as soon as I hit the pillow. If any action started up down the hall after I fell asleep, I slept right through it."

Chuck could have knocked one out of the park by relaying the story of how he had spent a large part of the night knocked up by the gorgeous woman. In Chuck's expanded-horizon thinking, the loss of the horizon he had glimpsed briefly carried far more weight than the fact that he had scored for one night.

Chuck didn't want to talk about it. At the moment, he wasn't interested in strutting his conquest and having his male ego inflated, when his sense of home and horizon had been drained out and left emptier than before.

The subject of the midnight bimbo and her orgasm chorus faded, and the conversation switched to the work that would begin later that morning.

"Do you know anything about the installation crew the South Carolina branch office sent over?" Ed Weinstein asked Chuck.

"I don't know anything about them," Chuck answered as he picked up his glass of orange juice to finish it. "I never met any of them. All I have is a list of names. We'll find out what they're like when we meet them. I suppose they're just another bunch of regular-guy techs like us. The only difference is that they have a female tech on their team, named Wanda something or other. I forgot her last name, but she's on the list."

"A woman tech?" Henry Archer said. It was more of a rhetorical sneer than a rhetorical question. "Oh, great. That'll stretch out the job twice as long as scheduled. We'll all probably end up putting in double overtime to straighten out her screwups and clean lipstick out of switching circuits."

Henry Archer was an older tech who had been with the phone company for almost thirty years and was nearing retirement. He had some lingering old-school male ideas about the ability of women to handle or understand technology. He could easily imagine women spending hours chattering inanely away and dishing the dirt over the telephone, but he had a harder time imagining a woman being able to understand or handle technology. In Henry's old-line thinking, the thinking of women wasn't circuited in a way that could understand complicated electronic circuits. To Henry, women would always be more proficient at understanding the function curve of a powder puff than delineating a logarithmic scale and were endlessly more oriented to looking at the pattern of their curves in a mirror than understanding an oscilloscope pattern.

"She'll probably put us two steps back for every one we take forward. We'll probably end up staying in this town long enough to earn squatters' rights."

"I don't think the company would have hired her if she didn't know what she was doing," Chuck said as he set down his empty glass. He had just come off a night with a woman who definitely knew what she was doing in the field Henry Archer thought was the only field women knew how to handle themselves in, but Chuck was magnanimous enough to give women credit for being able to understand and handle themselves in high-tech fields.

"She's probably a Jap," John Toman said. "Japanese women are the only ones who have any knowledge about electronics. They teach electronics and computers to everyone in Japan from the first day they start school. That's why the Japs are eating the American electronics and computer industries for lunch. In a couple of years, they'll control the entire market for consumer electronics in this country. Then they won't have to translate the instruction manuals for their consumer electronics into English. We'll all have to learn to read Japanese if we want to program a VCR."

"With a name like Wanda, I doubt she's Japanese," Chuck said. "That name sounds more like something from Oklahoma City than Osaka." He turned and looked at Paul. "But you won't have to wait until you get back to the hotel room porno channel in order to exercise your fantasies. Or exorcise them. You'll have something female to look at and drool over while you work. It should make the day go faster for you. Though it will probably make you work slower."

Paul looked over at Henry. "She's probably got a face that's less attractive than his unshaven ass," Paul said. "She may know what she's doing as a tech, but when it comes to looks, she's probably a real battle-ax.

Women techs probably go into the fields they do because they can't get a man and don't expect to get married and need a career to fall back on. Or they go into fields with lots of men to up the odds of landing any kind of man. She probably went to work for the phone company as a tech because she thought that with all the techs and linesmen in the company, there would be all sorts of men around her. She probably thought that working for the phone company would be the only chance she'd ever have to score."

The other techs sort of chuckled in agreement. They might not have shared Henry's low assessment of the technological aptitude of women, but they did more or less share the idea that women who worked as personnel in a male-dominated technical profession were either ugly or looking for a man. Probably both.

"She probably looks more like a reject from the Armadillo Breeders Association than a porno star."

The others chuckled again. Chuck didn't say anything. He had just come off, in all senses of the word, a one-night stand with his own personal porn star. In the light of the day the woman had left him in, all Chuck wanted to do was keep his love that dare not speak its name quiet. He just hoped the female tech from the South Carolina office was as good at her chosen profession as the woman he had known for the night and then lost in the morning had been at her chosen after-hours hobby. It would be small compensation if the female tech turned out to be as good all around as the woman he'd had and lost. In his prevailing state of mind, Chuck would have taken any positive surprise that came his way. But pleasant surprises didn't happen often in the world. When they did, they didn't stay around long. Chuck figured he'd had a big enough unexpected surprise last night to last him more than a year, if not a lifetime. He didn't expect any more pleasant surprises out of the rest of the trip.

As their breakfast meeting wound down, Chuck gave the group directions to the jobsite and the time to meet. The group broke up and went back to their individual rooms to get ready to leave. Chuck went to his room, where he had unexpectedly gotten what he had needed last night, to get what he needed for the day on the job. When Chuck walked into his room, he spotted the empty wine-cooler bottle sitting on the desk, where he had left it. It was the only physical reminder that the woman had existed and had been there—that and the messed-up bed.

Chuck wondered where the woman was now. If she was just finishing having breakfast, as he was, she might still be within a radius of only a few miles. If she had gotten on the road to put miles behind her and miles between them before stopping to eat, as she'd said she would, she might have been already be well over the horizon and moving farther away by that time, heading out for her next horizon. Either way, she had taken herself beyond Chuck's horizon and had placed herself over the horizon and out of sight of his possibility thinking.

But time, tide, and the phone company waited for no man to mope his way to maturity and come to the acceptance that he had loved and lost. Chuck had to get to the job he had been sent there to do. The maid would clean and straighten out the messy bed. He had to get his messy head together and acknowledge the fact that the woman would not appear on his horizon again.

But Chuck wasn't quite ready to make a full mental break with the woman and his memory of her. He picked up the wine-cooler bottle and stuck it in the drawer with his clothes to make sure the maid wouldn't throw it out when she straightened up the room and changed the messy sheets. He had to lay the bottle on its side to fit it in the drawer, but it was empty and wouldn't spill its contents on his clothes. Whether he kept the bottle as a permanent reminder of the woman was something he would decide later. To Chuck's way of organized thinking, there wasn't a whole lot of sense in keeping a souvenir of a romance that had short-circuited as quickly as it had begun and could not have been and of a woman who would never appear on his horizon again. Anywhere he left the bottle standing in his apartment or his life, it would only stand for what they had momentarily shared out of the bottle and the momentary love they had shared in bed afterward. It wouldn't stand for love that stood for all time or for the rest of their lives. The empty wine-cooler bottle would not stand as the symbolic representation of a triumphant achievement or even as a low-level sentimental memento of a chance meeting that sparked a lasting romance. The bottle would not be a memorial to a full life together. The empty bottle always be a memorial to loss, an empty hope, and an empty horizon. Looked at that way, the bottle, standing empty on a shelf, would stand as an empty negation of love instead of a monument to the triumph of love.

For the moment, he would hold on to the bottle. For the moment, his horizon thinking would hold on to his memory of the woman and imagine the horizons they might have visited and shared together. But in his organized thinking, Chuck knew that soon enough, he would have to acknowledge that he would never see the woman again.

The location of the new microwave relay station they were going to establish wasn't in the town itself. The site was actually several miles outside the town. It was a pleasant drive in the country to get there. It was a sunny and warm summer day in June. The sky was clear in the morning sun, with hardly a cloud in it. The route to the tower site took Chuck over an undulating two-lane blacktop country road that passed by houses and farms, fields, and woods. The bright blue of the country sky seemed boundless and borderless. The soaring, ethereal blue of the sky washed over the mottled and varied earthbound greens of the landscape below it.

Instead of using the car's air conditioner, Chuck had the front windows of the car open. He drove one-handed, with his left arm resting on the car door in the space of the open window, as he had often done as a teenager. Country smells familiar from his country boyhood blew in from the passing farm-and-field landscape outside. It was a country scene not unlike the one Chuck had grown up in. In at least one small way, Chuck had a sense of coming home. For a short period of daring thinking the night before, the woman had become part of Chuck's feeling and thoughts of home. Now his feelings of home and his feelings for the woman were drifting detached and apart from him like the country sky passing above.

Horizons were all around when one drove in the country. A person didn't have to have a poetic soul to be aware of horizons when in the country. It was just natural to be aware of horizons and think about horizons when driving in open country. Chuck was driving into a horizon that reminded him of home. It was probably only natural that he started thinking about horizons and home. Given that the woman had awakened his sense of horizons and home, it was only natural that he would think about her in terms of home and the horizon. More precisely, he thought of the woman and the horizon he had lost her to. When he thought of home, he thought of the home he'd thought he had with his wife but had lost. When he thought of the woman and home, he thought of the home that he had briefly glimpsed in her but that she would never be part of.

Horizons had been a big thing to the woman. She had talked about horizons incessantly. Somewhere out there, she was heading toward her next horizon. As he headed to the jobsite on his immediate horizon, Chuck wondered what horizon the woman was seeing now and what horizon she would be looking out on at the end of the day. If she had left while he and the rest of his work crew were having breakfast, she would have been in the next county by then. If she had left town about the same time and in the same rush as she had left his hotel room, depending on the direction she had taken, she could have been approaching the state line by then. If he had known where she was heading, he could have judged how far she had gone by that time. But trying to figure out where she had gotten to by then was a purely academic exercise. Chuck wasn't planning on doing something impetuously romantic, such as abandoning his work in the middle of the job and hiking out after her. The question of where she was going was as much of an academic unknown as was the question of how many miles she had already put behind her—or how many miles she had on her sexually. She hadn't told Chuck which direction she would be heading in when she left town. She guarded her horizons jealously.

Horizons defined the woman. She had said so. In more than one sense, horizons summed up and put their stamp how the woman had briefly related to Chuck. She had come unexpectedly out of the horizon when she came to Chuck in the bar. She had filled his horizon for one night. In that time, she had been all the horizon he could see. She had been all the horizon he wanted. She'd brought sunrise to a horizon that hadn't seen sunrise in a long time. She'd brought warmth to a horizon that had gone cold and empty. In one night, she had revived his horizon thinking, which had gone numb and inactive. For a short while, there had been light and warmth on the horizon of his life. For the same short length of time, he had thought of the possibility of a new horizon of love in his life. Then the woman had disappeared back into the horizon she had come out of, though he had tried to wrap a horizon around her.

The land rose up and plateaued on a relatively high plain. The outline of the newly completed relay tower jutted up into the sky in the near distance, between the tree lines of the semiopen countryside. In the light of the new morning, he would soon reach his immediate work horizon. Somewhere out there, the woman was moving farther away into the light of her morning, heading toward her next horizon. The sweep of passing countryside seemed to open and spread out to the horizons on all sides. The endless open horizons spreading out beyond and away from him only served to remind Chuck of the horizon he and the woman would not be sharing.

The turnoff to the access road that led to the tower was coming up. Chuck would soon turn off and stop at his immediate horizon. There he would direct and do the work he had been sent there to do. He would remain there until the work was done. For the next few days, the tower would be his horizon.

Chuck would soon stop at his near horizon. Somewhere out there, the woman would probably still be in motion to her more distant horizon. He had lost a horizon he had envisioned that the woman had said could not exist between them. Losing a horizon one thought he had in his hand could be more painful than losing the lover he had in his arms.

Chuck turned down the short quarter-mile access road that led to the tower. Ahead of him, the newly completed poured-concrete relay tower projected straight and clean into the air, inserting its straight, linear shape and its gray-brown color into the random and convoluted shapes and variegated greens of the trees behind it and the wash of blue sky it projected up into.

Though it would be equipped with the best and latest microwave equipment available at that date in the early 1980s, the tower was the last of its breed. No more of them would be built. They would come to be replaced by the ubiquitous narrow-framed cell phone towers held up by guy wires, with the equipment mounted at ground level. The bulkier towers would never come to be celebrated in story and legend, as the earlier steam-engine trains of the Casey Jones era of railroading had. They would eventually pass into history as unknown relics of 1970s and 1980s technology.

Though the tower somewhat resembled a squared-off lighthouse, it would have no resident lighthouse keeper living in it. No children would play within the fenced-in square around the microwave relay tower. No tower keeper's wife would hang out wash on a clothesline at the tower base. The electronic equipment in the tower was designed to function automatically and continuously without human intervention. When not being serviced by technicians, the tower would be locked, and the gate of the high chain-link fence surrounding the tower would also be locked, to be opened by phone company technicians only.

Since there would be no humans inhabiting the automated structure, the relay tower had been designed with a simple form-follows-function architectural ethos in mind. Its shape was as simple and functional as could be reasonably designed to elevate the horn and dish antennae and to accommodate the equipment and the function it was set to perform. The microwave receivers and transmitters inside were hardly simple in the formulas of their design and construction, but they would generate an outgoing signal that was designed to be as straight, clean, simple, and confined as the tower itself. Chuck and the two installation crews would finish the job with all the technological acumen and proficiency the designers of the tower expected for the tower to function. But unlike the upper walk of a lighthouse or the observation tower of a Florida hotel, the microwave tower was not a place that invited one to stay and survey the landscape spread out below. It was not a place designed to set one to thinking about the meaning of life or reviewing and celebrating his or her life.

As he turned toward the job he would dutifully do, Chuck's thinking took a turn back to the woman. The image of her leaving would weigh as much as the sum total of all the other remembered images of her combined. He couldn't put his life on hold for a woman he could never hold and who had no intention of being held. He couldn't sacrifice the horizons he could reach for a horizon that would forever remain out of reach.

He had been a passing fancy of the woman for one night. The desire for anything more between them had been a momentary wishful fancy of his horizon thinking. Life was a movable feast to the woman. The fact that she would always be in motion to another man, the next bed, and the next horizon was apparently the one immovable and immutable factor he or any man would have to come to grips with after coming to grips with her in bed. That she would be gone in the light of the morning was as inevitable as the coming of the sunrise. She had repeatedly said so.

The woman was centered on leaving as much as she was fixated on the next horizon. Leaving summed up the woman. Leaving summed up her philosophy and worldview. She'd had her leaving planned and set for the morning even before she came up to him in the bar. Leaving was all that ever could have been in their relationship. Even their goodbye had been short, truncated, and devoid of any of the proverbial lingering last looks and sad feelings that were supposed to romantically attend when a relationship ended. The woman had left with a wave of her hat.

But that was the way she had planned to leave. The moment she had first said hello to him, she had begun to say goodbye. The sound of the laughter they had never shared hadn't echoed in the sigh of parting they hadn't sighed together.

As Chuck pulled up to the tower, he saw that a single phone company service van was already there. The van was parked perpendicular to the high chain-link fence around the tower, on the far side of the locked gate in the fence. Chuck had left a little ahead of the other members of his crew in order to do the dutiful supervisor thing and be the first on-site. It looked as if someone else had arrived ahead of him. The phone company van was painted and labeled differently from the ones from his service office. The vehicle must have belonged to the Columbia branch service department and been driven to the site by a member of the work crew who were scheduled to meet them at the job, he thought. It seemed someone on the other work crew had been up as early as he had been.

As he pulled up to the fence, Chuck turned his car and drove parallel to the fence, heading toward the van parked farther down the fence line. There was only a grass access strip on the front side of the fence. Chuck drove slowly over the uneven grass surface as he approached the van from the other branch office. He didn't see the tech who had driven the van. The gate to the tower was still locked, so the tech couldn't have been inside the tower. Chuck figured he might have been out walking around on the far side of the tower, inspecting the structure and thinking about how to go about orienting the microwave feed-horn antennae. At least someone was thinking ahead in an organized manner.

The work wouldn't begin until both crews had assembled and coordinated their plans together. There would still be time for reflection before the first stage of the work started. As he finished the last yards of his drive to the job, Chuck used the time to complete the last-stage work of putting the woman out of his mind. He would simply have to go on with his own life and abandon his temporary passing fancy that he could have had a life with his temporary and passing-fancy lady and her philosophy of life on the road.

Chuck figured he would park on the far side of the van in order to allow the other tool- and equipment-carrying vans to be parked closer to the gate so the members of the work crews wouldn't have to walk as far to get stuff out of them. Chuck didn't want to take advantage of his position as project supervisor by parking in the closest spot and forcing the other workers to walk longer distances to get tools and get to their cars. As a supervisor, Chuck figured he could afford to walk a bit. He drove his car up to the van and prepared to pass behind it and go around.

As Chuck came up on the van, he said his last goodbye to the woman. He wished her well in the life she had chosen. As she had structured her life, it seemed a potentially empty and lonely life, but apparently, she had taken that into account. She would have the men and the horizons she wanted.

He would remember her. She would forever remain a warm and intriguing figure on the fringes of his memory. But a memory was all she would ever be. He would never see the woman again.

Then he saw the woman again.

As Chuck came up on the van, a familiar face and full figure topped off by a long mane of blonde hair stepped out from behind the far side of the van and walked around the back of the van. Once again, the figure of the movable feast of the woman was in motion in front of him. Except she wasn't dressed in tight leathers. The figure was dressed in a well-filled phone company uniform.

The familiar-looking figure turned the corner and walked down the left side of the van he was nearing. With his mouth gawking open, he turned his head and looked at the figure of the woman as he drove up on the back corner of the van.

The figure had her back to him, walking away. The full hips of the figure waved as she walked. The swell of hips stretched the dull khaki-colored slacks of her work uniform beyond their designed limit.

"Now, wait a minute!" Chuck said to himself out loud as he drove past the moving figure of the woman. His verbalized exclamation wasn't suave, but it was loud enough to be heard in his car. The window to his car was open, but apparently, the woman hadn't heard his surprise. She didn't look around.

The woman stopped at the middle of the van and turned toward the van. In a crisp and organized manner, she opened the door of one of the built-in carrying compartments in the side of the van. With the door open, she bent over and leaned her head into the open compartment. She seemed to be looking for something. Her bent-over posture emphasized the shape and fullness of her figure. Her large breasts weighed down the shirt of her drab phone company uniform. Her long blonde hair hung down the side of her head, obscuring the side view of her face.

The woman disappeared where she stood behind the van as his car moved by. Chuck's car continued past the back of the van, carried by momentum and by Chuck's not having put his foot on the brake. His mouth continued to hang open from surprise and disbelief. As the car continued to move under its own undirected volition, Chuck turned his head farther back. The inexplicable figure was still concealed behind the van. As the car moved, Chuck tried to put what he had seen together, stating with the way the figure was put together and how much the face and figure resembled the woman he had just put out of his mind and life.

It can't be the same woman. It simply can't be, Chuck thought to himself. *Things like that just don't happen in this world.* The woman had said she worked for a lingerie distributor, not the phone company. It sure looked like her, but it couldn't have been her. His overactive imagination was running away with him. The woman had gotten to him more than he had imagined. He had been thinking about her so much that his thoughts had overloaded and overflowed at all levels, high and low. His subconscious was sticking her face on anything that moved. He had the woman on the brain. He was seeing her everywhere. If this kept up, he would see her face on every waitress, every supermarket checkout girl, and every woman he came within fifty feet of in a bar. His life would be like a bad psychological thriller in which the paranoid, delusional victim saw the face of a nemesis or a departed loved one in the face of every person who passed by on the street. He would have to get control of his thought process and get his mind disciplined, or he would be ready to be fitted for a straitjacket and checked into a rubber romper room in a mental ward. Chuck figured he was losing it somehow. He assumed his one-night stand with the woman who had seduced him in the bar had so fixated his mind that he was imagining seeing her.

Chuck couldn't understand how something like that had happened to his mind. He had always prided himself on having an organized and rooted mind. He had never imagined himself as someone susceptible to hallucinations or momentary flashes of misperception, even about a woman he had made love to the night before. The vision he had had of seeing her again had been his imagination, he decided. He just hadn't been aware of how deeply the woman had affected him.

Chuck figured that apparently, there were quirks to his mind he hadn't been aware of. As the car continued to move, Chuck wondered just how far and deep his obsession with the woman had gone. It had hit an obsessive level if he was conjuring up images of her in everything that moved. Hopefully it had been a momentary lapse and slippage, a onetime mental hiccup that would fade quickly and wouldn't repeat itself. Hopefully it would go away the minute he saw the real face of the real person his imagination had superimposed the image of his dream woman onto.

At that point, Chuck realized he had driven quite a bit past where the van was parked. He was heading for the corner of the fence. In a few more yards, he would be out into the surrounding field. The person he had mistaken for the woman would have double reason to think he was crazy.

Chuck put on the brake, stopped the car, shifted into reverse, and backed up to where the van was. There, he backed around, straightened out the car, shifted back into forward, pulled the car up along the far side of the van, and parked. One of the doors to the storage compartment on the right side of the van was also open. Whoever his mind had stuck the image of the woman's face on seemed to be looking for something in the van.

I must have confabulated, Chuck thought to himself. *That's what I did. I confabulated.*

Chuck probably hadn't used the present or past tense of the word *confabulate* more than twice in his lifetime, but he was familiar with the concept and mechanism of confabulation. He figured his mind must have been so fixed on thinking about the woman that he had simply imagined her face on the face of another woman. The woman he had actually seen was probably the female tech who was part of the other team from the South Carolina office. He had seen a female face, and his mind had superimposed the face of the woman he had been thinking about intensely and continuously since the night before. The intensity of his lovemaking with the woman and the sudden growth of his feelings for her had provided the psychological energy that generated the image of the woman on another woman. Just how his overactive imagination had done a complete makeover job and given the female tech the figure and hair of the woman he had made love to was something Chuck wasn't sure about as he got out of the car.

Chuck figured maybe the female tech from the other office had a better figure and was better looking than Paul's speculation had given her credit for. If the service tech from the other office had a good figure, that could have been why it was easy for his mind to stick the face of his lover onto her face. The similarity in hair color and style could have been a coincidence or an extension of the confabulation. Either way, Chuck hoped that his mind had straightened itself out and that the mental aberration his mind had just sprung on him would be gone by the time he got to the female tech and looked at her directly face-to-face. But seeing the woman in the face of the female tech had been a mental aberration. The tech couldn't have been the actual woman. Things like that just didn't happen in the world.

Chuck rounded the back of the van, stopped at the corner, and stood there looking at the female service tech he assumed to be the projection screen of his mind's confabulation. The woman was still bending over with her head inside the storage compartment of the van. Chuck couldn't see her face. What he could see of her was definitely woman. The figure of the woman hadn't been a momentary confabulation of his disappointed-in-love mind trying to recapture something that was lost. The woman's figure was corporeal and as well contoured as when he had driven past a minute ago. It would have taken a really hyperactive imagination to confabulate a figure like that out of thin air or hallucinate the shape of a *Playboy* magazine centerfold onto the body of a battle-ax. The woman's large breasts filled her work shirt as if she were carrying two full wineskins concealed beneath her phone company uniform blouse. Her full hips strained the fabric of her uniform slacks. Even with the substitution of drab phone company work clothes for shiny leathers, the picture was curve-for-curve familiar. The woman's long blonde hair hung down past her face, which was half concealed inside the storage compartment in the side of the van. The color hadn't been a momentary confabulation. With the exception of not being quite as tangled as when he had last seen it, the wave and color of the woman's hair were as familiar as the curves of her body.

As Chuck stood there, the woman backed her head out of the compartment but continued to look into the storage compartment. As she brought her head up, her hair fell back and away from the side of her face. Even in only half-face profile, Chuck could readily see that the woman was no battle-ax. He could also see that this was no out-of-the-blue confabulation. The face, with full lips and all, was unmistakable. Chuck's mouth fell open. He leaned against the corner of the van and stared in incredulousness. It was the same woman. Apparently, things like that did happen in the world.

Without having seen Chuck approach, Wanda was aware that someone was standing there. She had seen the car pull up but hadn't recognized it as one of the cars belonging to anyone in her work crew. Whoever had come around the back of the van must have been a member of the work crew from the Memphis office, she thought.

"I hope the spectrum analyzer is in the other service truck, because it's not in here," Wanda said. "If they didn't pack it in the other van, I hope you guys brought one, or we're going to have to send out back to the shop for one."

The voice was as full and familiar from the night before as was her figure. The voice that had been so full of passionate cries the night past and so full of leaving at the door of his hotel room less than two hours earlier was once again standing only a few feet away from him, not long gone in the opposite direction toward a far horizon, as he had assumed. The combination of figure, face, and voice had been drummed into his head in one night as no woman had been imprinted on him in such a short time before. And the vision was no confabulatory hallucination. The figure was earthy and as real as they came. The woman was as real as she had come last night.

Chuck continued to stare in mounting incredulousness. He had no explanation for how the vision he had thought was lost and gone forever to a far horizon had suddenly been transposed back to standing a few feet in front of him. But the woman who had said she could never be part of his world and thought he could never be part of her world, the passing and ethereal woman he'd assumed he had already lost to the horizon of another world, was standing only a few feet away from him, dressed in the work clothes of his world. Now, standing at the back end of the van, he was standing on the side of the horizon he had thought he would never cross again.

"Hello, Ramona. Long time no see," Chuck said in a wry voice.

Wanda raised her head at the sound of the name she had used only last night and almost forgotten already. She had a quizzical look on her face. The voice had a familiar ring to it also.

"My name's not—" Wanda turned around and stopped in her tracks. Standing a few feet away from her, leaning on the corner of the van, wearing a big grin that could have been either sheepish or cheesy, was the lover she had left no more than two hours earlier. Along with the ear-to-ear grin he was wearing, he was also wearing a phone company uniform. In that instant, she found all the years of her organized and smoothly functioning approach-and-withdrawal strategy knocked into a cocked hat by a cocky smile.

341

"Oh shit!" Wanda said as full recognition and the full import of the person and the situation standing before her set in.

"Well, gee, I hope your name's not Oh Shit," Chuck quipped. "What kind of parents would stick their kid with a first name like Oh Shit? I'd sue my parents if they had given me the first name of Oh Shit. That's worse than Frank Zappa and his wife naming their son Dweezil. If your parents did give you the first name of Oh Shit, I can see why you would want to go under a different *nom de amour*. If you introduced yourself in a bar by saying, 'Hi. My name's Oh Shit,' everyone would think it was a joke. It could be quite a conversation killer. The night would go nowhere. I can see why you would prefer to use the name Ramona. It has a much sexier ring to it than Oh Shit."

At that point, Chuck noticed the name tag with the name Wanda sewn on the front of her work uniform. That jibed with the names of the work crew from the Columbia branch who were scheduled to meet with them there at the jobsite. The name didn't jibe with the name the woman had given him before and during their sexual workout session the night before.

"Even Wanda's a more romantic first name than Oh Shit. Using your real first name will avoid a lot of confusion. For the sake of avoiding confusion in our upcoming working relationship, I would just like to know what your real name is."

Wanda's mouth started to open and close like that of a catfish out of water. Her startled reaction provided Chuck with the final bit of confirmation that she was his lover from the night before. The question of where she had gone and whether he would see her again on any horizon had been settled for Chuck in a cosmically unexpected but pleasant manner. A whole new horizon of questions opened up.

Wanda pointed off in a general direction opposite the one she and the work crew she was with had come from. "You're from the Memphis office?" she asked in her own incredulous tone. "You told me you were a roving mechanic who repaired farm equipment. You lied to me."

"You're from the phone company?" Chuck said in an exaggerated tone. "You told me you were a fashion consultant for a lingerie company. We may be both guilty of telling white lies, but you were carrying around the bigger whitewash bucket. It wasn't a bucket; it was a whole trough. At least me saying I was a mechanic is somewhat in line with the work I actually do. It's all blue-collar, manual-labor, hands-on stuff."

Chuck thought to say that she was pretty good at her own form of hands-on work, but he had just gotten her back after he had thought she was lost to him forever. He didn't want to take the chance of antagonizing her by being crude.

"A fashion consultant is a whole different world than being a phone company service tech," he said.

The woman he had thought was from another world, a world he couldn't share and would never see her in again, had turned out to be a backyard kissing cousin in the main world he knew. But then again, Chuck knew a lot about kissing cousins.

Wanda put both her hands up to her forehead. "Oh, Jesus H. Christ!" she exclaimed.

"I'm a long way from being him," Chuck quipped glibly. "My name's Chuck. But you know that. I gave you my real name in the bar. However good you may have found me to be last night, I don't claim to be divine in stature. For the record, I'm not Jesus Christ. But you're hardly the Virgin Mary."

Chuck could have said something to the effect that as far as biblical personages and imagery went, she was a lot closer in comparison to the adulterous woman Jesus saved from the crowd about to stone her.

Chuck again glanced at the name tag on her uniform. Her real day job had been revealed. There was still the issue of what her real name was. "So what is your real name? Ramona? Wanda? Oh Shit? Or is it something else entirely? Since we're going to be working together, it would simplify things all around if I didn't have to guess at your name all the time."

Wanda pointed to the name tag on her uniform. "It's Wanda, OK?" she snapped. "Not Ramona, not Desiree, not Scarlett, not Grace Kelly, just plain old unromantic, hillbilly, countrified, hick-town Wanda. Can you handle that? Can we leave it at that?"

There was a lot about her that Chuck wanted to handle further. There was a lot about her he didn't want to leave.

"Oh, I can handle it all right," Chuck said. "As it goes, I'm not all that far from hillbilly. I'm a small-town country boy myself. As far as either of us being able to handle things, from the way you handled yourself in bed last night, I got the distinct impression you could probably handle anything."

Chuck had meant it as a compliment to get himself on her good side. He was wondering just how many sides she had to her. He was also starting to think about getting alongside her in bed again.

Instead of smiling, Wanda snorted at the compliment. She had been caught off guard and off script. She was still trying to sort out in her mind where the situation would lead and what the career and personal ramifications might be for her.

As far as leaving things where they were, now that Chuck had gotten her back, he had no desire to leave her just because her first name was a country-cracker name. He still wasn't sure if she had given him, or the phone company, her real name. But he wanted to get to know her better, even if her first name was Oh Shit.

Chuck pointed at the name tag on Wanda's uniform. The size and pronounced curve of her chest pushing out and up inside her uniform caused the name tag to angle upward at a forty-five-degree angle. As Chuck focused straight forward at her chest, instead of looking back at him directly, Wanda's name looked up at an angle out over the horizon.

"Well, it's at least gratifying to know I can trust the name on the uniform the company gave you," Chuck said. "If you can't trust the phone company, who can you trust?"

"Well, it looks like I sure couldn't trust what you told me last night," Wanda said.

"Which is a bit like the pot calling the kettle black," Chuck said, using a country aphorism the county woman should have been familiar with. "When you measure relative degrees of lie, it's more like the coal mine calling the kettle black."

"You could have worn your phone company uniform when you came into the bar last night, you bastard," Wanda snarled.

"I find that wearing a phone company uniform turns a lot of people off," Chuck answered. "It can be a real wet blanket when you go to start up a conversation. People accuse you of working for a big, impersonal monopoly out to overcharge them. That's why I don't wear my uniform into bars."

Wanda furrowed her brow for a second. "That's my excuse," she said.

"Besides," Chuck said, "the phone company might take it as a blight on their image if one of their employees was arrested in a phone company uniform for being drunk and disorderly in a bar or was seen throwing up on the company logo on his shirt. Phone companies like to think of themselves on an equal plain with the angels. Higher-ups wouldn't smile on that kind of negative publicity. It might not do very much to advance my career possibilities if I was caught swinging punches or vomiting a snootful all over a bar in a phone company uniform. The execs probably wouldn't like it if they knew I was in lowlife bars in a company uniform, even if I wasn't acting like a rowdy redneck beerhound. That's why I was out of uniform last night."

Chuck glanced at Wanda's drab phone company uniform and remembered the shiny, tight, form-fitting, and revealing leathers she had been wearing in the bar. "As for being out of uniform, I sure wasn't as far out of uniform as you were. I may have crossed over the line a bit when I stepped out of my uniform and dressed like an unspecific country redneck, but you went from a South Carolina phone company uniform to Frederick's of Hollywood. I was in my skivvies. You were a whole lot further out of uniform and a whole lot deeper into active disguise than I was. Not that I'm complaining, mind you."

He would have liked to mind her as much as he could. The short distance he was standing from her had knocked his remembrance and longing for his unfaithful ex-wife out beyond the horizon. "You looked a lot better in the uniform you had on, and off, last night than you do in a phone company uniform. The company should make the uniform you were wearing last night standard issue for all female employees. They should also hire more women techs who look like you. There's one guy on my team who thinks all women electronics techs are battle-axes. The company won't have to buy him lunch anymore. He's going to be eating crow for the rest of the job. He'll be eating so much crow they'll probably become an endangered species around here."

Wanda let the compliment pass without comment. She had a much bigger dead bird in her ointment to worry about. "If you had worn your company uniform last night, I would have figured you were with the team coming in from the Memphis branch," she said, giving vent to both frustration and spontaneous honesty. "It would have avoided a whole lot of complications for me."

"If I had worn my uniform and you had known I worked for the phone company, would the evening have turned out the way it did?" Chuck asked as both a rhetorical and a serious question.

"If you had worn your uniform, I wouldn't have even walked up to you," Wanda said truthfully. "I probably would have slipped out the back before you got a look at me."

"And I would have missed the best sex of my life," Chuck said in spontaneous honesty of his own. "I enjoyed every minute of our night together, and I'm not going to spend one minute here and now apologizing for not wearing my phone company uniform. I can see why you would want to wear what you were wearing instead of a phone company uniform. You looked a whole lot better in the outfit you had on than you do in a phone company nun's habit. But why the fake identity, and why would you have walked away from me if you'd known I worked for the same outfit you do? What do you have against phone company men anyway?"

Wanda started to wave her hands randomly. "It's just that when I'm on the road and I, ah, well, sort of, you know."

Chuck waved his hands in imitation of what Wanda was doing. "When you're on the road, do you, ah, well, sort of, you know, a lot?" he said in imitation of her uncharacteristic stammer.

"Copiously!" Wanda hissed defiantly, regaining her focus but not her composure. "But I only do one man at a time. Then I move on before they can get their hooks in me. I'm gone before they know my real name or where they can find me. I don't screw with the odds. And I especially don't screw where I work. There are way too many complications connected with that. Now I've got complications out the ass, which is the one place I haven't been screwed. Now I've come up screwed big-time all around. I've fallen into the first and main booby trap I've worked the hardest to avoid. I'm probably going to come out of this screwed—screwed in the negative sense, screwed harder than I've been screwed in all my years on the road." She shook her head. Her tone of voice lowered to a decidedly sarcastic growl. "This is great. Just fucking great."

"Oh, you were great all right," Chuck said in a rising tone of embellished, hyperbolic praise. "You were the best I've ever had." He spread his arms like an evangelical Pentecostal preacher with the Spirit really moving him. "I'll tell the world how great you are. I'll spread your praise throughout the country and the phone company."

Chuck had meant what he said to be an exaggerated compliment of her sexual ability and capacity. He hadn't meant it to be taken literally. Wanda didn't take it as detached, hyperbolic language, especially the bit about the phone company.

346

"That's what I'm trying to avoid!" Wanda hissed through clenched teeth. "I've got everybody in my department more or less thinking I'm celibate. It took a while to get the message across, but they leave me alone. Now I'll probably have every jerk in the company at all levels up to the board of directors hitting on me for a freebie. If I don't get fired for not going along with a supervisor or a paunchy vice president, I'll probably get fired because they think I'm going along with every man who comes along. They'll be afraid I'll develop a reputation that will dirty up the company's image: a bed-hopping, promiscuous slut on the payroll who's picking up men in every area code. That's not what they had in mind when they dreamed up the motto 'Reach out and touch someone.'"

Chuck hadn't really intended to spread the word about his sexual conquest and go about singing praises to her sexual ability throughout the company. But he realized he had been a little reckless in making a joke out of it. He could see how the prospect could make her feel nervous. He could also see how it could set a lot of slimeballs on her tail. Chuck figured the best course at the juncture would be to put her mind at rest.

"Your secret is safe with me," he said magnanimously. "I can't cross my heart and say, 'Scout's honor.' I was never a Boy Scout. But with all the country-boy sense of chivalry in me, I promise I won't tell anybody anything, either on your crew or mine. You may have Porno Paul on my team drooling over you, but he'd be doing that anyway. I will hold my silence."

Chuck wanted to comment on the fact that Wanda's lack of holding her silence during orgasm had come close to giving her secret away the night before. But he thought it would be a bit crude to make the point at the moment. Meanwhile, in the back of his mind, Chuck wondered if there could be more moments between him and the woman he now knew as Wanda but still didn't know at all.

His statement of intent had been meant to reassure her, but it didn't seem to have any effect. Instead of collapsing in a sigh of relief, Wanda looked at Chuck suspiciously.

"I suppose you'll be blackmailing me into bed with you as a price for your keeping your silence," Wanda said caustically.

Chuck could understand why she might be wary that he could plan to try to extort sexual favors from her through threats and blackmail. Such things had been known to happen in both high-up white-collar corporate settings and low-level blue-collar settings. The emerging feminist movement was making a big issue out of on-the-job sexual harassment of women. As far as sexual contact between coworkers went, Chuck's horizon thinking was focused on whether a return engagement could be arranged between them. But at the same time, he figured the slightest hint of blackmail or coercion on his part would anger her and drive her away. He had been given a seemingly miraculous gift in that he had found the lover he'd thought he lost forever. He still had copious desire for her, but he had no desire to drive her away.

Chuck knew the only chance he had to make love to her again was to step back from the woman he wanted to be sexually close to and forswear any sex that looked demanding or manipulative. Ironically, for there to be any chance of his making love to her again, he would have to be willing to forfeit sex with her until she came around to him on her own. That left open the possibility that he might still lose her all over again to another lover, especially her damned primary lover, the road.

"I promise I'll keep my dirty hands off you," Chuck said. "You may have Porno Paul's eyes going over you from top to bottom, but your bod will be safe from my prying hands. I also promise I won't come up with any backhanded dirty tricks or backdoor maneuvers to try to get you into bed—again. If you remember, it was you who took the initiative in that department. But I promise I'll keep your secret."

"I suppose you'll probably lose all respect for me, if you haven't lost it all ready."

"Along with respecting your secret, I'll respect you," Chuck responded. "My father taught me to respect all women." He didn't add that his father had taught him to treat even disreputable women with respect.

"Kudos to your father," Wanda said flatly. She still didn't sound convinced. She didn't look particularly reassured or convinced by his denial of intent.

Chuck figured a big gesture would be needed to convince her. "To prove what I said, if you're worried about me holding what I know over your head and blackmailing you with it, I'll give you something you can hold over my head and counterblackmail me with. If I try to blackmail you or I spill the beans and tell everyone about what you've been doing, I'll give you something even bigger you can threaten me with or hit me with. As far as me knowing all your secrets goes, here's a fungible secret of mine you can use. Remember that I said we didn't have a senior prom at my high school, and I didn't get laid on my prom night?"

Wanda remembered him saying that during their precoital conversation in the bar, but she didn't acknowledge it or say anything in response. She just furrowed her brow again. What did not going to a prom and not getting laid on prom night have to do with anything that could be used for blackmail?

"Well, I really didn't get laid that night. But I had already lost my virginity. The catch is who I lost my virginity to. If I get uppity and start spilling your secrets, you can tell everyone that I confessed to you that I was seduced by an older woman three times my age. She was fifty-seven at the time. I was eighteen."

"Do you have a thing for older women?" Wanda asked, not knowing what to do with the secret he had just handed her or whether it would be usable at all.

"She was my first," Chuck said. "But I wasn't her first. She had been there. She taught me what it was all about."

"Were you in love with her?" Wanda asked. She wasn't sure why she asked the question.

"I loved her enough to back away from her and not give her false hope that I would love her for life. Maybe I was being honest with her. Maybe I was being a jerk for loving her that one time, when I knew there would be no more love coming her way from me after that. You can use that against me. I won't deny it."

"I'll take it under advisement," Wanda said. She still had to figure out whether the fact that he had made love to an older woman was perverted or not. She guessed that depended on what the woman had thought about it. For all she knew, the woman might have enjoyed the hell out of it.

"How much I moved her back then, I'm not sure," Chuck said. "All I know is that you move me now. When we made love, you moved a lot nicer than any road ever moved for me. The same goes triple for you yourself. You moved for me better than the whole interstate highway system. Last night, you moved me more than all the roads I've ever been on or traveled over. I'd take you over any road any day. I'd take you with me on the road. I'd make love to you in any closed-in motel or out under the stars in an open field alongside any road in the nation. But I don't understand someone loving the road more than a human being."

The fact that she had been brought back to him and that they were going to be thrown together for a while made Chuck bold to challenge or at least question her life-on-the-road philosophy. Even if challenging her life philosophy reduced his chance of pinning her down in bed later, Chuck wanted to pin her down on her love for the open road.

He said, "Maybe I'm just an uncouth hillbilly about this kind of free-love thing. I guess there's supposed to be something sophisticated about free love and then leaving. My ex-wife was the original free-love-'em-and-then-leave girl. Poets are big on wandering and on the romance of the open road. Apparently, you fancy yourself some kind of poet of the road. So tell me what this love of the open road is all about and what wandering does for you. I've spent a lot of time on the road for the phone company. Being with the company has been good to me, but the road itself hasn't done a lot for me." Chuck's words trailed off rhetorically.

"It's about freedom. It's about liberation," Wanda said, going for the two standard, shopworn feminist canards of first resort.

Her words took Chuck back in time and back to familiar grounds: the grounds of the beds his wife had been slipping off to behind his back, the grounds of divorce court, and the grounds of his divorce. When he had confronted his ex-wife with her deceitfulness and adultery, she had used the same words as the first-order rationalizations of her unfaithfulness. It had sounded like feminist claptrap when Chuck heard it back then back in Memphis. It still sounded like claptrap now that he was hearing it years later in a different state and from another sexually roving woman.

"Freedom is the Declaration of Independence," Chuck said. "Freedom is the Bill of Rights. Freedom is Lincoln issuing the Emancipation Proclamation. Freedom is participatory democracy. Liberation is the Allied army blowing through Nazi-occupied Europe and grinding Fascism into the dirt they ground others into. What you're talking about and living sounds more like self-indulgence than freedom or liberation properly defined. I got the same casserole of crap about freedom and liberation shoved under my nose when I caught my ex-wife bouncing through every bed in western Tennessee."

Wanda was caught up a bit short by the direction and intensity of his response. It was sort of obvious to her that she had stepped on a raw personal nerve. She thought it would be a better strategy to take things in a different direction. "It's about being on your own without anyone controlling you," she said, going for the secondary principal feminist proverbial. "It's about being free to set the terms of your life for yourself without being tied up by the demands of someone else or being tied down to anyone."

"The way you're living sounds more like isolation than freedom to me," Chuck said. "There's quite a difference between the two." Since the woman he was dealing with had turned out to be as countrified as he was, Chuck went for another countrified analogy that a country girl should have been able to grasp. "It's like the difference between a mushroom and a toadstool. A toadstool looks like a mushroom, but mushrooms are edible and nutritious. Toadstools are poisonous. Isolation may look like freedom, but it's not the same thing. Real freedom is good for the soul. Isolation drains the soul and starves it."

Chuck didn't fancy himself a country Camus, but he was capable of his own existential flourishes.

Wanda wasn't getting anywhere. She didn't know where to take it next. She didn't even know why she was having the conversation. She had not expected to ever see him again after she shut the door of his hotel room behind her. She had expected a free and renewed field ahead of her to play in for the rest of the time she was in town. She hadn't expected to find herself standing in front of an academic board of review like a PhD candidate defending her thesis.

Wanda needed an argument that would end the debate. She needed an argument there was no defense against or a counter to, a subjective argument that excluded any point of view other than the subjective view of the person on the inside.

"It's not anything I can explain," Wanda said, going in defense of unshareable subjectiveness. "It's there inside me. It's part of me. It's been inside me for a long time. It's not something I can explain to anyone. I can't even explain it to myself. It's something I feel. If I have to explain it to you, you'll never understand it."

"If you have to hide behind the 'If you have to have it explained to you, you'll never understand it' dodge, maybe it's because it can't be explained at all," Chuck said, coming back by way of tautological logic.

But more often than not, the truth lay on the ground of the down-to-earth obvious than along the path of the contrived, esoteric existential.

Chuck continued. "Then again, the real explanation is often as obvious as it comes. The person hides behind vague and hazy pseudointellectual arguments that what they're feeling and what they want is somehow beyond explanation because they don't want to come out and state something more down-and-dirty obvious." He had and hadn't intended the references to being obvious and coming to be sexual puns. "I don't believe all this stuff

351

about the lure of life on the road and the romance of horizons, and I don't think you believe it either. I think you're just a red-blooded girl who's out to get all the sex she can get while the getting's good. I don't think it goes any deeper than that." Chuck hadn't meant the going-deep part as a sexual pun.

"So OK. Spot on," Wanda said. "You've outed me. That's what I am. Can we just leave it there?"

Chuck could see her point. Then again, he could see the outlines of the points of her breasts pushing tightly inside her dowdy phone company uniform.

"Now that you've exposed me, are you getting the idea that you can exploit the opening? Are you going to try to blackmail me? Are you going to threaten to report me to the company for what I do in my free time? What is it you want from me? Just exactly what do you think you're going to get off of me?"

"All I want from you is just a little up-front honesty," Chuck said. Given the size and measurements of her chest, he hadn't meant the up-front part as a pun. "You're so big on honesty and being honest. You didn't have trouble being honest about your plan to leave last night or this morning. Be honest with me now. Just say what you mean, and be done with it, instead of beating around the bush, using pseudoadventurous-sounding claptrap like you're Jack London talking about the romance of the open road and the call of the wild."

Regarding roads and horizons, Jack Kerouac would have been a more fitting literary-figure analogy to invoke. But due to the limited comparative-literature program in his small high school, Chuck's American lit background was somewhat limited. He knew just enough about literature to be dangerous.

He added, "If you like sex for its own sake, just say so. I can understand that. I can relate to you on that level. I've already related to you on that level. No pun intended. I'm not going to try to blackmail you into anything. I just don't understand this stuff about getting the hots for roads and horizons. I'd just like to know you a little better. Maybe I can figure out who you are."

"I don't live to be figured out by anybody," Wanda responded in a measured voice. "Whatever I am is what I am. I live for what I am and what's inside me. Whatever is in me has been in me for a long time. It's all part of me. Whether my horizons are low order or high order in your opinion, they're my horizons. I don't feel the need to defend my life. Like I say, can we just leave it there?"

He didn't particularly want to leave her under any circumstances, but he intended to keep his word about not trying to manipulate or force her. "You don't need to defend your life to me now, on the job, or after it," Chuck said. "If sex is as much of your life as you say it is, the only thing I'm curious about is this: What do you do for a life after sex?"

"For one thing, I don't spend my life answering questions that even I can't answer," Wanda said. "It's my life, and I'll stumble through it my way, no matter how many stumbling blocks there may be along the way. That's all you need to know about me. Now that you know me, there are one or two things I need to know from you, and I don't mean your phone number."

At the intersection of the road that ran past the tower and the short access drive that led to the tower, a mixed convoy of cars and phone company service vans were slowing down to turn onto the access drive. Chuck saw them out of the corner of his eye as the lead car turned onto the access road. They were the cars and vans of the crew from Chuck's office. They had carpooled to the site together. Farther back down the road, another group of cars and vans were approaching the turnoff. They belonged to the work crew from Wanda's office, who also had carpooled to the jobsite in convoy fashion. The two groups had started out close to the same time and had come together on the open road.

"How much are you going to be reading into what happened between us last night?" Wanda asked in a pointed voice. "Is what happened last night going to become personal with you?"

"Oh, it was personal all right," Chuck answered. "Last night was about as personal as it comes." He hadn't meant the coming part as a sexual pun.

"Whatever it was for you, last night was as far as anything personal goes for me," Wanda said. "It's as far as can exist between us. I follow my own path in life. I set my own course. I'm not going to give up my personal way in my life just because a man gets personal feelings for me. My life and the paths I set in life are the total of my life as I define it. Sex doesn't stop me in my tracks, and it doesn't lock me in. I'm not going to surrender my life and myself to the control of someone else, no matter how personal he might feel about me. I'm not about to step off the path of my life and walk someone else's path or the path they set for me."

To Chuck, it was a replay of the speech she had made when she left that morning. "Let's not start down that road again," he said. He hadn't meant the part about starting down the road as a pun about her love of the open road. *But if the pun fits, wear it*, he thought. When it came to wearing anything, Wanda filled out everything she wore quite well, including the dull phone company work uniform she was wearing. To Chuck's way of thinking, she could have worn a feed and grain sack and made it as eye-catching as a *Sports Illustrated* swimsuit.

"The only road I care about is the one I set myself on," Wanda said. "I'm just trying to make it clear that nothing has changed in my thinking or in my life just because we were intimate together. I wasn't in love with you when we made out together last night. I didn't fall in love with you, if that is what you were thinking. Don't flatter yourself that your masculine charms are going to make me swoon and fall into your arms and leave the road. The road is where I live. It's where I want to live. I intend to move and move on until I can't move anymore."

The convoy was coming down the approach to the tower.

"We'll work together, but when the job is finished, I'll be leaving, like I said. Don't try to follow me just because you know where I work and live. You won't be able to drag me or push me into following you or your path in life. I follow my own track. I'll always be out ahead of you or any man. Trying to follow me is like trying to follow the wind at night. Even if you do try to blackmail me, it won't work. I'll roll with the punches and keep on going, even if it isn't in the company. You can make of that what you will. For the moment, I don't know what to make of you."

"You can make of it that we'll work together at the job the company sent both of us here to do, and we'll get fired if we don't," Chuck answered. "What's passed between us won't come into wider knowledge or come into play."

But oh, how he wanted to play more with her.

Chuck held up his hand. The lead car was approaching the gate to the tower. "I meant what I said," he said. "I'm not going to blackmail you or try to force you to do anything you don't want. And I'm not going to try to arm-wrestle you off of any road you're on. Your secret and your horizons are safe with me."

Wanda didn't know where to go with it from there. They were going to have to work together whether she found it convenient or comfortable or not. She would have to wait and see if he was a liar. He seemed an honest and honorable sort. But then again, he had lied to her the night before. Then again, she had lied even more systematically to him. Then again, a lot of people didn't consider phone companies to be honorable by definition, and they didn't consider anybody connected with phone companies to be honest.

There was silence for a moment. The lead car in the convoy of Chuck's crew slowed down as it reached the gate and prepared to turn.

"So what do we do now?" Wanda asked rhetorically.

The car turned to park near the gate.

Chuck nodded toward the tower behind them. "We do the job we were sent here to do," he said professionally. "No demands on my part on you, except that you do a good job and show Henry Archer that women techs can do the job as well as men."

The other cars and vans pulled up and stopped at various parking spots on either side of the gate to the tower. When the techs from Chuck's crew got out and walked over to where their supervisor was standing, they found him and Wanda talking in technical language.

12

"This tower is supposed to be the epitome of modern high tech, and it doesn't even have an elevator. You'd think they could have put in an elevator," the tech said as he and Chuck maneuvered the heavy steel cabinet around another of the seemingly endless sets of stairs leading to the top room of the tower, where the cabinet would be mounted. "You'd think the company could have put one in when they built the place."

"They were probably trying to save money," Chuck said.

"You'd think they could have extended some consideration toward trying to save the backs of their techs who have to climb up here while lugging all this high-tech stuff with them like Sherpas on a mountain pass," the tech said.

The empty cabinet wasn't all that heavy in itself, but the length of it made the cabinet hard to maneuver around the interminable tight-right-angle turns the stairs made. In the narrow confines inside the square tower, there almost seemed as many turns in the stairs as there were stairs. They'd just get past one, turn, and be faced with another. The tower was more than ten stories high. The central shaft up to the equipment level was not particularly well vented or well lit. A series of small, unopenable windows went up on two sides of the tower.

"This is like climbing up the stairs of a Norman castle tower in medieval England. The only difference is that there isn't a comely damsel in distress being held prisoner in the top of the tower."

Actually, a rather shapely damsel would be joining them at the top of the tower. But she wasn't dressed like a princess, and she hardly gave the impression of being in distress about anything—except about keeping her secret.

"Take heart, me bucko," Chuck said. He was trying to talk as he imagined a Norman knight would have, but he ended up sounding like a pirate instead. "This may be the last time we'll have to lug everything up this high. From what I've heard, from now on, they're going to be going with open metal-frame towers with the reception and retransmission equipment at ground level, feeding into the horn and dish antennae at the top. We won't have to do any more lift-and-carry scut work like this."

"If the equipment is at ground level, at microwave frequencies, there's going to be a whole lot of signal loss with the RF running up and down that far. The line loss will nullify the height gain of the antennae."

"They'll run the signal through microwave waveguides," Chuck answered. "They're getting very good at designing microwave waveguides. There's hardly any signal loss in them. Or they'll pull the circuit panels up on ropes and mount the circuitry at the top of the tower, just below the antennae. Only the power line will run up from the ground. Either way, it will save us from having to do lift-and-carry grunt work like this."

He didn't say that instead of climbing up the stairs of enclosed towers to do installation, maintenance, and repairs, techs would have to climb up narrow, open-air metal-frame towers, exposed to the elements and held in place by safety belts—belts that could fail or were not attached to the tower when a tech slipped while climbing up or down. The danger of getting a sore back from lugging heavy equipment up flights of internal stairs would be replaced by the danger of being killed in a high fall from an open-air tower.

"You'd still think they could have put a freight elevator in this thing," the tech said.

"It's not much bigger than an elevator shaft now," Chuck responded. "If they put in an elevator, there wouldn't be any room for stairs. If the elevator failed or got stuck, we'd be trapped up at the top or in the elevator until someone got us out. Besides, putting in an elevator would double the price of the tower. It's not an office or apartment building. It's not like people are going to be coming and going all the time. I guess they figure that for the relatively few times anyone is going to be going up to the equipment level, stairs will do fine."

"Is that woman tech from the South Carolina section going to be here today?" the tech asked. "It's worth the climb just to get a look at her. Especially a full-body profile. I always wondered what a Frederick's of Hollywood model would look like in a phone company uniform. Now I know. As a fashion model who missed her real calling in life, she sure transcends the dumpy medium the phone company dressed her in."

"I don't know if she'll be here today," Chuck answered, thinking more forward thoughts than his coworker was. "She'll be here as soon as we get this equipment cabinet mounted and locked down. She's going to do most of the equipment installation. She's big on the electronics end. She's good at doing the electronic hookup." *As well as arranging other forms of hookups.*

"Does she really know the equipment?" the tech asked. "Or is she a decorative bimbo who was hired by the front office to show women's lib that the company is an equal-opportunity employer or because they wanted a decorative bimbo to drool over?"

"From what I've heard, she knows how to handle the equipment," Chuck said. From his personal experience with the woman of multiple names and free-charging libido, he knew how well she could handle her own personal equipment.

Chuck hadn't told the rest of his coworkers anything about how Wanda had aggressively seduced him the night before. He figured they would have just said he was making up a fantasy story. They wouldn't have believed him. He still didn't fully believe it himself.

Either way, he didn't intend to relate any of the story. As a natural-born gentleman, he didn't believe in spreading salacious stories about any lady, even if the lady in question was hardly chaste and ladylike. He would keep the promise he had made not to reveal to his coworkers what had transpired between him and Wanda. He would take the story no further with his coworkers at the phone company.

He had promised Wanda he would not take the story of how they had shared a bed, their bodies, and their passion for one night to anyone beyond her, so it was a moot point. She had said she had no interest in taking things any further with him. She had indicated she had no intention of taking things any further than one night with any man.

As the open room at the top of the tower came into view, Chuck caught a glimpse of a shapely figure in a drab phone company uniform walk past the open door on the other side of the equipment room. Seeing her again, Chuck resolved again that he would not take the story any further between himself and his coworkers. Being a natural gentleman, he was sure to keep his vow. He also sort of vowed that he wouldn't try to take things any further with Wanda, who didn't want to take things any further with him. But he wasn't fully sure he could hold up that end of his resolution without chewing his knuckles.

Inside the equipment room at the top of the tower, the cabinet was bolted down in place on the floor under the spot where the lead-in for the antennae ran in through the ceiling. The area of the equipment room was about the size of an office department room for lower-level employees that hadn't been subdivided into small cubicles yet. Except for the cabinet and a single desk, the room was mostly empty. The cabinet, which had been large and awkward when Chuck and the tech manhandled it up the stairs, seemed small and insignificant in the mostly empty span of the room at the top of the tower.

With dispatch, Wanda went about doing most of the work of installing the microwave relay equipment in the cabinet without the necessity of Chuck, the nominal supervisor, having to look over her shoulder and supervise. She proved she did not need supervision. Far from being a brainless bimbo hired for her looks, she was knowledgeable and efficient at her work. But then Chuck was quite familiar with her ability at doing pickup work.

Though he didn't need to check up on her work, Chuck found himself looking at her a lot. He tried not to be obvious about it. He would look away when she looked toward him. He would only look at her out of the corner of his eye. Once, out of the corner of his eye, he thought he saw her looking at him out of the corner of her eye.

When all that could be done had been done that day, the techs left, with the exception of Wanda, who was tweaking circuits, and Chuck, who was doing supervisory paperwork. The work was still in the beginning stage. Not all the equipment to be installed had been delivered. When it arrived, it would have to be mounted and hooked up. Following that, the equipment would have to be powered up and initialized. Then on-the-air tests would have to be done to see if the receivers were properly receiving the incoming signal, if the transmitter modules were transmitting properly, and if the critical circuit pathway to the next tower on the horizon was functioning with minimal signal degradation. There was still another two or three days of work left.

There was a used desk on one wall of the equipment room. It had been hauled up when the tower was being completed, with the intent that it would be used by phone company inspectors to sit and write reports when they came to inspect the tower and the mounted equipment. Chuck was sitting at the desk, doing his bureaucratic paperwork outlining where the project stood at the moment. From outside, he heard the last car of the departing techs start up and drive away. They had left behind him while he worked at the desk, saying, "See you tomorrow," as they departed behind him. He had grunted a reply as they said so long for the day. They had no plans to get together back at the hotel or meet in a local bar later that night. After he finished his bureaucratic paper-shuffling, he would go back to his room alone. He would spend the night alone. Sitting at the desk in the empty room at the top of the tower, Chuck felt alone.

Then he realized he wasn't alone.

Wanda, whom Chuck had left with the others, came up and stood alongside him at the desk.

"I hope you're only saying good things about me in your report," Wanda said. "If you louse me up in your report, they may use it as an excuse to cut off my pension."

"The company wouldn't do anything like that," Chuck said. Actually, he wasn't all that sure. "I'm saying only glowing things about you in my report. I just left the space where your name would go blank because I'm not sure what your name is." He turned to look at Wanda. "So for the record, what is your real name?" he asked rhetorically. "Is it Wanda, or is it Ramona, Desiree, or something you've never used straight up?"

"For the record, it's Wanda, like I said," Wanda replied. "I was being straight with you about that." That morning at least. "Given the situation, I couldn't very well bullshit you. For the other half of the record, you can count yourself as the first man outside the home office section I work for whom I ever let know my real name. And just in case you were wondering, you're the first man in the company who ever got into my pants."

Chuck thought to comment that she had jumped into his pants more than he had finagled his way into hers. But he didn't say it.

She continued. "Like I said, I don't screw where I work. There's a whole world of trouble in that. Now I've screwed up on two of my biggest points of avoidance, and I've done both within twenty-four hours. My lie has landed me in your hands."

"Let's just say that both of our lies have come home to roost before we even got back to the roost," Chuck said.

"What I want to know is where I stand with you," Wanda said.

"About three feet to my left and slightly at an angle to me," Chuck answered.

"That's not what I mean," Wanda said with her words coming out forcefully but uncertain-sounding. "Up till now, I've always been in control—in control of myself, in control of the situation. When I'm through with the situation and the man I've situated myself with, I'm up, out, and gone before the situation gets any more situational. Now I'm not in control, and I can't leave through any back door unless I leave the company; dump all my training, my career, and the position I've established for myself in the company; and start all over from scratch. You're in control—of me, of everything. I'm about as vulnerable as they come." She paused momentarily, and Chuck did not look up at her. "I just want to know what I'm looking at with you. Now that you've got me where you want me, what am I looking at? What are you going to demand of me? What are going to want out of me?"

This was a different woman than the one who had picked him up in the bar the night before. That woman had been confident, in control, free, and unbothered, ready to go forward decisively with what she wanted and ready to leave with equal confidence and decisiveness after she got what she wanted, which she had also proven she could do at the ending of their coming together the night before. The woman beside him sounded frightened. She seemed to feel trapped, with no exit door in sight.

Chuck looked up at her. He held up his hand and cut her off. "You owe me nothing," he said. "I seek no control or dominance over you. I'm not demanding anything of you beyond that you do the job and carry your own weight. I expect the same on-the-job performance I expect from the guys, but I don't expect or require personal performance from any woman. I don't go around taking advantage of women. I don't use women. I've been taken advantage of and used to varying degrees by different women, my ex-wife especially, before she became my ex. But I'm not out for revenge. Like I said outside, I won't hold anything over your head. I won't blackmail you for sexual favors. I won't spread stories. I'm not going to take advantage of you. I'm not going to come after you. Not even up here with the two of us alone where no one can see. So head on out back to where you're staying. I won't try to stop you. Just be back here on time tomorrow."

Chuck turned back to his paperwork. He assumed he would hear her turn and walk away. Instead of turning and leaving, Wanda stood where she was.

"Sounds good on the surface," Wanda said after a minute's silence. "Do you really mean any of it?"

"If I didn't mean it, I would have jumped you by now," Chuck said without looking up or making any move toward her. "I've never been of the mind to demand any sexual favors or any sexual reward from a woman."

Wanda was silent for another shorter moment. "I've more or less always been of the mind that any man who doesn't demand rewards is precisely the kind of man who should get rewarded," she said. "It's those who are arrogant, demanding, and overconfident to the point of arrogance who don't deserve to have their demands met or even have their demands heard. If a man comes at me like that, I'm already heading for the door. Some women find arrogant, demanding men to be a turn-on. To me, they're a turnoff from the first word out of their arrogant mouths."

The sun had been shining all day. In the midafternoon sun, the stuffy room at the top of the tower was starting to heat up.

Chuck stopped his paper-shuffling and looked up at Wanda. "I said what I meant, and I meant what I said," he said. "You don't have to reward me. I won't demand anything of you sexually. I won't chase you around this desk like a lecherous boss chasing his secretary. There's no room in here anyway." He turned back to his paperwork. "If you value being able to leave freely as much as you say, if you're of the mind to be leaving, you can leave. I won't run after you and tackle you."

"That's the third time you've said that," Wanda said. "Like they say, 'Third time's the charm.'"

She reached down and put her hand on his. It wasn't calloused from the work she did. At the touch of her hand, a jolt of sensual electricity ran through Chuck—a jolt equal in magnitude and direction to the one he had felt when she propositioned him in the bar the night before.

"You've got my appreciation and my attention," she said. "Undivided."

With a tug of her hand on his, Wanda pulled him to his feet. She didn't have to pull on him hard; there was no resistance on his part. He knew exactly what she was alluding to and what she was leading on to. There was no more uncertainty on his part as to what he wanted to do than there was on hers.

"In return for the way you've respected me, I'm both quite willing and quite ready to reward you till your eyeballs spin around in your head. And if you don't take it as bragging on my part, I also like to think I'm capable of showing my appreciation of you till we're both breathless."

It wasn't exactly the breathless acquiescence of a shy and demure heroine out of a romance novel. It definitely wasn't anything from Jane Austen. It was kind of crude even for Grace Metalious and her steamy Peyton Place novels. But it was straightforward and decided as to what she meant and what she wanted.

She wrapped her arms around him and pulled herself tightly against him. Her ample breasts pushed flat against his chest. Her pelvis pushed inward against his. Her long blonde hair hung over her shoulders and down her back. Chuck's body seemed to go weak. It seemed to vibrate from the inside out with an exponential increase of the sensual energy he had felt when she took his hand.

"Let's not waste any time on talk. There's no need for any talk at all. We both know what we want. Let's get down to it."

"Ah, should we meet in my hotel room like we did last night or at yours?" It dawned on Chuck that he didn't know where she was staying.

Wanda looked at him as if he were crazy. "I'm way too overheated," she said in a decisive voice. "I don't want to cool off, which is what will happen if I have to drive all the way back to your place. Besides, the guys you work with will see my truck in the parking lot of your hotel. They'll ask questions. It will be out at the company. We don't need to go anyplace or be anyplace but where we're at now."

"It's kind of hot in here," Chuck said.

"In the fired-up state we're in now, it won't be any cooler for either of us any other place."

"You mean now? Up here?"

"My mother always said, 'There's no time like the present.' Right now, for me, there's no time and place like the present we're in. I don't like to be kept waiting, and I don't like to wait. When I'm ready to go, I want to go. Besides, someone has to christen this tower. Might as well be us."

Chuck had figured the guys would christen the tower by breaking a beer bottle on its foundation base the way ship owners broke champagne bottles across the bow of a ship being launched.

"It's not like we haven't done this before. We did the same thing last night. It's not like we don't know what we want or what we're doing. I've been an old hand at this for a long time. You knew what you wanted and what you were doing last night. You seem to have been around the block yourself."

More precisely, he had been taken around the block by his ex-wife.

"While we're engaged in what we're going to be engaged in, don't go getting any ideas that there's more to it than what we're doing at the moment. And don't get the idea it's going to develop into anything lasting between us. When we're done and this project is over, I'm out of here and out of your life. We can have ourselves quite a time while it lasts. But when our time is over, I'll be on my way."

"You sound like that song I hear on the radio with a woman singing about singing in the sunshine while shacking up. And when she's done shacking up, she leaves."

The tune being referenced was the signature song of the melodic songstress of the period, Gale Garnett. The song opened its subtle melody and not-so-subtle message with the following lines:

> I will never love you.
> The cost of love's too dear.
> But though I'll never love you,
> I'll stay with you one year.

From there, it went immediately to the chorus:

> We'll sing in the sunshine.
> We'll laugh every day.
> We'll sing in the sunshine.
> Then I'll be on my way.

Given that the song advocated living together sexually, critics of the period said that instead of being titled "We'll Sing in the Sunshine," the song should have been titled "We'll Sin in the Sunshine."

Another relevant stanza of the song said,

> My daddy he once told me,
> "Don't you love you any man.
> Just take what they may give you,
> And give but what you can."

More prurient critics and aficionados of the song said that in the interest of honest consistency, the last line should have been amended to say, "Give what butt you can."

"Oh, you want it out in the sunshine?" Wanda said in a husky voice. She took Chuck's hand. "Follow me. I'll give you all the loving you can handle, and I'll give it out under the sun."

Chuck thought she meant to take him outside to make love out in the grass of one of the fields that surrounded the tower. "Won't people see us?" he asked.

"Not where I'm talking about," Wanda said. Holding his hand, she started pulling him away from the desk. "Unless they fly over in a helicopter."

Chuck started to head for the stairs, but Wanda tugged him toward the ladder going up to the roof. At the ladder, she stopped and looked up. "Follow me up," she said. "When we get there, follow me down."

Chuck didn't think she meant to jump off the roof.

Wanda started climbing the ladder. Chuck followed close behind. As they climbed, Chuck watched Wanda's full hips as they worked back and forth under the phone company slacks she wore. He was tempted to reach up and grab, but he didn't want to lose his grip on the ladder and fall.

At the ceiling of the equipment room at the top of the tower, Wanda pushed open the trapdoor and climbed through. Chuck followed. There were simple handrails set in the roof to hold on to as they climbed out onto the roof. In one corner was another short, open-frame metal tower with several microwave dish antennae mounted on it. In another quadrant of the tower roof were mounted free-standing horn antennae. They all pointed in their assigned directions along their assigned paths, waiting to be put online and start sending their signals out into the world and out to the horizons they saw.

The sky outside the partially lit equipment room was clear, blue, and bright in all directions. Chuck's eyes had become accustomed to the dim light inside the tower. They hurt for a moment as they adjusted to the bright light from the open sky above.

Wanda closed the trapdoor. There was no latch on it. It could easily be opened again. But Chuck didn't understand why she wanted to close it. He wondered if she feared someone would come back and catch them doing what they planned on doing.

"That's to keep us from wandering around and falling into the room below," Wanda said.

Standing in the open on the reinforced roof, Chuck looked around. From where he stood, he saw the view that had enthralled Wanda many times before. Stretching to the horizon in all directions, the land below was a multihued patchwork quilt of greens ranging in color from the emerald green of wooded sections to the varied lighter greens of the different crops in the fields. The sky was blue to the horizons. In one direction, a few fluffy clouds hung over the distant horizon. The contrail of a jet plane drew a thinning white line at the edge of the stratosphere high above. A hawk flew a meandering pattern at an altitude far lower than the airliner but higher than the tower.

"I love the view from up this high," Wanda said with a far-off sound in her voice. She looked out over the landscape and beyond with a faraway look in her eye. She glanced up at the hawk in flight. "I feel like I'm flying over the landscape like a bird on the wing." She looked straight ahead and out over the countryside spread out below. "I feel like I'm part of the world but above it. I feel I'm bound to the world but above the hurrying and strife and confusion down below. I feel like the world is there for me but doesn't have a hold on me. I feel like I own the world, but it doesn't own me."

She glanced at the hawk again. "I feel as free as a bird—as free as a bird that was tied to a perch but broke the cord that bound him down and flew away." She turned to Chuck. "Seeing the world from up here is incredibly stimulating to me, as stimulating as anything else. Right now, it makes me want to fly. I feel like I want to fly again." She spread her arms out as if she were unfurling wings. "I want to spread my wings and fly. Fly high. Fly fast. Right here. Right now."

"I hope you're not planning to jump off the building," Chuck quipped. "That could throw a monkey wrench into the whole project."

She started leading him away from the edge of the building. "As far as the two of us taking flight, I have something far more practical but equally soaring in mind."

Wanda turned and put her hand on Chuck's arm. From the railing, she led him to the center of the roof. There she turned and faced him.

With no hesitancy or uncertainty and with a practiced hand, Wanda started to unbutton Chuck's shirt. When she had it unbuttoned, she pulled it off him. Electricity ran through Chuck's upper body as he felt her long fingers and the palms of her hands run across and down his chest. When her hands reached his shoulders, she reversed direction and pushed the shirt down over his arms, and it dropped down behind him.

Then, with a coy look on her face like the look of a stripper undressing onstage, she unbuttoned the blouse of her phone company uniform. She held it up momentarily with two fingers the way a stripper would have and then dropped it. Her ample breasts, only partially obscured by her overtaxed, sheer, see-through bra, came into fuller view.

With no more hesitancy or uncertainty than she had ever demonstrated, Wanda closed the short distance between them. She threw her arms around him again and pressed herself up against him. Chuck felt the thin fabric of the bra with the spreading warmth of her breasts behind as they flattened out on his chest. The electricity kept flowing.

"Unsnap this thing for me," Wanda said, rubbing her chest on his.

Chuck draped his arms over her shoulders and ran his hands down her back. At the feel of the naked skin of her shoulders and back, the electricity flowed faster. He found the snap on the thin bra strap and tried to unfasten the bra, but working by touch without a direct visual view, he couldn't figure out the mechanism.

"Oh, you men are just never any good at snaps," Wanda said with a peeved voice as she reached around behind to unsnap the bra herself. It was a complaint voiced by women since snaps had been invented.

"Well, it's your bra," Chuck protested. "You're familiar with the mechanism. You've had the practice."

Wanda pressed her now naked chest against his and rubbed back and forth. The sensual electricity running through him was now complete. She groped down to his crotch and started to unbuckle his belt and unzip his pants. At the same time, Chuck went after the lower half of her clothing.

In a conjoined conjunction of thrashing arms with backs arched, locked at the top fulcrum in a kiss, the two full-charging rooftop hedonists, with arms scrambling, worked fast to pull down each other's lower clothing. Wanda had a moment of trouble in trying to work Chuck's boxer shorts over the large erection he had developed. As they pulled each other's clothes down lower, they had to arch their backs even more to maintain the kiss. The lower-shifting position was starting to become a little hard on Chuck's back.

When they got each other's clothes down to their ankles, they had to break their kiss to bend the rest of the way down, take off their shoes, and pull their clothing the rest of the way off. Chuck was so distracted he neglected to remove his socks. Wanda kicked at the pile of collapsed clothes at their feet. Not able to kick them away very far, she led Chuck more toward the center of the roof. The roof tar had been heated up by the bright sun. It was warm under their feet.

At the place designated in Wanda's mind for the completion of their joining, she stopped, pulled herself up against Chuck in an ardent clinch, and kissed him hard.

"Are you sure you want to do it down on the deck here?" Chuck said. "The roof tar's kind of sticky. Some of it may end up stuck to your back."

"If so, it will hardly be the first time I've dirtied myself up," Wanda said.

"Aren't you afraid someone may see us?" Chuck asked. He glanced around. From the lower position, he couldn't see the ground or the horizon.

"Don't worry," Wanda said. "With the height of the tower and the steep angle you have to look up at from the ground, no one can see the roof. No one on the ground can see us up here unless we're standing at the edge. If we stay toward the center, they won't see us standing. If we stay down low, they can't see us from the ground at all."

Wanda started to pull him down.

Though he had every intention of following her down, Chuck hesitated. "I thought you said your game plan and your maxim was one man one time and never more than once with any man. This will be the second time we've made love on the fly. Aren't you breaking your own rule by making out with me a second time?"

"Rules are meant to be broken," Wanda said. "At least mine are by me."

"But what does this do to your dictum of no continuing involvement or entanglements?" Chuck asked.

"Just because I fudge my routine with you doesn't mean I've changed either my make-out plan or my life plan," Wanda said, still pressing herself against him. "Just don't go getting any ideas that I'm going to fall in love with you, run off with you, and be your one and only. Don't get the idea I'm going to marry you. Don't get the idea I intend to marry anyone. I intend to keep on keeping on for as long as I can keep on keeping on. But I have no intention of letting myself be kept by any man. When we're done with whatever we do while together, I'm outa here and gone from you."

"I promise I won't fall in love with you," Chuck said to shut her up so they could get down to business—their business, not the phone company's.

"Enough said," Wanda said. "Now, are we going to get down to what both of us came up here for, or are we going to stand here with our jaws and our butts waving in the breeze?"

Wanda pulled him downward toward the roof. Chuck followed her as fast as she went. Flat on her back on the roof, Wanda spread her legs wide. Chuck had already worked out the relevant angles of her body and the axis of entry to her the night before. He penetrated her in a single smooth thrust without missing the target or having to grope around to get himself inside the entrance to her interior world. She was warm and wet inside. As he entered her, he felt her lower body go tense. Her arms wrapped around his back. As soon as Chuck was situated, he started thrusting rhythmically, picking up speed as he went. At his first thrust into her, Wanda's back arched. Then she started thrashing around, moving her body up and down as much as she could under his weight.

She started vocalizing as loudly as she had in his bed in his hotel room the night before. Her cries of pleasure spread out in an expanding sphere from the top of the tower. Chuck didn't think there was anyone close enough to hear, but he had visions of some farmer in the field picking up the faint sounds of sensual pleasure wafting on the breeze from somewhere he couldn't tell. To enhance the experience and to hold down the noise, Chuck covered Wanda's mouth and lips with his and kissed her. Guttural moans and groans continued to come from deep inside her throat. Chuck vowed again to himself that he would not tell any of the guys what they had done. However, he was not sure he would be able to keep his vow not to fall in love with her.

Wanda had talked about wanting to soar. On the wings and on the wind of their mutual surging pleasure, they took flight and soared above the top of the tower and out to the vista of their mutual pleasure. In the distance, the small clouds on the far skyline seemed to hang there. The hawk that had been circling a few moments earlier straightened his course and headed away toward the horizon.

13

"Do you want to have dinner together tonight?" Chuck asked, lying on his back, looking over at Wanda, who was lying on her back next to him and looking up at the sky. Lying on a bed of roof paper was not nearly as romantic a place for pillow talk as lying on satin sheets in a penthouse suite, but it was where they were.

"Everyone in my section is going to be having dinner together in the hotel dining room," Wanda said. "That includes me. I thought you and your guys were going to be doing the same thing."

Chuck was not surprised by her answer. Given what she had said about not wanting to get involved and about how she was always moving on, asking her for a date had been a faint hope he figured probably wouldn't pan out. It looked to Chuck as if the big kiss-off had started.

"But we can both sneak out and get together for a drink afterward when everyone's gone back to their rooms," Wanda added unexpectedly. "Meet me about nine o'clock in the bar where we met. Wait for me in the booth we sat in last night. If I get there first, I'll wait for you there. If the booth is filled, we'll find each other in the bar somewhere."

Chuck's immediate hope of seeing her again soon came back in full. His longer-term hope of seeing her on a repeated basis also increased to a higher degree of possibility. She was actually talking about seeing him again instead of doing another installment of the moving on she claimed to live by. Chuck thought to ask if it constituted another breach of her game plan and a contradiction to her life philosophy of always being in motion and moving on. But he didn't ask. The question might have reminded her and made her change her mind about meeting him.

Chuck pushed himself up into a sitting position. "We've been at this for an hour out in the sun," he said. "We're both starting to get sunburned. If anyone catches a glimpse of either of us tanned from head to foot, questions will be asked. Neither of us can say we went to a tanning salon. There isn't one in this town."

"What do we say if they see tan on our faces?" Wanda asked, pushing herself up into a sitting position.

"We'll tell them we were inspecting the antennae," Chuck answered. "We have to do that anyway tomorrow."

Wanda had flecks of dirt and dust on her back from the roof. Chuck reached over and brushed them off with his hand. Her back was not suntanned. She had spent most of her naked time lying on her back.

"Well, I'm ready enough to get off this roof and get going," Wanda said. "I've had enough lyin' around in the sunshine. I don't feel like singing in it."

In a flat seeming anticlimax to all the serendipity and free-running passion that had happened that day, they gathered up their clothes, got dressed, and exited the tower. Chuck wanted to pause and say a lingering goodbye, but Wanda drove off before he could. Chuck watched the taillights of the phone company van as it pulled away. He felt sort of let down that their time together was over and that they were parting. But he was heartened that he would have a rendezvous with her later that night.

If she showed up.

⸺⟨⟨⟩⟩⸺

"So what were you and little Miss Centerfold Refugee from the *Playboy* Mansion doing alone up in that tower after the rest of us were gone?" one of Chuck's coworkers asked in a prurient-toned voice as they sat around the table of the dining room in the hotel.

"What Ma Bell and the phone company pay both of us the big bucks for," Chuck said. "What we're going to be doing tomorrow. So get your head out of your jockstrap. It's been a long day. We've got another long day ahead of us tomorrow. No need to go walking around looking for a late-night good time. There's sure no night spot in this town worth heading out for. If your mind's still in the gutter and needs exercising, there's a porn channel on the in-house television entertainment network."

Chuck and the others went back to eating. When they were done, Chuck paid the bill with the phone company credit card he had been issued.

"So everyone turn in early and get some sleep," Chuck said as he stood up from the table. "That's what I'm going to do. Everyone meet here at eight in the morning. Meet at the tower at nine."

It was a lie, of course, designed to discourage them from leaving the hotel and bumping into him on the street as he headed for his meeting with Wanda or from going out to Jake's Bar and finding them together there.

Up in his room, Chuck waited. The time seemed to drag. When the time came and he was sure the others were in their rooms for the night, Chuck left his room and snuck down the back stairs and out the back door of the hotel. He went on foot and didn't take his car. If any of his crew saw him pull out or noticed the car wasn't there, they might get the idea that something was going on. On foot, he circled wide around the hotel on the far side of the street so as to present a small figure. In case any of his coworkers happened to look out a window and see him, at that distance, they would not recognize him. They would just think he was a local.

The town was small. The walk to the bar wasn't far and didn't take long. He got there ahead of the time they had set to meet. The same neon signs were lit. In the light of the signs, the thoughts that had been swirling around in his mind gelled and solidified. Chuck opened the door and stepped through.

14

The same crowd, or at least the same kind of crowd, who had been there the night before seemed to be there. Chuck didn't stand around looking. From the door, he stepped up to the bar counter and bought a bottle of beer, the same kind he had been drinking when Wanda first came up to him. Then he headed for the booth where he and Wanda had sat. He sat down in the same seat he had sat in when Wanda propositioned him. He sort of thought of it as his lucky seat.

His position in the booth faced away from the bar and the door. Chuck sat alone, looking straight ahead to the other side of the booth, where Wanda had sat the night before. But he wasn't seeing the other side of the booth. He wasn't seeing the rest of the bar. He was seeing a different horizon, one that started from the seat opposite him and stretched out to a distant horizon. The horizon he saw was crystal clear to him in its full length. At the same time, it was clouded with uncertainty to the point where it vanished.

Chuck sat nursing his beer, reflecting on the contradiction and the precariousness of his love for Wanda. It was the most real love that had ever entered his life. But it was a love he feared to speak, because Wanda might fear it was a love that, to her, would become a door, not a door to walk through but a door that would close on her and cut her off from life. However he tried to resolve the contradiction of Wanda and his love for her, he could find no way forward or through. Whatever direction he went in to try to straighten out a path to a life with Wanda, the contradiction was a Möbius loop that took him back to where he'd started. He could see the path to the life he wanted. But while he had been able to reach out to her in bed and on a rooftop, he had not gained the hand and love of the only life partner he had come quickly to want to walk through life with.

Accompanied by a faint bow wave of her perfume, Wanda stepped up alongside him. With a quick and smooth move, she sat down in the seat across from him. She wore neither her phone company uniform nor the hedonic huntress apparel she had worn the night before. Instead, she wore tight-fitting blue jeans and a country-style ruffled white blouse. Apparently, in her traveling ensemble, she had something somewhere in between her phone company uniform and her hot-tigress-on-the-prowl outfit. She wore red lipstick. Her long blonde hair hung down over her shoulders in the front and down her back, as it always did. She hadn't touched him when she passed.

"Well, fancy meeting you here," she said in wry voice. "Long time no see. Do you come here often?"

"Only when I do a crossover to the wild side," Chuck quipped.

It wasn't much of a stylish comeback or come-on line, but Chuck didn't care. He was gratified that she had actually shown up. He had been having visions of being left in the stood-up corner and being the last one to leave when the bar closed down. That she had come at all was another small hopeful sign that maybe she was coming around to him.

Or was she just looking to relive a wild night? The casual tone of her voice and the words she used didn't seem like the breathless, needful, deep longing of a woman engaged in a rendezvous with a man she had only recently made love to and wanted to love more deeply and passionately. Her response was a bit disappointing to Chuck. He wasn't able to judge or even get a hint of what her feelings were toward him.

Chuck stirred in his seat. "I'll get you a drink," he said, preparing to get up and go to the bar.

"I got my own," Wanda said, holding up the wine cooler she had bought at the bar while Chuck sat looking the other way.

By offering to buy her a drink, Chuck was just being polite. He didn't plan on plying her with drinks in an attempt to get her drunk. But he hoped that drinking might mellow her out and open her up.

Actually, no man had ever gotten Wanda drunk. No man had ever seen Wanda drunk. Wanda had never been drunk, not even when she had role-played a lone lonely woman sitting at a bar. It was a central tenet of Wanda's carefully crafted game plan that she would never get drunk in front of a man. It not only would have been a come-down but also would have constituted a terrible loss of control. Wanda felt that if she couldn't handle her liquor, she couldn't control anything in her life.

For about an hour, they sat and talked. They exchanged stories about jobs they had been on. From there, the conversation came around to their earlier years. Chuck told her he had been shy around girls when he was younger. For her part, Wanda didn't talk about or mention any of the lovers she had had in her life of making love on the run or her lack of shyness about picking them up.

When on the subject of their younger years, they talked about their parents. Wanda talked about her mother. From the way she described her relationship with her parents, she seemed to have gotten along well with her mother. Chuck had wondered if her sexual proclivities had developed and grown into what they were because she had come from an abusive or otherwise dysfunctional family and if her sexual needs were an echo of her home life, a constant, ongoing search to find the love that she never had felt and that never had been extended to her at home. But the stereotype didn't fit.

From her description, she seemed to have received a good amount of love from her mother. She seemed to possess a deep love for her mother. She said that she hadn't been back to see her mother for several months and that she wanted to get back home to visit but couldn't seem to find the time.

Her going off script and agreeing to meet with him again had given Chuck the hope that she might be coming to want to be with him on a long-term basis. That hope was further buoyed by the way she talked about her mother and wanting to return home to see her mother. At least she thought in terms of home and coming home. Maybe she could want to come home to him someday.

But contrary to what he hoped, in all her talk about wanting to return home to renew her ties with her mother, Wanda didn't mention, allude to, or seem to hint at wanting to maintain ongoing, repeating ties with him. As the evening wore on and the bar started to empty out, Chuck found himself no closer to any hope or indication that she wanted to maintain any contact with him after they parted at the completion of the job.

That she was apparently capable of loving in a deeper, ongoing, more committed sense, as revealed in her professed love for her parents, especially her mother, gave Chuck hope that she might be capable of developing deeper, continuing feelings for him. But in what she said, she extended no outward hope that those kinds of feelings might develop in her for him. Though he'd come to the bar hoping to determine what she might feel for him or if there was any chance she might develop the kind of feelings for him he hoped, he didn't bring up the question of whether the relationship could go any further between them than it had. He didn't even allude to the question indirectly. He was as afraid as ever that if he professed any kind of love for her, it might cause her to bolt and run.

As closing time at the bar drew nearer, Wanda's life philosophy seemed as intractable and set as it had from the beginning. No detectable dent or weakening appeared in the form and structure of her life philosophy of outlaw love on the run. Beyond the windows of the bar, the street outside was dark. Its structure and direction were hard to make out. The horizon was out of sight in the darkness. Inside the bar, though she sat only a few feet away from him, the horizon of his hopes was just as far away and hard to discern.

"Well, it's getting late, and I'm getting tired," Wanda said. "It's about time I get going. Starting time tomorrow is the same as it was today."

"I don't suppose you might want to, ah, you know," Chuck said.

Wanda put her hand on his wrist, and Chuck's hope jumped. "I'm pretty worn out," she said with a shallow smile. "We wore each other out doing double duty today. I've got to get some rest, or I'm not going to be good for anything tomorrow." She gave his wrist a little squeeze. "We'll take it from there and see what develops. But either way, let's find a more comfortable spot to sink down and get down to it. I don't want my butt rubbed in roofing tar again." She pointed at him. "Next time, I get to be on top."

"I'll walk you home," Chuck said, starting to get up.

"I came in the company van," Wanda said. "Besides, it's kind of a long walk back to where we've been put up."

"Where are you and your team staying?" Chuck asked, realizing he didn't know.

"In a motel out on the highway," Wanda said. "It's a bit seedy, but I'm used to seedy motels. I do my best work in them—after hours, that is. I guess our front office was trying to cut expenses by putting us up there instead of in the same hotel your front office put you and your team up in. The mattress in my room is a bit lumpy. But right now, I'm so tired I could sleep on a pile of old used phone cable."

Wanda smiled her shallow smile again and waved a little toodle-oo wave of her hand. "Good night," she said. She didn't say, "See you tomorrow," but Chuck figured that was understood. He still didn't understand any more about her than he ever had.

Without further ado or comment, Wanda turned and walked away toward the door. A short while later, he heard the faint sound of the van starting up somewhere outside. Through the window, he didn't see it pull away. The sound of the motor faded and was gone. Chuck sat alone in the booth, looking in no direction in particular.

Good night, he said silently to himself, his unspoken words trailing out after Wanda, whose direction he didn't know. *Nice dress. Great figure. Great hair. I love you. Will you marry me? Will you have my children? Can we have a life together? Can we grow old together? Will we be there together for each other at the end so we won't die alone? In the few short days I've known you, you've become the horizon of my life. Will you let me be the horizon of yours?*

As he sat alone in the booth, no answers came into his mind. No communications came to him from out of the darkness beyond the window of the bar. With no questions left to be asked; nothing further that could be discerned that night; nothing further to be delineated or brought into the open; nothing further to be gained that night, romantic or otherwise; and nothing further there to hold on to, Chuck got up out of his seat, left the bar, and walked away into the night.

The empty feeling that had come over him when Wanda left followed him out into the dark of the night. The only thing he had to hold on to was the knowledge that he would see her again tomorrow. Everything else had been left open and unresolved. Whether it would still be open and unresolved at the end of the next day or any day after that, Chuck didn't know. But as Scarlett O'Hara, who knew a lot about leaving situations open and unresolved, had remarked while standing in the wreckage left by the Civil War and in the wreckage of her marriage to Rhett Butler, tomorrow was another day.

15

"In another day, we'll be about done here," Chuck said in his supervisorial voice, addressing the two teams assembled in the equipment room of the tower. "The remaining equipment to be installed and hooked up goes in today. Tomorrow we do the pathway linkup. When the system's up, calibrated, and running and the home exchange office tells us it's all online and working the way it should, we're outa here and back to our respective home office sections."

That meant that at the dawning of the fourth day, after the third day spent on the road traveling in opposite directions—Chuck to his home section in Memphis and Wanda to her home office in South Carolina—he and Wanda would be separated by almost half the width of the continent, with no guarantee he would ever see her again.

In their conversation in the bar the night before, Wanda had expressed no commitment on her part that they would seek each other out or get together ever again. Along with that, there had been no outwardly expressed desire on her part to see him again beyond the horizon of the two days remaining. She had sort of promised him they would have another repeat engagement of the kind they had had in the hotel room and on top of the tower. But beyond that, the horizon was clouded and uncertain, with the clouds reaching all the way to the ground. Chuck didn't know if there was any kind of horizon beyond the clouds.

"After final installation, Wanda and I will be doing most of the system alignment ourselves. Depending on how far we get, if we don't run across any glitches in the system that we need help ironing out, the rest of you might be able to take off early."

Calling Wanda by her first name instead of using a formal technician name was a bit reckless. It could easily give the impression that the two of them were more familiar with each other than they let on. The horizon

378

of time he had left with her was shrinking. With it, all horizons seemed to be shrinking in around him.

"Everyone be here at the usual time in the morning," Wanda said. "Like he says, if we get the installation finished today, he and I can do the alignment and initializing ourselves. But do the install right. I don't want to be sent back here to straighten things out because someone screwed up and put tab A into slot B or because someone stuck a cable into a power conduit and blew out the stack."

"Where's Wanda?" Chuck asked as the last member of her crew headed down the stairs. It was the second time that day he had called her by her first name instead of calling her "your supervisor" or "your head tech."

"The last I saw of her, she was heading up the ladder to the roof," the tech said. "I guess she wants to check the antennae again."

As the tech left, Chuck climbed up the ladder and out onto the roof of the tower. But he didn't find her with her neck craned upward, looking at antennae. Instead, she was standing by the railing, looking out over the landscape. As he walked up to her, she waved to the members of her thine down on the ground, driving away. Whether they saw her waving from the top of the tower, Chuck didn't know. Given the steep angle they would have had to look up at and the fact that the roofs of their cars would have blocked most of the view, Chuck didn't know whether they saw them together at the top of the tower either. Given that tomorrow would be his last day with Wanda, he didn't particularly care whether they saw them together.

Chuck walked up behind Wanda and put his hands on her waist. It wasn't a grab-and-grope move, but what it alluded to was obvious enough. He figured the guys driving away were too far away to make out that he was laying hands on their supervisor, a supervisor who didn't want it known that she was screwing on the job. But again, he didn't particularly care if they saw.

"Like I said, not up here," Wanda said. "Meet me at the motel we're staying at. Ten o'clock tonight. Room seventeen. It's on the far end. The mattress is a bit lumpy, but I'm not laying myself down on tar paper again. Not even for you. Just park on the far end of the parking lot. Make sure no one sees you. Everyone should be in bed at the time, but stay in the shadows as you walk to my room." Once again, Wanda seemed to have everything worked out and arranged in her mind. "I get to be on top this time."

Wanda went back to looking out over the landscape. For a while, she stood there in silence with Chuck's hands still on her waist.

"I love the view from up high like this," she said spontaneously in a reprise of what she had said from the same spot earlier. Her voice had a serene quality to it, almost a longing. "From up here, I get to see a farther horizon than most people see in their life. I love this job. I love being able to see a farther horizon. I love setting my own horizon. I love being able to travel from horizon to horizon. I love not being tied down to one horizon or to anybody's horizon."

"You might not find climbing this high to be as much of a transcendental experience when they send you up an open-frame tower, held in place by gym shoes and a safety belt," Chuck said.

"I'll probably enjoy the job, the experience, and the view as much as I do now," Wanda responded.

"If you like a higher view, maybe you should put in for a transfer to a longlines outfit out west that works on systems that cross the mountains," Chuck said. "That way, you'll have a view not only from the tower but from the mountains as well."

"Who knows?" Wanda said casually. "Maybe I will."

Her answer and the casual way she spoke set Chuck back. He had said it just to say something. Instead, he found he might have put an idea in her head—an idea that would send her farther away from him, looking for a farther horizon.

As he looked out toward the horizon where Wanda was looking, for some reason, in the back of his mind, Chuck heard the flowing, drifting, winding, enigmatic lyrics from the song "Wichita Lineman" as sung by Glen Campbell. The song started out in simple technical terms of the kind Chuck was familiar with:

> I am a lineman for the county,
> And I drive the main road,
> Searching in the sun for another overload.

The song narrator was a dedicated phone company lineman out of a Kansas office who apparently worked rain or shine. Chuck was a lineman for the phone company. He and the nameless narrator tech of the song were fellow linemen; both were professional techs accomplished at their trade. Like his nameless alter ego, he also drove roads far from home—far from the home he didn't have. That was one of the reasons the song had stayed with him in his memory. In the back of his mind, it had become sort of his personal theme song.

Chuck was proud of his skill and proficiency at his trade. But even dedicated techs could grow tired of being on the road too much, even if they didn't have a home to return to after a stint on the road. Apparently, whether to rest up or to see a girlfriend, the narrator of the song felt he needed some time off:

> I know I need a small vacation,
> But it don't look like rain,
> And if it snows, that stretch down south
> Won't ever stand the strain.

Rainy days were often the only days other than Sundays when linemen caught a break.

There was another reason the song had doubled back on him and doubled down in his mind where he stood that day at the top of the tower.

> And I need you more than want you.
> And I want you for all time.
> And the Wichita lineman is still on the line.

That was where the song got personal for the narrator. For Chuck, what once had been a personal signature song had overnight become something far more personal for him.

Depending on how one interpreted the enigmatic lines, the nameless narrator of the song seemed to be speaking of his love for an even more nameless woman. For all Chuck knew, for all he had ever known about the song, the love the narrator felt for the unknown woman might have been unrequited. That would have explained the semimournful tone of the song and the longing in the lyrics. It would have explained the feeling of distance and separation that seemed to form the undercurrent of the song. As a love song, it was not an upbeat tune.

The most enigmatic part of the song came in a middle stanza, after the part about needing a vacation. At that point, the song became a bit mystical:

I hear you singing in the wire.
I can hear you through the whine,
And the Wichita lineman is still on the line.

The whine referred to was the interference that could develop on exposed telephone longlines, especially in adverse weather.

So why did the narrator of the song think he was hearing the voice of his distant lover? Had he tapped into the phone lines with the portable handset phone company employees often carried? Was he actually talking with her, or was the guy so lovesick that he was having auditory hallucinations, thinking he was picking up the voice of his phantom lover singing to him through the cable he was splicing? If the guy was having an auditory hallucination, it bespoke the power of love to unhinge even a straight-line, linear-thinking professional technician to the point he imagined he'd had a telepathic breakthrough and was receiving empathic impressions of his lover coming in to him from over the horizon. Or was the guy drinking on the job and having DTs?

Whether he was drunk, sober, or delusional and whether his hinted-at lover was real or imaginary, the Wichita lineman apparently didn't have his longed-for lover with him. Whether she was waiting for him at home or anywhere other than in his mind and in his longing was also unclear. At the moment, Chuck had Wanda there with him in his arms. But soon enough, she would be gone from him, leaving him with a need and want for her—a need, a want, and a woman unreachable out beyond the horizon, a horizon she would soon take herself away to and over without a glance back or a promise to return. After tomorrow, he still wouldn't have a home to return to, and he would be as far from love as the Wichita lineman.

"Why don't you just come to my hotel room like the first time?" Chuck asked, looking out over the landscape in the same direction as Wanda. The trucks and cars driven by the other techs had disappeared from sight down the road. "The mattress isn't lumpy. You can be on top there."

"Too many people around your place," Wanda answered. "I'd have to go through the lobby. Some of your people might see me. They'd know in a minute who I was there to see. The story would be all over the phone company grapevine as soon as they got back. Instead of being secret lovers behind closed doors, we'd be front-page news. It's safer if you come to me. Less chance of being seen."

But more chance of being heard. "If we use your room, you'd better hold the vocalizing down," Chuck said. "My crew heard you yelling your head off the first night. They just didn't know the sound was coming from my room."

Wanda laughed. "Yeah, I kind of got carried away and forgot myself. I'm usually more in control of myself."

"Those motels can have pretty thin walls. Your people might hear you sounding off. The story would be out from your end."

"If I start getting loud, stuff a pillowcase in my mouth," Wanda said. "If you get too loud, I'll stuff my panties in your mouth."

Chuck didn't think the thin thongs she wore would block much sound. But her thong had been part of her seduction outfit. Maybe she was wearing heavier underwear for work.

Chuck stood looking over Wanda's shoulder at the horizon in the distance beyond. The timeline and precautions for their upcoming return engagement that night were set. The timeline and the inevitability of their parting remained unaltered. The tower would endure for years. The landscape and the horizon he was seeing from the top of the tower would endure even longer. The life and future he hoped to have with Wanda would soon vanish over the horizon, the horizon he would not be able to hold to him.

The motel was of linear design, with rooms connected to each other in a straight line separated by common walls. It was the typical type of no-tell motel often used for the purpose of illicit liaisons. Aesthetically, its minimalist design left much to be desired. It was hardly a luxury suite overlooking Côte d'Azur and the Mediterranean. But when one was out for a low-rent rendezvous, any old love shack, however grubby, would suffice. It was the type of facility that, more often than not, had sufficed for the purpose of Wanda's intense purposes and connections—connections that vanished over the horizon with her the next day as she went on with her purposes and life.

The outside lights at the motel were few. Though guests could park in front of the motel rooms, there was an auxiliary parking lot at one end of the motel. The truck brought by Wanda's group was parked there. Chuck arrived at the appointed time Wanda had told him to come to her.

Though there was no one outside, he parked toward the back of the motel so as not to be seen. He walked around the inside perimeter of the parking lot, staying in the shadows, to minimize the chance someone might look out through a window and see him. Given that the view from any given room was pretty dark and drab, no one seemed to be looking out any of the windows. All the curtains on the windows were drawn. Faint light came from a few of the windows. The rest were dark. Either there was no one in them, or the occupants had gone to sleep.

At the end of the motel, Chuck stayed close to the wall. He peered around the corner and looked down the joined line of rooms. Not seeing anyone, he stepped silently around the corner and checked the number on the door of the last room. It was number 17, as Wanda had said. A faint light came from around the edges of the shades pulled shut. Chuck gathered his composure and knocked on the door faintly, trying to hold down the volume of the sound. From inside the room, Chuck heard a faint stirring. The light coming through the peephole viewer in the door went dark as a head blocked the view. Whoever was inside the half-dark room was looking out to see who was at the door. The lock turned quietly, and the door swung open, but there was no one in the opening.

"Come in quick," a familiar voice said from behind the open door. "And keep it down."

Chuck stepped quickly into the room. The door swung shut behind him, revealing Wanda dressed for sex. She was wearing the same overstretched see-through bra and narrow thong she had worn, and doffed, the first night they had spent together, when Wanda was operating under the alias of Ramona, a traveling fashion consultant, and he was under the professional alias of a traveling farm equipment mechanic. She didn't even have a bathrobe on. Apparently, she had all her moves choreographed and planned out in advance and all their allotted time together mapped out.

Wanda stepped around Chuck, closed the door quietly, and locked it behind her. Then she took his hand and led him deeper into the room. In the center of the room, she turned and faced him. Standing a close arm's distance from him, she unbuttoned his shirt, pulled it down over his arms, and tossed it to the side.

"Take off your shoes," Wanda said.

The obliging Chuck bent down, unlaced his work boots, and pulled them off along with his socks. The scene was starting out a bit like his sexual-initiation encounter. He couldn't say no to a forceful, dominant woman who took charge. Or to a sad, needful one.

As she had done before, Wanda unbuckled his belt and unzipped his pants. Then she quickly tugged them down. Apparently, she didn't want to waste time on what she considered needless preliminaries and desired to set her desire in motion. With his shoes off, Chuck was able to step out of his pants and boxer shorts with ease.

As soon as his cloths were off and cast to the side, Wanda stepped back. But she did not do so to admire her handiwork or his Adonis figure. She stepped back from him to gain enough distance to move freely. In a few quick, fluid moves, she removed her sheer bra and pulled her panties off. She handled her bedroom undressing routine in the same smooth and practiced way she handled her sex life and her life in general.

Wordlessly, Wanda took his hand again and led him the rest of the way across the floor to the bed on the far side of the room. The covers were already turned back.

Beside the bed, Wanda pulled him into a pressing full-body clinch. She kissed him hard. Chuck threw his arms around her. His lower hand landed on her naked back. His upper hand landed on her long blonde hair hanging down her back. He kissed her as hard as she kissed him, and he pulled on her from his side. Beneath the force of his grip, his body trembled at the feel of her full-length nakedness pressed against his. The feel of her body and his feel of want and need for her were the same and as intense as they had been the first time.

After a minute of hard kissing and body rubbing, Wanda broke the kiss. She removed one gripping hand from his back and waved it down in the direction of the bed.

"I know," Chuck said to the fired-up, ready-to-rumble Wanda. "I'll get in bed and lie down on my back. You want to be on top."

"Does it bother you to have a woman on top?" the all-business Wanda asked.

"Not really," Chuck responded. "I'm not one of those guys who think they lose their manhood if they aren't on top of a woman at all times. I just thought you might want to talk or something before we get going."

"I feast on sex," Wanda said. "Not on conversation."

She hadn't said a word since she directed him to take off his shoes. Apparently, precoital communication and meltingly expressed verbal expressions of want and need weren't a necessity on Wanda's part, nor were they on her agenda. Seduction was a practiced art with Wanda. But once she got up and rolling, foreplay was not something she felt the need to indulge in before the main indulgence began. If anything, she considered foreplay a waste of time. Once on a roll, she didn't want to practice anything that would break her stride. But she had never particularly practiced anything that slowed her down.

"What's to talk about?" Wanda asked rhetorically. "Talk is cheap, and talk is unnecessary. There's nothing that needs clearing up between us. We both know why we're here. We both know what we want. Let's drop the sexual Miss Manners stuff and cut to the chase."

There was a whole world Chuck wanted to talk about with her. He wanted to talk about the past, the present, and the future, especially the future and their future together, if only to determine if there was any future possible between them.

Wanda waved her hand at the bed again, directing him to lie down. Without further ado, Chuck complied and lay down on his back in the middle of the bed. The mattress was a bit lumpy. Wanda reached over and switched off the single light on the table near the head of the bed. The room went dark. Only a faint outline of light came in around the edges of the drawn shade. From there on out, everything would happen by feel and touch.

In quick follow-up, with no soft words of love spoken, Wanda straddled him. Her estimate of his position on the bed was unerringly accurate. It bespoke long practice.

In a single well-aimed move, Wanda thrust herself down onto him. Chuck's back arched in pleasure as he felt her warm wetness sliding down around and enfolding the full length of his erect love for her. With her on top and her full weight pushing down on him vertically, he felt as if he penetrated her farther than ever before. Wanda gave out a single gasp of pleasure of her own. Her body stiffened in response. Whether to position herself or steady herself, she reached down and grasped his upper arms. But she didn't freeze in a paroxysm of pleasure with her mouth open and her head thrown back. Without delay, the moment Wanda had herself sufficiently positioned, she started riding him, pumping up and down fast and hard. She had to bite her lip to keep from crying out in pleasure.

In the darkness, Chuck didn't see the move. He started to moan in deep male pleasure. He only got the beginning of one groan out before Wanda clamped her hand down over his mouth. He guessed she was afraid the sound might carry through the thin walls of the cheaply constructed motel. For all he knew, there might have been a member of her crew in the next room. The rickety bed had seen a lot of mileage. It squeaked a bit under the force of her lovemaking. That the bed squeaked didn't seem to alarm her. She kept up the pace. Chuck didn't know if the sound carried, but it seemed to fill the room. The room they were in was Wanda's reductionist territory. It was the kind of room she had cut her teeth in sexually. It was the kind of room she had consummated many of her conquests in. It was the kind of room she had made many exits from.

In short enough time, straining under maximum but silent effort, they both worked up a layer of wet sweat on their bodies. To Wanda, it was another sweaty engagement in a sweated-out, lumpy bed. That too was her territory. It was the kind of room in which she had left many of her lovers wondering where she was when they woke up the next day and found her gone. For a man to find her gone and not know where she was was Wanda's final reductionist territory.

For Chuck, time seemed to stand still. Like Wanda, he too was in final reductionist territory. But while Wanda was in the depth of her reductionism, Chuck was still skirting the outer edge of his reduction, unable to ask the questions he wanted to. He knew full well that any proposal of marriage on his part or any words that were marriage-related, hinted at marriage, or were vague extensions of the marriage question would send her running hard and fast away from him. If he mentioned marriage, the connection that would soon enough be broken anyway would be broken all the sooner. The same would happen if he uttered any words suggesting they live together in an exclusive way. That would send her running just as fast.

As if assured he would not make any untoward noise that might tip off others in the nearby motel rooms as to what was going on in her room, Wanda took her hand off his mouth and put it on his other arm to further steady herself. Except for low gasps, Chuck made no sound. The professions of love he wanted to make to her and the questions he wanted to pour out remained caught tightly in his throat and in his heart. He knew he dared not ask the questions pressing against him from the inside. If he asked them, she would be gone before his words stopped vibrating in the final gap left between them by her departure.

On and on into the night, Wanda and Chuck stayed locked in their straining, sweaty, intimate leather-and-velvet struggle, with Wanda on top, both straining hard against each other and straining hard not to shout out the vocalizations jammed in their throats. As on their first night, Chuck came several times inside Wanda. Wanda would shudder when he came but would quickly go back to pumping herself on him hard. For them, the world around the motel disappeared. All horizons disappeared except the horizons of each other. For an extended period of time, they went on in the same way, until they both finally collapsed from exhaustion.

Wanda reached behind her and pulled the sheet over them. They fell asleep in each other's arms, with Wanda still on top. Inside the room, the unasked question still hung in the air. The unapproached horizon hung in the dark night outside the room, as unapproached as it had been at the start.

——————

Chuck woke to the feeling of something poking him in the ribs.

"Hey, get up," Wanda's voice said in the dark of the room. He realized it was her finger poking him. "It's almost dawn. You've got to get up and get outa here while it's still dark, or someone's going to see you leave, and we're going to get caught."

He opened his eyes and looked toward the window. The faint hint of light of the approaching dawn filtered in around the edges of the window shade.

"Falling asleep together is all very romantic. It makes for great teenage songs. But we're both too old to do the 'Wake Up, Little Susie' bit," Wanda said.

She was referring to the 1950s song about a teenage boy and girl who fell asleep together in the balcony of a movie theater. Their reputations were shot. Their reputations would be converted from peaches-and-cream innocence to a naughty-girl-and-bad-boy pairing. Ever after, they would be subject to speculation, innuendo, sideward glances, local legend, clucking voices, and wagging tongues.

"You've got to get yourself in motion and out of here before the rest of my team see you. We've got to keep control of the situation and keep moving."

The personnel in the rooms around her were the men she worked with and shared nonsexual space with. If a man were seen sneaking out of her room in the early morning, her reputation would be compromised far more than Susie's. Though she was exhausted to the point of collapsing into sleep from their full-tilt-boogie sex, her instinct for survival, conscious and unconscious, had reacted to some internal clock in her body and had woken her up in time before it became full morning and the others of her team were up and stirring.

"Where are my pants?" Chuck said, straining to see in the dark room.

Wanda reached over and switched on the light. Chuck located his clothes and quickly redressed. Instead of sitting down to pull his socks on, he stuffed them into his pocket.

"We start at nine tomorrow," Chuck said as he stepped into his work boots and laced them. "One more day should get it."

"Go back to your hotel room, and get some more sleep," Wanda said. "I'll do the same here. If we both fall asleep on the job, they may ask questions."

Chuck walked to the door. As he opened it, Wanda turned out the light in the room so none would show as he walked out the door. He stuck his head out and looked around cautiously. No other lights were showing in any of the rooms. He stepped out the door and closed it quietly behind him. From there, he went to his car, started it up, and drove out the far side of the parking lot quickly but careful not to screech the tires, hoping to be gone before anyone could look out a window at the sound. It was the way Wanda would have done it.

At the front door of his hotel, Chuck had to buzz the night clerk at the desk to open the door and let him in. He ducked quietly into the hotel. There was no one in the lobby. As he buzzed for the elevator, he reflected that he had left Wanda without any long goodbye kiss or fond words of parting. As he rode the elevator up, he reflected that he had left without even saying, "I'll see you tomorrow." As he opened the door to his room, he reflected on the way he had left quietly and in the dark. He also reflected on how much he was coming to leave the way Wanda did. *Choose your lovers carefully. You soon come to resemble them.*

Given the time they had spent locked in their frenetic, orgasmic engagement and Wanda's rousting him out before the sun rose, Chuck had not gotten a full night's sleep. He needed to catch some more Zs in order to be fully rested for the work he would return to in a few hours. Chuck set the alarm on the clock radio in the room to wake him up in a few hours, in time to meet his team down in the restaurant for breakfast, and then laid down on the bed.

As Chuck drifted back to sleep, he looked out into the darkness of the room and reflected on the question unanswered and unasked. They hung further out in the darkness.

However Wanda might have been moved by their lovemaking, she hadn't given any indication she was moving away from her life metaphysics of outlaw love on the run. He had another chance to profess his love for her and pose his questions to her on the last day of the job and the possible final night they would share together. He hoped her answer would be different, but he didn't expect to get a more positive response from her.

At that moment suspended in time out over the horizon, as he lay in his bed, looking out at the horizon he could not see over, Chuck was conflicted as to whether he should ask the question at all. He didn't know if he would have the courage to ask. He knew even less if he would have the courage to face the answer he knew she would leave him standing with. More than one instinct told him it was probably better to leave the question unasked and resign himself to let it end quietly without fighting the inevitable and to watch her walk away from him forever. He was also sure that was the way Wanda would want it.

Either way, tomorrow would be the last day he saw her, his last chance to profess love for her and ask his question. They would have a partial day of work together during the day. They might have one more secret stolen night together that night. But the next day after that would dawn to separation, distance, and no further contact with her out over any horizon. It was not what he wanted. Wanda probably wouldn't have had it any other way.

After his wife had left him, he had been bereft of horizons. He hadn't believed in horizons anymore. In two short days, Wanda had become his horizon. But it was a horizon too far.

16

By early afternoon of the final workday, the system was up, fully initialized, and running. A lot of traffic had already been routed over the new path. Phone calls, important and banal, were flowing side by side without bleed-over over the multitudinous microwave frequencies handled smoothly and kept separate by the equipment that had been installed. With the work for all practical purposes done, some of the techs had already gone back to their rooms at the hotel and motel in preparation to leave the next day. Chuck and Wanda remained in the equipment room of the tower, doing final monitoring in case any last-minute glitches developed. Wanda stood by the equipment rack with portable telephone in hand, in contact with the tech department of the home base, checking to see if there was any signal dropout or if any channel had gone dead. Chuck sat at the desk, working on completing the installation report and putting the information down in the service logbook of the tower.

"I think we can wrap it up here," Wanda said, disconnecting the alligator clips that hooked the handset up to the phone system. "It's all running free and clear. It doesn't need us to sit on it and nursemaid it. It will do just fine running free on its own. We can lock the door behind us, lock the fence, and hit the road."

Chuck wondered if her words about running free and hitting the road had been chosen consciously or if they had been unconscious Freudian slips that reflected her inner philosophy. To Chuck, her work philosophy of promptly leaving completed jobs when finished sounded like her philosophy of leaving relationships. Maybe it was just her way of saying the job was done. But her work life and her love life on the road had always been joined at the hip.

She said, "You take one set of keys; I'll take the other. I'll turn in my keys back at my section. You turn the other set in back at yours. We all did a good job on this project. We won't need to come back here anytime soon. No tech will have to come back here for a long time. The company will probably give us both a bonus and then ship us both back out on new jobs. Who knows? We may even bump into each other again someday somewhere down the road."

Chuck went hollow at her words. He wondered if instead of making a simple statement that their professional paths might cross again, she was giving him the kiss-off he had known was coming.

"At least we won't be coming back here anytime soon," she said. With the handset in hand, she turned and headed for the stairs.

"Are we going to see each other again?" Chuck asked as she walked to the stairs.

"We'll see each other at dinner tonight," Wanda said. The two teams were getting together for dinner at the best restaurant in town. The bill for the dinners would be put on the expense accounts of the teams. The phone company would probably be good for both bills, as long as they were reasonable. The phone company frowned on expense-account padding— for low-level techs at least.

"I mean, are we going to have any time together alone after dinner?" Chuck asked as she reached the top of the stairs.

Wanda stepped onto the top stair. As she did, she turned her head toward him. Chuck braced himself for the big kiss-off.

"We'll see what we both have open," Wanda said in a noncommittal voice. She turned and started down the stairs. "I'll let you do the final lockup. See you at dinner."

She disappeared down the stairs. Chuck didn't know what she had meant by seeing what was left open between them. It might have been a way of putting him off until she was all the way gone. But at least it wasn't a "Goodbye, and don't slam the door!" statement or an "I'm outa here and out of your life, and you're outa mine!" final blow-off spit out in anger against a man she felt was trying to possess and control her. As Wanda walked down the stairs, their final parting hadn't arrived. At least he would see her again. They might even have one more night together. But whatever came of it would be only a temporary reprieve. When the sun rose the next morning and the teams went their opposite ways, the distance between Chuck and Wanda would open up and stretch out beyond the horizon.

As Wanda's descending footsteps grew fainter on the stairs, Chuck sat and looked at the empty stairwell. Once again, she was gone from him. Once again, she had left with dispatch. It wasn't their final parting, but that would happen. Again, there had been no lingering on her part and no backward glance. As he looked at the empty stairs she had vanished down, Chuck tried to sort out and discern the dynamic with which she thought.

Chuck turned back to his work at the desk in the room at the top of the tower. He completed it quickly and filed the service record logbook where another tech could find it and record any work that had been done. When he was finished, he took the second set of keys, walked down the stairs, and exited the tower. He locked the tower door behind him. Then he locked the gate in the tall chain-link fence around the tower. He would not be coming back any more than Wanda.

As Chuck drove away without looking back, he felt a twinge of sadness at leaving the tower, not because he had grown fond of the hot, stuffy tower, with its multistory walk-up stairs, but because it was where he had met the real Wanda, not one of her concocted alter egos, like Ramona. Coming to know the real Wanda hadn't kept her close to him. But at least it would be a real memory he would carry close with him for life, not a false and fading memory out over a horizon.

17

"Your turn to pay for the drinks," one of the techs on Chuck's team said as both teams got up from the restaurant table and prepared to leave. The expense accounts for both teams covered their meals while on the road on a job. The expense accounts didn't cover alcoholic beverages. The phone company didn't like the idea of their personnel drinking on the job, even after work hours, so booze was not included on the list of consumable items reimbursed. The techs, either individually or as a team, had to pay for their drinks. They took turns being the sacrificial lambs who picked up the bar bill for their group.

"Just my lucky day," Chuck said as he looked at the bar tab.

One of the techs on Wanda's team turned to Wanda. "Are you going to drive the van back to the motel, or are you going to ride with one of us?" he asked.

"Chuck and I are going to stay a little longer and have another drink," Wanda said. "He'll bring me back to the motel in his car."

Chuck was taken a bit by surprise that she wanted to stay with him in the restaurant after the others left and that she had said it openly. He was also surprised she wanted to ride back alone with him. They were both gratifying in and of themselves. It was equally gratifying and hopeful that she had initiated both. Along with what the gestures might mean about her wanting to be with him, they also held the promise of another night spent together.

She looked at Chuck. "Since you're buying, Mr. Lucky, you can buy me another drink. After getting through this job, I need extra fortification to recover."

Chuck smiled a little rueful smile.

Wanda looked at one of the techs on her team. "Didn't you carpool here in Frank's car?"

The man nodded.

"Then you drive the van back to the motel." She swept her gaze around the members of her team. "We'll all assemble in the parking lot at nine in the morning and convoy out."

Chuck looked at the members of his team. "We'll do the same," he said. "We'll meet in the hotel restaurant at eight in the morning, have a quick breakfast, and be on the road by nine. We should be back in Memphis by the end of the day."

The timing of departure from the site in mid-America was the same in both cases, the difference being that Wanda's team would be heading east to Columbus, South Carolina, and Chuck's team would be heading west toward Memphis. Once both teams started rolling, the distance between him and Wanda would grow fast, until she was far away over the horizon.

"We'll give them an hour to get back to the motel and into their rooms," Wanda said after the last techs from both groups had left the restaurant. "Then we'll sneak back into my room for one more go-round. We'll sort of tie the ribbons on it. We'll go out with a bang; you should pardon the pun."

It looked like he was going to have one more night with her after all. But she hadn't backed off on or softened her settled insistence that she would be gone after that.

"I'll get you up in time to make it back to leave with your team. If we play it smart and quiet, we can get in one more good, hard romp before we both split and head back to our home sections. No tears. No attempt on your part to try to hold on to me. No lies on my part about coming back to you, lies told by me to get away from you. No false spoken understanding on the part of either of us that we will ever see each other again. No lies. No promises that we both know will never be kept."

It looked like he would have one night more with her. But in the light of morning, any and all horizons he wanted to have and cross with her would vanish.

"The only promise I want from you is that you'll keep our secret to yourself. If you start bragging about any part of this, the story won't stay in your home office. It will go out as fast as and spread as far as if it were going out over a phone network. You know how male-centered the phone company can be. You'll probably be considered a real player. Your status will go up. You may even go up to a front office. My career will be ruined.

They'll put your picture up on the wall in every phone company office. They'll call me a slut and show me the back door."

"I've kept my promise and silence so far," Chuck said in a definite voice. "I'll keep it forever."

His answer seemed to satisfy and reassure Wanda. She nodded and said no more. Now that the others had left and they were alone at the table, it would have been the perfect time for Chuck to ask Wanda the questions he wanted to ask. But he would have been asking them in the face of the speech about no promises, no commitments, and no future together she had just delivered. Thus, Chuck shut down the question that had been pending and weighing there for two days. He shut down the horizon he had been seeing. In a short while, she would be out over the horizon. The horizon he hoped for in her would fold up and disappear.

They spent the next hour talking about light, noncommittal things. Nothing was said concerning the future. No words of togetherness were spoken. When Wanda thought enough time had passed for her team members to be back in their rooms, she motioned for him to drive her back to the motel. They got up from the table. Chuck paid the bar bill for his group. He and Wanda left quietly. To the people in the restaurant, they were just another couple heading into the night.

18

"Park close to the van but on the far side away from the motel rooms," Wanda said as they pulled into the motel parking lot. "The van will block the view. That way, if anyone gets up in the middle of the night and looks out the window, they won't see your car and know you're in my room with me."

Chuck complied with her directive, but the precaution wasn't all that necessary. The motel parking lot was so poorly lit it was hard to see anything in it.

Wanda led Chuck around the far side of the parking lot on the end of the motel, taking him to her room on the end the same way he had approached it on his own the night before. At the end of the motel, where Chuck had peered around the corner to see if anyone was outside, Wanda peered around the corner. There was no one outside, and all the shades on the windows had been drawn.

Wanda took Chuck's hand. She tugged him around to the door of her motel room, led him inside, and closed the door quietly. As she turned around in the room, she saw that the light on the telephone indicated there was a message for her.

"Someone's trying to get in touch with me," Wanda said. She turned to Chuck. "Did you call and leave a message for me for some reason?"

Chuck shook his head. He didn't answer verbally. He figured Wanda didn't want members of her team to hear a male voice coming from her room. She turned back to the phone.

"I'll call the front desk. Hopefully whoever called left a message. It's probably Mother. I gave her the number where we're staying. She likes to check up on me."

The phone system in the motel was comparatively primitive. There was no recorded message buffer to hold messages. She would have to call the front desk to see if they had taken down the name of who had called.

"Do you mind if I use your bathroom?" Chuck asked quietly as Wanda picked up the phone receiver. She waved him toward the bathroom.

Inside the bathroom, Chuck heard Wanda talking to the front desk.

"The front desk said it was Father who called," Wanda said as she pushed the button down on the phone. "This is a switch. It's usually Mother who does the checking up."

Chuck went on with what he was doing. From the bathroom, he heard Wanda dial her home phone number.

"Hello, Father," he heard Wanda say. "What's up?"

For some long moments, there was silence as Chuck finished washing his hands.

Suddenly, a piercing scream sliced through a startled Chuck. He dropped the towel and stepped over to the washroom door. Wanda stood seemingly frozen at the phone.

"Where did you find her?" Wanda said in an accelerating voice. "On the floor? Are you sure she didn't just pass out? You know her heart's been giving her trouble. Maybe it's just another episode. How long had she been there? Found her when you got home from work? You don't know how long she had been there? Could have been hours? Did you call the doctor? The ambulance. Did they rush her to the hospital?"

Wanda's mouth flew open farther. The pain in her voice went up an octave. Anger mingled with the pain in equal amounts. "What do you mean they pronounced her right there? Didn't they try anything? Too long? No vitals? They just carted her away? Was there any sign this was coming on? No sign? Nothing different? She seemed fine in the morning? Yes, I know what the doctor said."

Wanda became more animated. She almost seemed to bite at the phone. She stomped her feet on the ground and turned in half circles.

"No, no, no, no!" she cried into the phone. Then she seemed to regain part of her control. "When's the service? Yes, I'll be there. We leave tomorrow. I'll come right home. How are you? You're still doing better than me."

Wanda stopped turning and stomping. Once again, she stood motionless, but she seemed to tense up more. "I wasn't there," she said in a serious, self-accusatory tone. "I wasn't there for her. When I was home last time, she asked me to come back and live at home. But I said no. I just had to be out of the house and out to the four winds. Maybe if I had been there with her when it happened. Doctor said it was too big and involved? He said it wouldn't have made any difference if I or anybody was there? Nobody could have done anything? He may just be trying to make us feel better by saying nothing could have been done. But at least I would have been there with her at the end. I could have held her hand. She would have known someone was there with her as she slipped away. She died alone because I wasn't there. No, I don't blame you for not being there. I blame myself."

Her voice became sharp and bitter. "I'll damned well blame myself if I feel I'm to blame. You had to work. I could have been at home, taking care of her. I didn't have to be out over the horizon away from her, looking for more horizons. You were always a good husband, always with her. I spent half my life as an absent daughter away from her."

For a longer interval, she stood motionless with the phone receiver up to her ear. "All right, I'll let you go. I'll be home late tomorrow. I miss her too. I'll always miss her. I promise I won't forget her. I'll always carry her with me in my heart. I'll force myself to carry her in my heart, no matter how far of a horizon I throw my useless heart out over."

She stood there holding the phone receiver in her hand. Chuck came out of the washroom and walked over to her. Her father had hung up. As Chuck drew close, he could hear the dial tone buzzing in the receiver.

"What happened?" Chuck asked. As soon as he asked the question, he felt instantly stupid. He already knew what had happened from overhearing what she had said on the phone.

"Mother passed away," Wanda said in a low voice.

"Huh?" Chuck said, feeling even stupider.

"My mother died!" Wanda nearly shouted. She caught and steadied her voice. "Father found her dead on the floor when he came home from work. Probably from a heart attack. She had been having heart problems for a long time. She died alone with no one around to help her, comfort her, or even hold her hand."

Wanda slammed the phone receiver back down on the phone with almost enough force to break it. "I wasn't there! If I had been home, I might have been able to help her. I wasn't there. She was always there for me when I needed her. But I wasn't there for her when she collapsed. If I had been there, I might have revived her or at least called a doctor in time."

The end table with the phone on it was against the far wall of the room, the last room of the motel. There was no window looking out into the dark of night beyond. Wanda stepped quickly over to the blank wall with both of her arms raised and her fists clenched in grief and anger. She started beating heavily on the wall with both hands. "I wasn't there! I wasn't there!" she shouted as she pounded on the wall.

Chuck rushed up behind her, grabbed her flailing arms by the wrists, and pulled her back from the wall. "They don't have insurance in places like this," Chuck said. "If you punch a hole in the wall, they'll make you pay for it."

Wanda pulled out of his grasp, but she didn't head back to the wall. Instead, she turned toward the door. "I've got to get back home," she said in a decided voice choked with grief. "Father loved her. Loved her all their life together. Now he's alone without her. I don't know what he might do. He might take his shotgun. I may get home to find him dead on the floor where he found her. Even if he doesn't, I've got to be there for him."

She moved toward the door. "I've got to go now. I'll take the van. I'll get it back to the office somehow."

Chuck threw his arms around her and grabbed her from behind. "You're not driving anywhere in your emotional state," he said forcefully. "Especially at night. With your vision clouded by tears, you'll run off the road into a ditch and roll over. Your father will have two dead family members to mourn over. You don't want to do that to him." He pulled Wanda back toward the bed but not with the thought of getting back to what they had come to the room to do. "You're staying right here until the morning. I'll drive you back home. One of your guys can drive the van back. I'll take you home. I'll attend your mother's funeral with you. I'll be there with you."

"At least somebody will be with someone in this world," Wanda said, choking on her words. "But the funeral is days away. You'll be taking unauthorized leave."

"They can blow me kisses from a distance," Chuck said. "They can even fire me if they want. I'm not leaving you alone in the emotional state you're in."

He reached the bed and lay down on his back across it, pulling Wanda down with him. He continued to hold on to her as tightly as he had been.

Wanda didn't try to fight her way out of his grasp and run for the door. She lay there sobbing.

"I knew this could happen someday," Wanda said, gritting her teeth to get the words out. "Something gets every one of us someday. But I thought it would be somewhere down the line far away. She wasn't that old. She had always had problems with her heart, but she had lived with it. It hadn't killed her."

It only takes once, Chuck thought silently.

"I didn't think it would happen so soon and so suddenly, and oh God, I didn't know it would hurt so bad."

Chuck thought to say, "That's the way it always is," but he didn't think Wanda would find the statement comforting.

In an attempt to break the negative, vicious cycle of self-blame Wanda was descending into, he also thought to point out that had Wanda been living in her parents' house in her hometown, she would probably have been working and not at home when her mother had her fatal heart attack. Instead of her father, Wanda might have been the one to come home and find her mother dead. But he kept quiet, afraid she might, in her agitated emotional state, take it that he was trying to let her off the hook of self-blame she was trying to impale herself on. She might take both statements as somehow minimizing her mother's death. He didn't think she would appreciate that either.

He thought to speak some expression of sorrow and sympathy of the kind usually offered to the bereaved, but he didn't think anything he could say would be received well by Wanda in her emotional condition. Any sentiment he thought to utter dried up in his throat. It would have sounded like the trite and formulaic sentiments and pieties usually given at such times. Chuck figured anything he said would probably come out sounding phony and contrived. It would probably just make Wanda angry. So he held his tongue and just held her.

As he held her in silence and reflected on what had happened, Chuck found he was a bit surprised at the depth of emotion Wanda had demonstrated when she learned of her mother's death. In truth, Chuck had, to a certain degree, considered Wanda to be narcissistic and self-indulgent. Narcissistic and self-indulgent people usually didn't think as much of others as they did of themselves. They weren't hurt as deeply by the loss of loved ones around them. The hurt passed quickly, if there was any hurt there to begin with. The strength of emotions Wanda had expressed when she learned of her mother's passing seemed to indicate there was a depth of love and a capacity for love in her that he had questioned was there. To Chuck, it was a hopeful sign that she might come to love him and want to be with him. Her sense of loss might bring her around to where she did not want to be alone as much. Then again, he thought, her sense of loss might just take her deeper into her life philosophy of passing love and endless movement and send her out on the road, looking for more passing conquests over a horizon she would never return from.

Chuck held Wanda in his arms. Gradually, her sobbing ceased, and she fell silent. Some time later, Chuck realized the physically and emotionally exhausted girl had fallen asleep. If she had done so while driving fast over the open road in the dead of night, it could have resulted in a fatal crack-up.

He feared that if he slipped out and left her alone, she might wake up after he was gone and try to start the long drive home by herself, so he lay there holding her. Wanda was a practiced expert at slipping out on men, but even if he was asleep, if she tried to work her way out of his arms, he would wake up and renew his grip on her. Chuck also discarded any idea of asking her one last time if she would consider seeing him again. She would only have taken it as an attempt to use her mother's death as a way of manipulating her to his benefit. She would have been furious.

As Chuck held Wanda in his arms, he reflected on horizons present and past. As his reflection touched on loved ones past and now gone, he remembered Lucinda. Her memory had almost faded completely from him. Now reinforced by the death of the loved one of a lover, he knew he would remember her as long as he would remember Wanda.

In the half-lit room now darkened by distant family tragedy, any thought of sex disappeared. His thoughts of the future with her vanished. The only thought on Chuck's mind was to get her home safely. Once he got her there, he would leave her there and vanish over the horizon that had never been. As for horizons close in, the only horizons were the confines of the room and the approaching day tomorrow. As he contemplated the horizons that were and weren't, Chuck fell asleep.

—⟶✺✺✺⟵—

"Your office has given her compassionate leave to attend the funeral of her mother," Chuck said to the assembled members of Wanda's team.

They had come to her room and unexpectedly found him there. A quick explanation had convinced them it hadn't been a case of hanky-panky.

"But she's in no mental state to do a long drive like that. I'll take her back home in my car."

"One of you is going to have to drive the van back to the Columbia office," a partially recovered and stabilized but still depressed and melancholy Wanda said, and a member of the team raised his hand to indicate he would drive the van. "After my leave is up, I'll catch a ride into the section, probably with Chuck here. My car is there, not at home. Once back, I'll be looking to get back to work and put all this behind me."

"I'll be attending the funeral with her," Chuck said, outlining the sudden change of plans to his team assembled in the parking lot of the hotel. Wanda waited in his car. "I'm not sure how long it will be before I'm back at the section. If the higher-ups in the Memphis office want to dock me a few days' pay, that's their business. But for now, I'm not letting her drive alone. Not even in convoy."

Wanda's group had already left. They were far ahead down the road. Chuck's group left in the opposite direction, to the west. Chuck and Wanda drove away together by themselves in Chuck's car. Wanda, who had always thrilled at the sights of open country on the open road, taking in every detail as she drove over it, sat with her head down most of the way. Up ahead over the horizon, half the home she had started out in was gone. The road no longer seemed her home.

Chuck had wished for more time with Wanda. Suddenly, he found himself presented with the extra time he had wished for. He wondered if God had somehow arranged the timing of her mother's death as a way of granting him the extra time he had wished for.

Oh God, if you had anything to do with it, I didn't want it this way, Chuck prayed silently as he pulled out of the parking lot. *If you were involved, did you have to do it this way? I didn't wish for this to happen just so I could hold on to her a little longer. I didn't pray for this. If you got that idea, you misread my mind. I'd rather never see her again than have her go through this kind of pain.*

Chuck meant what he said. He knew God would see through any hypocritical, self-serving prayer. He also knew if he even hinted at what he had wished for, Wanda might grow insanely angry and explode all over him in thinking he had somehow prayed to God that her mother would die so he could take her back home and be with her for a few days more.

Chuck didn't think God worked that way. But despite being a sophisticated girl versed in high tech, Wanda was a southern country girl. Country folk could be quite superstitious at times. If he told her he had wished for more time with her, she might get the idea he had hexed her mother and caused her death. If she ever got that idea, she would drive him away in fury.

19

The road to Wanda's home went over both superhighway and two-lane country blacktop. It was new territory for Chuck. He had never been that far east in his life and career. He had once been sent to work on an extensive repair job on a telephone exchange facility in New Orleans that had been damaged in a fire. He had been farther south than where he was heading, but he had never been as far east as Wanda's hometown. He wasn't sure what to expect. But he had never been sure what to expect from Wanda.

For the better part of the day, they pressed on toward Wanda's former home, a home now bereft of one of the two people who had made it home while she lived there. They traveled mostly in silence, with only the road noise filling the interior of the car. For a long time, Wanda sat looking at the floorboard under her feet, not saying anything. People said talk was good therapy.

As they traveled on, Chuck did not try to engage her in conversation or get her to talk. He felt she would probably have taken it as a phony attempt to cheer her up in a situation in which nothing would suffice to cheer her up to any degree. Chuck also was afraid that if he came on with a lot of phony cheerfulness, she might think he was minimizing her mother's death, which might make her angrier than any bumbled words of cheer or sympathy he could offer. The only way he could think of to honor Wanda's mother was to maintain the solemn silence.

They drove on in silence, not stopping to eat or get gas. After a long time, Wanda raised her head and looked down the road ahead. She didn't look to the side, and she didn't say anything. Her expression didn't brighten or change. She didn't seem happy to be viewing the open road, which had been such a compelling aspect and prospect of her life. The miles opened up before her and fell away behind her with no apparent enjoyment in her recognition of the miles stretching out ahead and falling away behind. Nor did she give any sign of pleasure in the miles coming and passing on her silent part.

They did not share the driving. Chuck drove all the way. The long drive was tiring, but he still didn't want her behind the wheel in her damaged emotional state.

Wanda's hometown wasn't Cannery Row. It wasn't Tobacco Road. It wasn't Moonshine Alley. It wasn't redneck hell. Her hometown was a reasonably pleasant town of about seven thousand in population. There was a business district with numerous standard stores of the kind one could find anywhere. The town was neither bustling with economic dynamism nor decaying rust-belt funk. There was a clean and modern-looking police station. The town hall was an older-style brick building built in an earlier-era baroque style. But it was clean and looked well maintained. There was a good-sized, modern-looking high school with a full-sized athletic field that looked to contain dedicated sections for football, baseball, track, and other sports. The town was not out front and heading dynamically into the future, nor was it mired in a stagnant and dispirited past.

"Turn here," Wanda said, pointing to a side road coming up on the far side of the town. It was the first thing she had said since she gave him directions to get to her hometown when they left the hotel parking lot. They drove about half a mile over the crumbling blacktop to where Wanda indicated for him to turn off onto a dirt road that ran perpendicular to the road they were on. The side road was more a classic country road composed of two parallel ruts worn into the ground by countless numbers of cars and pickup trucks, with a grass strip down the center. On either side of the road were scattered wood-frame houses that looked as if they had been built in the 1920s or '30s. Most of them needed paint and maintenance. Some of them looked as if they should be torn down and rebuilt.

Wanda pointed to a house at the end of a dirt driveway connected to the dirt road. The house was of the same architecture and age as the others, with a covered front porch. Chuck pulled the car into the dirt driveway and stopped close to the steps of the porch.

"I hope there's a gas station in this town," Chuck said, looking at the low state of the gas gauge. "We're almost out of gas."

"There was Rollo's Texaco at the corner of Standard and Pierce Street," Wanda said, opening the car door. "You could have stopped there. You drove right past it."

It was the most she had said since the trip started. At least she was talking again.

"I wanted to get you home," Chuck said. "We can get gas later." *Depending on how much later there will be between us.*

They both got out of the car and walked to the steps to the porch. Wanda moved faster than Chuck. The steps creaked as they walked on them. At the top of the stairs, the front door opened, and a late-middle-aged man stood in the door. Chuck assumed he was Wanda's father. He had probably heard them drive up and had come to the door.

Wanda rushed up to him, hugged him hard, and buried her face in his shoulder. Chuck couldn't tell if she was crying. Her father hugged her back and buried his face in her shoulder. No words were necessary. It was a gesture of both love and grief at their mutual loss. Chuck didn't introduce himself. He stood back and looked on. It wasn't his house. It was Wanda's home, but it was a home with half the soul gone from it. It wasn't his grief being poured out at the front door. It was Wanda's grief. He couldn't feel the depth of Wanda's grief as she felt it. He felt shallow. He felt like a phony and an interloper.

Wanda turned partway toward Chuck and pointed at him. "This is Chuck," she said. She used only his first name because in all the time and ways they had been together, she had never asked his last name. She had never inquired of the last names of any of her conquests. "He's from the phone company. He's the supervisor of the other installation team we were working with. When you told me about Mother, I wanted to jump in the van and take off to get home. He wouldn't let me go. He said that in my emotional state, I would probably run off the road and kill myself. I was so wrought up and out of control at the time I just might have. You might have ended up burying me alongside Mother."

"Well now, that is quite an accomplishment in itself," her father said. "When she gets her blood up, gets the bit in her teeth, and gets going, no one can stop her or even slow her down. Her mother couldn't. I couldn't. You're the first man who's been able to take her in hand and rein her in. I thank you for keeping my daughter safe. She says she's good at keeping herself safe, but I don't think she's as good at it as she thinks."

Wanda looked at him. "Chuck is going to go to the funeral with us," she said.

"If it's all right with you, sir," Chuck said. "I'm not family. You may not want anyone who's not family there at a private personal service."

"My wife would want you there," Wanda's father said. "She always liked to have people around. I'm sure she'd especially like someone who looked out for her daughter there."

"You look kind of peaked," Wanda said, looking at her father. "Have you had anything to eat?"

"I haven't had much since lunch yesterday," her father said. "I spent most of today making arrangements. Earlier, I grabbed a leftover hard-boiled egg. But beyond that, no."

"I'll fix dinner for the both of you," Wanda said. "Is there anything to eat in the house?"

"There are some catfish in the refrigerator left over from the last time I went fishing. Your mother never like cleaning fish." He looked at Chuck. "Martha did most of the cooking. Wanda helped some. But she never took over the job."

Wanda looked at her father. "While I'm here, I'm taking it over," she said in her supervisor and organizer voice. "I'll make dinner tonight." She looked at Chuck. "You bring in the suitcases." She looked back at her father. "I'm going to put him on the cot in the guest bedroom upstairs, the one with my old radio station in it."

"Maybe the stuff in there can get some using once again," Wanda's father said. "It's been sitting there for years, waiting for you to come home. It will probably be happy to see someone coming back to it."

"I don't even know if it still works," Wanda said.

"I can try to get it working for you," Chuck said.

"Even if you can, I still don't have a license for it," Wanda answered. "I'll have to bootleg a call. I've done that enough."

"We can use my call," Chuck said.

"You have an amateur radio operator's license?" Wanda asked with a small tone of surprise in her voice.

"Yes. I haven't been on the air a whole lot in the last few years. I kept vowing to install a two-meter-band VHF mobile radio in my car, but I never got around to it. The license is still valid, though."

"You never told me you had a ham license."

"You never asked, and the subject never came up. We were always otherwise preoccupied. Do you have an antenna up?"

"I had one up when I left home—single-band dipole. Made it myself when I built the transmitter. Water may have gotten into it by now. I don't know if it still works. I don't know if it's still up." She looked at her father. "Is it still there?"

"I think so," her father said. "I never found it lying on the ground. If I had, I would have thrown it out. I never liked clutter lying around in the yard."

"He's a neat freak," Wanda said to Chuck.

"Your mother was the neat freak," Wanda's father said. "She always kept the house just so. That included picking up after me. I was never much at keeping things neat. Had her for that. Got lazy. Now that she's gone, the housekeeping around here will probably go to heck."

At the words "she's gone," Wanda bit her lip. Tears formed in her eyes. She turned her head away as if she didn't want to be seen crying. Her father pulled her in to him again.

"I'll get the suitcases," Chuck said. He turned and headed to the car, not wanting to be seen as gawking at their sorrow.

—————

"Sorry I burned the dinner," Wanda said, picking up the plates. "Too much heat. Not enough butter in the pan. I'm out of practice."

Chuck had a feeling she had never been in that much practice. "It was only burned on the bottom," he said. "The rest of it was pretty good."

Actually, the fish had tasted a bit smoky all the way through. Chuck was trying to be magnanimous. He wasn't surprised that Wanda wasn't a particularly accomplished chef. A girl who spent the better part of her life trying to escape and avoid domesticity wasn't likely to give Julia Child a run for her money in the kitchen.

"I'll do the dishes," Wanda said.

"Leave them for later," Chuck replied. "Show me your amateur radio station. Maybe we can get it back in operation."

"I suppose that means I'll be getting static on the TV screen again," Wanda's father said. He looked at Chuck. "Every time she used that thing when I was watching television, it would wipe out the picture. When she was younger, her playing radio scrambled out parts of our favorite programs we were watching. It's one of the reasons I took up fishing. But Martha and I just smiled and put up with it. Our daughter was doing something none of the other teenagers her age knew how to do. It made her special to us. We didn't want to discourage her. We wanted her to go on being special, so we encouraged her to keep on with her hobby, even if it did occasionally mess up a show we were watching."

"That rasty old TV set we had back then had no RF shielding," Wanda said. "Everything got through. A little more metal case shielding around the receiver front-end circuitry would have solved a lot of problems. But TV manufactures are always trying to save a few pennies by cutting corners. Maybe the one you have now is better shielded, but I'm not sure they're doing a better job of shielding today."

The phenomenon was called TVI, for *television interference*. Back in that era, it was often a bone of contention between radio hams and television viewers. The problem would pretty much go away when television transmission later switched from analog to digital format.

"Besides, we won't be on the air that much, and any interference problem will go away when my leave of absence is over and I go back to work."

The family dinner around the worn dinner table with the oilcloth tablecloth had been a pleasant and intimate gathering, even if the catfish had been scorched on one side. What Wanda had said reminded Chuck that in a few days, after the funeral was over, the togetherness that had warmed him around the dinner table would be over. From there, he and Wanda would go their own ways, probably never to see each other again.

The radio room was in a small guest bedroom on the second floor. The floor was wood. There was an old bed along one wall. There was a wooden table with a drawer that served as a desk. A wooden chair sat in front of it. What looked like amateur radio equipment sat on top of it. There was no placard proclaiming the call sign of the station. There were no QSL cards recording contacts pinned to the walls. Some stations of amateur radio enthusiasts filled whole walls and whole rooms; QSL cards and certificates of ham communication accomplishment covered the walls. For a ham shack, the room was a modest affair. But Chuck was reminded that it was an unlicensed pirate operation using false call signs and false or no names—sort of like Wanda's sex life.

Chuck bent down and looked at the receiver. It was a high-quality, commercially built professional-grade receiver with heavy-duty knobs. Chuck looked at the name. "Wow. This is a Hallicrafters SX-24 Skyrider Defiant receiver," he said in a respectful tone. "It's a bit old—1930s vintage—but it's a classic. Does it work?"

"The case and the hardware may be 1930s, but most of the insides are new," Wanda said. "When I got it, it didn't work. It had probably been sitting in a garage or attic for years. I cleaned it up. I replaced the high-value power supply filter capacitors. They were all bad. Then I replaced all the rest of the old lower-value original capacitors in the circuit. I replaced a lot of the original resistors. Many of them had deteriorated and gone out of value, as listed on the resistance codes printed on the bodies. I got the dust out of the main tuning capacitor and the band switches. The dial cord was broken. I restrung it. I got it up and humming. I wasn't about to let a real piece of work like that sit on the shelf and dry out. With or without a license or approval, I was going to put it in circulation."

It was sort of like Wanda's sex life, he thought again. Chuck didn't know if the name of the receiver model had directly influenced her sexual proclivities. He didn't think so. But the word *Defiant* in the name did fit with Wanda's defiance of social and sexual convention.

"You don't need a license to operate a receiver," Chuck said. He looked at the other piece of equipment sitting on the table. It was more amateur-looking. It looked more like what hams called *home brew*, meaning it had been assembled by an amateur radio operator in a home workshop. It had no outer cabinet like the receiver. It consisted of an open chassis with a power transformer and a single tube that looked like a 6L6 mounted on the top. It didn't look to have been commercially manufactured. "You do need a license to operate a transmitter on the air. This doesn't look like the audio code practice oscillator you said you made. This looks like a transmitter."

"Single-tube CW oscillator and transmitter for the twenty-meter band," Wanda said. CW stood for *continuous wave*, or unmodulated Morse code transmission. "About twenty-watt output. Enough to get out all over the country when the band is open. I built it from an article in an electronics magazine. I put up an antenna and got it on the air as soon as I had it working and started racking up contacts. Had to be careful about how I went about doing it. As I didn't have a call, I bootlegged calls. To keep out ahead of the FCC, I never used the same call twice. I don't remember how many contacts I made over the years. I never kept a logbook."

Chuck was quietly impressed. It was a testimony to her skill as an operator that she could make that many contacts with such a limited system. But Wanda was a skilled operator in more ways than one. When it came to making ham radio contacts, Wanda was working with an

411

underpowered apparatus. When it came to making sexual contacts, she had first-rate equipment to work with.

"Never did get a license for it."

"Don't worry. I won't report you to the FCC," Chuck said. He touched the transmitter, another extension of Wanda that went out over the horizon. "If you want, I can help you put your station back on the air. We can work on it tomorrow. But it's past sunset. The twenty-meter band is a daylight band. Propagation closes down after dark. The band will be dead. Maybe we can get it back on the air tomorrow."

"The funeral is tomorrow," Wanda said.

20

The church was a small-town wooden-frame church with a brick base. There was a minister's pulpit at the head of the church, but there was no raised altar platform. The body had been prepared the day Chuck and Wanda were on the road to Wanda's hometown. The body lay in a simple open wooden casket at the front of the church. It was a limited affair, but Chuck didn't feel that Wanda's father was being disrespectful or cheap by not having a more elaborate service. Funerals could be exorbitantly expensive. Chuck figured the service and arrangements were all Wanda's father could afford.

The funeral was a simple affair. The minister was a short man with a small build and a kind face. He praised Wanda's mother as a good and beloved member of the congregation and the community. That her mother had been a member in good standing and acceptance was attested to by the number of people who attended the funeral. The small church was nearly full. Wanda sat and cried silently during the service with tears rolling down her cheeks. Chuck took her hand. She gripped it and didn't let go until the eulogy and service were over.

At the grave site, the pallbearers took the casket out of the hearse and set it on the heavy straps of the mechanism that would lower it into the grave. The minister gave a final invocation, and the casket lid was closed and secured. Wanda looked away as they closed the coffin. Chuck figured Wanda would have said something to the effect that she had said goodbye to her mother too many times and didn't want to say a final goodbye. Chuck also figured that once the casket was closed, Wanda would touch it fondly one last time before it was lowered away from her. He had heard that a lot of people did that at the interment of their deceased loved ones.

But Wanda held back from approaching the coffin any closer. As the burial crew started to turn the crank handle on the lowering mechanism,

Wanda turned and walked away. Given all the wrenching emotionalism she had displayed, Chuck didn't take her walking away as a sign of anger or rejection. He figured she thought if she didn't see the final acts of burial, it would be as if her mother wasn't really gone. Chuck and Wanda's father caught up to her. Wanda's father put a hand on her shoulder but not to stop her and turn her back to the service.

"I don't want to see this part," Wanda said, confirming what Chuck had thought she was feeling. "You go back to the service. I'll walk home. I'm not walking away forever. In the future, I'll visit the grave and pay my respects. I just don't want to see her being covered up."

"I understand," Wanda's father said. "We all came to say our goodbyes together."

Chuck thought he was going to try to stop her and pull her back to the service, saying she was showing disrespect for her dead mother by walking away. Instead, he kept walking with her.

"We'll all go back home together. This is no time for either of us to run off and be on our own," her father said.

"I promise that when everything is settled and over, when I'm settled about it, in the times when I'm back home, I'll stop and pay respects at the grave," Wanda said.

Chuck wondered how many times that would be. He had a bit of a hard time imagining Wanda the wanderer remaining tied to and returning to any one place, especially a grave. He also had a hard time imagining Wanda remaining tied to any part of her past life. Wanderers could feel hurt and loss like anyone else, but they kept on wandering.

"Right now, I just want to hide my face and not see it anymore," she added.

What better place to hide and forget, Chuck figured, than away over the open road with nothing but horizons ahead and all horizons of the past cast away behind you? He wondered how long it would be before she was back on the road. He didn't imagine it would be long.

Wanda said no more. With Wanda out ahead and her father and Chuck following, they walked out of the graveyard. It was over.

"Mind if I talk to my daughter in private?" Wanda's father asked Chuck.

Chuck and Wanda were sitting on the high-backed wooden outdoor bench on the porch. Neither Wanda nor he had been talking. Chuck didn't think Wanda would like it if he tried to force conversation out of her. When they had returned to the house, instead of going inside, Wanda had sat down on the bench. Not wanting her to be alone, Chuck had sat down beside her. They had sat in silence for close to half an hour. Wanda had sat with her head down, not saying anything. She didn't cry, but she looked as if she would never smile again. Later, she raised her head and looked straight out across the yard, still not saying anything.

"Sure," Chuck said, getting up. He turned to Wanda. "I'll go up into your radio room and check out your station. Maybe tomorrow we can get it on the air."

He started to walk away. Then he stopped and turned back to Wanda. "Unless you're leaving tomorrow. How much more leave time do you have?"

"I have two more days," Wanda said. "I have to be back at the section the day after that. That gives a full day tomorrow. But the day after tomorrow, I'll have to be back at the Columbia section office I work out of. I'll pick up my car at the section office. I just have to get there."

"I can drive you in my car," Chuck said.

"Why would you want to do that?" Wanda asked in a quizzical voice. "That will take the better part of the day. Unless you want to drive at night, you'll have to spend the night in Columbia."

Even if they didn't have sex, the prospect of spending a night at Wanda's apartment in the city was intriguing to Chuck. At least it would be one more night with her.

She continued. "It will just put you out further in getting back to your section. You'll be stretching out your unauthorized absence. I doubt they'll fire you over the time missed. You're too valuable of an employee. But they may dock your pay."

Chuck appreciated her looking out for his employment interests, but he was looking forward to one possible last night with Wanda in her apartment. He would lose that if she went on her own. He would also lose his one last chance to try to talk her into staying with him.

"I can take her," Wanda's father said. "It's not that far of a drive, and I have truck parts I have to pick up in Columbia."

Chuck appreciated Wanda's father's offer, but he wished her father wasn't so helpful. If Wanda's father drove her back to her apartment, Chuck would lose his possible last night with her. He would also lose the chance to ask her one more time if she would stay with him.

"When we leave, you can head out your way," Wanda said to Chuck. "But unless you want to end up driving part of the way at night, you'd better get an early start in the morning. It's an all-day drive from here to Memphis. You'll need a quick start without any delays."

Early morning goodbyes were not usually lingering.

There was no use in making an issue of it with Wanda's father or with Wanda. Once again, it came down to leaving. With Wanda, it always seemed to come down to leaving. Wanda was the one who did the lion's share of leaving. The next morning, both of them would be leaving, with Wanda going one way and Chuck going another.

Chuck nodded numbly and went upstairs. In the radio room, he stood for a moment, looking at the amateur radio station he and Wanda would try to put back on the air tomorrow. He didn't know if any of the equipment worked. He wanted to test it out. But instead of moving into the room, he stood just inside the doorway, held in place by the thought that he had only one more day with Wanda. After that, he might never see her again.

To distract himself from the thought, he walked up to Wanda's ham radio station. He turned on the receiver. It was tuned to the twenty-meter band, where Wanda had left it. For a short while, there was an acrid whiff of a burning scent as the tubes heated up and burned off the dust that had settled on the glass envelopes of the tubes from years of not being turned on. Modern transistor radios were low voltage. The tube radios of the design era when the receiver had been built were high-voltage affairs, using two hundred to three hundred volts on the plates of the tubes. The power supply transformer and capacitors had to supply the high voltage that powered the tubes. The high operating voltages made the power capacitors prone to shorting out, especially when they were old and the electrolytics inside them had dried out and gone bad. Chuck wondered if the new power supply capacitors Wanda had installed when she had done her rebuild of the receiver were dry from age and were about to burn out from the unaccustomed load and fill the room with the acrid smoke of shorted and flamed-out power capacitors. But the capacitors held.

Presently, sound started to crackle through the speaker. Off to the side of the frequency the radio had been left tuned to, garbled voices from stations off frequency came through. Chuck turned the main tuning dial.

The voices cleared and became understandable as he tuned through them. Stations came and went as he tuned across the band. The band was open, and propagation was good. He heard W2 stations from New York and W6s from California coming in. A W7 from Washington state came in with a five-over-nine signal. The guy was probably running a kilowatt. Stations were coming in from everywhere. He heard what sounded like DX coming in from across the ocean. The whole country—the whole world—seemed to be coming in. Chuck was sure Wanda would appreciate the broad sweep of horizons out there calling. He paused in his tuning when he realized that soon Wanda would answer the call of the horizons inside her and go back out to take herself away over those horizons.

———⌘———

"What's up?" Wanda asked as her father sat down beside her.

"Does something have to be up for me to talk to my daughter?" Wanda's father asked.

"I know you," Wanda said. "You don't sit down with me to have a heart-to-heart talk unless you've got something weighing on your mind. Besides, you've got that something-serious-to-talk-to-me-about look in your eye. It's the same look Mother always had when she had something on her mind concerning me."

"When you needed serious talking to, it was your mother who took you aside and did the talking," Wanda's father said. "I was never good at it, so I let your mother do the serious talking. Now that she's gone, I guess I'll have to do the serious talking for her."

At the words "she's gone," Wanda looked away again.

"Like I said, between your mother and me, I'm not the one of us who was good at serious talking. But then again, neither of us could outtalk the serious talks you had with yourself." He paused.

Wanda looked back at her father. "You're like a hound dog sniffin' around when he's on a scent he's after," she said. "Is there something you're trying to get at?"

"The first thing I want to know is how much longer you're going to be around," Wanda's father said. The question was as much rhetorical as it was a factual inquiry.

"It's like I said," she answered. "I've got all day tomorrow and the day after. Then I've got to be back at the station the next day. Whether you take me or Chuck does, it doesn't matter. Is that what you wanted to talk to me about?"

Wanda's father paused again. He seemed to be collecting his thoughts. "The last time you were here," he said, starting out slow, "after you left, your mother came to me and said she had had a talk with you."

Wanda looked away toward the horizon beyond the lot. "We talked for some time," she said. "Then I headed out. I didn't know it was going to be the last time I saw her. I never spoke to her again. I didn't even call. I guess I'm a poor excuse for a daughter."

"I'm not trying to dump some kind of guilt trip on you," her father said. "I just want to tell you what we talked about."

"Somehow, I don't think you sat down with her to talk about the weather or the state of repair of the house or to tell her the catfish were biting," Wanda said. "I get the feeling you were talking about me."

He nodded. "Pretty much so."

"Well now, I suppose I've been giving a lot of people a lot to talk about around here," Wanda said. "Depending on what you told them. So what were you two talking about concerning me? Was it about how your wayward daughter was carrying on and causing tongues to wag and how I was embarrassing you by being wayward out on the road?"

"Your mother and I pretty much knew you were out there sowing wild oats, as they say. We talked about that part of it among ourselves, but we never talked about it with anybody else. For all the rest of the town knew, you were just a telephone linesman. Lineswoman."

"So what did you say about me in private between yourselves?" Wanda asked with an edge coming into her voice. "Did you tell each other you didn't know how I came out such a wild, randy, out-of-control bad-seed hussy, when I came from a quiet, conservative household like this one? They say, 'Breeding will out.' Did both you and Mother wonder why breeding had come out so backward and different from you in me? Did you wonder how two God-fearing, churchgoing, solid citizens managed to turn out such a tramp?"

Wanda's father raised his hand but not to hit her. He raised it for her to stop. "Your mother and I never considered you to be a tramp or a slut. We never called you anything like that."

"Then what did Mother say about me when you and her had your little talk about me?"

"She said she had hoped to talk you into coming home and living here with us."

"She did," Wanda said. "I mean, she tried."

"She didn't really think she would get anywhere with it, but she said she had to try. It didn't work out the way she wanted. But she had kind of figured it wouldn't. The next day, you were up, out, and gone again."

"How did Mother know the way I was living my life out on the road? I didn't tell her. I never bragged about it. I didn't deny it when she said it. She just seemed to know. I didn't tell you either. I'm not sure how she got onto what I was doing."

Wanda looked away at the horizon, a horizon now forever behind her. "Mother was kind of intuitive," she said, answering her own question. "She did kind of have a sixth sense about things. I suppose that was how she divined what I was doing in my spare time out on the road."

"I don't think it was sixth sense," her father said. "Nor was she consulting a crystal ball or reading tea leaves. She just knew you. She had spent her early married life with me raising you. She knew your ins and outs. She knew how you thought, though you didn't think she knew. She knew you when you didn't even know yourself. That's not a sixth sense. That's just instinct rising up to where you come to know someone deeper and draw impressions from them because you know them, love them, and care for them. If you want to call that something psychic, I guess you can. That may be the only real psychic phenomenon there is."

Wanda looked back at her father. "Did Mother have any kind of premonition that she was going to die soon?"

"None she told me about," her father said. "If she had any feeling that she was going to pass, it may have simply come from living with a damaged heart for so long. She had lived with it since she was a young girl. But it had been kicking up more than usual for the past few months. I guess she figured it was getting closer to going all the way out on her."

Wanda bit her lip and looked away again. Tears formed in her eyes. "If I had been here, I might have seen it coming and could have gotten her back to the doctor in time and kept her condition from catching up and getting out past her," she said in a strangled voice. "At least I could have been there in her last moments."

"Like I said," Wanda's father said, cutting in, "I don't think anything could have been done. Don't blame yourself for not being there."

"I'll damn well blame myself if I think I'm to blame. And no one's going to stop me or tell me otherwise!"

To Wanda's father, that response was pure Wanda. No one could ever tell her or convince her otherwise of anything, not even when it came to unjustified self-recrimination.

"If I had been here, I might have made a difference. Instead, I was off over the horizon, making a difference in my different life." Wanda wiped the tears from her eyes with her fingers. She turned her head to look at her father. "When you had your talk with Mother, did she say the reason she wanted me home was because she had a feeling she was going to die, and she wanted me home to look after you in your old age? Or are you just making the story up because she's gone, you're alone, you don't want to be alone, you don't want to grow old alone, and you're making the story up out of whole cloth as a way of trying to manipulate me into coming back home and living here with you so you won't be alone? Are you thinking of me, or are you thinking of yourself?"

Wanda's father was silent for a moment. "When we talked that time," he said finally, "your mother wasn't thinking about premonitions. She wasn't thinking about me or even about herself." He looked straight at Wanda. "Her concern was for you. She was worried about what the way you were living was doing to your soul."

That her mother had been thinking of her wasn't a surprise to Wanda. Her mother had always put others above herself, especially her husband and her only child, her daughter. It was one of the things that made her mother's death so hard on her. Nevertheless, what her father had said caught her up short.

"How do you mean?" Wanda said.

Wanda's father paused. "She just didn't think the way you're living was going to end well for you. I don't mean your working for the phone company. She was talking about your bed-bouncing and sexual adventurism. She figured that in the end, it would take you nowhere, and you would end up alone and would come to the end of your life alone."

"She said as much," Wanda said. "It's nothin' I haven't said to myself. I've always assumed I would come to the end of my life alone. I've pretty much had my life planned that way. I'm used to the thought that I will end up alone. It doesn't bother me to be alone."

"Maybe not now," her father said. "It's when you get there that counts. Your mother felt that when you got to the end of your life and found yourself alone, you wouldn't like it near as much as you think it won't bother you. By then, it would be too late to backtrack. She was fearful you'll end your life in regret, not in self-congratulations. That's the thing about being alone. From afar, it can seem seductive. When viewed from a distance, it can appear like a mountaintop experience. When you actually get there, you find it's not a peak but a pit. Your mother was sure it was all going to fall in on you someday, and in the end, you would find being alone to not be one bit as attractive as you think. I can testify to that. Now that I find myself alone without your mother, I don't find being alone one bit attractive or stimulating."

"But you and Mother were together more than half your lives," Wanda said. "You were acclimated to each other. You were imprinted on each other. You were one. You were used to being together. I'm used to being alone. After all the time I've spent alone, I don't think it's going to bother me to close the door on the final chapter of my life by myself."

"Your mother was afraid it would hurt you far more than you think. She feared for you in that way. She was afraid you would end your life on a lonely, sour note."

"So what did Mother want me to do to keep from being alone and keep from being a sour and lonely old maid?" Wanda asked pointedly. "Join a convent? Become a missionary?"

"Nothing quite like that. She was just hoping you would—you know."

In the back of her free-form mind, Wanda was starting to think her life was just a long and meaningless string of you-knows.

"I can guess," Wanda said. "She was hoping I would meet a nice man, fall in love, drop my wandering ways, settle down, get married, and have grandchildren we would bring around and take home with us at the end of the day. Is that what you mean? It was what she meant. She said as much the last time I talked to her. Mother was a country-girl romantic. She thought that finding the right man was the end goal of and only ticket to happiness in a woman's life."

"Where it comes to finding the right man for you, you seem to be halfway home," her father said. "The guy you brought home with you seems like a decent sort. He sounds like he cares for you. If he didn't, he wouldn't have come all this way out of his way to get you back home safe. You can hear in his voice that he cares for you. Your mother would have heard it too."

"Chuck is a great guy; I'll give you that," Wanda said. "He may be a bit impetuous. He doesn't always pick up on what I'm saying to him. He doesn't pick up on what I'm saying to him about me and how I don't want to be picked up on. But he's not a jerk. I don't think he has a jerk bone in his body."

"That sounds like a good recommendation for any man," her father said. "If he's that great and that much of a nonjerk, you should pick up on him right away. And you should do it quick. There are a hell of a lot of women out there looking for a decent, nonjerk man. If the word gets out how much of a nonjerk he is, they'll swarm him in a minute. If he doesn't get anywhere with you, he'll go off with one of them. And he won't be back. Your chance for a life with him will disappear. Forever. Forever can be an awfully long time. Especially near the end."

"I just don't think I can spend a life with one man," Wanda said. "I don't know if I'm capable of it. I don't think I have the strength."

Though he didn't show it outwardly, Wanda's father was a bit surprised by his daughter's equivocal statement that she didn't know if she could do it. He knew his daughter pretty thoroughly. If she still had been as firm in her commitment to her wandering lifestyle, the statement would have come out as strongly as it ever had. There would have been no trace of subtle doubt in her voice. This time, the tone of her voice and the strength of her words weren't as strong as they always had been. Something had changed. The conviction wasn't there.

"Loving one person for life and staying with them for life isn't a superhuman feat," Wanda's father said. "It doesn't require the strength of Superman. It's not hard to love one person for a whole life. It actually comes easy once you get used to it and get going at it. You could do it as easy as me. You could love one man for life. You could do it easy if you just put your mind to it. I know you well. You can do anything you put your mind to. For you, it's just a matter of putting your mind to it. And keeping it in one place. I never had any trouble being with your mother all our lives together. I never grew a roving eye. I never stepped out on her. I never had any desire to wander. I was happy with her all our lives together. I never went out like a roving cat at night, looking to howl. I never had a thought to. When you love someone deep and real, you don't have any thought of running around behind them. You don't have the need for running around."

"That's you, and more power to you for being able to do it," Wanda said. "I don't know if I can do anything like that. I don't think I'm capable of doing a life with any man, even the best nonjerk in the world. I'm not sure I can love one man that way. While Mother was alive, I spent an untold number of hours secretly telling myself that I just couldn't spend my life in the keeping and possession of one man. I spent as many hours telling myself that kind of deep love is a trap that would smother my life and any love I felt for him."

"Love like that doesn't smother life. Love for life enhances life. It makes it a more real life. It helps greatly to get you through life. Your mother would have told you that loving deeply makes love and life come alive."

Wanda turned her head away at the invoking of her mother. She also turned her head away from the depth of emotion she hadn't thought she could ever reach but had more than reached in the death of her mother. Her sorrow over her mother's death was real enough. But she was sorry for herself as much as for her mother.

"She did," Wanda said. "But I've spent a whole lot of hours since Mother's passing wondering if I'm capable of any kind of deep love. I've spent so many of my years living and loving shallow and on the run that I'm not sure if I could break myself out the mold I set myself in, even if I wanted to. I wouldn't know how to go about beginning to love deep like that. I've had no track record at loving deeply. I sure haven't had any practice at it. With the exception of Chuck, I've never been with any man more than once. And in his case, it was only because fate took a hand and threw us together. It wasn't my doing or my idea. Where it comes to loving one man for life, I wouldn't know where to begin."

"You begin where you're standing and go forward from there, like you do in anything in life," her father said. "Where it comes to lovin' for a lifetime, you've had your mother's example all your life. You had her example and her ways being imparted into you long before your ramblin' ways set in on you. Just go back to her example, and live it out in your own life."

"So what am I supposed to do?" Wanda asked. "What does going back to Mother's ways entail as far as me and my life are concerned? Am I supposed to give up my career and all my training, give up all I've made myself, give up working for the phone company, give up my pension that

I'm not fully vested in, and move back into this house, where Mother used to live but is gone from now, just so I can live in Mother's memory?"

"Well, I didn't mean it that way. I was talking about your personal life and your personal lovin' and—"

Wanda held up a hand and cut him off. "I'll make a deal with you. When I've reached retirement age and the phone company puts me out to pasture by forcing me to retire, if you're still alive at the time, I'll move in here, live here, and look after you the way I didn't look after Mother. That should make both you and Mother happy."

Even that minor concession on his daughter's part to come home instead of remaining on the open road surprised Wanda's father. It was a breakthrough; it just wasn't quite Wanda.

"In my will, the house was slated to go to your mother if I died before her," her father said. "I'll change the will to put the house in your name. One way or the other, the house will be yours. You can do with the house what you like. If you want to live here before or after I'm gone, you're welcome back home. If I'm gone and you want to sell the house, you can. If you want to turn it into a bordello, Mother and I aren't going to haunt you one way or the other. No hard feelings by either Mother or me. This home won't mean much to us anymore. We'll both be together in a better home."

In the back of her mind, Wanda heard the choir of their church singing the old spiritual "When the Roll Is Called Up Yonder, I'll Be There."

"Our love wasn't perfect here. Nobody's is. When we're both together in our final home, our love will be complete and perfect. I'll be joining her soon enough."

A frightened Wanda turned toward her father. With the combined strain of her mother's sudden death, the funeral, and the burial, Wanda wasn't thinking fully straight. People who weren't thinking straight misinterpreted things.

"What do you mean you'll be joining her soon?" Wanda said, her fear becoming noticeable in her voice. "You're not thinking of forcing the reunion by taking yourself to join her by your own hand, are you?"

Instead of turning his head away or becoming agitated, Wanda's father smiled. "No," he said calmly. "I'm not going to second-guess God, break his laws, and mess with his plans. If he wants to hold me over and keep me here awhile longer, I'll go along with him. It's not that I'm afraid of dying or that I don't think I'm ready to meet my Maker. I just don't feel qualified to take over his role, yank everything out of his hands, and take his will and plans into my hands. Right now, I'm at peace with it either way. He can keep me here awhile longer, even years longer if he wants. He can take me out of here tomorrow. I'll follow his plan without substituting my will for his."

Wanda relaxed a bit. She had never been a deep theological thinker. Now, within the space of a few short days, she had found herself confronted by some of the biggest issues of any and all times: God, God's will, life, death, mortality, the loss of love, and the loss of a loved one. The once certain Wanda, who had formerly confidently planned every step of her life, found herself stumbling around in a dark region she didn't know the size and scope of. She didn't even know where the boundaries were. She also found herself in the imploded center of runaway emotions she had thought she had gotten under control a long time earlier.

"Well, that's good to hear," Wanda said. "I came apart when you told me that Mother had passed away. I haven't gotten myself back together yet. I may never be back together all the way. If you went away on me, especially by your own hand, I'd probably come apart completely. I'd never be able to get myself back together. I might not even want to."

"We all leave this life one way or the other. One day or the next," her father said.

"But Mother left too soon," Wanda said. "Even if she had a bad heart, she died too soon. If not too soon for God, then too soon for me."

Wanda's words caught in her throat. She was sure her father was going to ask why, if she'd loved her mother the way she said she did, she hadn't stayed closer to her but had stayed so far away on the road.

Wanda bore her gaze and her words into her father. "You've got to promise me you won't leave me by your own hand," she said in her decisive voice.

"I promise."

"You've got to promise me you won't leave me. At least promise me you won't leave me anytime soon. Promise me you'll be here for me when I come back home."

"Are you planning on coming back home at all anytime?" he asked rhetorically. "No matter how far in the future it might be? When you left, you said not to expect you to come back ever—that the open road was your home and your future. The road was where you said you would end your days."

"Oh, that was just a lot of my talk back then," Wanda said. "Especially the part about my dropping dead alongside the road. That was just a lot of silly romanticism of the kind I indulged myself in back then."

It was the first time Wanda's father had heard her classify her chosen and constructed lifestyle as an indulgence. But he didn't say anything, fearing that if he did, it might get her fired back up, and she would take it back.

"Like I said, when my career is over and I'm retired from the phone company and living on a pension, I'll come back here to live. You've just got to promise me you'll be here when I come back, or else my being here won't mean anything. If both you and Mother are gone, it will hurt worse to live here surrounded by nothing but memories than it would hurt to live alone on the road. If you want me to come back home, you've got to promise me you'll be here when I get back."

It was the first time Wanda's father had heard her speak about coming back home to live as a pensioner. But he didn't say anything, fearing she might get her pride up.

"I'm not the One who sets times and seasons," her father said. "He sets times and seasons for nations. He sets them for people. If you come home, I hope I'll still be here. But that will be the Lord's doing, his plan."

"Do you think God has some kind of plan in all this?" the neophyte, entry-level theologian Wanda asked. "And if he does, what do you think it is?"

Wanda had never been much of a theologian. The only time she had ever thought much about God and heaven was when she assumed that neither of them would have gone very far in approving of her chosen lifestyle. By thinking even entry-level theology, Wanda was entering unfamiliar territory.

"I used to think that God's plan for me was to love your mother, look after her, and stay with her," her father said. "Now that she's gone, I don't know what his plans are." He paused. "Some people say God plans out everything in detail. Others say he lets this world lurch around on its own, lets us lurch around on our own in it, and sorts out the pieces in his heaven. I don't know which formulation applies best to him. I don't know if anyone can apply any simple formulation to God."

Wanda's father paused again, longer this time. "I don't know why God took your mother and left us both without her," he said finally in a slow, considered voice. "If there is a divine plan being worked out here concerning my life, I have the feeling that in one way or the other, it concerns you and looking after and guiding you. For all I know, that may be the only plan he has for my life. If that is his plan, it's only a continuation of the concern your mother had for you."

At the invocation of her deceased mother buried only earlier that day, Wanda went silent.

"She told me more than once that she was afraid the way you were living your life was going to end badly for you. She even said that if it was necessary for her to die in order to get you to rethink the way you were living, she would be willing to die to do it."

Wanda recoiled in shock at what her father was saying. She was still in deep emotion at the death of her mother. People in deep emotion often misinterpreted what others said and turned it around.

Wanda twisted in her seat to the point that she almost fell off the bench. "Are you saying that Mother committed suicide in order to get me to come home?" she asked in a shocked tone.

"I'm saying nothing of the kind. Your mother's heart was damaged from a bad case of scarlet fever when she was a young girl. It nearly killed her then. She survived, but it left her heart damaged. She lived most of her life under the cloud of having a damaged heart. It just finally caught up with her. I don't know if God kept her alive and let her grow up so I could marry her later. I don't know if God had anything to do with her dying or whether it was just the inevitable working its way out. But she didn't commit suicide and make it look like a heart attack. I don't think one can do that anyway. She wouldn't do anything like that to me. She wouldn't do anything like that to you. She loved us both. Even with its damage, your mother had a big heart. She wouldn't have deliberately hurt either of us that way."

"Are you saying her heart gave out from worrying about me and how she thought my life would turn out badly for me?" Wanda asked, still on the edge of her seat.

"I'm not saying that either," her father answered. "I'm just saying that your mother's concern was for you, not herself."

Wanda got up off the bench and walked over to the railing around the porch. She put her hands on the rail and leaned out a bit. She looked away at the horizon, but the only horizons she saw were the ones inside her. Standing in place, Wanda turned back to her father.

"Do you blame me for Mother's death?" she asked in a forced voice. "Did she die because I wasn't here?"

"Like I said, she died because her heart gave out," her father said. "I'm just glad it lasted as long as it did and gave us the time together we had. But if her heart gave out, one of the reasons it gave out may have been because she gave so much of it out to both of us."

"If I had left the road and come home to live, would her heart not have given out, and would she not have died?" Wanda asked. "Do you blame me for her dying because I wasn't here with her?"

The question was more or less rhetorical and self-justifying. Wanda expected him to say again that he didn't know.

"If you had been on the road and had had some kind of vague premonition that something bad might happen to Mother if you didn't come home—but nothing definite and nothing you could put your finger on—would you have left the road, left the life you had been living on the road, and come back home to stay?" he asked. "On the strength of only the feeling that it would have made your mother happy, would you have left the road and come home?"

The question caught Wanda up short, mostly because unlike with the other carefully construed and rehearsed answers she had constructed her life and her life narrative around, she was not prepared with a completed answer for it. She didn't have the beginnings of an answer for it.

Wanda looked at her father for a moment and then looked away. "I don't know," she said. "I never thought about it that way. I suppose if I had known she was dying, I would have rushed home to be with her when she passed. But I don't know if I would have given up my life and come home on the off chance that my being home might have made her feel better and might have kept her alive a little longer. I don't like thinking that I wouldn't have come home, but I don't think I would have. Mother never asked me to do that."

"And she wouldn't have. She would have never tried to manipulate you that way."

"What about you? Are you going to keep me home to replace Mother?"

"I'm not going to do the first thing of that. I'm not going to try. I'm not even going to think about it. So there's no need for you to jump the fence and run off into the woods. I'm not going to try to hold you here. Your mother wouldn't have had it. She knew you had to find your own way in life. She just hoped it would be one that would not cause you pain.

To that end, she let you go, always hoping you would come back one day. In the final end, she loved you and your life more than her own."

Those were the best of words and the worst of words. The words were intended by Wanda's father to assure her of her mother's love for her and that she had not rejected her anywhere along the line. Though not intended by her father, his words drove a knife of guilt into and through her heart.

"And I'm the ungrateful child who disowned her and her love for me and threw that love back in her face."

Feeling as if she had been slashed through by a saber of her own making, Wanda bolted into motion. Instead of running to the two stairs down to the ground, she leaped over the porch railing. As a teenager, she had leaped over the railing many times just to prove she could do it. She hit the ground running. With fast steps, she circled around the front of the house and disappeared off the side. Her father neither tried to stop her nor called her back.

Wanda circled around behind the house and headed off diagonally across the backyard. As she did, she passed close by to the antenna of her outlaw radio station. Chuck was busy with the equipment. He wasn't looking out the window and didn't see her or hear her pass by soundlessly on the ground.

On the far side of the yard were scrub woods. The woods went on for a distance, and where they ended, the land opened up into the cultivated farm fields on the outside of town. Wanda had wandered around the woods an untold number of hours as a child and teenager.

She thrashed through the brush of the woods until the houses along the road disappeared behind the brush and scrub trees. Eventually, she came to a small partial clearing where she was sure no one could see her. There she sat down heavily and folded her legs in front of her. Sticks and twigs scratched her legs, but she didn't feel them. She buried her head in her hands and cried. Her self-control hadn't left her completely. She cried silently. No one heard the voice crying from inside the woods. But she couldn't stop crying.

"Oh Lord, what good am I?" She sobbed quietly into her hands. That she invoked a power higher than her in the ordering of her life was a new and unexplored horizon that had opened when she asked her father whether God had been involved in her mother's death.

"All my love is a lie. Where it comes to loving, I'm nothing but hollow pretense. All my loving has been nothing more than shallow indulgence. There's never been a minute of real love in any of it. I have loved no man for real. No one has loved me for real. The only two people who've loved me for myself are Mother and Father. I don't know if you took Mother from me, but I had taken myself away from her a long time ago. I went over the horizon away from her. I would come back to her. I would have her come back to me. I would have her and her love for me back again. But neither of them can come back to me. I am left in an empty circle made of myself and nothing else. What good am I? What good am I?"

Like ice breaking off the wing of an airplane and falling away behind, Wanda's philosophical basis of her carefully planned, self-indulgent life shattered and flew away in the slipstream of her sorrow. At that moment, she entered a new, transcendent world she was unaccustomed to. She just didn't realize it at the time. That new world would take some time to gel.

When Wanda had started out planning her life on the run, she had known it was a life that could end up with her being alone, the kind of life that could end up empty and regret-filled for others who didn't have the same grit in their craw that she did. In preventative preparation for that contingency, she had thrown off the smothering weight of emotions, especially the emotions of sorrow and regret. She had willed to herself they would not get her down or get the better of her, and they would definitely not knock her off her track.

Now sorrow and regret, the emotions she had thought she banished from her life without ever having felt them, were on her in full force—with more force than she had thought they could carry. They folded in on her like a heavy asbestos curtain, weighing her down to the point she could hardly move. Her self-vaunted control of her life and emotions had been stripped from her and thrown out the window in a flash by the death of her mother. All her imaginings of love and all her self-inspired illusions of control of her life and herself had died suddenly and been interred with her mother.

With no one around to hear her, the unapologetic Wanda, so proudly unapologetic about her life, cried unapologetically. When Wanda remembered the way her mother had held her when she cried as a young girl, she cried all the harder.

"Where's Wanda?" Chuck asked, looking around, when he came downstairs from checking out Wanda's radio station.

"She had another attack of the blues about her mother," Wanda's father said with understatement. "She had to get away and be by herself for a while. You know how she is about needing to be alone."

As well as any man she ever stepped away from, Chuck thought.

"She went off on her own for a long walk."

"Should I go out looking for her?" Chuck asked. "I don't think she should be alone in her state. If she's walking around in emotional distress, she might get lost. Or hit by a car when she isn't looking."

"You've never been here before," her father said. "You don't know the area. You'd get lost. Wanda knows every inch of country around here like the back of her hand. She's rambled it all. If you get lost, she'll have to go out looking for you." He leaned back in his seat a bit. "Don't worry about her. She's not going to get lost, and she's not going to wander into the path of an oncoming truck. She'll come home when she works out what she's got to. Depending on what she's got to work out, she could be gone for hours or for days."

Chuck had only one full day left with her. He didn't want to lose any time with her due to an attack of wanderlust on her part.

"She'll probably be gone only for a few hours, but she won't be out all night. She'll be back by dinnertime."

Wanda's father thanked Chuck for his concern and offer to help. Chuck nodded and went back upstairs to Wanda's bootlegged ham radio station. Wanda's father watched him as he went. He still considered Chuck to be a good catch who could stabilize and look after his headstrong girl if only she would pick up on him and not be so thickheaded and stubborn that she walked away. Unfortunately, the prospect of his wandering daughter giving up her wandering ways, staying in one place, and calling any place but the open road her home wasn't a high-probability scenario.

Inside the radio room, Chuck looked out the window. Wanda was not visible anywhere. Even in her own backyard, Wanda was again gone from him, away over a horizon out of sight.

Maybe it was the thought of Wanda out over the horizon that gave Chuck the idea to take the station on the air. If she could be out over the horizon, he could go out over the horizon himself.

He turned the receiver back on, but instead of passively listening, he also switched on the homemade one-tube transmitter Wanda had constructed to be the other half of her bandit station. Unlike the tunable receiver, the transmitter was a crystal-controlled single-channel unit set for the code portion of the band. He read the frequency printed on the hard case of the body of the crystal and tuned the receiver to that frequency.

Fortunately, Wanda had thought to construct a manual TR transmit-and-receive switch that, when thrown, muted the receiver and connected the transmitter to the antenna. Out of proper protocol and consideration for other hams who might have been on the frequency and on whose transmissions he might end up stepping, he listened for a few moments.

The band was open, but the frequency was clear. Chuck pulled open the drawer in the table desk, looking for something to write with. Inside the drawer, he found an electronics magazine with a cover that featured an article on how to build a single-tube ham radio transmitter. It was likely the one Wanda had built the set from. Along with it he found a yellowing pad of paper and a pencil. He didn't find a station logbook with contacts entered into it. But not keeping an incriminating logbook was not surprising for the operator of a pirate radio station.

The Morse code transmitter key was connected. Chuck pulled it around into a better position on the table. He threw the main switch, pounded away at the key, and started calling CQ in the code portion of the band. CQ was the code signal for a general call asking if there was anyone out there who wanted to talk to him. He used his own call instead of making one up, as Wanda had done. For all he knew, it was the first time a legitimate, nonbootlegged call had gone out over the air from the station. He didn't know how far Wanda's low-powered peanut-whistle transmitter could get out. But if she had worked as many contacts as she'd claimed, the crude setup had worked in the past. It could easily get out as far that day.

The twenty-meter band was the premier DX band for amateur radio. When the band was open and the skip was running hot, it only took a few watts of power and a simple antenna hanging out the window to work the world. As a young ham operator, Chuck had thrilled at being able to send his presence through the air, out over the horizon. Apparently, Wanda had enjoyed it just as much—until she had found another way of taking herself out over the horizon.

After sending out a few short CQs, Chuck switched back to the receiver and listened. No answering signals came back to him. Either no one had heard him, or the signal from Wanda's transmitter wasn't strong enough to carry far. Or he hadn't called long enough to attract attention. Then again, he wondered if he was getting out at all.

Wanda hadn't bothered to build a watt meter that would give a power output reading. For all he knew, only a faint, weak signal was going out from the jury-rigged transmitter to the improvised antenna that had weathered so long in the elements that the antenna contacts had corroded away to the point where the antenna wasn't connected anymore. For all he knew, he wasn't even getting out past the backyard. For all he knew, instead of sending a signal out through the ionosphere, he was overloading the tube by transmitting without a load connected. It would have been ironic if the tube had sat unused all those years, waiting to be put back on the air, only to be destroyed in a false hope that it was putting out a signal that someone would hear.

As he thumped away at the code key, Chuck wondered if his attempt to establish a long-distance contact with the reluctant system was a metaphor for his failed attempts to establish a long-term relationship with Wanda, a contact that had one more day to run before she disappeared over the horizon by staying in place and he disappeared over his horizon. Chuck resolved that if he didn't get any response on the next call, he would shut down and not call anymore. Not expecting to hear anything come in to him from out of the bright and distant sky, Chuck stopped transmitting, switched the receiver back in, and listened, ready to shut down the system and leave it to go back into its limbo of disuse.

From out of the air and the distance, a signal came in, calling him by his call sign. The signal wasn't particularly strong. It didn't pin the signal-strength meter. But it was in the clear and was readable. It was a W7 station coming back to him but not from Washington state like the one he had heard earlier. This W7 was in the south end of the seventh call district in the state of Arizona. The Rube Goldberg contraption Wanda had lashed together as a young teenager had stood the test of time and gone the distance he had doubted it could. Wanda's creation was sort of like Wanda herself. But then, as far as durable creations were concerned, Wanda was a creation of herself.

Chuck worked the contact. He and the other operator exchanged signal-strength reports and QTH locations. When he was finished, he wrote the contact down on the pad of paper he'd found in the drawer of the table. He thought Wanda might like to have the information that her station still worked. It couldn't get her into any kind of trouble with the FCC. He was the one who'd worked the contact. His call was legitimate.

After the contact was over, Chuck held the frequency. He called CQ again and made another contact, this time a W6 in California. California was such a big state with so many hams that the state was a call district unto itself. As he was out of practice with a code key, Chuck's sending was a bit rusty at first, but it smoothed out and became more flowing as he went along as the old muscle memory and rhythm came back to him.

Working the contact brought back the remembered thrill of being a young boy sitting in front of his big Hammarlund receiver, working contacts with his commercially made Globe Scout transmitter. With only a single 6146 tube operated at relatively low voltage, it hadn't been all that much more powerful than Wanda's home-brew set. As he had grown up, he had sort of drifted away from the hobby. When he had become married and divorced from his unfaithful wife, his radio equipment had gone into a closet. His mothballed station had followed him from closet to closet in several moves and come to rest in the closet of the small apartment he currently rented in Memphis. He hadn't put it back on the air. He vowed to do so once he got back home, but he wasn't sure how he would go about doing it. Apartments were notoriously tricky places to run antennae out of. Chuck stopped transmitting in the middle of a CQ when he remembered he would be heading back to his apartment the day after tomorrow. Wanda would be heading back to her apartment the day after that. Like his ex-wife, she would become just one more broken contact fading over the horizon of memory.

Chuck put the thought aside and went on working contacts. The skip was coming in from all over the country. The contacts included a W1 in Maryland, a W2 in New Jersey, a W3 in Pennsylvania, a W4 in Florida, a W5 in Texas, a K7 in Idaho, a W8 in Ohio, a W9 in Illinois, and a W0 in Colorado. Wanda's little pirate transmitter-that-could was standing up and working the whole of the country. Once, he thought he heard the faint call of a KH6 station in Hawaii trying to get through to him. But the signal was too weak and down in the noise to copy.

The band was open strong. With so many faraway stations seemingly so close to him, in the back of his mind, Chuck had a glimmer of a thought that maybe Wanda wasn't that far away from him. She just wasn't there in the room with him.

Lost in the rediscovered thrill of making connections over the horizon, Chuck went on making and recording contacts. Along with stateside, one of the contacts was a VE7 station in Canada. The whole of the North American continent was available to him and coming to him as he sent his radio-frequency presence out to it. He paused to wonder if what he was feeling was a lower-level analog to what Wanda felt when she sent her much more physical presence out to work the motel bedrooms of the country. The day after tomorrow, she would be gone over the horizon again. He would have her with him one more day, but she wasn't there in the room. Her presence was off elsewhere. He wondered where she was at the moment.

"Does that thing still work?" Wanda's voice said from behind.

He turned around to see Wanda standing in the open doorway. Her face appeared to be damp. Even in the less-than-full light of the room, Chuck could see the wetness and the transparent streaks of tears on her cheeks. He assumed she had been off somewhere by herself, crying for her mother, whom she had seen buried only a few hours earlier. He didn't mention it to her. Hoping to make her feel better and get her mind off all she had been through, he tried to take the subject in a different direction.

"It works fine," Chuck said. "You did a good job of putting it together." He picked up the pad of paper he had listed the contacts on. "I wrote down the stations I worked, so you can see how far it gets out. I didn't work all the states, but I worked or at least heard all call zones, except Alaska and Hawaii."

"Wow," Wanda said. She sounded impressed but distracted.

"If you ever get a logbook, you can put down theses contacts in it. While you're at it, you might think about getting a license to make it legal."

Wanda glanced at the pad but didn't offer any further comment.

He dropped the pad back onto the table. "Given that you're so good at electronics, I don't see why you didn't build a phone transmitter."

"Even a simple AM transmitter has more sections and is a lot more complicated than a code transmitter," Wanda said. "And you have to build an audio modulator for it. A single sideband transmitter is even more complicated. And they both take a lot more parts to put one together. My access to parts was rather limited back in those days."

Chuck still wanted access to all of Wanda's parts. "Where did you get the parts for it out here?" he asked out of curiosity. "Is there a Radio Shack in town?"

"When Father went into Columbia, I would go along with him," Wanda answered. "I picked up the parts I needed at electronics stores. I didn't have the technical knowledge back then that I do now. So I stuck with building a code transmitter. They're a lot simpler. Besides, if I had used voice transmission, some OO might have come to recognize my voice and might have tracked me down. So I stuck with code. It's a lot easier to hide your identity."

The acronym *OO* stood for *official observers*. They were the Miss Manners and snitches of amateur radio—volunteer hams who monitored the ham bands, listening for irregularities and crude and illegal operating practices to report them up the line to the FCC.

"If I'd used voice, I could have ended up getting a pink slip from the FCC. If I'd gotten identified and caught, I could have been fined—a fine my parents would have had to pay because I couldn't."

At the indirect allusion to the things her mother had done for her as a child, Wanda's words caught in her throat again. She stopped talking. She bent her head down as if to prevent him from seeing that she was crying.

"I'll let you take over and work contacts of your own if you want," Chuck said, trying to change the subject.

With her head still down, Wanda waved her hand quickly back and forth. "No," she said in a stifled voice. "You go on. At least the old set is getting used again. It must feel like old times. Maybe it won't think I deserted it like I deserted Mother."

She raised her head and regained control of her voice. "It's getting late in the afternoon. I'm going to have to start preparing dinner pretty soon. I'll make spaghetti. It isn't as easy to burn spaghetti, though I'll probably find a way. I'm getting pretty good at burning my way through life and burning bridges behind me and leaving those who knew me behind."

Chuck didn't know that Wanda knew how to prepare spaghetti. At least she wasn't going all the way back to her country roots and fixing chittlins and turnip greens.

Wanda turned around. As quickly as she had appeared, she was gone from the doorway. Chuck heard her walking away down the hall.

"Maybe tomorrow you can get back on the air," Chuck said to the vanished Wanda, though he couldn't see her and didn't know if she heard him. He listened for a moment. Then he heard water running in the sink in the upstairs hall. He figured she was washing the tears off her face. A short while later, he heard her go down the stairs.

Chuck turned back around and sat down at the makeshift station again. But he didn't go back to transmitting. Instead, he sat and listened to the contacts going on between others, not really hearing them. Given that he would soon lose the one contact he wanted to maintain, he lost his interest in making contact with others out there. Whether Wanda would ever use the station again, he didn't know. All he knew was that the day after tomorrow, Wanda would be back in the air and away from him. Their final separation would have already happened if the tragic death of her mother hadn't intervened.

At least he would have tomorrow with her. After that, it would be over and in the air behind. But he would have one more day to state his case. He figured it would be an exercise in shouting over the horizon. But tomorrow he would be with her. After that, it would be only open horizon as far as he could see.

The twenty-meter band was a daylight band. It shut down after dark, when the ionosphere cooled and dissipated because it was on the dark side of Earth, without the energy of sunlight falling on it. It faded out and stopped being reflective until the sun rose over the horizon again. As the shadows on the backyard lawn started to grow longer, signal strength on the band grew weaker. Soon enough, it would shut down for the night.

For an indeterminate length of time, Chuck sat there listening and thinking in the gathering twilight, out over the horizon he would go back into without Wanda. It was a dull and colorless horizon with the light behind him. There was no horizon ahead that he particularly wanted to go into. He was still sitting there when he heard Wanda call him to dinner from the foot of the stairs. She did not come up to bring him down. Chuck shut down the equipment and his thoughts of what would come the day after tomorrow and headed downstairs.

21

"The stereotypical view of the Thing from the Audiovisual Department is a nerdy loser who can't get a date and who sends all the girls running away from him screaming because he's such a geek," Wanda's father said. "When Wanda was head of the school audiovisual department, she reversed that stereotype and stood it on its head. She had half the boys in high school standing on their heads, wanting to be her assistant."

"They especially wanted to lend me their hand and get things up and running in the dark storage room where the equipment was kept," Wanda said. "But it wasn't the equipment they were looking to put their hands on in the hope of getting things turned on. If the boys saw me going into the storage room to bring out the equipment, a moment later, there'd be a boy standing in the doorway, asking if I wanted any help in getting things set up and turned on. They were already turned on."

Dinner was over. Wanda hadn't burned the spaghetti. The sun had set. It was dark outside. For some time, Wanda's father, Wanda, and Chuck had been sitting around in the living room, talking. Mostly, Wanda's father and Wanda were reminiscing about Wanda's childhood in the town. Both Wanda's father and Chuck prompted Wanda to recount stories about her youth in the hope of getting her mind off the sadness of the funeral earlier that day. To some degree, it seemed to be working. Occasionally, Wanda would smile a small, momentary half smile as she recalled some particular memory of her small-town childhood. It might not have been a perfectly idyllic childhood, but it seemed to have been reasonable.

"I was the head of the high school AV department in those days. In an attempt to be modern, the school had audiovisual equipment that was occasionally brought out and used for teaching in classes. The school AV equipment consisted of an early-model tape-reel video player, tape recorders, and a black-and-white television on a wheeled cart. When it was needed for a presentation or as part of a class, I was the one who would bring it out, wheel it down to the room where it was to be used, set it up, play the tape, and bring it back to the storage room and put it away afterward. When I brought the stuff out, I made a habit of getting the cart with the AV equipment out through the door before any boy could get in and close the door behind him. Sure enough, half the time, when I pushed the cart out, I would run it into a boy who had seen me go into the room and was hoping to get into the room with me before I could get out."

Chuck wondered if that was where and how Wanda had developed her skill at keeping her foot in the door for a quick exit.

"When I was in the hall between classes, wheeling the stuff down to a classroom, half the time, a boy would come up to me and ask if I needed help in setting it up, which I didn't. Either way, I don't think any of them figured a girl knew anything about AV equipment, let alone how to run it."

"She knew so much about electronics even back then that she could run the school AV department all by herself without any help," her father said. "She knew more about it than the teachers."

"The electronic skill set of most of the boys didn't run much beyond tuning the radio of a pickup truck. Their physical interest set didn't run much beyond football, baseball, and necking. It didn't make our high school an academic trendsetter, nor did it produce any standout breakthrough individuals in any field. Our high school didn't produce any captains of industry. Our high school didn't produce any breakthrough scientists. Our high school didn't produce any Newtons, Pasteurs, James Clerk Maxwells, or Einsteins. It didn't produce any Edisons. It didn't produce any computer designers. For that matter, it didn't produce a Bill Gates or Steve Jobs.

"Even when the boys faked offering to help, they weren't of any help. Most of them just wanted to follow me back to the storage room, hoping to catch me there alone, hoping they might catch a break from me and do some pawing and necking. They said they wanted to lend me a helping hand. The only helping hand they wanted to extend to me would have been shoved up under my dress. I wasn't about to stand still for that from any boy, and I wasn't about to stand still for this town."

That statement fit Wanda, the love-'em-and-leave-'em slip-out artist who never stood still for a man, not even long enough for him to learn her real name.

439

"Were all the boys in that school out in the halls, wandering around?" Chuck asked. "Didn't any of them attend class? You make the place sound like an out-of-control ghetto school."

Inner-city schools in ghetto areas of big cities were starting to become that way. School discipline was breaking down. Teenage boys, often gang members, wandered around the halls, disrupting classes, dealing drugs, and acting in a threatening manner. The seeds of what would become a wider, systemic breakdown of inner-city education were being laid. He assumed discipline was still being maintained at small-town schools in that day.

"It's not like my school was *Blackboard Jungle*," Wanda said. "The boys were at the age where they were on testosterone overload, and in their sweaty, overheated little minds, they imagined that all girls were sweaty and ready to sweat with them in the sack. And whether it would have been in a bed, in the bed of a pickup truck, in a hayloft, or in a storage room, I had more than enough of them ready to sweat it out with me."

That statement fit Wanda, connoisseur of sweaty beds in sweaty motels of the open road.

"Not to go bragging on myself, but I had the looks. With looks often comes exaggerated, inaccurate, unearned, overheated reputations. Though I hadn't been giving any of the boys a tumble, they assumed a girl who looked like me just had to be loose and hot to trot. I was also a cheerleader. The boys probably figured cheerleaders are loose, because any girl who can throw her legs apart as wide as a cheerleader is probably throwing them as wide apart in bed. It didn't dawn on them that I had a lot planned for my life. I was already in the process of planning out my life, and I wasn't about to let those plans be derailed by losing control and letting myself get involved in any teenage drama. And I for sure wasn't about to do anything stupid and reckless that would keep me stuck in this town for the rest of my life, like getting pregnant and marrying the local bad boy who got me pregnant. I saw that happen to some of the girls in my school. I wasn't about to let it happen to me. So I kept the boys at arm's length. I kept the bad boys at double arm's length."

That was interesting coming from Wanda, a bad-girl juggler of bad boys.

"I guess most of the boys, and a lot of the girls, probably figured I was just playing hard to get. I got accused of it by both the boys and the girls. But I was playing hard to get. Mostly because I didn't want to be gotten. It was my life as well as my body the boys were trying to get at and get their jollies off of. I figured that letting that happen would make for a whole lot harder life to end up living than living hard to get. Like I said, I had a lot of plans for my life. I had them all lined up and ready to go. I wasn't about to deal away my life and my plans by dealing in with them or with this town. If that's playing hard to get, so be it. I was the hardest-case girl who ever walked away from this town."

Wanda looked at her father. "Like I said, when I'm retired and can't work anymore, if you're still around and need help, I'll come back to this house and live with you. But it will be because I love you, not because I have any love for this town or any great desire to return to it."

Wanda looked at Chuck. "Tomorrow I'll take you on a tour of the town. There's not all that much to see. Half an hour should do it. Then we've got the rest of the day. We can drive around in the country on the open road. After that, I'm back to the open road. There's a lot I want to put behind me."

She stirred in her seat. "Right now, I'm tired, and I want to get to bed. This hasn't been a very pleasant day for me. The sooner I can get to sleep and forget about it the better."

Wanda stood up. The gentlemanly Chuck started to get up, but Wanda held up her hand to stop him. "Don't bother to get up on my account," she said. "You don't have to do the gentleman thing on my behalf." She looked at both her father and Chuck. "The two of you stay here and keep on talking. You can talk about me if you want. I won't feel that you're talking behind my back. Soon enough, I'll have the wind at my back, and it won't matter what you or anyone says about me."

Wanda turned and walked out of the room. After they heard her walk up the stairs, Chuck and Wanda's father sat in silence for a moment. Wanda's father offered no further anecdotes about his daughter.

Chuck stood up from his seat. "I think I'll hit the hay too," he said, using what he thought was a country aphorism.

"I'm not sure how comfortable you'll find that bed," Wanda's father said to Chuck. "It's probably kind of saggy. But it's only for two nights."

Chuck said good night and headed for the stairs to the second floor.

Inside the auxiliary bedroom that was Wanda's radio room, instead of going to bed, Chuck stepped over to the receiver and turned it back on. Instead of listening on the band he had been listening on earlier, Chuck tuned the receiver to the eighty-meter amateur band. The light was off in the room. The translucent half circles of the dials of the radio, with their curved black lines of radio bands and frequencies printed on them, were lit from the back by the dial lights behind them. The glowing dials were the only color in the room.

The eighty-meter band was a nighttime band. It was the opposite of the twenty-meter band in that it didn't open up fully until after dark, when the twenty-meter band shut down. Chuck tuned around. Signals were coming in, but they weren't particularly strong. Eighty meters was much lower in frequency than twenty meters, which Wanda's antenna was cut for. On HF, wavelength was inversely proportionate to frequency: the lower the frequency, the longer the wavelength. Eighty meters was close to one-fourth the frequency of twenty meters. A resonant antenna for eighty meters was almost four times the length of an antenna cut for twenty meters. Given the length limitations, Wanda's antenna wasn't very efficient as a receiving antenna on eighty meters. But it was enough to pick up transmissions.

Signals were coming in, though not as strongly as they could have on a resonant antenna. He heard only W4s coming in from the call zone he was in. He heard a few W8s from the eighth call zone, north of the fourth call district. He heard one W0 coming in from Missouri, in the tenth call district to the west. But that was the farthest out he could hear. Chuck didn't turn on the transmitter. It was set for the twenty-meter band, which had gone silent from lack of propagation arriving. There was no one on that shut-down horizon to talk with.

Chuck tuned through several QSOs on the phone portion of the eighty-meter band. He could have listened on the code portion, but he wanted to hear human voices instead of dots and dashes. He finally stopped on one of the QSOs. He stood there listening, but he wasn't really hearing it. In the back of his mind—and the front of his mind and the other parts of his mind, remote and close in—he knew he had only one more day with Wanda. That would give him one more chance to try to persuade her to stay with him or at least remain in contact with him, even if from over the horizon. But he had no idea how and had no opening strategy to go about convincing her to stay close to him.

From what she had said, Wanda still seemed implacably set against the idea of remaining not only in the town but in any one place. She also seemed as implacable as ever against the thought of staying with him or with any man on a permanent basis. He had no idea how to begin. There was no strategy or trick he could use that she wouldn't see through and reject.

Stratagems came and went in his mind. He thought of being subtle. He thought of being romantic. He thought of being bold. He thought of going big, going all out, going for broke, and asking her to marry him. Maybe if he seized her in his arms and pledged his all-out, undying love for her, she might be so overwhelmed that everything would invert, and she would fall into his arms, saying yes. That was the way it worked in romance novels, wherein the masculine hero swept the initially reluctant woman off her feet and off to bed and, from there, off to the altar.

But Wanda was Wanda—the Wanda he had always known, for the short time he had known her. She wasn't a formulaic romance-novel heroine. She was the same Wanda with the same thoughts and was settled in her convictions—the same Wanda she would probably always be. She would be unimpressed, unshaken, and unmoved by such an obvious, clumsy ploy. If anything, she might become angered that he thought with a shallow, romantic come-on, he could negate everything she was and could easily turn her around and turn her to him. She might slam the door on ever seeing him again, even over a distant horizon.

Chuck heard the bathroom door open and close. A short while later, he heard the door to Wanda's bedroom open and then close behind her. A short while after that, he heard the faint sound of the bed creaking as Wanda climbed in. At no time had she extended any invitation for him to join her behind closed doors in her room. Chuck longed to try to ease her pain in some way, if only by lying silently next to her. But he knew full well that he dare not go into her bedroom. She would probably explode into full-fledged fury at him, shouting that he was trying to use her sorrow at the death of her mother as a way to manipulate her so he could score. She would probably throw him out of the house then and there.

Chuck turned back to the radio. He listened for a short while but without any interest in the voices coming in from over the darkened horizon. Horizons didn't mean much to him anymore. The day after tomorrow, the only horizon that meant anything to him would close down and go away, leaving him alone. He switched off the radio. Inside the dark room, he closed the door and lay down on the bed. It did sag.

For some time, he lay there contemplating the future, which held nothing for him as far as Wanda was concerned. At least in the morning, she would still be with him. He would have the day with her. Then the horizon would shut down. Somewhere in the indeterminate time of the room, his imaginings faded into the dark void of sleep.

———✦———

"If my clothes look like I slept in them, it's because I did," Chuck said as he sat down at the breakfast table. He had woken up to the smell of bacon and eggs wafting up from the kitchen.

"You timed your appearance just right," Wanda said as she carried a big frying pan filled with bacon and eggs fried in the fat from the bacon. "It saved me the problem of having to go upstairs to drag you out of bed."

That was interesting coming from Wanda, who had practically dragged him into bed in the first place.

Wanda started to apportion out the eggs and bacon. "And I didn't burn them. That's the secret of cooking good fried eggs and bacon: just have enough grease or fatback in the pan, and they won't stick."

Chuck wondered if it was an old country culinary trick Wanda had gotten from her mother. But he didn't ask because he didn't want to bring up her mother. She might break down and start crying again.

"Tonight I'll take you for dinner at Hanley's Family Restaurant," Wanda added as she put the last of the eggs and bacon on Chuck's plate. "They don't serve pâté de foie gras. They don't serve pâté anything. But they're reasonably priced, and the food is pretty good." She paused for a moment. "At least it used to be pretty good. I haven't been in there for a long time. I hope it hasn't gone downhill."

"It's as good as ever," Wanda's father said. "I don't know how much longer it will be around, though. Ben Hanley is getting on in years. He's older than me. His children don't have any interest in taking over the business. They don't even live in town. Ben doesn't have all that many years left in him. When he's gone, his children will probably sell off the restaurant. Maybe it will become a drugstore—that is, if they can find a buyer at all. Either way, they'll probably just close the doors. Whether it will reopen as a restaurant or different business is anybody's guess." He looked at Chuck. "If it opens as anything at all. It may just sit there locked up. This town may not be rust-belt America, but it's not exactly a high-growth, fast-turnover business-opportunity environment."

"Well, if Hanley's goes out of business, I'll be sad about it," Wanda said. "I had a lot of good times in there with you and Mother and with the other girls when I was a teenager."

That she would be sad to see the restaurant go was a bit of a hopeful thought to Chuck. If she could be nostalgic about a restaurant and sad to see it go, it might be a sign that she would be nostalgic about him and would be sad at the thought of seeing him go and being apart from him—perhaps enough that she would want to stay with him and give up her wandering ways.

"I'm glad I won't be around to see it. I don't care that much about this town, but I care even less to stay around and see it fall apart. It's just another reason why you're not going to find me hanging around this town." Wanda looked at Chuck. "After breakfast, I'll take you on the sightseeing trip of the town I promised. It's so small we can see it on foot and still have the other half of the day left open. We can take a driving trip around the area outside the town. I'll show you all the places I wandered as a young girl and a teenager."

It was a hopeful sign to Chuck that she wanted to spend the whole day with him. Maybe she had more of a sense of wanting to be with him than she knew. She might even have been edging toward the point of not wanting him to go. The more realistic lobe of his mind told him any hope he had that Wanda would want him to stay with her might be nothing more than wishful thinking. But wishful thinking had carried him from the beginning, ever since Wanda had come up to him in the bar. As far out over the horizon as his wishful thinking might have been extended, he had no desire to let it or her go. He had one more day to hope, and then the horizon closed down. He listened for any hint that her thinking was turning around to where she would ask him to stay.

"While we're out driving, before you take off tomorrow, you'd better stop to get some gas in your car, or you'll run out before you get to the county line."

⟞◦◦◦⟝

"And there's my old high school," Wanda said, pointing to the side. "I can't call it my high school. It was my high school and high school for all the teenagers here. It's the only high school in the town. Hallowed halls of memory. Setting for urban academic legend, high hopes, and high personal social expectations of being a player on the teenage scene and, above all, being popular. All followed in turn by disappointment, fading hopes, and the lowering of expectations. All sung to the tune of coming of age and other forms of teenage angst."

The building was square and functional in design, neither low-slung and modern nor aged and archaic. It was Saturday. There were no students coming and going, milling around, or knotted in groups, talking. Off to one end was what looked like a multiuse athletic field. Boys in football uniforms were scrimmaging on the field. Chuck assumed it was a Saturday practice, maybe in preparation for a big game coming up. Instead of turning in at the main walkway leading to the front door, Wanda kept walking straight.

"Don't you want to go in and walk your old halls of ivy once more?" Chuck asked.

Wanda kept walking straight, not looking at the school. "Nothing in there for me," she said in a flat voice. "Nothing I care to see. No dusty memories I care to conjure up."

"You might run into some of your old teachers," Chuck said.

"I doubt it," Wanda answered. "That was a long time ago. They're probably all gone by now, retired or dead."

"You might run into some of your old high school cronies," Chuck said. "You could exchange stories and catch up on memories."

"There aren't any boys I care to catch up with," Wanda said in the same flat voice. "I didn't spend any time trying to catch up with them when I was in school. I spent a lot of my time trying to stay out ahead of them."

"What about the other girls you knew and rubbed shoulders with?" Chuck asked. "You might run into one of them."

"Like I said when we drove in," Wanda said, "one of several things happened to the girls in this town in my day. The lucky ones got married to someone from outside and left the town. There weren't many of those. Others married someone from inside the town, had children, went into domesticity, and faded into the background of the town. Others got pregnant by a boy of the town, married the father of their child, settled into a rocky marriage, and faded into the background. Later, they got divorced. Others got pregnant but didn't marry the father. They kept their child and moved in with their parents. Or they put their child up for adoption and left the town. That's about it for the girls of my generation in this town."

Chuck picked up on Wanda's comment that the girls who got married were the lucky ones.

"One way or the other, the ones who stayed here got swallowed up and went into one form of domesticity or another. I don't know about the current generation, but no girl from my generation went on to college or any higher education. I was the only exception in going away. And I do mean going away. I learned going away in this town. In my mind, I was gone from this town before I knew where I was going. I was gone from this town as soon as I could transport myself out. I've been going away ever since. I intend to keep on going."

"It doesn't seem like such a bad town to be from," Chuck said.

Chuck wasn't sure why he made the comment. Mostly, he was trying to feel Wanda out to see how nostalgic she was, if she was nostalgic to any degree. Nostalgic people were nostalgic about places they had fond memories of and fond feelings for. They wanted to return to them. Nostalgic people were nostalgic for people they had fond memories of and fond feelings for. They wanted to return to them. They wanted to stay with them. Wanderers didn't come back and didn't stay. They just kept on wandering.

"*From* is the operational word," Wanda said. "I was from this town. I stopped being from this town when I got myself out of this town. I'm not coming back to this town. I'm not coming back to any life that would tie me to any deadpan place like this or any kind of deadpan life that's lived in places like this. Any place you get tied down to is deadpan. I've got the life I want now. I've got the open road. It's fine with me. It's the only kind of life I want."

It was not the favorable hint of nostalgia Chuck had hoped for. Wanda's voice trailed off. They walked on in silence for a while. The school fell away behind them.

"Did you ever think about having children?" Chuck asked. "In this town or anywhere?"

He wasn't sure why he asked the question. He knew it was a risky one to ask Wanda, who had often said she thought of all domesticity as a poisonous trap and had just reiterated it. But he was running out of time. He had to chip away at her hard carapace of disdain for domesticity and any form of convention to see if she could possibly be persuaded to go into something even remotely resembling a conventional and ongoing relationship with him. He was gambling on the conventional wisdom that women, even wandering ones, melted at the thought of having children.

"Mother always hoped I would settle down and have grandchildren I would bring her," Wanda said. "She would have made a great grandmother. She thought I would have made a good mother. But I would make a lousy mother. Unlike Mother, I don't have the instincts for it. I don't have the inclination for it. I don't have the desire for it. I especially don't have the desire to leave the open road for a child, which I would have to do if I had one. Wandering is a great life for a mature woman who knows herself and what she wants out of life. It would be a miserable life for a child—no home, no family, no friends. Just movement. It would be a life I wouldn't want to inflict on a child—the child I won't have."

It was a warm and bright summer day. Wanda's long blonde hair caught the light as it swayed as she walked. Her swelling chest stretched out her blouse to the point that the buttons threatened to pop. Her swelling hips pushed out full and rounded to the stretch limit of her blue jeans. The innate sexuality that had drawn the boys to her, which she had withheld from them under her real name but had extended to men on the open road under an endless index of assumed names, was back, now on full mature display in the town where it had all started. Back on her first block, she walked as if she didn't care if anyone saw her and didn't care what they might think of her or the provocative way she was dressed. The prodigal daughter of the town had returned, if only to say she was leaving again.

Wanda looked at Chuck. "Why did you ask that question?"

"I was just wondering," Chuck said. "But I agree with your mother. I think you would make a great mother."

"Any theoretical children out in the great theoretical beyond would do better for their pregerminated selves to pass me over and find another womb to be conceived in. I wouldn't be much of a mother to a child of either sex. If I had a daughter, the best I would be able to do for her would be to encourage her to be a rootless wanderer like her mother. She might or might not find the open road as stimulating as I have, but in her wanderings, at least she wouldn't be tied down to a stunted, stifling, nonmoving life in a town like this."

By saying that the hypothetical daughter she didn't intend to have might not find being on the road to her taste, she had just conceded that not everyone viewed life on the open road as the nirvana she had always considered it to be. For Wanda, it was more than a little concession. But

Chuck was preoccupied and focused on the closing time window he had left to be with her. What Wanda had said kind of went against her grain. But it kind of went over his head. He didn't pick up on it.

"I still think you would make a better mother than you think you would," Chuck said.

Wanda thrust her arms out to both sides in a gesture of telling him to quit. "Just drop it!" she said in a borderline-angry tone. "Since I don't intend to go there, don't you go there. Just leave it."

Chuck knew the sound of the decided Wanda's voice. He said nothing further on the subject. It was a moot point anyway. If he had been married to Wanda and she hadn't wanted to have a family, he would not have pushed her to have children. In the stage of thinking he had come to in his mind, he wanted Wanda to stay with him even if they didn't have sex. As far as the horizons crossed that day, it was Chuck who had crossed the furthest.

Wanda took him by the arm, pulled him off the sidewalk, and started to tug him across the street. "If you want to go someplace, I'll take you to Main Street and the business district," she said in the middle of the street. "It's a long way from the Magnificent Mile, but you may find it quaint. At least you can get a beer at one of the two bars in town. If either of them is still there."

Wanda led him down a side street between rows of simple one-story houses built of clapboard and low-grade cedar siding. A few of them had minimal brickwork around the base. A number of them needed paint as much as the houses in Wanda's suburb. Some of the houses had children's toys scattered around the small backyards. A few were boarded up, with grass and weeds growing in the unmowed yards and For Sale signs with the name of a real estate agent on them in the front. The same agent name was on all the signs. Apparently, there was only one real estate agent in the whole town. There were no Sale Pending signs on any of the houses for sale. Whoever the agent was, the person had a monopoly on a dead zone.

Wanda didn't cluck her tongue at the deteriorating look of her hometown. She didn't point to any house boarded up or for sale and say that she had known the people who used to live there or that it was a shame they were moving away. She just kept walking straight ahead, not appearing to take notice of the signs of decline in her hometown. Chuck wondered if it was all invisible to her and if she saw only the open road beyond the town.

There was no new construction going on anywhere Chuck could see. The town wasn't a hot growth zone. It wasn't what one could have called *small-town picturesque. Small-town funk* was a better description. Stasis and stagnation seemed to be the prevailing motif. Still, the town couldn't quite have been called a rust-belt town. Clapboard didn't rust.

The side street they were on ran perpendicular to the main street. It ended and opened up onto the business district. Shops of varying sizes and ages lined the sides of the main street. Though it was a prime business time on a prime business day, some of the former shops were locked, with no light on inside. Their front windows stared blankly out onto the underpopulated street. The shelves inside were empty of anything except gathering dust.

The town wasn't a ghost town. A few scattered cars were pulled up along the curb. A few scattered people walked the dull sidewalks in front of the dull stores that had life in them. All the shops and stores were of an older-generation design and construction. Some had wooden steps leading up to wood-framed glass doors. The only modern-looking building was a clean and fairly new-looking drugstore of a large and well-known national chain positioned on one corner. Wanda said it had been built after she left home. Apparently, the front office of the drugstore chain had considered the town to be worth the gamble of at least a midsized store. The gamble seemed to have paid off. There were a few people inside the drugstore. Chuck didn't see any other drugstores anywhere on the main drag of the town. Like the lone real estate agent trying to dispose of the unwanted vacant property of the town, the drugstore appeared to have a monopoly on business.

As they walked past the stores, Wanda pointed out various establishments, living and dead, and recounted incidents and memories of her early childhood that had taken place in them. The now vanished five-and-dime where she had bought small toys for herself. The vanished sewing shop where she had bought thread and fabric for her mother. The still existent wood-floored hardware store where she had bought tools and mechanical parts to build her radio projects.

The main street of the town was a scene that George Bailey, the main character of Frank Capra's movie paean to small-town life and values, *It's a Wonderful Life*, would have been familiar with as he walked the streets of his hometown, wanting to get out of the town as much as Wanda had wanted to get out of her hometown. Both of them were sworn and committed wanderers. George Bailey was eventually persuaded to stay in his hometown by an outpouring of love and sentiment from the people of the town. Wanda had long ago shaken the dust of her town off her shoes and left. No outpouring of love by her parents or anyone in the town had kept her from departing where she didn't want to remain. It didn't bode well for Chuck's hope that he could negate the wanderlust that had defined her life and hold her in place. But he wasn't trying to hold her in place in the town. He just wanted to hold her to him wherever they went, on the road, in a tower, or in a motel. Unfortunately, Wanda had gone forward out of the town and was still going forward on the settled belief that being held by one man was as poisonous as being held in the town would have been.

It was noon and lunchtime. Hanley's Family Restaurant was open.

"We'll be going here for dinner," Wanda said as they walked by. "I'll take you to the Round Robin diner. It's the only other eating place in town. I hung out there a lot as a teenager when I was in my *American Graffiti* stage. It's over on the other side of town. If it's still there."

When she said she wasn't sure if it was still there, Chuck didn't know if she was referring to the diner or the other side of town.

They were both still there. Round Robin was a classic 1950s-style diner and malt shop that had served as a teen hangout in Wanda's student days and before. As a retro joint, it was complete with a jukebox and functional remote terminals in the booths. But it hadn't been built as a retro motif. It had actually been built in the 1950s and had managed to survive largely intact and unchanged since then, one of the more picturesque ways the town had remained in dead neutral.

They sat down in a booth and ordered. While they were waiting for their order to arrive, Wanda put a quarter in the jukebox remote terminal and punched in the code numbers for a song. The song she chose was "The Wayward Wind" by Gogi Grant. The song was a sad little ballad about a woman who was in love with a wandering man. The lyrics described how the unnamed wandering man tried to settle down but eventually gave in to his wanderlust and went back on the road, leaving the narrator woman with a broken heart. It was the only song Wanda played. Chuck didn't know if she had chosen the song as a calculated reminder to him or if it just appealed to her as a theme song for wanderers. Either way, her choice of song did not bode well for Chuck's hopes.

"Come on. Let's get out of here and into some open space," Wanda said as they walked to the door after Chuck had paid the bill. "I'm tired of walking around in circles in this town. I did enough of that when I lived here. Let's jump in your car and go for a drive. I know just about every mile of area around here. As a child and teen, I walked it on foot or rode it all on my bicycle. I know all the ins and outs around here."

She also knew the ins and outs of getting in with a man and getting out the back door when she was through with him.

"Most girls would feel nervous walking alone on the side of the road this far away from anything," Wanda said. "I actually felt safer alone out here than I did back in the town. The boys in town who might have been of the mind to jump me if we were alone together weren't with me. They were back in town. Walking by myself, I could see what was coming down the road from a good distance. I had plenty of warning time. The woods around were thick. If I saw one of the boys from town walking toward me or if I saw a car with a man in it slow down as he came toward me, I could duck into the woods and lose myself. I knew how to sprint through the woods and get away without leaving a trail. I suppose that's why, since I grew up, I've always felt safer in motion on the open road than tied down in any one place anywhere a man could hem me in and get control of me."

They had been driving around at random for some time in widening circles on all sides of the town with Chuck at the wheel and Wanda directing. Wanda kept them mostly on the two-lane blacktop county roads and farm roads. As they went, Wanda pointed out landmarks.

"I started out wandering close to home on foot. When I got older, I traveled out farther on my bicycle. I always had it in the back of my mind that when I got older, I would get myself a motorcycle. Not a wimpy little Vespa like the girls ride in Italy but a full-sized hog. A Harley or something with a motor bigger than a sewing machine. But I couldn't begin to afford it. When I got started in my job and was finally making real money and could afford a real bike, I was too busy. I was out on the road like I wanted to be, but it was in a phone company repair van. I couldn't possibly have carried all the equipment on a bike."

Wanda had bragged that she knew every mile of the roads around her town. With every mile they traversed, with Wanda describing it in familiar terms, the boast seemed less and less hollow. She had been there. Chuck was becoming impressed with her record of wandering. In her early wandering phase, she had covered a lot of ground. As a grown woman, she had covered a lot wider ground—across the country and through motel bedrooms.

"If you'd had a bike, you would have had to get yourself some black leathers like the bikers wear," Chuck said. "You look good in leathers."

Chuck tried to imagine her dressed in black leathers like the biker gangs wore. But even with the top buttons unbuttoned, showing off lots of her generous cleavage, and her long blonde hair hanging down, contrasting the black leather, his mental picture of her in basic black leather was kind of flat. She had looked far better and more sensuous in the shiny red leather she had been wearing the night he met her in the bar. Besides, real biker women were tougher and more hard-bitten-looking. Wanda was too drop-dead gorgeous to make a convincing biker girl. She would have been far better as a scantily clad model splayed out over bikes in motorcycle advertisements.

Wanda didn't pick up on his compliment. She kept talking in the vein she had been. "However I did it, all my wanderings set Mother to worrying. She was afraid that nothing good was going to come of it."

As soon as she mentioned her just-deceased mother, Wanda fell silent. She looked off to the side, as if she were going to cry again. Chuck wondered if Wanda was imagining her mother looking down from the Great Beyond and thinking that all her wayward daughter's wandering would come to the sad end she had worried it would.

Up ahead, the intersection of the gravel road they were on and a two-lane blacktop road appeared. Wanda saw it and looked forward. She told Chuck to stop at the intersection.

"This is the road you'll be leaving on," she said in a tour director's voice. "It's easy to pick up from town. Father will give you directions. It's the same way we came in. Once you get on this road, you stay on it until you hit US 20. You take 20 west past Augusta, Georgia, to Atlanta. In Atlanta, you pick up US 75 and take it to Chattanooga. In Chattanooga, you pick up US 24 and take it to Nashville. From Nashville, you take US 40 into Memphis. It's superhighway all the way. But from Nashville, you kind of have to double-back on yourself and head southwest. As an alternate route, you can pick up Route 64 outside Chattanooga and take it straight west into Memphis. It's shorter and more direct, but it's not superhighway. It's mostly two-lane blacktop."

Chuck nodded and grunted his understanding. He hadn't been planning out his route back to the home he didn't have in Memphis. He hadn't even looked at a map. He had been preoccupied with trying to find a way to bring Wanda into some form of home with him, even one on the road. He hadn't planned his exit. It seemed the organized Wanda had planned out his route from the town for him, the town that had once been her home but that she didn't want anymore. She was sending him out to the open road, where she had no fixed address where he could find her later. She was sending him back to his apartment, which was a fixed address but wasn't a home. Wanda had always been good at arranging her departure from men. Apparently, she had his departure from her all arranged.

A ways out from the town, they drove through a wooded area that hadn't been cleared and turned into farmland. Wanda pointed to a small dirt side road and directed him to turn off and drive down it. Chuck followed her instructions, turned off, and drove down the rutted road, bouncing as they went. About a quarter mile in, the road came to an end at a small lake no more than sixty feet in length and forty feet wide. The woods were behind them. A large cultivated farm field spread out on the other side of the lake.

Chuck stopped the car. Wanda got out, walked over to the shore of the lake, and sat down and looked out over the lake. Since she looked as if she intended to stay for a while, Chuck shut off the car, got out, went over to where she was sitting, and sat down beside her. Wanda sat there silently looking out ahead.

"Nice lake," Chuck said in an attempt to make conversation. It wasn't much of a lake.

"It's not a lake," Wanda said. "It's a retention pond. It catches the rainwater runoff coming off the field. It's part of Old Man Spencer's farm. At least it used to be. I don't even know if Old Man Spencer is still alive. He was already pretty old when I was a teenager. He's probably dead by now. I don't know who owns the farm."

The sky was blue and bright. A few scattered, fluffy clouds drifted by lazily high up. Except for the lower altitude, it reminded Chuck of the way the sky had looked when he made love to Wanda on the top floor of the tower.

"Other than backyard plastic pools you could only sit in and splash like a little kid, this was the only body of water close by town where you could actually swim any distance in a straight line. The other girls and I would sneak in here as teenagers to go skinny-dipping. At least we did until the day we saw Old Man Spencer hiding behind his tractor in the middle of the field, looking at us through binoculars. We grabbed our clothes and ran back into the woods. Kind of freaked us out. After that, we were too wary that he might be doing a Peeping Tom, spying on us and drooling with who knew what on his mind. I guess we were afraid that if we came back, we might find him on this side of his field. So we didn't come back again. Wrecked a good swimming hole and put a pall over all my happy memories of being here. I haven't been back here since that day. This is old-home week all around."

While it was not exactly Walden Pond, Wanda's story of her memories reminded Chuck of what Garrison Keillor had written about in his paean to small-town life and experiences, *Lake Wobegon Days*.

Wanda fell silent and went on looking around and out toward the horizon beyond the far side of the field. "I can't say I miss it," she said, breaking her silence. "But in a way, I do. Not enough to leave the road and move back home here. But I really should get home more often."

Hearing Wanda use the word *home* so much, Chuck felt a surge of hope go through him that maybe she could be persuaded to think in terms of a home with him.

Wanda looked around rapidly from side to side. Then she jumped up onto her feet. "The hell with it, and the hell with the ghost of Old Man Spencer, even if he is watching," she said. "I'm going in for a dip."

Wanda kicked off her sneakers. She unfastened and pulled down her blue jeans. Her full hips bobbled free. She was a barefoot country girl with butt cheeks of tan. She unbuttoned her tight blouse and pulled it down her back and off her arms. Wearing only a minimal thong and her overloaded and straining sheer bra, she put her arms up over her head in a diver's stance, dove headfirst into the pond, and disappeared in a big splash—one more splash of the many she had probably made in the town.

The water of the pond was less than crystal clear. Farm retention ponds usually didn't have the sparkling water quality of mountain springs in Switzerland or Tahiti. Apparently, the pond was deeper than Chuck had thought. For a moment, Wanda was lost to his sight in the semimurky water. Then he saw her figure coming up, sleek and fast, from the depth.

Wanda broke the surface and started quickly and athletically swimming the long axis of the pond. Like an Olympic swimmer in a competitive match, she touched the bank at the far end, reversed direction, and swam back the full length of the pond. The pond wasn't as long or as wide as an Olympic-size swimming pool. At the speed she was moving, it didn't take her long to reach the opposite end. She touched the shore there, kicked off, and headed back. The muscles of her arms, shoulders, and legs worked in fast-paced synchronization. The off-color water was tinged a peat brown. Chuck wondered what gave the water its brownish hue. He figured it was probably mostly caused by decaying plant material in the rainwater that had run off the land around. For all he knew, it might contain fertilizer and pesticide-residue runoff from the farm fields nearby.

Whatever gave the water its coloration, the reddish-brown water of the pond flowed hydrodynamically around and over Wanda's back and the curves of her full but sleek, athletic-figured body. Esther Williams never had looked so much like a full-figured centerfold from *Playboy* magazine. Though *innocent* was hardly the word for Wanda, in its own way, it was something of an idyllic scene of country innocence, one that Garrison Keillor never had penned.

Wanda stopped in the middle of a lap and waved to Chuck on the shore. Though she didn't say, "Come in; the water's fine," Chuck wondered if she was inviting him to join her in skinny-dipping. He reached to take off his shoe. "Do you want me in there with you?"

Wanda waved her hands to dissuade him. "You'd better not. Water that's not moving can be dirty and loaded with germs. I'm acclimated to it. You're not. I've had about every childhood disease you can pick up in here. I'm immune. You might pick up some kind of bug that will knock you on your ass and have you puking the day after you get back. You'll miss more work. And that's just for starts. For all I know, there may be leeches in here. You stay put. Don't come in here."

"I don't think I'm going to come down with malaria or typhoid," Chuck said weakly.

"Maybe not that," Wanda said, "but you may pick up something that will tie your stomach up in knots and have you sitting on the toilet for a week."

Chuck had been looking forward to one more nearly nude encounter with Wanda, even if it didn't end in sex. However, mostly at her invoking of leeches, Chuck decided to take her advice and stay out of the unmoving brown-tinged water. He pushed his shoe back on. Inwardly, he appreciated her epidemiological concern for his health. But by saying that any bacterial nemesis he might pick up in the pond wouldn't hit him until the day after he returned to Memphis, she had reminded him he would be leaving in the morning. He had only one more chance to try to convince her to stay with him as a lover or in any capacity. The sun would rise the next morning, but the horizon would close off.

"It's getting late," Wanda said, looking at the position of the sun in the sky. "I've got to clean up before we go to dinner."

Wanda swam over to where Chuck was sitting on the sloping shore of the pond.

"Give me a hand out," she said, extending a hand to Chuck.

The slope of the wall of the pond was nearly vertical below the surface. What footing there was below the surface was mud. Wanda had a hard time climbing out of the pond. She kept slipping back. Chuck reached out with his hand and took hers. Digging in with his heels, he helped pull her up onto the shore. She scrambled up, digging in with her feet and knees, getting all of them muddy.

Up on the bank, Wanda stood up. She started pulling her wet hair off her face. With her arms above her shoulders, she stood there pulling the tangles out of her hair and straightening it out. As she did, water dripped off her body.

Women don't always appreciate how well the wet look works for them and how good it looks on them, Chuck thought. *When a woman's body is wet, it seems to shine. It makes her look like she's been rubbed down with oil. It makes her look sleek. It makes her look like a wet otter. It makes her look like she can move fast. It makes her look like she's ready to go. It makes her look like she's ready to keep on going. It makes her look like she's been going on for some time. It makes her look sweaty. It makes her look like she's getting sweaty by thinking about being in tight and sweaty contact with you. It makes her look like she's been sweating from exertion. It makes her look like she's ready to get sweaty by exerting herself in having sex with you. It makes her look like she's getting sweaty while thinking about getting sweaty with you. When a woman's body is wet and her hair is wet and tangled, it makes her look wild, untamed, free, and unmanageable. It makes her look like she's ready, willing, and able to engage in an unmanaged, tight, sweaty, rolling encounter with you down in the dirt or down anywhere.* That day, it made her look more Wanda.

As Chuck watched her, he wondered if he should throw himself at her. He wondered if she was about to throw herself at him. He started to get a bit humid in thinking about having a moist and intimate struggle with her down and dirty on the ground by the edge of the pond, an encounter that would leave the whole of her back dirty and mud-streaked, not just her knees. He knew this could be and probably would be the last chance he ever had to be locked in a tight and sweaty, passion-throbbing embrace with her before the horizon rose up between them.

But she didn't make any come-on moves toward him. She didn't say any come-on words to him. She didn't give him any come-on looks. The moment passed and faded out over the pond, out and away over the fields.

Standing up, Wanda pulled her jeans back on and then put on her blouse. The water on her skin made her blouse cling. It also made it semitransparent. The outline and seams of her bra showed through. Instead of putting her shoes back on, Wanda picked them up, tossed them into the car, and went barefoot. Chuck followed her to the car. From the pond, they drove back to Wanda's house. Wanda's father was still at work.

"I've got to take a shower and wash this pond scum and mud off of me and outa my hair," Wanda said as they reached the second floor. "I shouldn't be too long. Wait for me."

For the first time he could remember, she had actually said, "Wait for me." Chuck was careful not to read too much into it. But on a lower level, he took heart from it.

"I'll be in the radio room," Chuck said. He didn't plan to leave the house to go for a walk. He had done enough walking that day. Other than sitting on the front porch, he didn't know where else he would have been waiting for her.

Inside the radio room, Chuck retuned the receiver to the twenty-meter band from the eighty-meter band, where he had left it. Though it was getting late in the afternoon, the twenty-meter band was still open. Signals were coming in from a range of places as wide as the day before. Chuck tuned the receiver through the phone band, trying to gauge what distance it was open to. Again, he heard several different call zones. The radio horizons were still out there. That night would be his last chance to try to convince her to stay within his horizon. He had no idea how to go about it or if it could be done.

In the background of the radio, Chuck heard voices coming in from over the horizon, voices that would soon disappear as the band faded and closed down. In the background of the house, Chuck heard the water running in the shower.

Chuck went back to listening to the receiver. He stood there in silence for some time, listening to the signals coming in and gauging their strength. The band would die out and close down for the night not long after sunset. It would open back up tomorrow to the same distant horizons. Tomorrow

Chuck's horizon with the woman he wanted to share horizons with would shut down and not open up again. He wouldn't know what horizon she was seeing. He wouldn't even know where she was.

"Ten-four, good buddy," Wanda's voice said behind him. "You got your ears on?"

Chuck turned around to see her standing behind him, dressed in a short terrycloth bathrobe that stopped halfway down her thighs, drying her hair with a towel.

"That's CB talk," Chuck said. "Real hams don't use CB slang."

In the world and thinking of many licensed amateur radio operators, citizens band radio was often considered to be déclassé, a ghetto for technologically challenged louts, barroom babblers, and grade-school dropouts who were too incompetent or too lazy to learn the code and theory to pass the test necessary to get a ham license. CB operators were often loud, obnoxious, and verbally assaultive. Language heard over CB channels could be crude, coarse, sexually explicit, and pornographic. CB language and the subjects aired over the CB airwaves were sometimes under the radar of polite conversation and often just plain over-the-top. The language was also occasionally downright racist, with the N-word being thrown about from the safe anonymity of the airwaves. To many licensed hams who had done their homework and run the gauntlet of taking FCC-administered tests, CB radio was an outré imitation of real amateur radio, a poor and vulgar, downscaled country cousin to the real and accomplished world of amateur radio.

CB radio was also restricted to a single band known as the eleven-meter band. The band had at one time been an amateur radio band but had been taken away and given over to the newly created citizens band. It formed another reason why, in their technological and radio-frequency class-think, hams didn't always harbor generous estimates of their downsized cousins, whom hams often saw as being like layabout family members who didn't work, lived off the rest of the family, ate up family food, drank beer while sitting on the couch and watching television, took up space in the house, and contributed nothing to the family while they consumed family resources and took over their space.

Possibly with some of this in mind and in the hope of keeping the CB band from becoming a howling cacophony of crudity coming in on skip from all over the country, the FCC restricted CB radios to a power limit of five watts, which was sufficient to work skip if the band was fully open, whereas the maximum output allowed for amateur radio was a thousand watts. That didn't stop some more technologically accomplished CB operators from building high-power amplifiers to extend their reach over the low-power radio horizon. Hams often saw CBers as cheats in more ways than one.

As a general rule, hams tended to take more pride in their accomplishments and in paying their dues to get on the air, whereas they often saw CBers as a welfare class who were given radio privileges as a freebie and treated the privilege accordingly. As a general rule, in terms of over-the-air operational behavior, hams were more quality-conscious, politer, and more considerate as operators, though there were occasional clumsy, inconsiderate, or poor operators, known as *lids* in ham jargon.

Then again, there were occasional out-and-out pirate operators, such as Wanda.

"Is anything going on out there?" Wanda asked.

"The band is still wide open," Chuck said. "Plenty of contacts still to be made. Sit down, and I'll help you get back on the air like I promised."

He waved her over and directed her to sit down at the desk. As she did, he tuned the receiver back to the code portion of the band. The spoken voices of the phone frequencies disappeared, to be replaced by the dots and dashes of Morse code in the code portion of the band. Chuck put the receiver on the same frequency as the transmitter. The frequency was clear.

Wanda discarded the towel she was drying herself with and sat down in front of her homemade transmitter, which had proven to work well the day before.

"The frequency is open," Chuck said. "Go ahead and put out a call. I'll tune the receiver for you."

By that date, most of the ham equipment being used on the air were transceivers. Transceivers were a transmitter-receiver combination that transmitted and received on the same frequency, unless the operator set it for split-frequency offset work.

"Use my call sign. That way, it will be legal, because I'm here controlling the transmission. If you get back on the air on a regular basis, you might think about getting a license of your own. That way, you'll be legit, and you'll keep yourself out of trouble. If you keep on bootlegging calls, one day you might get caught. Then not only will you get a summons from the FCC, but the ARRL will subject you to torture by the Wouff Hong."

The Wouff Hong was a piece of ham radio urban legend. It was a nonexistent instrument of torture joked about and said to be used by the grand pooh-bahs at the headquarters of the American Radio League, the watchdog agency that organized ham radio contests, coordinated amateur radio activity, kept the bands clear of bad conduct, and reported illicit operations to the FCC.

"I'll keep it in mind," Wanda said, referring to getting a license. Chuck hoped she would take his advice. But down inside, he had a feeling that even with legal sanction hanging over her head, Wanda, being the woman she was, might go right on operating illegally, trying to keep herself under the FCC radar—not because she was too lazy to get a license or because she was too technologically challenged to pass an amateur radio operator's license test, which she could have easily, but because she actively preferred the stimulation of a bandit life lived in the shadows and on the run. If she did get back on the air, she might carry out her radio life the same way she carried out her sex life.

"If you do go back to bootlegging, don't use my call. If you do something out of line and someone reports it, the FCC boys will come after me."

"I've never used the same call twice," Wanda said. "I won't use your call at all. Don't worry. You've done so much for me to get me through this. I wouldn't do anything like that to you. If the FCC ever does pick me up, my lips are sealed as far as you're concerned."

The next day, she would use those lips to kiss him and say goodbye for the last time.

"If the FCC traces me down, I'm not going to cop a plea and say you put me up to it and slip away and leave you to face the FCC."

The next day, she would slip away and leave him to bootleg sex on the open road.

"I won't send you up."

The next day, she would send him away.

"On the off chance the FCC boys hassle me and start taking names, I'll keep your name out of it."

As far as taking names went, Chuck still had a feeling that she hadn't become any more amenable to taking his last name or even remaining on the same horizon with him. He doubted she would reverse the direction she had been going in since he met her—the direction she had been going in all her life—and respond in a favorable manner if he asked her to stay with him in any capacity. But as long as the odds were, he had to try.

"Put out a CQ, and see who comes back to you," Chuck said, switching on the transmitter. The filament of the single tube lit up and glowed as the tube warmed up.

Though Wanda had been absent for a long time, she still remembered how the system worked. She threw the TR switch and started pounding out code, using his call sign. After putting out a call for a reasonable enough time to be heard, Wanda threw the switch back to the receive position. The receiver unmuted. Radio noise came over the speaker. Chuck stood silently, listening. Wanda sat there listening. For a moment, they heard nothing but the soft hiss of radio static.

Then, out of the ether, the dots and dashes of a Morse code signal came to them from over the horizon, using Chuck's call sign.

"Got someone!" Wanda said, whooping it up. For Wanda, it was a renewal of the remembered thrill she had gotten when she worked out over the air and the horizon as an unlicensed pirate operator. Chuck was gratified to see her recapture the old feeling she had once had from making contacts. At the same time, he remembered it would probably be the last time he ever saw her excited.

The station was a K0 station in Kansas. From South Carolina to Kansas was hardly world-record DX. Her twenty-watt teapot-whistle transmitter was hardly a professional DX hunter's big signal rig. But it was enough to do the job. The little rig-that-could and its mistress who had built it were a lot alike in that when they set their minds to it, both could accomplish a lot more than others estimated they could.

For about half an hour, they worked several other contacts. Chuck stood by the seated Wanda, encouraging her to make more contacts—not to fill up the logbook she didn't have but as a way of stretching out the time he had left with her. All of the contacts they worked were in the fourth call district, the district they were in, and in the tenth and fifth call districts to the west. They heard nothing farther out. Gradually, the signals grew weaker and more distant-sounding. The band was fading out for the night. The radio horizon was closing down. The next day, he and Wanda would go their separate ways over separate horizons.

When he had married his ex-wife, he had believed in love. He had believed in love for a lifetime. He had believed in faithfulness. He had believed in staying with the one you loved for a lifetime. He had believed in the continuance of love. He had believed in home. His ex-wife had betrayed and scattered those beliefs. She had drained out of him his sense of love and the continuance of love, to the point that he hadn't really believed in either of them.

His sense of love and belief in love had slipped into the background of his thinking. Love had faded out over a horizon so far he didn't think he would ever see over it and see or even think in terms of love again. However, he had met a woman who, in a short while, had rekindled the sense of love he'd thought he lost forever. Ironically, he had fallen in love with a woman convinced to the core of her being that love, faithfulness, and love for a lifetime were a poisonous venom that would drain her life out of her and leave her shackled to an empty and circumscribed life that would not be her own. She believed she would feel she had lost her world. He would have to convince her of a different way of thinking, an alternate world of thinking. He didn't know if he had anywhere near the ability to do so. He didn't know if it could be done by anyone.

Chuck could assemble, repair, reassemble, orient, boot up, and get working a complex microwave relay terminal, but he hardly had the first hint of an idea regarding how to go about reorienting Wanda's internal world—if it could be done by him or anyone. Wanda's thinking defined her. It defined her the way she wanted to define herself. Wanda's thinking was a world unto itself. It was a world apart—a world that, as of tomorrow, would be apart from him forever. Chuck knew which direction he would be taking in the morning. He knew the direction Wanda would be taking. However, he didn't know the direction his sense of love and belief in love would be taking.

"Well, I've got to take myself out of here and get dressed," Wanda said, standing up from her seat in front of the desk where she had been working contacts. "You go on hamming for a while. You've got the license. You're legit on the air. When you're done, come downstairs and find me. We'll go to dinner at Hanley's."

Wanda turned and left the room without a sideward glance at him. The lower half of her short bathrobe curved out over her full hips. The bottom seam of her bathrobe touched on the upper half of her thighs as she walked across the room and out through the door.

Thus, it was over. It wasn't over forever, at least not then and there. He would see her when they went to dinner together. But in Chuck's mind, their forever separation began when she casually walked out of the room without touching him or giving him a longing look. Again, Wanda hadn't said one word or dropped one hint that she might be rethinking or refeeling her life on the run and on the road. There didn't seem to be the slightest hint of daylight between her and the wandering she had always believed and lived by. Wanda the wanderer was still intact and unchanged. She seemed as emotionally unmoved by the thought of his departure from her as she always had been. The dream that had started the night she walked up to him in the bar died for him there in the room. It died a little more than a week after it had begun. For her, the dream had never begun.

Chuck stood listening to the fading signals of the band as it closed down. He resolved that when they were at dinner, he would ask her to stay with him. He would ask her, as he'd planned. But it would probably prove to be little more than a perfunctory act. He had already discounted the prospect that she would say yes even to living with him, let alone marrying him.

Chuck listened to the fading signals for another minute, and then he switched off the equipment, left the room, and headed downstairs. When she came into the room, she would find him gone. When she came downstairs, he would meet her there instead of her meeting him there. It would probably be the only time in their brief, cobbled-together, improvised, horizon-crossing-but-now-concluded relationship when he ever stole a march on Wanda. The next day, she would steal a march out of his life.

———⚬/⚬/⚬———

"Before I go tomorrow, I've got to remember to disconnect the antenna from the receiver," Wanda said. "If a bolt of lightning hits nearby, even if it doesn't hit the antenna directly, it could ride in on the antenna lead-in wire and burn out the receiver."

As an electronics expert, Chuck knew that the heavy static discharge of a high-voltage lightning strike even blocks away could burn out unprotected electronic circuits, especially the sensitive circuits of a receiver front end. As a ham radio operator, he knew not to operate during an electrical storm and to ground or disconnect the feed line from the antenna to the radio.

"Why don't you take your station with you to your apartment in Columbia and set it up there?" Chuck asked.

"To do that, I'd have to string an antenna out the window over to another building or mount a vertical antenna on the roof," Wanda answered. "I don't think the manager of the apartment is going to let me do that."

"Since you're good at building antennae, you could make yourself a short vertical antenna with a large loading coil at the base to compensate for the shortened length," Chuck said as Wanda took a drink of apple juice. "When you wanted to operate, you could open the window, stick it out, and start cranking."

Chuck had brought up the question of whether she planned to take her home-brew station with her when she went back to her apartment as a way to segue into the questions of whether she would stay with him and whether he could take her with him when he left the next day.

"Those little shorty base-loaded apartment-dweller special antennae are too short to be efficient," Wanda said. "They don't get out very well." Wanda knew all about getting out far and wide. She took a drink of her apple juice. "Besides, for all I know, the FCC may have a monitoring station in Columbia like they do in other big cities. I'd be operating right under their noses. They'd triangulate where I was. They'd pick me up in a heartbeat and drag me in for a hearing. It kind of defeats the purpose of being a pirate operator if you work out of an alley that runs behind an FCC monitoring station."

"You could get around all of that if you got yourself an amateur radio operator's license," Chuck said. "You wouldn't have to worry about getting caught, and you wouldn't have to go sneaking out into the country to do it. If you can master electronics the way you have, getting a license should be easy for you. Most of the questions on the ham tests are pitched to the Boy Scout level, even the tests for advanced-level licenses. You could get out from under all the problems of being an unlicensed operator and all the dangers of getting caught if you'd just get yourself a license. You're not technologically incompetent, and you're not lazy. There's no reason for you not to get a license. If you're going to go back on the air, you don't have to run the risk of being a bandit."

"The thrill of being a bandit on the bands and on the road is what it's all about," Wanda said.

22

While not fancy or particularly upscale, Hanley's Family Restaurant was a pleasant enough family-style establishment with tables and a counter separating the kitchen entrance from the rest of the restaurant. Patrons were finishing dinner at their tables. There was one person sitting at the counter.

The restaurant was clean. There weren't peanut shells on the floor. There weren't loudmouthed rednecks guzzling beer and whooping it up at the bar. The place didn't have a bar. The food was tasty and well prepared. The salad at the salad bar was fresh. The waitresses weren't old and surly. They were all youngish-looking pre-college-age girls apparently from the generation who had come of age after Wanda left the town. Wanda didn't seem to recognize any of them. She didn't wave at any of them or call out their names. As he looked at the smiles on their faces, Chuck wondered if behind the smiles, they too were planning how to get out of town the way Wanda had in her youth.

"Or do you enjoy being a bandit operator out on the edge of the band?" He wanted to add, "In the same way you enjoy being a bandit sexual operator operating out beyond the edge of social norms and acceptance," but he didn't. Instead, he asked, "Is it stimulating to you? Do you get a charge out of being a bandit? Do you want to keep on being a bandit operator for the rest of your life?"

The radio-related question was just a stand-in for the real question he wanted to ask about her bandit sex life. He had thought of the question many times before but hadn't asked it openly, fearing it would put her off or make her angry. It was an equally risky question to ask now at a time when he needed every bit of warm feeling for him on her part in order for him to ask the real question that was hanging fire in his heart and in the air over their last time together. But time was running out. Their time together was almost over. It was pretty much now or never.

Wanda looked at him as if surprised by both the direction of his questions and the intensity with which he asked them. "Maybe I'll get a license; maybe I won't. Maybe I'll continue to be a radio bandit. As for my station, I'll probably just leave it here at home and use it when I'm home visiting—not enough to attract FCC attention. I'll probably be too busy and on the road to get home and around to using it very much anyway. Why all the concern? I'm glad you think enough of me not to want to see me get in trouble with the FCC. But I don't think that's going to happen. If you're so worried about me catching an FCC summons, maybe I'll take the time to get a license."

It was another minor victory for Chuck. At least he had convinced Wanda to do one small thing she otherwise would have felt bothered to do.

"But then again, maybe I'll just go on being a bandit." Wanda took another drink of her apple juice and set the glass back down. "In one way, you're right about me. I do enjoy being a bandit, on the air and on the road. Always have. Probably always will. Either way, it's not worth getting so worked up over. If you're worried about my station sitting there going to rust, I'll give it to you. You can put it on the air legal-like back in Memphis. You can think of me while you're banging out contacts with Tahiti, Paris, and Gondwanaland."

The usually informed Wanda thought Gondwanaland was a country in Africa. Actually, it was a supercontinent that had existed millions of years ago on prehistoric Earth.

She continued. "I don't know how much or how often I'm going to get back home to use it. Like I said, if you're worried about my station deteriorating from disuse, I'll give it to you. When you leave, you can take it with you. At least it may feel that someone cares for it. That way, it may not think it's been abandoned."

Some ham radio operators felt sentimental about their radios. Sometimes they attributed feelings to them.

Chuck reached across the table with both hands and took one of Wanda's hands in his. Wanda looked at him with an uncertain look.

Chuck said, "What I was hoping to take away with me when I leave is you."

"Is there a point to this?" Wanda asked.

"The point is that when I leave, I wasn't thinking of taking orphan ham radios with me," Chuck said. "When I leave, I was hoping you would leave with me."

Wanda recoiled. She leaned her head back a bit, but she didn't pull her hands out of his.

He added, "I was hoping you would come away with me when I leave and would stay with me and that we would be together for the rest of our lives."

"Are you back to that again?" Wanda said with an edge coming back into her voice. "You're like a dog chewing an old bone. I've told you enough times that I like you, but I don't want to marry you. I don't intend to marry any man."

Instead of coming out decidedly and certainly, Wanda's words trailed off.

"We don't have to get married," Chuck said in a tone of concession. "If you don't want to get married, we can live together. I just want to be with you."

"What that gets for you is obvious," Wanda said in an obvious tone. "But what does it translate into for me? Am I supposed to give up my career, give up my freedom, give up my life, become your appendage, and ride along with you wherever you go?"

It was the heyday of expanding feminism. The same question was being asked in similar form and content by an increasing number of women of all ages and predispositions.

"You don't even have to leave where you are and come away with me," Chuck said. "I can wangle a transfer to the Columbia office you work out of. I'm not leaving anybody behind. My parents live in California now. They retired to a retirement community in the Palm Springs area. I don't have any brothers or sisters. We can live in your apartment together. We can go on the road as a team and work together like we did at the tower."

"That's not what the phone company means when they say, 'Reach out and touch someone,'" Wanda said. "If the word got out that we were running our own shack-up road trip, jump-starting each other when we were supposed to be jump-starting phone company equipment, it would make the phone company look like something out of *Hustler* magazine or a Hollywood scandal sheet instead of a staid, professional, conservative organization, the kind of image they like to project. It would make the company look like a bordello. They'd fire both of us to avoid the bad publicity. We'd both be out of a job. We'd be blacklisted, unable to get a job with any phone company anywhere. Even if it only got out internally, they'd probably still fire us because they don't want their employees screwing in-house. They probably have an unwritten policy against employees of the opposite sex fraternizing with each other and screwing each other, even in privacy behind their own closed doors. Like I said, there are too many problems involved with screwing where you work. There are just as many problems involved with bedding those you work with. Even if it takes place after hours, the company probably has an unspoken policy against that. They'll probably think up a reason to can us both."

"I don't know of any company policy, official or unofficial, against employees getting married," Chuck said.

Wanda shot him a "Don't start that again" look.

Chuck realized he had stumbled, and he changed direction. "I'm not trying to take over your life. I'm not out to control your life. I just want to share life with you until the end of our lives. I just want to keep you from ending up the way your mother feared you would."

Chuck caught himself. For all he knew, he had blundered badly by invoking the mother Wanda had just buried a short time earlier. She might think it was a crude attempt on his part to manipulate her by her feelings of sorrow for her recently deceased mother.

"What's that supposed to mean?" Wanda snapped.

The sharp tone of her voice made Chuck think he had been right to suspect he had verbally blundered. "Well, you said," Chuck said, stumbling over his words, "that your mother said she was afraid for you—afraid that the way you were living your life was going to turn out bad for you."

"In what way?" Wanda asked pointedly.

"She was afraid that when the thrill of living a runaround life, especially the thrill of continuing to run yourself through the mill by running yourself through motel bedrooms on the open road, wore off, you'd be left alone and unhappy, and you'd end your life alone, not celebrating but regretting the way you had lived your life. I mean no disrespect to your mother. I more or less agree with her on that one."

Chuck stopped there and said no more. Everything he was saying sounded clumsy, bumbling, and manipulative, especially when he invoked her mother, whose death had so broken her up. It might only provoke the decided girl, who was easily provoked but almost impossible to dissuade once she had set her mind and her life to an idea she built her life around.

"And how do you propose to save me from all the tribulation, heartache, and loneliness you see coming upon me because of the lack of romance you see in my life?" Wanda asked in a grindingly sour and ironic voice. "Do you propose to do so by taking me into your life and supplying the romance you think I'm lacking in mine? Do you imagine yourself as the one who will save me from stumbling in life and through life? Are you looking to monitor my life and deliver me from my own folly and bad judgment? Do you propose that you are the only one capable of injecting into my life the romanticism you think my life is short on?"

The tone of her voice was turning hard and impenetrable. "If that's what's involved for me in the life you want to take me into with you, the life you would extend to me and then pull into yours is going to be little more than a life of you molding my life into yours. The hand you are offering to extend to me is a condescending hand holding and controlling me. That's not the kind of life I want. It's not the kind of life I've ever wanted. It's not the kind of life I'm prepared to accept from any man, not even when it comes wrapped up in a romantic love-for-a-lifetime package. That kind of life would be death to me. It would smother me. It would shut down all horizons for me except one: the horizon of you. I'm not ready to accept the shutting down of all my horizons for a horizon set for me by someone else."

"I wouldn't try to smother you," Chuck said. "I wouldn't try to dominate you. I wouldn't try to control you. I wouldn't try to shut down your life."

"Oh, I believe you," Wanda said. "On all counts."

Chuck had been struggling to get one small concession out of the concession-resistant girl. Unexpectedly, she was granting him an across-the-board concession. What, if anything, it meant he didn't know.

"I don't believe you'd try to smother me. But the situation and the compromises necessary to maintain the relationship would have the same effect. I don't believe you would deliberately try to dominate me. I don't believe you would try to control me out of some ego-driven need to control that some guys have. I can pick that up in a man in a heartbeat. But the compromises necessary to make the relationship work would have the same effect of controlling me. You might not consciously try to shut down my life and change it around, but the compromises necessary to live a shared life with you or any man would force me to reorder myself and my life. Especially the part of my life I live under the sheets on the open road. I know you wouldn't put up with that on my part any more than you put up with it from your cheating wife. But that part of my life is as much a part of my life and what I am as any other part is."

A waitress handed a couple at a nearby table their check. They got up and prepared to leave.

"If we were married or living together, the call of the open road would still be in me as strong as ever. The call of love on the run would still be in me as strong as it ever was. Eventually, it would win out. Eventually, I would betray you. And that eventuality probably wouldn't come about all that far down the road."

"I would never betray you," Chuck said.

"I know that too," Wanda said. "You're not the cheating type. You just stumble all over and fall for women who are. But I know you'd be faithful. You're the faithful type. Faithfulness is in your blood. It's all through you. It's part of your great-guy nature. I'm sure you wouldn't betray me. I know you'd stay with me for life. You're the faithful-for-life type of guy. I'm just not the faithful-for-life kind of girl. I'm nowhere near that kind of girl. Never have been anywhere near that kind of girl."

Chuck was a great guy. He was also a great technician who could pick up on complex circuitry with a single look. But often, an enhanced ability to pick up in one area left one deficient in the ability to pick up in other areas. Like much of the human race, Chuck didn't pick up well or respond accordingly with what he didn't want to hear. The relevant end-stage, reductionist parts of what she was saying were kind of going over his head with room to spare.

"If you believe that I won't betray you, why won't you stay with me?" he asked. For Chuck, it was the crux of the matter. For Wanda, it was getting repetitive.

"Faithfulness is you," Wanda said. "But it's not me. I've never been faithful to any man. I've never thought to be faithful to any man. I've never wanted to be faithful to any man. I've never planned to be faithful to any man. I've never tried faithfulness. I've never believed in faithfulness. I wouldn't know where and how to begin being faithful. I'm probably not capable of faithfulness. If I tried to be faithful, I doubt I could keep at it. I'm exactly the type of woman whom great and faithful guys like you shouldn't get involved with but always inevitably do. In the end, they end up hurt. They end up hurt because the innate goodness in them leaves them vulnerable to being hurt. They end up hurt by women who can't be hurt and can't feel hurt. They pour their good-guy nature, their good-guy souls, their trust, and their faithfulness out on women who cannot be trusted, don't have a faithful bone in their body, treat their good-guy faithfulness with contempt, and throw it back in their faces—women who can't be trusted for an inch of faithfulness. Women like your ex-wife. Women like me."

Wanda wrapped her hands around his hands and squeezed them. "You can't trust me. You wouldn't be able to trust me any more than you could trust that cheating ex-wife of yours. If we were married or if we were even living together unmarried, I'd be restive, wanting to get back to roaming again. I'd be looking at the back door, wanting to get out and go back to my old wandering ways, not just on the open road but in the bars alongside the road. You'd know what was going on in me. I wouldn't be able to hide it. There would be constant tension between us. There'd be arguments and fights. I'd feel trapped. I'd feel hijacked. I'd feel that my life had been drained out of me and into you. Even if we were on the road together, I'd be looking to get away from you farther down the road. I'd be looking for a horizon beyond you. I'd be looking for a life apart from you. I'd be looking for a bed apart from you. I'd be looking to get back to the way I was living before we got thrown together."

Wanda's voice had grown louder. She glanced around to see if anyone was looking their way and lowered her voice. "I'm telling you this for your own good. I'm telling you because I'd only hurt you, and I don't want to hurt you. If you tried to hold me close to you, the closeness you would hope to find in me and have with me would stretch out into a bitter distance between us. The happiness you would hope to find with me would be quickly gone. If it ever even developed."

A waitress walked past. Wanda paused until she was out of hearing range.

"I can't give you love. I don't think I have any real love in me to give. I don't think I ever had any real love in me to give. The only thing I can give you that's real about me, the only thing I can give you from out of what little depth I have in me, and the only thing I can give you out of my shallow little heart with any real value to it is honesty. It may not be what you want to hear. It may leave you feeling empty. But in the end, any lie I told you, especially any lie I told you about spending a life with you, would leave you far emptier."

No more people had come into the restaurant. The dinner crowd had reached its small-town peak.

"If I professed any deep love for you, a love deeper than I have for living my life as I define it, it would be a lie, pure and simple. If I told any lie, if I made any pretense about staying with you for any length of time, I'd soon enough go back on my phony words. In the end, the end that would be inevitable from the beginning, after being kicked in the teeth for a second time by a woman, your ability to feel love or even believe in it would be gone. The only feeling that would be left in you would be bitterness. Your love would be gone as fast and as far as I would be gone. That's the only future you'd face if you tried to hold me to you. That's why we shouldn't start. That's why you shouldn't even think of trying to start up with me. It wouldn't work. Being with me, knowing me, with me being what I am, would poison your life. In the end, the strain of knowing me might even shorten your life. Being married to you; being bound to you or to any man, even loosely; and being unable to move would smother my life. It would take all the meaning out of my life. It might end up shortening my life as much as it might shorten yours."

"They say married people live longer," Chuck said, not knowing what to say at that juncture. "Statistics are supposed to bear that out."

"That may be true for other people," Wanda said. "It will probably prove true for you, provided you find and choose a better, more faithful love-for-a-lifetime woman than your ex-wife. But I'm not that woman. I don't think I'm remotely capable of being that woman. Being married to each other wouldn't be a door to a wider and longer life. It would be something of an emotional suicide pact for both of us."

At the front desk, a couple finished paying their bill and left the restaurant. The crowd was beginning to thin out.

"When it comes to your wanting to go with someone for life, don't try to go there with me. For the good of both our lives, don't try to have a life with me. Like I say, you trying to have a life with me could drain the life out of both of us. It could even work in reverse and shorten life for both of us."

The last patron sitting at the counter got up and prepared to leave.

"So let's just say a quiet and mutually beneficial goodbye to each other and go our separate ways. We can live in fond memories of each other, but we shouldn't try to force those feelings into what could only become a hardscrabble reality between us. Even though we're apart, living in our memories will be far easier on our lives than if we break ourselves against each other by trying to force together and hold together what can't be joined or can't be sustained if joined. So let's just leave things where they are and not try to cross horizons that can't be crossed. Living in good memories is better than living in a bad reality. It will be better for our lives all around."

A long-forgotten line from the song that had been playing in the lobby of the motel where her new alternate, wandering life had begun, inspired by what she had overheard next door, came to mind.

"We'll both live a lot longer if you live without me." Her voice trailed off and stopped.

"I've never wanted to live with or be with a woman as much as I want to be with you," Chuck said. "I didn't want to be with my ex-wife, even before I married her, as much as I want to be with you and have you be with me. I never wanted to be with any woman as much as I want to be with you."

Wanda said nothing.

"You're all I ever wanted to find in a woman and more. You're all I ever hoped to find in a woman. I had pretty much given up on finding anyone like you. I had given up on love. Knowing you restored my belief in love. Before finding you, I had gone empty. You brought me back from the edge of emptiness. Now you're about to walk away. When you go, I see nothing ahead but a return to emptiness. You are the woman I always dreamed of and more than I hoped to dream of."

Wanda held up a hand and cut him off. "Your dreams and your love just won't work with me," she said in a quiet, halting voice. "I'm not the girl you hope for. I don't think I have it in me to be that kind of girl. I can't change, even if I wanted to. I can't be what you want me to be. I can't be what you need."

Chuck started to say that a determined girl like her could be anything she set her mind to be. She had said the same of herself many times. But Wanda held up her hand again.

"You're a man of soul. I poured my soul out on the open road a long time ago. It hasn't come back to me since. You're a man of substance. You deserve a woman of substance. I'm not a woman of substance. I'm shallow, superficial, hollow, and passing. I'm a shadow of a woman. Shadows are shifting and passing. You need a woman who will stay. I'm not capable of staying." Wanda's voice trailed off again.

"I'm capable of staying with you," Chuck said. "That puts us halfway home. Staying with you would be right for me, as right as it seemed to me at the beginning. If you stay with me, in time, you may find that everything else fades away, even the call of the open road. Instead of being a horizon that is unreachable, staying will seem right, natural, and easy. Instead of seeming like death, staying will seem like life to you. Staying with you came to seem like life to me the first time I made love to you. I loved you then. I love you now."

"You didn't fall in love with me," Wanda said in a still-low voice. "You fell in love with an image you imagined in your mind. I didn't ask you to fall in love with me. I'm sorry you did. But I'm not the woman you think you love. I can't be that woman. You need a far better woman than me. One who's worthy of your soul and your substance. One who will stay with you and all that you are. That's the kind of woman you need. I cannot be what you need. I cannot be what I'm not capable of being."

"I still don't want to lose you," Chuck said.

"You lost me from the beginning," Wanda said, looking down at the table, her voice still low. "You never had me. Not because of anything you did or didn't do but because of what I am and what I can't be." She looked up from the table but only halfway. She didn't look him full in the face, as she usually did. "I can't be what I can't be. What can't be can't be. I can't leave the road. I can't leave being what I am. Let's just leave it here. I'm sorry I hurt you. I don't want to hurt you any more."

"You haven't hurt me," Chuck said.

Wanda held up her hand again and pulled away the hand he had been holding. "Please. Just don't say anything. Just leave it alone. You're a great guy, the kind of man every woman dreams of finding, the good ones and the bad ones. Someday you'll find a great woman who'll be everything you're looking for, everything you want and need. I'm not that woman. I'm not." Her voice trailed off.

Chuck did what she asked. He fell silent and didn't say anything further.

As she'd stated, Chuck was a great guy. But being a great guy didn't necessarily give a man deeper insight. Sometimes great guys could miss subtle things. In his case, Chuck was a bit slow on the uptake. He heard Wanda's words, but the weak tone and hesitancy in her voice didn't quite register on him. Her words of goodbye were soft and sad. Others might have found her words halting and uncertain. Her weak words weren't the decisive words he was used to hearing from her. The words were there; the fire wasn't.

Romantically oriented people might have said that if he had been more forceful and pushed harder, he could have broken down her resistance. That was the way it worked in formulaic romance novels.

But Chuck could do nothing. However equivocal her feelings might have been inside, with her words, she had slammed the door and nailed it all around the perimeter. Chuck was afraid if he pushed harder, it would just get her back up, and she would push back as hard as he pushed. She would grow angry. She would slam the door harder and drive in more nails.

Thus, it was over. Chuck paid the bill, and they left the restaurant. They drove back to Wanda's house in silence. When they entered the house, Wanda went straight upstairs and into her room. Chuck followed slowly, but he didn't follow Wanda into her room. Instead, he went back into the guest bedroom and radio room. He sat down at the table. With slow movements, he turned on the receiver.

It was getting dark. The nighttime bands were already open. But instead of tuning the receiver to the eighty-meter band, he tuned it to the forty-meter band. The forty-meter band was a nighttime band midway in frequency between the eighty-meter band and the daytime twenty-meter band. He tuned across the phone portion of the band. Ham stations were coming in from all over the country out to the radio horizon. Even the distant stations he noted briefly and with little interest. The only horizon he had any interest in wasn't on the far radio horizon. It was right down the hall, in another room. But it was a horizon further away than any on the radio spectrum.

Chuck shut off the radio and went to bed. It was relatively early, but he had to get an early start in the morning. He knew Wanda was in another room close by down the hall. He wondered if she was sleeping or was awake and staring out into a lightless room, as he was. He wondered what she was thinking. As Chuck lay in bed, staring into the darkened room, he wondered how far apart they would be at that same time the next night and where Wanda would be.

"Where's Wanda?"

"She left about half an hour ago," Wanda's father said. "She said she was going for a long walk. She said she needed some open air. I think the real reason was that she doesn't want to see you leave."

Chuck stood inside the front door of the house with his small travel bag in hand, talking with Wanda's father. He didn't know whether her not wanting to see him depart was a sign that she loved him and didn't want to see him drive away or whether she was afraid there might be another emotional episode like the one in the restaurant the night before. He had wanted to see her one more time before he left and was disappointed she didn't want to say goodbye to him. But he could understand how she might want to avoid a tearful scene. Maybe she didn't want to feel herself cry.

"Do you think she'll be back anytime soon?" Chuck asked. "I wanted to say goodbye to her."

"She's not very big on saying goodbyes," her father said. The statement was accurate enough. When it came to slipping out quietly, disappearing, and leaving men to wonder where she had gone, Wanda was practiced at the art. In the light of the new morning, she had practiced it one more time. As Chuck stood preparing to leave, not knowing where she was, the knowledge set in the rest of the way that Wanda was still Wanda. All the professions of love and staying he had spoken the night before hadn't made the slightest dent in Wanda.

"You can wait if you want. But she probably won't come back if she sees your car is still here. Around noon is when I planned to drive her into Columbia. She'll have to come back before that. You can say your goodbye to her then. It's a relatively short drive from here to Columbia, but it's a long drive for you from here to Memphis. I'm not trying to get rid of you, for her or for myself, but you'd better get an early start if you don't want to be driving long after dark. If you want to wait until she gets back, I can fix breakfast for the both of us."

"I'll grab something on the road," Chuck said. "You can say my goodbye to her for me. But I don't want to drag out my leaving any more than she wants a prolonged goodbye. So for both of our sakes, I'd better get going. If she's nearby watching, I don't want to leave her standing out in the woods, waiting for me to go."

Chuck walked out through the front door. Wanda's father followed. Chuck stepped down onto the front porch steps. Wanda's father stopped at the steps.

"I'm going to be sad to see you go—not for me but for her," her father said. "You would have been good for her. You're the kind of man her mother always hoped she'd find, settle down with, and drop her wandering ways for."

"Yeah, well, Wanda didn't see it that way," Chuck said as he stepped off the bottom step.

"My daughter has always seen things through her own eyes," her father said. "No one else's. Like you, I hoped she would think with her heart where you were concerned. She may think with her heart more than her head, but my daughter's heart has always belonged to her. I don't always know what's in my daughter's heart. I don't always know where her heart will be or what state it will be in from one day to the next any more than I know what state of the Union she'll be in from one day to the next. I had come to think her heart had become tough and hardened to love. For a long time, I didn't think her heart could be broken. But it was when her mother died. I can't say where her heart is at any moment or where it will be tomorrow. All I know is that her heart can't be stolen, and it can't be forced."

How well Chuck had come to know that.

Chuck didn't comment. He started walking toward his car.

"There's an old saying," her father said to his back. "'What goes around comes around.' Who knows? With her heart as unpredictable as it is, maybe someday she'll come around to love and staying. Her mother always hoped for that."

And she had died with the hope still in her.

"She might even come around to you."

Chuck wondered what decade that might happen in. Science would probably perfect and understand the unified field theory before he or anyone understood Wanda, he thought. Trying to work out a unified field theory had defeated Einstein. Wanda's thinking and wanderlust had defeated him. He stopped and turned around.

"She pretty much closed out that possibility," Chuck said. "From all angles and directions and in no uncertain terms. Second-guessing her didn't work. Neither did thinking that she really didn't mean what she said and that she would come around. I've got nothing left but to take her at her word. I don't know any other way to take her."

"That's about the only way you can take my daughter," Wanda's father said. "At her word. You may not like what she says, but she says what she

478

means and means what she says. She may not speak the words you want to hear. She may not give you the hope you want, but if nothing else, she'll give you honesty."

Wanda might give a man partial honesty along the way to an empty horizon, Chuck thought, but it was a dubious honesty.

Her father continued. "It may not mean that much to you, and it may not mean all that much to her, but you got through to her more than any man has."

An extra step further along the way to nothing was still nothing. Chuck did not comment on any of this. At the car, he turned around again. Before getting into his car, he waved goodbye to Wanda's father. Wanda's father waved goodbye to him. Chuck would have liked to say something like "See you the next time around," but Wanda had made it clear there would be no next time, nor did she seek a next time. His horizon with her was as empty as it was shut down.

Chuck got into the car, started it up, and drove away. The landscape that had become familiar and felt like home with Wanda as a guide fell away behind him.

Instead of taking US 20 west, as Wanda had recommended, Chuck took side roads until he got to US 26 North, away from Columbia. At Asheville, North Carolina, he picked up US 40, which would take him the rest of the way to Memphis. The route was a bit more indirect than the one laid out for him by Wanda. It was a bit harder to drive, often twisting and turning through mountain passes. But it was a more scenic route, passing through the Great Smoky Mountains. Chuck didn't mind the extra time and mileage. He hoped the scenery would take his mind off Wanda.

West of the mountains, the land flattened out into the rolling countryside of midland Tennessee. Chuck took the bypass around Knoxville. West of Knoxville, he picked up US 40 again. From there, it would be pretty much open ground and uninterrupted driving until Nashville. Though distracted by his thoughts of Wanda and his love for her, which had died almost as soon as it had been born, he remained conscious of his speed, carefully keeping it no more than five over the speed limit. He had no need to be stopped by some ticket-hungry state trooper looking to fill his quota. He didn't need to lose his license on his way back to his apartment, which was only nominally home and which he wouldn't be bringing anyone home to.

Chuck wanted to put as much distance between him and Wanda as he could in as short of an order as he could. It really wasn't Wanda he was trying to distance himself from. He was trying to put distance between himself and the dream that had been born in him when he met Wanda. That dream had become his horizon. Now the only horizon ahead of him was the one containing the empty miles of the state of Tennessee.

The dream that had been born in him had not been born in Wanda. They had become lovers to the full degree in his view, but in Wanda, it had been only to the degree of a door cracked open to a salesman. Her father had said Chuck had kindled a certain degree of love in her, more love than any other man had come close to. But that love had been stillborn. Whatever degree of love she might have passingly felt for him, it hadn't transformed Wanda or her life. Wanda the lover hadn't been sufficient to overcome Wanda the wanderer.

There was an old saying: "Once burned, twice shy." One would have thought that after being burned twice by women—first his unfaithful wife and then Wanda—Chuck would have been on the brink of giving up on women and abandoning the hope of love and any further pursuit of love. In Chuck's case, the adage worked in reverse. As he drove on at his steady pace, Chuck did not want to give up the dream of love and of staying in love and staying with the one he loved. He had come too close to the dream with Wanda. He didn't want to give up the dream, even if Wanda had never shared it.

After having loved Wanda to the degree he had, he wanted to rekindle the dream of love. He preferred to rekindle the dream with Wanda, but Wanda had abandoned the dream she had never really embraced. He wanted to rekindle the dream and the love in himself, but it would have to be with another woman. That he had now been hurt twice only accelerated his desire to find a life partner. To that end, he was ready and willing to risk himself as a victim of unrequited love a third time. Instead of withdrawing from life, he would head back into the romantic fray and get right back on the horse.

Chuck reached Nashville around rush hour. Even the through highways, including the one he was on, were crowded with local rush-hour traffic. Cars crept. Horns blew. Given that he was in no particular hurry to get back to the empty apartment that was his empty home, Chuck didn't grumble, complain, or get honked off and honk. He went with the flow, as slow and halting as it might have been, and kept composure, which other drivers were losing, even though they had been through the same thing for years. With no one waiting for him, the ordeal of being stuck in traffic had little sting or meaning.

As the traffic crept along, Chuck felt like just another Mr. Average disappointed by love, stuck in traffic, going along with the flow of traffic, going along with the flow of his life, and going nowhere fast with either.

West of Nashville, the traffic thinned out and picked up speed as drivers pulled off at exits that led them to the suburbs they lived in and commuted from. From there, US 40 angled slowly south, angling toward Memphis. It was pretty much a straight shot into Memphis without any traffic delays. The only traffic problem might come on the bypass around Jackson. The FM country station grew weaker as he pulled farther away from Nashville. He reached down and turned off the radio.

It had gotten dark by the time he reached Jackson. AM radio on the broadcast band propagated farther at night. Chuck had grown tired of the country music coming out of Nashville FM and had turned off the car radio. As he drew nearer to his hometown, he turned the radio back on, switched to the AM band, and tuned in his favorite hometown radio station. Chuck was not a fan of hard rock or rockabilly. The station he tuned in was an obscure station that played a combination of contemporary, soft rock, oldies, folk, and ballads.

As Chuck listened to the station, a familiar song started playing: "Back on the Street Again" by the Sunshine Company. Though the song was mournful, it was one of Chuck's favorites. The familiar lyrics rolled out of the radio:

> I'm back on the street again.
> Got to stand on my own two feet again.
> I'm walking that lonely beat again,
> Rememberin' when, mmm.
> Rememberin' when.

Chuck had never been sure what the lyrics referred to. He could tell only that they seemed to have something to do with sadness and loss. The part about walking a lonely beat again made the song seem like something sung by a cop who had experienced a loss in his life, possibly the loss of a lover or the death of a partner in the line of duty. He had never really thought that was what the lyrics referred to. But whatever the hidden meaning of the lyrics, now that he'd lost Wanda, the lyrics had a force in him in a way they never had. They also had an immediate application to him. He was driving a lonely beat back to his empty apartment, remembering Wanda almost every mile.

> I remember a time
> When I thought the world was mine.
> The world belongs to someone else now,
> And I'm just standin' in line.

Chuck had thought he found his world in Wanda. Wanda didn't belong to another man. There was no rival man for her hand or her world. For her part, Wanda had made it clear she belonged to the world she had chosen and had made for herself. Though he wasn't standing in line behind other men, Chuck was standing outside the door Wanda had never opened.

> Got a tear in my eye again
> To remind me that I might cry again.
> Feelin' bad, wonderin' why again.
> Rememberin' when, oooh, oooh.
> Rememberin' when.

Chuck wasn't about to cry for his loss of Wanda. It wasn't because he thought it was unmanly for a man to cry. Crying just never seemed to solve much of anything. He would not collapse into ineffectualness and romantic longing over his vanished lover. He would stand on his own two feet. He would go on with his career. He would move on in life, hopefully to another woman soon.

> So I'm thinkin' of me again.
> That's the way it's going to be again
> Till the day I can be again.
> Rememberin' when, oh, oh.
> Rememberin' when.

On the stretch of road he was traveling, the last stretch before his exit, Chuck wasn't thinking as much about himself as he was about Wanda. He knew he would continue to think about her. He knew he would remember her. At the same time, he was determined not to become a recluse living in his memories of Wanda. Her memory would remain with him, fading into the background, growing dimmer and further away with the passage of the years ahead. He would not wear his love for Wanda and his loss of Wanda on his sleeve for the rest of his life. He would go on with his life without Wanda as if she had never been part of his life, which she had never wanted to be. But he would not systematically banish his love for her from his thoughts and memory entirely. He would not live out his days in memory of Wanda, but he would not forget her.

By the time the exits to Memphis came up ahead of him, Chuck had pretty much said his goodbye to Wanda. He took the exit nearest his apartment and turned off. From there, he navigated the city streets of Memphis, which were familiar even in the dark, until he arrived at his apartment building. He parked his car in his parking space, grabbed his small suitcase, and went inside and up the stairs to his floor. The lock on the door of his apartment turned to his key, as it always had. He opened the door and went inside. The familiar apartment felt the same and different. In one way, it was like landing on a new planet. In another way, he felt as if he had never left.

Inside his apartment, Chuck closed the door. The lock clicked shut on what was behind him. Instead of turning and going into the bedroom, Chuck set down his suitcase and, without turning on the light, walked to the window and stood looking out. The apartment was on a floor high enough to accord a limited panoramic view of a portion of the Memphis skyline. The scene outside was neither seedy nor upscale. The lights of buildings glowed steadily. The lights of cars moved on the grid work of streets below. A few stars were visible in the sky.

Chuck stood in front of the window, thinking. He wasn't sure what he was thinking about. With Wanda banished from his mind, there was a large gap where his thoughts would have been. The only thing he could think of at the moment was what the future might hold for both of them. That too was largely a blank. Thoughts and feelings swirled around in and through him like a spinning gyroscope. He couldn't sort them out any better than he could sort out what the future might hold. The only stabilized center of the centrifuge of his thoughts was that he had loved Wanda.

The next morning, he would resume his life and his job when he checked back in at the maintenance headquarters of the phone company.

For all he knew, they might have a new assignment waiting for him to go out on. There was no rest for the weary, but it might take his mind off Wanda. Unless they sent him back to the tower where he had met her or one like it.

Standing by the window, looking out at the darkened and uncertain horizon beyond, Chuck thought about how a significant part of his life had appeared and come upon him unexpectedly in the form of an unexpected woman—serendipity personified.

That significant part of his life had gone from him almost as fast as it had come. But in the short time it had lasted, that unexpected portion of his life had lasted long enough and been significant enough that his life would not and could not be the same again. He had tried to reach the horizon, but the horizon had retreated away from him, and he had not been able to grasp it. Whether any horizon of equal significance would present itself to him again he did not know.

As Chuck stood looking out the window over the half-lit Memphis skyline, he elevated his gaze a little higher. The close-by vista didn't grow any brighter, but it expanded out to the horizon and beyond. What was taking place within and beyond the horizon, he didn't know, nor did it have much immediate meaning to him.

He didn't know what awaited him in the new day that would dawn in the morning. All he knew at the moment was that it was a world of chance encounters, limited chance, lost chances, disappointment, dissolution, no return, and lost dreams. He was back on his feet again. But that only meant he was on his own to wade through and try to find happiness and meaning in a world that would probably always be one step ahead of him. Either way, if he wanted meaning in his life, he would have to go out and look for it. It was unlikely any good thing would seek him out and come to him out of the unexpected blue the way Wanda had. Things like that only happened once in life, if at all.

There was a sad old country song titled "Will the Circle Be Unbroken?" The circle he had wanted to form with Wanda was broken. It had never closed, not on her part. The song ended on a note of hope that the circle of lost love and lost loved ones would be restored in heaven. Wanda would not return. She would not circle back to him or anyone. Wanda wasn't a circular girl. She was a linear girl who went in a straight line through, past, and beyond. There was less chance of her circling back to him than of many of the equally chanceless things in that chancy world. Wanda would always be the Wanda she wanted to be. He would never close the circle with her. Wanda's circle would always remain a closed circle open only to herself.

23

Wanda looked down at the damp circle left on the bar by the condensed moisture on the glass she held in her hand. She took a drink and set the glass back down off-center from the circle. When she picked it up again, it had formed another circle on the bar's surface. The two circles formed a pair of interlocking rings that would remain until the bartender wiped them off with a bar rag. Wanda held her glass up off the bar so as not to set it down and disturb the conjoined rings. She sat there with a dissolute look on her face and one arm on the bar, looking at the rings.

A casual observer looking at the morose look on her face and her hunched-over, motionless posture might have gotten the impression she was drunk and growing drunker, had consumed a large amount of hard liquor, and was on the verge of nodding off or passing out. Actually, it was only Wanda's second drink, which was one more than her self-imposed control-maintaining limit of one drink. She wasn't planning on ordering a third drink. The two she had already had had given her a buzz and put her into a disconnected, floating state.

Wanda was back on the road again. As she had assumed it would, the phone company had sent her out on several jobs since her return to work following the death of her mother. This time, the assignment was in the reaches of the western tip of Virginia, near the town of Big Stone Gap, installing a relay tower that would increase phone coverage in western Virginia and in the rural areas of the states around it. The phone tower was an open-frame tower with the antennae at the top and the electronics down in a fenced-off shack at the base. Wanda didn't have to climb the tower to work on the installation. The area was green, with low, rolling hills. It was Wanda's kind of scenery. But the lower altitude didn't allow for the panoramic view she had been accorded from the top of the tower she had worked on with Chuck. The restricted view took a bit of the pleasure out of the job.

Wanda was back at the bars again, dabbling around the edges and superficial form of her old game. But the old sense of illicitness, zest of bandit love on the run, thrill, and anticipation weren't there for her anymore. At first, Wanda had figured that the lingering effect of her mother's death was draining the feeling out of it and that it would all return to her in time.

But after a long dry spell, the old feelings and thrill had not returned. The empty feeling that had overtaken her remained. The old feelings were growing further from her. The stimulation hadn't returned either. She hadn't made a single pickup since Chuck. The desire to make pickups had tanked along with every other part of her old life. It was getting so that she didn't even want to go to bars anymore. Some nights on the road, she would stay shut in her motel room and watch TV or listen to signals coming in from over the horizon on a transistor portable shortwave receiver. At least the quiet thrill of radio communications was still there. She resolved to get herself a ham license. Even unlicensed pirate operation on the ham bands no longer held an appeal for her.

The nights when Wanda hit the bars on the road, she often had to force herself to go into them. Sometimes she would turn around at the door and go back to where she was staying. That night, she had made it through the door of a local bar and had gone inside, mostly with the thought of getting a drink. She had thought that maybe drinking would restore the old feeling. But booze wasn't getting it back for her.

However clouded her thinking and forward vision might have been, her peripheral vision was still functioning. Out of the corner of her eye, she saw a man get off his stool down at the other end of the bar. He had a fixed look on his face, and it was focused on her. He walked toward her. His gaze was still focused on her. He wasn't wearing a phone company uniform. He wasn't any of the other phone company techs she had seen on the job. He was probably a local from the area.

When he was out in the middle of the aisle in front of the bar, Wanda got a better view of the man. He was dressed like a farmer, farmhand, or grain-elevator operator. He was about her age. He wasn't quite as good looking as Chuck, but he fell on the spectrum of Wanda's standards of acceptability.

But Wanda had no desire to offer the man anything or pick up on what he might have to offer. Wanda tensed up as the man approached her. She thought to get up off her barstool and head for the door, but it might not have been necessary. For all she knew, the man might simply be heading for the bathroom. She hoped so. It would have been the easiest option for both of them.

The easy option was not to be that night. The man sat down on the barstool next to her and leaned over toward her. His face was inches from hers. "And who might you be?" he said in a smarmy, country-accented voice. "I haven't see you in here before."

It wasn't the most original of opening lines. At least the man hadn't started out with the dumb-assed opening remark of "Hey, good-lookin'" or some variant, and he hadn't gone on to say, "Do you come here often?"

"The reason you've never seen me in here before could be because I've never been in here before," Wanda said, looking straight ahead across the bar. "There's a certain logical progression between the two propositions."

Wanda realized she might have goofed by using the word *proposition*. Her long experience with men in bars had tuned her senses to where she could tell which way the situation was going to go before the man had finished his first sentence or, in some cases, before he had even opened his mouth and spoken his first line. By her instinct for tone of male voice and her sense of male body language, she could tell the man was probably thinking of propositioning her. By using the word *proposition*, she had probably opened a link to the man's libido, a link that needed to be shut down in a timely manner. The man leaned in closer to her.

"Do you see a For Rent sign on my face?" Wanda said, still looking forward and away from the man.

"Ah, no," he said in a still-smarmy but somewhat confused voice. It was not a line he had heard a woman use in a bar before.

Wanda turned her face toward his. "Then don't move in until you're invited." She turned her head back forward.

"I've never seen you in here before," he said. "Before I go any further, let me say that you're the best-looking woman I've ever seen in here. You've certainly got the best figure I've ever seen on a woman in here."

"The boobs are real," Wanda said, looking forward away from the man. "Any smile you see on my face is fake."

"No offense intended," he said in a still-smarmy voice. "I just wanted to say hello."

"With that, it's long past time for me to be saying goodbye," Wanda said.

With a quick move, Wanda got off the barstool on the side away from the man. Just as quickly, she circled behind the man at a far enough distance away that he could not reach out and grab her by the arm without getting off his barstool. She moved toward the front door, hoping the man would not follow her. Luckily, he did not get off his stool.

"Leaving so soon?" he said as she moved toward the door.

"As fast as my little ole legs can carry me," Wanda said, glancing at him as she passed him.

"But I wanted to meet you," he said in a smarmy voice. "I wanted to get to know you. There's a lot I don't know about you. There's a lot you don't know about me."

"And nothing I want to learn," Wanda said, looking forward. Like a shot, the fully sober Wanda headed toward the front door with a quick step. She opened the door and stepped out of the bar. The man looked after her with bemusement mingled with disappointment on his face. He got up, walked slowly toward the front door, opened it, and looked around in the parking lot. If he could get the license plate number of the vehicle she had come in and look up the registration, he thought, he could find out where she lived.

The sound of an engine caught his attention. Looking in the direction the sound was coming from, in the lights of the parking lot, he saw what looked like some kind of utility truck with an out-of-state plate pulling away. He didn't think the woman had come in that. He figured she was some kind of honky-tonk queen from a nearby town who had decided to wander afield of her hometown and had come into his. Or she was a bored farm wife who had snuck away from her dull farmer husband and come into town for a night of drinking and cheating. He figured she had probably come to the bar in a pickup truck and left in the same. But the only vehicle he saw pulling away was the boxy van he doubted she had arrived in. He figured he had been too slow in getting to the door, and she had pulled out of the parking lot before he opened the door. If so, she was a fast-exit artist.

The man wondered if she was a honky-tonk queen, a bored wife out on the cheatin' side of town, a nympho on the prowl, or just a barfly. Whatever she was, he had been prepared to show her a proverbial good time. He had enough of an ego that he'd thought she would be an easy pickup for him. Instead, she had blown him off and walked away, leaving his ego confused and deflated. He wondered why she didn't want to give him the tumble he had been looking for and had thought he found in her.

Oh well. Too bad. Gorgeous women alone and unattended at bars, giving the impression they were not only available but actively looking to get picked up, were a time-honored male fantasy. Either way, they didn't come along that often. He'd thought he had scored big-time. It might have proven to be the biggest score of his life.

The man still didn't know why she had walked away from him in such a quick manner. In his simplistic male thinking, he figured some women put out gangbuster signals but developed cold feet when crunch time came and ran out the back door. He had been ready to give her the best of himself. The old Wanda would have given the man the best of herself.

As she drove away down the road through the gathered darkness that night, Wanda was no longer sure what the best of her was or if there even was a best of her.

◦◦◦

Chuck was on the road himself that night. This time, he was in Colorado, working on a maintenance job. It was the farthest west he had ever been in his personal travels or on the job. The distance from the part of the country he was familiar with, coupled with the rough western landscape, made him feel isolated and alone.

Unlike Wanda, he wasn't on the road in his car, nor was he in a bar. He had thought many times to go to bars in the hope of finding a woman he could form a relationship with and build a life with, either through marriage or by living with her, if that was the way she wanted it. But instead of making the scene at any bar, every time so far, he had changed his mind at the last minute and stayed put where he was, whether on the road or in Memphis.

Unlike Wanda in motion on the road, he was holed up in a roadside motel, the closest one to the jobsite. He lay on the motel room bed, reading the layout and technical manuals for the equipment he was working on with the other members of the crew he was with. Next to him on the nightstand sat the old Zenith Trans-Oceanic battery-powered shortwave receiver he had had since he was a young boy interested in electronics. It had been given to him as a present. He had the radio turned on. But instead of listening to foreign broadcasters coming in on shortwave from over the horizon, he was tuned to the standard broadcast AM band. That night, he was listening to WLS in Chicago. WLS was a high-power clear-channel station. Clear channel meant that at night, when the propagation on the broadcast band opened up, the weaker local stations on the same frequency had to go off the air so the higher-powered stations designated as clear channel could broadcast all across the nation.

As a boy in isolated rural Tennessee, Chuck had spent an untold number of hours at night listening, not only to shortwave stations but also to clear-channel AM broadcast band stations, such as WLS in Chicago, WLW in Cincinnati, and WNY in New York. That night, he was tuned to WLS. It was the closest clear-channel radio station to him. The closer proximity of the station wasn't needed. The AM broadcast band was wide open. The station he was listening to filled the frequency solidly.

Chuck didn't particularly believe in telepathy. He found it an interesting phenomenon to contemplate. There were some scattered apocryphal reports of the phenomenon. But as a phenomenon, it seemed too poorly understood, too chancy, too scattered, too random, and too unduplicable to be of any practical use. *Besides, who needs telepathy when you have radio?* As far as mind-to-mind communication, telephones, Handie-Talkies of the kind they used on the job, and ham radio were infinitely more reliable and replicable than telepathy. Besides, many purported examples of telepathy proved to be little more than coincidences, or at least they could be explained along those lines.

Maybe it was the remoteness of the location and the road the motel was situated on, but for some reason, Chuck started to think about remote and open roads winding through remote locations. From there, he thought of Wanda, who had made open roads and the romance of the road into her life story. At that moment, he became aware of the lyrics of the song playing over the radio. A male voice was singing,

> For I don't know where you are,
> And I don't know what you do.
> Are you out there feeling lonely,
> Or is someone loving you?
> Tell me how to win your heart,
> 'Cause I haven't got a clue.

But let me start by saying,
"I love you."

Chuck had disciplined his mind not to think of Wanda. He felt he had been doing a pretty good job of it. But the lyrics of the song knocked all of his mental discipline into a cocked phone company hard hat. All the feelings came flooding back to him as if they had never left.

But instead of being a montage of random memories and visions, his thoughts tracked with the words of the song. He wondered where Wanda was. Was she out in the dark, heading down a remote road somewhere? He wondered what she was doing at that moment. Was she heading to a bar? Was she at a bar, running her game? Was she lonely, or had she already transcended the prospect of spending the night alone by making yet another barroom conquest? Was some man loving her already? A man whose name she hadn't asked, whom she hadn't given her real name to, and who would wake up in the morning and find her gone with no calling card left behind? Was Wanda being the Wanda she had always been? He assumed that was the case. There were some constants in the universe. Wanda was one of them. That kind of change wasn't in Wanda or within any of her horizons.

He didn't bother to follow the song and rhetorically send the question out into the night as to what he could do to win her heart. He had given that his best shot and come up empty against Wanda's determined wanderlust. Inside his mind, he whispered, *I love you*, out into the dark. Nothing came back to him from the dark outside the room or from within him.

Chuck switched off the radio. He lay back on the bed and switched off the light. In the dark, he slowly started building his wall against thinking of Wanda back up. One by one, he closed off and closed down the memories that had flooded in on him.

He didn't know if Wanda was on the road that night. He assumed by that hour, she had settled in with whatever man she had chosen as lover for the night. The next day, she would be back on the road again. But as usual, she would be traveling in a straight line away from the man. She would not circle around back to the man. Wanda had never circled back to any man. Chuck knew she would not circle back around to him. The circle she had never closed with any man would not be closed with him.

In the fight for her heart, Chuck knew he was outmatched. When it came to love, romance, and following what called to her heart the strongest and promised her the most, the romance and call of the open road would always be stronger in Wanda than any other romance. He knew he could never win.

24

"OK, Mother, you win," Wanda said as she laid the flowers on her mother's grave. "You got your wish. I hate the road. I don't want to go back to it, like you hoped I wouldn't. I used to love the road; now I hate it. It's been my life. Now it's taken all of my life. I poured my life out on the open road, to no real benefit of anyone. Least of all myself. I thirsted for a life on the road and all that went with it on the side. I drained my life out into the road as if it were rainwater soaking into the dust of the road. The road took all I had to offer and gave back little of value. The road soaked my life up, leaving it as dry and thirsty as ever. You said that in the end, the road would leave me with nothin'. You didn't say it in so many words, but that was what you meant. Now the road has left me with nothin'. Nothing was all it had to offer from the beginning. In the end, I got the nothin' that lies at the end of the road. Wherever you are now, I don't know if you're hearing me. But you were right."

People often talked to their departed loved ones in graveyards, even if they didn't think their loved ones were there or anywhere around where they could hear. Some did it to say goodbye. Some did it out of guilt for what they had done or not done for the departed ones they were addressing. Some did it to say they were sorry. Some did it to say what they had been unable to say when their departed ones were still alive. Some did it out of self-justification. Others did it out of self-loathing. Many did it as a way to unburden themselves of any number of things. Some did it as a way of kicking themselves while they admitted their departed ones had been right all along. Some did it in the hope that God would hear and forgive or that when they died, God would send someone to say goodbye to them over their grave so at least they wouldn't pass into eternity alone and unremembered.

"I loved the idea of life and love on the run on the road. I did a lot of lovin' on the run. None of it ever came back to me in a real way. But I never wanted real love. I said so to myself enough times. Now I find myself left with the nothing kind of loving you always said I'd find myself left with. You were right about that too."

It was a Sunday, the day customarily and traditionally reserved for thinking about life, death, eternity, and the beyond. Wanda was off work. She had returned again to the graveyard to place flowers, as she had done several times since her mother's interment. There were already flowers there in a vase. Wanda recognized it as the vase her mother had kept flowers in in the house. The flowers looked fresh. She figured her father had been there earlier in the morning and placed them there. Wanda put the flowers she'd brought in the vase alongside the flowers her father had left.

"Life and love on the run on the road used to be the most meaningful thing in my life. Now the meaning's gone out of both of them. I'm not sure it was ever there. I probably only thought they were the same. For you, love and meaning were always one. The meaning never went out of love for you."

Wanda sat back on her haunches. "Love was always simple and straightforward for you: one husband; one home; one family; one love for life; no outside affairs to juggle; no circles that didn't close; and one wayward prodigal child you worried about, whose affairs you thought would get her nowhere, bring her nothing but grief, and, in the end, leave her lonely."

A graveyard was kind of a strange place to talk about oneself in the third person. But a lot of weirder sentiments and confessions had been offered in cemeteries.

The graveyard served mostly the population of the town. The farmers in the districts outside the town had their own scattered cemeteries. Wanda's mother had lived all her life in the town and had died there, never wanting to be anywhere else.

"Love has never been simple for me. It's never been a simple part of my life. That's probably because real love was never a part of me. Except for you. Now you're gone, and what little real love I had in me has gone, if it was ever there anywhere to begin with."

A small colorful bird perched on one of the tombstones. It eyed the ground as if looking for seeds to eat.

"For you, love was the key to heaven. For me, *love* and *loving* were just window-dressing cover words for lust and self-centered self-indulgence. You worshipped the God of love. I worshipped the god of sensuousness. You looked to heaven for love. I looked for heaven in passion."

The tombstones were a variety of multicolored stone hues. Her mother's tombstone was a simple vertical slab of gray granite on a flat base. The stone was divided into two sections, with her mother's name and dates on one half. The other half was blank. When her father died and was buried in the adjoining plot, his name would be carved into the stone next to his wife's. It was a limited memorial arrangement, but her father couldn't afford a more elaborate one.

"You will see heaven. You're probably there now. You will see heaven as God intended it to be. You found enough of simple heaven here on Earth. You will be with God in heaven because you lived by his love in life. In heaven, you will walk the flowered fields you loved to walk in life. When I pass the final horizon, I'll probably find myself on a dirt road that stretches out forever, a road choked with brambles, briars, thorn bushes, and thistle. I'll walk the path barefoot. It will be the only road I'll get in the hereafter. My eternity road. It will be the road I deserve for the degraded definition and practice of love I carried with me through life. I'll walk it forever."

The grass of the cemetery was manicured, watered, and green. Above the green of the cemetery, the sky was clear and bright blue from horizon to horizon.

"As mother and daughter, we were as close to each other as we could be. At the same time, we were polar opposites, as far apart as we could be. You were content with your life. I was never content with mine. You loved the place you were in. I was never happy being in one place. You were content to live your life here. You were content to die here. You always knew where you were. You always knew where you wanted to be. You always knew you wanted to be here and stay here. I knew I had to be moving all the time. For you, being in constant motion would have been like death to you. Staying in one place has always seemed like death to me. The open road was meaningless to you, a place to get lost on. The open road—and moving down it—was the only meaning to me. At least it used to be. Now the road holds no meaning for me. I don't know what the meaning of my life is or where my life is going."

The grave site was near the edge of the cemetery. Wanda wasn't in the center, where she would have been readily seen by the small handful of other people tending the graves of their departed. If she hadn't wanted to be seen, a quick step would have taken her in among the trees, in the unused but manicured section that ran along the outside edges of the cemetery. Future graves would be placed in among the trees, but for now, the land was clear. The section was the one Wanda had walked through when she left the graveyard after the final graveside benediction, not wanting to see her mother's casket sealed and lowered. That day in the cemetery, Wanda vowed she wouldn't run from her mother again.

"I always thought you would be there in the background of my life as a defense against the time when the road no longer had any meaning for me and I wanted to come home. Your passing from this life has brought it home to me just how much of a nothing a good part of my life has been and the nowhere it's heading into. At least my love for you was real, as opposed to the phony and self-indulgent, counterfeit love I spent my free time pursuing in sleazy motels on the road."

Wanda stood up. "As I said, love has never been simple for me. Many people would have found your life to be boring. To my eternal discredit, I somewhat thought the same thing."

Some people who talked to the dead in graveyards did so to vent against the ones buried at their feet. Others vented against themselves.

"Chuck once asked me what I would do for a life after sex. I had no answer for him then. I have no answer for you now, for any part of my life. I have no answer for myself. Your life was a love story. My life has been a leaving-love-behind story. Your love will go on through eternity. The false front of love I put forth will be interred with my bones. No one will remember it. My life has had little to offer anyone beyond that. I have nothing to offer myself. I probably have nothing in me that goes beyond me or anything. I have nothing to offer heaven. You looked to heaven for love and the Author of love. I looked for heaven in passion and far horizons. I found plenty of passion. I wandered all sorts of horizons. Heaven still eludes me."

For a minute, Wanda stood looking at the grave. "Well, I've got to get going," she said. "I'll be back to pay my respects more than I've been doing. I promise I'll also visit Father more. I'm still on the road, working. I'm not going to quit my job. I worked too hard to get it. But the road isn't home to me anymore. This is home. I promise I'll get back home more often."

Wanda's mother had lived all her life in that town and had died there, never wanting to be anywhere else. Wanda wasn't sure the town would still be home if and when her father died. After he was buried next to her mother, the town would become little more than an empty circle of fading memories. An empty circle of passing memories wouldn't mean anything more than an empty road. After her father was gone, she probably wouldn't come back again.

Wanda looked at the grave of her mother, which would one day also hold her father. As a young girl who hadn't yet had any close personal experience with death, she had often meandered among the gravestones, pretending she was on Easter Island or was an explorer exploring the stony peaks of a mountain range. But that day, she had had enough of graveyards. She had come to her hometown planning on visiting home, but she suddenly felt a need to talk with her father. She exited the graveyard, got in her car, and drove to the house she had shared with her parents, where only her father now lived.

But when she went inside, her father didn't respond to her call. Becoming panicked that her father might have died suddenly the same way her mother had, Wanda raced through the house, but she didn't find him collapsed on the floor or dead in his bed. After going back downstairs, she looked in the kitchen closet. His fishing pole and tackle box were not there. Wanda breathed a sigh of relief. After paying his respects at the grave, her father must have gone fishing, she thought. At least he knew what he was doing and had an idea of where he was going to be going from there on out.

Wanda stood in the doorway of the empty house, wondering what to do. She didn't know which fishing spot her father had gone to. There were several he frequented. They were all a fair driving distance from the house. It would have taken way too long to drive around making the rounds of them all. She could wait for him to come home, she thought, but that might not be until late that afternoon. She could end up waiting half a day for him. She was too agitated to sit and wait.

That day, she had to keep moving. She would catch her father the next time she was in town. She didn't know when that might be, but she reminded herself to call first to see if he would be in. After all, she worked for a phone company. Wanda got back in her car and drove away, heading back to her apartment in Columbia. The town of her childhood fell away in the rearview mirror. By the time she reached the open road, it was gone from sight. She vowed to herself again that she would return. She just wasn't sure when.

Thus, Wanda's wanderings ended, not with a bang of decision but with a whimper of lost home and love. Wanda the wanderer had been born looking at horizons. The main horizon that once had loomed large for her had been the horizon of sex. From its nascent beginning, sex had grown to become a guiding horizon of her life to be pursed over and through all horizons of her life. Now, on the far side of the horizon that had started long ago in her motel room next to the amorous couple in the adjoining room—the night that had formed the outline and goal of her life and set her on her sexual life quest, a quest that had taken her away from home and her mother, who was now gone from her, and brought her to abandon any thought of home—suddenly, sex, which had shaped her formative youth and formed the biggest part of her world afterward, now seemed a lesser part of life.

The air-conditioning in Wanda's car didn't work well. To keep herself cool, Wanda drove with the windows open. The swirling air currents in the car whipped her long blonde hair around. It often flew in her face. Sometimes she would pull it away. Sometimes she would let the next gust of road wind do that.

When Chuck had asked her, "What do you do for a life after sex?" the question had seemed loaded and intended to blow up in her face. Her mother had asked her the same question, though not in such a pointed manner. She had ducked and dismissed the question. She'd considered it to be off-base. She also had considered the question to be an absurdity. To her, sex had been her life. It had been life itself. It had been the loadstone that drew her onward, the compass that set the direction of her life, and the light that shone out over the edge of the horizon. It had been the river of life she drank from and hoped to drink from more. Now it was a mudhole in a dry and parched land.

The question of the end of life and mortality had always been something out beyond the horizon. Now the unexpected death of her mother had brought mortality home to her with a force deeper, stronger, harder, and more real than she had imagined it would ever come home to her. But mortality had come home to the home and mother she had left behind for a life of wandering and indulgence on the open road. Now both the open road and sexual indulgence were in suspension. She had not had sex since the last time she made love to Chuck. She hadn't tried to have sex or even been back to a bar since her failed attempt to restart her old randy, pick-up-and-get-picked-up life, when she had beat it out of the bar after the man came at her with the intent of picking her up.

Wanda knew her mother had thought she had her life direction wrong. She had said so more than once. She had also hinted that she would be willing to die if that was what it took to make her wayward but loved daughter reconsider her life and path in life. Wanda didn't think her mother had somehow willed herself to die as a way of forcing her to rethink her life and life priorities. She didn't think God had conspired to take her mother from her for that purpose. But she could imagine her mother bargaining with God, telling him that he could take her home if doing so would bring her daughter to the point of questioning her life.

If that was what her mother had bargained and hoped for, it was working. Big-time. The passing from life of the one who had given her life had irrevocably changed the direction of her life, a direction Wanda had assumed couldn't be changed. Wanda didn't know if her mother was looking down on her from the Great Beyond. She didn't know if her mother had made a deal with God to take her home to heaven if it would bring her randy daughter to reevaluate her life. Either way, Wanda figured her reevaluation would make her mother happy.

If getting her to the point she had come to had been her mother's intent, Wanda wanted to curse her mother for the unanswerable question left hanging in her mind. But she couldn't bring herself to curse her mother for anything. She thought to curse Chuck for leaving her with the same question. She thought to curse God for filling the background of her life with the question. If it was God's doing, he had posed the question the way only he could, leaving her with a question hanging over her life that was bigger than she was and bigger than her life. Her mother, Chuck, and God had posed their question out of love, not judgment. She couldn't curse any of them for their love, no matter how much their questions were now tripping up her life.

Then there was *meaning*, a word as loaded as and often used interchangeably with the equally loaded word *love*. Her life of bandit love on the run once had held life and meaning for her but now felt like a series of tawdry indulgences devoid of quality, love, and meaning. At that juncture, Wanda wondered if she herself was as void and meaningless as her life now seemed.

She pressed her foot down harder on the accelerator. The car sped up. A short burst of speed later, she was over the limit. That in itself didn't alarm her. She was used to living beyond the limit while maintaining control of her progress over the limit. Despite her speed, she maintained control of the car. The wind whipped through the open window faster. Her hair flew more.

Despite dicing with a speeding ticket from the highway patrol and dicing with death by losing control of the car, Wanda arrived back in Columbia in one physical piece but in scattered mental pieces. She negotiated the streets of Columbia and came to her apartment building. She parked the car and went up into her apartment. It was getting later in the afternoon. The shadows were growing long. Inside her apartment, she stood in her bedroom, looking out over the city of Columbia the way Chuck had stood looking out on the streets of Memphis. But she wasn't seeing the streets of Columbia.

The reversal was complete now. It hadn't happened all at once. It had been building up for some time, since her mother's death. It had progressed through her storming out of the bar when the nameless man tried to pick her up. It had proceeded from there to the self-lacerating speech she had delivered over her mother's grave. Now, as she stood silently looking out her window, at that hinge moment, the world of her self-indulgent past finished caving in on her with as much force as her mother's death had crashed down on her. The open road died for her. The once bittersweet feeling of longing for and moving toward horizons was now just a bitter aftertaste. The horizons she had lived for, which had seemed sweet and full to her, were now void of life and feeling. The open road that had seemed so endless and beckoning trailed off into a weed-choked dirt path that disappeared into a stand of thorny bramblebush of the type she had been unable to get through as a child. The horizon beyond was dry, barren, fragmented, and empty.

Like Chuck, Wanda knew she would go on. She just wasn't sure of the direction. The only direction she resolved she wouldn't go in was backward. She would stay with the phone company. Electronics had been her coequal interest along with sex. It was still her primary interest. Her career and her technical acumen were big accomplishments in her life. She wasn't about to give it all up to become a secretary or a nun or for any job that kept her in one place. She would still go on the road as the job demanded. She just wouldn't love the road for itself. Nor would she go back to her freewheeling, free-loving, self-dissipating ways. That lifestyle was as dead to her as was the open road for the open road's sake. She had looked into the abyss when her mother died. As she looked back at her randy life, she saw an abyss vacant of anything. Vacant of quality. Vacant of real love. Vacant of life. It was an abyss she had no desire, in terms of sexual desire, wanderlust, or otherwise, to immerse herself back into.

When Wanda had looked out earlier from the tower she had been working on, she had liked the view of her life. Now there was nothing in her life she liked. A hole of emptiness had opened under her feet when her mother died. Since her mother's death, she had felt isolated and alone. To Wanda, it was starting to feel as if she would end her life that way. She had been unafraid of living alone while alive. She had been unafraid of dying alone. However, the death of her mother had knocked the old Wanda out of her and left her feeling more alone than she ever had, more alone than she had thought she could feel. As she stood looking out the window at the darkness, the feeling of being alone closed in around her like a shroud. She had always enjoyed the feeling of being alone and passing through life alone and on her own terms. Now she found she didn't like the feeling. There were no feelings around her or in her that she liked.

Her mother would stay dead and buried behind her. Her randy life of rolling from one meaningless, passing, momentary hedonistic encounter to the next, heading down the open road toward a vanishing horizon that retreated from her, finished dying within her. There at the window, she abandoned the life that had been born in her and had begun in her the night she heard the amorous couple in the next room, the life she had crafted. That life had been the only life she wanted. Now she stood at the far terminus of a life that seemed empty and meaningless. It was not a life she had any yearning to return to and take up again. But abandoning even an empty and meaningless path didn't by itself open a path to the future or even show her what a real life path was. Standing by a window and looking out didn't open up the future to her any better. As Wanda stood looking out the window, she didn't know where to go to find a real life or even where to begin looking for one.

Wanda looked out over the cityscape spread out around her. In the background, her portable radio was playing. A softly sad but familiar female voice started to sing. Wanda recognized the singer as Linda Ronstadt, her favorite female singer, who had sung the signature song of her earlier career phase: "Different Drum." It was the song that had been playing in the background as Wanda surged through and out of the lobby of the motel where she had lain in bed listening, enthralled, to the passionate sounds in the next room. With Linda Ronstadt's randy-girl signature song at her back and adding weight in the back of her mind, Wanda had gone forth from the motel determined to replicate in her life what she had heard happening in the next room.

As Ms. Ronstadt's melodic voice sang, the song unwound over the radio in the switching-circuit room. The plaintive words flowed out and faded into the room.

> Somewhere out there,
> Beneath the pale moonlight,
> Someone's thinking of me
> And loving me tonight.

"Not me, sister," Wanda said under her breath. "You've got the wrong bimbo. Ain't nobody thinkin' much of me, not next door or out there. I made sure of that."

> Somewhere out there,
> Someone's saying a prayer
> That we'll find one another
> In that big somewhere out there.

"I doubt anyone's out there sending any prayer my way," Wanda said in a suppressed voice. "No one's praying for me, not in church or out in the moonlight. I'm not about to be found. I'm not about to be found because nobody's looking for me, around the block or in anybody's county. Even if someone was looking for me, they couldn't find me. I made myself hard to find. Oh, I let myself be found well enough for my purposes. I let myself be found all over the map, all over the road. I put myself out for real. But I never let myself be found in any real sense, and I never let myself be found in anything resembling real love."

> And even though I know how very far apart we are,
> It helps to think we might be wishing
> On the same bright star,
> And when the night wind starts to sing a lonesome lullaby,

> It helps to think we're sleeping
> Underneath the same big sky.

"I preferred motels myself," Wanda said. "They're easier to slip out of and get away from. The only time I slept underneath the open sky was on top of a tower, in the roof tar. For all the good it did me. For all the good any of my lovin' ever did me."

> Somewhere out there,
> If love can see us through,
> Then we'll be together
> Somewhere out there,
> Out where dreams come true.

The song repeated the last two stanzas and wound to an end. Wanda continued looking out the window. She didn't reflect any further on the song. The time for reflection had passed. She had let any reflection on her life go past her throughout most of her life. There wasn't any time left or any reason to circle back and start reflecting on what she had let go past and what was now gone from her.

"Oh, God," Wanda said quietly to herself, "if you're always havin' your Son, Jesus, go around looking to forgive people like Mother said you and he do, you'd better get him workin' for me. Ain't many others who are going to bless me and recommend me to the angels. If you won't be a horizon of forgiveness for me, there aren't a lot of people out there lookin' to do so."

She wasn't any more sure where her life was going or would be going any more than she had been after her mother died. Her life would go on from there till it came to an end. She was sure, however, that no one would be coming from somewhere out there to give direction and meaning to her life.

———∽⌀∿⌀∽———

Sitting on a barstool with a longneck beer bottle in hand didn't provide much in the way of meaning for the present or progress into the future. As a life option, it was a static position not given to forward motion. But occasionally, something resembling possible progress came out of the blue.

It was called serendipity. Serendipity occurred when something came to you that you weren't expecting and weren't even looking for. At that point of unexpectedness, something came to you even if you thought you weren't going anywhere. Even if you thought you'd never be going where you wanted to be again. Sometimes it sounded like the call of the future. Sometimes it was a tin echo of the past.

Chuck's crew were west of the Mississippi again, this time doing an upgrade on the cell phone system to increase coverage in the southeast corner of Missouri, where the state bulged out to the east, not far from his home state of Tennessee, on the west side of the Mississippi River. The area around was largely undeveloped rural farmland. The only cities of any size were Cape Girardeau some fifty miles to the north and Paducah, Tennessee, to the east across the river. The only other close big town of any size and name was Cairo, Illinois, where one could be thrown out of town for pronouncing the name of the town like the capital of Egypt instead of "Kayro," the way natives of the town insisted it be pronounced. Cairoians (Kayroians) were sensitive as to how their city's name was pronounced. According to one apocryphal story, a disc jockey newly arrived at a radio station in town was fired on his first day on the job and sent packing because he pronounced the name wrong.

Chuck was also not far from the New Madrid area, which, although normally geologically inactive because it wasn't anywhere near a mountain range or tectonic-plate boundary, ironically, had given the country its two biggest earthquakes in recorded American history in the early 1800s. Chuck wasn't thinking of earthquakes that night. The earth hadn't moved for him since he lost Wanda.

The bar was a country roadhouse bar not all that different from the one he had been in when Wanda came up to him, with wood floor and all. Chuck couldn't remember if the bar he had met Wanda in had had a jukebox or not. If it had, it hadn't been playing. The bar he was in now had a jukebox playing somewhere in the background. Instead of a countrified cryin'-and-dyin' song, the tune playing was a light, upbeat tune by country singer Hank Williams. Chuck was familiar with the lyrics. He didn't sing along but listened abstractly as the song played:

> Say, hey, good lookin',
> What you got cookin'?
> How's about cookin' somethin' up with me?

Hey, sweet baby,
Don't you think maybe
We could find us a brand-new receipt?
I got a hot-rod Ford and a two-dollar bill,
And I know a spot just over the hill.
Soda pop and the dancin' is free,
So if you wanna have fun, come along with me.
Hey, good lookin',
What you got cookin'?
How's about cookin' somethin' up with me?

Chuck took another drink from his nearly empty beer bottle while debating whether to have a third beer. He wanted to have a third round, but driving back to his motel on an unfamiliar road in the dead of night with a two-beer buzz slip-sliding down into a three-beer intro-level drunk could become problematic. He could easily miss his turnoff and end up lost and driving around in the darkness of a rural Missouri night, growing more lost and farther away by the minute. At the same time, he wanted another beer. The song playing on the jukebox faded into the background. In the back of his mind, he remembered the words of another country tune: *Longneck bottle, turn loose of my hand.*

"I'd have used the same 'Hey, good lookin'' line to introduce myself," a female voice said from behind Chuck, "but since it's playing, I won't use it. It might make me sound like a twit who's so unimaginative that she has to plagiarize lines from songs to approach a man."

Chuck turned his head. As he did, a woman came up and stood beside where he was sitting at the bar.

"The line's so hokey most men would probably just laugh it off and think the woman was a dumb hick. I doubt that line would work on a man."

"It would probably work on a whole lot more men than you think," Chuck said. "Us guys are suckers for come-on lines like that. They work on us. Because lines like that work on us, it makes us think they will work on women. That's why we use them on women. It probably just makes us sound like jerks. I doubt it works on women near as much as we men think. Would you fall for a line like that from a man?"

"Well now, it depends entirely on the man who's asking," the woman said with a country-accented voice. She moved up closer and stood with her hip pressing on the barstool next to him. "Hi. My name's Delia."

"That's not much of a country name," Chuck said. "I thought all country girls had country names, like Sandy or Dolly or Wanda. Delia sounds more like a New York name."

Serendipity, thy name is woman. Though nowhere near a twin or a clone, the woman resembled Wanda enough to jolt Chuck out of the two-beer-assisted semicatatonic slump he had drifted into. The woman was an inch or two shorter than Wanda. She had longish blonde hair a shade darker than Wanda's. Her face looked a bit like Wanda's, but her facial features were somewhat coarser than Wanda's. Her chest size was about a third the size of Wanda's or Dolly Parton's. She was dressed country-girl style in a lavender blouse that, instead of being tucked in under her leather belt, had the two bottom sides tied together, which left part of her midriff showing. She wore tight blue jeans. Her hips were as full as Wanda's. While not as buxom as Wanda, in a way, she was sort of a scaled-back version of Wanda.

"Delia is about as country a name as they come." The woman protested Chuck's ethnic displacement of her country name to the Big Apple. "There's nothing New York about it."

"You're probably right," Chuck said apologetically with his empty beer bottle still in hand. "I wouldn't know. I've never been to New York. Then again, I haven't been around here before."

"Well, that saves me the trouble of using the equally dumb opening lines 'Do you come here often?' and 'I haven't seen you in here before.'"

"For that matter, this is only the second time I've been west of the Mississippi. The other time was out in Colorado. Most of the times I've been on the road have been in the Midwest. I'm based out of Memphis. The territory we cover is mostly to the east."

"Does sound like you do get around," Delia said. "It sounds like you've been more far flung than I've ever been. If you've never been west of the river but twice, I've never been east of it. The only times I've been out of the state is twice: once to Arkansas and once to Kansas. By comparison, you've been all over the country. You do sound like you have get-up-and-go."

"Don't credit that to any great sense of adventurism or wanderlust on my part," Chuck responded. "Credit my job. Being on the road is part of my job. If it wasn't for my job, I'd still be back home, being the Tennessee provincial I started out as."

"Well, now I know where you're from and where you've been," Delia said. "That still leaves me not knowing anything about you. You've got my name. What's your name?"

"My name is Chuck. My mother gave me the name of Charles. I always hated my full name. It sounds like one of those snooty English butlers. I shortened it whenever I was out of Mother's earshot. Thankfully, Father used my nickname."

"Hello, Chuck. Mind if I sit with you?"

"Go ahead," Chuck said. "But in my present state of inebriation, I don't know how much lucid company I can be for you." He waved his nearly empty beer bottle. "I've been drinking kind of heavily. I may start babbling and end up collapsing in a drunken stupor with my face on the bar. Guys do that kind of stuff."

Chuck hadn't been drinking that heavily. It was only his second beer. He had a bit of a buzz going, but he was far from falling down drunk. He was trying to discourage the woman because he had come to the bar in an attempt to forget Wanda. Being approached in a bar by a down-scaled Wanda clone the way Wanda had approached him not only was ironic but also kind of defeated the purpose of forgetting.

"I'll take my chances," Delia said. She sat down on the stool next to him.

"Are you from around here?" Chuck asked the reciprocal question after she sat.

"I'm from Charleston," Delia said.

Chuck kind of froze when he heard the name of the other major city in Wanda's home state. "You mean South Carolina?" he asked. This was carrying irony too far. But then again, how could the woman have been from South Carolina if she had never been east of the Mississippi?

"Hardly," Delia said. "I mean Charleston, Missouri, the first town north of here, on the far side of I-57, not far from where it dead-ends into I-55. The town's a dead end in itself, at least for me. I've lived there all my life. Haven't been able to work up enough money or enough smarts on my part to get out. Haven't found anybody to take me out. I'm still looking for a white knight in shining armor to ride to my rescue and take me out of the town. If not a white knight in shining armor, at least a traveling insurance salesman with a big car or a farm-equipment salesman with a big pickup truck who will take me on the road with him. Any old road out. Any old time."

She paused and sat there looking at the phone company uniform he was wearing. When he had gone to bars in the past, he had taken off his uniform and put on street clothes that looked like the kind of clothes worn by people in the area. That allowed him to blend in with the locals. He was afraid if people knew he was with the phone company, they might get mad, saying their phone service was lousy or their phone bill was too high. That night, he had thrown caution to the wind and had not changed clothes before going to the bar. Identity concealment hadn't worked with Wanda. She had seen through it quickly enough. He figured Delia would see through any lie he told. And he was tired of lying.

"Are you some kind of cop?" Delia asked. "Highway patrol or some multistate police department? Is that why you've been to so many states?"

Chuck gave a confused look. "Why do you think I'm a cop?" he asked in a confused voice. "Do you see a badge on my chest or a gun on my hip? I'm not carrying a star or packing heat."

"Then what's that uniform you're wearing?" she asked.

Chuck turned on his stool to give her a clear view of the phone company logo, which had been out of sight on his far shoulder. "I'm with the phone company. I'm an installation and repair technician for Ma Bell. We're doing a system upgrade in the area. I've been working on the tower on the hill by the river. To answer the question you're probably going to ask, I don't know if what we're doing is going to increase your phone rates or not. You'll have to take that up with the front office. I'm just a soldering-iron jockey. Now, if you want to hit me with a beer bottle for being with the phone company, you can have one of my empties. Just don't use a full bottle. You might break it on my head, and the beer would run off onto the floor and be lost."

"I promise not to get mad and start shouting about greedy utilities overcharging the public," Delia said. "I also promise not to start swinging with a bottle. Your beer, your secret, and your head are safe with me."

Maybe it was because she resembled Wanda. Maybe it was because she had approached him in a bar the way Wanda had. Maybe it was the isolation and emptiness he had felt since Wanda broke up with him. Maybe it was the beer he had drunk. Whatever the reason, Chuck decided to throw caution to the wind a second time that night.

"In that case, would you like a beer?" Chuck asked. "I'll buy. I can afford it. I have money to spare. I work for a big, heartless utility overcharging the public."

Delia laughed and agreed.

Chuck ordered two more beers: one for Delia and, despite the buzz already on him, one for himself. Chugging a third bottle of beer when one was already sliding into the buzz zone was not the best drinking strategy. Buying drinks for and moving closer to a woman who looked like a woman he was trying to forget was not the best forgetting strategy.

They sat and talked. Things edged into the personal. He learned Delia had lived in the town all her life, as she had said. At seventeen, being young and, in her own words, not very insightful, she had married a local bad boy in his early twenties. Instead of giving up his wild and irresponsible ways and settling into responsibility as the head of a newly formed household, he had gone deeper into irresponsibility, not seeking gainful employment and carousing with friends, drinking, and getting into drugs, both doing and dealing. He and his like-minded cohorts had gotten into petty theft and graduated to stealing cars and stripping them to sell the parts to fly-by-night auto parts dealers in order to get money to support their drug habits. He had been busted for drug possession and grand theft auto and sent to prison. She'd divorced him and moved back in with her parents. When released from prison, he had not returned home. She had gotten a job as a clerk in a local drugstore and had worked there ever since. She had no children. At one point, she made a point of saying she had no children and was free to pick up and move without being tied down by the baggage of children. She specifically used the word *baggage*.

"You're not going to be able to move on very far in life if you spend your free time sitting on a barstool, holding on to a beer bottle in one hand and holding on to whatever emotional baggage you brought to the bar to try to drink away," Delia said. "Is it a woman?"

Chuck paused with his hand in midair, bringing up his beer bottle. He looked at her with a confused look. "What makes you think there's a woman involved?"

Delia waved her hand in a thus-and-such gesture. "You can tell when men have a woman on their mind. They get a certain look on their face. They have kind of a lost and faraway look in their eyes. You have that look. I could see it the minute I came into the bar. I didn't think you had the look because your hometown professional sports team lost in the playoffs, and I don't think you're here looking blue and drinking because phone company people don't get no respect."

There was little Chuck could do or say. Delia had him pegged better than he had himself pegged. He had actually halfway convinced himself he had come to the bar to work off the strain of a long day on the job. But he had drunk too much to speak without somewhat slurring his words, let alone speak a plausible-sounding denial.

"Never let it be said that you're not an insightful woman," Chuck said. "As a matter of fact, I am here drinking to forget, and in point of fact, it is a woman I'm drinking to forget."

"Men don't drink to forget women," Delia said. "They drink to forget war. They drink to forget that their pickup truck or motorcycle broke down and that they can't afford to have it fixed. They drink to forget their losses in the stock market. They drink to forget they're bankrupt. But when it comes to women, men don't drink to forget. They don't want to forget. They drink to remember. They just drink to ease the sharp edges of remembering the woman they want to go on remembering or can't let go of remembering while they sit in bars and drink and remember while they claim they're trying to forget."

To the increasingly alcohol-influenced Chuck, Delia's statement did seem to have a logical progression to it. He just had too much of a buzz on to read it step by step the way he read complex electronic circuit diagrams.

"Then, more properly stated, it's a woman I'm drinking not to remember," Chuck said.

"Do you want to talk about it?" she asked. "About her? If you're looking to get out from under your memories of her, you might find that the quickest way out is through."

Chuck figured there was a certain logic to that proposition. At least there was a certain amount of country-girl common sense to it. He had been trying to discipline himself not to think about Wanda anymore. But after two and a half longneck bottles of beer, thoughts of self-discipline were becoming mushy and fading down behind the horizon. But even through a beer haze, his remembrances of Wanda were sharp and distinct.

"I suppose there's something to what you're saying," Chuck said with a beer-loosened voice. "It's not like I made a vow of silence not to talk about her. It's not like I promised I would never talk about her, even in the third-person past tense, not using her name."

Wanda was gone from him. His love for her hadn't departed from him as fast as she had. In that sense, he figured he didn't owe Wanda anything. She hadn't wanted his love, but she hadn't thrown it back in his face and treated him or his love for her with contempt. She had just explained quietly and almost tearfully why she loved the road more than any man, wasn't able to change the way she felt, and didn't think she could. She had been honest with him from the start. Along with still loving her, he respected her for her honesty, even though that honesty had left her away and gone from him. He would talk about her to Delia. But he would talk respectfully. He would be honest, but it wouldn't turn into a drunken swearing-and-venting fest. But it would be as honest as a man could be on three beers.

"What can I say?" Chuck said rhetorically. "She was just a woman I knew and fell in love with. We both worked for the phone company. She was a tech like me."

"You met on the job?" Delia asked.

History had a way of repeating itself, first in sorrow and then in irony.

"Sort of," Chuck said, looking away. "She worked for the phone company like me, but she was based out of a different city. That's why I had never met her before. But when we met, neither of us knew the other worked for the company."

Irony, thy name is woman.

Chuck turned his face to Delia. "Actually, we met in a bar like this one. She came up to me like you did. She was dressed the way you are. We started talking. I was lonely. She was horny. She put the two together. She seduced me there in the bar. We went to my hotel room and made out for half the night. We fell asleep together. Come the morning, she was gone. I figured she was a female love-'em-and-leave-'em artist and I'd never see her again. But I ran into her on the job the next day. It created quite a rumpus between us, but we kept it quiet from the others. Later, she came to feel that since we had been thrown together and had to work together for a time, she might as well put the time we had together to good use, sexually speaking. She seduced me again, up on the roof of a phone company microwave relay tower. After that, we started up a short-term affair.

"When the work we were there for was completed, she went on her own way. Which was something she had been doing all her life. By then, I had fallen love with her. When I professed that love, she made it clear she wasn't interested in my love or any man's love. She wasn't interested in any love that would tie her down. After that, she was gone."

"Did she break your little heart?" Delia asked in a cloying voice.

"More accurately stated, I broke my own heart by trying to break into hers," Chuck said. "We had a quickie affair. We both got some sex off of each other. For me, it turned into head-over-heels love and thoughts of a life together going forward. For her, sex definitely wasn't the last thing on her mind, but it was the last stop before the back door. I professed my love for her. I told her I wanted to spend my life with her. I put my all into it. For my troubles, I got a few words of regret on her part, but what I mostly got were explanations of how it wouldn't work, how it couldn't be, and how she wasn't and couldn't be the kind of woman I was looking for and wanted. She wasn't a woman of that many words, but she had plenty of words to spare when it came to the way things were with her."

He spoke with the beginnings of a beer-induced stumble. His narrative didn't proceed smoothly or in a fully logical progression. But at nearly midnight in a country bar far away from the home he didn't have, Chuck wasn't thinking in terms of correct grammar or syntax.

"Before she dumped you, did she lie to you and lead you on and string you along?" Delia asked.

"Of all you can say that she did to me, the least she did was lie to me," Chuck said. "She was up front, open, and honest from day one that it wasn't going to be and couldn't be with a woman like her. In some ways, it would have been easier if she had lied to me—a nice, painless lie, like she was in love with a man who didn't love her, and she would spend the rest of her life loving him and had no room in her heart for any other man. That way, I would have turned back before I even got to her door. Instead, I just beat my head in against her door and against my own door of loving her, neither of which was going to open."

"You said she said that it couldn't be with a woman like her and that it couldn't be with her for any man," Delia said. "If she was that antimale, what kind of woman was she? Was she a closet lesbian?"

"She was closeted when she needed to keep things under wraps and under control when it came to her sex life," Chuck said. "She was flat-out open and unapologetic when she was going after what she wanted out of a man." He took a drink of his beer. "Sex was no problem for her. Sex was her hobby. Her avocation."

"Was it her profession?" Delia asked.

"Her day job was working for the phone company," Chuck said. "Sex was the way she unwound, or wound herself up further, when she was on the road. But sex wasn't her profession. The only time she took any money for sex was once when she wanted to feel what it was like to feel like a hooker. But she only did that once. For her, the transporting impetus was getting herself pleasure and racking up a score. Not money."

"Was she some kind of free-love advocate?"

"Free love," Chuck said in a wry voice. "Free loving. Free form. Free floating. Free flying. Free on the road. I think she loved being free on the road as much as she loved making love in a soiled bed in a seedy motel off the road. In the end, the open road was as much of a lover and a mover to her as were all the erstwhile onetime, one-night bedroom partners she picked up along the way. Me included. She probably had it in her mind to get herself a man at every mile marker along Route 66."

"Busy girl," Delia said in an impressed-sounding voice.

"I'm exaggerating a bit on that," Chuck said. "But to her, a life of love on the open road was the only life she wanted. Love shared for a night and then left behind was the only kind of love she wanted. I was willing to give up my more settled life and share life on the road with her as long as we could be together. But she only wanted to walk the road alone. I would have followed her on the road. I would have shared love with her on the open road, but to her, love shared was love restricted. Life shared was life limited. She would have felt tied down and tied up. She said it all enough. I was willing and ready to spend a life with her. She only wanted a life on the road."

"If someone was willing to take me out of the nowhere life I've been living and take me with him on the road, I'd be off with him like a shot," Delia said. "I'd be gone all the quicker if it was you taking me on the road with you. You're the first man I ever wanted to go away with. You've got all sorts of reasons for moving on. I've got no reason for staying here. I think we could put those reasons together real easy."

Chuck sort of froze in position on the barstool he was sitting on. Her words were starting to sound like the opening gambit of a pickup, if not the opening line of a seduction.

"You've got a woman you're trying to forget. Sitting at a bar and moping for her isn't going to get you beyond remembering her. It takes a woman with you in the here and now to forget a woman from the past. I could be that woman for you. We could help each other forget that we aren't with the lovers we started out with and that we aren't where we really want to be. We could create our own space in the world and in the night. We could go on from there to keep a place in the world that would be all ours from then on."

Chuck froze again. It was a speech Wanda could have given and probably had given in similar form and content many times but with no hint of continuance beyond. Even through three beers, Chuck heard what Delia was saying. She was talking about permanence and staying—all the traits he had wanted in a woman and in a life with a woman, all the things his ex-wife had taken away when she betrayed him behind his back, and all the things Wanda had disavowed and run away from when she ran from him.

"Ah, we've only been talking for an hour, and now you're talking about wanting to spend a life with me," Chuck said. "Not that the concept of spending a life with a woman bothers me. But it's all kind of fast. I don't know anything about you, and you don't know anything about me. For all you know, I could be a closet psycho."

"I'm a pretty good judge of men," Delia said. "I can tell by instinct just by looking at him and listening to him for five minutes whether a guy is a jerk or dangerous. I don't sense any of that in you, and you aren't coming on like that. It may be a big gamble on my part, but from what I can tell about you, you're worth taking a chance on."

Chuck's self-effacing nice-guy personality had scored again without his trying or even looking to score. "Don't you think we should get to know each other before we plunge right in?" he asked. "Especially into a lifetime commitment?"

"I'm not talking about us heading out to find a justice of the peace," she said. "Getting to know each other is what I'm talking about us doing. I'm just not talking about doing it through a series of church socials. I'm talking about not doing any more talking. I'm talking about getting started from right here and heading out. The usual question at a time like this is 'My place or yours?' Since your place is in Memphis and mine is just over the hill, let's make it my place. You could follow me to my place in your car, or if you're too drunk to drive safely, I could take you with me in my car. In the morning, I could bring you back to pick up your car.

"We could get together while you're working in the area. After you're done here, you could come up and spend the weekends. You said you're based out of Memphis. Memphis isn't all that far away. It's a short drive up I-55, on superhighway most of the way. You can get here easy. After a short few weekends spent together, instead of a state-line-crossing affair, you might find real easy that you want to keep me with you all the time and take me on the road with you. Like I said, for you, I could leave all the nothin' I've got now behind me and go off with you.

"I may seem like I'm coming on pretty fast. But in a short while, you're going to be gone. Not just from this bar but from the state. If I'm going to get anything going with you, I've got to get that something started—something that might bring you back around. If the way I'm coming on makes me sound fast and forward, I've got to get myself in quick. If that makes me fast and forward, well, you can't blame a girl for trying."

Actually, you can, depending on what she's trying and how hard she's trying it, he thought.

A great number of men had fantasized about meeting a woman who would throw herself at them the way Delia was and the way Wanda had. The self-effacing Chuck had never fantasized that way. To do so would have made him feel arrogant and chauvinistic. Even after Wanda, he still hadn't really imagined a woman throwing herself at him the way Delia was. Though he had always wanted a life with a woman, he hadn't imagined a woman throwing herself at him proactively and saying she wanted to come away with him on the spot and spend a life going forward with him from there. As a result of not having imagined anything like that, he had never imagined what words he would say in response to the offer he thought improbable.

"Madam, we've hardly been properly introduced," Chuck said in an ironic voice, slurring his words to sound more intoxicated than he really was.

"Proper has nothing to do with it," Delia said. "This late at night, in a country bar far away out on the open road, miles from the nearest nowhere town, for two people with the same needs, proper is off in another county. Proper is off over the horizon. Proper doesn't come into it. In a spur-of-the-moment encounter like this, there's no proper form. There's no proper introduction. There's no proper approach. There's no proper interval. There's no proper proper. We both know what we want. We both know what we need without saying it. You need to forget a bad love. I need some good lovin'. There's no reason to be proper with each other. There's no reason to be proper about any part of it. There's no proper needed. There's only us and our needs and where we go from here with them. There's no one around to explain proper to us. There's no one we need to explain ourselves to. There's no one we should explain anything to, including ourselves. There's no one to apologize to, no one we should apologize to, and nothing we need to apologize for. We may go on for life. We may not go beyond one night together. But we're not going to know until we get going."

Chuck found himself on the verge of setting foot on a road. It was a road he had gone down before. It was a road he wasn't sure he was ready to start down again then and there. It wasn't because he thought she would send him out alone the way Wanda had. It wasn't that he intended to live the rest of his life in memories of Wanda. It wasn't that he was incapable of loving another woman after Wanda. But his life felt empty after Wanda, and the emptiness hadn't gone away. He wasn't convinced in his own mind that taking up with a downscaled Wanda clone was going to cure that emptiness. If anything, taking up with a Wanda afterimage might only worsen the emptiness by continuously outlining what hadn't been and what couldn't be. He would be living with an imitation of Wanda, all the while knowing that the real Wanda would never come back to him. Instead of being a palliative for Wanda, a woman who looked like Wanda might be an ongoing reminder of what he had lost.

Perhaps the better idea would be to just not go down the road at all, he thought. *Do the proverbial start-all-over-again routine.* He could leave the past totally behind. Find a woman the opposite of Wanda. Find a new road to go down with a new woman, a woman who didn't keep him circling back in his mind and memory to Wanda. Find a woman who would stay.

Through an expanding horizon lubricated by beer, Chuck wondered if the woman now sitting beside him could be that woman. Perhaps the woman would prove to be the antidote to Wanda. She looked like Wanda. In a way, he would be going back to Wanda, a relationship on which he thought the door was closed forever. In a way, he might be grasping at straws of the past. But then again, once the straws were grasped, he might find himself in the open field of his future. Some people might have looked askance at the whole thing and said it was a road going in the wrong direction and a path littered with stumbling blocks.

But was there something wrong about taking a lover who looked like a former lover? Did it violate sexual etiquette? Would Dear Abby have turned her nose up? Would a counselor have waved red flags, saying it was a risky move that would lead to a relationship filled with baggage and land mines, a relationship bound to fail? Was becoming involved with a lover who looked like a past lover an obsessive-compulsive neurosis that Freud would have frowned upon?

Whatever deeper truth might have been in it, psychoanalytical theory could be pretty arcane. Life could be arcane for some, but Chuck saw no reason it had to be arcane for him. Delia was there and real, and she was anything but arcane. She might be the way into the future he was looking for, he thought. Though she was something of an afterimage from the past, she might be the key to the future. She might be a replay of the past, but she might be a replay who played out right this time. She had come out of the night the way Wanda had. She had sat down next to him the way Wanda had. She was propositioning him the way Wanda had. But she was talking more about staying than about moving alone along the open road the way Wanda had. She could be a Wanda who cared more for him than the open road, he thought. She might be the Wanda who would stay.

An old country song asked, "Will the circle be unbroken?" Inside Chuck's mind, a circle broke. The circle was the circle of love he had drawn around Wanda and had left open for her to come into with him, a circle he had opened with his wishful love in the face of Wanda's love of being free and unattached on the open road. His circle of love for Wanda broke apart and a new circle closed, leaving him inside the circle and Wanda on the outside. There in a bar that resembled the bar where it had started, his love for Wanda ended. It was over. He would not open the circle of his heart for her again.

At the same time, a circle opened. It was a circle connected to the past but that led out of the past into the possible future. It was the circle Delia was offering to open for him with her, starting in her bed and going from there to he knew not where. For all he knew, it might be to a life with a woman he wanted. A life with a woman who would stay for life.

At the moment he might have jumped to his feet and taken off with her, Chuck's feet and mind dragged. It wasn't because he was still hopelessly in love with Wanda and wasn't able to think about or respond to another woman. By that emotional point in his life, and well into his third beer, he felt he no longer owed Wanda anything, let alone giving up a life with a woman who was professing willingness to share life with him the way Wanda hadn't.

But at the moment, he wasn't sure about the situation or about the woman, nor was he sure he was sober enough to discern the situation accurately or discern his future with Delia.

"It's all a very interesting proposition," Chuck said, feigning being drunker than he was. "One I would like to pursue."

Any lingering pull of Wanda notwithstanding, he wasn't ready to begin the pursuit of a lifetime commitment from off a barstool on such short notice and in such an impromptu manner, especially in his present alcohol-influenced condition.

"But in my present condition at the present moment, I'm afraid I wouldn't be very much good for you. I'd probably fall asleep or pass out on you before I could do much of anything or even get it going. It could prove to be a very unsatisfactory scene all around. Perhaps it would be a better idea for me to give you a raincheck and for us to get together at a later date when I'm sober."

It was sort of a lie. For one thing, he wasn't that drunk. Beyond that, the job he had been sent to do was almost completed. Only a few final systems checks were needed. He would probably be through with his work by midday tomorrow. He had two days left in the time allotted to do the work. He could easily get to and meet Delia after she got off work in her nearby hometown just down the road.

"I'll be around a few more days," he said. "We can get together a short way down the road."

Or he could just quietly fade away and disappear from the scene. He would be back in Memphis, maybe off on another job, by the time she realized he wasn't going to call. He would be gone out the back door that Wanda had been so proficient at using.

Delia reached into her purse and brought out a slip of blank paper and a pen. She proceeded to write her name, address, and phone number down on it and gave it to Chuck.

"Are you going to stay any longer?" she asked as she handed the paper to him.

"I think I'm about done here," Chuck said. "I know my limits. If I drink any more, I won't be able to drive safely, let alone accomplish anything for you under the sheets." He turned on his barstool and started to get up.

519

"If you feel you're not up to driving, I could drive you," Delia said again.

"Thanks," Chuck said, "but I can make it. Besides, on the way back, I've got to check in with the section chief." It was sort of a lie. He didn't have to check in with the section chief. He was the section chief. "I'll let you close down the bar."

It wasn't the best getaway line he or any man had come up with. But he needed fresh air blowing in his face through the open window of a moving car to sober up, and he needed movement and distance to think clearly.

"I've closed down bars too many times, including this one," Delia said. "I don't want to hang around here until closing time. I'll walk out with you."

Their departure was an anticlimax. Chuck did the gentlemanly thing and walked her to her car. Her had figured a country girl like her would drive a red or black pickup truck, if not some kind of garish Bigfoot truck jacked up high on tractor wheels. Her car turned out to be a white low-end, midsized import of some kind and nationality Chuck couldn't make out in the dark. At the door to her car, she asked him again if he felt OK to drive. Chuck said he was all right.

"Call me before you get away to Memphis," she said as she opened the door to her car.

Chuck didn't make a definite reply or say they had a date on. He gave only a noncommittal response, saying he had her address and phone number. He closed her car door for her and stepped back. Delia started up her car and drove out of the parking lot. Chuck stood in the parking lot and watched her drive away into the night.

Chuck went to his car, got in, and drove off. There was only a single road. He was going in the same direction as Delia, but he did not follow her closely. He could see the taillights of her car in the distance ahead, but he did not close the gap. He didn't want to frighten her by making her think he was chasing her with thoughts of running her off the road, dragging her out of her car, and assaulting her in the dark in a field alongside the road. He also didn't want to get too close, as it might give her the idea he had decided to take her up on her offer to meet again. He had her phone number and address, but he hadn't made up his mind whether he would call her or not. He wasn't going to make up his mind there in the dark on the road. That was for another day and another horizon.

Chuck drove away through the dark. He drove away from the bar, from the woman, and from his past memories. He also drove the last stretch of open road away from Wanda. In his mind, he finished saying his last goodbye to her, the goodbye he had been saying in increments since they broke up. That night, on an unknown mile on the darkened night highway, he closed the door on the last of his memories of Wanda and of the future that he had hoped to share with her but that she had wished to share only with the road. He was moving away from that portion of his past. Whether he was moving into his future, he wasn't sure. He would probably contact Delia, he thought. At least she had talked about sharing a future with him. With the horizon of Wanda closed off behind him, Delia was presently the only woman he might be able to share a future with. She wasn't perfect, but by that stage, he didn't know what perfection was in the world or if it was achievable. But he might have a reasonably happy life with her. When all hopes for fireworks and grand passion in a relationship fell through or didn't materialize, sometimes reasonableness was what was left. At that point, one abandoned thoughts of sweeping passion and settled for reasonableness. Reasonableness started to look good. Or at least reasonable.

Chuck was into his thirties. He had no family. He had no children. His ex-wife hadn't wanted children. She had considered them to be a drag on her life and a redirection of her life. Chuck hadn't caught on to the possibility that his ex-wife's belief about children slowing her down and redirecting her life might eventually come full circle to her belief that their marriage was doing the same. She was like Wanda in that respect. The difference was that his ex-wife was a liar who had feigned love and staying. Wanda had thought the same, but she had been more honest and up front about it.

On the darkened road Chuck was traveling, with the wider landscape out of sight in the night, living and dying alone seemed neither reasonable nor attractive. He had come closer to perfection with Wanda than he had thought he ever would. It had turned out to be a road too far, a road that had no end. But his brief encounter with Wanda had left him feeling that his life had been empty before he found her. Or before she found him. When she'd left, it had left him feeling emptier than he ever had felt.

But that was in the past. The past was a scant landscape to live in. As Chuck drove on through the uncertain night, he resolved again that he would not revisit the past. Many times, he had lapsed from that earlier resolution. He resolved to do a better job of holding the resolution. He would not live in memories of the past. He would live in the uncertain future, not the empty past. He would not return to the past, a past that would not return to him. He didn't know which direction the future would take him in or where he would be taking his life in the future.

25

"Where you're going to be taking it is just over the border to Charlotte, North Carolina," the section chief said to the assembled group of techs. "They had a fire in a major switching facility. A lot of equipment got destroyed; a lot of phone service was knocked out. They need to get full service back as quickly as possible. They've asked for our help on this one. I'm sending you. The replacement equipment will arrive in a day or two. I want you there and ready to go when it gets there. Be here tomorrow morning at seven, awake and ready to roll. You'll convoy again the way you did on the last installment job. Shouldn't take you long to get there. The company will make hotel reservations for you near the jobsite. It probably won't be the Ritz. But it won't be Cannery Row."

In the past, Wanda would have wondered about the bars she would find nearby in which to present herself, how to go about making an entrance, and how best to dress to attract attention. Now her mind was a flat blank on all those once important past accounts.

"Either way, you're up at bat again. You're back in the saddle again, back on the road again."

Wanda nodded like the rest and walked away with the other techs when the group broke up. As she walked away, the emptiness that had dogged her since her mother's death followed her. In the near past, Wanda would have been thrilled at the thought of being on the road again, even on a short-distance trip. Now it was just another job. She would do the job and do it to the best of her ability. She was a professional. She was proud of her professional ability. On the road, she had been a professional pickup artist. She had been proud of that too. But now it was a horizon she would not return to.

In the empty quarter of her mind that had once been filled with the thrill of being on the open road, thoughts of the road itself did not come alive in her anymore. The open road no longer called to her the way it had. It held no call for her at all. She had lived for the feeling of moving on toward the horizon over the open road. Horizons once had shone brightly in her life, when moving on to new horizons had formed the basis of her life, but there were now no horizons of any color or brightness. There was only a void where horizons had once held sway for her. She had yet to find any other horizon to fill the void and find a direction to take life in.

⌀⌀⌀

"OK, this is where we're going to be taking it," Chuck said, straining his neck to look up the full height of the tower. "All the way up to the top."

They had unlocked the gate in the chain-link fence around the tower and walked up to the cement base it was mounted on. Chuck turned to the stronger-looking of the other two techs with him.

"Pete, it's you and me up the tower," Chuck said to the tech, who was about his size and build. In the three-man group, they were the best tower climbers. "We'll do the installation. We can't all be up there. There isn't enough room for more than two guys on the electronics platform. There's barely enough room for one man. It doesn't look like there's enough room for one man to squeeze past the other. When we're up there, we'll have to coordinate our moves so that one of us doesn't knock the other off the tower." He turned to the more slightly built tech who was the third man on his team. "Rudy, you stay down here. I'll drop the line to you from the platform. You attach the line to the bags with the modules. We'll pull them up."

The three techs stood at the base of the open-frame tower. The bottom few feet of the tower tapered down to where the tower was joined to the concrete base by a single pivot that the tower had been pulled up on. The tower was made of four sets of heavy-gauge steel pipe held rigidly in uniform spacing by a zigzag arrangement of angular and horizontal steel braces welded to the vertical risers. There was a minimal ladder on the tower; its steps were made from D-shaped metal-rod sections welded to the tower. From the seemingly contradictory and unstable base arrangement, the tower rose more than three hundred feet, held rigidly vertical by two four-wire sets of heavy-gauge guy wires pulled taut and anchored firmly to the ground. Near the top was an expanded section that contained the microwave relay equipment. There was a small platform around the

524

equipment section just wide enough for one man to stand on but not wide enough for two men to pass each other. Farther up at the top were the microwave antennae. Looking up the tower from the base was like looking up the straight face of the Matterhorn, which climbers had been scaling for generations—and dying on.

"It's not like I don't want to be part of this, but thanks for leaving me here on the ground," the shorter tech said. "I don't mind the old-style enclosed towers, but these open-frame, open-air jobs give me nosebleeds just looking at them, let alone trying to climb them. I'm glad it's a clear day. For your sake, I just hope an electrical storm doesn't blow up while you're up there."

"The tower is grounded," Chuck said. "Any surge will go straight down past us into the ground."

"And will blow you off the tower on its way down," the tech said. "Either way, if it starts to cloud up, get down fast. I don't want to be the one who scrapes your carbonized bodies off the grass and drags them back to section headquarters smelling like fried bacon."

"You have no sense of adventure," Chuck said, looking up the tower.

"I have a sense of high-voltage arcs coming down out of the sky and the gravitational coefficient coming up out of the earth," the tech said. "I've got enough respect for both of them to know that neither of them has any respect for any of us."

"We didn't come here to be killed by either electricity or gravity," Chuck said. "We came here to do a refit-and-upgrade job, not to leave ourselves dead on the ground. So let's be careful. Do the job. Don't dawdle, but don't do a rush job. Do it right the first time so we don't get sent back." Chuck looked up the tower. "I don't want to have to go up this thing more than once. So let's get going. This is what we came here for."

———

"OK, this is what you're here for," said the section chief of the fire-damaged Charlotte, North Carolina, switching facility where Wanda's repair team had been sent to replace the equipment destroyed in the fire.

Some of the other techs secretly thought Wanda should have been the section chief of their group. But the phone company of that day was still an old boys' network. Despite her knowledge and experience, which put her a head above the male techs, Wanda was just another midlevel tech and would probably remain so for some time. Maybe at some unknown and unknowable time in the future, she might break through the silicone ceiling to a higher-up general office position. At the moment, she was just another one of the guys—with a figure that set a lot of the guys to drooling.

"The replacement units are on their way. I don't know when they will arrive, but we can use the time before they arrive to pull the damaged stuff out and clean up. So let's get started."

———

"OK, let's get started," Chuck said to the tech who was going to climb with him, throwing a coil of light but strong nylon rope over his neck. "Hook up your safety belt whenever you're not moving. That's what they give them to us for."

The two started climbing the tower, with Chuck in the lead and Pete a few yards behind him. They maintained the separation so as not to step on each other's fingers and so that if one fell, he would not grab the other and bring them both down.

They climbed slowly and deliberately, not rushing, making sure of every hand grip, and setting their feet securely on each horizontal bar. At the level of the first set of guy wires, there was a gusset plate welded to the four vertical bars on the inside of the tower frame to provide additional strength. As Chuck put his hand on the plate, instead of feeling the familiar touch of metal, he felt what seemed to be a collection of twigs and grass. As he touched it, with a rustle of wings, a bird flew away. The collection of grass and other ground debris hadn't been blown up there and deposited at random by the wind. It was a bird's nest, built high off the ground. The positioning of the nest had been good thinking on the bird's part. It was up high away from ground-dwelling predators that fed on the nests of ground-nesting birds, such as weasels and feral cats. As he passed the nest, Chuck looked inside. There were several newly hatched chicks hunkered down in the nest with perplexed looks on their faces.

"Sorry, Mama Bird," Chuck said to the departing bird. "Didn't mean to scare you. We'll be careful not to overturn your nest. We won't dump your babies. We won't even touch them, so they won't have our scent on them."

Chuck was afraid if the mother bird detected human scent on her nest, she might abandon it and her chicks. He otherwise worried that he might have scared the bird so much it wouldn't return to its nest ever.

He looked down at his climbing partner. "There's a bird's nest here. There are live chicks in it. Watch out you don't knock the nest off where it's sitting."

Pete called out an affirmative. Chuck climbed quickly past the bird's nest. He took a double step over the nest so as not to step on it with his boot. Looking back down from a higher altitude, he saw the bird fly back to its nest. He noted with satisfaction that they had not scared it away. The baby birds would not be left to starve.

At the electronics level of the tower, Chuck pulled himself up onto the narrow walkway that ran around the microwave relay units mounted below the antennae and moved out of the way so his partner could get up onto the walkway. While Pete was climbing up, Chuck stood looking out over the landscape. The view was as panoramic as the view had been from the top of the tower where he and Wanda had met, under her real name, and worked together. Though as tall as the narrower open girder he was on now, that tower had seemed solid and immovable. The platform he was standing on now moved perceptibly when walked on. It seemed flimsy and precarious. The roof of the first tower had, by relative comparison, been far more spacious. The platform he was on that day was a tiny percentage of the size of the roof of the tower where they had made love out of sight in the sunshine. The walkway he was standing on had barely enough free room to turn around on. The railing was only waist high. One could easily have toppled over it.

As Chuck stood there looking out, thoughts of Wanda and how she might have reacted to being on that tower filled his mind. He figured she would probably have found being at the apex of the narrow open-frame tower to be adventurous and would have found the view sublime. He found himself wondering where she was and what she was doing. Then he shook his head as if to clear his thoughts of Wanda. Once again, he reminded himself that he had vowed not to think of her. He needed to restore his self-discipline in that respect.

Besides, he had a pending date with a local woman. He touched the piece of paper in his shirt pocket with the name, address, and phone number of the woman he had met in the bar. He hadn't called her yet. He still hadn't decided whether he would call her or keep his distance and quietly slip away.

———⁂———

Halfway across the continent, Wanda worked in a focused and deliberate manner. Her work was an anodyne to the feelings of loss and emptiness that had followed her since the death of her mother. The feeling hadn't faded or dialed down. If anything, it had slowly grown. She hadn't been to a bar since the time the man tried to pick her up in the bar in the western reaches of Virginia. She hadn't even been to a bar within walking distance of her apartment. She would sit in her apartment and watch television or sit in the dark and contemplate she knew not what or contemplate her unknown future. All she knew of the future was that she wasn't going to go back to cruising the bars. She didn't have the enthusiasm, the heart, or the soul for it anymore. Work gave her both an anodyne that let her forget her emptiness and a way to concentrate her mind.

She had also abandoned her once shining philosopher's stone of sex. The philosopher's stone of legend was a magical stone that could turn lead into gold. For her, sex had turned to dross. When it came to sex, she had given it her personal best. In return, her personal bests in all the beds she had made love in and then slipped out of while feeling buoyed up had let her down. Those feelings had given her a feeling of freedom and movement. Now those once prized feelings had deserted her and left her feeling as if she were standing unmoving in the middle of nowhere, off any and all roads, with no love, home, refuge, or future in sight. Even the road was out of sight. The world of sexual sensations and feelings that she had lived for and that had been the meaning of her life had left her feeling drawn up inside herself, within her soul, which had become a small, enclosed room with no door. She did not know where her future lay. All she knew was that she didn't have a high view of her life.

———⁂———

"I think my ears are going to pop from the altitude," Pete quipped. "Either that, or I'm going to get a nosebleed. You don't really know how high these things are until you look down."

"Don't look down," Chuck said.

528

"There's only open sky above you, no room to move, and no place to sit. Now I know what flagpole sitters feel like."

Chuck didn't comment further. He tied one end of the line firmly to the railing and let the coil drop. It unraveled as it fell. It barely reached the ground. Using his Handie-Talkie radio, from up on the tower, Chuck called to Rudy, the tech at the tower base, saying which module he wanted. Rudy tied the end of the rope around the carrying straps of one of the canvas bags that held an upgrade module. Chuck and Pete, on the tower, pulled it up. Before they did, they hooked up their safety belts in case the weight threw off their balance and caused either of them to fall.

Chuck and Pete removed the old module, replaced it with the new one, and hooked it up. Then they lowered the old module back to the ground. Chuck called over the radio for the next piece of equipment he wanted. Rudy sent it up for them. Several times, they did the same.

By the time they were finished, it was getting late in the afternoon. Chuck untied the end of the rope and let it drop. Then they began the slow, deliberate climb back down the tower. At the level of the nest, the bird took flight again but returned to her nest after they had passed.

"We're done here as far as you two are concerned," Chuck said to the others as he climbed the final few feet back to the ground and stepped off the tower. "We can all head on back for the night. Tomorrow I'll do the final system alignment and calibration."

"Don't you want someone to help you?" Pete asked.

"This is a one-man job," Chuck said. "No use in two of us going back up that tower. You'd just be standing around on the ground with your thumbs up your butts. You might as well head for the barn and report in. I'll be along after I do the alignment tests tomorrow. No need for you to hang around here in Dixie Siberia. I can do one more night in that fleabag motel we've been staying at."

Besides, staying would give him one more day to decide whether to call Delia. If he did, staying would give him a night to be with her in a bar of her choice. Or a bed of her choice. His mind went back to how she had come up to him and boldly propositioned him. From there, his mind went back to the night Wanda had come up to him in the bar. But he was trying to forget Wanda.

"How are you going to know if the equipment is working, the circuit pathway is open, and the signals are getting through?" Pete asked.

"I'll call into the nearest switching office with my handset," Chuck answered. "They can run continuity tests to see if the circuit path is open, what the signal strength is, and whether it's getting into the landlines."

"OK. Just don't fall. I won't be there to grab you."

"You could fall just as easily as me," Chuck said. "If either of us tried to grab the other, then one of us could pull the other down. There'd be two graves at the base of this tower." Chuck didn't think the company would bury them where they fell. He just said that to make a point.

"If you fall from the top, you'll bury yourself in the ground by momentum alone," Rudy said. "Headfirst six feet down."

"I don't intend to take a header off this thing," Chuck said, glancing back up the tower. "I'll remember to hook up my safety belt."

The other techs didn't look fully convinced. But no more was said. The three headed back to the motel they were staying at. The two other techs checked out, and Chuck went back to his room.

Chuck went to dinner in a small restaurant in the town where Delia lived. He didn't see her there. He didn't use the number she had given him to call her from the restaurant or from his motel room. Back in his room, he went to bed early. He turned off the light. It took a minute or so, but his eyes became accustomed to the dark.

He lay in his bed, staring out into the darkness of the room, trying to discern the face of the future. In the darkness, he could see the faint, blurry, random patterns the brain's visual cortex created to stimulate itself, which many people saw when they stared into darkness. In his imagination, the blurry images coalesced in sequence into two faces: the face of Delia and Wanda's face. Delia's face faded and passed from him in less than a minute. He didn't try to hold the image. Wanda's face lingered. He didn't try to drive her image out of his mind. He was breaking training by not trying to actively push the image of her face out of his mind. After all, he was trying to discipline himself to forget her. But he was far from any place he knew or had known or anyone who knew him. His lapse of self-discipline would go unreported and unnoticed. What happened in his mind in a motel outside Caruthersville, Missouri, would stay in Caruthersville.

As Chuck watched, he saw Wanda's face in shifting patterns of remembrances. He saw the come-hither look she had given him when she came to him in the bar. He saw the sensual expression she had worn before she made love to him in his hotel room, where they had made love for the first time. He saw the startled face she had worn when she saw him the next day at the tower jobsite where their two work teams met. He saw the faraway look she had worn as she looked out over the surrounding landscape from the top of the tower and at the horizon beyond. He saw the sensual look she'd had when they made love on the roof of the tower. He saw the wrenching, painful look she'd had when she learned of the death of her mother. He saw her face as she cried silently as she sat beside him at her mother's funeral. He saw her water-streaked face as she emerged from swimming in the retention-pond swimming hole outside her hometown. He saw the sad but decided look on her face when they sat at dinner in the restaurant in her hometown and she told him that she could not love him and that there would never be a coming-together between them or a future together. He saw the look he imagined she had been wearing when she left her house in her hometown because she didn't want to see him go and didn't want to say a teary goodbye.

Once again, he circled back through his memories of Wanda. His memories were full and sweet, even though they had ended in parting. Once again, he could neither curse nor bless her.

But a life lived in a circle of memory is a life going in circles, he thought. *It's not a life moving forward. It's not a life moving anywhere. It is a life spent looking longingly at a door you know will never open again. No matter how sweet the memories, no matter how sweet a life lived in memories might seem, it is a life you have to get out of.*

Though it was not an intense repentance, Chuck repented of his lapse of self-discipline in allowing himself to think of Wanda, especially in such a full way. His visions faded back into the random patterns of shifting, faint light that his visual cortex was giving his brain as something to look at where there was nothing.

In one of his novels, author Thomas Wolfe penned the well-known and oft-quoted words "You can't go home again." Lying in a bed in a motel room far from the home he didn't have to return to, staring into the darkness he could not banish, Chuck once again pushed his memories of Wanda out of his mind. He didn't drive them out violently. He just turned his back on them. He vowed again he would not return to them. The woman he had met in the bar had said the only way out was through. He had gone through his love for Wanda and had come out on the far side. He would not circle back to it. He would continue in a straight line away from it. In time, the memories would fade over the horizon behind him.

He was not sure he liked the idea of losing his memories of Wanda. But he was not about to give up the future and all it held, good and bad, to look fondly on a horizon fading behind him. He would not look again on a past he knew was closed and would not return to him.

As the patterns of false light and memories shifted in his mind, Chuck slipped into a dull sleep, a sleep neither fitful nor pleasant. Only one dream intruded into his sleep. In the dream, he saw the tower he would climb the next day. Then the dream shifted in altitude, if not location. In his dream, he was looking out over the landscape from a high place. He couldn't see what he was standing on, but he was up high. From his high view, the landscape below expanded out to the horizon. It was a familiar-looking landscape. In his dream, he knew he had seen it before. He couldn't tell whether the landscape was the one he had seen that day or the one he had looked out over from the top of the tower he had shared with Wanda.

In the half-conscious twilight horizon between wakefulness and sleep, just before he crossed the boundary, for a quick instant, Chuck wondered if the images in his mind were coming in from outside or were coming from inside his mind and were being projected outward over the landscapes he was dreaming about.

⎯⎯ ⦾⦾⦾ ⎯⎯

Half a continent and a time zone away, Wanda wasn't able to achieve even a state of dull, fitful sleep. She didn't toss and turn, but she wasn't able to find a sleep-inducing position. It wasn't because the room she was in was junky or squalid. The hotel the phone company had booked for the work team in Charlotte was tidy and accommodating. The room was, in ways, cleaner than her apartment. Nor was she unable to sleep because thoughts were coming into her mind from an unknown source. The thoughts intruding on her mind didn't come telepathically from a mind outside hers. The thoughts intruding on her mind all came from within her own mind.

The anomie, depression, and disconnect she had felt from her past, from her life, and from herself after her mother's passing had not faded since her mother's funeral. The feelings were with her still and were doubling down. Since the one brief, idyllic interlude with Chuck in her hometown, the feelings of emptiness and meaninglessness had dogged her every step. The feeling that she herself was an empty, hollow, meaningless cipher, a scraggly shadow in life and love, had also stayed with her and was growing.

As the weight of her self-accusations piled up, laying the weight of their substance against her, paradoxically, she felt increasingly hollow and empty. She felt like the head of a dandelion weed that had gone to seed and was blowing away in the wind. Any substance she had felt for her life and herself seemed drained, dry, and nonexistent. Repeatedly, she wondered if there had ever been any real substance to her life and her love.

Oh, she had loved. She had made love to more men than she could remember. She hadn't bothered to remember any of their names. She hadn't wanted to remember them. She had made love under more aliases than she could remember. She had run through so many men and so many aliases she couldn't remember which alias she had used on which man. She had run from one quickly passing affair to the next, panting to get to the next affair almost before she had finished the affair she was running through at the moment. Now she felt as if she had run through life so fast that she had run out of her life into a void of nothingness.

She had loved sexually. She had given herself sexually, but she had never given real love. She had felt love physically in her body, but she had never felt love in her heart, not real love. She had practiced the art of seduction and counted it as love. She had pushed herself and extended herself in the acts of physical love, but she had never extended herself to any man in real love. Real love had never been extended by any man to her.

Wanda paused momentarily in her pity party to remember that one man had loved her for real. He had loved her for herself and loved her in spite of herself. But she had sent him away. He would not return to her. She doubted real love would ever return to her, even if it passed by just out of reach.

She had performed love physically and had been good at it. But it had all been a performance. She had given herself to be taken sexually. But she had never been taken by real love. She had never gained real love. She had never lost real love. She had never had real love on the giving or receiving end. She had never had it because she had never sought it. She had never wanted it. She had resolved never to be taken in by, taken over by, or submerged by love.

The only real and transcendent love she had ever felt was for her mother. But that love had been smothered and pushed to the side of her life by her pursuit of love on the run. Her love for her mother had been further submerged by her love of the open road. She had vowed she would never be hurt by love. But since her mother had died, she had been taken by surprise by how much the loss of real love could hurt. She knew now that real love could hurt. That in itself could constitute a reason not to pursue or hope for real love. Doing so was a defensive strategy that could keep a lot of hurt out of her life. But creeping in upon her was the thought that without real love, life was not real life.

Wanda tried to get to sleep, but sleep did not come to her. Finally, she gave up the fight, went into the kitchen, and fixed herself a cup of warm milk. It was a bit distasteful to drink, but her mother had always told her that warm milk would help a person sleep. She went back to her bed. Instead of tossing and turning, she lay still on her side, looking into the darkened room, trying to discern the shape of her future. She wasn't able to make out anything distinct.

As she finally drifted off to sleep, all she knew was that one more day's work would do it. Tomorrow would be the last day of work at the facility she was helping to repair. Then she would be gone from there. For all she knew, as soon as she got back to the home office in Columbia, she might be sent right back on the road again to another job. As she approached and started to cross the boundary into sleep, she wondered if that would be the story of the rest of her career with the phone company and the direction of the rest of her life: always moving on, pausing at one place, and then leaving, pausing at one momentary point in her life and then moving on. Each stop was just one more horizon she would momentarily glimpse, and then it would be gone from her.

26

"Just one more thing we need you to do, and then you're gone from there, and you don't have to come back," the voice coming over the handset said.

Instead of "gone from there," Chuck figured better words to use would have been "safely down from there." With one slip, he could find himself heading toward the ground at an accelerating pace, drawn downward by the gravitational coefficient.

"What's that?" Chuck asked. The air was as clear and the sky as bright as they had been the day before. The view from the top of the tower was as elevated and panoramic as it had been. Chuck sat on the narrow walkway around the equipment compartment near the top of the tower. His handset was patched into the phone company circuits by alligator clips on the ends of the wires of the handset. Like a daredevil schoolboy, he sat with his legs dangling over the side. He had his safety belt attached.

Chuck had finished the necessary alignment checks and had called in to the nearest switching office to run a check on whether the signal pathways were open and how well the signals were getting through. One by one, he had checked with the nearest switching centers to get reports on whether the signals from the tower were getting through and how well they were getting through. Everything was nominal.

"We need you to get in contact with the main switching center in Charlotte, North Carolina," the voice on the handset said. "They had a bad fire that knocked out a big section of the grid. They're just getting things cleaned up and back online. They asked us to run a pathway check to see if the signals from the tower you're on are getting through the system and are connecting up with them."

"What's the number there?" Chuck asked, looking at the push buttons on the handset.

"We'll call them and patch you in," the voice on the handset said.

"Roger, D," Chuck replied. He had been about to disconnect and climb down from the tower. It looked as if his departure would be delayed a bit. It didn't bother him to wait. He didn't have another job to get to. He wasn't going anywhere fast. It was a great view from where he was sitting on the tower.

Chuck sat back and looked out over the landscape. The nearby fields were a patchwork of different shades of green. On one horizon, he saw the deeper green of woods. On the horizon to the east, he could make out the muddy gray of the Mississippi River. It was a pleasant enough sight. Unless he was sent back to the tower in the future, it would be the last time he looked out over the particular landscape he was seeing.

In earlier years, from such an altitude, he might have imagined he could see the future. But any such vision escaped him that day. He could see the pleasant green land spread out around him, but the future was out of sight over a far horizon. He would leave the tower soon, and the vision he was seeing he would not see again. It would be another pleasant landscape he would not return to and would not see near him again. Pleasant landscapes and views of the future had been escaping from him at an accelerating pace.

27

"Hey, Wanda," a voice called out.

Wanda recognized it as the voice of one of the techs who worked there at the Charlotte exchange. "Yo," she said, not looking away from the circuits she was inspecting.

"Check the ABBE circuit," the tech said, standing in the doorway between the outer office and the banks of switches. "Give me a signal-strength report."

"Who wants to know?" Wanda asked casually.

"Some guy from the Memphis branch," the tech said. "He says he's sitting on top of a tower out in the boonies in Missouri, talking on a handset. He wants to know if his tower is making the trip to us through the system. He says he wants to get finished and get down. He says he's had enough of towers."

Wanda stepped over to a panel of gauges and meters. She scanned until she found the one for the named circuit. "Looks nominal," she said.

The tech stepped back into the office. A moment later, she heard him talking on the office phone.

Wanda stood motionless for a few moments. There was something reminiscent about it all. She walked to the door. By the time she got there, the tech had hung up the phone.

"Who was that tech?" Wanda asked from the doorway.

"Didn't give his name," the tech said. "He just said he was from the Memphis section and wanted to get off the tower and back on the road. I guess he doesn't like towers. But he said he would like to have a tower that tall to mount his amateur radio antennae on."

To Wanda, it sounded familiar. She was silent for another moment.

"What's the number on the handset he's using?" Wanda asked.

"Here," the tech said, reaching for a piece of paper. "I wrote it down in case I had to call him back."

Wanda walked over and took the piece of paper. The number was a designation number of a handset. She didn't recognize it.

"Do you need to talk to him?"

"Ah, yeah," Wanda said. "Something I have to check out."

"Well, if you want to talk to that guy specifically, you'd better hurry. You probably won't get him. He said he was finished and ready to leave. He's probably disconnected his handset by now."

Wanda walked back into the circuit room and sat down beside an open circuit rack. She connected the alligator clips on the loose ends of the handset wires to a convenient tap-in terminal.

The phone company motto at that time was "Reach out and touch someone." There had once been a someone out there for her. They had touched briefly and then gone off down separate roads. Their taking separate roads had been her idea. At the time of their parting, the past had been sealed off, apparently forever. Now, for one fleeting moment, a crack had opened in time and space, a crack into the past sealed off from her. The past she had sealed off. Maybe she could reach out into the past and touch someone who had been there for her and wanted to be there for her but was gone from her. Someone she had sent away.

Wanda paused for a second. She sat feeling conflicted, looking at the handset in her hand. She didn't know if calling was a good idea. It could open a lot of floodgates she hadn't wanted to open. It could bring up and out a lot of bad feelings. It could open a door better left shut.

Then again, it could open up the only door she wanted to open all the way in her life. The considerations were innumerable. The consequences were not easily calculable.

But it was all a moot point she had no time to think about and calculate upon. In quick sequence, she started pressing the buttons on the handset. As she did, a feeling of uselessness came over her. The narrow window had probably closed. It was most likely too late. If it was him, he had probably disconnected his handset after the tech had hung up the phone. He was probably climbing down the tower at that moment. As she pushed the last button and held the handset up to her ear, Wanda assumed she would hear nothing.

A ringing sound came through the earpiece speaker of the handset.

Chuck was sitting on the walkway of the platform, looking out over the view he would probably never see again. A pleasant breeze was blowing at the top of the tower. He didn't know if it was blowing at ground level or was a higher-altitude wind. He felt neither particularly regretful nor contemplative. It was a pleasant view, but there would be other views that he would see and experience and that would then be gone from him. He was getting used to that. For the present moment, he sat looking at the horizon so near around and so far from him. In that moment of horizon glimpsing, Chuck put away his final faint remaining connection with the past and looked toward the future.

But it wasn't a distant horizon beyond reach that Chuck was thinking about. It was a much nearer, more accessible horizon. The only immediately relevant consideration going through his mind was whether to call the woman he had met in the bar. Maybe it was the altitude, but he decided to call her and ask her out someplace, to a bar or nightspot in the town she lived in and was familiar with. He didn't know where it would go from there. He had Delia's phone number on the piece of paper in his pocket. He decided to call her from where he was on the top of the tower. She would probably find that amusing, he thought. Besides, it was the only phone or phone access for miles.

Chuck pulled the piece of paper with her phone number on it from his pocket and looked at the number. Then he put it back in his pocket. His handset was still tapped into the phone lines. He raised the handset and prepared to push the buttons to dial. At that moment, the handset rang. Chuck pushed the connect button.

"What's up?" Chuck said into the mouthpiece of the handset. He figured it was his home office in Memphis calling him back with something they had forgotten to tell him earlier. He expected to hear a familiar voice come right back to him over the handset. For a moment, all he heard was silence.

"Well, speak of the good old boy, and up he pops," said a familiar voice that neither distance nor the technological limitations of the handset lash-up nor his wish to forget could hide. It was a voice he'd thought he would never hear again.

"Ah, Wanda?" the surprised Chuck responded.

"Speak of the not-so-good old girl, and up she pops," Wanda said.

"Where are you?" Chuck asked, looking down at the base of the tower as if he could see her there with her own handset, tapped into the same line he was. Then he looked out over the distant horizon as if he could see her out there somewhere.

"I'm in Charlotte, North Carolina, working on the rebuild of the exchange destroyed in a fire. I was the one who took the reading and passed on the signal report you asked for when you called in from the tower you're on. I assumed it was you."

"Ah, yeah, it's me," Chuck said, not knowing where to go at that juncture. "It's a surprise hearing from you. How did you know where I was?"

"When I asked who had called, the super at this exchange said it was someone from the Memphis branch. He also mentioned that the guy said he wished he had a tower as tall as the one he was on to mount his amateur radio antennae on. Putting the two together, I figured it had to be you."

Chuck still didn't know where to go at the unexpected juncture. He had vowed he wouldn't spend the rest of his life pining for Wanda. He had vowed he wouldn't try to contact Wanda, and he hadn't. Wanda had told him not to attempt to contact her. He had vowed to discipline himself concerning her. He had vowed he wouldn't think about her. He had been doing an increasingly good job of not thinking about her. He would have been within his right to simply hang up on her. But in that moment, self-discipline was not withstanding. Nor did it have any compelling grip. He didn't know where the situation was going, but hanging up on her was the last thing he wanted to do.

"I must say, hearing from you is a surprise," Chuck said, not sure what to say or what he should say.

"Why is it a surprise?" Wanda said. "We both work for the phone company. There was a good enough chance we'd meet again someday on the job, if not on the lines; it just happened sooner than I thought. Go figure fate and Ma Bell's worksheet. Go figure the god of former lovers or God himself or at least the god of good timing. Whatever deity may or may not be involved, I wouldn't have known where you were if I hadn't been here when you called in. I was wrapping things up and was about to leave. If you had called in an hour later, I would have been gone. I wouldn't know where you were. I would have been thinking about something else, not about you. We would have both gone our separate ways without thinking about each other. This conversation wouldn't be happening."

Chuck looked out over the horizon again, as if trying to see her.

Wanda continued. "But it is. I don't know if it's fate or not. But it will do until the real thing comes along. Whatever has intervened, without it, we wouldn't be speaking now. We might have never spoken again. As timing goes, that would be far worse timing."

"The surprise is that you're talking to me at all," Chuck said. "I thought you didn't want to speak to me again. You told me not to try to contact you."

"If you will remember, if you want to remember, I didn't exactly say that I didn't want to talk to you again or that I wouldn't talk to you again."

"Close enough," Chuck said.

"What I said, maybe not in exact words but close enough, was for you not to pursue me and try to get me to fall in love with you, because it wouldn't happen, I was too set in my ways to change, I probably couldn't change if I tried, and I was probably incapable of feeling or giving real love. I said I was telling you what I told you then for your own good, because you would just end up hurt and sad if you loved me and tried to make me fall in love with you. That's why I broke it off and told you not to contact me."

"And I didn't," Chuck said, wondering if this was the point when he should hang up. He felt it was his right to do so. He knew it would be the best thing to do to maintain his discipline and resolve not to think of Wanda again, which was what he had been trying to do and had been getting better at. Now all that was out the window. Just hearing her voice brought all the old feelings rushing back as if they had never gone away.

"Are you angry at me for dumping you?" Wanda asked.

"You didn't dump me," Chuck said. "It wasn't like that."

"For sending you away then. For turning my back on you. For turning my back on your love for me. Are you angry at me for not returning the love you had for me?"

"You were under no moral or romantic obligation to love me just because I loved you. You were free to feel love for me or not feel love for me. Maybe you turned your back on me, but it was your back to turn. I have no right to get my nose out of joint because I loved you but you couldn't love me."

"The question was and still is whether I'm capable of giving or receiving real love. I came out of the night to proposition a lot of men to make love to me on my terms, you included. But as far as the proposition as to whether

I'm capable of giving or receiving real love goes, I've been looking at myself in the mirror of my mind, and I don't see a lot of evidence for either."

Chuck was silent for a moment. "Are you sure this is the same Wanda?" he asked rhetorically. "The same Wanda I knew? You're nothing but a big ball of contradictions and self-doubt. The Wanda I knew never had a minute of self-doubt."

"I'm the same Wanda you knew. I'm just a new Wanda looking back at the old Wanda and not liking what she sees."

"When did this transformation take place?" Chuck asked in the same rhetorical voice.

"You were there when it began," Wanda said. "You saw the beginnings. You were there at the inception."

"When was that?" Chuck asked. "I don't remember any big change coming over you."

"It started when Mother died. You saw how hard it hit me. You do remember that, don't you?"

"I remember." Chuck recalled holding the sobbing girl who had become hysterical when she received the phone call from her father informing her of her mother's sudden death.

"That's when it began," Wanda said. "But it didn't happen all at once. While you were there with me after Mother's funeral, it took my mind off what had happened. What you weren't there to see was how much harder it hit me later. After you were gone, after I sent you away, it hit me hard again. I not only had lost Mother but also started to feel I had lost myself. Everything in my thinking turned around. It all turned upside down. I no longer felt like the free spirit I had made myself. I felt like a slut. I felt like a tramp. I felt like all the things I was afraid Mother had feared I would become, even though she said she wasn't thinking those things about me. The pain of losing Mother didn't go away. It kept on hitting me. It built up. Finally, it blew apart every bridge back to my old life. It just went on. Alongside the pain of losing Mother, I started feeling the pain that I had wasted my life."

A fast breeze blew past Chuck. Though his safety belt was fastened, he took a firmer grip on the tower.

"For a short while, I tried going back to my old ways. I tried going back to bars. I tried going back to the open roads and the open encounters of my rambling life. I thought if I could get back to my old life, it might make the pain go away. But none of it worked. I didn't even get started. I already hated myself for living a life that had pained my mother to see me living. And when I tried to take that life up again after her death, I only ended up hating myself all the more."

The breeze tugged at Chuck again.

"It took Mother's death to make me realize how much of a washout my life has been. Since then, I've been stumbling all over myself, trying to sort out what my life has been about, not finding much of anything to recommend it. The only thing that keeps me stumbling on is that I know now how much I've been stumbling through my life, not knowing if there's been much of anything to it, thinking maybe something will turn up that will give substance and meaning to my life. When I heard you were on the line, something came over me. I just had to tell you that you were right. I already told Mother that she was right. I said it to her over her grave. I don't know whether she heard me or not." Sitting on the floor of the telephone exchange switching room, Wanda looked around to see if anyone was listening. "I like to think she did."

Chuck was growing a bit alarmed at the hard and nihilistic way Wanda was describing herself and at the growing intensity of the way she was describing her life as a failure. Her reference to her dead mother added another degree of worry. In the back of his mind, he wondered if she was thinking of joining her mother.

"You're running yourself down unfairly," Chuck said from the top of the tower halfway across the country from where Wanda was sitting on the floor of the switching room. "Why are you telling me this? Are you trying to apologize for what you think you've done?"

"Look," Wanda said in a halting voice, "this isn't easy for me. Yes, I'm trying to apologize. There's a lot of people I have to apologize to—Mother, Father, God, you, the phone company who gave me an expense account to use on assignments, the expense account I tapped into to cruise bars and get myself picked up. There's a lot I have to apologize for. I just don't know how to go about it. I'm not experienced at apologizing to anyone for anything."

Chuck shifted his position on the walkway of the tower. The vibrations spread out through the metal walkway.

"I've spent my life not apologizing to anyone for anything or thinking I need to apologize for anything. I've spent an equal portion of my life not thinking I could be wrong about anything and not caring whether anyone thought I was wrong about what I was doing. What I was doing to Mother's view of me and to myself. I've spent just about every day of my life up till now thinking I didn't need to rethink anything about my life and myself. Now I don't think I've spent one day of my life up till now thinking anything out straight. I set myself deep into my own thinking and ran with it. I did the same with my pride. I set my pride and locked myself into my pride a long time ago. My pride hasn't done me any good any more than my lifestyle has. It's time to cut both my pride and my old lifestyle loose and find myself a real life. But like I said, it isn't an easy thing for me. I'm bucking a whole life of self-programming. Now I have to kick a life of self-programming down the road the way I used to kick cans down the street when I was a young girl."

Another low rush of breeze brushed past Chuck where he sat near the tower's top.

"Don't try to cut me a break. Don't go easy on me. Don't spare my feelings. Just this once, don't be such a Mr. Nice Guy. I don't deserve *nice*. I didn't deserve you, and you didn't deserve the way I used you. So go along with what I'm saying. Agree with me that I've been a self-centered, self-indulgent jerk. Rip into me hard—as hard as I'm ripping into myself. Agree with me that I've trashed my life and that doing it hasn't done anything for my life. Don't sugarcoat me. Don't schmooze me by telling me not to run myself down. Just rip me up by agreeing with every bad thing I say about myself and the way I've been living my life. If you try to soft-soap me, it might make me rethink my rethinking and push me back toward the way I used to think, though I don't think anything is going to do that."

"I don't need to run you down," Chuck said. "You're doing a very good job on yourself. That's why I asked if you're the same Wanda. The old Wanda I knew would have never run herself down as hard and as thoroughly as you're doing. Even if you didn't love me and you sent me away, I think I like the old Wanda better."

"The old Wanda was a jerk," the distant Wanda on the line said. "For now, act like I'm the same old Wanda who sent you away. Don't be Mr. Nice Guy and go easy on me. Be angry with me. If you get angry with me, it will make me feel better than if you try to soft-stroke me. I deserve to be gotten mad at. So don't ease off on me. Be angry with me."

Chuck gripped the handset harder. He held his grip on the tower harder. "I don't have any right to be angry with you," he said decidedly. "You were always up front with me about what couldn't be between us. I

544

especially don't have any right to let my ego get out of joint because you didn't want to go off with me. You have every right to be with who you want and every right to not be with someone you don't want to be with, even if they want to be with you. It would be just my ego running away with me if I was mad at you for telling me we couldn't be together. I'm not asking you to apologize to me for that. I'm not asking you to apologize for anything. You have nothing to apologize for. I can't accuse you of being a liar. You never lied to me. You were always honest. You weren't very big on staying around, but you were honest that you wouldn't be staying. That honesty has to stand for something."

"Oh yes, my much-fabled, oft-exercised honesty," Wanda said in a sour voice. Words started to pour out of her. She tried to keep her voice down so she wouldn't be heard in the outer office, but the volume of her voice increased despite her efforts to keep it down. "My honesty that lets every man I pick up and manipulate into making love to me know up front, 'It's only passing love for one night, and then take your lovin' self away from me, and don't slam the door on your way out.' You know what it's like. You got caught up in my passing love before it passed on down the road and left you standing on the corner. Passing love is all I've ever given. Passing love is all I've ever felt. My honesty that you find so vaunted does is to let everyone know how far apart I stand from them. My honesty lets everyone know that my heart belongs to me and will never be extended to them in any real way. My honesty lets them know up front they will never get close to me. My honesty says I will always be moving on, away from them."

At a lower level of the tower, the nesting bird flew away from its nest in search of food for its chicks.

"My honesty hasn't done me or my life any better than my roving eye and rambling ways have. All the good either of them did me was to show me where the back door was so that I could get out and away quick and tell everyone not to be surprised when they found me gone. Now it's all left me outside the back door of love and life, looking at a closed door with no way to go back through or to go forward in life. My old life is over. I'm not going back. It was never a real life. From here on out, I want a real life. I just don't know how to get to a real life or if I'm capable of living one. I'm not sure if I would know a real life if it walked up to me.

"I walked up to you in lust, looking to use you for more passing pretend love. All the others I had been with used me as I used them. They made love to me as I arranged it, but they didn't love me. You were the only one who really loved me. I turned my back on you and sent you and your real love down the road away from me. I would have both you and your real love for me back. But real love is fragile and easily damaged beyond repair. Once it goes away or is driven away or sent away, real love doesn't return, not to the one it is given to or to the giver."

There was an old saying: "What a difference a day makes." In the days he had lived since Wanda broke it off with him, up to the present moment atop the tower, Chuck had seen the world he wanted move further away from him, moving in the direction opposite the one he had wanted to go in since he met Wanda. Maybe the lofty vista he could see from the top of the tower was distorting the world, but now the world had reversed direction. He saw the world he had wanted since he met Wanda coming back to him. He read the world in the few thin words she was speaking. Was the reversal real on her part? Or could her reversal reverse itself when it sank in on her how much of her life path it would reverse? If they got back together, as she seemed to be hinting at, would it last? Or was she just feeling down and blue? When she came out of the funk she had fallen into, would she go back to her old ways of thinking, her old ways of wandering? Would the call of the open road return to take her and his world away again?

The possibility that she would go away again notwithstanding, until that day arrived, did it make a difference now?

"Ah, are you saying you want us to get back together?" Chuck asked hesitantly, looking out over the world with its now new vista. "Are you sure that's what you really want? Are you sure it would work?"

"I'd like to imagine it would," Wanda said, sitting on the bare concrete floor between the banks of switching circuits in the telephone exchange office. "But it's all probably just a figment of my dreams. That kind of romantic reversal is the stuff of romance novels. As much as I want a real life, it's not the stuff of real life. It's not the stuff of the real world. I've always lived in the real world. Once you stamp out the frail blossom of real love, it doesn't spontaneously regrow. It's gone, and it stays gone. You're gone. Your love for me is gone. The only reason I'm talking to you at all is to give you the satisfaction of letting you know that you were right all along."

What a difference a horizon crossed makes once you've crossed it. What even more of a difference it makes when the horizon comes to you, Chuck thought.

She continued. "Once real love is kicked out the door, it doesn't circle around to return to the door it was sent away from. It just keeps on moving away down the road. You're gone far from me, and your real love is gone as far from me as you are. I acknowledge that as much as I acknowledge that you're not going to be coming back. As I said, real love dies easily. It does not live past the rejection that sends it away. It dies there and is buried at the feet of the one who loved and had their love kicked away."

At that moment, Chuck wondered if Wanda was saying she felt that she had lost his love forever and that there was nothing left to her but to fade out of his life forever after she said her final goodbye. Or was it a desperate roll of the dice at long odds—and distance—to get him back? And what difference did it make if it was the latter?

"Real love, when kicked in the teeth, remembers forever. It does not give itself again to the one who kicked it, even if their repentance is real."

"The Bible says that real love does not hold grudges," Chuck said, trying to remember the exact quote but not able to remember the exact wording or the chapter and verse. "It is patient, kind, and forgiving."

"I closed the door on your love," Wanda said. "The end is the end. The door doesn't open again for someone who put herself outside the door."

"And I'm saying the door isn't closed. Love doesn't kick down doors, but it does stand there and knock. You can still open the door and let love come back through it—if you really want to. Is that what you're saying?"

Chuck wondered if she had come to a whole existential turn of mind concerning love and her love for him. Or was he just her save-her-hand wild card in a deck she felt was stacked against her in a life she felt was falling in on her? And what difference did it make if she did?

Wanda said, "I'm not one of those women in romance novels who go all weak and blubbery, saying, 'I need you,' to the confident men they collapse in front of and collapse their lives to. I've never been that kind of girl. I don't think I could be that kind of girl if I tried. It's not in my nature. But I've come to the definite decision that sometimes life is a whole lot easier if you walk through it with someone who holds you up while you hold them up."

The reversal was complete, as complete as it was unexpected and unimagined. On a day when he had finished putting the past behind him, expecting not to see it or think of it again, a fleeting past he had believed would never and could never return to him, suddenly, the past was all around him everywhere. But now the past was talking about going into the future with him.

It should have been a moment of existential and romantic triumph. The lover he had wanted more than any other—the lover who had walked away from him, apparently never to return, saying she couldn't be what he wanted and couldn't, in any romantic circumstance, give up the life she was living—was seemingly coming back to him, saying her leaving him had been the biggest mistake of her life.

But as the exhilaration soared in him, alongside the exhilaration rose doubts that were equal and opposite in strength and depth. Taking up with Wanda and falling in love with her had been a dicey proposition during the brief and passing time they had been together. Chuck had more than a few real-time, real-world questions as to whether taking up with her again would prove to be as dicey and unstable a proposition as it had been in the first instance. Had she really changed? Had she changed as much as she said she had? Had her mother's death really delivered an existential blow to her view of life and love on the open road, which had so captivated and formed the life she had been living when he met her, or was it just a speed bump that had temporarily thrown her offtrack and off her form?

"Are you saying you want to marry me?" Chuck asked, not sure he would get an answer and not sure she knew the answer herself.

"If you would have me in marriage," Wanda said. "That or some reasonable facsimile of it."

The reversal was complete. She was reversing the whole of her life, the path she had followed long before he met her. But the underlying question was still pointing the way it always had.

"When it comes to marriage, the question is not whether I would have you," Chuck said. "The question is whether you would have it. Since I met you, from the first, you always said that your life was free on the road and that marriage would be like a cage for you. Until a minute ago, the only thing you ever said about marriage was that it wasn't for you and never would be for you. You said it wasn't a fit with you and didn't fit in with you, your life, or your plans for your life."

Chuck shifted the handset against his head, pulling the earpiece in closer. "You've had a roving eye ever since you hit the open road. You said so yourself. I was married to a woman who turned out to have a roving eye. I was betrayed and left by a woman with a roving eye and a roving mind. I was divorced once. Even though she betrayed me and I had every right to be mad at her and to divorce her and had every right to satisfaction that I divorced her, divorcing her was not a happy or satisfying experience. It hurt. I don't want to go through divorce again. If we got married, what guarantee would I have that after a while, the road wouldn't start calling to you again? What guarantee would I have that once you heard the call of the road and outlaw love on the road, as soon as you got the itch again, as soon as you got the longing again, you wouldn't be out the back door right away and back on the road and back in the bars and motel bedrooms?"

"If you don't trust me to stay in a married state, if you don't want to take the chance of being married to me, we can live together. That way, you won't be walking around worrying what will happen if it comes to divorce. You won't be hurt if the marriage breaks apart. No marriage. Just a relationship. No pain if the relationship comes undone."

"If your positional and sexual wanderlust came back on you and the relationship broke up, the breakup would hurt as much as if it were a divorce. I love you that much. It would all be the same to me. Either way, it would hurt."

At the other end of the jury-rigged hookup, Wanda said nothing.

"Though it may hurt to let you go now that you seem to be coming back to me, the hurt of a second breakup might be far worse than the first. For the emotional good of both of us, it might be the far better idea to just leave things where they lay between us and not try to put back together something that will fall apart all the harder if the open road and your one true love, the love of wandering, call to you. You'll start thinking, *What am I doing hanging round?* and you'll be gone."

"All that was the past," Wanda said. "That was yesterday. Now the time has come when yesterday don't mean nothin'. Neither does the road. They were the only thing real to me once. Now you and the real love you had for me are the only real things to me."

Chuck glanced out at the horizon beyond the river. "You based your whole life on the narrative you set for yourself. Are you really ready to throw the narrative out the window after following it for so long?"

"I thought I was great at setting out and setting up and defining the narrative of my life." Wanda's voice came back over the handset. "But I find that I'm not very good at the narrative of anything. Maybe you can help me find a real narrative of life."

"Your path, as you defined it, has been the centerpiece of your life," Chuck said. "It's been part of you for a long time. You've invested a lot of your time and strength in it. Do you have the strength to throw it all behind you over your shoulder and walk away?"

"I've already done that," Wanda said. "I'm not going back to the way I used to live. If I had any desire to go back, I would have done it by now. And I don't have any latent desire to go back hiding under my skin, fighting to get back out. There's nothing there to blow up in your face. My past is all dead to me—as dead as Mother is. I hope to see her again one day in another life. For now, knowing she's no longer around for me has left me empty in this one. I have no desire to revisit the empty way I was living. I have had enough emptiness to last me more than a lifetime. I don't need to add more emptiness by trying to return to a life that now feels like I was running on empty the whole time I was running myself through it. There's nothing real to me in my earlier life, especially in the love I practiced and received. The only real love I ever received or felt from anyone other than my parents was from you. Now I want to kick the back door I walked through back open. From there, I want to leave my old life behind and walk the rest of the way through life with you. The road be damned."

"And how do I know that a short time after we're married, the road won't start calling to you again and call you away back to your wandering ways? How do I know you'll spend the rest of your life with me like you're promising to do?"

"The only way I can prove to you that I'll spend a whole life with you is to spend a whole life with you. Then, when I die, if I go first, you can look down at my grave and say, 'By golly, she was as good as her word.'"

Chuck sat there at the top of the tower, looking out at the horizon, wondering if she had really crossed the horizon and come to him and would stay or if the horizon would reach out and pull her back.

"It all sounds good on the surface," Chuck said. "Especially the part about you wanting me in your life and wanting to be part of my life. Having you in my life has been the only thing I've really wanted out of life since my wife left me. I want a real life. I want a life with you. But how do I know you won't be gone in a flash back to your old ways if you realize that's the only way you want to live? What real-world guarantee can you give me, and what guarantee can you give yourself, that the call of the road and your own wanderlust won't rise up in you again and hit you so hard that you don't want to give it up?"

"There aren't a lot of full guarantees on anything in this world." Wanda's voice came back in a decided tone without pause or hesitation. "I can't fully and unequivocally guarantee you in full honesty that my old ways of thinking won't rise up again to try to seduce me back into my old wandering ways. I can only say that my old way of thinking and feeling is gone from me, and I don't see it coming back, not tomorrow or ever. All I can tell you is that I have come to hate the old self-indulgent, atomized, isolated way I was living. I've already left it behind, and I'm not going back. It doesn't satisfy me anymore. It never really did satisfy. That's one of the reasons I had to keep moving: to stay out ahead of the void I saw opening behind me and eating away the ground under my feet. I just didn't acknowledge it, not even to myself. I didn't dare to acknowledge it. To acknowledge it would have been to take a knife to the jugular vein of my whole worldview and life philosophy. I don't believe any of my old personal metaphysics anymore. I can't believe it anymore. Like I said, none of that is real to me any longer."

The breeze at tower-top altitude stirred again.

"I want a real life, not another installment of the alternate-world imitation of life I was living on the outside fringe of life. I want a real person to share a real life with. Like I also said, you're the only real thing that's ever come along for me. I want back the real life and real love I momentarily had with a real man, a real man and life I sent away before my old way of thinking completed dying, the real horizon opened up for me, and it hit me how stupid and self-dissipating I was being. Now all of that is gone from me, gone beyond a horizon I can't get back over and have no desire to recross."

The breeze tugged at him again. He looked away in the direction of the horizon her voice was coming from.

"I'm not going back to the way I was. For me, that's a given. There's only one way I want to go and plan to go. That's into the future. I prefer to go into it with you. But I'll go alone if I have to. Life just won't mean as much if I don't go through it with you. But I won't give up in life, and I won't give up on life. I won't hide from life. I won't curl up into a ball. I won't become a recluse. Like the saying goes, I won't promise you a rose garden. I can't say it will be happily ever after in all categories and at all times. But I'm determined that I'm going to knock myself trying to take it to a reasonable approximation of happily ever after and keep it there."

The tower creaked slightly in the increased breeze.

"I can't give you a full guarantee that there won't be any pain in our life together, provided you still want a life with me. The only place where anyone is free of all the pain of life is in the grave. In the end, a perfectly pain-free life ends in the grave just as much as a more involved life. But in the former, when you come to the edge of the grave and look back, you feel like you never really lived."

The sky above the tower and the land it stood on were clear and blue. They reminded Chuck of the sky and land surrounding the tower where he and Wanda had met. Out on the horizon, beyond the river, a small cloud moved slowly past.

"Trying to avoid all pain, especially by staying isolated and not being involved with life and love, is a defensive strategy. It may avoid some of the depths, but you never reach the heights. In the end, you're left empty—safe and empty. I should know. I wasted a good but empty portion of my life by running free and running away from real love and life by running my way through empty love and empty life, down empty roads. Since then, the scales have dropped off my eyes, and I see the light. The light hurts my eyes now that I see it and look at it and know how much and how hard I ran from real life. But one of the reasons I ran so fast, hard, and far was that in the back of my mind, I knew the light of the way I was living would burn a hole in my soul if I stopped to look at it. So I kept on running hard and fast down any road I could find, any road that kept me out ahead of myself and the truth at my heels."

The breeze blew again. The tower creaked slightly again but not threateningly so.

"But like a wolf, the truth ran me down. Now it's dragging me back and is chewing me up. One way or the other, I'm going to break through to real life and real love. You're the only one, outside of my parents, who really loved me for me. The only way I see through to real life and love is with you. My past is gone from me. I don't want it back. I'm available to move into the future with you if you still want me to go with you, like you did once. Or have you shut any thought of me out of your heart and mind? Have I shut down any thought of the future and horizons for you? Is there no horizon left that you want to cross with me?"

There was an old saying: "Time to shit or get off the pot." For Chuck, it was time to commit or get off the tower. Everything he had thought was lost never to return was coming back to him stronger and more real than ever before. At the same time, he wondered just how real it was and whether the reality would last. Despite her repeated affirmations that she had changed and wanted to have a life with him, Chuck hesitated to extend himself and grasp the hand she extended to him from over the horizon.

What he had thought unimaginable was there for him just over the horizon at the end of the line. She was coming back to him, claiming he was all the horizon she wanted. She had been all the horizon he wanted. Now it looked as if he could reclaim the horizon he had thought he lost. But he still wondered if loving her and hoping for her to love him and stay with him would turn out to be a false horizon and a horizon too far.

Wanda said, "Am I beyond all horizons to you? Is there no return for me? Is your anger with me set in stone forever? Are all doors to your love closed? Have you found someone new?"

Chuck fingered the piece of paper with the name and address of the woman he had met in the bar. "Ah, no," he said. "No."

A heavier breeze blew past. The tower creaked and swayed slightly. Everything had changed. Everything he had hoped for was coming to him. It was the reality he had hoped for, the reality that had vanished from him. Now she was back, saying that the road was gone from her and that she wanted to be with him forever. Her statement as to how she had changed and now wanted to share a life with him sounded decided and decisive. But he had no guarantee that at some point in the future life they shared, the call of the open road wouldn't come back. He had no guarantee she wouldn't be gone. Before he committed to the commitment she said she was now willing to share with him, he wanted a guarantee that she would stick to her newfound commitment to him and a life together. At the same time, if he backed away from her because he didn't have a perfect guarantee, in the end, he could find her gone and himself left with nothing.

She had taken the initiative to come to him in the first instance. She had taken the initiative to make them lovers. She had taken the initiative when she left him. Taking the initiative was all Wanda all the time. Now she was taking the initiative in coming back to him. Now it was up to him to take the initiative, or the moment, the future, and any horizon it contained could slip away forever.

"We should definitely sit down and talk about this," Chuck said. "But I don't want to talk with you long distance, with my butt perched a couple hundred feet above the ground on a tower. We've got to meet in the middle somewhere. I have a few days' leeway before I have to report back in. Can you get away from your section for a couple of days?"

"I can arrange it," Wanda said. "Where do you want to meet?"

"Remember the bar where we first met?" Chuck asked. "It's close to halfway between us. We can meet there."

For a moment, there was silence.

"I've got a better idea," Wanda said. "There's a certain motel. It's closer to the midway point between us. It's nothing swell—kind of sleazy, actually. But it played a central role in firing up my pubescent drives, shifting them into high gear, and setting me out on the life path I followed after that. I used it again in a more advanced stage later on down the road. It would make for just the right spot to christen my new life."

"Whatever you say," Chuck said. "But, ah, where is this place?"

"Not far off the junction of two back country roads," Wanda answered. "The kind I used to travel. It was still there the last time I was in the area. If you get there before me, rent room nineteen. If you get there after me, look for me in that room. If the room is rented, ask what room I'm in at the desk. If all the rooms are taken, go to the nearest motel or hotel, and call me through the phone company. One way or another, we'll meet up somewhere out there."

Wanda gave him directions to where the motel was located. She said, "See you there," and then hung up.

Chuck turned off the handset and quickly disconnected it, as if he were afraid she might call back to say she had changed her mind.

Instead of climbing down the tower straightaway, Chuck sat there for a minute, looking out over the horizon, a horizon he would cross over. He was already halfway there.

He reached into his pocket and pulled out the piece of paper with the phone number and address of the woman who had propositioned him in the bar. He glanced at it and then threw it out over the side of the tower. It floated away on the breeze, falling as it drifted away.

Chuck unfastened his safety belt and started climbing down the tower. The bird that had flown away returned to its nest, coming home.

28

"The place hasn't gotten any more high tone since we were here last," the woman said. A varied, undulating series of moans, groans, and other assorted sounds of a couple actively engaged in passion filtered into the room. "If anything, the walls have gotten thinner since we were here."

"The place must have been built by the Japanese," the man said. "I think they made the walls out of rice paper."

The squeaking of an old bed frame that had probably seen considerable hard use was interspersed with the sounds of human passion. The bed in the adjoining room must have been placed on the other side of the wall from the bed the couple were in. At times, it sounded as if the headboard of the bed in full-tilt use hit the wall.

"If the guy doesn't take it easy, he's going to crack the plaster," the man said. "At least he hasn't knocked anything off the wall in here."

There were no pictures or other decorative trimmings on the wall to knock off. Low-caliber motels like that one were rented for beds and closed mouths of management, not for art deco accompaniments.

"I wonder if it's the same bed we used," the woman said.

"Could be," the man said. "Places like this are designed for fast turnover of patrons, not for scheduled replacement of old furniture for new." The headboard in the next room hit the wall again. "Though whoever they are, if they get going any harder, they may break the bed. The manager will probably charge them for a new one."

One of the age-old questions of sexual etiquette was who paid for furniture broken during the dynamics of full-out sex.

"They're sure getting the most out of the bed and the room, despite the limitations of each," the woman said. "Or I should say, they're getting the most out of each other in the room."

"The room worked just fine for our purposes back then," the man said. "It sounds like it's working just fine for them tonight."

In the dark, the woman glanced in the direction of the wall through which the undulating sound of passion was penetrating, apparently with minimal loss of volume. For a short while, she lay quietly listening, remembering.

"I wonder if anybody heard us when we were carrying on in that room," the woman said.

"Maybe," the man said. "We didn't make any more effort to keep it quiet than they are. The sound probably carried as far that night as it's doing now. If there was anyone in this room and awake that night, they didn't knock on the wall and tell us to hold it down."

"If there was anyone in here that night, I wonder what they thought about it."

"If they thought anything about it, they probably thought that it was just some hooker who had brought her john to the motel to conduct her business and that she was putting on a big show for him in the hope that maybe he would give her an extra tip on top of the agreed-on price," the woman's husband said in a suppositional tone.

"You're so romantic," the woman said into the darkened room.

"Places like this aren't devoted to high-order romance, my dear," the man said. "Places like this are made for low-order, get-naked-quick, get-down-and-dirty, get-it-on, get-it-done, and get-moving-the-day-after sex. Places like this are dedicated third-rate-romance, low-rent-rendezvous establishments. You don't find swooning romance in places like this. You don't find Jane Austen or Charlotte Brontë in a no-tell motel. Besides, if someone did overhear us way back then, what difference does it make now?"

"No real difference," the woman answered. "I just wondered if they wondered who we were."

"If anybody heard us, they probably dismissed it as being just another fuck-'em-and-move-on encounter," the man said. "The kind that probably takes place here every night. They probably forgot about it and about each other by the end of the next day. I doubt anybody took anything away with them from it. If they thought anything, they probably thought we were just two randy fornicators who had picked each other up for the night and would be going our separate ways in the morning."

"Well, in a way, we were just randy fornicators," the middle-aged woman lying in the bed next to the man said. "At least at that stage we were. We weren't married. That came later on down the road. We weren't even engaged. It was the first time between us."

Another series of moans filled the low-rent motel room the couple had come back to in order to remember the start of the affair that had led to their marriage and the life they shared.

"But I was already thinking about everything I hoped would come of it beyond. I wasn't thinking about leaving and going my separate way in the morning. I wasn't thinking of you as a one-night stand and then on to the next." She turned to the man and looked at him. It was difficult to pick out his features in the dark room, but the silhouette of his face was familiar. "Was that what you were thinking?"

The couple in the next room were occupying the room she and her husband had occupied the night they started the affair that led to their marriage. The couple in the next room were also occupying the same quantum sexual energy level they'd had that night.

"I'm not fully sure what I was thinking that night," the man said. "I was distracted. I wasn't really thinking about what direction it would go afterward. But by the end of the night, I had pretty much decided I didn't want to go in any other direction than you."

The woman was well satisfied with her husband's answer. The man paused. In the dark, he glanced toward the wall that separated them from the action in the other room and the action it had seen from them in the past, a past that was growing longer and further behind them as they aged.

"They sure have the same energy we had back on that night," the man said, impressed by the unseen couple's strength, stamina, and staying power.

"They also have our room," the woman said. "Wasn't that the room we had—room nineteen?"

One of the reasons they had taken this sentimental journey was to make love in the same room they had first made love in.

"I believe it was," the man said. "The position is the one I remember: next to the last in the row. When we checked in, I asked for the room, but it was taken." Another drawn-out moan came through the wall. "By them, apparently."

"I wonder who they are," the woman said.

"They're probably teenagers," the man said. "Or wild local rednecks. That's why they have the energy we don't quite have anymore."

"What kind of car is parked outside the room? That may give us a clue as to who they are."

"There isn't any car parked outside the room. If they're redneck locals, they probably came in a pickup truck." The man glanced at the window with the blinds drawn. "When I looked out earlier just before we went to bed, I didn't see any pickup truck parked outside. The only thing parked outside the room is a telephone company service van."

"The phone company?" his wife asked in a surprised voice.

"Yeah, but I don't think it's telephone service people in the next room," the man said. "Low-level phone company personnel are technogeeks working for the higher-level technogeek bureaucrats in charge. They're all pretty staid and boring. They don't go in for no-holds-barred, yell-your-head-off sex. Besides, one of the two people I can hear in our old room is a woman. Except for operators, I don't think the phone company hires women as technical servicemen."

His wife did not respond. She lay there in the dark, listening to the sounds of pleasure coming through the wall. What she heard did sound like pleasure, but somehow, in a way she could not be sure of, it sounded like more than just low-level fornication. It sounded deeper than that. Somehow, it sounded like fulfillment and love fulfilled. It sounded like a horizon beyond sex alone.

The woman was silent again for a longer moment. She lay listening to the sounds like the ones they had made in the adjoining room more than a silver anniversary ago.

"I wonder if the room is enchanted," the woman said.

The man looked in the direction of his wife in the dark with a "What brought that on?" look on his face, which his wife could not see in the dark. He put her words down to the romance novels she occasionally read. His wife had otherwise never been a hard-core romantic. He had never heard her say anything along that line. *But women can surprise you as to what they're really thinking and have been thinking underneath all along*, he thought.

"What brought that on?" the man said, looking at his wife, whom he could not see clearly, even next to him, in the dark.

"We fell in love after falling into bed in that room," she said. "It sure sounds like the couple in the room now are on their way to falling in love big-time, if they aren't there yet. It just made me remember a story I once read about an enchanted cottage reserved for newlyweds that was filled with the lingering spirit of love left from the couples who had stayed in it before. I was just wondering if some kind of spirit of love fills that room."

Women can come up with the strangest ideas, the man thought. "I don't think so," he said in an unromantic tone. "I've heard stories of enchanted cottages—or you have. I've heard of enchanted forests. I've heard of enchanted castles and enchanted kingdoms. I believe Disney has one."

"I think that's the Magic Kingdom," she said.

"But I've never heard of an enchanted sleazy motel," the man said. "Enchantment and sleaze don't go together well. They aren't in the same category. If any deeper love comes into that room or any of the rooms in this place, it's because the people who use it bring love into it. But I doubt the room magically imparts love into anybody who doesn't already have it inside them when they come into it."

The man listened again to the sounds of passion wending their way through the thin wall from the next room. "They certainly seem to have the physical part of lovemaking down well. Whether they have anything spiritual to back it up and carry it on beyond tonight and out into a life together, I don't know and can't tell from their sound alone any more than anyone who heard us that night could have been able to tell that, despite some rough spots, we would go on to have a life together."

Another heavy moan of excited, passion-thumping, hard-driven female stimulation came through the wall.

"We kept it together. But just because they sound like we did back then doesn't mean they're anything like us when it comes to staying together. They might not follow the same path we took forward from that room and on out through life together. For all I know, they may break up and go their separate ways in the morning light. They may have planned it that way from the beginning."

The woman continued to listen to the passionate sounds coming from the next room over, especially the throaty pleasure sounds being made by the woman—the same kind of sounds she had made in the room so long ago.

Her husband continued. "Like I said, places like this are dedicated to fast turnover and anonymousness when it comes to sex on the run. They aren't dedicated to establishing commitment, bonding for life, and living happily ever after."

"From the sound of it, they're already there," the woman said. "They sound like they're very much into each other." She paused when she realized she had just made a terrible sexual pun, at least when it came to the unseen man.

"Don't let the decibels fool you," the man said. "The level of noise made during sex just indicates how much they're enjoying what they're feeling physically. It doesn't automatically translate into depth of feeling or into the kind of deeper love that holds a relationship together for a lifetime. There may even be a negative correlation. There's an old adage that people who have no thought of commitment beyond make more noise during sex. Not because they're dirtier, though that may be part of it, but because, since they're not distracted by thinking in terms of a life together beyond, they can put all their energy into enjoying a good fuck without any thoughts of love, commitment, ever after, or responsibility getting in the way and slowing them down."

The woman listened in silence.

"Just because we found depth of feeling and commitment for life doesn't mean they will or that they're thinking about it or even care to think about it. Tonight may be all there is for them. All horizons may disappear in the morning. There may be no horizon together for them beyond tonight."

His wife listened in silence for another minute and then said, "Somehow, I think they will go on beyond tomorrow. More than that, I have the feeling they'll go on to a whole and full life together like we did."

"Because you still think the room is enchanted?" the man asked.

"No. I never really did think that. I was just waxing poetic, remembering that story I read."

"So what makes you think there's more to it than just another random pickup and one-night stand? What makes you think they have a lifetime horizon together? What makes you sure they even want a horizon beyond the one they will cross while going their own separate ways tomorrow?"

"I can't really say. Maybe it's some kind of intuition. Maybe it's just wishful, romantic thinking. But somehow, I have the feeling that when they leave for the horizon in the morning, they will leave together and will cross any horizons together."

"You surmised that from the sounds they're making?"

"Sort of. The sounds are like the sounds we made in that room way back when. We're still together. Like I said, I don't know how I know this. I don't even know if I really know this. But somehow, I have the feeling they've been through the horizon and won't be looking to walk away from each other and disappear from each other over a horizon. I don't think they'll be walking any distant horizons. It sounds like they're coming home."